Alfred Herbert Palmer

The Life and Letters of Samuel Palmer

Painter and Etcher

Alfred Herbert Palmer

The Life and Letters of Samuel Palmer
Painter and Etcher

ISBN/EAN: 9783337016616

Printed in Europe, USA, Canada, Australia, Japan

Cover: Foto ©Raphael Reischuk / pixelio.de

More available books at **www.hansebooks.com**

THE

Life and Letters

of

SAMUEL PALMER

Painter and Etcher

WRITTEN AND EDITED BY

A. H. Palmer

Illustrated

LONDON

Published by *Seeley & Co., Limited*

Essex Street, in the Strand, 1892

CONTENTS

PREFACE

ABOUT ten years ago, when I was writing a short memoir of my father, it occurred to me that a companion volume of his letters might be published. I knew that many of these were preserved by his friends, and esteemed not only on account of regard for the writer, but for what was thought considerable originality. Yet I was not prepared for the extent of the collection which was most courteously placed at my disposal, carrying with it, by virtue of its very existence, the evidence of some merit. The publication of the volume was postponed; but the delay was by no means unfortunate, inasmuch as it gave me leisure to sift the material and reject that which was unsuitable, while applying myself, at the same time, to a closer and more unprejudiced study of my father's life.

There being an analogy between writing dashed off, for the most part, without the slightest thought of publicity, or of literary precision, and rapid sketches from nature done with a purpose and a will, I thought there would be as much danger in tampering in the one case as there always is in the other, and that it would be best to leave the selected letters to stand or fall on their own merits, without the manipulation such collections have sometimes received. Nevertheless I deemed it well to omit passages that were of no interest whatever except to my father's correspondents, the omissions being indicated in the usual way. A few explanatory comments were necessary; but I compressed these within the narrowest possible bounds. I was unable to fill up the gap between the years 1839 and 1848, having no letters of any interest at my disposal written within that period. Should any such exist I should be grateful for the loan of them.

As time went on, I became more and more impressed by the inadequacy and unworthiness of the memoir I have mentioned (a tyro's work, superficial, and in some respects misleading), and I thought it would be well to accompany the letters with a new biography which should be more worthy of its subject, and which, above all things, should be true. I therefore began a careful study of all my father's memoranda, artistic and otherwise ; of his numerous old pocket-books, his business papers, and particularly of what I will call (for want of a better term) his shorthand notes from nature. These consisted in innumerable little blots and scratches and hastily scribbled hints or impressions, which, slight as they were, bore a far more important part in the artist's professional career and in the growth of his best works than might be supposed.

Many of the rejected letters contained, like the memoranda, passages of biographical or artistic interest, and I decided to quote these passages freely, that, even at the risk of an appearance of patch-work, my father's story might be told as far as possible in his own words.

To those who have read the old life I wish to commend the new, because the relations of the two may be compared to the relations of a somewhat inaccurate and meagre table of contents to any work and the work itself. Even my father's most intimate friends will find that there is something to be learned of his career which is new to them, for much that I have quoted no eyes but his own ever saw before, while of those struggles with adversity which did so much to shape and to ripen his character, few persons knew the full extent.

When the manuscript of the *Life and Letters* was finished I availed myself of the valuable help of Mr. Allan J. Hook, to whose just and pertinent criticisms I consider myself very greatly indebted.

The list of my father's exhibited works and etchings I believe to be fairly accurate and complete ; and for this completeness I am much beholden to Mr. F. G. Stephens and Mr. Allan J. Hook, who kindly searched the Royal Academy and some other catalogues. For the list of the works exhibited by the Royal Society of Painters in Water Colours I am responsible myself.

The illustrations in this volume were chosen with some difficulty, and with the advantage of Mr. Seeley's advice, from a large mass of material. As much of my father's work is most difficult to render by any photographic method, we thought it well to choose such examples as could be dealt with with some prospect of success, and which at the same time should be fairly representative.

The portrait is a reproduction of a life-size stump drawing which, as the crude work of a student, will perhaps escape very harsh criticism. It is given as the only portrait in existence showing my father at that age—an age when, mentally, he was in the prime of life.

The device upon the cover is taken from the statue of Endymion in the British Museum. This beautiful figure is mentioned by my father (by the name of " The Sleeping Mercury ") as a test of taste and of the imaginative faculty. See the *Letters*, pages 183 and 261.

A. H. PALMER.

TILFORD, SURREY. *October*, 1891.

LIST OF ILLUSTRATIONS

THE LIFE OF
SAMUEL PALMER

THE LIFE OF
SAMUEL PALMER

CHAPTER I

1805 TO 1826

EIGHTY-SIX years ago Surrey Square, in the parish of St. Mary's Newington, was not severed by interminable streets from every country association. From the upper windows might be caught pleasant glimpses of sylvan Dulwich, and the southerly wind came fresh from many a neighbouring copse and meadow, long since forgotten.

At that time a young bookseller lived in the Square. His father (a prosperous City tradesman) was the son of Samuel Palmer, a pluralist divine of Sussex, and the grandson of Samuel Palmer, a Wiltshire Rector.[1]

Although the bookseller could trace his descent still further back, and no doubt was proud to be able to claim kindred with Richard Hooker (not to mention a certain Sir Stephen Fox), Fate had denied him the ancestral orthodoxy. He was, I believe, a Baptist of the strict old school; and ultimately obeyed a "call" to exhort the members of a Baptist congregation in Walworth.

His wife, to whom the slightest expression of his decided will was an unalterable law, had figured as "Lavinia" in a frontispiece designed by Stothard for some work of her father. This literary gentleman had also achieved a book on "Domestic Happiness"; but, as I have always understood, he was a domestic martinet of the first water. He had written books, and the books had been printed, so he was the pride of his family, who meekly obeyed his orders, and worshipped him (at a very respectful distance) under the title of "The Author."

On the 27th of January 1805 (the bookseller being then thirty years old) there was born to him his first child. This was my father who,

---

[1] An inscription and a coat of arms upon an old brass within the altar rails of Wylye Church, still testify that the Rector's bones lie beneath. He was presented to the living by Archbishop Wake (whose niece he had married), in 1708, three years before his death.

in due course, was registered at Dr. Williams' library, under his forefathers' Christian name. Like many first-born children he was supposed to be delicate, and was the source of needless anxiety, but he always asserted that he owed his life to the very original gastronomic notions of his young nurse. She found him pining on pap and other baby diet, and boldly substituted more substantial and unusual nutriment. However this may be, he certainly owed to Mary Ward something more than a precocious appetite for salmon. She was one of those faithful and affectionate servants of a race which seems to exist no longer, and although for the most part unlettered she was not only " deeply read " in her Bible, and in *Paradise Lost*, but was acquainted with other poetry. For instance, when the child was between three and four years old, Mary and he stood watching at a window while the full moon, rising behind the branches of a great elm, cast a maze of shadows on the opposite wall. As the shadows changed, the girl repeated this couplet :—

> " Fond man ! the vision of a moment made !
> Dream of a dream, and shadow of a shade ! "

My father never forgot those shadows and often tried to reproduce them with his pencil. There are not many nurse-maids who are capable of intelligently quoting poetry to such purpose as to fix an incident like this permanently in the memory of a baby, and I think it is evident that both must have possessed a rare faculty.

My paternal grandfather was a methodical, punctilious, and very simple-minded man, whose words were generally wiser than his actions, the wisdom being otherwise than worldly. He was not without originality, and though his natural bent was evidently towards the exact sciences, he had considerable literary taste. So far from becoming indifferent to the books with which his trade made him familiar, or regarding them as so much merchandize troublesome to dust, he seems to have felt for them a deep regard, unlike that of the mere bibliomaniac, and to have delighted in their constant presence. Inside the last of his little home made pocket-books that exists I find these words (written by my father when he gave it me), " He loved knowledge for its own sake." His letters certainly bear this out. They are feats of legibility, are sensible, and are sometimes seasoned with a little dry humour, but they are not the letters of a man who is likely to be successful in much besides the neat storage of innumerable facts, gathered indiscriminately.

Considering his boy rather weakly and the fragility a good reason for deferring his schooling, he determined to lay the foundations of his education himself, in his own way. Thus at an exceptionally early age, the child was encouraged to fall to upon his Greek and Latin, and was allowed at the same time "free pasture through a wide range of English literature"—literature of such variety, that bigotry does not seem to have been one of his father's failings. Every day a portion of the Scriptures was learnt by heart, and every day were repeated with the other lessons, these words :- "*Custom is the plague of wise men, and the idol of fools.*" This was a rather subversive maxim for the nursery, but one for the learning of which (as I have often heard him say) my father had cause to be thankful all the days of his life. When a son of his own was beginning his career he gave him this very similar advice, "If we once " lose sight of goodness as the principal thing we are adrift without an " anchor. *If we merely ask ourselves ' What will people say of us ?' we are* " *rotten at the core.*" It will be presently seen how thoroughly these precepts were put into practice, even to the verge of fanaticism.

The exceptional eagerness my father showed in following his early studies caused the months to pass away very pleasantly : and from time to time, by way of holiday, he paid visits with his mother to relations at Green-wich and Margate : this last journey being made, I believe, in one of the old "Hoys" owned by a distant kinsman. It was in Margate, perhaps, that his delight in the supernatural had its origin : weird stories of murder and of unquiet spirits which roamed in some of the ancient houses being common.

My father never spoke of his childhood as having been unhappy or dull, but although some young cousins tempted him into a few boyish pranks, it seems to have lacked the boisterous frolic so essential to the well-being of children. It was for the most part a sedentary and prece-ciously grave childhood, which proved deleterious to the body, and, for a time, to the development of a healthy mental condition. It was all very well to nestle in a corner with his cat "Watch" and a glass of home made wine, there to pore over the pages of a favourite author, but it was such habits as these that led to his becoming physically unlike the average English boy—small of limb, soft handed, and lacking in activity. They also helped to produce a sensitiveness which he would have been better without, and a strange liking for shedding "delicious tears" at performances on the organ.

After the birth of a second son, who afterwards received the smatterings of an artistic education, my father was sent to Merchant Taylors' School —a life for which he had been carefully unfitted. Before he had begun to find his level, and to profit by the inestimable advantages of that well-known process, it was discovered that he had "a taste for art." He tells us that his parents misinterpreted " an instinct of another kind—a passion-" ate love (the expression is not too strong), for the traditions and monu-" ments of the Church : its cloistered abbeys, cathedrals, and minsters, which

" I was always imagining and trying to draw : spoiling much paper with pen-
" cils, crayons, and water-colours." This might have been an unfortunate
instinct for the elder son of a very earnest Baptist to possess, and it is not
surprising that it was at first "misinterpreted." We have my father's
authority for the fact that he was what he calls "a free-thinker" at
fourteen, and we know that he afterwards became and remained a staunch
churchman. What part, however, my grandfather's arguments and influence may have played in the growth of his son's religious opinions —
whether he opposed them, or simply left them to grow unchecked, I do not
know.

No one has realized more thoroughly than my father afterwards did
the priceless value of a liberal education, and the serious responsibility
resting on those who take away the opportunity of acquiring it except
for the gravest reasons. "It is too commonly the case," he wrote,
"that when my young master prefers scribbling over paper to his Latin
and Greek, he is supposed at once to have a 'taste for painting.'" In my
father's instance, the result did not seem to justify the step of removing
him from school. He began his artistic studies heartily, but for want of
proper teaching they were altogether misdirected. Instead of being made
to attack the all-important rudiments of draughtsmanship and anatomy (a
discipline of which he afterwards well knew the value) he was allowed
to copy laboriously, prints of the Campo Santo frescoes, engravings of
"botanical minutiæ," and even architectural drawings.

When he was nearly thirteen years old these ill-advised attempts were
interrupted by his first great trouble. He was paying a visit to his grandfather "The Author" early in the year when he was told that his mother
was dead. He had dearly loved her, for he says "she was the counterpart
of her who has charmed us all in Cowper's verse," and the news "pierced
him like a sharp sword." It is doubtful whether he recovered the shock
for many years, and to this cause may be partly attributed a morbid and
melancholy tendency of mind which grew upon him to no small extent,
although its attacks were fortunately intermittent. His capability of suffering in this and other calamities cannot be gauged by his age, or by the
usual standard of susceptibility, but only by his own abnormally sensitive
temperament : and it will be seen, by and bye, how terrible a scourge that
temperament became.

Father and son were now thrown more together, and they turned for
their recreation to the diligent study of English literature. The bookseller, in
spite of his avowed contempt for custom was, as I have said, a punctilious
man, and he loved to do everything with the orderly deliberation that sometimes degenerates into an iron routine. He made himself little vellum-
covered memorandum-books just the size of his waistcoat pocket, and filled

them with elaborately written notes, ranging from the solution of an algebraical problem, to a quotation from some favourite poet or divine. If the daily walk with his son proved wearisome or unattractive, out came the little book to shorten the homeward journey.

The artistic studies were still continued to small purpose, but as it had been definitely decided that the boy should become a painter he received some lessons from a Mr. Wate ; an obscure artist, but a man whose sterling and unostentatious character, together with his methodical habits, impressed his pupil not a little.

Good news greeted the student not as he says himself on his fourteenth birthday, but just after it, and this was the letter he received. "Mr. Young presents compliments to Mr. Palmer informing [him] that "Mr. Wilkinson of No. 4 Beaumont Street, Marylebone has purchased his "picture No. 169 marked at 7 guineas, and Mr. Wilkinson wishes to see Mr. "Palmer, being disposed from the specimen he has seen of his abilities, to "give him further encouragement. British Gallery, Pall Mall. February 2, "1819."[1] In the same year he was represented at the Royal Academy by three subjects.[2] It is less remarkable that so young a tyro should have tried to grapple with the difficulties of painting from nature and the difficulties of design, than that he should have ventured to send his first attempts to the leading exhibitions of the day, with encouraging results. Perhaps we may conclude that crude as these works were, they were not without sterling qualities which the kindly Academical veterans detected. But the standard of those days was, of course, quite a different thing from that of the present time.

The Academy exhibition of 1819 was the first my father had seen, and he was at once deeply impressed by Turner's *Orange Merchantman*. This was the origin of his admiration for the great painter : and he says that afterwards, when "Mr. George Cooke the engraver would sometimes drop "in of an evening for a talk about art, the engravings of the brothers from "Turner formed part of the pabulum of my admiration—lunacy I may "almost say, before the popular expositors of that wonderful man were "born . . ." The frame of mind which forced the lad of fourteen to stop before the *Orange Merchantman* and to carry away with him such a vivid impression of that one picture was probably due partly to the kind of literature in which he had enjoyed "free pasture," and partly to the same predisposition which fixed the moon-cast shadows in his memory. Faculties which at that age are generally rudimentary appear to have been already fairly developed.

[1] This picture was either *Bridge scene, composition*, or *Landscape, composition*.
[2] 257. *Landscape with ruins ;* 259. *Cottage scene. Banks of the Thames, Battersea.* 414. A study.

In 1820 he was again successful in getting a picture accepted at the Academy, and we find from the index of the catalogue that the family had migrated to No. 10, Broad Street, Bloomsbury.

The boy began now to flounder into the deep waters of his profession; but he was not altogether without encouragement. It was long before the days of the westward tide which left the stone stairs and lofty rooms of Newman Street high and dry on the shores of unfashionable life, and in that street dwelt Stothard, who must have known something of the family as he had drawn my grandmother. From Stothard plenty of good advice was forthcoming, together with occasional tickets of admission to the lectures at the Royal Academy, where Flaxman then discoursed on sculpture. But my father was without the healthy emulation of the schools, where he might have profited by seeing the workmanship of those more experienced than himself. So, at a time when he should have contented himself with the alphabet of art, he was full of theories and speculations more suitable to the most learned professors; and full also of boyish certainty about things of which he knew very little. As far as art was concerned he continued to misuse his days, but at the same time, be it remembered, to exercise very diligently his mental faculties, till he became acquainted with Mr. John Linnell, who was his senior by twelve years, and in full career as a well-known artist. The healthy influence of this remarkable man came just at the right moment, and I shall presently have to allude to it more particularly. According to Mr. Richmond the acquaintance arose through Mr. Linnell admiring some of my father's small sepia landscapes, and it soon grew into intimacy. The new friend introduced the student to John Varley and Mulready: and just as Turner's work had appealed to one peculiarity of that student's mind Mulready's thoroughness and love of conscientiousness appealed to a second. As my father wrote afterwards, Mulready "was one of the few who realized Lavater's advice to devote ourselves to each new undertaking as if it were our test—our first work and our last." Mulready's maxims were much to the mind of a youth who, in spite of his admiration for Turner, was now struggling to imitate the very texture of the marble statues at the British Museum; and we shall find that, in after years, my father handed them on in his own way by harping on the importance of Patience, Elements, and Accuracy.

He was now about to enter upon the first of the five eras into which his career naturally divides, by falling under a peculiar influence which seemed to him almost supernatural.

My uncle Mr. John Linnell Junr., writing to me touching an erroneous date in Gilchrist's *Life of Blake*, says that his father "first became ac- "quainted with William Blake when he (J. L., Senr.) was living in Rathbone "Place (1818) to whom he paid a visit with the younger Mr. Cumberland·

" Blake lived then in South Molton Street, Oxford Street (2nd floor), and
" J. L. employed him to help him with the engraving of his portrait of Mr.
" Upton, a Baptist preacher. This is stated thus in his autobiography by
" J. L., and the first entry referring to Blake in J. L.'s Journal is dated
"*June* 24, 1818, when he took Blake the picture of Mr. Upton and the
" copper plate to begin the engraving upon." This was the beginning
of an intimate friendship between Blake and Mr. Linnell Senr., and it was
through the latter that, six years later, my father became himself intimate
with Blake, though he had doubtless known his works for some time.
That these works were inspired by the spirit of the purest and noblest art
and were worthy to be ranked with the greatest works of the greatest
masters he soon became convinced, and neither he nor Mr. Linnell
appeared to see in them any other peculiarity.

The first records of my father's acquaintance with Blake occur in 1824,
and that the two friends visited the Academy exhibition of that year together seems probable from a passage in Gilchrist's *Life:* " Mr. Palmer
" well remembers a visit to the Academy in Blake's company, during which
" the latter pointed to a picture near the ceiling by Wainwright, and spoke of
" it as ' very fine.' . . . ' While so many moments worthy to remain are
" fled,' writes Mr. Palmer to me, ' the caprice of memory presents me with
" the image of Blake looking up at Wainwright's picture : Blake in his plain
" black suit and *rather* broad-brimmed, but not Quakerish hat, standing so
" quietly among all the dressed-up, rustling, swelling people, and myself
" thinking " How little you know *who* is among you.' " According to Gilchrist, this picture was a scene from Walton's *Angler,* and upon referring
to the Academy catalogue we find it entered thus. " No. 268 *The Milk-
maid's Song,* T. G. Wainwright, *H.* ' Come live with me and be my love.'
From *The Compleat Angler.* Isaac Walton and Venator listening.' "

Now my father more than once described a certain interview with Blake
at Fountain Court as a first interview ; but no doubt through his having
mislaid and forgotten the memoranda he made at the time his descriptions
differ. I have been fortunate in finding among his papers the very book in
which the notes (together with some others relating to Blake) were entered,
and, assuming that the incident of the picture is correctly related, we are confronted with a difficulty on account of the date assigned to the first interview.
These notes, however, being evidently written very near the time of the
occurrences with which they deal are more likely to be accurate than my
father's recollections many years afterwards. They open as follows :—

" On Saturday, 9th October, 1824, Mr. Linnell called and went with me
" to Mr. Blake. We found him lame in bed, of a scalded foot (or leg).
" There, not inactive, though sixty-seven years old, but hard-working on a bed
" covered with books sat he up like one of the Antique patriarchs, or a

"dying Michael Angelo. Thus and there was he making in the leaves of a
"great book (folio) the sublimest designs from his (not superior) Dante.
"He said he began them with fear and trembling. I said 'O! I have
"enough of fear and trembling.' 'Then,' said he, 'you'll do.' He de-
"signed them (100 I think) during a fortnight's illness in bed! And
"there, first, with fearfulness (which had been the more, but that his designs
"from Dante had wound me up to forget myself), did I show him some of
"my first essays in design : and the sweet encouragement he gave me (for
"Christ blessed little children) did not tend basely to presumption and
"idleness, but made me work harder and better that afternoon and night.
"And, after visiting him, the scene recurs to me afterwards in a kind of
"vision : and in this most false, corrupt, and genteelly stupid town my
"spirit sees his dwelling (the chariot of the sun), as it were an island in the
"midst of the sea— such a place is it for primitive grandeur, whether in the
"persons of Mr. and Mrs. Blake, or in the things hanging on the
"walls. . . ."

    The authority of the Academy catalogue for 1824 on the one hand,
and that of my father's notes on the other leave no way of reconciling the
conflicting dates, except by assuming that either he or Gilchrist was in
error as to the title of Wainwright's picture, and that it was one of those
exhibited by that notorious and accomplished criminal in 1825. This is
the more probable because we find that it was not till October 9, 1824,
that my father showed Blake some of his "first essays in design," whereas
there were two works of his [1] hanging in the very exhibition Gilchrist refers
to —works which he would not be likely to refrain from bringing under his
companion's notice.

    I must return to the time preceding these notable events in my father's
life, reminding the reader once more that (as he himself freely acknowledged) his early professional career, as far as technical training went, was
very ill-advised. It seems that his artistic feeling and taste were at first strong
and acute, then decadent, and then, temporarily, almost extinguished; a state
of things probably caused chiefly by this misdirected practice. But all
this time there was a steady intellectual advance —the steady influence of
the best literature upon a mind naturally susceptible to all good influences,
whether moral or poetic. The first crop may have failed, but the soil was
mellowing.

    Just at the time when a dangerous propensity might have arisen to
wander off on bye roads leading to idleness or pleasant dilettantism there
came upon the scene the decided, uncompromising character of John
Linnell—a courageous artist who had fought many a tough battle, and

---

[1] 504. *Landscape Twilight :* and 706. *Study of a Head.*

who knew the dispositions and strength of the enemy. He was remarkable for individuality; and happily, he was full of admiration for some of the old giants who tower above all the painters of their own and after times. " Look at Albert Dürer," he said; and he said it so imperatively that the words are quoted more than once in my father's early memoranda. He urged the study of Michael Angelo and Bonasoni—the study of the figure, and particularly of Antique sculpture. His twelve years of seniority went for a good deal, but not for more than his great strength of character and originality. All who knew John Linnell intimately must admit that he belonged to the order of men who, if they fail with one weapon or with many, coolly and doggedly fight on to victory. His convictions were strong, deeply rooted, and, as might have been expected from an entirely self-made man, accompanied by a great intolerance of any convictions of a contrary kind. He was by nature so painstaking and so extremely industrious that it needed not the precepts of his friend and master Mulready to turn him towards an honest and sterling professional ideal. Of this ideal as it existed then some notion may be gathered from his early engravings in line and mezzotint, after his own pictures : particularly the fine plate after his portrait of John Martin, the stern old Keppel Street Pastor.[1] A reverent regard for truth is shown in every touch, and those essential characteristics which distinguished the sitter from his fellow-men are evidently grasped intuitively, and made the most of.

At the time of his first acquaintance with my father Mr. Linnell was living at Cirencester Place, Fitzroy Square, in the midst of a career equally remarkable for determined industry, indomitable energy, and for eccentricity. He was to be found at one time elaborating with exquisite delicacy of touch the dainty ivory miniatures in which connoisseurs professed to see qualities worthy of some of the Old Masters : at another taking a turn with his great, bony hands at his own flour-mill and kneading-trough, kept going to supply the appetites of a family which repudiated baker's bread. He would turn from the labour of love and enthusiasm on his excellent engravings to receive some fashionable or distinguished sitter ; and then, perhaps, to give a lesson to a pupil, in whose plethora of accomplishments, drawing had to be included. Moreover, by the irony of Fate, he was then practising as an " unremunerative luxury " that branch of art by which he afterwards gained renown and wealth. He had, in a

---

[1] It used to be a favourite story with my father that this old gentleman was once invited to a grand dinner given in his honour by some rich member of his flock, who held him in great awe and esteem. When the guests were assembled at the table, and he was pressed to partake of the choicest, he cast his eyes around him with these words :—" There is nothing here that I can eat." Consternation followed, and assiduous inquiries as to what could be got for him. " Bring me," he said, " an onion, and a pot of porter."

pre-eminent degree, the knack of turning everything—his friendships, his natural gifts, and his opportunities, to the greatest possible advantage : while his stern self-denial, and contempt for conventionalities of all kinds, made it a greater pleasure to save and to hoard up his savings than to spend them on personal comfort and personal appearance.

Now it was only natural that such a man as this with his extraordinary versatility, vitality, energy, and executive powers, together with his eminent friends, and his fine old books, should attract a student much younger than himself, who was possessed of some characteristics complementary to his own ; and, having attracted him, it was also natural that he should give him an impulse in a right direction. But before ascertaining by means of my father's written records what this impulse was like we should remind ourselves that the phraseology of these records will altogether mislead us if we attempt to compare it with that used by any average man. My father's reverence for anything that even distantly approached greatness of character was as exceptional as his own self-abasement ; and, throughout his life, his tendency was always to take people at their own valuation of themselves, and sometimes even above it.

He inherited from his father the habit of committing to paper whatever he considered worth remembering, and he had formed another habit of carefully writing down the exact nature of any difficulty he encountered, because, in doing so, he found that the solution often suggested itself. More than twenty of the large, clasped pocket-books in which these memoranda were made have been preserved, and they also contain so many sketches, poems, essays, and columns of accounts, that the series, as far as it goes, forms a kind of skeleton autobiography.

Among the earliest of these memoranda are the following :—

" *November*, 1822 to *June* 9, 1824.—Now it is twenty months since you
' began to draw. Your second trial begins. Make a new experiment.
" Draw near to Christ, and see what is to be done with Him to back you.
" Your indolent moments rise up, each as a devil and as a thorn at the
" quick. Keep company with the friends of Publicans and sinners, and
" see if, in such society, you are not ashamed to be idle. Ask Christ to
" manifest to you these things ; Christ looking upon Peter (called *Repentance*)
" and Peter's countenance. Christ's promise to the dying thief—the looks
" of both. Christ leading His blessed to fountains of living waters (which
" being the union of all vision, should be done as the artist's Prince) :
" Jesus weeping at Lazarus' tomb. The three first are the chief, and
" are almost unpaintable—quite, without Christ. Lay up, silently and
" patiently, materials for them in your sketch-book, and copy the prints to
" learn such nicety in pen sketching, or rather, making careful studies, as
" may enable you to give the expressions. But smaller subjects of separate

" glories of Heaven might be tried —hymns sung among the hills of Paradise
" at eventide ; . . . a martyr, having painted his murder, laughing, or
" rather smiling at his torments.   A family met in Heaven . . . ."

" *January 2nd* [1825].—Now is begun a new year.   Here I pause to
" look back on the time between this and about the 15th of last July.   Then
" I laid by the [*Holy*] *Family* in much distress, anxiety, and fear ; which
" had plunged me into despair but for God's mercy, through which and
" which alone it was that despondency not for one moment slackened my
" sinews ; but rather, distress (being blessed) was to me a great arousement :
" quickly goading me to deep humbleness, eager, restless inquiry, and
" diligent work.   I then sought Christ's help, the giver of all good talents
" whether acknowledged or not, and had I gone on to seek Him as I
" ought, I had found His name to me as a civet-box and sweeter than all
" perfume.   Notwithstanding, as it was, I think (by Him alone) I improved
" more since I resolved to depend on Him till now, than in the same time
" ever before ; and have felt much more assistance and consolation.   For
" very soon after my deep humblement and distress, I resumed and finished
" my *Twilight*, and quickly took up my *Joseph's Dream*, and sketched in
" my new sketch-book.   Mr. L. [Linnell] called, and looking at my *Joseph*,
" sepias, and sketch-books, did give me indeed sweet encouragement.   Soon,
" by his desire, I went with him to Mr. B. [Blake], who also, on seeing my
" things, gave me above my hope, over-much praise : and these praises from
" equally valued judgements did (God overruling) not in the least tend to
" presumption and idleness, and but little to pride ; for knowing my own
" stupidness (but not alas, to its full) I gave back the praise to God who
" kindly sent it, and had granted to me desponding, that at eventide it
" should be light . . . ."

In another of these note-books (including a period from November
1823 to July 1824) this is the first noteworthy entry :—" N.B. in my
" attempts to copy the Antique statues to try and draw most severely, and
" to cry out for more and more form : and then I shall find in the Antique
" more than I can copy, if I look and look and pry into it earnestly for
" form.   I shall not be easy till I have drawn one Antique statue *most*
" *severely*.   I cannot execute at all.   The least bit of natural scenery
" reflected from one of my spectacle-glasses laughs me to scorn, and hisses
" at me.   I feel, ten minutes a day, the most ardent love for art, and spend
" the rest of my time in stupid apathy, negligence, ignorance, and restless
" despondency ; without any of those delicious visions which are the only
" joys of my life—such as Christ at Emmaus : the repenting thief on
" the cross : the promise to Abraham : and secondary visions of the ages
" of chivalry, which are toned down with deep gold to distinguish them
" from the flashy, distracted present."

But in following Mr. Linnell's advice to study the antique, my father
had pried too closely; and hence (as we gather from his subsequent
statement) his "sedulous efforts to render the marbles exactly, even to
their granulation," led him "too much aside from the study of organization
and structure." Nevertheless, by this kind of discipline, he acquired the
invaluable habit of looking at things with concentrated attention, and with
certain definite reasons for that attention. He writes :—"Look for Van
Leydenish qualities in real landscape, and look hard, long and continually.
Look for picturesque combinations of buildings, and elegant spires and
turrets for backgrounds."[1]

At the end of a year of close study and investigation, that was now
applied to better purpose than before, he briefly sums up his artistic career
as follows :—

"As it seems reasonable to divide the soul's journey into stages and
"starting-points, and to stop and look back at certain intervals, and at
"each fresh stage to go back to the primitive and infantine feeling with
"which we set out ; and to lay in such a store of humility, simple anxiety
"to get on, and diligence in the great, nay stupendous pursuit of grand
"art as may stand us in stead for a year's journey or so, I divide my life
"with respect to art into two parts. First, my very early years, in which
"I distinctly remember that I felt the finest scenery and the country in
"general with a very strong and pure feeling ; so that had I then seen the
"works of the very ancient Italian and German masters I should have ad-
"mired and imitated them, and wondered what the moderns could mean
"by what they call their 'effects.' Then, when I gradually learnt arithmetic
"and grammar, my feeling and taste left me, but I was not then completely
"spoilt for art. But when I had learned to paint a little, by the time I had
"practised for about five years I entirely lost all feeling for art, nor did I
"see the greatest beauties of even the Dutch Masters, Cuyp, Ruysdael &c. ;
"so that I not only learnt nothing in this space of time that related to
"high art, but I was nearly disqualified from ever learning to paint. But it
"pleased God to send Mr. Linnell as a good angel from Heaven to pluck
"me from the pit of modern art : and after struggling to get out for the
"space of a year and a half, I have just enough cleared my eyes from the
"slime of the pit to see what a miserable state I am now in. . . . I have
"now made my first struggle—alas, with how little success. I shall now
"begin a new sketch-book, and I hope, try to work with a child's simple
"feeling and with the industry of humility. . . ."

---

[1] In the same volume as this, there is a rough pen and ink sketch, apparently intended
for St. Christopher bearing the sacred Child ; and beneath it is written, "My first
attempt at figure-designing, 1823."

Among many visits to the Dulwich gallery at this time of great impressibility, one is recorded as having been made in Mr. Linnell's company.

" Memoranda, day after going to Dulwich. Cox is pretty—is sweet, " but not grand, not profound. Carefully avoid getting into that style " which is elegant and beautiful but too light and superficial : not learned " enough—like Barret. He has a beautiful sentiment and it is derived " from Nature ; but Nature has properties which lie still deeper, and when " they are brought out the picture must be most elaborate and full of " matter even if only one object be represented, yet it will be most simple " of style, and be what would have pleased men in the early ages, when " poetry was at its acme, and yet men lived in a simple, pastoral way.

" Girtin's twilight, beautiful, but did he know the grand old men ? Let " me remember always, and may I not slumber in the possession of it, Mr. " Linnell's injunction (delightful in the performance), ' *Look at Albert* " *Dürer.*' In what a simple way Landscape impressed the mind of Raffaelle : " yet his little bits make me despair.

" How superior is Mr. Linnell's style of colouring to that of any other " modern landscape painter, and yet not half so captivating to an ignorant " eye as others.

" Look at Mr. Blake's way of relieving objects, and at his colour.

" The copy of Leonardo da Vinci at Dulwich is merely a head and " shoulders. How amazingly superior it is in style to any portrait there. " The tone of the flat blueish sky is wonderful, though it is nothing " of itself. It is the colour of the soul, not vulgar paint. Ruysdael, " Hobbema, Paul Potter, and Cuyp—how intense, how pure, how profound, " how wonderful ! "

After a singularly comprehensive list of " fine things " seen during this journey to Dulwich, once again comes—" *Look at Albert Dürer.*" The writer is evidently entering that early stage of discovery when the mind, naturally short-sighted, takes up for the first time the telescope of knowledge.

A few months later, the following entries were made in the new sketch-book just referred to. After describing Michael Angelo as " The Salt of Art," and speaking enthusiastically of the old German and Italian Masters as compared with the " Venetian Heresy," the writer continues :—" I sat " down with Mr. Blake's Thornton's *Virgil* woodcuts before me, thinking to " give to their merits my feeble testimony. I happened first to think of " their sentiment. They are visions of little dells, and nooks, and corners " of Paradise ; models of the exquisitest pitch of intense poetry. I thought " of their light and shade, and looking upon them I found no word to " describe it. Intense depth, solemnity, and vivid brilliancy only coldly " and partially describe them. There is in all such a mystic and dreamy

" glimmer as penetrates and kindles the inmost soul, and gives complete
" and unreserved delight, unlike the gaudy daylight of this world. They
" are like all that wonderful artist's works the drawing aside of the fleshly
" curtain, and the glimpse which all the most holy, studious saints and
" sages have enjoyed, of that rest which remaineth to the people of God.
" The figures of Mr. Blake have that intense, soul-evidencing attitude
" and action, and that elastic, nervous spring which belongs to uncaged
" immortal spirits . . . Excess is the essential vivifying spirit, vital spark,
" embalming spice . . . of the finest art. Be ever saying to yourself
" ' Labour after the excess of excellence' . . . There are many mediums
" in the *means*—none, O! not a jot, not a shadow of a jot, in the *end* of
" great art. In a picture whose merit is to be excessively brilliant, it can't
" be too brilliant : but individual tints may be too brilliant. . . . We must
" not begin with medium, but think always on excess, and only use medium
" to make excess more abundantly excessive. . . . I was looking with
" Mr. L.: [Linnell] at one of Bonasoni's emblems, a rope-dancer balancing
" himself with this motto, *In medio est salus*. ' Yes,' said he emphati-
" cally, ' for a rope-dancer : but the rope-dancer only keeps the middle
" that he may be not a middling, but an excessive fine performer. . . .' "

" Well would it be, if those who hope at last to produce works of
" exquisitest beauty were constantly haunted. . . . urged, and lashed by
" this truth, that the more quietly they take things now, the more pleasures
" they allow themselves, the less distressful the anxiety of weighing but a
" little too light in the balances, the less rigidly sublime the ideal goal, by
" so much will be the vale of life the gloomier—the murkier the sunset
" with the thickening horrors of a stormy night. Sometimes for weeks
" and months together, a kindly severe spirit says to me on waking in the
" morning the name of some great painter, and distresses me with the
" fear of coming short at last : and I think it is then I do most good."

His creed, he says, must not be judged by his work in 1825, but by his
present sayings :—" Though I hope," he continues, " we shall all be severe
" outlinists, I hope our styles of outline may all be different as the design
" of Michael Angelo from his equal, Blake, and the outline of Albert
" Dürer from that of Andrea Mantegna. There is no line in nature,
" though excessive sharpness. Nature is not at all the standard of art, but
" art is the standard of nature. The visions of the soul, being perfect,
" are the only true standard by which nature must be tried. The cor-
" poreal executive is no good thing to the painter, but a bane. In pro-
" portion as we enjoy and improve in imaginative art we shall love the
" material works of God more and more. Sometimes landscape is seen
" as a vision, and then seems as fine as art : but this is seldom, and
" bits of nature are generally much improved by being received into the

" soul, when she thinks on such supernatural works as Mr. Linnell's picture
" by Lucas Van Leyden. . . . Often, and I think generally, at Dulwich,
" the distant hills seem the most powerful objects in colour, and clear force
" of line : we are not troubled with aerial perspective in the valley of
" vision. . . . Genius is the unreserved devotion of the whole soul to the
" divine, poetic arts, and through them to God : deeming all else, even
" to our daily bread, only valuable as it helps us to unveil the heavenly
" face of Beauty. . . ."

Following several rather lugubrious unfinished poems in the note-books,
with imagery far superior to the unmusical diction and halting metre, there
comes a copy of a very characteristic business letter :—"Samuel Palmer,
" having completed Mr. Bennett's very kind order, begs to state that the
" pictures and drawings now delivered, being somewhat different in style
" from those he used to paint when Mr. Bennett gave the commission, he
" shall not feel the least reluctance to taking back any of this set that Mr.
" Bennett may disapprove. S. P. will be happy to listen to any suggestion
" from Mr. Bennett, towards the improvement of this set of pictures and
" drawings." [1]

After another interval of poetry, the writer adds :—" It was given me
" this morning (16th October, 1825), to see that I had done wrong in
" seeking for Mr. Bennett's pictures, visions more consonant with common
" nature than those I received, at my first regeneration, from the Lord. I
" will no more, by God's grace, seek to moderate for the sake of pleasing
" men . . ." Further on he continues :—"The artist who knows propriety
" will not cringe or apologize when the eye of judgement is fixed upon his
" work. And the artist who knows art, ere he bring his work forward to the
" envious world, or hope for the admiration of the few select discerners, will
" elaborate it to his utmost thought ; if indeed, material tablet can receive
" the perfect tracings of celestial beauty . . ."

It is not easy to find among the works of this period which have
survived instances of the moderation which Mr. Bennett's " order " seems,
for the time being, to have produced, or of work which the world would be
likely to covet. In all is excess : in many, " excess more abundantly exces-

---

[1] These are entered as follows :—

	£	s.	d.
Windsor . . .	5	5	0
Twilight	3	3	0
Scene from Kent .	7	7	0
Rustic Scene . . .	7	7	0
Harvest Moon	7	7	0
6 Drawings .	1	10	0
	£31	19	0

sive," but it is just this very quality that gives them their undoubted hold upon the minds of " the few select discerners" who can manage to understand them.

The execution, as in Blake's *Pastorals*, is often primitive, the design archaic and simple : but the result is so clearly the offspring of a mind swayed almost solely by poetical and imaginative faculties of uncommon development, that the technical blunders, and the anomalies, and the absurdities, find forgiveness with those who have mastered at all events the alphabet of this strange unwritten language.

Still turning the leaves of the same volume from which I have quoted, we arrive at a list of subjects taken from the books of *Ruth, Daniel*, and *Jonah*, which it was evidently the writer's intention to attempt : and we find also a prayer that God might prosper him in painting his " visions" of the story of Ruth and Naomi :—" Young as I am," he continues, " I know—I " am certain and positive that God answers the prayers of them that believe, " and hope in His mercy. I sometimes doubt this through the temptation " of the Devil, and while I doubt I am miserable : but when my eyes are " open again, I see what God has done to me, and I now tell you, I *know* " that my Redeemer liveth."

Pages of description would not give so good an idea of the aspect of my father's mind at this time as the passages I have quoted. I have quoted them reluctantly : firstly, because they were never intended to be seen ; and secondly, because they show a mental condition which, in many respects, is uninviting. It is a condition full of danger, and neither sufficiently masculine nor sufficiently reticent. It is, however, not without hope, and everything depends on the actions which next follow—on the strength of character available to bolt the flour from the bran.

As regards external influences, on the one hand there was the outspoken, practical counsel of John Linnell, enforced by the examples of such splendid and typical energizers as himself and Mulready ; and on the other hand was the mystic and parabolic teaching of old, neglected William Blake, driven home by what seemed an unaccountable force which enslaved those who were willing to give themselves up. Deeper in the young student's mind than either of these influences had yet penetrated, there were a few passionate longings and loves,[1] and an ideal of which its owner, though conscious of its presence, could hardly have given a coherent explanation. To foster these there was, so to speak, the exotic

---

[1] He writes thus to Mr. Valpy, June 23, 1880, "I can remember nothing which so "agreeably disturbed my male lethargy, except perhaps my first reading of Fletcher's "*Faithful Shepherdess*. But when there I found, in black and white, all my dearest "landscape longings embodied, my poor mind kicked out and turned two or three "somersaults. . . ."

atmosphere of a secluded and peculiar home life. In an ordinary family, or in an ordinary school or college career, all these strange doings and opinions would have been modified. They would, to a great extent, have simply died out, if they had come into existence at all, as we feel a solemn or pathetic impression die out before an hour or so of bustling, business activity, or the uncongenial remarks of a hostile critic.

The counsel of Mr. Linnell, we must remember, was in some particulars rather supplemental than antagonistic to that of Blake ; and it is probable that the young man who was now courting the society of these two very dissimilar men had qualifications which enabled him to reconcile many of their opinions.

I think it is easy to see the influence of Blake and his works in much that I have quoted. Art is described as the standard of nature : the " visions of the soul " as perfect, and therefore " the only true standard by which nature must be tried." " Excess " is " the essential spirit . . . of the finest art." " Delicious visions " are sometimes granted, sometimes withheld, and much prayer is made that the visionary may be prospered in painting them. Some of these seem to have been so vivid that they led to more than the crude sketches in the pocket-books, and at last (as I shall show), to a complete change in the course of my father's career.

There is a peculiarity to be found in most of these early note-books of his which in some cases would have augured ill for the future success of a young man. The poems and essays are seldom completed. The beginnings of all of them are drafted, revised, elaborately re-revised ; and at each stage there is a neat elaboration which invariably changes, sooner or later, to untidy scribbling. But I take it that this simply showed the result of a series of impulsive struggles towards an ideal which was almost out of reach, rather than the descent of apathy, or the failure of energy. It is the action of a mind not yet broken to the determined fight with the difficulties of real life, and may be likened to the plunges of a colt before he has learned to economize his strength, and to throw his weight steadily against the collar.[1]

Returning for a moment to a topic upon which I have touched already, and referring to the short autobiography of my father which was published in 1872, we find these words, " . . . but I was unacquainted with artists, " and time was misused until my introduction to Mr. Linnell, who took a " very kind interest in my improvement, and advised me at once to begin a " course of figure-drawing. . . ." Now whether it was these words them-

---

[1] Real eccentricity of a decided type is to be found in one of these volumes, in the guise of a treatise on " Household Government." This is a collection of masterful opinions on the enforcement of male authority ; and the ideal is a domestic martinet, who rules an utterly impossible household in an utterly impossible way.

selves, or their interpretation by the occult science of criticism, which led
to the making up of a fiction touching the relations of the two artists, it is
hard to say, but after my father's death it was asserted that :—"Samuel
Palmer . . . was a veteran water-colour painter of the school of Blake
and Linnell, from each of whom he borrowed much that made him singular
among his fellows." Wherever "the school of Blake" may have flourished,
and apart from the difficulty in imagining a "school of Blake *and* Linnell,"
it seems to me that this criticism was misleading. It would easily lead to
the conclusion that my father was a copyist, and successful as an artist
only because he was so. I must admit that the few autobiographical words
I have quoted do not convey an adequate idea of the kind and invaluable
help and encouragement my father received at his friend's hands ; and I
have taken pains to give such extracts from his writings as will place that
matter beyond a doubt. But in reading these extracts, it is essential to
bear in mind what I have said about his unusual reverence for anything at
all approaching greatness of character ; and also not only that his gratitude
was far more easily moved than is usual, but that he habitually expressed
it in somewhat profuse terms. He speaks of Mr. Linnell as having been
sent to him by God as "a good angel from heaven," and on one occasion
he writes to the angel thus :—"Those glorious round clouds which you
paint, I do think inimitably, are alone an example how the elements of
nature can be transmuted into the pure gold of art." I must admit that
I possess one little picture of my father's, painted about this time, the sky
of which is very suggestive of Mr. Linnell's manner, and even of his colour ;
and further, that another picture known as *The Bright Cloud* may suggest
the same painter in the treatment of the sky. Nevertheless, judging by
the hundreds of other examples I have of my father's work, executed before
and since he became acquainted with Mr. Linnell—judging by the most
characteristic of his works of any period, it is possible to maintain that what
made him "singular among his fellows" (that is to say the best of his
etchings and water-colours), was not borrowed from anybody, but was
essentially his own. Further, that his art is particularly remarkable for
belonging to no school ; and that its "pictorial genealogy" cannot easily
be traced through any other artist. That the genealogy of a certain portion of his early works can be traced through one or two of the Old Masters
and through Blake is very true. Even in the two pictures I have quoted
as undoubtedly savouring of Linnell, there is much that is thoroughly
original in conception, sentiment, and execution.

The sympathies, and I think I may say the ideals, of the two artists
were as totally distinct as their characters, and although my father was
beholden to his senior for some technical instruction in oil-painting, besides
his counsel and encouragement, it was not long before (disregarding Mr.

Linnell's definite advice) he struck into a course of practice as entirely independent as his course of thought. Except that both were diligent students of nature, and (each after his own manner, and in his own time) full of vigorous industry, I, who knew them both so intimately, find it difficult to imagine two men more unlike and even antagonistic. It was this dissimilarity that made their intercourse, as Mr. Richmond says it was, mutually beneficial.

If it could be proved that Samuel Palmer became John Linnell's copyist, and drew from that source his inspiration and technique, the whole story of his life, his ideals, and his struggle to realize them, together with half his artistic memoranda, would have to be thrown aside in a heap, as a shameless and fatuous series of falsehoods.

I think we may liken my father's acquaintance with Mr. Linnell to a favourable breeze filling the canvas of some craft carried out of her course by contrary winds, and then becalmed : but the acquaintance with Blake may be compared with the first haven, after a voyage full of doubt, and danger, and delay. Long after Blake (as my father put it) "was taken away from the evil to come" and his body had been huddled into a "common grave" at Bunhill Fields, his disciple wrote of him as "The Maker, the Inventor, one of the few in any age," and described him as a fitting companion for Dante and Michael Angelo—the language of a man who knew the value of the comparison he was making. None of the young artists who also fell, one by one, under Blake's influence would have challenged the opinion, and the only survivor of them all (a man whose whole life has been spent in intercourse with persons of the greatest eminence) emphatically endorses it. Yet the influence was that of a man who lived in "comparative neglect and noble poverty," who worked without ceasing to maintain himself and his wife in severe frugality, and whose very sanity has been doubted, denied, and defended so often, that his name has become a kind of artistic Shibboleth.

This last vexed question has a good deal of interest for one who has studied my father's life—perhaps the staunchest and most affectionate of all Blake's followers : and the interest is increased when we find that the influence over those followers was to some extent personal : that they derived a certain part of their reverence and admiration from an intimate personal intercourse. It might be suggested that "birds of a feather flock together," and that a man's disciples, themselves not without eccentricity and full of the rash enthusiasm of youth are not the jury before whom to try him. But we find not only that these were all undoubtedly sane men intellectually above the average, and men who, for the most part, made their mark in after years, but that, in every case, the allegiance survived their youth, and lasted in undiminished strength to the end of their days. Even so practical and wary a veteran as John Linnell, was held in the same bonds. An insane man of any ordinary type would not have been likely to become the cynosure of such as these. He would not be described by fairly competent judges as possessing "great powers of argument," a kindly and equable disposition, and as having a ceaseless pleasure in his work. We hear nothing, even from unbelievers in Blake's sanity,[1] of periods of moroseness, of idleness, of physical violence, or of melancholy. With one singular exception, I believe all have been obliged to admit that his life was a cheerful, consistent, industrious, and self-denying life. With none of the advantages of education, or of the hard polish imparted by friction with society, he had sufficient natural ability to accomplish much that has been handed down to us with a respect we are compelled to share.

The bluntest accusation of insanity with which Blake's admirers ever had to deal is an assertion made by Doctor Richardson in an essay on hallucinations, which was quoted in a paper in *The Cornhill Magazine* of August 1875, and it culminates in these words " . . . he became actually insane, and remained in an asylum for thirty years."[2] This fiction was met by an emphatic denial from three of Blake's personal friends,

[1] These unbelievers will be pleased to hear that my father was once supposed to be of unsound mind himself, and that by his own house-maid. He was in the habit of soliloquizing and of repeating fragments of his favourite poets. The girl's former master had also soliloquized, but had ended his career in a lunatic asylum. Naturally, therefore, after the first day or two in her new place, she bewailed her fate to her fellow servant, as of one destined to enter the service of gentlemen who were "queer in their heads." I think this was the same girl who expressed her astonishment that her master should have two frames of tailor's patterns hanging up in the drawing-room, the "patterns" being Blake's *Pastorals*.

[2] The passage referred to is as follows :—" There can be no doubt that some persons " possess the power of forming mental pictures so perfect as to serve all the purposes of " objective realities . . . . The same faculty is exercised by the artist who draws either " from memory or by a sort of creative talent which enables him to conceive suitable " forms or attitudes, and copy them as though the conceptions were realities. Dr. " Richardson, in an interesting essay on hallucinations, mentions a singular illustration of " this faculty in the case of Wm. Blake. This artist once 'produced three hundred " portraits from his own hand in one year.' When asked on what this peculiar power of " rapid work depended, he answered, ' " that when a sitter came to him, he looked at him " attentively for half-an-hour, sketching from time to time on the canvas : then he put " away the canvas and took another sitter. When he wished to resume the first portrait, " he said, I took the man, and put him in the chair, where I saw him as distinctly as if " he had been before me in his own proper person. When I looked at the chair, I saw " the man." ' It may be well to mention that the exercise of this faculty is fraught with " danger in some cases. Blake, after a while, began to lose the power of distinguishing " ' between the real and imaginary sitters, so that ' (the *sequitur* is not quite manifest, " however) ' he became actually insane, and remained in an asylum for thirty years. " Then his mind was restored to him, and he resumed the use of the pencil ; but the old " evil threatened to return, and he once more forsook his art, soon afterwards to die.' "

Mr. Richmond, Mr. Linnell, and my father. Mr. Richmond speaks thus :—" What a strange assertion ! I must say, I think Dr. Richardson is more deluded about Blake, than dear old Blake ever was about anything himself." Mr. Linnell treated the matter with characteristic impatience, as " idle stuff " akin to other "lies" about Blake which had been circulated. But my father supplemented his exertions to secure the publication of the truth by writing to *The Athenæum* as follows :—
" Without alluding to his writings, which are here not in question, I
" remember William Blake, in the quiet consistency of his daily life, as one
" of the sanest, if not the most thoroughly sane man I have ever known.
" The flights of his genius were scarcely more marvellous than the ceaseless
" industry and skilful management of affairs, which enabled him on a very
" small income to find time for very great works. And of this man the
" public are informed that he passed thirty years in a mad-house ! " These three vindications made forty-eight years after Blake's death by men grey in years and not without experience of the world carry some weight, and form as strong an argument in favour of Blake's sanity (in his friends' sense of the word), as any we shall meet with.

But on the other side of the question there are many difficulties. Blake is admitted to have had imagination so vivid, powerful, and " disproportionate " as to " overshadow every other faculty." But it would seem that imagination pure and simple, however vivid it might be, could hardly call up the shades of " Moses and the Prophets, Homer, Dante, Milton :
' All . . . majestic shadows, grey but luminous, and superior to the common height of men,' " and converse with them comfortably by the sea shore. Nor can imagination pure and simple have much to do with a tiny fairy's funeral which troops from beneath a leaf of a flower in the garden, after " a low and pleasant sound."

There is no doubt that Blake believed that he saw and asserted that he saw " visions." He described them, conversed with them, and even drew them, transferring his eyes from the paper to his strange sitter and back again just as he did when he drew his wife's portrait. The credulity of the nineteenth century not following this precise channel it became necessary for his admirers to explain the matter, which they have done more or less ingeniously : but I think we may assure ourselves that had he possessed that " balance of the faculties," which constitutes true sanity, and which his most ardent admirers are obliged to admit that he wanted, the actual appearance of a " vision " after he had conceived it would have been met by incredulity justified by some reasoning process.

There is another phase of Blake's visionary faculty which is more attractive because it is not so abnormal as the one of which I have been speaking. He had, he said, a " double vision " or power of seeing always

in action, which with the rapidity and clearness of the photographer's lens
changed many outward and visible objects to clear and often beautiful
mental pictures.[1]   In this way a tall thistle changes to an old man grey in
years ; and the stars to all the heavenly host shouting for joy.   It is therefore no wonder that seeming trifles filled him, as he says, "full of smiles
or tears."   If we are repelled by his spirits and spectres, we can turn with
relief to this transmutation, and find there a wider and more natural field
for a powerful imagination such as his.   The precise point, however, at
which this imagination outstrips the most powerful kind possible in
a sane man it is not quite easy to see.   A sane man conceives or sees
within him an exquisite landscape—conceives it so clearly that he is able
to paint it ; but he does not step forward to enjoy the shade of his groves,
or to listen to his sylvan musicians.   His Galatea remains a cold impassive
statue.   With Blake, on the other hand, the mental and bodily vision appear to have been permanently confused, and confused so completely, that
he was not aware which were the objects beheld by the corporeal, and
which by the mental eye.   The point of divergence from sanity would
appear to be the belief in the reality of the mental picture, and the apparent
power of projecting it in such manner as to enable it to be drawn
as any other external object would be drawn.   The sane man can see his
imaginary objects within, and it is immaterial whether he shuts his bodily
eyes or not, but when Blake sat down to draw one of his ghostly portraits
and glanced to and fro between his imaginary sitter and his paper, he
would appear to have been using first one sense of sight and then the
other without being aware of any difference between the two.[2]   So it was
that when Blake was making a drawing of " The Ghost of a Flea " the
sitter inconsiderately opened his mouth.   The artist being thus " prevented

---

[1] There is a curious passage somewhat illustrating the *modus operandi* of this faculty,
in the concluding notes in his copy of Lavater's *Aphorisms*.   " As we cannot experience
" pleasure but by means of others who experience either pleasure or pain thro' us, and as
" all of us on earth are united in thought, for it is impossible to think without images of
" somewhat on earth.   So it is impossible to know God or heavenly things without
" conjunction with those who know God and heavenly things.   Therefore all who converse
" in the spirit converse with spirits.   For these reasons I say that this Book is written by
" consultation with Good Spirits because it is Good, and that the name Lavater is the
" amulet of those who purify the heart of man."   After this, we may say to ourselves : —

            " Such tricks hath strong imagination,
            " That if it would but apprehend some joy,
            " It comprehends some bringer of that joy ; . . . . "

[2] He once said to Mr. Richmond, " I can look at a knot in a piece of wood till I am
frightened at it."   That he sometimes adapted himself to his company is proved by an
anecdote I had from the same source.   One day Flaxman called on the old painter and
said in the course of conversation,—" How do you get on with Fuseli, Blake ? I can't
get on with him at all.   He *swears* so."   " Why," said the other, " I swear at him again."

from proceeding with the first sketch" listened to the Flea's conversation
and made a separate study of the open mouth.

But for such anecdotes as this we might bring ourselves to think that,
as there is an enormous difference between the distinctness of the mental
pictures conceived by the highly imaginative and the highly unimaginative
man, Blake possessed merely some extension of a normal faculty ; and as
we read that, in days of old, men's eyes were sometimes opened for a time
upon the invisible world, so, in a degree, it might have been with
him.

Whatever the solution of this question of Blake's sanity may be it was
a question which never once occurred to my father during the whole time
of his acquaintance with that human enigma.   He saw in him something
which, in his opinion, separated him entirely from all but the greatest of
the great, and to everything else his eyes were shut.   Of the deep and
lasting impression made by Blake there were other instances.   Besides
Mr. Linnell, three artists became fascinated much in the same way and
I believe quite independently of each other.   These three, Messrs.
George Richmond, Edward Calvert, and Francis Oliver Finch, were well-
informed men with no lack of individuality, but they did not seem to
be disturbed by any suspicion, or to see in the industrious old engraver
even any startling eccentricity.   Nevertheless their minds may have been,
and probably were, by natural bent as well as by training in accord with
his on many points : so that if they had never encountered him they
might have followed ideal art at all events in sympathy.   Their minds were
also so exceptionally well furnished as to enable them very often to
read between the lines of Blake's conversation.   Yet after all, their devotion may have been an instance of that mysterious and almost magnetic
attraction which, since the days of the prophets and their disciples, has
occasionally knit men together in far closer bonds than those of ordinary
intercourse.

My father wrote of Blake that, "he saw everything through art, and
in matters beyond its range, exalted it from a witness into a judge."   I
think this may perhaps be the key to what the uncharitable would call the
disciples' infatuation.   As enthusiastic and by no means unprejudiced
artists they saw in Blake's art something which, in their opinion, so
excelled as to separate it and him from all else : and seeing this, they
intuitively shut their eyes to other things as a mother is blind to the
ugliness of her child.   Whether (granting equal personal intimacy) they
would have fallen so completely under his influence or believed so completely in his sanity if they had never seen one of his artistic works is
much to be doubted.

In December 1870 my father wrote to Mr. Richmond touching the

Spiritual Form of Pitt guiding Behemoth, a picture by Blake which was then being exhibited at Burlington House, "Supposing for a moment "that we have been under a delusion, and that he differed from others "not by excellence but by eccentricity, would not the merest glance have "popped our paper bag, seeing him in juxtaposition with the Old Masters "which, through your arrangement, flank and surround him?" With no cause for partiality and with no pleasant memories of happy hours spent with the kindly visionary, we must admit that he differed from ordinary men by excellence *and* eccentricity—eccentricity so great that it may be said to have verged upon, if it was not identical with a species of insanity. We may conclude that this was an extraordinary and exceedingly rare phase of mental aberration in unique conjunction with an artistic genius capable of giving birth to works sometimes endued with a grace, a grandeur, and a spiritual beauty of colour, which sets them apart from the creations of ordinary men. That they do so stand apart by themselves (for better or for worse), it is almost impossible to deny; and we cannot deny that, for the most part, they seem to have been evolved without any direct reference to nature, or to the canons of art, being stamped with a very peculiar kind of originality. It may also be granted that there is something about them which places them beyond the range of ordinary criticism; just as there is in certain touching kinds of music a quality altogether beyond the learned analysis of the most highly-skilled musician. Both appeal to a subtle and deeply-rooted faculty quite distinct from any which depends on education, and to this faculty, such art or such music never appeal in vain.

If Blake was insane, we may yet congratulate ourselves that there was such marvellous method in his madness and especially that he was poor. Freedom from conventionalities, an intellect, like some spring days, all the brighter for the passing clouds, a ceaseless industry, and a "noble poverty" —all these combining enabled him to bequeath to us some handiwork which is strangely beautiful, and some poems both musical and pathetic. Works such as these show "a happiness which often madness hits on, which reason and sanity could not so prosperously be delivered of."

The possession of a common centre gave unusual cohesion to the little group of enthusiasts. The "House of the Interpreter," as they called Blake's dwelling, became their rendezvous, and he encouraged their friendship with the never-failing geniality which seems so different from the changeable moods of insanity. After they had become intimate one with another they began to hold regular monthly meetings at their own homes, for the purpose of comparing their sketches and designs. In these designs, Blake's sway over them is very evident, although it by no means obliterates individuality. The opinions and actions that grew out of the allegiance to their master needed some courage, for they involved a separation from those of most other men, the deliberate renunciation of the " main chance," and the certainty of incurring that deeply-dreaded ridicule which is so potent a factor in human life. " Take here," says Lavater in the *Aphorisms*, " the grand secret—if not of pleasing all, yet of displeasing none—court " mediocrity, avoid originality,[1] and sacrifice to fashion." " *And go to hell,*" writes Blake in the margin. To Lavater's description of "heroes with infantine simplicity" Blake adds " *This is heavenly.*" Even from these two passages it is possible to judge in what direction Blake would endeavour to lead his young followers ; and we find accordingly, that they courted originality and affronted fashion with a zest worthy of their teacher : while, at the same time, they showed not a little of the child-like simplicity of character so dear to him. They inflicted on each other abundant good advice, and in some cases were even known to follow such advice. For instance, my father (then about twenty) belonged to some amateur musical society, and became so fascinated by his violin as to steal precious daylight hours from his painting. But he was warned at last that he was ruining his prospects as an artist, and thereupon he not only immediately withdrew from the society but thenceforth " sang and fiddled only in the evening."

About this time, Mr. Linnell was living with his family in part of a small farm-house near the " village " of Hampstead, still keeping on the house at Cirencester Place for professional purposes. The walls of the five little rooms were encrusted with works of ancient art, and there was a pleasant, homely sentiment of country seclusion about the place. Although Blake professed to hate Hampstead, here he might often be found, standing at the door to enjoy the summer air, or playing with the children, or listening to the simple Scotch songs sung by the hostess, the ready tears falling from his eyes the while. Here too, he would often plunge into some animated argument with John Varley (another frequent guest), in whose favourite judicial astrology he found a topic that interested him. A pencil sketch by Mr. Linnell shows them thus occupied. Varley is pointing upwards, and his fine animal physique contrasts very strongly with the peculiar physiognomy of his adversary.

Fortunately for my father, Broad Street lay in Blake's way to Hampstead, and they often walked up to the village together. The aged composer of *The Songs of Innocence* was a great favourite with the children, who revelled in those poems and in his stories of the lovely spiritual

---

[1] Endymion, writes Lord Beaconsfield, " was intelligent and well-informed, without " any alarming originality or too positive convictions. He listened not only with patience " but with interest to all, and ever avoided controversy. Here are some of the elements " of a man's popularity."

things and beings that seemed to him so real and so near. Therefore as the two friends neared the farm, a merry troop hurried out to meet them led by a little fair-haired girl of some six years old. To this day she remembers cold winter nights when Blake was wrapped up in an old shawl by Mrs. Linnell, and sent on his homeward way, with the servant, lantern in hand, lighting him across the heath to the main road.

It is a matter for regret that the record of these meetings and walks and conversations is so imperfect ; for, in the words of one of Blake's disciples, to walk with him was like "walking with the Prophet Isaiah."

I have introduced to the reader by their names several of Blake's artistic disciples, and it is strange that these more intimate followers of his should have been distinguished by dispositions in some respects quite unlike the dispositions of ordinary men. At the same time they all possessed in a very high degree a rare faculty. My father writes of one of these early companions, Mr. F. O. Finch (a friend of his boyhood), " He had imagination, that inner sense which receives impressions of beauty as simply and surely as we smell the sweetness of the rose and the woodbine." It is natural that persons having so much in common between themselves and so little in common with the world at large should become unusually intimate. Among them none was more-remarkable than Mr. Edward Calvert—so original a genius that he is worthy of a closer acquaintance.

" A philosopher to whom I am indebted for some rudiments of civilization," wrote my father in 1872, " stood still suddenly one day when we were walking and talking, and uttered these words —' Light is orange.' They have never been forgotten." This philosopher was Mr. Calvert, who was, I believe, the same " accomplished friend " (then a young man) who, " in the pleasant vale of Bickley . . . sat down under a tree, and solaced himself by repeating aloud in the sonorous original passages from one of Virgil's *Eclogues*," to be greeted by an acquaintance with the exclamation " O you poor lost creature !" To this friend, my father says he was indebted for some of the happiest hours of his life, and it was to him that he sent the first words written after its most crushing sorrow. A few months before his death, he writes again to the same gifted person :—" Your kindnesses to " me are among my few pleasures of memory. They were of a rare quality ; " for, as my wife and I love to say, they never varied with my circumstances " which, though never prosperous, were sometimes much the reverse. You " hated me for three days for singing you ' The British Grenadiers' and " that was all !" [1]

---

[1] Such was this gentleman's refinement of taste, and such his love for ancient Greece and its heroes, that the infliction of 'The British Grenadiers' must have tried him seriously. It was sung by my father precisely for this purpose. He really disliked the sentiment of the song well nigh as much as did his friend. See Letter LXII.

Speaking of one of Mr. Calvert's works, my father says, "I don't set up for a judge, but like a blind baby feeling for the breast know the taste of milk, with a somewhat precocious appetite for cream. I *find* the cream in your *Cider Press*, which, in poetic richness, beats anything I know, ancient and modern."

Making all due allowance for the writer's way of expressing himself, just as we must do in the case of his expressions touching Mr. Linnell, it is easy to see that the person to whom the passages I have quoted were addressed was no ordinary person, and that the friendship between the two was no ordinary friendship.

Edward Calvert, thus alluded to as a philosopher, a consummate artist, and a true friend was born in Cornwall about 1803. The son of a naval officer, he began life in a ship commanded by Sir Charles Penrose (as Mr. Richmond relates) where, in the "dim light of the midshipman's cabin" he pursued, as best he might, those artistic studies of which he became more and more enamoured. An intimate friend having been killed by his side in an action, he soon afterwards abandoned a career for which he was little fitted. He then qualified himself by a course of private instruction, by the curriculum of the Royal Academy schools, and by a study of anatomy at one of the hospitals, for a painter's life. But all this instead of leading to the sharp professional battle ended in a dreamy, intellectual dallying with art which his private means permitted him to enjoy. He introduced himself to Blake (with whom in many respects he was naturally in harmony), and succumbed in his turn to the spell I have described. This, no doubt, was partly caused by his possessing in no small degree that "innocence and humility of heart" which the old man loved to find. Many of his works showed Blake's influence as clearly as others reflected the influence of the literature and art of ancient Greece, a country to which he afterwards made pilgrimage. Some were exhibited at the Royal Academy and unhappily (owing to his most fastidious taste), many more were destroyed by himself before their completion :[1] for, as Mr. Richmond says, "he was always stretching out his hand to grasp that which he could not attain." The few of his productions that survive are so striking and show such a profound poetic feeling that had he denied himself the luxury of his "learned leisure" and possessed such unfailing energy as distinguished Blake and some of Blake's other followers his name would inevitably have become widely known.

Among these surviving works are a few impressions from the wood-

---

[1] On leaving his former home for his final residence in Hackney, he is said to have destroyed even the few blocks and plates that remained.

engravings [1] he cut with his own hand at a "dreamy time" when ancient philosophy and poetry vied with ancient art to beguile the happy days. The engravings are such that they naturally associate themselves with some of Blake's finest work, and they have also an affinity with certain work of my father's to which I shall presently refer as forming a perfectly distinct phase in his art. To prove these blocks Mr. Calvert set up a press in his own house, No. 17, Russel Street, Brixton Road, and it was there that his equally enthusiastic friend spent so many of those happy hours of which he speaks. There (as it is recorded), Mrs. Calvert was known to rise from her bed in order to prove a "Pastoral" over which the two young artists had been brooding far into the small hours.

Among the wood engravings, perhaps the most striking is the *Christian Ploughing the last Furrow of Life*, a work described by Mr. Richmond as being of "great beauty in the print, but as drawn upon the block before it was cut, of *superlative* beauty." The merit, however, is of a kind that appeals only to those few who can understand such art as Blake's and a very quaint form of allegory; and furthermore, who are susceptible to the appeal of latent subtleties of sentiment, quite indescribable by words and undemonstrable by any comparison. As a true wood-cut, the brilliancy, feeling, and power of the work are great. *The Cider Press* I will not venture to describe, because the words I have quoted about it raise the expectations of its excellence so highly that unless the beholder possessed my father's special qualifications to judge of this excellence and the same standards of comparison he might condemn the verdict as being as absurd as the verdict (which he will find hereafter) on Giulio Romano's *Nursing of Jupiter* may appear to be. Language is as powerless to describe what my father saw to admire so ardently in the one case as in the other ; but from the consideration of the whole of his biography and correspondence a clue may be found by those who care to seek one. *The Cider Press*, in my opinion, is not superior in sentiment to a little "pastoral" which has as its subject a youthful couple retiring to rest in their tiny, ancient cottage. Seen through the lattice and upon the right-hand side of the design is a glimpse of a twilight landscape with a crescent moon and brilliant stars, which is doubly condensed poetry.

Of Mr. Calvert's original opinions, equally original delivery, and a few curious perversities- of his habit of walking to and fro with his fingers on his mouth before his utterances. I have often heard my father speak, but always with respect, as for the opinions and foibles of a true philosopher. Naturally a somewhat silent man, his utterances when they came were regarded by

---

[1] The dates of publication (for nearly all the wood-cuts were " published as the Act directs " by the artist himself), on the impressions in my possession include a period from September 1827 to September 1831.

the hearers as Sibyllic. Of his personal appearance Mr. Richmond writes, "he was short and squarely built, with a forehead rather broad than high, with an expression rather contemplative than observant." Mr. Linnel (whose words were usually as incisive as his portraits were faithful) described him as resembling "one of the old prophets"; by which Mr. Richmond thinks he meant "a Seër of much that was hidden from others."

To use his own words, spoken of Mr. F. O. Finch, Mr. Calvert "pursued his way and his work undiscouraged by neglect and undiverted by example," till on the 14th of July, 1883, he died as quietly as he had lived, leaving in the portfolios of his old friends a few relics of his refined taste and peculiar genius. He left also only one survivor of that happy and enthusiastic "little band who reverenced Blake as their chief, and very sincerely loved art for its own sake."

CHAPTER II

THE reader will have gathered that although my father's first steps in his profession were ill-advised, there had been a precocious and rapid intellectual growth, and it would be natural to think that as he recovered the lost ground and became more and more engrossed by art, his literary pursuits would have been neglected if not altogether abandoned. Moreover, the fathers of most young men are not backward in contriving that their sons shall become "useful," that is money-getting, members of society as soon as possible. But there seemed to be none of this feeling in the methodical old Baptist. He loved knowledge, we are told, for its own sake and not for what it would fetch in the market, and how warmly this disinterestedness was appreciated the following words, written by his son beneath the score of a musical composition, will serve to show :—" I dedicate this work to my
" Father, because, not choosing to sacrifice me to Mammon with the mum-
" mery all the while of Christian prayers, with an affection rare in this day,
" he led my erring steps where Faith, Temperance, and Study evermore
" resort and wait to take the hand of those who love their charming company.
" And because he supported me, never once murmuring, long after that time
" when our fathers use to thrust their offspring from their bosom at the first
" crude opportunity, that they may clutch their gold alone and gorge a richer
" feast."

This breathing-time allowed by the father's kindness was invaluable ; and the "free pasture" in the rich fields of literature had a beneficent influence which is to be traced through nearly the whole of the student's artistic career. According to his own account, after he had diligently read the satirists and learned from them to "despise vice and folly," he passed on to the authors of the seventeenth century, where he "found matter to admire and to imitate—sanctity and ideal beauty." Although I think he was naturally better fitted for a scholarly career than for any other, he was now engaged with equal avidity in two different quests. It is a matter of opinion whether this was a wise course—whether art and literature ought to be or need to be so widely separated as they usually appear, still less so hopelessly estranged as they are often found. But we shall presently see how greatly he was beholden to literature not only for his art but his happiness, and consequently how passionate his hereditary affection for books became.

From 1819 (the year of his first success as exhibitor) to 1826 his name continued to appear in the catalogues of the exhibitions at the British Institution and Somerset House.[1] In 1826 he entered upon another new era in his life; an era which impressed itself as distinctly upon his future artistic and mental career as his acquaintance with Blake had done hitherto.

One of his early ambitions had been to attempt a series of designs to illustrate certain stories of the Bible, and he speaks of "visions of the story of Ruth and Naomi," apparently regarding them as legitimate mental off-spring he was anxious to nurture. Referring again to the old pocket-books, we find among other devotional writings a prayer which was indited about April or May, 1826, "On going to Shoreham, Kent, to design from *Ruth*." It is an earnest prayer enough, and proves that the writer's art was in close relationship to religion of a fervid and emotional character. This decision to leave London was also caused by some temporary break-down of health ; and it is evident that the absence was intended to be a long one. The same volume contains a cash account of the Shoreham expenses, from which it appears that a young sculptor and disciple of Blake's, Mr. Frederick Tatham, accompanied the *Ruth* enthusiast, and that between them they mortified the flesh not a little. The cost of board and lodging for the two roughly averaged eight shillings a week ; and my father seems to have lived almost entirely on milk, eggs, and bread and butter. The extras include postage, books, gold paper, pencils, ivory tablets, and very rarely, just a taste of meat. The visits to London were evidently made on foot : but whether the attractions of Russel Street, Brixton, and of Fountain Court made these visits frequent, I do not know. A short, fragmentary journal contains the following :—

"At Shoreham, Kent, August 30, 1826. God worked in great love with "my spirit last night, giving me a founded hope that I might finish my "*Naomi before Bethlehem*, and (to me) in a short time. . . . . That night, "when I hoped and sighed to complete the above subject well (it will be my "maiden finished figure drawing), I hoped only in God, and determined "next morning to attempt working on it in God's strength. . . . Now I go "out to draw some hops that their fruitful sentiment may be infused into "my figures. . . . . August 31. We do or think nothing good but it has "its reward. I worked with but little faith on my *Naomi before Bethlehem* "this morning and succeeded just in proportion. After dinner I was helped "against the enemy so that I thought one good thought. I immediately "drew on my cartoon much quicker and better. . . . Satan tries violently "to make me leave reading the Bible and praying. . . . . O artful enemy,

[1] Some thirteen of his works were hung at the Royal Academy, up to and including 1826.

" to keep me, who devote myself entirely to poetic things, from the best of
" books and the finest, perhaps, of all poetry. . . I will endeavour, God
" helping, to begin the day by dwelling on some short piece of scripture, and
" praying for the Holy Ghost thro' the day to inspire my art. Now, in the
" twilight, let Him come that at evening-time it may be light. God bless
" my father and brother and poor dear old nurse ; who, though a misled
" Baptist, shall sing among the redeemed for ever. . . . The last 4 or 5
" mornings I thank God that He has mercifully taken off the load of horror
" which was wont so cruelly to scare my spirits on awaking.[1] Be His great
" name ever blest : He persists to do me good, spite of myself, and some-
" times puts into my mind the unchangeableness of His promise, the reality
" of future things. Then I *know* that faith is the *substance* of things hoped
" for, the *evidence* of things not seen. . . . Wednesday. Read scripture.
" In morning, ill and incapable, in afternoon really dreadful gloom ; toward
" evening the dawn of some beautiful imaginations, and then some of those
" strong thoughts given that push the mind [to] a great progress at once,
" and strengthen it, and bank it in on the right road to TRUTH. I had
" believed and prayed as much or more than my wretched usual, and was
" near saying 'what matter my faith and prayer ?', for all day I could do
" nothing : but at evening-time it was light : and at night, such blessed
" help and inspiration ! ! O Lord grant me, I beseech Thee grant, that I
" may remember what THOU only showedst me about my *Ruth*. . . . .
" Thursday. Rose without much horror. This day, I believe, I took out my
" *Artist's Home*, having through a change in my visions got displeased with
" it ; but I saw that in it which resolved me to finish it. Began this day with
" scripture. Friday. So inspired in the morning that I worked on the
" *Naomi before Bethlehem*, which had caused me just before such dreadful
" suffering, as confidently and certainly as ever did M. Angelo I believe."

The remarkable rhapsody from which I have quoted is laboriously and
crabbedly written, and shows no signs of being otherwise than honest. It
is needless to point out how strongly it savours of Blake ; and assuming
that it is the honest expression of mental action, it must create no little
wonder that even Blake could have infected any healthy mind to such a
great degree with his own nebulous way of regarding simple things. I
must not be understood as making any reflection upon the unmistakable
tone of piety that runs through the whole, but merely as deprecating a
certain morbid and effeminate tendency of thought, and the strange
hallucination that difficulties arising from want of knowledge or want of
physical energy arose from want of direct inspiration from on high.

The works to which this very unstudent-like student was labouring to

---

[1] This is probably the same visitation as that of the " kindly severe spirit " mentioned
previously.

give birth and for whose sake he turned his back. on London are remarkable for exaggerated attitude, unwieldy muscular form, and a nightmare composition for which even the teaching of Blake could not be held responsible. The spectator is repelled before he has time to discover little nooks of landscape which, in repletion of detail and their pleasing sentiment suggest some of Albert Dürer's backgrounds. Still further light will be thrown on the state of mind from which such remarkable conceptions grew by some notes written by my father in his copy of Payne Knight's *Analytical Inquiry into the Principles of Taste.*

[TEXT].—"Though not to be compared even with a third rate artist of " Ancient Greece in knowledge of the structure and pathology of the " human body, he [Michael Angelo] appears to have known more than " any of his contemporaries ; and when he made his knowledge subservient " to his art, and not his art to his knowledge, he produced some com- " positions of real excellence." [NOTE].—"He produced some composi- " tions of real excellence !! Michelangiolo produced some compositions " of real excellence !!!!! O ! Knight, had you spent your time in making " works yourself instead of writing about other people's, you might have " known better."

[TEXT *continued*].—"Such are almost all those, which he designed for " others to execute ; such as the Raising of Lazarus, the Descent from " the Cross, and the Entombing of Christ ; in which he lowered the tone " of his invention to meet the capacities of the colourists, Sebastian del " Piombo, and Daniel di Volterra ; and thus, through mere condescension, " became natural, easy, and truly sublime." [NOTE].—"What original " Inventor but can assert the impossibility of this. with respect to " Michelangiolo and anyone else ! He became truly sublime by lowering " the tone of his invention !!! Was this a descent to Parnassus or an " ascent to the Bathos ?"

[TEXT]. ". . . there has always appeared to me more of real grandeur " and sublimity in Raphael's small picture of the Descent of God, or " Vision of Ezekiel ;[1] and in Salvator Rosa's of Saul and the Witch of " Endor, than in all the vast and turgid compositions of the Sistine chapel. " Salvator, indeed, scarcely ever attempts grandeur of form, in the out- " lines of his figures ; but he as seldom misses, what is of much more im- " portance in his art, grandeur of effect in the general composition of his " pictures. In the wildest flights of his wild imagination, he always exhibits " just and natural action and expression ; of which the picture above " cited is a remarkable instance." [NOTE].—"Those artists who are " so base that they do not attempt grandeur of form and yet lyingly

---

[1] This picture is alluded to by my father in one of his letters, as an instance of the " condensing power of art."

" pretend to grand effect are now called modest : but those who, as
" William Blake, do attempt and achieve both will, with him, by blind
" cunning and stupid wilfulness be set down impudent madmen : for our
" taste is Dutch : Rembrandt is our Da Vinci, and Rubens our Michel-
" angiolo ! This is not an over-sounding of the depth of our degradation."

[TEXT *continued*].—" The visionary spectres in the background are wild
" and fantastic in their forms, as such fictitious beings might naturally be
" supposed to appear : but *the mixture* of horror and frenzy in the witch, of
" awe and anxiety in the monarch, and of terror and astonishment in the
" soldiers, *are* expressed, both in their countenances and gestures, with all
" the truth and nice discrimination of nature ; and with all the dignity and
" elevation of poetry. The general effect of the whole, too, is extremely
" grand and imposing ; and it is this general effect that pre-engages the
" attention, and thus disposes the mind to sympathize with the parts." [The
" italics are my father's.] [NOTE].—" As if he had said, ' You see,
" artist, what a light and trivial superfluity is grandeur of form in the out-
" lines of your figures, for here are produced without it not only more real
" grandeur and sublimity than are in all the Sistine Chapel, but here are
" individual figures wild and fantastic in their forms—here is a witch in
" whom are mixt horror and frenzy : here are awe and anxiety in a monarch ;
" here are terror and astonishment in the soldiers—here are all these
" express'd both in their countenances and GESTURES—mark ! their
" GESTURES—and that too with all the truth and nice discrimination
" of nature and with all the dignity and elevation of poetry, by one
" who scarcely ever attempts grandeur of form in the outlines of his
" figures !' Passions express'd not only in countenances but in gestures
" with all the dignity and elevation of poetry, by one who scarcely ever
" attempts grandeur of form in the outlines of his figures ! ! ! ! "

[TEXT *continued*].—" Those painters who, in their zeal for the grand
" style, affect to despise what they are pleased to call tricks of light and
" shade do in reality despise the most powerful means, which their art affords,
" of producing the effect, which they profess to aim at ; as will abundantly
" appear by the works of Titian, Rubens, and Rembrandt : who without
" any pretensions to grandeur of form, or dignity or elevation of character
" or expression, have produce grandeur, and more imposing pictures [Note
" ' or impositions '] than any of those, who have sought for grandeur in
" vast outlines and unusual postures" [Note " Was this intended for
" Fuseli ? "] [NOTE].—" Those painters who had a zeal for the grand
" style and practised it however they might despise tricks certainly never
" despised chiaroscuro. Michelangiolo's and Da Vinci's works are models
" of light and shade so profound, subtle, intense. and commanding that
" after *their* contemplation, the Venetian and Flemish pictures present only

" in their effects the miserable varieties of imitation, spiritless and castrated,
" blind wanderings and glaring impudence. To prove this, any perceiving
" mind need only carry before the works of Rembrandt the recollection of
" the copy of Da Vinci's Last Supper, which copy is at the Royal Academy,
" or look over Rembrandt's original etchings by the side of the *Illustrations*
" *of Job* by our most lamented William Blake."

It is easy to see from these notes what importance the writer attached
to grandeur of form, and it seems from his contemptuous allusion to our
" Dutch " taste that there had been a considerable change of opinion from
the time when he spoke of his so entirely losing all feeling for art that
he did not see "the greatest beauties of even the Dutch Masters."

At the end of the Payne Knight memoranda the following was written
some forty years later :—" I knew the positive and eccentric young man
" who wrote the notes in these pages. He believed in art (however
" foolishly) ; he believed in men (as he read of them in books). He spent
" years in hard study and reading and wished to do good with his know-
" ledge. He thought also it might with unwavering industry help towards
" an honest maintenance. He has now lived to find out his mistake. He
' is living somewhere in the environs of London, old, and neglected, isolated
" —laughing at the delusion under which he trimmed the midnight lamp
" and cherished the romance of the good and beautiful ; except so far as
" that, for their *own sake*, he values them above choice gold. He has
" learned however not to 'throw pearls to hogs' ; and appears, I believe,
" in company, only a poor good-natured fellow fond of a harmless jest."

Now if we turn after reading these notes of my father's to the most
singular of the works upon which he was engaged just after the time he
left London, we shall find it pretty evident that he himself "sought for
grandeur in vast outlines and unusual postures "; and that he spurred
his hobby onwards by means of his unmeasured admiration of Michael
Angelo, Fuseli and Blake, till in some instances, in seeking the sublime
he sank to the ridiculous.

In the first of the examples before me (all of them being in monochrome), two inordinately brawny female figures, one young, the other
older, are crammed into the opposite sides of a design measuring about
17 inches by $11\frac{1}{2}$. Between them is a low table bearing some small fruits,
and on the sward just beyond the barn or cottage where they sit, dance
four men and women in a measure which would do honour to the orgies of
any savages correspondingly muscular. A few sheep (in the conventional
rows affected by Blake) browse behind, and behind them again is a cottage
bosomed in rugged but abnormally fertile country. On one side, an open
manuscript shows certain biblical writings. Parts of the figures, such as the
extremities, are elaborated with evident pains and show some knowledge.

A still more remarkable design is one probably identical with the *Naomi before Bethlehem* which caused so many mental throes. The wildest conceptions of Blake and Fuseli combined with the most extravagant symbolism of early art could not be more wild and extravagant than this. It is of the same size as the drawing last described, but much more elaborate, and there are crowded into it seven or eight figures. Upon the right, staring fearfully and fixedly at the spectator, stands a woman. She points towards a kind of symbolic city which is half concealed by the flaming rays of a portentous sun, and her extended arms separate a heavy, shroud-like cloak. Leaning on her bosom in a somewhat graceful attitude is a girl in classical drapery. On the left and also in the foreground are two old men with limbs so huge, attitudes so contorted, and countenances so forbidding, that it is difficult to associate them in any way with the story of Ruth. They are reapers, and one holds in his hand an archaic sickle, his foot resting on bundles of corn. Behind them walks another reaper, and behind him again appear the grotesque heads of two oxen. In the middle of the background a sleeper pillows his head upon the abundant grain, while over him seems to hover a female spirit possessed by some great emotion. Close to the sun and just rising above the horizon, a crescent moon and six stars of astounding size blaze in the sky.

Such are the works for which the young painter bestowed his prayers and his energy during the first summer's residence in Kent, but it is art which is hardly of the kind suggested by some of the extracts I have quoted. Although intense of its kind. it does not look as if it grew so much from prayer, fasting, and thanksgiving as from inexperience lashed on by an ill-controlled and powerful imagination which, in its own turn, was nurtured by some strong and strange influence. If nature has been consulted, it has been consulted as it were in a distorting glass ; and the canons of an artistic fanaticism have prevailed against all else.

Now although the benefits of this strange practice were probably very small in proportion to the time expended, the results were not indefinite or doubtful. Had the same time been spent at an academy, or under the direct daily influence of any artist, the ideal which all this while steadily kept its place in the student's mind might have been extinguished, the search for the fuel which fed that ideal abandoned, and that unconscious plagiarism which gradually tempts the beginner to follow some school, or style, or individual might have become possible. By retiring to a lovely and secluded spot and there wrestling with difficulties which must have been appalling for the sake of this preconceived ideal the young artist risked professional extinction, but happened upon a tangled and disused path in art—one which he knew had been trodden by illustrious feet.

It was natural that the eremitical and uncouth form of artistic enthu-

siasm which I have described should be put down by any prosperous
London painter who concerned himself about it at all as professional
suicide. Accordingly, in the midst of the Shoreham accounts, there is a
rough draft of a letter to Mr. Linnell, part of which runs thus :—" I am
" startled by this sentence in a letter just received from my father, ' Mr.
" Linnell . . . foretells that your voluntary secession from artists will end
" in the withering of art in your mind. He has known it to be so . . . . ' "
Nevertheless, in spite of this warning, either the book of *Ruth* or the beautiful scenery of Kent held its own against the artists of London, and instead
of rejoining them my father made up his mind to leave town altogether.
A very small income, recently inherited, made him feel comparatively independent, but he had no intention of separating himself from his father.
While the student had been passing his time as we have seen, the bookseller
had determined to relinquish an unremunerative business, being willing no
doubt to leave a dingy house and the rattle of incessant traffic for a peaceful
and beautiful valley. So, taking with him his private library, and Mary Ward
as housekeeper, he joined his son at Shoreham, there " walled about with
books " to begin a long sojourn. It was to this period of his own life that
my father in his old age dearly loved to look back, and from the reminiscences of those seven glorious years, illustrated by the contents of a
portfolio devoted to the art of the same period, his hearers were able to
form in their minds a vivid and characteristic picture.

The neighbourhood of Shoreham is lovely still ; for by some fortunate
caprice of Capital, it has not only remained unfashionable, but has survived
with less devastation than usual the advent of the inevitable railway and
the attendant villa. The village is still adorned by much that is ancient,
and nestles in a hollow between two shapely shoulders of the chalk range
near Sevenoaks. It is threaded by the cheery, trout-haunted little Darent,
winding its way past old Lullingstone to Farningham and Dartford, through
old demesnes and water-meadows : while, here and there (to make it
pay its way as even the gayest rivers should), there rumbles a venerable
mill.

London is only twenty miles away ; but years ago, a distance now
disposed of by a few puffs of steam kept back that foul tide that has crept
little by little over so much of Kent and Surrey. No unsavoury crowds defiled
the sweet air with their ribaldry, and no shrieking engine startled the hares
from their twilight supper, or the herons from their patient watch over the
shallows. Everything connected with the little village in those happy
times seemed wrapped about with a sentiment of cosy, quiet antiquity,
full of associations that carried you far back into the pastoral life of
merry England, years ago.

Lingering on in the ancestral parks stood many a " shattered veteran " of a thousand winters' gales, glad enough at last to rest his aged limbs upon the ground they had shaded for centuries. Dingles and combes clothed with tall brakes or the wayfaring tree and whitethorn teemed with living things. Indeed, some of the ancient peasants stoutly maintained that snakes " of the bigness of a man's leg," and deadly lizards basked sleepily on out-of-the-way banks where men never passed. Moreover, a stout old yeoman, jogging home from market through the valley at twilight, once saw a flying reptile which, by dint of whip and spur, he overtook and slew ; and there, they said, it was to be seen by unbelievers the next day, lying on a wall at Otford, wings and all !

Spring clothed the innumerable orchards with clotted blossom, and Autumn never failed to fulfil this fair promise by lavishing the fruits in such profusion that the very leaves seemed in hiding, and the boughs were bent lower and lower till their treasure rested on the grass. Rich too were the harvests that the kindly soil gave to her sunburnt children, whose dress was beautiful and whose every implement was archaic. No grudging machinery clawed away the gleaner's perquisite, but they toiled on till the harvest-moon gilded their faces and the hungry owl gave them shrill warning of his supper-time.

As for the jovial time of hop-picking, the whole village made "sunshine holiday" then ; and age and youth and childhood, merrily singing as they worked, garnered in the fragrant crop without the help of strangers.

When winter came and great drifts lay upon the hills for weeks together, those happy countrymen plied their flails amain in huge, thatched barns where, centuries before, the good-natured goblin may have drudged with all his "awful strength" to earn his cream-bowl. Then, tired out, they betook themselves to the snug chimney-corner and listened, as the storm swept down the valley, to the old people's tales. For village superstitions lingered then in plenty, and as to the haunted chamber at the Grange, its dread secret was a topic for generation after generation of the rustic wiseacres.

Who shall picture in his mind the hues of those summer sunsets—the deep amber twilights throwing out into sharp and solemn relief the densely-wooded hills, with here and there a sailing heron, or a few belated rooks? Who shall describe those impassioned notes sung " so wild and well" in the May starlight, while each brake and coppice rang with an answer from a feathered throat? The tempests too, that burst upon the valley after days of sultriness, were far more terrific than ever afterwards, and once the lightning fell, it is said, like a very rain of fire.

The Moon herself bore little resemblance to the pallid, small reality we see above us nowadays. She seemed to blush and bend herself owards men (as when she stooped to kiss Endymion in olden time) casting a warm, romantic glow over the landscape that slept at her feet.

The village church, sixty years ago, was an example of the ineffable beauty time sometimes bestows on human handiwork as if to make amends for the short span of human life; but from this condition it has long since been effectually rescued. Rich and poor, gentleman, yeoman and labourer joined their lusty voices, led slowly by stringed and wind instruments. The cheery bells pealed year after year across the fields for gay weddings and national thanksgivings, but now the deepest of them all has tolled for each of those village worthies, who have rested side by side so long that the yellow lichen and tendrils of ivy have crept over their once familiar names and blotted out their virtues.

Such then was the "valley of vision" as my father saw it, and such the village where he took up his abode. He left London with a devoutly serious purpose, and with the certainty of failing in that purpose partly because his ideal was inaccessible, and partly through ascribing his failures to the wrong causes. A diminutive "independence" was made to stretch to the meagre limit of the most frugal habits, and his ignorance of the ways of the world well-nigh amounted to the childish simplicity of Blake's ideal. None of his ambitions and few of his wants seemed to be those of ordinary men, and it is therefore a small wonder that the life on which he was now entering should altogether differ from ordinary lives. His art, his writings, many of his tastes, and even his dress at this period were all strikingly peculiar: and the friends who afterwards frequented Shoreham having "congenial taste," they formed altogether a remarkable little clique which no doubt set the whole village agape.

When my father was no longer responsible for the Shoreham house-keeping the almost austere privations of his previous stay were in some slight degree relaxed, and a few recipes for savoury but always economical dishes found their way into the memorandum-books. The family allowed themselves one expensive luxury, and only one. Tea, costly as it then was, added such cosiness to the long evenings—such zest to Chaucer and Ben Jonson that it was irresistible. My father often began the winter's day with a plunge into the Darent and a breakfast of bread and apples; but when the moon looked over the woods of the eastward down, and the latten-bells of the last team had jangled by in the frosty air, the two enthusiasts and their friends put the steaming tea-pot by the fire and reached down the tall folios from the book-shelves.

"Waterhouse," the scene of these literary revels, still stands. It is close to the bridge, and has, over the meadows and long straggling village street, a pretty western prospect bounded by yews and beeches which cap the opposite hill. Behind, rises the larger down, which rolls far away till it opens again for the River Medway at Rochester.

Most of the frequenters of the "House of the Interpreter" (and the "Interpreter" himself, I believe), found their way to "Waterhouse" (journeying sometimes by coach, sometimes on foot) and often stayed there while they filled their sketch-books. Even Mr. Linnell felt the common enthusiasm when he looked down upon the village and wrote a characteristic letter to my father, dated August, 1826 :—" I have found so much "benefit from my short visit to your valley, and the very agreeable way in "which we spent the time, that I shall be under the necessity of seeing you "again very soon at Shoreham. I dream of being there every night almost, "and when I wake it is some time before I recollect that I am at Bayswater.[1] ". . . . How I shall recompense you for your kindness I know not, but I "am so set upon the thing that I am induced to run the risk of imposing "upon it to the utmost, until time affords me some opportunity of testifying "my sense of your hospitality, for though I have been at many places on "visits, I never was anywhere so much at liberty . . . P.S. Pray squire me "no squires. It is not my desire to be ever called 'squire.'"

The friends called themselves "The Ancients," and their watch-words were "Poetry and Sentiment." Their personal appearance was as strange as their habits. My father, for instance, has been described as "remarkable for a certain baldness over the forehead which, added to a flowing beard (a thing to be looked at in those days), together with a cloak down almost to the heels, gave him to passers-by the appearance of an apparition, by no means an unpleasant one, but certainly not youthful."[2] All this singularity, of course had sorely puzzled the villagers, who called the new comers "Extollagers" and looked upon their camp-stools (hitherto unknown in those parts), as the appliances of some dark science. This is not surprising, for my father writes that "summer nights were spent under the open sky to watch the Northern glimmer and the flushes of early dawn," —that Locke's *Macbeth* music was "sung by night in hollow clefts and deserted chalk-pits," and that sometimes the climax of a tragedy was roughly improvised in a certain Black Lane, a dark, lonely place, and the scene of a half-forgotten murder.

The party often walked by night to distant villages, or carefully chosen spots far away among the hills, whence they could see the sunrise over the flower of Kentish scenery. They were also especially fond of those effects that gather in the sky with great summer tempests, and at the first mutter of approaching thunder, whether by day or night, they hurried out and revelled in the thickest of the storm.

[1] He had left Hampstead and had built a house at Bayswater.
[2] *Memorials of F. O. Finch*, p. 47.

A crew so nocturnal would have tried the patience of anyone less amiable than my grandfather ; but Mr. Richmond still remembers that he would get up even at one o'clock in the morning to make tea for the young men ; and would give up his own bed if any of them arrived on an unexpected visit, dead beat with walking.[1]

In the course of time " The Ancients " made many acquaintances among the villagers, none the less welcome for horny hands and plain manners. The very idiot (an original idiot withal), who basked away his life upon the bridge in sunny weather, looked for their coming, for one and all stopped for a few words of greeting.

In the churchyard of neighbouring Otford, hard by the ruins of the old castle, we may now read these words upon a goodly headstone. " Here reposes in Jesus Christ, the body of Richard Lipscombe late of this Parish." Now " Dick " was the ostler of Otford Inn, but by reason of his quaint wit and his aptitude for making impromptu verses he became an especial favourite with the whole party. They never forgot each other, and many years afterwards one of the number (Mr. John Giles), not long before his own death raised this grave-stone in the old man's memory.

Dick recorded my grandfather's ministrations to the neighbourhood in a poem which opened thus :—

> " A gentleman to Otford comes,
> Led by the love of Souls,
> Which Muster Bradley don't believe,
> Nor neither Muster Bowles."

It seems that these ministrations did not lack energy, for the minstrel sang :—

> " Palmer is a man of God,
> He *is* a sound divine,
> For when he doth expound the word,
> His face doth always shine."

Space forbids me to recall all the stories I have so often heard when the few survivors of " The Ancients " foregathered in my father's study at Red Hill. Among them there was one touching a meek and grievously henpecked baker whose jealous wife furtively tracked him as he went his rounds among the village maids and matrons. He had a tame jackdaw which had learnt by heart most of her favourite conjugal admonitions, especially this, " *Ah!* Thomas V——, Thomas V——, You hadn't a shirt to your back when *I* married you, Thomas V——." Placed thus between two fires, the man, meek as he was, wrung the bird's neck one day, in self-defence. He was given to unusually emphatic prayer at chapel,

[1] My father's journeys to London were still, for the most part, on foot, but were sometimes shortened by a lift in the carrier's cart, or in a lumbering fruit-waggon bound to the Borough market.

of which his wife disapproved : so when he waxed very fervid, she clapped her handkerchief upon his mouth.

It was either literature or music that wiled away my father's hours of leisure ; for neither he nor, I think, many of the clique ever acquired the smallest interest in the time-honoured country sports, for some of which there must have been opportunities. There was a curious absence of the innate and almost universal instinct which makes these sports so peculiarly the solace of an Englishman. He rode and drove a little, but the somewhat disastrous results detailed in his descriptions of these experiences were not flattering either to his skill or to the cattle on which he tried it. But his substitute for exercise was so unusual a capacity for enjoying a quiet hour spent over a favourite author or design that it appeared to usurp the place of ordinary active recreations. He certainly suffered physically from this peculiarity, and there is little doubt that, even mentally, he would have been none the worse for a measure of exhilarating outdoor exercise. The lugubrious poetry and morbid prose upon which he sometimes spent his time would have been better unwritten ; and the troubles which caused him to give way in that manner would have appeared less formidable if he had found some healthy distraction other than mere walking, or an occasional jolt upon a superannuated cart-horse.

As it was, he had plenty of leisure to read very attentively such solid works as Butler's *Analogy*, Barrow on the Creed, and the Lives of the Saints and Fathers, books which deepened his natural piety not a little. He writes :—" I mean to get the print of the Venerable Fisher and his fellow-" martyr Sir Thomas More, and hang them cheek by jowl in my little chapel, " that they may frown vice, levity, and infidelity out of my house and out of " my heart." This office the pair seem to have performed very effectually, as my father approached even his painting almost in the spirit of a Fra Angelico, or as some devout young monk would have set him down to illuminate a breviary. Few undertakings were begun without prayer or finished without thanksgiving, both of these being sometimes committed to writing. If the fits of melancholy to which he was subject made invention tedious or difficult, inspiration was invoked, as it had been invoked by Blake, humbly, and I think quite sincerely, from above. In Blake's own words, it seemed as if ". . . God who loves all honest men " led " the poor enthusiast in the paths of holiness." Nevertheless, many of the writings and doings of this period are so strange that, but for the strong vein of sincerity which runs through them, they would be a laughing-stock, instead of deserving respect as the growth (however erratic) of a naturally simple and sincere character.

I have spoken of troubles that marred a time of otherwise unbroken tranquillity. Rather more than a year after he left London, my father was

In Lullingstone Park, near Shoreham.

told that William Blake had died. It was a loss he must have felt very keenly, but he was able even thus early in life to embalm the memory of the dead with the hope of a reunion in an unspeakably fair land where tears will fall no more. After a time of another great sorrow in 1829, he wrote thus. "The allurements of this world promise much and reward " little, but the studies and exercises of wisdom, virtue, and holiness, seeming " at first crabbed and dull, hold in their hard shell endless and unsating " variety of true pleasures."

It will perhaps have occurred to the reader that, hitherto, I have been describing the career, not of an artist likely to "make a mark" in his profession, but rather, the career of a misled, mystical fanatic, who, in spite of warnings and in spite of good examples, persisted in his strange beliefs, impossible ideals, and in a course tending to professional extinction, or to a life marked by "deepening neglect," such as the life of Blake. A certain passage, however, in the note book of 1824 that I have more than once quoted should be remembered. "Look for Van Leydenish " qualities in real landscape, and look hard, long, and continually. Look " for picturesque combinations of buildings, and elegant spires, and turrets " for backgrounds." My father never for one moment forgot how essential to a painter is the close and devoted study of nature. Little of Linnell's or Mulready's advice on this point was thrown away on him, and now that he was surrounded on all sides by beauty, that advice began to bear fruit an hundredfold. With the occasional interposition of a careful, life-size portrait, or an elaborate, still-life study, he was continually sketching out of doors ; and as for the atmospheric phenomena known to artists as "effects," they had long been, and continued always to be, the object of constant and earnest observation. Lullingstone Park, lying between Shoreham and Eynsford, was a deservedly favourite sketching-ground, for its lovely glades were shaded by trees so huge and old that some of them may have lived long before the first pious pilgrims wended their way along the neighbouring hills to Canterbury. Among my father's Lullingstone studies is one in pencil of two trees, which (as the reader may see) is worthy of note.

The youth who drew these trees so conscientiously, although he was somewhat fanatical and given to nebulous theories (besides over-much melancholy), was, in fact, worshipping nature : and he was looking "hard, long, and continually" at what he called "real landscape." He had said, moreover, "In proportion as we enjoy and improve in imaginative art we shall love the material works of God more and more." Having assured ourselves of these facts we will turn to a letter he wrote to Mr. Richmond about 1829—that is, in the third year of the Shoreham era and in the 24th year of his age. There, we shall find the following singular declaration :—

" I will not infringe a penny on the money God has given me, beyond
" the interest, but live and study in patience and hope. By God's help I
" will not sell his precious gift of art for money; no, nor for fame neither,
" which is far better. Mr. Linnell tells me that, by making studies of the
" Shoreham scenery, I could get a thousand a year directly. Though I
" am making studies for Mr. Linnell, I will, God help me, never be a
" naturalist [1] by profession." Although there is a tinge of grandiloquence
about these words, they express a resolution which, however much it was
temporarily modified by circumstances in after life, was really the key note
of the whole of the artist's career, from the day when he fixed his gaze on
Turner's *Orange Merchantman.* To quote his own words, he " lived to find
out his mistake "; and " old, neglected, isolated," to laugh " at the delusion
under which he trimmed the midnight lamp, and cherished the romance
of the good and the beautiful." But, nevertheless, the resolution did not
cease to exist, and lasted on till the day came when he took up his pencil
for the last time. It will be seen reflected as clearly in his last works as in
any of the innumerable designs which he did in his " valley of vision."

We may ask ourselves what it is that separates these designs so
completely into a class by themselves—which makes them hold so much
together, and yet, collectively, stand so utterly alone. Even the Shoreham
studies from nature, faithful as they are, show much besides the mere
difference of handling and their particular degree of skill which separates
them from the studies of any subsequent period. The problem is a hard
one. Among the reasons we may find (we can never find them all), besides
the resolution I have quoted, I think are these. A primitive and old-
world sentiment, allied to a somewhat analogous execution. A brooding
peacefulness, and a certain sentiment of surpassing fruitfulness. The
absence from the artist's mind of any prudential or sordid check on a
superlatively poetic bent and on a superlatively strong imagination. The
continual recourse to the finest literature, and particularly to poetry
mellowed by time. Lastly, there were those strong " loves of the mind,"
and " dearest landscape longings," which were the cause of his being
" entranced " by certain things he met with from time to time in nature.
Be all this as it may, every example of the Shoreham art is stamped, so to
speak, with a peculiar hall-mark; and I think that those who are qualified
to judge will find that it is a mark which guarantees sterling metal.

Among the oil pictures of this period (painted for the most part on
thick panels) *The Harvest-moon,* which was exhibited at the Royal Academy
in 1833, is a typical example; as although it is so small ($10\frac{3}{4} \times 8\frac{3}{4}$ inches)

---

[1] My father does not mean a naturalist in the common sense, but a popular kind of
painter who makes his living—often his fortune—by copying pretty bits of scenery
warranted to sell, and ingeniously sprinkling them with figures and animals to taste.

it is full of the Shoreham sentiment, and is not without some of the accompanying peculiarities. The moon has risen behind some lofty timber, driving back the mysterious shadows from the cornfield below, till all is bathed in rich, amber light. Few other scenes would accord so well with the profound peacefulness of the deep azure sky, jewelled by a brilliant constellation—with the repose of the mysterious landscape threaded by a winding river. There is nothing out of place in the laden waggon with its team of oxen, or in the harvest labourers, for their dress proclaims them labourers of long ago. *A Landscape Twilight* is a picture of the same diminutive size as *The Harvest Moon*, but one in which the " condensing power of art " impresses the eye with a feeling of space and fulness. A team of oxen drag a laden waggon past an old farm or manor-house, and, from one of the lattices, a stream of ruddy light falls on a hillock in the foreground, where a flock of sheep rests for the night. The waggoner, leaning on his staff, stands with his back to us, looking across a deep, wooded valley towards distant hills which sleep under the last gleam of departing day. The wild, gloomy sky I have already referred to as savouring of Linnell's influence. Both these pictures, like all of the same period, are remarkable for their suggestiveness, calling forth our own more timid imagination, and leading it away to explore the recesses of a romantic country without allowing us to realize the fact that our explorations are really bounded by a little paint upon a wooden panel.[1]

Of the seventeen works that were admitted to the Academy from 1826 to 1833 (the years of the Kentish sojourn), five are described as twilights. Twilight was a time always intensely loved by the painter, who made it his constant study ; especially when the moon, with some attendant planet, softly asserts her supremacy over the amber or crimson sky, and village lights begin to glimmer. The preference is natural, for it is a time which, in very beautiful country, conveys a pleasure very much akin to that given by solemn and stately music of the highest order.

One of the largest and most characteristic of the Shoreham pictures is upon a thick panel measuring twenty-eight by twenty inches. The doors of a great barn (on the floor of which we stand) are open before us, and form a kind of frame to the subject. In the chequered shade of some trees outside, a group of men and girls are busy over their sheep-shearing. Beyond and far below them an expanse of undulating country rolls away, glowing in a flood of sunshine. Within the barn on our right is a group of admirably painted rural implements, together with a rustic hat which

---

[1] Many of the best of these pictures, after half a century of neglect, were sold to my father's cousin, Mr. John Giles, the most appreciative purchaser they could possibly have found—one who remembered their progress. At his death, they realized prices at Christie's which would have astonished painter and former purchaser alike, if they could have been foreseen at the time the pictures were being painted.

was one of my father's most treasured possessions, occurring over and over again in the works of this time. A striking feature in the picture is the bold colouring peculiar to this era in the painter's life.

Of the Shoreham water-colours I have many that are notable, from among which I will mention a couple as examples of the attempt to convey a sentiment of extraordinary fruitfulness and lavish prodigality on the part of nature. The first shows an apple-tree standing in an old-fashioned, walled garden. The tree is in blossom, but the ordinary sense of this word fails to convey any idea of the clotted masses of white and pink that hide the branches and leaves, and glow in the stream of glorious sunlight that pours down upon them. The whole subject, from the white cumulus cloud above to the flowers of the garden, forms a sparkling, gorgeous mass of colour, almost tropical in its intensity. The technical handling is as noteworthy as the conception for, although in water-colour, so thickly are the various blossoms painted that the drawing may be compared to a cameo of low relief. An autumnal design forms a fitting companion. Between the banks of a hollow, shady lane, a shepherd pipes to a few sheep as lazy as himself. Over these and beyond them is a church spire bosomed in trees, and in the background there abruptly rises a hill thickly covered with ripe corn which blazes in the sun like burnished gold, against a very dark and thunderous sky. Overhanging the lane is an apple-tree loaded to the extremity of every twig with bright crimson apples so numerous and so enormous as far to surpass the utmost stretch of possibility.

These two drawings are evidently based upon actual scenes; but the artist's passionate love for Ceres and Pomona has led him from the land of plain fact into fairy-land. Throughout his life he revelled in richness and abundant fruitfulness, and it is easy to see from the two subjects I have just described, how he was attracted by such a sentiment as that conveyed by the concluding verses of the sixty-fifth Psalm. Therefore, when he encountered in nature any instance of prodigal profusion, whether of foliage, blossom, or fruit, his delight took his imagination by the hand and led it far away from beaten tracks. The result is either impressive or ridiculous according to our capacity of understanding and appreciating the qualities aimed at, and the earnestness of the attempts to embody them.

My father, early in his Kentish sojourn, had "beheld as in the spirit such nooks—caught such glimpses of perfumed and enchanted midsummer twilight," that he wished he could paint them on ivory as backgrounds to figures. Where he attempted to accomplish this, the result is very peculiar. In the example before me (measuring about 3½ inches long), we have the head and shoulders of a very dark and heavy-browed young man who gazes at us out of the picture. The intense colour of the flesh and hair is height-

Ruth Return'd from Gleaning.

The Bright Cloud.

ened with real gold, and behind the red and green drapery that swathes his shoulders—behind his long black locks is a small space into which are compressed a solemn, twilight sky; a landscape with a church, a castle, and a windmill: and, on a foreground knoll, a few Druidic remains brilliantly lighted from the same source as the face itself. The painting is so thick that even the transparent tints stand up after the manner of bas-relief. If such performances as this were in any degree inspired by the Shoreham scenery, as there is every reason to believe, they are forcible evidence that Blake's "double vision" had descended very liberally upon his disciple.

By far the greater number of the Shoreham water-colours were painted in monochrome, such as bistre, sepia, or ivory black. They include several separate series of subjects which are alike in size. The pastoral element largely preponderates, moonlights or twilights being very common. The earliest of these series is remarkable for a Chaucer-like quaintness, and for a somewhat primitive and pre-Raphaelite handling. The Blake tradition is evident, and there is the same indescribable affinity I have pointed out before, between these and all other contemporary works of the young painter. Next in succession come a considerable number of careful but exceedingly bold drawings in sepia or ivory black, which show a greater feeling for nature than those last mentioned without any sacrifice of poetry, while, at the same time, there is no lack of variety of subject and originality of design. One of the boldest of this group has for its chief feature a huge bank of cumulus clouds which look (as Mr. Hook says of the cumuli of Cadore) as if you could knock your head against them. They are lighted by a low evening sun which has already left a middle-distant, woodland valley in dense shadow. Some sheep repose upon a foreground knoll, and a girl fingers the pastoral pipe relinquished to her by a young shepherd. The execution is a compound of pen and brush-work, and varies from the most emphatic boldness in the nearer trees to delicate modelling in the clouds above. This was the precursor of that oil-picture of the same subject, previously mentioned as one of those which shows a Linnell-like treatment in the sky, and it was perhaps inspired by the "glorious round clouds" in painting which my father thought Linnell so excelled. A series of very small designs in sepia also done about this time is singular for poetry of subject, graceful composition, and for more delicate handling than the predecessors.

Of the monochromes I have two which were exhibited in the Royal Academy in 1829. Of one, *Ruth returned from Gleaning.* I am able to give a small reproduction. A "sketch" was exhibited with the *Ruth*, under the title of *The Deluge.* Beneath a dark lowering sky, an illimitable waste of waters bears the distant ark, and surges round a few isolated, foreground rocks which it will soon cover. Stretched supine upon them either dead or dying lies at full length a tall and beautiful undraped woman. One arm rests on her dead child, the other falls, together with her long hair, into the waves. The treatment of the figure is an immense advance upon such crude and jaundiced imaginations as the *Naomi before Bethlehem*.

If we hurriedly turn over the mass of these Shoreham productions we shall probably be struck first by the predilection shown for moons, church spires, flocks of sheep, twilights, and cornfields, and then by the fact that there is so little sameness or repetition in design. A fondness for certain effects and certain objects has not impaired the fertility of the inventor's imagination in representing them. Thus, we are shown more distinctly than by a hundred written ratifications how genuine was the resolution expressed in the letter to Mr. Richmond. Had the artist depended for his material solely on the fields, and woods, and hills around him, and had he used that material in a sordid way he might have given us faithful representations of those he selected, but there would have been inevitable repetition, and he would never have shown us as he has undoubtedly done the very spirit and quintessence of the loveliest and most poetic pastoral scenery—scenery which we may imagine as that of ancient England, when shepherds piped upon their pipes, and the clouds dropped fatness. There is no slavish allegiance to what is usually and often falsely called "Truth to Nature;" and to this freedom, strange as it may seem, we owe a fascination which, although it cannot possibly be described in words, has been felt even by artists who are themselves realistic. There is a passage in a letter to Mr. Richmond dated October 16, 1834, alluding to a certain visit made by that artist to Devonshire, which is very significant. The writer was probably deeply impressed by his friend's reminiscences—those (it must be remembered) of a highly imaginative artist, and he evidently kept them before him while he was at work.

Thoroughness stamped everything that was done at Shoreham, and there was that love and concentration of spirit which will generally pluck a man from the deep and dismal ditch of mediocrity and set him on his feet. There were no smatterings, and there was no sub-division of energy into a thousand little channels. What was worth doing at all was considered to be worth doing heartily, and consequently both work and recreation (such as it was) were enjoyed to the full. Technically, there is evidence of a vigour of manipulation equivalent to the vigour of a somewhat wilful but eminently original mind ; and just as an impassioned orator will carry his audience with him more easily than one far more correct but calm and mechanical in delivery, so this strong colour and fearless draughtsmanship take hold of the spectator, and compel his attention more authoritatively than many an exhibition water-colour with unexceptionable qualifications for the ornamental cord and rosette of the Philistine drawing-room.

Even as early as this Shoreham period, the pen was a favourite implement, and it is astonishing with what vigour and certainty my father plied it. Attacking the core of each design, he drew it boldly in with black, or bistre, or sepia ; sometimes with little, sometimes with great regard to minute detail. Upon this firm basis, colour as bold and significant was fearlessly superimposed. The finish was never equally distributed, but was always focussed on the kernel ; each subject being evidently chosen in the first instance with peculiar care from a teeming mass of mental material.

The oil pictures, like many of their companions, were often begun in tempera[1], and were wrought not only to a great extent in the technical manner, but also, as we have seen, in the devout spirit of some of the mediæval pictures. Although purchased with difficulty out of the most scanty means, none but the very choicest materials were used, even to pure gold and ultramarine ; for brilliancy and durability were considered as above all things imperative. The pure, white grounds (touching which remarks will be found in the letters), and the preparation of the heavy panels to receive them were matters of especial solicitude. The former were laid with " Blake's white," a pigment for making which Blake gave my father the recipe. As for the capacious brass syringes (a cumbrous and costly invention which succeeded the bladders used for holding paint), many a laborious day was spent in filling them ; and not far from where I am writing rests the great marble slab, grinding on which the enthusiast used "to swette and swinke" till the colours reached an ideal refinement of texture.

As a contrast to the peacefulness of the life I have described there came an outbreak of political fever, but it was at a time of such great public agitation that the infection of the village is not extraordinary. In Kent and elsewhere machinery had been destroyed, barns and stacks burned, and threatening letters dispersed. It was just after the passing of the great Reform Bill that my father wrote *An address to the Electors of West Kent* which was printed in considerable numbers : though not, I should imagine, at the author's expense. That he partook of the vehement excitement of the time is shown by the fieriness of his arguments : and it is strange that, in spite of his wide reading, in spite of the almost universal misery of the agricultural classes—misery of which he must have heard even in thrice happy Shoreham, his arguments should have leaned in the most party-spirited manner possible to the side opposed to reform.

---

[1] Sometimes drawing-paper was glued to the panel, and the picture painted upon that.

Although the uncompromising opinions and language of this squib afterwards became a source of some amusement to its author, it is by no means without power, and it is evidently the offspring of a cultivated mind warped by a strong bias.

With the exception of this political episode the seven years' residence at Shoreham, as described by "The Ancients" themselves, is most pleasing to contemplate, for it is not saddened by any evidences of the wide-spread agricultural distress, and it almost savours of the pastoral age. "Over-pressure" had not then reached the village school-room; the ploughman's boy was innocent of a hundred ill-digested smatterings, and sylvan peace was rarely broken by the clank of machinery. A "lenient penury" chained my father to the valley, laying the foundation of the wholesome tastes and quiet manners of his after life, and he had time to drink deeply of the knowledge Nature bestows on such as are worthy of her confidence. Perhaps there may be some, even in these more enlightened days, who would gladly relapse into a time of like tranquillity, with leisure to follow a refined and thoughtful calling unjostled by the crowded ranks of an army of competitors. The quietness of the young artist's life, quite as much as the great beauty of the surrounding country, had a most beneficent influence upon his art and, as I have said, his Shoreham works, whether on paper, ivory, or panel—in monochrome or colour are impressed more or less distinctly with peacefulness—with a peculiar archaic and poetic sentiment. A hostile analysis would reveal great peculiarities, but there is nothing common-place and there is no mere affectation of pre-Raphaelitism. If any feel within them even the faintest vibrations of a responding chord, they will be moved quite as much by the work the young village enthusiast produced at this time as by any efforts of his after life. To the man who would disdain to wile away a summer among those hop-gardens and orchards, to saunter at twilight over those romantic hills, it is art that appeals utterly in vain.

There is an analogy between the writings and the art of this period of my father's life which those who are familiar with each will detect easily. We find in both, often united with much quaintness of expression, the evidence of certain opinions which are rare and unpopular. These opinions steadily grew, and there were few, if any, of those abrupt changes of method, purpose, and belief, commonly associated with youth, especially youth unrestrained by any scholastic discipline. A very young mind which is not only its own disciplinarian but a martinet in self-discipline is rare, and in my father's earlier letters much occurs which, considering the writer's age, is remarkable. The opinions of his riper years on many subjects may be likened to mature timber whose seedlings sprouted in the Kentish valley. Time pruned them here and there with the keen knife of experience, but the stems increased and remained firmly rooted through all life's storms.

As we turn from these simple and happy days of earnest but unhurried energy, perhaps we shall feel a tinge of the regret with which my father looked back to the old cottage by the Darent when the time came to bid it farewell. No longer would the hours be wiled away with "literature, and art, and ancient music." Disappointment after disappointment was to be met, and bereavements to be borne which nearly broke his heart. Only by eschewing much that is considered essential to happiness, by refusing much that is demanded by society, could be preserved untainted to after life the benign influence of this time of probation — a period of rest mercifully given on the eve of life's battle.

CHAPTER III

1833 TO 1848

PROBABLY it was quite of his own free will that my father broke up the country home, and brought to a close a period which he afterwards regarded as, on the whole, the happiest of his life. Being now 28 years old, he may have begun to feel that a manly career involved something more than mere enthusiasm for art and literature—more than a practice such as his had been for the last seven years. He still "believed in art (however foolishly); he believed in men (as he read of them in books);" he had "spent years of hard study and reading, and wished to do good " with his knowledge. He thought also it might, with unwavering in- " dustry, help towards an honest maintenance." At last even some prickings of ambition may have prompted him to join the ranks of the stern mercenaries who are eternally thronging to the front, there to fall or become honourable. The little "independence," as he called it, upon which he had so long contrived to live in contentment and even in a kind of luxury seemed to shrink into its true proportions ; so, at last, he determined to return to London. He settled in a small house he had bought with the proceeds of a bequest, in Grove Street, Lisson Grove, where he was within easy reach of Mr. Linnell at Bayswater, and of his old friend Mr. Edward Calvert, then living at Park Place, Paddington.

Whether my grandfather accompanied his son to Grove Street at this time, I do not know ; but as we find him soon afterwards following the profession of a schoolmaster, I think it is doubtful, and I have met with no allusion to any other companions in the little house, save the faithful Mary Ward and a favourite cat.

My father, towards the end of his stay at Shoreham, had discovered that " the expenses of one person living as an epic poet should live " could be cut down to 5s. 2d. a week : but the old memorandum-books reveal that he found it no easy matter to achieve this economy. For instance, the poet's estimated nightly allowance of one candle grievously curtailed the nocturnal talks and readings to which all " The Ancients " were so much addicted. My father was also perturbed by faults which he now began to discern in his practice and style, and he catalogues them as follows. " Some of my faults. *Feebleness* of first conception through bodily " weakness, and consequent timidity of execution. No first-conceived,

" and *shapely* effect. No rich, flat body of local colours as a ground. No
" first-conceived foreground, or figures.

| " Whites too raw. | Greens crude. |
| " Greys cold. | Shadows purple. |

" RIDGES OF MOUNTAIN ALONG OPEN COUNTRY.

This list is followed by suggestions for his future practice :—

"(1) Base the subject on a neutral-tint effect like Varley's little drawing,
" so that at the beginning the great shapes of the lights shall be forcibly
" announced. (2A) Invent at once the great masses of Local Colour,
" and aim at once at a splendid arrangement. (B) Blocks of local colour
" before the small varieties. (3) Carry on the drawing till real illumination
" be obtained. Investigate on some simple object what are the properties
" of illumination and shade. (4) If possible, complete at whatever struggle
" the foreground and figures at the time. (5) Let everything be colour,
" and not sullied with blackness. Think of some of Titian's things, as
" *The Entombment.* (6) CLEANNESS OF TINT. Try to get something
" beautiful in the first design."

Written in the same place are the records of many and elaborate experiments in oil vehicles which evidently consumed a large amount of time. We find also long tables relating to colours, and (for the first time) some particulars concerning pupils, from which it appears that, even thus early, my father had secured a good, though small teaching connection.

It so happens that most of the " faults " he confesses to are not to be found in the works of the six or seven preceding years. They show neither "feebleness of first conception," "timidity of execution," nor any lack of " shapely " effects. We must therefore conclude either that he accused himself falsely or that prudential motives had led to a temporary retrogression which he soon endeavoured to check.

Six subjects were exhibited at the Academy in 1834, all evidently chosen from Kentish scenery ; but in the following year we find a *Scene from Lee, North Devon.* This is the first record of a series of visits to a country which, even before he had explored it, seems to have commended itself to my father's affections, and afterwards became his ideal of English scenery. I have not seen any letter of his referring to this particular journey, but he tells us that it was brought about by some third-rate print of Combe Martin Bay which he saw in a shop-window. Stirred up by that, he went westwards till he found in the "heaped up richness " of the loveliest of counties nearly all he desired in landscape.

To those familiar with his works it will be unnecessary to point out how, in some of his later designs, he idealized Devonshire just as he idealized Italy—how it enriched his imagination and influenced his choice of subject. Perhaps the best example of this is a drawing of the Milton Series (painted towards the close of his life), known as *Morning.* He says of it, "If my moor remind the spectator of anything North of South Devon I have laboured in vain." He even went so far as to place his "habitable latitudes" "south of the railings of Hyde Park, and their kernel in Devonshire." It was in this way that he expressed an unaccountable prejudice against Scotland, a country which he never saw or desired to see : regarding it with an antipathy worthy of Dr. Johnson himself.

In the year of this Devonshire journey, my father accompanied Mr. Calvert in a North Wales sketching-tour, being joined on the way by another of "The Ancients," Mr. Henry Walter.[1] It was the first sight of mountainous country, and though it was a country that, in his opinion, contained "the finest prospect in the principality," it failed to gain such a hold on his affections as that which was fruitful and abounding in the rich, pastoral and agricultural sentiment he loved so dearly. The weather was, for the most part, unfavourable for fine effects ; and save for a glimpse or two through rifts in stormy cloud hanging about the mountains, the travellers were not fully recompensed for their journey till they were well on their homeward way. As a child he had "a passionate love for the monuments and traditions of the Church, its cloistered Abbeys, Cathedrals, and Minsters ;" and now he saw, "rising from a wilderness of orchards and set like a gem amidst the folding of wooded hills," the remains of Tintern Abbey. To a mind toned by a secluded life and by the works of the old fathers and divines, such a place was far more than a subject for a sketch, or an archæological curiosity. Its grey walls and crumbling mullions were eloquent of ancient days when the chanted vespers deepened the solemnity of the twilight, and the glimmering lamp or taper dimly showed forth the hues of the tall windows. Touched to the heart he sat down before the ruins and, as he plied his pencil, recalled the times of old when the Abbey and its library of illuminated manuscripts were a fair oasis in a desert of ignorance and violence.

Especially fond of studying the phenomena of water, he had already secured (in spite of the unfavourable weather) a series of careful sketches of the finest falls ; but at Tintern he was abruptly checked by want of money. The Welsh expenses, simply as he had lived, had surpassed his expectations and had left him at last even without the means of getting home. Mr. Walter happened to be in the same predicament and hence arose the

---

[1] This artist resembled Mr. Calvert, inasmuch as his talents justified a far greater measure of professional success than he seems to have achieved. He was an animal-painter of no common merit, and though my father greatly treasured a number of examples of his old friend's skill which he possessed, those examples show that, of all "The Ancients," Mr. Walter was perhaps the least influenced by Blake.

appeal to Mr. Richmond which will be found in its place among the letters. The incident was typical of what was to come. Henceforth, prosaic and ruthless necessities dispelled as fast as they arose most of my father's day-dreams and reveries, but at the same time spurred him onwards towards the attainment of a professional standing.

About this time or rather later he writes to a friend as follows, " . . . hav-" ing for the last two or three years used the brush incessantly, " almost to the exclusion of the pen, I scarce know what to write about " or how to write. It is sad that surrounded by so many glorious pursuits " —painting, music, eloquence, and the Heaven-descended sciences—such " continual and almost exclusive attention is necessary to proficiency in " any one of them as, in some measure, shuts one up from the rest. " Painting, however, does not harden the heart or obliterate the remem- " brance of intellectual intercourse. But we are the servants of time and " space which cut off, sometimes for life, the most delightful intercourse ; " and we should be the slaves, but for the mellowing influence of memory, " which has many a time brought back to me the happy hours in which " I was favoured with your society. I passed Ryde in a steamboat the " summer before last, on my way to Wales, and wished to pause in vain.

" As I believe you take a very kind interest in my welfare, I will tell you " what has been my manner of life since we met, at the risk of egotism. I " have forsworn other loves and devoted myself exclusively to my Art— " have made two long tours in Wales which have been the means of making " me some useful connections and gradually improving the aspect of my " circumstances, and what I value much more, of laying the foundation, " I hope, of solid attainments. Meanwhile the cranium becomes stuffed " with gallipots and varnishes ; the blessed winter-evening talks are " curtailed ; and with the exception now and then, of a whole play of " Shakespeare at a gulp and now and then your favourite *Christabel*, " matters go on much more prosily and orderly.

" It is very much easier to give vent to the romantic by speech than to " get it all the way down from the brain to the fingers' ends, and then " squeeze it out upon canvas. However, I should be sadly grieved to for- " swear all the nice, long, old-fashioned talks. . . . . . and know of no one " with whom I should more enjoy a revival of them than with yourself. " The little knot of friends remain united as you left them, only, if possible, " more closely cemented than ever. We talk, now and then, of old times " and wish you were with us ; which desire, no one feels more sincerely " than, my dear Sir, Yours faithfully and affectionately, SAMUEL PALMER."

As my father's knowledge of nature increased, he began to turn over in his mind the possibility of making a pilgrimage to see the master-pieces of art in Italy, and at the same time, of feasting his eyes on landscapes so replete with old associations—on antique cities whose every stone told the history of heroes, philosophers, and poets. He even expected, he says, to see Claude's "magical combinations." Before the days of photography (for it wanted two years or more to the introduction of even Daguerre's process), all that an impecunious student was likely to secure to whet his appetite for the wonders of foreign art were perhaps a few conventional line engravings, or an etching or two. As to the expenses and discomforts of travel, they alone were enough to deter any poor man from leaving England. Nevertheless for two years after he had evidently made up his mind to find his way to Italy, my father bided his time, working on with redoubled energy and contributing, meanwhile, to the Academy exhibition a few of his newly-made Welsh and Devonshire studies.

Early in 1837 he wrote this in his pocket-book, " My dear nurse, and most faithful servant and friend, Mary Ward, died at five minutes to five o'clock, 18th January, 1837." She died, as she had lived for so many years, devoted to her young master and in his house. He tended her to the end, and as a parting gift received at her hands her old Tonson's Milton, whence she had often read to him when he was a child. Her death, no doubt, hastened a great event in his life. His long intimacy with the Linnell family had led to an engagement to the eldest daughter Hannah, once the little child who so merrily headed the troop which welcomed him to the Hampstead cottage. Although now only nineteen years old she was full of artistic enthusiasm. From her babyhood she had been surrounded by artists and, times out of number, had sat on Blake's knee while he repeated his poems and stories so beautifully that she remembers them to this day. She had been trained to look upon art, not only as a passable profession, but as an occupation worthy of the greatest and the best. Every moment she could snatch from innumerable domestic distractions she employed with pen or pencil in copying prints from the Old Masters or in making original designs. She and her sister Elizabeth had already joined the Church of England, and my father used to take them to the services at Westminster Abbey and St. Paul's, or some other favourite place of worship. It was proposed that, after the marriage, the couple should spend some time in Italy, painting from nature, and executing commissions from Mr. Linnell for certain copies from Old Masters that he was anxious to secure. Accordingly, my father, with characteristic energy, began to set his house in order. Materials were renewed and arranged, superfluities were pruned away with almost military rigour, and a pistol with ammunition was actually purchased wherewith to protect the bride ; while at the same time, I believe, some curious modifications were introduced into the bachelor wardrobe with the view of securing more durability and simplicity, even at the cost of

appearance. But there were obstacles in the path, and the most formidable
was found in that time-honoured stone of stumbling, the future mother-in-
law. Accustomed to an habitual dread of all sorts of dangers even in ordinary
London life, Mrs. Linnell seems to have regarded the Italian project as
little better than a madcap journey to a land of fever, volcanic catastrophes,
banditti, priests and (perhaps worse than all), of indigestible food. Her
qualms were at last, but with the greatest difficulty, overruled, and the
knotty question of expense yielded to the expedient of contracting a
temporary debt to Mr. Richmond. Therefore, on September the 30th,
1837, the adventurous pair were married by Mr. Linnell's express desire
at the Registrar's office at Marylebone. It was a civil marriage, and
as such must have given a staunch churchman like my father no little
pain.[1] They left England four days later, with Mr. and Mrs. Richmond
as their companions, who were also bound for Italy.

My father's first impression appears to have been one of unalloyed
delight in the architecture and rich interiors of the continental churches,
each with its throng of poor worshippers : but perhaps the pages of *Udolpho*
and *The Italian* had prepared him for the heavenly music and slow mediæval
reverence which he looked for in vain. If his staunch though somewhat
high-church protestantism had been shaken in the least degree (as I believe
some of his friends predicted that it would be), by the ritual of Rome, the
irreverence with which he saw this ritual marred would have established
him as firmly as ever in his early faith. But in his theological views he
never wavered. Never for one moment, even when Gregory XVI. blessed
the vast, prostrate multitude in St. Peter's, with every soul-stirring accom-
paniment, and with music which was at last celestial, was my father's
allegiance to the Church of England undermined. The result of all he saw
and heard in Italy was just the same as the result of the fiercest of
Mr. Linnell's arguments in favour of dissent.

The omission of some bribe to an official led to delays in Paris, and
gave the travellers an opportunity of seeing the pictures in the Louvre, but
my father was glad to turn his back on a city with which he had evidently
small sympathy, to begin the then formidable journey towards the Alps in
the cumbrous *diligence*. The "brutal, butt-end horsewhipping" and other
cruelties by which the miserable team were tortured did little to increase
the rate of travelling, and he was often able to snatch a sketch or two of the
effects of dawns and sunsets over scenes so new and strange to him. At

---

[1] Among some details connected with his family which he wrote in the last volume
of his commonplace-book is this sentence. "Register of Samuel Palmer's birth is
at Dr. Williams' Library, Red Cross Street, London. His parents were married at
St. Mary's, Newington, Surrey about the year 1804. S. P. was married at the Court-
house, Marylebone ; he, a churchman !"

last when the horses began to creep up the slopes of the Jura mountains and he saw archaic tumbrels full of grapes drawn by cream-coloured oxen with "faces like poets," and guided by ideally picturesque peasants, all the weariness and discomforts of the journey were forgotten in a moment. Fairyland had once again revealed itself, and some of the young enthusiast's brightest visions of fruitfulness, grandeur, and beauty were realized.[1]

Just four weeks after leaving England he entered Rome, that "wilderness of wonders," as he calls it. A letter he wrote to Mr. Richmond in September 1828, shows that even then he was keenly sensitive to the associations in the midst of which he now found himself, and in after years he wrote, "Rome is a thing by itself which, once seen, leaves the memory no more. A City of Art which one had dreamed of before, and can scarce believe that one has really seen." But the time of dreams and reveries was gone by, and though, in his short autobiography, my father speaks lightly of this Italian sojourn as his "wedding trip," never have those words been so singularly applied. He and his young wife set themselves tasks whose difficulty and laboriousness might have daunted the strongest and most accomplished veteran. Every hour seems to have had a labour of its own : and almost every form of pleasure-taking was made impossible by a penurious economy. Enthusiasm for the associations and admiration of the beauty of what they set themselves to paint carried them through ; but the girl, so fresh from her mother's nervous guardianship, broke down at last from the sheer hard, unhealthy, drudgery of working early and late at copies from the Old Masters, including the *Stanze* of Raphael, and the frescoes of the Sistine Chapel.

While his wife was thus engaged, my father chiefly devoted himself to out-door work — devoted himself so enthusiastically and diligently that, in time, he was able to complete in about five sittings even the most elaborate of his studies ; such, for instance, as the *Ponte Rotto*. The term "five sittings" is somewhat elastic, but in this case it probably meant five determined and vigorous attacks of as many hours as the lighting of the landscape admitted.

On the 27th of January, 1839, he wrote thus in his pocket-book :—
"Was brought by the goodness of God into my 34th year. Now I
"must either at once produce fine finished works, or 'live a fool and die a
"brute.' After wandering through labyrinths one comes back to first prin-
"ciples. The outline, after all, I believe to be the great difficulty ; the
"only first step and great accomplishment of art. When a pure and
"expressive outline is on the paper, the prey is caught. The rest is like
"cooking and garnishing it."

[1] *A Dream in the Apennine*, exhibited in 1864, recalled the impression formed by these scenes of mountain beauty.

The best of the Italian studies show the fruits of these resolutions. They show a greater mastery of principles, more forbearance from dogma — more draughtsmanship and technical skill than the time which divides them from the later Shoreham work fully accounts for ; but the qualities which made that work so remarkable and, in its own way, so fascinating are to be found not at all, or in only a very modified degree. The hand and the imagination are alike in subjection to a mind that has been vigorously disciplined, but at the same time so wisely that it avoids, what is so difficult to avoid, any approach to running from one extreme to or towards another. This painter who was even yet fresh from a life of seclusion and so peculiar a practice seems to have determined on a wise eclecticism. He stables his hobbies ; but he does not forget that some of them have carried him over timber which, on quieter animals, he would have failed to pass. For these reasons, the studies he was able to show to the Roman connoisseurs met with as much approval from them as they have invariably done from critics and artists in England. On turning over the portfolios which contain them, the careful observer is struck at once by the fact that the greater part represent a golden and glittering Italy ; and it is equally obvious that the many allusions met with in my father's letters and memoranda to that long sojourn refer to a favoured land of sun and of splendour. We hear and see little or nothing of that monotony, sadness of colour, and absence of brilliancy, which some artists have asked us to accept as the attributes of Italy, and which are undoubtedly to be found there at certain times and places. That a few of the studies do certainly show these less pleasing peculiarities proves, I think, that my father encountered them ; but the fewness of them suggests that he far preferred the other aspect, and made as much as he could of those effects and those scenes which most strongly appealed to "the loves of his mind."

Not the least interesting feature in the two years' Italian residence was a series of letters to the travellers from Mr. Linnell, who wrote to them once a fortnight. It is impossible to read these letters without forming a high opinion of the sound sense, and manly, straightforward character of the writer ; or without amusement at the narrowness of some of the channels into which his mind is pent, and at his combative nature.

On certain points connected with religion, literature, and art, my father had his own very definite opinions and held to them with bull-dog tenacity. Mr. Linnell had also his own opinions and equal tenacity in holding them against all comers and all argument. It was unfortunate that the new relatives differed on several of these essential points, particularly on religious matters, as these last invariably " produce arguments of that torrid heat, which no subject save theology can engender." These differences, how-

ever, serve to give at all events a piquancy to the correspondence ; intro-
ducing an occasional clash of arms into epistles otherwise peaceful. Mr.
Linnell is moreover continually divided between a very strong desire to
secure the copies of the Old Masters he had commissioned his daughter to
make, and a desire to allay his wife's constant tremors by prevailing upon
the young artists to return forthwith to Bayswater. My father, on the other
hand, had made up his mind to return when he had done the work he had
set himself and not before ; and he did not feel himself justified in cutting
short so golden an opportunity—one which would never recur—on account
of the anxiety of his mother-in-law.

I will give a few extracts from Mr. Linnell's letters :—

"*April* 29, 1838. [To my father.] . . . I am very busy, and pretty
" successful in my pettifogging way, pleasing those most who know but
" little of Art, but who are kind enough to employ me. I endeavour to
" learn contentment, notwithstanding a deep sense of professional insuffi-
" ciency, because I know how much worse I should be, if I sacrificed the
" best interests of my family for professional aggrandizement. If you can
" make money enough without going much out of the path which your
" genius and taste prompt you to pursue, consider yourself most happy
" and blessed. Endeavour, by pursuing this path, to obtain sufficient to
" preserve your independence and keep up a fair price for your work, and
" if you can accomplish that for a few years, and at the same time lay in
" a stock of knowledge of the phenomena of nature and the principles and
" practice of Art, you will be a Turner some day without turning. . . . .
" The Exhibition is all in the Great Room this year, for there is nothing
" of first-rate interest in any other. The picture of the Exhibition, if one
" may judge by the number round it, is *The Queen's Council* by Wilkie,
" and the picture or pictures of the Exhibition if you judge by what is
" said, are Mulready's *Seven Ages*, and Turner's *Ancient and Modern Italy*.
" I have heard many say of Mulready's, when I was standing near it, that
" there was no one in the world could paint it but himself; indeed it
" appears to me to be a wonderful result of the humble and unostentatious
" imitation of nature, connected with pure and elevated taste, and great
" knowledge of Art. The color also, which you know I generally assert to
" be much more a piece with the drawing &c. than is usually supposed
" in all works of Art, is here as good as any quality in it. . . . Let
" nothing tempt you to lose your time or your money to obtain mere
" acquaintances, which often are only the means of losing more time and
" money. Those are the most valuable friends which are made by your
" exertions in the Art ; and do not forget that the battle is to be fought at
" your easel. . . . "

"*June* 26, 1838. [To my father.] . . . Well, I do not know what else

" to say, except about my own affairs ; and one thing I learn by looking at
" yours is that, being a grumbler like you, I have no doubt my affairs
" appear to another in a better light than to myself. In fact there is no
" obtaining any peace, I find, without looking at the whole, and caring little
" about some things, provided principal things are well. A man may have
" as much vexation about the color of his carriage or temper of his
" horses, as a poor man about the point of his pickaxe, or expense of his
" wife's cap."

" *September* 23, 1838. My dear daughter Hannah, I am very glad to
" find that you are struggling with the real difficulties of the Art ; as I have
" no doubt but, with Mr. Palmer's assistance, you will accomplish enough
" to produce some beautiful works ; and, what is of more consequence,
" increase your capability of receiving those inspiring impressions of beauty
" and sublimity which nature was intended to produce. This, I think, you
" will find to be a more important part of the education of the mind, than
" mere scholastic teachers and pupils can believe. It is that to which science
" is only auxiliary. Science does not necessarily elicit perception, for a
" person may know and be able to repeat whole volumes, but like the monks'
" prayers, the stringing the beads shows how little the mind has gained in
" perception. You cannot, however, produce a beautiful work without
" perception of beauty. Go on therefore, with as little exertion as you can,
" always trying to attain your end by skill rather than hard labour—by a
" perception of the principle upon which nature delights you, and not
" attempting more of the varieties of nature than are essential to your
" object. You know, however, that I do not mean to encourage a negligent
" or bald style, for there is nothing I like better than a good fag at the
" variety of nature ; but I am persuaded you will accomplish much more
" by perceiving the principle upon which a little work may be made
" effective. Unless this is constantly remembered, you exert yourself
" more than is necessary ; like trying by force to disentangle a skein of
" thread ; or, as people say, to ' kill the Devil with a little hand-saw.' No,
" try how by skill you can make a little labour express sufficient, even
" when you labour most economize. Wrestle skilfully, for you wrestle
" with an Angel, and though you may halt all your life in your opinion
" of yourself, recollect it is no small honour to have wrestled with an
" Angel, and prevailed to the obtaining of a blessing. I promised you
" some professional news. Now I will tell you. I have sold my *Emmaus*
" picture. That, I hope, is news ; for an Artist to sell an historical
" picture. Aye, and sold it too to the Committee of Taste. ' Stand out
" my shoon, up higher get my bonnet.' The purchase voted unani-
" mously by the Committee of The Art Union Society. Master John
" has a plate in hand of it, of which I have etched the outline. I

" hope to do something better of the same kind, but I am too busy
" at present.

" I dined the other day at Mr. Sheepshanks' where I met Messrs.
" Mulready, Collins, Robinson . . . . &c. When we had finished our
" wine, &c., Mr. Collins let out that it was his birthday, which started
" Mr. Sheepshanks in quest of a bottle of sack, and wonderful stuff it
" was, and in addition to what we had had, went nigh to make us tipsy.
" Being, however, in civil, godly company, I thought there was no harm in
" being drunk, and so took my share. We got to Deptford by a fly, to
" London Bridge by railroad, and to Bayswater by 'bus, *all right.* Mr.
" Sheepshanks is a capital fellow. He is as enthusiastic as a young Artist ;
" has a huge collection of the best modern pictures with which he is ready
" to jump out of his skin with delight. You leave his society with the
" strong impression that the Art is worth ten times the exertions you have
" ever bestowed upon it. Mr. Mulready's last picture is the crown of his
" collection. I hope next year to accompany you to see it."

" *November* 2, 1838. [To my father.] . . . I feel a doubt from what
" you say about your drawings, whether you do not compose too much. I
" would venture to advise you to endeavour to do as much as possible by
" simply laying an emphasis on the beautiful, and leaving agreeable blanks
" or breadths where the objectionable matter comes. And if you think
" a foreground in one place is applicable to a sketch made in another,
" I would make the studies separate, but I would not try to marry them
" on the spot. If, however, you feel otherwise, don't mind what I have
" said. I only mention it as a thing I should be very careful to avoid
" doing on the spot, for fear of injuring the veracity of a drawing from
" nature. I think the remark is of most consequence when you begin
" with a beautiful distance and middle-distance. For, if you start with a
" foreground, you may venture to insert a distance from nature without
" so much danger of injury; as, in that case, you will in all probability
" make it sufficiently subordinate; whereas, if you have elaborated a
" drawing of everything but a foreground and, as will be most likely,
" exhausted all your strength of color &c. in parts, it will be impossible
" in that drawing to make the *whole* true by adding a foreground ; and it
" would be better to make a separate drawing of any foreground or figure
" you think may be good for it, and afterwards in another drawing, put
" them together. Take care therefore ; for though complete subjects may
" be more like a collection of pictures to look at and reckon upon, they
" will not yield so much in the long run as separate studies. Get as many
" figures as possible, and if you set them near some bit of ruin, or with
" some landscape behind them, you are sure to make a picture by finishing
" your figure *first,* and then adding as much or as little as you please of

" what you see beyond, and you will be sure to have the figure and
" background relatively true, besides having a study applicable to other
" backgrounds. Let me therefore again say, draw figures out of doors,
" with the background you wish, as near as you can."

"*November* 23, 1838. [To my father.] . . . I am persuaded there is
" no departing from truth anywhere, either in poetry or painting, without
" losing by it ; and here I do not lose sight of imaginative Art ; for where
" for the sake of a more full expression of the grandest qualities of nature,
" some exaggerations are indulged in, or allegorical figures made use of, it
" is evidently to obtain more truth thereby than can be expressed by the
" mechanical transcript of nature, which, in many cases, would be un-
" intelligible . . . It appears to me, a beautiful and divine necessity that
" right feeling is necessary to a perception of the true means of expression.
" It will show itself in spite of the meanest powers of execution, though it
" will lead to the greatest ; but no subtlety can hide the effects of wrong
" feeling . . . Remember you are not only at liberty, but I invite you to
" be as plain in your criticisms upon my conduct when there is opportunity.
" Not that I think that my practice will bear scrutiny as well as yours, for
" I feel that all I have said above applies to myself, and I wince from the
" sight of my own weapons when I see their point towards me. Neverthe-
" less, I think it most useful to be reminded of such things by a friend ;
" and if done in a friendly spirit, it cements friendship by evidencing
" sincerity, which I assure you does not provoke me at any time like secrecy.
" It is freemasonry that I detest—secret oaths and vows extracted, kid-
" napping of the intellect, and Burking the perceptions. How many
" active-minded, clever people carry about with them a load of fetters
" which they try, too often successfully, to fasten upon their friends under
" the plea of ornamenting them. Some are golden chains to be sure.
" but most are iron gilt. O for spiritual power to burst those bonds by
" which we are confined in 'uncouth cells, where brooding darkness
" spreads his jealous wings' instead of exulting in the healthy atmosphere
" of divine light and truth. As, however, evil is to be overcome with good,
" let us cultivate a perception of the beautiful in everything. for when that
" is perceived and loved, we easily part with the deformity which has
" previously satisfied us.

" . . . I have seen Mr. Varley this morning. who brought me Hannah's
" horoscope, all drawn out very curiously. He seems much interested in
" your welfare, and brought the nativity to show me. as Hannah is in her
" twenty-first year and he considers it an important period. I have asked
" him at what period she was ill during your present journey, but he would
" not tell. Perhaps some one will tell him before he consults his books,
" and then he will know. However, it is kind of him. and I must tell you

F

" what he says of the future : and there can be no harm in taking care.
" Well, you must take care, he says, all next month (I say every month till
" you return, and then too), particularly of indigestion. If anything is the
" matter, it is Mars' and Saturn's fault, he says. I say if it should proceed
" from a cold room and carbonel, it will be your fault, Mr. P., so mind
" your Ps and Qs, or I shall tickle your toby, and comb your head with
" a knob stick, as Mrs. Francis used to say to her husband. To be
" serious : do not, my dear fellow, run any risks now for the sake of
" saving. . . ."

" *December* 23, 1838. [To my father.] . . . for landscape studies, or
" the application of figures to landscape you should sometimes choose a
" light and shade which is very striking and vivid at a distance, as the
" figure relieves entirely by such qualities in landscape very often, taking
" care that the shapes of the lights are picturesque in every part. If a
" face is in shadow, let it be well lighted by reflection and, generally, let
" the light show the action of the figure as plainly as possible. [sketch]
" I think those are qualities particularly requisite in figure as introduced
" into landscape and always distinguish the figures by the landscape-
" painter from those introduced into landscapes by a figure-painter who
" does not paint landscape. But the treatment should depend chiefly
" upon the expression of your subject in effect, colour, &c., and that should
" rule the figures ; and if you fancy a central light and soft shadows, and
" your landscape accords, let nothing prevent you from attempting it ; only,
" remember, you will not escape so easily as upon the other tack. N.
" Poussin is a fine example of vividly constructed plan, though not always
" vividly painted. Titian finer still, . . . but you find the more difficult
" and more beautiful only in Raffaelle -sometimes in Titian and Leonardo
" and in A. Dürer, and perhaps in many others which you have seen
" since your sojourn in Italy, but of which I am unhappily ignorant—I
" forgot : in Julio Romano, you have both qualities—those of vividness
" and picturesque choice and arrangement of light, seen with a Poetic
" Imagination, straining nature through his mental sieve till everything
" mean or vulgar was excluded. Such a man as Julio seems to have taken
" nature into his mind as ore is taken into a kiln, where it is so digested
" by internal heat that nothing but pure metal escapes into the mould
" intended for it ; but I must stop, for that way a long letter lies . . . .
" When you are grinding colour, try some of the yolk of egg . . . I think
" it is better than glue. You may set a palette by this method at any time
" for water-colour, by mixing a few dry colours with egg—the yolk only,
" and as Cennini says, as much egg as colour. Spread the colour when
" mixed, on the palette thin, and it will wash up again with water easily,
" especially if a little sugar be added. Do not carry a bottle of egg-

" mixture [1] in your pocket, as in Rome the breaking of it might be the
" cause of breaking the peace ; particularly if you went to wash at a public
" fountain."

" *March* 8, 1839. [To my father.] . . . I have sold my picture of
" *St. John preaching*, which I sent to the British Gallery, to Sir Thomas
" Baring for 150 guineas with the frame. It has been very well spoken of
" by the press, among whom you know I have scarcely an acquaintance ;
" so that I may feel it a compliment, as I have always rather shunned
" them and despised their hireling principles, generally speaking. I am
" now and then able to devote a day to a picture or two of a similar
" description, and if I could prevail upon Mr. Richmond to communicate
" some of his discoveries, who is entirely devoted to spiritual Art, I should
" feel encouraged. Any one like Mr. Richmond, leaving the Vanity Fair
" of Art, and entering the wicket gate to go to the New Jerusalem is
" such a reproach to those who stay behind, from whichever cause, that I
" could despise myself for not following him, if I did not feel that my
" family is an excuse which I have no right to evade. Besides, I am too
" old, and shall content myself now if I can be the means, any way, of
" assisting others to attain that excellence which craves a whole life of
" concentrated exertion. You, I feel, are in the right road to distinction,
" and need not care about present and immediate return so much ; for
" though, in this age, more perfection is required to obtain notice, yet,
" when at your age, to have mastered so much will ensure the rest . . . .
" Tell Mr. Martin he must write me a long letter, and tell me all the
" gossip of Art. He will be able to afford the time, which I cannot ask
" you or Mr. Richmond to do; though nothing would gratify me more than
" a long sincere letter upon Art from him, because under such circum-
" stances, I feel the best of thoughts would be expressed, and the most
" valuable hints to a person in my condition given. I am like a servant
" who has only over-hours for study, whereas you and Mr. Richmond are
" at college—at the great University of Art. He ought therefore to com-
" municate, for auld lang syne . . . "

---

[1] I have mentioned my father's numerous experiments relating to chromotography.
He had already largely experimented in egg vehicles, and the letter alludes to an amusing
incident in connection with these trials. He had manufactured some precious emulsion by
means of yolk of egg ; and, perhaps to secure more liberal shaking, had deposited the
tightly-stoppered bottle in one of his capacious pockets. The bottle was forgotten, and
the coat was daily worn, till one day when a detachment of " The Ancients" were walking
through London, there came an explosion and a stench so unspeakably foul, that all of the
party but one lost their presence of mind. This one, however, hastily taking out his knife,
ripped out the pocket and its contents and cast them into the gutter. They had not gone
far when, chancing to look back, they saw a Jew dealer in old clothes approaching, who
made a greedy dart at the pocket, but straightway flung it from him with such a dramatic
action of disgust, that the young men never forgot it.

" *May* 10, 1839. [To Mr. Martin under cover to my father.] The " exhibition has opened without a picture from Sir A. Callcott. Nothing " from Hilton. Mulready, smaller ones only. It is a good exhibition " though, notwithstanding, as the new hands are strong. A Mr. Redgrave " has a capital picture of the daughter of the Vicar of Wakefield returning " to her home, when she is met at the door by her sister ; and the affec- " tionate look of the sister into her face is so pathetic that it excites the " feelings as much as a very touching piece of acting. Mr. Severn's " pictures look extremely well. I like them much. . . . I had an applica- " tion the other day from Mr. E. Landseer to lend him my shop to finish " his large picture of the Queen in. Mr. Collins told him he thought I " would lend it him, as he believed I made no use of it myself. I think " Mr. Landseer will build one similar himself eventually, he likes mine so " much ; and very likely in this neighbourhood."

" *June* 11, 1839. [To my father.] . . . Your plan respecting ' little, " oil pictures and drawings painted in a day, at once from nature,' requires " some explanation and reconsideration. I do not like it. It savours " too much of the practice of some who have stocked the market with " cheap pennyworths of Art, to their own pecuniary disadvantage and " degradation as Artists. Don't think at present of doing anything of the " pot-boiling description. Better to teach for money, and take pains with " some finished works for reputation. You are in a good position for such " a line of practice, and will, I think, succeed in it. Take care of all you " have done, and do not undervalue your works now, because others " have not appreciated them. One successful picture in the Exhibition, " will raise the value of all you have by you 100 per cent. ; and that " success repeated, will again raise them 500 per cent. Wait until you " return, and we will talk over these matters, when I think *we shall agree.* " Our sense of interest in such things sharpens our perception of truth : " not but it is equally to our interest to cultivate just and liberal opinions " upon all subjects, however remote apparently from our present concern. " Some very important event sometimes turns upon a step which, if taken " upon a previously adopted false principle, is most ruinous ; but is often " taken upon that principle, even contrary to the man's perception at the " moment of action : for if the principle has been maintained with party " feeling and bigotry, the perception of its pernicious quality comes too " late, and for consistency's sake it is acted upon, in spite of the mortifying " truth apparent at the moment. We each admire many things which " are beautiful : and perhaps if we were to begin from some point wherein " we are quite agreed, we might extend the base of our mental union " by proceeding carefully to examine how many things we could " agree in. We each profess to be conservative of everything good

" and beautiful, and we only differ respecting the mode of effecting
" our object. . . ."

"*July* 30, 1839. [To my mother.] . . . The completing a tour like
" yours is something like completing a picture. It may be spoiled by
" dwelling too long upon it, and should be ended suddenly; for going
" on proceeds often from the habit of going on, rather than a clear per-
" ception of advantage. To know when to leave off is a great art in
" everything. If you can make your escape now, do not lose the oppor-
" tunity, but come over the first bridge that presents itself to your notice.
" I wait, however, in despair of being able to influence the Governor,
" whose immoveable walk-through-rivers disposition, which he inherits from
" his no-thoroughfare-path-papa, I too well remember. I ought, however,
" to say what I can to cheer him up in his troubles, though I only say these
" things about rivers to help him over the bridge if I can ; but he is such
" a neck-or-nothing man. . . . The whole machine of our family goes on
" pretty well, but I feel as if I were in a treadmill sometimes, obliged to
" go faster than I wish, and that if I did not keep step, I should be in
" danger of breaking my shins, or something worse."

" *August* 21, 1839. [To my mother.] . . . All of us (except mamma and
" the twigs), went to Hampton Court the other day. I went to meet Sir
" A. Callcott and some friends of his and mine. While we were comparing
" Dorigny's prints of the Cartoons with the originals, who should appear at
" the other end of the gallery but B. R. Haydon Esqre., swelling like a
" turkey-cock : and, after some marching and counter-marching, without
" being noticed by any of the party, he went out with arms akimbo as
" grand as Pistol."

" *September* 30, 1839. [To my mother.] . . . Pray tell Palmer that I will
" talk to him about the drudgery he mentions which he says he will be glad
" to do, when he returns. It is a mistake, I believe, to suppose that any
" great progress can be made in poetic landscape unless the whole mind and
" time is devoted to it. He ought to take warning by my pettifogging prac-
" tice, lest he fail of accomplishing the best he is capable of, as I have fail'd.
" I say fail'd because I am too old to rally sufficiently to improve much."

The foregoing extracts contain, I think, much that is interesting. Mr.
Linnell represents even himself as condemned by expediency to a certain
line of art, from which he evidently desires to break away, and eventually
did break away. My father for his part, keenly sensitive at last to his own
narrow circumstances, is driven to suggest an expedient for bringing in
what, in one of his letters to Bayswater, he pathetically calls " small monies."
To this my grandfather replies, " I do not like it." Probably, nothing
short of the thought of his unpaid debt, and the recollection that the cost
of the homeward journey would nearly reach the appalling sum of £50,

would have driven the staunch Shoreham enthusiast to dream of "little oil pictures and drawings painted in a day, at once from nature," as a means of adding to his income. He is very properly advised not to think of "doing anything of the pot-boiling description"; but rather "to teach for money and take pains with some finished works for reputation."

Tempted no doubt by this same poverty, and naturally very fertile in designing power, he seems at one time to have contemplated "composing" in his sketches, and he receives from Mr. Linnell some admirable counsel touching the importance of not "injuring the veracity of a drawing from nature."

Part of the extract dated November 23, 1838, is particularly interesting, as it touches on the vital and vexed question of realism in art, and the extent to which nature may be transmuted in the mind without the sacrifice of "truth" in its noblest and largest sense. My father's own opinions on this point will have been partly gathered from the description of his earlier work, and from the passage in the letter to Mr. Richmond already quoted.

Mr. Linnell seems to have made up his mind that he was condemned by his age, as well as by the demands of his large family, to a practice which he twice characterizes as "pettifogging"; but his ideal is far different, and is made apparent by the advice he gives his son-in-law. He sees that the study of "poetic landscape" will demand "the whole mind and time," and he longs to devote himself to more "spiritual art" than that which he is forced to pursue.

Unfortunately, nearly the whole of the letters from my father and mother to the family at Bayswater have been either lost or destroyed ; and with them the written record of their labours. Briefly epitomized, their proceedings were as follows. Leaving their travelling companions at Rome for a time, they journeyed southwards to Naples, which they saw "glittering like a mosaic of gems, but with innate, living light from a sea of beryl." Thence they removed to Pompeii, where they stopped a month, living in one of the ancient buildings which had been occupied by some superintendent of the works who was then absent. If the sentiment of such a place had wanted poetry or pathos, both would have been added by the story of Glaucus and Ione. This the travellers read for the first time in the evenings, while the remote thunder of Vesuvius (then in eruption) shook their door as if the dead, roused from their centuries of sleep by that solemn sound, were once again seeking shelter in their desolate homes. At Pompeii my father made many studies, and among them one of the amphitheatre, which is a particularly pleasing work, and notable as showing a complete mastery of technical difficulties, besides great knowledge. My mother was equally industrious.

Vesuvius, 1838.

A Storm on the Cornish Coast.

By way of Corpo di Cava and various out-of-the-way places they returned to Rome, the record of their journey being one of incessant painting and the conquest of innumerable difficulties at the cost of a Spartan self-denial.

In a letter from my father to Mr. Linnell, dated Papignio, August 23, 1839, is the following passage :—" . . . As we are now on our homeward " march and it will be important to finish our journey successfully, I am " anxious to get the benefit of your advice as to our next movements ; as " everything we do now will bear upon our London settlement and our " preparations for the exhibition next spring. On the one hand it appears " important that, immediately on my return, I should begin one or two " pictures of a moderate size (? perhaps), which, *if successful*, would be " likely to bring me into notice ; and I am endeavouring at this moment to " secure this point having just finished two most beautiful foreground " subjects, which are at the same time highly poetical and full of the realiza- " tion which connoisseurs look for.   Now as I shall also, at the same time, " have to teach and use all other means to get small monies, the sooner we " are in London the better . . . On the other hand, our travelling expenses " from England to Rome (to say nothing of Naples), came to £50, and " though we may come back rather cheaper, will be considerable ; and it is " worthy of consideration whether, when on the spot at so great a cost, and " where we may perhaps never be again, we ought not to seize the advantages " held out to Anny in such a place as Florence, so as to enable her to make " a small and very select set of recollections from the choice things there, " which we can obtain nowhere else ; such as picked specimens of Andrea " del Sarto, Masaccio, Fra Bartolomeo and John of Fiesole, which could not " be done in less than three months.   This would bring us to the end of " November before leaving Florence, and land us in England at the begin- " ning of January ; and then, though there would be two months before us " for painting for the exhibition, this would not suffice, because of preparing " our drawings for inspection &c., teaching perhaps, and other unforeseen " obstacles ; so that I should have little to exhibit but studies or drawings " in water-colours ; but still we should have secured other advantages offered " by Florence, which we have paid much to come at and may never reach " again.   I lay these two plans of proceeding before you . . . I now earn- " estly desire to do something effective for the exhibition next year which " would give me standing as an artist, or at least widen my connection among " the patrons of art.   At the same time, I do not wish, having struggled " hitherto conscientiously for the best, to throw away a great continental " advantage . . . Now, when I speak of exhibition preparations, I do not " mean to the exclusion of all possible means to get small cash in every way. " Of course I shall be anxious immediately on my return to mount and put

" the last touches to several drawings which I have with me, and which are
" ready for inspection, and to teach &c. &c. ; but I should like, as I have
" two ¾ frames not much the worse for wear, to paint at least two really
" effective *pictures*, besides exhibiting some of my drawings. Now, whatever
" others can do, *I* cannot attempt this in a desolate, dirty house, such as
" mine was during Mrs. Hurst's administration [after Mary Ward's death],
" with clothes hanging to dry in the passage ; therefore I think and indeed
" feel sure that the only way will be, if the house is swept and garnished
" ready for us, to go into it at once with Anny. . . ."

It will be readily seen from this letter that my father wished and
intended to earn a name not as a painter in water-colours, but a painter in
oils   This was always his ambition, and that he was always thwarted was
a source of constant regret to him.

At the end of two years the labourers returned from their " wedding
trip " laden with the fruits of their toil—returned from a sunny and beautiful land to the dreary darkness of a London winter.   Often and often my
father spoke of the contrast between the brilliant skies and the marble
buildings they had left behind, and the filthy Thames warehouses, looming
through the fog in which they landed.   Indeed he ascribed to this change
the origin of the acute asthma which sorely troubled him in after life.

Although his early career had been that of a hard worker not without
griefs and disappointments, and anxieties on account of his mental and
professional progress, these anxieties had little to do with worldly matters.
But now the studies he had once pursued for their own sake had to be
submitted to the touchstone of utility.   He had before him the unspeakably weary struggle against the neglect and contempt to which education
and gentle manners only serve to make a poor man painfully sensitive.
Every old anxiety was redoubled and multiplied.   Will his allegiance to the
principles so enthusiastically followed ten years before survive the grip of
poverty, or will they melt away (as such principles are wont to do) under
the enervating warmth of popular favour bought at the usual price of
that article ?   An answer is found partly in memorandum books—in the
accounts and other private papers of the next twenty years, and partly in
the works which were produced in the same period.

For the first year or two after his return to England my father's income
was increased by the sale, at a good price, of the sets of prints of the Sistine
Chapel Michael Angelos engraved by Mr. Linnell, which had been taken to
Rome and coloured from the originals, and also by the sale of my mother's
copies from the Old Masters.   When this source of supply was exhausted,
my father, in accordance with the intention expressed in the Papignio letter,
fell back upon his oil-painting.   He intended to take up the thread of his
Shoreham studies, and to pursue them with the great additional knowledge

and experience he had gained in Italy. But whether the two years of almost unremitted water-colour practice had, for the time being, made the other method difficult or uncongenial, or whether (as I imagine was the case) discouraging personal influences besides the influences of other untoward circumstances were at work, the oil pictures of this time (judging from all I have seen) were weak and timid to a degree surprising to those who are familiar with the crisp touch, glowing colour, and bold impasto of the best Shoreham panels. The composition might be graceful, the light and shade well studied, but the love of higher qualities than these—the "double vision" so peculiarly evident in those works appeared no longer. That matters were not prospering, is shown by the solicitude with which every trivial item both of receipt and expenditure was entered in the accounts, and by a feverish anxiety to increase his teaching connection. In the midst of the entries for 1840, appears this significant passage :— "Supposing lessons stop, and nothing more is earned—avoid snuff, two " candles, sugar in tea, waste of butter and soap . . . But it is more difficult " at present to get than to save. Query. Go into the country for one month " to make little drawings for sale?" Two candles a night are not a remark- ably liberal allowance for a hard-working artist and his wife, but he is prepared to go back to the still narrower rations of the " Epic Poet." Alas, for the "Great Reads," of which he had spoken so hopefully in a letter to Dr. Williams from Italy !

I am glad to say that he did not go into the country for the purpose of making "little drawings for sale"; but in September 1844, he passed some time at Lady Stephen's in Dorsetshire, teaching, and painting some pictures which did not sell. The examples I have of these are highly finished, but are monotonous in colour and generally uninteresting.

Two unconnected memoranda in 1842 have, when taken in conjunc- tion, a certain grim irony. At the head of the entries of the year he writes, " Income, God willing, of 1842 ✠. He giveth food to all flesh, for His mercy endureth for ever." Later on, " Our professional experi- " ence, 1842. February 3, I went to the British Gallery, and found both my " pictures and one of Anny's rejected. March. Mr. Ruskin and others were " shown our drawings. Mr. Nasmyth was to name me as a teacher to " Admiral Otway. I offered Miss B——, Addison Road, to teach one " pupil for 10s. per annum. [This was a school.] Went to British Artists, " and found one picture hung near the ceiling, another rejected, and Anny's " *Job* rejected. Mine were the same pictures I sent to the B : Gallery, " for the new frames for which I had paid £5 8s."

This struggle with difficulties and the attendant temptations and mis- givings might possibly have been averted. My father was wont to lament in after years that a little encouragement and help at this critical time would have enabled him to paint in oil from the figure, to acquire a more complete mastery over solid colour and, as he so earnestly wished, to follow the career of an oil painter. But he met, instead, with discouragements and obstacles without end. Deliberate promises of such help which had been made to him again and again were disregarded, and the golden dreams he had dreamed under the bright Italian noon faded away into the cold realities of a disappointed life.

It may be well to mention in passing a notable exception among the weak handling and colour to which I alluded as characteristic of some of the oil pictures finished after the return from Italy. *The Rising of the Skylark* is a small panel picture which was painted *con amore :* and although it was completed some years later than the period we have reached, it was begun before all hope of a return to oil painting was abandoned. Foreshadowed by a sepia sketch of a much earlier date, and followed some time afterwards by an etching bearing the same title, though of a different composition, this little work shows that the Shoreham power and the feeling for the most poetic aspects of nature had not failed : but, although forced to lie dormant, were always ready to awake in their full strength under genial circumstances.

Upon his own birthday (the 27th January) in 1842, my father's eldest child was born. He named him "Thomas More" after the great Chancellor. whose portrait had hung at Shoreham, "check by jowl" with the portrait of Bishop Fisher. to "frown away vice and levity and infidelity." The event led to a temporary migration from Marylebone to Thatcham in Berkshire. where the family remained from August to October, much to my father's benefit. Here he painted two water-colours which were exhibited the following year at the Gallery of the Old Society ; and the visit led to the production of an admirable drawing which appeared at the same exhibition under a title whose accuracy no one appears to have challenged. *At Donnington, Berkshire : the Birthplace of Chaucer*, a work now in the possession of the Linnell family, is without exception one of the best examples of my father's subdued manner that I have seen. It seems astounding that a painter as accomplished as this drawing proves him to have been should ever have been concerned about "small monies" or the number of "dips" allowable for an evening's study.

He had now drifted perforce more and more into the practice of water-colours ; and in 1843 his future career was virtually determined by his election as Associate of the Old Society. As my father was one of those who are liable to be depressed by failure and exhilarated by success far more than is usual, it is probable that Napoleon after Austerlitz was less elated than he, when the Secretary's letter arrived. At last the painter had achieved a standing in his profession, and his name was enrolled among some of the elect of art. His pleasure was enhanced by the sale from the Society's gallery to The Art Union (then, by the bye, an illegal institution), of a drawing entitled *Evening—the Ruins of a Walled City.* The £30 he received for this work was for him, at that time, a large price.

In September 1843, he again visited North Wales; and not only the studies he made there, but the copious memoranda show to what purpose he had employed his time, in spite of discouragement and failure, since the return from Italy. It did not suffice him that he could skilfully choose and accurately copy any beautiful portion of landscape or foreground. He had acquired and constantly exercised the power of analyzing what he saw and of arranging the whole of the phenomena under the laws which he discovered and studied. He also made illustrated notes on detached sheets of paper which he accumulated in a special portfolio labelled "Written Memoranda," many more being secured in his never-failing sketch-book. In these researches consisted one branch of his artistic studies. The other, and in his opinion by far the most important branch involved the solution of the difficulties connected with composition and design. Here, on the high altar of his own ideal, was practically sacrificed the best of all his other researches put together ; and also that " potentiality of growing rich " which has allured many and many an enthusiast away from his own track into the more pleasant paths of popularity.

The sketching expeditions were not made in at all a luxurious manner. The apparatus carried was as simple as it was complete. A deal case or a portfolio slung round the shoulders with a strap held a good supply of paper, together with two large but very light wooden palettes coated with home-made white enamel and set with thick clots of colour so prepared as to be readily moved by the brush or the finger. A light hand-basket held a change or two of linen, reserve colours, an old campstool which had seen service in Italy and, when necessary, the lunch or dinner. The coat was an accumulation of pockets in which were stowed away the all-important snuff-box, knives, chalks, charcoal, coloured crayons, and sketch-books, besides a pair of large, round, neutral-tint spectacles made for near sight. These were carried specially for sunsets and the brightest effects on water ; and, together with a small diminishing mirror, completed the equipment. The minimum of the plainest clothes and boots heavily nailed furthered the sketcher's object, which was to travel on unfrequented tracks or mountain paths, in any company or none, and utterly unfettered. A good constitution and the training of his youth made him indifferent to rough quarters and rough diet. He writes, " In exploring wild country I have " been for a fortnight together uncertain each day whether I shall get a bed " under cover at night ; and about midsummer I have repeatedly been

" walking all night to watch the mystic phenomena of the silent hours."
He seemed as much at home in clambering down a Welsh mountain
towards dusk after a hard day's work, guided only by the roar of a
neighbouring torrent, as in joining the evening gossip in the chimney-
corner of a village inn, after explaining to some who took him for a travelling
pedlar that he had nothing to show.   He tells how he read a seven-volume
edition of Sir Charles Grandison for the second time while weather-bound
in a wild district in Wales : how he foregathered with Crabb Robinson
whom he met on one of these occasions ; or how he lay in bed while his
drenched clothes were being dried for him at a kitchen fire of the inn
where he had taken shelter.

He sketched rapidly, though not so rapidly as in after years ; while to
save time, he used a great deal of warm middle-tint paper and body-colour,
a practice he eschewed in most of his finished drawings.   Many of the
sketches show a more or less advanced preparation in black chalk or
pencil, or in a colour such as bistre, used with a pen.   Pens, indeed, of
all sizes were resorted to as at Shoreham, from the little crow-quill to
the reed.   His execution varied from delicate stipple or most minute
draughtsmanship to the bold sweep of a brush two inches broad, filled
from the thick masses of colour on the wooden palettes.   These large
clots of easily-moved colour were a distinguishing peculiarity in his
practice. both in and out of doors ; and he had many small china
saucers which he filled to the brim with the pigments of which he
used the most, so prepared as to set, without becoming hard.   He
recommends an advanced pupil to take out " whole saucers full of
colour, great reed pens, vast brushes, and bottles of brown ink," but he
takes care at the same time to reiterate his watch-word—" Exactness."   He
seldom attempted to attain in one sketch more than the pith or kernel of
the subject ; but upon a separate paper, or on the margin, he made
memoranda of appropriate figures, cattle, or clouds which happened to
appear, together with notes explaining the deficiencies of the sketch in
peculiarly subtle or exquisite passages.   The immense mass of material
and knowledge he accumulated therefore is not to be measured so much
by the actual sketches, as by the system of shorthand notes (as we may call
them) in pen, brush, and pencil, which almost invariably accompanied
them.   These notes he was able to read and make use of many years
afterwards. and in a peculiar manner.

In the course of a minute description of his sketching method given to
a friend, he says, " Very transitory effects, *e.g.* sunsets.   These are generally
" quite lost through trying to do too much.   Long before a palette can be
" taken out of the portfolio, the cloud has passed off the mountain, or the
" golden gleam has become dingy shade.   Therefore a scratch with pencil in

" the sketch-book is the first thing—writing what there is no time to draw.
" Then get out the crayons; and with the scene before you, and the remem-
" brance fresh, try to make something like it. If this comes like, it is
" enough: if not, keep it with the water-colour. It is best done small—half
" or a quarter size of your portfolio paper [probably ¼ Imperial] is enough.
" Then make a separate, careful outline of the scene, going on if you have
" time, and adding the local colour &c. &c.

" It is surprising how few sketches of transitory effects painters bring
" home which, after a lapse of time, reproduce the effects to their memory.
" Perhaps because they do not confine themselves to the characteristics of
" the effect—that very something which made them get out their paper :
" perhaps because they go on with it after the effect goes off, trying to get in
" some detail, instead of taking another piece of paper. I can paint better
" from my pencil memoranda of effects than from any other. If an effect
" be *very* fine, I think we should, beside what I have recommended,
" make a little coloured sketch of it immediately on going home.

" Effects, less transitory, of sunshine on beautiful matter. Little, careful
" sketches about ¼ of the portfolio size, in water-colours on white paper.
" How many beautiful recollections might be brought home from a fine
" country, if we would but limit our attempts to the measure of our time and
" means, and try, at all events, to secure the characteristic features and hues,
" instead of making ambitious attempts where time and opportunity are
" small."

The following note is taken from my father's commonplace-book, and
seeing that it was written at a time when, in spite of the encouragement of
his election as Associate of the Old Society, his circumstances were by no
means prosperous—when, in fact, he was in the midst of a fight to make
both ends meet, it will bring to mind that old Shoreham determination to
pursue art for its own sake :—

" *Monday*, April 17, 1843.—Taking-in day at the Water Colour. Thoughts
" as to my next year's painting if my unworthy life be spared. Try to make
" my things first Poetic ; second Effective.

" POETIC.	" EFFECTIVE.
" By doing subjects I love and greatly " desire to do. BRITISH; ROMANTIC; " CLASSIC : IDEAL."	" By studying phenomena in the country, " laying the great stress upon small—very " small sketches of effects ; always making, " at the same time, at least a small pencil " outline of the matter ; and that I may " not be solicitous to produce showable " pictures in the country, let me now, at " home, do all I can for the next Water- " colour exhibition."

The last of the notes written in Payne Knight's *Principles of Taste*, and quoted already, forms a somewhat pathetic commentary upon this. The resolution was not without a courage of its own, for my father knew from experience that the kind of art he expresses his intention of following was either repudiated by nine-tenths of those to whom an artist has to look for his daily bread, or put aside as we should put aside a book in Sanscrit. The Romantic and Ideal were dangerous reeds to lean upon even in the year of grace 1843. But sanguine, simple-minded enthusiasm, though meeting again and again with its rebuff, revived just as often, and clung just as unreasonably round the old loves of the mind.

Early in 1844 a daughter was born to my father, and whether or no the happiness of this event led him to look on all things with more cheerfulness than usual it is certain that when he came to the then peaceful and quiet neighbourhood of Guildford, in fine September weather, both his notes and his sketches spoke of unusual splendour of illumination and variety of colour. As these notes are of considerable interest if they are taken as forming part of an artist's mental career—part of the history of the evolution of his own peculiar manner, I will quote some passages :—
"Guildford 1844. The lights in nature are more distinct from the shadows
" (however modified by reflection) than in pictures. The shadows are very
" deep relatively to the lights, yet seem clear and full of reflected light.
" This quality is worth a most serious effort. It is much seen in shady lanes.
" The want of it gives a dismal, indoor look to the picture. Cast shadows
" across lanes &c. are not hard, or cut out, or all of a depth—some very
" dark and sharp winding up to the emphasis against the brilliant light.
" With these are intermixed tender, transparent shadows, and half-shadows,
" in every variety of intermixture and gradation. But the first thing that
" struck me on coming here was the POSITIVENESS, INTENSE
" BRIGHTNESS, and WARMTH of the LIGHTS ; and that the
" SHADOWS are full of REFLECTED LIGHT, though very deep."

Next to this we find a note upon the margin of a slight but pretty sketch of distant country basking in quiet, autumnal sunshine, and seen over a green hill whose trees cast a maze of shadows on the smooth grass :—"The cast shadows
" travelling over the figure-like ground develop the forms and emphasize
" them. They do not so here, from the slightness ; but in nature, the living
" chequer-work of the shadows and their pungent lines often develop and
" emphasize the principal forms, while they light up the whole with a dance
" and dazzle of splendour." The writer has evidently become fully aware that the splendour and yet superlative delicacy and variety of nature's colouring, where nothing is crude and nothing out of place, can only be faintly adumbrated even by the most skilful and daring colourist ; and it will be seen by his subsequent memoranda and practice, that he was also aware of one potent cause of this unapproachable splendour—the transmis-

sion of light *through* coloured objects to the eye. This is one of the reasons, if not the chief reason, of a characteristic arrangement of subject he affected in after years.

The notes continue as follows :—" The shapes of the focal lights and " touches must be thoroughly understood and drawn to give any chance of " imitating the vivid splendour of nature's lights. The shadows in nature " are very deep compared with the wonderful light ; and themselves, never-" theless, are clear, beautiful, and clean in colour, and full of reflected light, " warm or cool. The smiting of the light upon the shade is accompanied " by its opposite, viz. endless play and gradation. Nature seemed " WARMER than ever, but with a perpetual interplay of greys.

" Some of the conditions of the glitter in sunshine IMPORTANT : " Holes of dark. Cast shadows : as well as the incessant play of the " common shadows.

" To a black or dark animal and a white one, all the landscape —except-" ing stubble fields and suchlike—will be a MIDDLE TINT.

" Glitter of a white or very light object will be helped by its SQUARE-" NESS of shapes, GENUINE MIDDLE TINT of its BACKGROUND. " a mass of something relieving dark near it, and the play of CAST " SHADOWS and HOLES of dark, which are the enrichment of nature's " breadth. These, I think, govern and mass the varieties of colour in " banks of wood &c., and make smooth, enamelly hills precious."

These and many like observations appear to have been condensed, and the result entered as follows on a slip of cardboard :—" 1844. WHITE in " FULL POWER from the first. Remember blazing days wherein it makes " middle-tint colours in sunshine seem dark, AND GRAYS COOLER " THAN WHITE. WHITE NOT TONED WITH ORANGE, but in " juxtaposition with the PRIMITIVES.

" DEADLY DARK BROWNS LAID ON AT ONCE.

" FLASHES of LIGHT, or BLOW of DARK
" To get vast space, what a world of power does aerial perspective open ! " From the dock-leaf at our feet, far, far away to the isles of the ocean. " And thence—far thence, into the abyss of boundless light. O ! what " heavenly grays does this suggest !

" Stothard spoke of the value of flat tints. One flat tint relieves very distinctly from another."

There then follows a list of things to be attained in his work or im-pressed on his memory, and among them the following " Think, more than work upon distances." " If spared to September, 1845, a batch of imitation." " Rigid imitation of relative and neighbour darks and colour."

From Guildford were sent many letters to the little boy Thomas More. Some were elaborately written, regardless of time and trouble, in Roman type, to serve as early reading lessons ; and one of them describing a fair on St. Martha's Hill (the subject of a study or two) is illustrated with very pretty and careful little pencil drawings. All show the same anxiety that the child should give his heart to God and learn to love wisdom.

From Surrey my father went on to Wales, and there continued his painting and memoranda for three weeks. Pecuniarily the results of the year's work were unsatisfactory, his income for 1844 being smaller than in any year since his return from Italy.

In 1845 he spent a great deal of time at Margate, where his family remained from May till October, and this period was spent to much purpose, chiefly in studying effects and sunsets. In addition to this he passed upwards of a month at Princes Risborough in Buckinghamshire ; where he appears to have carried out his intention of devoting himself to "A batch of Imitation." *A Farm-yard near Risborough* deserves the heartiest praise as a true, graceful, and unaffected study from nature—lovely English scenery, in its most sober aspect. The colouring is gentle, the execution faultless, and there is no special appeal to exceptional qualities of mind— no hobby ridden into the china-shop of popular ignorance. The subject is dear to all lovers of the country, and its treatment (from the flock of sheep in the foreground to the downs in the distance) will not fail to please those who love art also. This drawing was exhibited in 1846—one of seven English subjects, the seven exhibited in the preceding year having been all Italian. This is a circumstance that is probably more than mere accident. Imitation cannot be achieved unless the object to be imitated is at hand. Moreover, Italian colour and Italian themes, dear as they were to the artist, were perhaps unsaleable at a time when he was little known. It was possibly just about this time that my father began to turn over in his mind what he calls "Designs prudentially considered." *Designs*, mark ; not scraps of nature more or less skilfully transferred to canvas or paper, without previous refining in the mind—I might almost say, in the heart. Some undated memoranda under the title I have just mentioned run as follows :—" 1st. SUBJECTS. A subject should be interesting either from " its BEAUTY, or ASSOCIATIONS, or BOTH : OBJECTS or SCENES, " intrinsically BEAUTIFUL.

"Claude brought together things in which all men delight. Majestic " trees, sunny skies, rivers with gentle falls, venerable ruins and extensive " distances. His ground was soft for pasture or repose. The accident which " most quickens such beauty, is LIGHT.

" 2nd. SUBJECTS in which ELEMENTS, or their combinations or " secondaries, are the principal matters, as such in which are expressed

" DEW ; SHOWERS or MOISTURE ; THE DEEP-TONED, FERTIL-
" IZING RAIN-CLOUD ; DROUGHT, with its refuge of deep, hollow
" shade, and a cold spring ; the BROOK ; THE GUSHING SPRING,
" or FOUNTAIN ; AERIAL DISTANCE.

" 3rd. LIGHT either produced by its great enforcer cast shadow, or
" by great halved opposites, as when the sun is in the picture.

" 4th. DARKNESS, with its focus of coruscating light, and a moon or
" lanthorn. The precious and latent springs of poetry are to be found
" here.

" FIGURES, which in landscape are an adjunct, should if possible be
" in ACTION, and TELL a STORY.

" PRUDENTIALLY it is important (1) to ATTRACT the EYE.
" These attract the eye—BROAD EFFECT ; STRONG CONTRASTS,
" as warm and cool, bright light and deep shade ; VIVACITY :
" SPARKLE : FRESHNESS : EMPTY and FULL.
" (2) TO FIX THE ATTENTION by FULNESS and INTRICACY :
" (3) TO AWAKEN SYMPATHY by doing what WE STRONGLY
" LOVE.
" (4) TO DELIGHT by close IMITATION, at least on the points which
" first meet the eye, and by EXECUTION."

The reader will no doubt see that, in the case of an artist such as I
have been trying to describe, considerable difficulty was likely to arise by
his endeavouring to awaken sympathy by painting what he strongly loved,
that is, the " Romantic and Ideal," and by attempting to incorporate with
it " close imitation " and glib execution. We shall find in the works by
which he is best known neither imitation nor execution in the ordinary
sense ; but the foregoing notes, carefully studied, point to the conclusion
that, with the eclectic taste often co-existing with wide knowledge, their
writer was capable of loving very strongly widely different things—things
different alike from the Shoreham panels and the later Red Hill imaginations—and of extending his vision to either pole of art.

There is a simplicity in these memoranda—a taking it for granted that
the public would respond to his appeals and concessions, and learn to
love what he loved, is not without pathos. It seems (to quote Payne
Knight's words once again) that he still " believed in art (however
foolishly)," and " believed in men as he read of them in books."

In one of the old note-books will be found the following :—" April 1845.
" When huffed by bad hanging retreat for strength, not to popular style,
" but to NATURE. . . . Plan of 1845 D.V. Paint from *Effect* and *Colour*
" sketches. An elegant subject for *Florence* frame in hope of SCREEN.[1]

---

[1] A coveted position at the Society's Gallery.

" Carrara mountains and distant Florence. Twilight, blue cloud Welsh effect,
" . . . A scheme for next exhibition D.V., after my annual comparison of
" *my* works with others of W.C.S. exhibition. Effects independently of
" subject matter. 1. Cool sunrise with sun. 2. Do, without sun, in ¾ light.
" Italian coast like Callcott's *Spezzia.* 3. Effect like my little *Bay of Baiæ,*
" being an attempt to do it better. 4. The tender moonlight seen at Mr.
" Calvert's."

Part of the notes made at Princes Risborough are of especial import :—
" Collins's, Princes Risboro', Bucks, 1845. After having studied here for a
" month, my general impression with regard to effective painting and the
" conduct of picture is this.

" The bask of beautiful landscape in glorious sunlight is in nature
" perfectly delicious and congenial with the mind and heart of man, but the
" imitative power is so limited—particularly so as to the lowless of the light
" pigments with which we imitate—that the above, when upon paper or
" canvas, should perhaps only be considered as the corpse which is to be
" ANIMATED.

" The ANIMATOR is CHIAROSCURO. HOLES of DARK,
" BOLD CAST SHADOWS—the same PLAYFUL and INTRICATE
" sometimes, when cast from trees like (blueish) soft, cool gray, blotting
" or dappling over the finished matter (figures most beautiful under this
" effect). Where figures or sheep come in nearly front light against holes
" of shade under trees they are like plates or bassi-relievi of wrought gold.

" If it be judicious to follow the manner of working sketches from
" nature in the working of pictures, then remember, that though the sketch
" becomes finished beyond comparison sooner, yet that the process seems
" slow and the means delicate. The use of a violent colour immediately
" shocks one, and it is dappled about and melted into delicacies.

" PROCESS. 1. Chiaroscuro copied from sketch of effect. 2. Some
" realization of the solid matter, in which delicate drawing must take the
" lead, and ever accompany colouring. The working up of the pattern
" and textures is a slow work, even in drawing from nature, and this I think
" should not be hurried.

" How is that wholesome, clean, and unpicturelike appearance to be
" obtained, which on every side delights one in every country walk ? 1st
" by a more fresco-like treatment, not spreading juicy colour too widely.
" Secondly perhaps, also by remembering that the greater proportion of
" matter out of doors is a medium far removed from the coldest blue and
" the most gaudy yellow and orange. Hence a gray cottage side and a
" yellow tree tell in nature and have their just value. Thirdly by patience,
" in ripening the masses of illuminated matter : for what would nature be

" without its delicate playfulness of things into each other ; its infinity and
" endless suggestiveness. Now this can be imitated in a hurry neither in
" copying out of doors nor in painting at home. Fourthly by keeping the
" variety of the palette ALIVE. For a bit of nature, however small, refuses
" to be copied by any impatient dab or idle spread of one colour. Think
" of a gray stem with lichens and mosses, rich as a cabinet of gems, or
" think of a single piece of rock. Now how contemptibly do we imitate
" this with a few dabs and patches of colour.

" And all this is only one little corner of Art. The conclusion of the
" whole matter is this, that it is almost impossible to do rightly or wisely.
" That conceit, self-complacency, and indolence, should be incessantly
" hunted out of the inner man. That everything we do should be done
" with all our might, and that rest and recreation should be proportionably
" separated and entire. What a blessed thing is sleep to a mind always on
" the rack for improvement ! "

Not many years before this was written the writer was speaking of
" glimpses of perfumed and enchanted midsummer twilight." of " nooks "
spiritually beheld, and of his being " so inspired " that he worked as
confidently as if he were Michael Angelo himself upon a design that had,
just before, caused him " dreadful suffering."

The Risborough memoranda foreshadow what we may undoubtedly
regard as an approaching change in his practice—a change well marked
and possibly prudential, but one (if I read it aright) which did not affect
his inmost ideal. He appears, at this period of his life, to have been
swayed by two contending impulses ; the one brought about by a very
keen admiration of nature as it is viewed simply by the outward eye ; the
other, by the action of a different and to him a more natural kind of
vision which added to nature a supernatural beauty. For the time being,
" juicy colour " seems to be forsworn altogether ; and although he delights
as much as ever in " the bask of beautiful landscape in glorious sunlight "
he is becoming far more keenly sensitive than of old to subtle ways of
enhancing such splendour and securing some of the variety of nature's
colouring by means of a palette kept " alive." Nevertheless, many of the
water-colours that followed show a distinct and well-marked stage of
transition from early enthusiasm to a circumspect prudence, partly brought
about, no doubt, by the discovery of the unpopularity of enthusiasm for
nearly everything he esteemed, and partly by the difficulty of converting
pictures above the comprehension of the average art " patron " into beef
and mutton. No doubt he realized ruefully enough that most of the
qualities he was attempting to secure, most of the delicate subtleties of
nature's forms, and the exquisite variety and interplay of nature's colouring,
together with all the laws and the principles he was so laboriously

mastering, were as utterly beyond the comprehension of that patron, as of a blind man.

In letters of a far later date written after a good many more of life's bitter lessons had been mastered, we find him asking whether sight is considered the lowest of the senses, that its proper culture is so much neglected ; and he speaks of the " illiterate eye of a senior wrangler."

A good example of the temporary change in his practice is a water-colour exhibited in 1845, and entitled *Tivoli and the Cypresses of the Villa D'Este*. It is a replica of one of the best and richest of the Italian studies, but so much of the vigour and spirit has been evaporated that the drawing looks as if it had suffered years of exposure to bright sunlight.

Another of the memorandum-books contains a full and careful record of my father's labours about this time as a teacher, and we find that he had now what some have delighted in calling a " large and fashionable connection." In this branch of his calling, as in all others, his energy, system, and order were conspicuous, and where he met with good material to work upon he was proportionably successful. But although, after 1845, there was an improvement in his income chiefly brought about by this teaching (the sale of drawings being small and the prices low), his fight was still a hard one, and his expenses were increasing apace in spite of luxuries of all kinds having been ruthlessly cut off. At one end of this book, in bold but now faded writing, are extracts made at Shoreham, from Shakespeare, Spenser, and other poets, with remarks upon them : and at the other end is a list of engagements with pupils, the amounts received, together with some informa-tion from my father's friend, Mr. F. O. Finch, touching the starvation terms usually arranged with schools. In the middle of the book are columns of personal accounts laboriously and minutely entered in pencil, but anything but perspicuous, and remarkably unbusinesslike ; this being invariably the case when my father attempted such matters. Among other items is one of £21 received from Messrs. Bradbury and Evans for a set of four illustrations to the first edition of Charles Dickens's *Letters from Italy*, an undertaking which led to a brief correspondence with the author.

It is difficult to imagine a more dreary commentary upon my father's life than this old book of memoranda and cash accounts. It shows how that life began in studiousness—without idleness, yet with leisure to see, to read, to think, and be happy : then, how it drifted little by little into a determined and continuous struggle against adverse circumstances ; with the ever-present fear that if, through illness or otherwise, that struggle were for an instant remitted, the lost ground could never be recovered.

Taking up the book next in order to this we find the story saddening still more. It opens with many extracts (copied as before, at Shoreham, with painstaking elaboration and evident delight) from favourite works of devotion, and from religious discourses. Then we come to a "List of pictures sold" from 1843 to 1853, including several in oil—altogether five and forty works [1] at an average price a little short of £16. Against this income, were to be debited the expenses of a London house and household! It can thus be realized how much depended on his unremitted exertions as a teacher, and upon good health and spirits. As has been well said, "The most painful and frequent form of the inter-dependence of dual " conditions, is when a man must have money to get health (by rest and " ease) and must have health to get money." [2]

That my father regarded his teaching as a necessity from which he would have escaped if he could is shown by this extract from a letter to my mother. "June 14, 1847 . . . What use I could have made in the " country of these three weeks of fine weather! If I could but stand the " loss of the first disentanglement from teaching I think it would be a " hundred times overpaid : but it is full of difficulties."

Returning to the book, we find at the end of some notes of a doctor's attendance on More, and probably connected with it in the writer's mind by the anticipation of the inevitable bill, these words :—

"I must, D.V., strike out at once into a NEW STYLE. SIMPLE " SUBJECT ; BOLD EFFECT : BROAD RAPID EXECUTION : " rounding the chiaroscuro without timidity as to blotting out little lights. " when the leaving them precise and sharp would involve premature " niggle—using the Globe Principle with power and boldness. On " Tuesday, March 3rd, [1846] I called, as I had long intended, at Mr. " Colnaghi's. I was no sooner there, than Mr. Scott asked me if I had " heard from Mr.———to whom he had spoken in my favour respecting " Mr.———'s sons at Willesden. I called on Mr.———coming home- " wards. He gave me a note to the tutor, Mr. Clarke, and I was engaged. " I gave the first lesson Saturday March 7. If DIVINE PROVIDENCE " PLEASE, how easily is employment obtained. October 8, I have had " the above teaching ever since, blessed be God."

On the other side of the same leaf as the foregoing entries of 1846 is this : "December 15, 1847. My dear daughter Mary Elizabeth *died* at " 25 minutes to 6 p.m. The above was written on the evening of her death." Eleven days later, my father wrote below this the particulars of the child's last illness. It is a sad, simple story of suffering borne by a mere baby with touching patience ; and also, as it seems, of the incompetence of the doctors who might with a little more attention have saved her life. The story ends as follows :—". . . . Her mother was sitting at the end of the bed when Mrs.

[1] A good number of the drawings are of a size then a favourite one with the artist and known to him as " Little Longs" or " L. L." They measured from 16 × 7¼ to 16¾ × 7½.
[2] *Etching and Etchers.* P. G. Hamerton.

" Linnell said 'I think she is gone.' Anny put her face close to Mary's, but
" could hear no sound of breathing. Her eyes were open and fixed, but her
" face turned deadly pale . . . . SHE WAS DEAD. Mrs. Linnell closed
" her eyes. The last I saw of her dear gray eyes was in the afternoon, when I
" watched them. The lids closing a little over them made it seem like a
" mournful and clouded sunset. She had appeared for the most part un-
" conscious for two or three days, but on the morning of the day she died
" Anny was going to bed, when she held up one trembling arm and then the
" other. Anny put her head down between them, when she held her tightly
" round the neck for about a minute, and seemed to be thus taking a last
" leave of her mother. She had done so to me about two days before.
" She bore her sufferings and took her physic with the greatest patience,
" saying in the early part of her illness, 'I will take it to please you, dear
" Papa,' and sometimes said the same to her Mama before I came up.

" Six weeks back from this evening, Sunday, 26th December, we spent a
" happy afternoon together, reading Schmidt's story of Antony, and before
" she went to bed she was playing at magic music . . . . "

My father's agony as he wrote these words must be gauged not by the
ordinary standard of susceptibility to mental pain. What he felt was an
intense, ceaseless, and insufferable torture to which, but for that one hope
of ultimate reunion which forms so strong and beautiful a feature of
Christianity, death would have been far preferable. His grief was also
the harder to bear by means of his almost childish inability to restrain it.
He had to go about his work and to keep his teaching engagements with
eyes bleared and a voice often choked by sorrow.

The poor baby had been her father's pet, for she was unusually gentle
and affectionate, and intelligent far beyond her years. Unspeakable
dreariness seemed to drop upon the house like a black pall when the
golden little head and cheery voice were there no longer. That staunch
old friend Mr. Calvert did his best to console the mourners and spent
every evening with them, but at last they determined to leave Marylebone,
and in March, 1848 they removed to 1.A, Victoria Road. Kensington—an
old detached cottage overlooking the Riding School.

THE removal to Kensington in the spring of 1848 was a wise step. The little house in Marylebone was now in the midst of surroundings among which few professional men would care to be found, and to the clay soil my father attributed much of his ill-health since his return from Italy. The chief benefit of the removal was that though it increased his distance from one or two of the companions of his youth it brought him into the very midst of an artistic circle whence arose invaluable friendships. Moreover, Kensington Gardens formed a better apology for the country than dank Regent's Park, and gave him some opportunities (such as they were) of studying foliage and sylvan effects.

Having wavered between Yorkshire and the south of England in choosing the place for his summer campaign his old prejudice against the North prevailed, and he spent the greater part of July in Cornwall. Here, on this and other occasions, he accumulated a large number of pencil, chalk, and water-colour sketches of the coast, including a three weeks' series of sunsets painted each day with precisely the same foreground of sea and rock ; "a piece of study" which he afterwards quoted as having been of great value to him. The sunsets were boldly and very rapidly executed, some on white, and some on tinted paper : and for this work he wore the large neutral-tint spectacles. Such of these studies as I have seen are skilful ; and particularly so in the most difficult part—the scintillating track of sunlight upon the water. In the whole of this Cornish work Mr. Linnell's ideal of studying from nature is realized ; that is, the end in view is attained "by skill rather than hard labour"— by "a perception of the principles upon which nature delights." There is not a touch too much, and every touch is as significant as the symbols of stenography. The knowledge gained by this especial attention to sunsets over the sea was afterwards utilized in many works : among others, in *Robinson Crusoe* ; *St. Paul landing in Italy* ; and *The Brother come home from Sea.*

On the 17th of December (almost the anniversary of little Mary's death) my paternal grandfather died, being then seventy-three years old. Writing of this loss with the characteristic freedom with which my father spoke of his emotions he says :—" The first gush of tears came with the

" thought, ' How he loved my childhood's soul and MIND—how he
" laboured to improve them, sitting in the house and walking in
" the fields !' "

In 1848 nearly two-thirds of my father's income were derived from
teaching. His drawings, considering the time, and thought, and devotion he
lavished upon them were still selling at almost absurdly unprofitable prices
—prices which were kept down as much by his want of courage as want of
capital, although he was occasionally comforted by friends' assurances that
they were " moderate." He says however, " This year I made a great
advance in the estimation of artists by my mottled-sky drawing begun at
Margate." He was perhaps at this time not fully aware that the estimation of artists is no gauge whatever of the estimation of the public ; but
had he been so, he would have far preferred the former. This notable
" Margate Mottle " as he called it, is to be met with elsewhere amongst his
designs and memoranda.

The drawing alluded to was not sold (in spite of the high estimation of
artists), and is now in my keeping. [1] The execution is somewhat slight, but
the composition and light and shade are pleasing. The sun sets in the
midst of that beautiful dappled glory sometimes described as a " mackerel
sky." Tall and graceful middle-distant trees cast their shadows over the
cattle which are cooling themselves in a mill-pond after the day's heat, and
over wheat reddening for an early harvest. Nestling beneath the trees and
in their deepest shade sleeps the old mill ; and beyond them stretches a
wild, woodland country with hills that, here and there, seem to attain to the
dignity of mountains. The sky (although it is luminous), judged by the
standard of my father's later works is somewhat faint and vapid in colour,
giving the impression of the fading of some pigment such as Indian yellow,
which he certainly used about this time.

The chief interest of this drawing to the artist himself afterwards lay in a
small oil copy which was painted in his presence in June 1852, by Mr. Reed,
an intimate friend learned in the history and mysteries of oil-painting, and
with whom it was my father's delight to discuss the practice of the great Venetians and other masters. In a note-book devoted to oil-painting my father
writes as follows :—" Mr. R. most kindly painted in one day before me an
" oil sketch from my ' Margate ' sunset—the mottled sky—to *show* me his
" method and processes, of which he had before, with the same kindness,
" imparted the general principles. His sketch seemed to me to possess some
" of the finest qualities of Venetian painting ; and some of those points on
" which, before, I had felt doubtful (particularly the cool reds and the
" heightenings with white, afterwards toned, during the progress of the work),

[1] Like a good many works painted at this period it measures **28 × 20½** inches. I have
hitherto supposed the title to be *A Landscape—sunset*, but that work was exhibited in 1847.

" I saw to be important points of a great scientific whole." My father after
wards writes at the beginning of his notes, " Inferences from the following
" combined with my own notion. A brilliant white ground. First painting.
" white, black, and grey. A little copal and spike oil, with very stiff white,
" painted freely and boldly with hog-tools, so as to get a permanent thread
" and texture, from which the successive paintings should become less and
" less impasted, filling up to a rich, solid, waxy, surface (in appearance).
" Second painting by various means got up to the intended colouring as
" soon as possible, only cooler than intended, and the blues and greys
" kept very fresh."

This note-book forms conclusive evidence that as late as 1852 my father
still clung to his old hope of practising, at all events occasionally, as an oil-
painter : and there is an allusion to the beginning of a picture he had also
exhibited as a water-colour in 1849, *Farewell to Calypso.* Indeed my late
researches among the lumber of our old home at Red Hill revealed enough
canvases, stretchers, panels, and even pictures in various stages of completeness, to convince any one of my father's devotion to a branch of art which
the disappointments of his later life left him so little opportunity of
practising.

Christian descending into the Valley of Humiliation. a drawing of some
size exhibited in 1848, did not repay an unusually ambitious treatment.
In colouring it ranks with the works which constitute what I have called
the " transition stage " in my father's art, but the sky shows great knowledge.
It returned unsold from the exhibition to take its place with those unfor-
tunates a few of which many a discouraged artist hides away from his own
and other people's sight.

For the summer months of 1849, my father took his family to Red Hill
in Surrey ; then a quiet and pretty neighbourhood whither, not many years
before, the Porchester Terrace veteran had removed. Here Mr. Linnell
now ruled his small dominion of " Redstone Wood " as independently as
an eastern chief. Designing his own house, and personally supervising the
fitting of almost every block of stone in its strong walls, he had so placed it
on the brow of a well-timbered hill sloping towards the west that it served
as his observatory for those effects for which he was soon to become celebrated. He had, as it were, fortified a stronghold in the midst of the
placid and conventional country society, and there revelled in his art. pored
over Greek and Hebrew, ground his corn, baked his bread, brewed his ale,
and thundered forth his denunciations of men and opinions that displeased
him ; being aided and abetted in all that he did by a family to whom, for
the most part, every word of his was an irresistible ukase.

Religious differences had long since diminished what sympathy had
once existed between his son-in-law and himself : and although the younger

artist's respect for the veteran's genius, earnestness, and other sterling qualities had decreased not one whit, there was an imperceptibly widening breach between them. It could hardly have been otherwise when the one had become an implacable enemy to sacerdotalism and the champion of Liberalism in politics, while the other still firmly held to the religious faith of his youth and had little sympathy with Radicals, although he no longer railed at them with the intolerance found in The West Kent *Address*.

In his innumerable letters to my mother her father ceased not to argue energetically and ingeniously on the side of nonconformity ; or to attack with characteristic contempt and violence the faith she had embraced before her marriage. It was these circumstances that led my father in one of his letters to his wife, to speak as follows :—

" . . . That we may never have in future to misspend time in the " deplorable mischief of religious controversy, pray understand, as I " thought I often mentioned, that I am no Puseyite, but a most unworthy " member of the Church of Christ, in common with every one of those " poor children 'at the Philanthropic Farm School ; that if I have any " ' religious views '—if I may use that disagreeable expression—they are " about equally unfavourable to the Manning School and to Puritanism.

" I have no doubt that the worship of the primitive Christians was a " musical service, and therefore always should prefer a chanted ritual to a " read one ; but I should not frequent any church, nor have ever done so, " where I thought that such ritual was accompanied by false doctrine, " unless it were the only church within reach.

" I believe that our cathedral service is more like that of the Christian " Church at Jerusalem under the episcopate of St. James, than any other " I have ever heard of. As to worship in any societies not under the " authority of our own bishops, or attendance at them, I can truly say that " I have hitherto set an example of self-denial ; and [I] think in serious " things of this kind it is always best to be on the safe side. Merely as " an intellectual treat it would be a strong attraction to know that Dr. " Newman is coming to London and will preach on the Sunday evenings, " but I have hitherto forborne. . . . "

This is the most distinct declaration of my father's religious opinions with which I am acquainted ; and it was a subject upon which, in after life, he was particularly reticent. The circumstances which led to the writing of the foregoing words were not without their influence on his subsequent history, and led to others which served to embitter the more effectually, much of his future life.

It will be seen that, personally, he had little inducement to linger at Red Hill, and he did no more than pay intermittent visits from London to his family. He plied his brush and pencil on these occasions as assiduously as ever ; but a neighbourhood, however pretty, which was almost entirely without running water and the rich pastoral sentiment he loved—one daily suffering more and more from railway extension was not much to his mind.

To this period, or perhaps to a time rather earlier, may be ascribed some undated memoranda on a small sepia sketch :—" The principle of " the Borghesi Titian, viz. 1st, globose lights contrasted with *sheets* of dark, " and 2nd, *Added* INTENSE spot of light and dark on figure ; as, for " instance, black and white cow. Remember this, O thou dull brute ! " Under a small sepia design of a Welsh castle and town, with the sun setting behind them, are these words :—" Looking at a town in the late " twilight the lightness and darkness of the local colours of the trees and " buildings classify themselves and become breadths 1. 2. 3.

" The gradations between them are a secondary matter, though " exquisite, varying in size and brightness. Some of middle-tint. Some " glittering through dark recesses or trees. The variety in *candle-* " *LIGHTS* is most beautiful."

Beneath a sketch of the sun setting behind a near, dark, wooded hill is the following. " Where the scheme is a great mass of dark under the " sun, then cool local colours below are called for, as ruins or gray rocks. " And I think the one vivid light on water from upper sky, as observed at " Guildford among the deep middle-distant woods, very important where it " can be introduced. I think so bright a light as the sun should be " echoed somewhere ; and for a more important reason, it is wanted in " orange twilight as otherwise there is no focus—the sky affording no " *point* of focus when the sun is gone." Upon the same piece of paper, but beneath a sketch of the sun setting behind a more distant down, with an expanse of country between that down and the spectator is written. " Middle distance not lighted by the sun has, after the manner of " twilight after the sun dips, a delicate, warm light, from the golden " horizon. Cover the sun, and you find it not confused but clear, " though very broad and delicate, so that a little white might be used. " Tempera would do it."

It is in his cash accounts for 1850 that I find my father's first allusion to The Etching Club. This was a small society which flourished most when the art of etching was comparatively little known in England, and it was originally formed of a few more or less well-known Royal Academicians and water-colour painters who were mutually acquainted, and who supped every month in a jovial but simple fashion at each other's homes. From time to time, exchanging the brush for the needle, and beginning in 1841 with *The Deserted Village*, they had illustrated some beautiful poem, or had brought out a portfolio of independent subjects. The slender profits accruing from these works were allotted by ballot ; each member's vote, I believe, being distributed among his fellow member's etchings in varying proportion according to his opinion of those etchings. The result of this was that each plate was valued according to its degree of merit and its degree of completeness, so that a slight sketch upon the copper was valued at a lower sum than a ripe and highly-finished etching.

Years afterwards, when a new art, resembling the old one chiefly in name, became the rage there was a considerable infusion of new blood into the Club ; and new opinions were introduced by the etchers who did not carry their work as far as the older hands, upon the question of the method of payment. Dissensions arose, and these disputes were the beginning of the end. The Club lived long enough to be told by a new school of critics which also had arisen that it had done very little for the true art of etching—had been in the dark touching the resources, the scope, and the legitimate field of that art. Then, after a futile struggle to keep pace with the achievements of the "true etcher," as displayed in the last work, the Club quietly ceased to exist.[1]

As my father belonged, and was proud to belong, to this little society,[2] and firmly believed in the traditions which were current among some of the older members, I will briefly describe the essential points of difference between those traditions and the usage of the more modern school of etchers, which has now, as it would seem, so completely eclipsed the old in the esteem of the general public, and even in the esteem of some connoisseurs.

The etcher who believed in those old traditions approached his work as a work of difficulty, uncertainty, but of supreme fascination. He came fresh from his pictures or drawings—from a positive process and a flexible point, to a negative process, where each line had to be scratched with a small steel point upon a hard, shining metal, previously covered with a kind of dark varnish : and scratched too, the reverse way to that in which it was finally to appear in the proof, all the lines of course being, in this stage, of very nearly equal tenuity. As he hoped to achieve upon the copper some of the highest, loveliest, and most subtle qualities in art ; to perpetuate and

---

[1] It is some consolation to believers in the old tradition to find that, although such of the early publications of the Club as find their way into the hands of the second-hand booksellers still fetch good prices, this last work fetches less than a quarter of the price at which it was published ; even although every proof is signed by the artist.

[2] He was also one of those who stoutly supported the old rules of the Club, and failed to see why a plate which had taken him months to complete, upon which he had lavished all his experience and knowledge, should be valued by fixed rule at the same figure as a slight sketch done in a few hours, instead of having the value appraised by a consensus of the members.

distribute a design that should be as good as he could make it, and do him
no dishonour, he was content to dwell day after day, and perhaps week after
week, upon the work : till, to the uninitiated, the plate was a glittering chaos.
It was then immersed in an old-fashioned mordant or acid, which "bit in,"
or ate away to a certain degree, all the exposed lines, without touching the
surfaces of copper still protected by the varnish. Timing the first biting as
accurately as he could, the etcher removed the plate from the mordant, and
very carefully "stopped out" (that is, covered with varnish) such lines as
he intended to appear faintest in the proof. He then reimmersed the plate
for another carefully timed period, and again "stopped out"; repeating
these processes again and again,[1] according as he desired more or less variety
of tone, gradation, and other high qualities, in the finished etching.
When all the lines except the deepest, or last bitten, had been covered with
stopping-out varnish, the etcher removed the ground and betook himself
(not without qualms) to his printer, who was to furnish him with the first
"trial proof." The printer of that day was an unambitious and often a very
unintelligent mechanic, firmly bound to the petrified traditions of an inflexible routine. He did no more, and was rarely asked to do more, than to
show the etcher the real extent and condition of his work ; which he accomplished first by inking the plate all over, and then by wiping it with canvases
and polishing it with whiting till all the ink was removed, except that in the
excavations caused by the acid ; and the untouched surfaces between the
lines were consequently represented in the proof by absolutely clean paper.

The etcher, lacking the prescience and infallibility of the practised engraver, was often humiliated, sometimes horrified to find that, in spite of all
his labours and all his calculations, he had fallen more or less short of his
intention—that his plate was empty, and lacked the variety, finish, and
gradation he had anticipated. He found perhaps, or was led to suppose by
unusually execrable printing, that he had miscalculated the activity of the
acid : and that, consequently, certain passages had been over or under-
bitten. The printer, accustomed to the certainty of the professional, looked
upon this poor amateur with pity, and pulled him an extra proof or two,
each more or less identical with the first.

The artist then took up his work afresh. He laid a new ground, and
by means of patience, and care, and the higher branches of artistic knowledge, achieved, little by little, the result he sought : visiting the printer from
time to time, till he saw before him a proof which fulfilled his ideal—a
proof that, having been produced by fairly simple and straightforward
printing, could be repeated indefinitely.

The result achieved in this manner (presuming the etcher to be an ex-

[1] A justly celebrated etcher is said to have given 70 distinct "stoppings out" to one
plate : that is, to have created seventy varieties of depth.

perienced artist) possessed certain qualities not to be found elsewhere within the whole range of art. It was a happy mixture of "art and accident"; and the accident had been turned to such account by art that, in certain respects, the result eclipsed the master-pieces of the most highly-skilled line or mezzotint engravers. There was infinite variety of tone, with brilliant sparkle and interplay of light and shade. The lights scintillated or gleamed ; the shadows were at once transparent, shadowlike, and rich in colour ; the half-tints were full of variety, together with subtle and charming gradation. The workmanship itself varied from bold lines deeply excavated in the metal, but still instinct with life, feeling, and draughtsmanship, to the most tender and delicate manipulation that human fingers guided by human love could compass. The etcher had concentrated all his enthusiasm and all his knowledge upon these few superficial inches of steel or copper. He and he alone was responsible for the exact degree of the mutual relations of every tone, the shape and intensity of every light, and the perfect harmony of the whole.

This was the tradition of the old-fashioned etchers as I have known them ; and it is easy to pick out examples of its fulfilment from among the earlier works of the Club.

It will be seen, of course, that one of the chief characteristics of this kind of work was its honest and genuine originality. What it professed to be it was. There was no more difficulty in distinguishing between the work of the artist and the work of the copper-plate printer than there is in the case of a proof of a line engraving. Nothing more was deputed to the printer than he was, as a mechanic, fit to undertake, and no iota of the difficult task of ripening the workmanship to the ideal perfection was eluded in anticipation of help from other hands. Indeed, whether help were or were not desired, it was not forthcoming.

With the usage of the modern etcher, the case, for the most part, is different. Although he begins just in the same way, and with the same materials : and though, in some instances, he may even be equally careful and solicitous in the choice of his subject, he soon reaches a point at which his resemblance to his devoted elder brother ceases. He has learnt to anticipate extraneous help, and this anticipation leads him to depute to other hands some of the very matters which the old type of etcher would have made an especial point of keeping in his own.

The nearer the simple old trade of copper-plate printing has approached the borders of the occult sciences, and the more it has tempted the etcher by offering him cheap substitutes for his own careful labour, the more has that temptation been yielded to, till a point has been reached when it is not unusual for an hour or even more to be spent by the printer upon a single proof. This time is chiefly devoted to processes which were unknown to the old printer, and which more or less vitally effect the balance of the light and shade, the shapes and intensity of the deepest shadows and highest lights, the quality of the half-tones, and in some cases, even the drawing of prominent objects. Inks of different colour are sometimes used for different portions of the same subject, in order to convey a certain kind of illusion, and even skies (not to mention sun, moon, and stars) have, after a manner, been manufactured, where the etcher has preferred to save himself the trouble.[1]

It is true that, anticipating this assistance, the etcher may have planned its direction and extent beforehand in his own mind, and that he may endeavour by personally superintending the printing of a sample proof and strictly enjoining the printer to imitate that proof to secure the fulfilment of those plans throughout the edition. Were printers in general possessed of any artistic education, or familiar with the rudiments of draughtsmanship, or of the laws of chiaroscuro and aerial perspective, it is possible that such sanguine anticipations might be realized to a certain extent, but only so far as it is possible for one artist to interpret the mind of another. For the most part, however, they are without any such education, are petrified by their apprenticeship and early training, and are nearly always working against time. It is therefore nearly as preposterous to suppose that the printer can safely be trusted to materially increase or diminish or to transpose the intensity of the lights and darks, or otherwise to supplement or alter the etcher's workmanship time after time through an edition, as to suppose that an artist's frame-maker could be trusted to usurp the palette and brushes on " varnishing day," or his colourman, to complete a black and white cartoon.

That the etcher's difficulties who trusts to his printer's skill so far from being diminished by either printing himself, or getting some master of the art to print him, a sample proof for an edition are often greatly increased is a fact that has been abundantly proved. The greatest master-printer of the age is well aware of this. A proof that he himself can produce in a few minutes as he smokes his cigarette is often unapproachable by any less skilful and supple-fingered person ; and he will decline to pull a sample proof for an edition so good that he knows his staff will be incapable of copying it successfully. A well-known publisher who had been continually confronted with this difficulty of getting a sample proof successfully imitated throughout an edition (or indeed imitated at all) told me that. in his opinion, the difficulty arose from the fact that the average printer is incapable of seeing the difference between an execrable proof and a superb one—incapable of analyzing the causes of his success or failure. It is

[1] That skies have proved a stumbling-block to many a member of the modern school would seem probable, from the innumerable instances in which they are altogether omitted.

obvious that if it is impossible to make the manipulator see *why* a wipe in a certain place or direction makes the difference between a good proof and a bad one—if the language in which you can best convey your meaning is unknown to him, you cannot expect that wipe to be given intelligently : and you may cudgel your brains in vain for the mechanical equivalents to such terms as "breadth," "delicate half-tone," "vivacity," "sparkle," "richness," or "gradation."

In this consists one of the chief stumbling-blocks of the modern etcher, and it arises from his deserting, in certain all-important particulars, the older traditions of the art. He has learnt to rely on help of a very material kind (a kind that makes or mars his own work as an artist), from a man who is not, and never can be an artist—a man who, by training and necessity, must, does, and will, always work as a skilled mechanic. And the evil does not end here : for in many cases a sample proof is given to this mechanic which has depended upon its success in the artist's eyes upon certain qualities which no one who is not also an artist is capable of understanding. These qualities the mechanic endeavours to imitate, and in doing so he produces those remarkable results which have, of late years, appeared by the dozen in print-sellers' shop windows, under the title (and sometimes the fraudulent title) of "Artist's Proofs."

I have Mr. Hamerton's permission to quote one of the strongest protests I have seen, against the printing of etchings by mere tradesmen. Writing to my father in January, 1872, he says : -"What a murderous thing bad printing is, for etchings ! A new edition of a book of mine with 37 of my own little plates has just been published in America. The plates were printed . . . . in London, and so ignorantly, stupidly, and hideously that I was quite unable to bear the sight of the book and stuck it into the fire where I would stick every other copy of the same edition if I could only get at them all. I will never trust an etching again in the hands of any *tradesman printer.* To print an etching a man ought to be an artist."

The tricks and dodges of printing are very fascinating and very beautiful in themselves, but the etcher of the older school who tried such few dodges as existed in his day found sooner or later that, in trusting them too implicitly, he was leaning on a broken reed. Taken broadly, and compared for the sake of illustration with the best earlier etchings of the old Club, many modern plates are monotonous in tone, and lacking in brilliancy. Their chief faults appear to be a flatness and lack of variety which is mainly brought about by what is technically called the *retroussage* of the darks and shadows ; this, besides making them all of equal depth, *makes them all of the same quality.* The modern printer rarely achieves a skilful focus either in his lights or darks, and if he does achieve a focus it is very often in the wrong place. Such partnership productions do not show the true

genius of an exquisite and essentially autographic art ; and although they
may be, as their admirers assert, "true etchings," or "done at a sitting," or
done with "a few lines sternly clear," they kick the beam as works of art
and of love, when fairly weighed by impartial and competent judges
against such plates as Mr. Hook's[1] *Egg Gatherers*, his *Fisherman's Good
night*, or the late Frederick Taylor's inimitable little plate entitled *What
shall he have who killed the Deer ?*

To such a pitch has the confusion between the work of the etcher and the
work of the printer risen, that criticisms have been written, and written too
with all the authority of the specialist, in which the former has been credited
with effects due entirely to the latter. In the eyes of such of the public as
are learned enough to know that "etching" is not drawing in pen and ink,
the confusion is still more completely confounded ; but the admirer of one
of the old etchings ("false" I suppose we must call them, if we wish to be
up to date), had at least the consolation of knowing whose handiwork it was
which he admired. This is a consolation which is denied to the purchaser,
and denied, it seems, even to the critic of to-day.

The etcher of the older school was by no means without the vexation of
spirit arising from his printer's inflexible adhesion to ancient tradition, but
his work gained rather than lost by those eternal laws which govern the
British workman, because he was led to a distrust of mere machinery, human
or otherwise—led to that patient, thoughtful, and devoted ripening, to that
solicitude of mind, upon which all high excellence depends, in picture or in
poem.

The printing of that day could be done badly—even brutally ; and in
common with his brother members of the Club my father suffered much from
work which was not only unintelligent, but which seemed almost vindictive.
Indeed it sometimes approached that "thorough scouring with a cloth" mentioned, I believe, as the usual method of wiping etchings by a critic in *The
Pall Mall Gazette*. Over and over again my father had striven for ink which
was not cold but warm in tone, and he had always been defeated by the
surreptitious mixture of a little blue with the black. He had stood on the
watch, hour after hour, to prevent the inevitable and equal "scouring" of the
surface of the plate with whiting before passing it through the press. He
had mourned over cheerless tints of India and other papers, and had covered
the margins of many a proof (now in my keeping), with pathetic adjurations
that might just as well have been addressed to the press as to the man who

---

[1] Of modern etching Mr. Hook writes to my father thus :—"Some etchers, nowadays,
"dip a daddy long-legs into the ink, and start him on an adventure across a continent of
"*papier vergé*. A glowing eulogy appears in *The Times*. 1st state proofs, before
"daddy fluttered his wings, 5 guineas ! After flutter 8 guineas !!! and so on. Poor
"Rembrandt !"

turned the wheel. He knew nothing then (and the printers of that day knew as little) of the possibilities latent in the grimy and relentless paraphernalia of the printing-office. But time passed on, etching became popular, and at last, under the auspices of the best printer of the day, my father introduced a press into his own house, where blueing, and "scouring," and inflexible routine, no longer tormented him.

With his liking for ideals, he had always aimed at ideal printing, but even when all the resources of the art were at his command he did not abate one jot of the time, and care, and patience he bestowed upon his plates. I will quote a paragragh of a letter I received from him when I was very carefully printing a series of *remarque* proofs of one of his plates, at my own press in London :—" Success in the printing of this etching depends on delight " in solitude and *locked doors*, a *contemplative mood*, and intense con- " centration ; indeed, these are the conditions of all high excellence. . . . " I say again, consider of *your kind* of printing (as Sir Joshua says to " the painter), that you must work with THE BALANCES IN YOUR " HAND ; that whosoever balances must attend—whosoever attends " must, during that mental operation, ' *be quiet.*' " In another letter he writes thus :—" For myself, I doubt whether etching, in the old " sense of the word, is not almost superseded by the new art of " *retroussage*, added by the printer upon a comparatively slight fabric. " Sometimes it has been very effective, but in most instances is so " inferior to linear etching as to become quite another art : but then, " as it produces an effect quite as satisfactory to the public in about one- " fifth of the time,[1] it beats linear etching out of the market. It seems to " me that the charm of linear etching is the glimmering through of the " white paper even in the shadows, so that almost everything either " sparkles or suggests sparkle. Now this is somewhat like the effect of a " purely white ground under an oil painting. The demonstrable differ- " ence may be small, but the real deterioration of a dark ground is " universal ; and, not to quote irreverently, it is a ' darkness that may " be felt ' if it cannot be proved. Well *retroussage*, if not kept within " narrow bounds, extinguishes the thousand little luminous eyes which " peer through a finished linear etching, and in those of Claude are " moving sunshine upon dew, or dew upon violets in the shade."

In the slight biographical sketch I published in 1882 I spoke of my father's practice in the technicalities of etching as combining " successful calculation," and " deep knowledge of the materials employed," with " inexhaustible patience," and " marvellous manipulative skill." This, I

---

[1] Here my father is in error. The darks produced by *retroussage* can be achieved in very much less than a fifth of the time they would take if produced by the action of the acid.

regret to say, is not accurate. He himself speaks of his earlier practice as " a scramble of uncertainties from beginning to end : " and when I recall all that I have seen him do, and all the notes he made upon the subject, I must admit that although we may freely grant him his patience and manipulative skill these were more often displayed in overcoming the results of inexperience and mischance than in aiding those of "successful calculation." His greatest skill lay in the matchless art with which he not only turned accident, and often very untoward accident, to account, but produced from it latent qualities which far eclipsed any qualities that would have arisen from greater precision and certainty. For example : he writes :—" . . . I used to sit down to etching with becoming gravity, " though the work had sometimes a rather negative bearing : for I re- " member once spending a whole day in nearly burnishing out a sky that " was overbitten. The perverse acid *would* bite skies and nothing else : " but being spared to attempt another, I humbly trust to go half through " the copper." This plate was *The Skylark*, and what I so much admire in it· the delicate upward flush of early dawn over thin vaporous cloud, was the result of the day's elbow-grease directed, not by knowledge of any etching technicality, but by knowledge of one of the most beautiful effects in nature.

To quote him again on this question of uncertainty, he says :—" . . . I " spent several days working and proving in London in a ghastly frame of " mind, owing, for once, not to my own clumsiness, but to the detestability, " both as to thinness and quality, of the old, scraped, Club copper on which " [my etching] was done. I gave myself up for lost on Saturday at 5.30, " but, by a desperate perseverance, had singed the last neck of the hydra " by 6.15, and hope to send you soon, one of the very best impressions. " . . . My wretched plate bent up like an earwig disturbed in an egg- " plum." I think it is natural to wonder a little, first at the notable economy which served out to a member of the Club a plate thinned down by the removal of a former etching, and secondly at the innocence of technicalities which cheerfully accepted that plate and produced upon it so elaborate an effort as *The Morning of Life* in happy ignorance that, in the hands of a printer who seems to have been equally innocent of technical knowledge, it would curl up "like an earwig disturbed in an egg-plum."

The Willow, my father's probationary etching, was not at all ambitious. It was the first essay and an honest one, in an art which was once considered difficult. It will be seen that some of the lines in the sky have been ruled, a fault that led to a timely admonition from that superb etcher Mr. Creswick, and to my father's study of the sky of that tiny masterpiece *Evening on the Common*. The great technical advance from *The Willow* to the three little plates known as *The Herdsman's Cottage, Christmas,* and *The Skylark,* is in some degree accounted for by the help and encouragement received from my father's old friend the late Mr. C. W. Cope, and from that eminently kind and skilful artist, the late Mr. T. O. Barlow. *The Skylark* reproduces the theme though not the details of the small picture I have mentioned as having been painted *con amore* some years before.

My father was not content with transcribing on copper (as he did in the case of *The Willow*) some sketch or study, but having thought out and matured a congenial subject in his mind, he seemed to plunge at once and by preference into a combat with the greatest possible difficulties. Among those he successfully overcame (besides the effect I have mentioned in *The Skylark*), are the contrast of the cold sheen of the moon with the cosy glimmer of candle and firelight : and the full blaze and dazzle of the sun, setting behind trees which cast a dancing maze of shadows on the grass. Such effects are hard enough to deal with by means of all the resources of pencil and colours, but when they are attained by processes such as directing the attacks of a powerful corrosive upon steel or copper we may permit ourselves to admire.

My father's sheet anchor was that beautiful refinement known as "stopping out." This is a process so vitally important that it was shrewdly said by a well-known engraver that one day devoted to it was worth five devoted to the needle. It will be seen by an examination of such plates as *The Herdsman* and *The Rising Moon,* what an amount of thoughtful work was bestowed upon them in this respect.

A pithy saying of Mr. Hook's concerning etching, "Lose your line and you lose your light," my father kept constantly in mind. *Retroussage,* unless very sparingly and skilfully applied to his plates by an artist's hand, would destroy that clearness of line, and with it half their subtlety, their atmosphere, transparency of shadow, and variety of tone.

Those who have seen him sitting, sable in hand, hour after hour behind the tissue paper, pencilling in varnish silver cloudlets round a moon ; or have seen him revelling in the ferocity of the seething mordant with which he sometimes loved to excavate an emphatic passage will not wonder that he achieved only thirteen etchings : and they will think, perhaps, that the measure of his celebrity, in this his favourite branch of art, is well deserved.

Of these thirteen plates, eight were finished at Kensington, but both *The Morning of Life* and *The Early Ploughman,* though begun there, were finished elsewhere.

Having lived three years in the old cottage in Victoria Road, early in 1851 my father moved into Douro Place, a neighbouring street. Number six was about the most complete antithesis to his ideal of a residence that could have been devised. It was a hideous little semi-detached house, with a prim little garden at the back and front, and an ample opportunity of profiting by the next door neighbours' musical proclivities. One end of Douro Place was occasionally honoured by royalty, and by the other lesser luminaries who visited the well-known sculptor John Bell: and the other end was blocked by a high wall. By all the sights and cries peculiar to a surburban cul-de-sac Douro Place was favoured, and many an organ-player well used to sudden ejectment from other lairs of artists played with impunity near Number six, little thinking what happy memories of the sunny South his dark visage was calling up.

There was no studio, so my father painted, as best he might, in the "drawing-room," purposely chosen by him for certain reasons on account of its direct *south* light, in spite of the out-look upon the opposite houses.

Perhaps the chief of these reasons was the saddening influence upon an artist's colouring of a North light—an influence which (especially in London) my father thought had been very detrimental, chiefly to figure-painters.

The rent being higher than that of the old cottage his fight became still harder, and do what he would to economize his expenses steadily increased. His patience, however, kept pace with his vexations. Years ago, when half a dozen pictures out of eight sent to the Academy were rejected, he had resolved "with the patience of an ox" to paint an equal number for rejection the following year and, "if need be, the year after that." Now, when his son was rapidly growing towards boyhood, and the temptation to abandon his unprofitable ideal and to court popularity was redoubled, he quietly and firmly put it away from him. He sought to become, as he put it, "a Christian bull-dog:" and every day brought abundant opportunities of emulating the virtues peculiar to that tenacious quadruped.

The following passage is significant, and although it was written later in his life it describes his present convictions :—" Many very striking qualities " may be rapidly secured, but those which touch the feelings and the imagina-" tion cannot be tossed off; so that when there is, as at present, a ready " art market at high prices, no artist can do full justice to himself but by " foregoing thousands of pounds which are within his reach." This frame of mind was not new, for twenty years before, Mr. Linnell had vainly pointed out a quick and easy way to independence. Nor was the renunciation of popular art an example of what is known as "sour grapes." A glance at almost any of the best Italian, Welsh, or south-of-England studies leads to the conclusion that had the artist who could produce such works, and produce them so easily, chosen to watch the weather-cock for every flaw and shift in the fickle breeze of public taste—if he had chosen to tint and stipple up the traditional drawing-room water-colour he might by this time have steered into a snug harbour. Although he was failing to realize his inmost ideal it existed still, and it saved him from that sordid and miserable bondage to ways and means in which so many toil the best of their lives away—it saved him from the blight of mediocrity.

A phenomenally bad man of business he still not only put a very low price upon his very best work, but often failed to get even that ; and he was indifferent to the time he bestowed in ripening a drawing, even after it had been exhibited, bought, and paid for. There were thus several causes, besides his unwavering allegiance to poetic landscape, tending to decrease his income, and had it not been for his teaching he must either have forsaken his ideal altogether, or come to a dead-lock in his affairs. His exceedingly simple personal habits and rigid economy removed some of the usual temptations to extravagance, but it may be imagined that a man with so devoted a love of books and fine old prints must have had, from time to time, many a burning shilling in his pocket. The paraphernalia of the little room which did duty for a studio were eloquently simple. Such matters as frames the worse for wear, a common student's easel, plethoric, home-made portfolios, or a kitchen chair half hidden beneath a pile of unmounted sketches are not lost upon the astute dealer, accustomed to the sumptuous luxury in the studios of the popular R.A.'s., and he deals accordingly. Unless with the boldest men nothing succeeds like success, because of success is born that confidence and health that carries the diffident and painstaking man through difficulty ; but, on the other hand, no heart sinks so low as the heart of an enthusiast who does his best to produce refined and excellent work, regardless of time and of labour, when he finds its very refinement its chief drawback and its price gauged chiefly by his own necessity.

Driven by necessity as he was on the one hand, and tempted by the certainty of making money on the other, it is wonderful that my father's loyalty to his old choice of subject remained unshaken, but the titles of many drawings he exhibited after he became an Associate of the Old Society proclaim that loyalty. Nevertheless, the colour of some of the works of this time leads to a suspicion that the untoward external circumstances were not without an influence : and it is easy to see that the Princes Risborough resolutions as applied to strong colour are in force, though the " plates and bassi-relievi of wrought gold " are not to be found.

The following notes in a design-book are of import. They speak of seeking a " new style," involving less manipulative finish ; and also, for the first time, of lowering his themes :—

" Never hurry for exhibitions, but from the Autumn of 1850, D.V.,

" carry on a continuous movement of works for sale. Endeavour after oil
" pictures. What are the secrets of a proper rapidity. 1st? Decision in the
" first design—seeing the *whole at once.* Trying after indicative formation
" of the central difficulty. After a studious and careful preparation, instead
" of aiming at finish aim to execute the mental vision with as little
" manipulation and as much inventive energy as possible ; doing only what I
" see . . . . A more large and general system of study from nature ; less
" task-work and fatigue. Investigation of effects, WAITING till they present
" themselves ; then trying to catch them thus : -

" 1st. (A) A very small sketch of the Proportion of Darks in pencils or
" chalks : (B) A small coloured sketch of the same, merely for use, but the
" more complete the better as a *specimen* of the class of effect. Have an
" eye to the above this year, D.V., but let the ETCHING be the point of
" most painstaking.

" 2nd. Sunsets or the like on some bold principle, or one sunset and one
" moon and firelight of the same story. Look carefully over Devon and
" Cornwall sketches for smaller subjects.

" A deep, Gray Day a good subject. Coincident with other things will
" be an attempt at a New Style.

" Forswear HOLLOW compositions like *Calypso* and *St. Paul,* and
" forswear great spaces of sky. TAKE SHELTER in TREES and try
" the always pleasing arrangement of white cloud behind ramification, and
" reflex in water ; also sheep foregrounds.

" Even Mr. —— finds that the directly poetical subjects are less
" saleable ; so if I go upon this tack and lower the themes I must
" endeavour to compensate for contraction of span by intensity of expres-
" sion and development.

" I am inclined to think that a sketch in one colour, with all the principal
" parts and striking completed effect, would be a very sure foundation, and
" the painting from it comparatively easy. Try something like the solid
" BLOCKS of sober colour in De Wint.

" Why do I wish for a NEW STYLE? 1st. To save time. 2nd. To
" govern all by broad, powerful chiaroscuro. 3rd. To ABOLISH all
" NIGGLE. The MEANS. 1st. To work from a bold sepia sketch carried
" on so far that figure and everything should be already decided. 2nd. Not
" to be solicitous about the brightness of little specks of light, so as to
" hinder the full sweep of a great brush by which should be attained the
" full and right effect at a distance.

" My chance of standing with others in execution will be to find my
" way to it by certainty of effect and parts in first design. 2ndly. By not
" in any way evading *FORM.* 3rdly. By painting with large and
" broad gradation (v : Gaspar Poussin), suggesting minutiæ by large

" work.   NEVER   FORGET   TINTORET'S   scheme   of   CAST
SHADOW.

   " Try to have in progress a number of small subjects in which extreme
" fewness shall be the charm—for I fear that I have neither power nor
" inclination to do anything which is not in some way or other strongly
" characterized. . . .   Subjects to have ACTION.

   " Action.   HUNTING.   DRIVING of SHEEP, Parting the flocks.
" STORM in HARVEST.   FORDING THE BROOK.   Steadying the
" cart.   The fall of the Oak—felling.

   " THE PRACTICAL SUGGESTION of 1850 is to open, D.V.,
" some connections for PRIVATE SALE ; and 2nd, to collect and keep by
" themselves all [the works] that I have for sale."

   It is noteworthy that after a four years' interval the writer of these notes
once more cautions himself against too great a solicitude about the " little
specks of light."   For these he had a weakness, and he knew their priceless
value in what he was accustomed to call true etching.   His later method of
using some pigments much drier than is usual in water-colour, and of
dragging one colour dryly over another led to a sparkle and brilliancy which
was largely due to the little specks he refers to.   Such characteristic
qualities were conspicuously absent in certain drawings which I believe to
have been the outcome of this hankering after a method whose primary
object was (as he honestly admits) to save time.

   After reading the foregoing notes there is a feeling that it would be
more desirable to possess a work executed before they were put in force,
than afterwards.   However charming " extreme fewness " might be made,
or however desirable it might be to economize time, it was not such things
as these which increased my father's reputation ; and it was fortunate for
that reputation that it was neither within his power nor inclination to do
many works at all events latterly, which were not characterized by fullness
and above all by ripeness.

   As it was to teaching drawing that my father at this time of his life owed
the possibility of painting his favourite themes at all, it might be supposed
that there, at all events, he courted popularity and economized his time by
the most approved means.   He knew perfectly well what such means were.
He knew precisely what degree and kind of efficiency rich parents expected
the drawing-master to impart, and he knew precisely how some of the most
fashionable masters had become so.

   He wrote in the latter years of his life :—" What inspired young ladies
" think they may accomplish after a course of lessons is what can barely be
" approached by a life-long study."   And again :—" In nine cases out of
" ten people don't want real teaching for their daughters, but some fine
" touched-up drawings to show in which they do not reflect themselves but

" their masters.   I have no reason to complain, having always in London
" as much teaching as I could desire, but it is my full conviction that a good
" bold quack, with plenty of tact, a comely presence, and well-cut, Hoby boots
" would beat any real artist out of the field as a teacher—I mean as to the
" figure he would cut on Schedule D."   He also complains that the higher
the rank of his employers the more surely he found the domestic school-
room resembling, as far as art was concerned, "the operating-room of a
third-class hair-dresser's shop :" and this leads him to wonder, (as I have
mentioned before) whether sight is considered "the lowest of the senses,
that education does not deign to recognize it." [1]

Now, in spite of the enormous temptation to follow the usual fashion of
teaching he took as his watch words two of the very last things which are
palatable to most of an artist's private pupils, namely "Elements and
Accuracy."   As in his own artistic practice he worked on sound principles,
these he taught, and in these he remained unshaken.   He writes thus to a
young lady who was a favourite pupil and friend :—" My plan with you
" and Laura has been from the very first to have you make really good
" drawings, instead of a parcel of half-studied fragments ; but if you
" wish for any great success, repeat to each other when you meet in the
" morning the word EXACTNESS.   All who draw from nature *must* be
" exact.   Talent is shown by rapid exactness.   Genius is developed
" through slow exactness at first : but whether fast or slow it is exact,
" and is called genius when it most *exactly* embodies sublime conceptions.

" All educational acquisitions which have not exactness are in my
" opinion worse than useless : so much injury is done to the mental
" structure by the bad habits acquired in the obtaining of these so-called
" acquirements.   I would rather see young people play at marbles, for
" then they do manage to be as exact as they can : and so far, it is a true
" educational exercise.

" I believe you will be exact : and let me tell you it is a very rare gift
" indeed."

With a reckless disregard of the financial consequences he guarded
his pupils against too sudden a conceit of proficiency because they might
be able to make a tolerable copy of fruit, or flowers, or a rustic cottage by
setting them to draw an egg in black and white chalk ; an undertaking

---

[1] Few professional men can at the same time be more amused and more galled by the
public ignorance of their craft than artists.   Every one whose daughters can daub a
cottage or a bird's nest assumes a half-contemptuous equality of knowledge with the
man who has spent the best years of his life in mastering a few of the problems of art.
Both the ignorance and the assurance reach a climax in certain country society, as can be
readily seen on such occasions as church decoration, the distribution of awards for table
decoration at flower-shows ; and last but not least, in that crucial test of taste, the
modern " drawing-room."

which the beginner will find rather humiliating. Indeed, he himself
would sometimes "go to school to a potato," as he expressed it ; because
the making a good and unmistakable chalk likeness of such an object
severely taxes the draughtsman's power, and tends very much to his
advantage.

Much to the astonishment of his neighbours my father often allowed
the weeds and grass of the little back garden to reach maturity, in order
that his pupils might draw them from the window ; and the laurel-bushes
did duty in the same manner.   Underneath a chalk sketch of his own of
some dandelions and grass-tufts on the back lawn are these words :—
" Farewell, soft clusters—the only pretty things about the premises—ye
" are to be mowed this evening, and to leave a scraped scalp of
" " RESPECTABILITY !" May, 1856."

For the sake of dear old Kent he had planted a root of hops among
the lilac bushes, and in one of his letters he laments that, just as its
clusters were fit for sketching they had been ravished by the baker !

Between 1848 and 1858, my father visited Devon and Cornwall four
times, on each succeeding occasion becoming more enthusiastic in his
admiration.   His luggage and paraphernalia were simpler than ever, and
after describing a beautiful South Devon route he says :—" This would
" be a thing to do very leisurely ; no luggage, but one spare shirt.
" Sketching portfolio with *thin* plate-paper, and Richard and Wilson's
" thin brown paper, which would weigh lightly.   In pocket, case of
" pencils and black and white chalk, and light little box for reserve black
" and white chalk, and the three chromes,[1] and blue and browns for slight
" indications of local colour on the brown paper.   This, on the whole,
" I find the most rapid method of sketching."   He says elsewhere " If
" I am spared to go again into the country I hope to begin a new plan
" —not sitting down to local matter, but WALKING and WATCHING.
" I ought to see Chiddingstone three miles from Hever, or some very
" picturesque village, for lines about mills, old forges, or cottage doors,
" as these things are so useful where husbandry figures are introduced.   I
" ought to watch the operations of husbandry.   The MONTHS would
" make a good book of etchings."

He also writes thus about the same time :—" . . . I coasted round as
" far as Ilfracombe—waterfall into the sea—then back, and landed at
" Combe Martin, walking home to Berrynarbor.   We must take the
" trouble to map out and paint with the different local colours arable land
" and garden, which come in every variety of rows and patterns.   Also

As in the case of Indian yellow, he appears to have been unaware of the unreliable
nature of the chromes.   He afterwards rejected all these pigments from his list of " safe
colours."

Mouth Mill, near Clovelly.

Clovelly Park.

" woods and woody hills must be juicy and rich : real TREE COLOUR,
" not anything picture colour. Detached, elegant trees sometimes stand
" out into the glade [sketch]; and above the woody or arable hill-tops, a bit
" of much higher hill is sometimes visible, [all] heaving and gently lifting
" themselves, as it were, towards the heavens and the sun. It is of no use
" to try woody hills without a wonderful variety of texture based on the
" modelling.

" In the solemn moor-tops, the furze &c. is the dark, and the barer
" ground a graduating half-tint—but all dark and solemn. WHAT CAN
" BE THE REASON that they delight so much ?

" NEVER FORGET THE CHARM of running water. In Berry-
" harbor valleys it gushes everywhere. O ! the playful heave and tumble
" of lines in the hills here."

Another time he writes to a friend :—" We had a glimpse of South
" Devon—loveliest of lands ! And, but for the rain, we should have tracked
" its infinite richness till it becomes the enamelled footstool of Dartmoor.
" May the utterly South-Devon stricken one who is now solacing his South
" Kensington exile with your Murray keep it a *little* longer, till he has
" time to get another and an ordnance map of that sweet place ? No
" wonder that Reynolds painted richly (we visited his birthplace), or that
" Johnson, in that lap of nature's luxury, forgot himself over the Devon-
" shire cream."

In nearly all his sketching my father aimed first at a careful selection
of subject matter which would add to his knowledge or supply a record of
some valuable phenomenon : next, at rapidity of execution ; and he preferred amassing a store of knowledge by a kind of shorthand which was
intelligible only to himself to wasting time on work more elaborate and
intelligible to other people. As I shall have occasion to reiterate, everything done thus was not an end in itself, but the means to an end.

His repeated allusions to the importance of these annual campaigns
(holidays in no sense), his anxiety to get away in time for his favourite
effects, and his reluctance to attempt to paint the most difficult of
these effects merely from memory show that, even by an avowedly
imaginative painter, a direct and constant reference to nature or rather
an intense, absorbing, and lifelong study of nature was considered
absolutely essential. This is to be found in the Princes Risborough
notes, and over and over again elsewhere. He was aware that the deep
study of nature has given to many an immortal work of art and literature
at once its truth, its grandeur, and its wonderful perennial freshness : but
he was also aware that those who see in a superb sunset little more than
an interesting chromatic phenomenon, and in the richest nooks of wild
country merely so much material for the landscape-gardener and farmer

of the future do not study nature to the greatest advantage. He knew that the "naturalistic school" of painters, as he called them, became popular chiefly because, in their appeals to those whose sense of sight (mental and physical) had not been cultured, they made themselves easily understood. Painting (and often painting very admirably) objects that are universally familiar, they produce a picture in which nothing startles, or perplexes, or offends. But the poor, shrivelled, half-starved faculties, that the imaginative artist seeks to reach and to awaken remain untouched.

Although my father was beginning to see more clearly than ever that the country was the most profitable home for a landscape-painter such as himself, there was a certain part of his London life which he enjoyed very keenly. In one of the early note-books dealing with that most peculiar form of male domestic despotism which he called "Household Govern- ment" he lays down the law that the hours of evening must be held absolutely "sacred" to literature and music ; but though he still revelled in this kind of quiet, cosy seclusion, he was often tempted abroad, even in those sacred hours, by the attraction of thoroughly congenial society. A real anxiety to improve himself was one of his most distinguishing characteristics, and he was habitually watchful to learn something from *all* with whom he was brought into contact. Self-assertion and the exposition of personal opinion not being rare, he had innumerable opportunities of gathering his mental honey. How he revolted at a very common opposite tendency to gather evil rather than good, and against the treachery that abuses kindness and hospitality by making it an opportunity for the storage of scandal and ridicule is shown in one of his letters to his elder son.

By this time, and notwithstanding that his anxieties had been increased by my own birth, the chief interest and solicitude of his life had centred in that elder son. The provision of the means for his education was his chief inducement to work, and to watch his mental growth his chief pleasure. For all grief and labour, past, present, and to come there might be one rich reward—to see this son grow up a good, learned, Christian gentleman.

Few have been better fitted than my father to prepare the ground for such a harvest. There was no looseness of purpose, no indecision, no doubt as to the essential points. There was one guiding principle, and a bright pharos to steer by. "Let me advise you," he wrote to my brother, "amidst all you meet with, gay or grave, pleasant or irksome to remember "that there is also RIGHT and WRONG—never to forget that."

The boy promised well. Inheriting not only his father's precocity, but the musical tastes which had accompanied it, he worked hard and did well at school. Each successful achievement, and each addition to the row of prizes on the shelves at home warmed his father's heart, and fanned the flame of his one great ambition. Like the father and son in the old days at Surrey Square and Bloomsbury, these also were much together, talking as they walked of their pleasant labours in the mines of poetry and philosophy, and of the associations abounding in the old London streets.

On Sundays they often attended the services at St. Paul's and Westminster Abbey, glorying in the music, and gazing their fill on the tombs of the heroes and poets whom they seemed to know so intimately through their works. Whatever my father dearly loved seemed to find a natural place in his son's heart, and there was no thought of the dangers of precocity stimulated by over culture.

In June 1854, my father was elected a full Member of the Society of Painters in Water Colours, having contributed to the Exhibition in Pall Mall in the eleven years of his Associateship seventy works. In the first three years he had sent a large proportion of Italian subjects, but the themes of nearly the whole of the drawings that followed appear to have been derived from British Pastoral scenery.

It has been gathered that, at one time, it seemed as if he curbed his natural impulse in the direction of strong colour and daring composition from prudential motives ; and he speaks of "designs prudentially con-sidered." But, from time to time. he allowed himself more freedom. As regards composition, this was the case in *The Dell of Comus* (1855), a notable and very original drawing, full of wild poetry. The theme was evidently congenial, and the whole mind was thrown into the execution. *The Brothers in Comus lingering under the Vine* (1856) is a work which shows more characteristic colouring and an arrangement much favoured by the painter, in which the direct rays of the sun are partly veiled by thin, intricate foliage. This drawing, and its companion, *The Brothers discover-ing the Palace and Bowers of Comus* which was exhibited at the same time were very well received by my father's fellow artists : but, in spite of a moderate price, returned unsold from the exhibition—another significant hint that he dolorously took to heart. These two subjects are in the matter of colour so totally dissimilar. that they suggest an attempt to gauge the public taste by offering an alternative. *The Brothers under the Vine* is as rich and vivid as the other is what admirers of my father's most characteristic work might probably call vapid.

In 1855 Mr. Alexander Gilchrist introduced himself, full to overflowing of interest in Blake : and he must have been somewhat astonished to find in his new acquaintance an enthusiasm equal to his own, and no whit the fainter for long lapse of years. My father and mother spent several memorable evenings deep in the rich collection of well-remembered works which the biographer was busy in describing ; and once they became so absorbed that day broke when they thought the evening scarcely ended.

In the following year my father again undertook some drawing upon wood, namely nine illustrations to the story of "The Distant Hills" in a new edition of Adams's *Sacred Allegories*. Three other designs had appeared in *A Poetry Book for Children* two years before, and two more are to be found in *The Book of favourite Ballads* published some time afterwards. This appears to have been the last of his work on wood, and the result cannot be regarded as satisfactory. He seems to have been unaware that any special treatment was necessary to secure a good translation by the engraver, and to have worked on the block just as he would have worked on a pencil drawing not intended to be reproduced at all. As he expected impossibilities in translation and was inexperienced in this kind of drawing, it is no wonder that the outcome was disappointing to himself and to others. Had he persevered in some early attempts to cut a block or two with his own hands the result would no doubt have been notable in some way or other ; for in wood-cutting, as in everything else, he had a high ideal. His ideal will be found embodied in Blake's own blocks for Thornton's edition of Phillips's *Pastorals*. These, in my father's opinion, were "perhaps the most intense gems of bucolic sentiment in the whole range of art," and "utterly unique." He spoke of them as his "heart's delight," and contended that, unlike the skilful modern wood engravings, they showed the true genius of the art—those essential qualities which should distinguish it from other arts. One of the chief treasures of his "Curiosity Portfolio"[1] was a sheet or two of early proofs from these little blocks, printed and signed by Blake in his presence.

Turning to my father's technical water-colour practice about this time, we find that fortunately it can be described pretty much in his own words, by means of his letters and his common-place book.

In 1830 he had written :—"Let not the painter say ' I have done many "pictures, and therefore should be able to do this less carefully ; ' for each "time invention is a new species though of the same genus. . . . If the "painter performed each new work with that thirsting of mind and humility "of purpose with which he did his first, how intense would be the result." I have arranged a few passages chronologically to show that a quarter of a century had not diminished the solicitude, or dulled the enthusiasm. The original notes are interspersed with lists of good subjects or "spines of subjects," and are often illustrated by highly significant little "blots" (as he called them), which in many cases were the germs of future works :—

[1856. Written to my mother from Kensington.] " . . . I have now

---

[1] This portfolio, besides containing a few of the choicest specimens of the art of "The Ancients" and their master, Blake, held certain etchings of Claude, some portraits, and a few other works which made the collection altogether of exceptional interest.

" no difficulties about the egg, which seems a material exactly suited to
" me . . . You had some grand sunsets last week. I got some lines of
" them, straining my neck out of Ann's [the attic] window. Pencil lines of
" effects with the colours written are now of the greatest use to me, as
" I *have* coloured sketches from nature to supply the want of colour
" where it cannot be got . . . I have now got in the egg a delightful
" material, and if I could gain knowledge as to more rapid completion of
" works I should be very glad. . . ."[1]

[1857.] "CONDUCT of a PICTURE. After reading in *Black-*
" *wood's Magazine* of December 1857, a quotation from Fergusson on
" Hindoo Architecture ('They built like Giants, and finished like
" Jewellers'), and after thinking of the Gothic cathedrals and the vast
" amount in both of absolute work and labour, it seems that landscape-
" painting is worth such labour, and that the moment for beginning is
" when the general effect has been obtained. Then should come the finish
" and enamel of the figures and the tracery of the near boughs and grass-
" flowers. The best place to begin with will be, I think, the high lights of
" foliage, getting the principal ones right by elaboration and *design*. This
" will prevent them being carelessly covered down and at once give
" mystery to the darks. First, general effect secured. Second, the tracery
" work, beginning with the lights. . . ."

[1858. Over a sketch of twilight.] " Finest twilights (with moon) of
" all, I think, which add to full splendour of colour the mystery of
' transparent vaporous gloom. Observed in Cornwall and at Margate
" after evening Church, July 18, 1858. In these days, there is an *immense*
" *power of light;* searching, vast depths of gloom, and woods are *very*
" *deep*. Do not forget ; all is full of colour."

[1858. Over a pencil sketch.] " Obs : 1. Golden light catching on
" hillside of fine country with Rembrandt gradation and emphasis of woody
" hill in shade, of itself material for picture. Very *light* relatively to shade.
" Very full of rich golden colour, and velvety and real in texture.
[Sketch.]

" 1st day at Hartland. In valley towards Abbey. In wooded glens
" the most brilliant sunshine is very beautiful And where the effect and
" arrangement are very vivid, one sees on half closing the eyes that the
" light is in detached *shapes or patches*.

[1] I quoted in the last chapter a letter from Mr. Linnell written in 1838 advocating
the use of yolk of egg as a vehicle, and the allusion to the breakage of a bottle of the
mixture refers to still earlier experiments of my father's. I have several beginnings of
his in this material, in which I believe he completed a good many drawings ; but he
subsequently abandoned it, probably on account of its softness and susceptibility to
damp.

" I am equally impressed by the vividness of light and vividness of
" colour. These imply that the shadows must be struck on an intensely
" deep key, and then one must get their clearness. Sky-gray lights and
" reflected lights as one *can*."

" 1859. I think I have hit the WHY, or at least the FACT of the
" most powerful effect structure for me. A mass of shade in centre, with
" one side hard and the other soft, [sketches] as my *Morning of Life ;* [1]
" but in this kind where the clash is between distance and sky, dark must
" be somewhere else ; and, I think, best organized thus [sketch] : and the
" 2nd might differ from the principal by broken against smooth, figure
" against landscape, thus [sketch]. Perhaps I had better in future, D.V.,
" do my designs more neatly than heretofore and in sepia. . . . Besides
" the above, I think that although one side must (perhaps alternating) be
" sharper than the other, yet that the leading mass should be a SHAPE,
" telling at a distance."

[1859.] " I mean never to do a landscape without some little figure
" story."

" 1859. D.V., Sketches for Mr. Craven at once, and of use for other
" exhibition drawings. BEGIN at once. Try figures with bright local
" colour (pre Raffs :) : compose more carefully ; then at once paint the
" masses with oil-colour-like sweeps. Make washed gamboge and raw
" Sienna the key of yellow. If I can, get a foreground or two from nature.
" Try a silver morning, perhaps sunrise. Rich twilight. Remember
" principle [sketches]. By models or otherwise, avoid looseness in the
" focuses. Think of subjects which have for some time been discontinued,
" as sheep under trees, or in fold ; descending stubble-fields with village in
" deep distance, but always with figure story. Think of some passing
" event now India [2] is done. Why did the moonlight etching please every-
" body ? Partly by structure and effect : partly because the matter was not
" above comprehension, whilst it was a kind of matter which I most strongly
" feel. N.B. It grew out of a most simple thing—houses at Margate with
" bars of moonlight. Could I find among my *effects* things as simple
" which would develop ? "

[1] He probably refers to the water-colour drawing exhibited in 1859.
[2] In the Water-Colour Exhibition of 1859, among eight drawings, two were entitled
(186.) *Returned from India*, and (232.) *A Letter from India*. In the preceding year
No. 256, was *Going to India*. It is unnecessary to remind the reader of the events which
made any allusion to that country of interest at that time, and led my father to choose
such realistic titles for drawings that had nothing realistic about them.

"1859. What must I do to attain excellence?

"Increase what I love.
"What do I heartily love? Much!
"Figures of antique grace and sentiment,
"and rich picturesqueness.

———

"Intense depth of shadow and colour.
"Mystery, and infinite going-in-i-tive-
"ness.

———

"The focus, a well-head of dazzling light.
"The utmost deep and heaped up
"Devonshire richness.
"EFFECTS. Midsummer glowing
"Twilight, and rising moon, with trees of
"intensest depth. . . .

———

"Moonlight with firelight.

———

"Sunsets. Dawn. Silver Sunrise.
"Sunset through trees.
"Cloudy, fresh, dropping, spring morn-
"ing. One focus of cream white cloud."

Supply Deficiencies.

"Where am I weak? (or rather alas!
"where am I *not* weak?)
"Design figures vigorously. Consult
"model *early*. Paint them neatly.

———

"Conduct picture, so that from the first
"it may be sightly for its state. At the
"moment when I would shudder to show it
"let me pause and ask, 'why?' I ought to
"keep the shadows and half-tints flatter.
"Let me try to make the getting in exactly
"resemble OIL painting, with that broad
"suggestive smear in the half tints and in
"the landscape part of the lights. *Painted*,
"not glazed; as *e.g.* yellow ochre and
"emerald green for smooth grass—laid
"smooth, so as just to cover the paper.
"Even in skies—still more in landscape,
"lay the TINTS as nearly as I can of the
"relative intended depth, like a wood-
"cutter—leaving the gradations for the
"finishing."

[On the outside of a paper portfolio.] "Little Long, Exhibition, W.C.
"1860. Thoughts on RISING MOON, with raving-mad splendour of orange
"twilight-glow on landscape. I saw that at Shoreham. Above all this,
"one pinnacle might catch the fire of the last sunlight."

"*August* 1860 . . . I am *thinking* of North Devon with light luggage
"in travelling-bag, but the weather is not tempting so perhaps it will not
"transpire. For the future I mean to inquire wherever I go, after old
"manor-houses and mansions, and farm-houses which have been such.
"They are quite the gems of a neighbourhood : and, if possible, we should
"always see the interior."

I think it is obvious that a great deal of what I have quoted, would not
have occurred to what is generally understood as a water-colour painter :
and the contemporary drawings show much in their handling that suggests
the traditions of oil-painting, rather than those of the sister art. The
palette, as I have pointed out, was set with thick clots of easily-moved
colour. For emphatic touches and bold foreground work the pigment
thus prepared was laid upon the paper or cardboard,[1] sometimes with very
large, flat, camel-hair brushes, sometimes with a palette-knife, sometimes

———

[1] Paper was ultimately abandoned for cardboard of a particular kind, namely "Six
sheet London-board" on account of its marked deficiency in bearing out the pigments.
See Letter XLVII.

I

with the finger, in "oil-colour-like sweeps." On the other hand, in the
extreme distances and more delicate parts, such as the faces of near
figures, there is the stipple peculiar to water-colour carried to a great
degree of refinement, and in nearly all finished drawings the use
of body-colour for the lights was forsworn. A notable example of
this peculiar handling exists in the beginning of a "Large Long"
drawing [27¼ × 12¼ inches] which hung in the posthumous exhibition
of 1882 under the title of *The fallen Tree*. Across the foreground
lies the moss-grown trunk, broken off by some great gale. Against it
leans a girl listening to a youth who sits near her. From the mountain
side the eye wanders over an expanse of wild and romantic country
watered by a river threading its way towards the sea, and jewelled by
glittering cities. Among the cliffs on the left stands a partly-ruined
fortress, frowning over the woods at its feet upon a deep ravine where the
evening sunshine has already been blotted out by shadowy mist. Some
mountains on the nearer sea shore gleam yet in the rosy light, and the
view is closed by a chain of gigantic jagged peaks covered with snow.
This drawing is chiefly interesting on account of the remarkable execution
of which it is a typical example. In the girl's head, in part of the lower
buildings of the fortress, and in the more distant country we find tinting
and stippling almost delicate enough for a miniature; but in the outline
and shadow of the tree-trunk there is the boldest and most emphatic work
capable of being produced by great pens, and fat "oil-colour-like sweeps"
applied with the palette-knife: the pigments being bistre of full depth
mixed with gum. One kind of work is in close juxtaposition with another,
but had the drawing been finished they could, no doubt, have been harmonized. Several of the principles set forth in the notes I have quoted
are exemplified; such, for instance, as "broken against smooth, figure
against landscape:" and the shadows are "struck on an intensely
deep key."

Turning our attention from my father's purely artistic practice to his
social life at this time, we shall find a few passages from his letters to my
mother worthy of attention. [Kensington, 1856.] "I have risen at 7—
"breakfasted at ½ past . . . so I have begun, in a small way, to reform,
"and mean to get it all half an hour earlier if I can, and to keep to it
"inflexibly, so far as I am concerned.

"... Of all things, early bed and early rising are most distasteful to
"me; but believing myself to have been ill-used and unjustly neglected as
"an artist, as well as in many other ways, I am willing to tax my strength
"to the uttermost to benefit my family; and, perhaps, by not over rating
"my own powers of will but cultivating them to the last, may make this
"house a model of morning industry. . . ."

[Kensington, 1856.] . . . "I feel that I cannot neglect family
" reading and prayers without positive sin, and trust some plan may
" be devised by which it may be continued. The master of a family
" is, in a measure, responsible for the souls of his wife, children,
" and servants ; and cannot answer at the Judgment Seat, 'Am I my
" brother's keeper?' . . . I think, if possible, it will be best for me to
" go out of town with More directly his holidays begin, which I think is
" the middle of June ; but then we may have bad weather. On the other
" hand, NOW seems to be the time for weather useful to me. It is always
" a perplexity. It is quite true, as your father says, that my subjects are
" wasted upon such little drawings, but then comes the difficulty—not one
" large drawing was sold at our private view.

" How very touching and beautiful are the collects and psalms just now.
" I trust you will prepare for Holy Communion on Whit Sunday. It is
" specially a day of grace and sanctification to the faithful. In the bustle
" of life we see nothing but illusions : getting to church in good time and
" reading the psalms for the day before service begins, the poor world-
" withered heart begins to open like shrivelled leaves in a gentle summer
" shower ; and then we see things as they are, if we have kept our evil
" passions under discipline during the week, living in love and charity with
" ALL MEN. For this is the condition ; If *from your heart* 'ye forgive
" not men their trespasses, neither will your Father forgive *your* trespasses.'
" 'With what judgment ye judge ye shall be judged.' You know Herbert's
" lines, 'The Sundays of man's life,' &c.

" If we duly weighed God's blessings we should see and feel that the
" greatest of all was in the ability to go to church ; whether a cathedral, or
" the humblest of those grey turrets which are, to the Christian's eye, the
" most charming points of our English landscape—gems of sentiment for
" which our woods, and green slopes, and hedgerow elms are the lovely
" and appropriate setting. Landscape is of little value, but as it hints
" or expresses the haunts and doings of man. However gorgeous, it can
" be but Paradise without an Adam. Take away its churches, where for
" centuries the pure word of God has been read to the poor in their
" mother tongue, and in many of them most faithfully *preached* to the
" poor, and you have a frightful kind of Paradise left—a Paradise without
" a God. For the works of creation will never lift the soul to God until
" we have been taught that our Lord Jesus Christ is the 'Way,' and that
" 'no man cometh to the Father' but by Him. Let not our thoughts
" wander to queer architecture like that of good Mr. G. . . .'s church, or to
" the dresses of the people. Ever remember when inclined to criticise
" persons or places, our Lord's 'What is that to thee? follow thou me.'
" We cannot be too severe upon our natural censoriousness and imperti-

" nent curiosity—our profane levity, and longings after something new.
" My son, fear thou the Lord and the King; and meddle not with them
" that are given to change.' . . ."

[Kensington, 1856.] " . . . As to improvement in art, the whole disposi-
" tion of my time at this invaluable season which is now beginning, if it
" were arranged and invented on purpose to prevent it could not do it more
" effectually. My summers are literally *wasted*, while almost all other land-
" scape-painters are reaping some harvest from the country. I fully believe
" that *now* my choice in art is pretty well settled, I could make a much better
" income by living in the country than here, as my teaching is very little and
" for the last few years has been rather decreasing than otherwise. But
" whenever I have had an opportunity it has always been crossed, as it is
" now, by the difficulty of providing for the first year. There is also
" education of children for which London is the best place. . . . I am
" prepared to lead a life hopeless of any earthly good, and to persevere to
" the utmost of my power in patient well-doing, unappreciated and
" ridiculed, and with a daily and hourly opposition which will no doubt
" shorten these days of mine, which have been most emphatically ' few
" and evil.'

" In about a week or ten days I must try to get out of town for a
" fortnight, that I may not lose this weather, which is my only chance of
" art renovation. . . .

" Nothing but house-cleaning has been going on since you were away,
" and I have let them clean out my study closets; preferring the risk to an
" accumulation of dirt. Indeed there has been for a long time such a
" gradual diminution of books &c., that I am getting used to it, and
" have ceased to feel much annoyed at the reckless destruction of casts &c.
" in the attics, till at Mr. Cooke's the other day I saw in a prominent
" place over one of his parlour doors, a bas-relief [the same as that] which
" with several others of mine has long ago been destroyed. . . . What
" egregious blockheads we must be if we ever more attempt to vie with
" people who have fifty times our income ! . . . . .

" . . . . It is, I believe, an invariable truth that the better we are
" ourselves, the better shall we think of others. Satan is called the
" accuser of the brethren. Let us beware. Let us ' study to be quiet, and
" to mind our own business,' and not only talk of the ' charity which
" thinketh no evil.' but for once and for good, try to make our lives
" and our talk its embodiment. . . ."

[Kensington, August, 1858.] " . . It will require such undivided atten-
" tion to maintain and. D.V., improve the step which I have for the last two
" or three years, by the kind providence of God, made in public estimation,
" that for the future, when I settle down to my exhibition work it will not

" do for you to be absent. Therefore if you wish to *stay* at Redstone this
" year, it must be *before* I get my peep at Devonshire. I must therefore forego
" the harvest, and take my chance for a shot with the partridges over the
" stubble ; and in the meantime with my increased power of making use of
" nature, I believe I am losing hundreds—eventually, perhaps, thousands of
" pounds. For were I now in some healthy country place with my materials,
" I might be making, partly out of doors, besides my more complicated
" exhibition drawings, some of those a positive commission for which I
" refused, leaving the matter open."

[Kensington, 1858.] " . . . I can *begin* my subjects better in London,
" but when *Italian* weather sets in I should like to go out of town directly,
" if it were only for a week, and take my drawings with me. The weather
" from which I get my subjects and my suggestions for the remainder of the
" year is that dazzling weather when all the air seems trembling with little
" motes. A week of that is, to me, worth three months of ordinary fine
" weather. It is then I see real sunsets and twilights.

" My little drawings seem to have done me real good with the artistic
" public. The secretary of one of the great provincial exhibitions called
" the other day to *beg* me to send something, and really I felt a little con-
" fused, as Lord Palmerston could not have been approached with more
" respect. This, of course, drew forth all my *native loveliness !* So it was
" ' sweets to the sweet.' "

[Hastings, 1859.] " I feel a strange relief since the squally, strange
" change in the atmosphere. Before the two thunderous days, it was what
" I call gasping weather ; but since, although very close for this airy place,
" there is a delightful humidity in the air. I felt while the rain was pouring
" down, the refreshment which I suppose a plant feels under the same in-
" fluence, after drought. I DREAD the DUST of town, which withers me
" whenever I get out ; and if I could have my choice would prefer a
" month's incessant rain. You must see what an affliction it must be to
" me, anxious as I am after high excellence, to be as it were dodged and
" disappointed in all my attempts to get a sight of beautiful nature and
" strength to use it.

" I hope, D.V., when I return, to make a struggle for regularity as to
" the breakfast-hour ; to get four hours clear, good work before dinner ; and
" then, for the *present*, to take the rest of the day easily ; and when I get,
" D.V., stronger, to adopt Mr. Cope's plan of a Saturday holiday. But
" again I dread the dusty drought. Dr. Bell [1] will order me out, but I feel
" like Cain, ' Whither shall I go ? ' What a mockery to go out for health
" and refreshment into that dreadful granite-dust. And am I to see no-

---

[1] My father was, at this time, a firm homœopathist. It was an epidemic of credulity
which was then prevalent in Kensington.

" thing of that external loveliness which is my spring of successful work ? O !
" that I were nestled among those granite taws of dear Devonshire, 1500
" feet high. As soon as the Turners come [to the South Kensington
" Museum], I shall be out enough you may be sure, in the direction of
" Brompton, but I must see some out-door beauty, or my mind will
" perish. . . . . "

[Hastings, 1859.] "I have been very quiet and undisturbed here, which is
" much in my favour. I do not care about these things on my own account.
" I could go quietly like a poor sheep under the first hedge and lie down
" and die, so far as that goes ; but as a living flour-mill which has to grind
" corn for others, it is a source of alarm to feel that the machinery is quite out
" of order . . . I seem doomed never to see again that first flush of summer
" splendour which entranced me at Shoreham; for what with east wind and
" mist I have seen little but Indian Ink. . . . I have begun some designs
" to send to Manchester, [in sepia] but determining not to work much yet,
" have made little way. I was quite hurt to hear about poor dormouse's
" death. His life was too like what my own will be—short and unquiet.
" . . . Joy and thankfulness, or a broken-hearted old age, a man must look
" for from his children. I have only just enough strength to discharge my
" duties if everything goes well and rightly ; but domestic sorrows will
" soon break me up utterly . . . "

[Kensington, 1859.] " . . . I work quite as much as I ought as to the
" time spent, and vary my work ; but I feel as if I were repeating myself, and
" have very little impulse or enjoyment in it. I don't know whether it pro-
" ceeds from body, or mind, or both, but my feeling all day is that of
" Macbeth. . . . 'The wine of life is drawn,' the lees alone left. This is
" very important when one's calling is to amuse the public. There must be
" vigorous and intense feeling in works which are to make others feel, and
" after all I have gone through my work is a yoke and a burden which I
" would gladly shuffle off.

" I send you a very fine stanza from Mrs. Barbauld's *Life*, a poem
" written when she was very old. Madame D'Arblay used to repeat it to
" herself every night before she slept :—

> " Life ! we've been long together,
> " Through pleasant and through cloudy weather ;
> " 'Tis hard to part when friends are dear ;
> " Perhaps 'twill cost a sigh, a tear ;
> " Then steal away, give little warning,
> > " Choose thine own time ;
> " Say not Good-night, but in some brighter clime
> > " Bid me Good morning.

" I would rather have written this, than whole volumes of descriptive
" poetry such as the press now abounds with. . . ."

[Kensington, circa 1859.] "On Friday the 19th and Sunday the
" 21st, More officiated as organist at the temporary church at Earl's
" Court, playing them out on Sunday with the Hallelujah Chorus. He
" got through very well indeed. One of the psalm tunes he had never
" seen before. You have sometimes remarked that organs are a favourite
" topic here, but just now I do not know what you would say, as Mr. L——
" is going again to the Continent, and has given More leave to practise on
" his beautiful instrument! So our talk is of fugues, stop-diapasons, open-
" diapasons, double-diapasons, the swell, swell-couplers, principals, fifteenths,
" sesquialteras, bourdons, and double sets of 32-feet pipes! . . . I think
" the eagerness with which More takes up and perseveres with a favourite
" study is a very good sign, although I wish the subject had been painting
" rather than music, but boys sometimes take a sudden turn."

It will be seen that there is a considerable difference in tone between
the passages I have quoted from my father's purely artistic memoranda,
and these contemporary letters. In the former there are many evidences
of unabated enthusiasm—many hopeful plans and an abandon of delight
in the superlative beauty of nature. The latter speak of disappointment, unjust neglect, wasted summers, and at last of his very work itself,
as "a yoke and a burden which he would gladly shuffle off." He seems
to be alternately building up castles in the air, and mourning over their
ruins; sanguine one hour, desponding the next. He begins to long for a
country life, not only for the sake of his profession but because he dreads,
on account of his asthma, the dusty London summers, and the dark yellow
fog of November, in a neighbourhood where the fields and market-gardens
had retreated, little by little, before dreary rows of mansions. But an
exodus that was so easily accomplished in 1826 is quite another matter
now. He sees that he would be swamped by the want of capital before
he could recover himself from the loss of his first year's teaching. As it is,
any calamity such as prolonged illness would find him in evil case. He
therefore remains where he is, fretting over his troubles, perplexities, and
wasted time, and finding his only consolation in the growth of his eldest son.
He had apparently given up the hope of the boy following his own profession,[1] but the school successes promise so well, that he begins to think
of a university scholarship, and of holy orders. To this hope he sacrifices
everything; and he is half prepared, if More goes to Oxford, to follow him
and begin life afresh.

It was thus that matters jogged along till the wintry spring of 1861.
More was now nineteen years old, and next but one to the head boy at
school. He had become a fair classic and a good musician, while he had

---

[1] He had given him his first drawing-lesson when the boy was two years old!

a genuine love for the best English literature. He had always been full of energy which my father stimulated by every means in his power, and he had been encouraged by every possible persuasion to work his hardest. But just about this time he complained of lassitude and weariness, and he longed for a quiet country holiday. Accordingly my father (after sending in his drawings to the exhibition) started with his sketch-book and carpet-bag, in quest of lodgings. After much exploration in well-remembered neighbourhoods he finally lighted on a lonely farm-house some miles from Abinger in Surrey, and six or seven from Dorking. "High Ashes" was a lovely spot lying on the slope of a valley between Holmbury Hill and Leith Hill. The homestead itself stood at an elevation of some 500 feet, and from its windows might be seen a splendid prospect. Many miles of wooded country, enriched by ancient farms, stretched far away, till all vanished in a faint grey line revealed by those clear days that foreshadow rain, as the sea itself.

Everything was so happily quiet and bucolic—the scenery so beautiful, that my father's anxiety to turn his back on the vapid suburb where he craned his neck out of the attic window to catch a glimpse of a fine sunset between the chimney pots, was redoubled. He had returned to Kensington after he had settled his family at High Ashes, and he writes as follows to a lady friend.

[*April*, 1861.] . . . "You will be pleased to hear that poor More is " really better. They are all crammed into a little farm house just on the " top of Leith Hill, the summit of which is 900 feet above the sea-level ! " More just crawls about and vegetates, and has taken my violin—is " perhaps at this moment frightening the pigs with his first scrapings. Of " course he can get no teacher there, but then he pegs very earnestly into " anything he undertakes. He says he is living discreetly "*à la cabbage*," " and is going to press and preserve flowers.

" He has taken a *huge* chest of Latin and Greek books down (I " forget how much they cost by railway), to attack by and bye, if it please " the Divine Disposer to restore him."

In May my father writes thus to my mother from Kensington :— " To-day, Thursday, is like yesterday—thorough influenza weather. East " wind, damp, cold, and fog. The houses in Albert Place loom through a " dirty yellow fog, and the top of a tree in Kensington Gardens is but " just visible. The gloom just now is overpowering. The London smoke " is hovering over like a pall. The cold makes one's fingers ache after " washing.

" A horror came upon me this morning lest I should have killed More " by finding so cold a place as High Ashes. . . . Since the *balmy* weather ceased (balmy !) we have been obliged to have winter fires ; and as to

" outlining, designing, inventing, it has been quite out of the question.
" Depressed as I am, I have still the English *will* about me—to fight to
" the last and die at my post. I think, D.V., I may yet conquer by taking
" in a whole system-full of new blood from nature.

" Half-past eight. The darkness increases, and the foul smells of
" London come in through every crevice. . . ."

[Kensington, May, 1861. To my mother.] " I am too poorly to work
" any longer here, and should spoil everything I touch, so I think I had
" better come, and then we can all consult as to what is best. . . . The
" spare room will do very well for me if it become warm enough to
" work in it without a fire. . . . I think the thing to save us, D.V.,
" would be four months, or five, of my work in the country. . . . If
" I cannot come after all, and settle to work, I ought to know at
" once ; but *dreadful* waste of time seems to be my lot, much as I desire
" the contrary. . . . When will it all end ? I really think, much as I hate
" rash steps, that poor Kensington is no longer the place for us.

" I have yet, thank God, stamina enough left to work *hard* and
" vigorously in the country, and why should not I, as well as others with
" the degree of reputation I now have, raise it *very very* much. Then we
" might perhaps afford two houses. . . . O ! my poor work. Guineas are
" being lost by hundreds, in losing the spring."

[Kensington, May, 1861. To my mother.] " . . . Without positively
" *taking* an extra room could you try what sort of bargain you could
" make. . . . A decent painting light, not overshadowed by trees, is
" essential. I do not intend, in my present vexed and feverish state of
" mind, to *rush* to work, but to walk gently round and see what there
" is, so as to get calm if I can. I *do* want to *try* what I can do, having
" nature at hand."

[Kensington, May, 1861. To my brother.] " . . . The month of
" May is always more prolific in the effects I paint than any other :
" and as my drawings are *avowedly* hung out of the way because they
" are said to kill everything else, I think of trying one or two cool ones
" this year ; perhaps of early mist clearing up over the distant country
" (but my kind of cool effects do not last beyond the month of
" May), nor will anything but wide prospects and a range like that
" of Leith Hill suit me. I am therefore anxious to come down as soon
" as possible . . . perhaps there is some room, or unoccupied granary,
" or such-like, in which they would let me work. This is a matter for im-
" mediate consideration, as the picked effects will soon be over, and
" everything settle into summer heat. Is there any loft in those barns you
" enter by ? "

Finally my father's wish was fulfilled and he joined us at " High

Ashes," where he found more genial weather and an abundant supply of subjects. Notably, there was a day's sheep-washing in a beautiful old mill-pond to which we walked through great pine-woods. The shearing in the barns, the branding, and many other farming occupations kept him busy with his sketch-book, and he also began two or three water-colours of his then favourite long proportion.[1]

As for the invalid, his rambles in the knee-deep heather, or in the cool brook-threaded valleys, however great a contrast to the Kensington constitutionals, had not done so much for him as was hoped, and the chest of books remained unopened. My father wrote out a long statement of the case for the use of the doctors and it sets forth that, about the middle of May, there had been a change for the worse, but that after this the young man was able to " walk slowly with a stick." Then they got him a donkey-chaise : and twice a day, with my mother walking beside him, he rode propped up with pillows in the shade of the sighing pines. It was about this time, that my father wrote thus, to his old friend Mr. J. C. Hook :—" . . . I have been three weeks helping to nurse my elder son, who " has over-studied and exerted himself, and who is so seriously ill that, " unless he mends, it will not be right for me to leave ; but the ever-pleasant " memory of the days spent with Mrs. Hook and yourself at Hambledon " will urge me to come again, unless duty says ' no.'

" They have so built us up with great houses at Kensington as to " destroy the elasticity of the air, and to make a climate always tepid, " muddy.

" I find I cannot breathe there, nor do half the work I could get " through elsewhere, and so I am looking about for some large cottage or " small farm-house near a railway. I explored Guildford, but in vain, and " I do not like it. I came here, and in a week felt well. My wife also " has derived great benefit from it, but I am quite disheartened at the " difficulty of finding anything at once pretty high, with a dry soil, and " near a railway station. I suppose there is no hope of [succeeding] in " your neighbourhood, but I *have* sometimes cast longing eyes to the vicinity " of Hindhead . . . ."

It is useless to give a full history of the succeeding weeks. As June passed and the warm hand of summer daily clothed the beautiful country with new loveliness, it became evident that my brother's brain, long over-taxed, had severely suffered. Yet there was hope, and on the 2nd of July he wrote hopefully to a friend, of having turned the corner of his disease and of looking for a return of health. Nine days later the pale shadow that had once been the " hope and ornament " of my father's existence kissed

---

[1] These were " Large Longs," measuring 27¼ × 12¼ inches.

A Churchyard View.

him for the last time, and very early in the morning of the following day, bade a weary life farewell.

That awful cry that rang out of old over all the land of Egypt never echoed more mournfully than at " High Ashes " farm. It was very gently that they prepared the father for the news that his first-born was dead ; but he rushed from the house in bewildered agony and never re-entered it. One of the doctors, seeing his critical condition, drove him in his carriage to the house of his brother-in-law, Mr. James Linnell, at Red Hill, and he saw Abinger no more from that day.

The mother followed her son for the last time through the shadows of the pines, and laid him beneath the yew-tree in Abinger Churchyard, near the ancient woods known by the familiar name of Evelyn. Not long before he had sketched the very spot where he was buried, while he was on a walking tour with a school-fellow, little thinking how soon he would repose in that quiet place.

In resuming the story of my father's life after the death of his son we have to do with the life of a changed man—a man whose most cherished hopes had been dashed to pieces; whose remorse and deadly grief shook the very foundations of his character. I say remorse because, now that it was too late, it undoubtedly dawned upon him that he had done unwisely in taxing to the uttermost a willing and precocious intellect unprotected by a strong physique. It was a secret remorse for he would never acknowledge, and indeed he denied that he had, in any way whatever, forced his son along the fatal path. I have heard my father described, and by one of his warmest admirers, as a man "full of theories." Of all these, his theories on the subject of education and the management of the young were perhaps most often in his mind, and were those upon which he had most prided himself. The result (as may be guessed by an allusion or two in his letters, written after the calamity) added a refinement of bitterness to what he was called upon to suffer. The "finger of scorn," as he says, could be pointed at him as one who had egregiously failed in that very thing of all others in which he had promised himself success.

Strange as it may seem, in the descriptions my father wrote of his suffering at that time there is no hyperbole. Even reason itself must have had a struggle for the mastery and, for a moment, the darkest forms of despair cast a sombre shadow over the faith that half a century of trial and trouble had not shaken. Even two months after the death my father wrote, "yesterday was the *only* day a part of which I have not passed in bitter weeping."

Much did he owe at this dark time to the generous help and touching kindness of those true friends he was so fortunate in possessing. To the end of his life he remembered this kindness as vividly as the cause; and, when he could, repaid it.

The parents returned to Kensington only to prepare for immediate removal, and then there arose the miserable question, whither to go? The country had lost its charm. That "eternal loveliness" which my father had found "the spring of successful work," and that "first flush of summer splendour" which had so entranced him at Shoreham had vanished for

ever, and to seek them any more seemed utterly vain. He writes :—" My
" loss has made me so incapable of *personal gratification* from external
" objects, that what is called a beautiful view gives me no more real
" pleasure than the contemplation of a kitchen sink." On the other hand,
if he was to take up the now grievous burden of his work to any purpose
he must be near London. Here again, although his friends did all they
could for him, it was in vain ; so it came to pass at last that we found
ourselves, for the time being, in a little lodging on Red Hill Common.
Early in September 1861, after some fruitless explorations, he took a cottage
in the old town of Reigate, near which two friends of his youth had settled.
The neighbourhood was chosen almost entirely on my mother's account,
because it was near Mr. Linnell's house, but my father would certainly have
preferred almost any other. Excessive damp soon drove her to " Redstone,"
crippled by rheumatism, and she was forced to leave her husband to a
nearly solitary and inconceivably miserable sojourn of six months.

While still in the lodgings at Red Hill Common he had made this
entry in his common-place book :—" If it be the Divine will that I
" live on after this calamity I must try to do my DUTY—my duty
" towards God and my duty towards my neighbour. My wife and child
" are my nearest neighbours. I must use my calling for their support.
" How can I make works which will cheer others when quite cheer-
" less myself? Perhaps thus. 1st, choosing themes I *loved*, for I love
" no art themes now; 2nd, very simple and massive in effect ; 3rd,
" getting in whole effect (after the figures are well designed) at a heat ;
" 4th, sufficient model realization ; 5th, delicate pencilling. Can etching
" be made productive ? Vanity of vanities. August 28, 1861."

This awakening from the stupor of grief to a sense of duty was
followed by a struggle to check a relapse by hard work, and as the result,
no less than five drawings appeared in the summer exhibition of 1862.

Far from his artist friends and his favourite haunts, it is little to be
wondered at that the instant he laid down his brush or pencil he seized
upon a book. In this old and favourite consolation he found some relief
from the bitter thoughts that every unoccupied moment loosed upon him.
He wrote thus to a young lady :—" I don't suffer much from solitude in
" the evenings. I *spring* upon my books. I always spoke a good word
" for solitude, and it is grateful to me. Books ward off the ghastly
" thoughts."

My father had one devoted companion—a little black cat. It was a
strange preference, and the same as that of his friend Francis Finch who har-
boured all stray cats that would stop with him. He writes :—" I never
" think of London without one pleasant reminiscence—its fecundity of
" cats. A fine cat is often the one beautiful ornament in a drawing-room.

" Then he does not set up for somebody else, make capital out of
" philosophy, or stick at inflicting capital punishment on a noisy canary-
" bird.[1]   Nor does he eat by accident, or affect an odious indifference to
" the quality of his food.   He masticates vigorously, which Cobbett said
" was so good a sign in 'young ladies.'   Give him fried fish and he
" purrs as he masticates."   There is certainly an undoubted sentiment of
cosiness[2] which a cat embodies as it basks before the fire, which my father
loved.   The rackety, demonstrative, though utterly disinterested affection
of a dog, and especially the tendency to fidget, would not have harmonized
so well with the old volumes which beguiled the winter evenings at " Park
Lane Cottage " as " Trot's " complacent purring.

The letters and memoranda written at this time seem to me to require
some explanation on account of their showing an apparent want of self-
control.   We are accustomed to see men, and even women, suffering from
the most cruel bereavements, and yet going about their duties calm, reticent,
and dry-eyed.   We must, however, make due allowance for differences of
temperament, and differences of physical robustness.   Those who are
endowed with an unusually large amount of the imaginative faculty are
sometimes peculiarly susceptible to the influences of joy, grief, or disappointment.   Although, like children, they are more easily moved to joy
or to sorrow than the average of men, these emotions should no more be
condemned as shallow than the temperament of the others should be condemned as callous and phlegmatic.   " How well so-and-so bears his loss,"
is one of the commonest expressions of every-day life ; but it would be
equally to the point to say, " How strong is So-and-so's nervous system."
If my father be judged by the usual standard of reticence and self-control
he will be judged unjustly.

Although books were a great consolation, out of despair itself a consolation still greater had arisen.   He wrote :—" If we will but be still and *listen*,
" I think we shall hear these sad trials talking to us ; saying as it were,
" 'You have known life and enjoyed it, you have tried it and suffered from
" it ; your tent has been pitched in pleasant places among those of dear
" relations and tried friends, and now they are disappearing from around
" you.   The stakes are loosened one by one, and the canvas is torn away,

---

[1] My father, loving conversation, loathed canaries.

[2] How my father valued cosiness the following words show. " I have often
" sympathised with such of the poor dear Irish as destitution has plucked from their cabins
" into the well-ventilated unions.   That these cabins are smoky, dirty, and painful to the
" olfactory nerves we know, but then they are SNUG, and how much lies in that little
" word, to poor benighted Englishmen, callous to France, and progress, and glory.   Did
" you never put your feet in the fender and, as it were, fold yourself up, and wish you
" could *roll* yourself up like a dormouse ? . . . I have bathed day and night, summer and
" winter, but confess that a cosy corner is the thing to sit down in."

" with no vestige left behind, and you want something which will *no* be
" taken away. You want something large enough to fill your heart, and
" imperishable enough to make it immortal like itself.   That something is
" God.   Having Him, you will possess all things ; having Him *not*, you
" will be impoverished for ever.   You feel how earth's sweetest pleasures,
" love and friendship, bequeath a legacy of anguish when they leave us :
" then, for the years which remain, TRY THE GREAT EXPERIMENT,
" and take up the cross of Jesus Christ.'

" Thus it is that calamity seems to speak to *me*, and thus it has spoken
" to others in all ages.   .   .   I detest cant as much as any one, but am
" drawing near to the end of my race : and although anything but credu-
" lous—rather too sceptical perhaps [1]—yet I do heartily believe that union
" with Jesus Christ in the Sacrament is the one thing upon the planet
" which is true, rational, and real ; that most other things are temporary
" fallacies, very well in their way, but very vain."

The Reigate cottage having proved unsuitable, my father, once again,
had to begin a search for some permanent and healthy home.   But not
being well fitted at the best of times for business-like investigations, or the
complex problems of a house-hunt, he felt himself helpless.

He was at this time frequently corresponding with his friend Mrs.
Gilchrist, who had just lost her husband.   Resolute and brave in the midst
of her sorrow, she had " tramped it wearily over nearly all that angle of
country between the Hog's Back, Guildford, and Hindhead," in search of a
new home.   With her London house let over her head and each day
bringing with it " fullest measure of labour and suffering," she had tramped on
till she lighted on the lovely village of Haslemere where she ultimately
settled.   My father knew it well, and delighted in the gradual blending of
the rich, cultivated land with the moor above.   He himself seems to have
had serious thoughts of settling down there, having vainly explored, he says,
the whole of the rest of Surrey near the railway.   Nevertheless, he seemed
tethered to the neighbourhood of London by prudential motives, and
he lacked the enterprise that discovers and appropriates the choicest
homes of the earth.   In May, therefore of 1862 he decided on a small
detached house [2] at Mead Vale, Red Hill ; not by any means his ideal
residence, but a pleasant contrast to the damp cottage where he had spent
the dreariest winter of his life.

Hardly a mile away and near the well-known Red Hill Junction there
stood, on flat, swampy ground, as ugly a town as you could find, with no
history beyond the history of the railway, and no old association.   West-

[1] My father was fond of saying this, greatly to the amusement of some of his friends.
[2] After living there nineteen years, he describes himself as being " in the midst " of
what is to him " the most emphatic solitude, a growing railway town."

wards, however, a pretty valley opened out, formed between the same great downs which cradled Shoreham and an uneven, sandy range which, at a lower elevation, runs parallel for a long distance.

Perched upon this range of sand, and about four hundred feet above the sea, stood " Furze Hill House," a solitary vedette of the neighbouring brick and mortar army. It had not long been built and was what house-agents, for some inscrutable reason, call a " Gothic villa." Pretentious outside and inconvenient within, it was undoubtedly "genteel"; so the new tenant immediately gave a grand name to everything. The drawing-room he called " The saloon ": one bedroom " The boudoir "; another, which was damp, " Bronchitis Bower ;" and a little downstairs closet (where some of his old books had to be stored away), " The Butler's Pantry."

The terraced garden was less pretentious, and was divided by a holly and laurel hedge (greatly beloved of nightingales and whitethroats) from a steep furze-field, where there were to be seen, according to the season, clots of golden blossom, masses of brakes far taller than your head, or the blush of heather. Two sloping lawns with cedars and deodaras round which the rabbits chased each other led the eye downwards to a copse of larch and beech, which seemed to teem with birds and squirrels. This was so far below that, but for a dark crown of Scotch fir, one could see above the topmost sprays, stretching far away without a break, many miles of Surrey and Sussex ; till, with the quiet gradations of English scenery, the landscape merged in the grey outline of the great South Downs full thirty miles away. After heavy rains, and much to my father's joy, the " Sullen Mole " revealed itself as a veritable river, winding in and out among the meadows. To the eastward, the hills of Kent bounded the view, and nine miles on the right in the opposite direction, a great spur of sand culminated in the summit of Leith Hill.

By degrees my father became accustomed to his sorrow, but he writes thus about this time to an old friend :—"I fancy you can " hardly enter into the feeling with which I rise in the morning; not a " murmuring against Providence, but the painful stooping, as it were, to " take up the burden of the coming day—a longing to be let off; a " feeling of utter incompetence to the task ; no hopeful motive and no " strength."

It was, however, a very strongly-marked peculiarity of his temperament that, in spite of the terrible reality and permanence of his grief, the time came when a superficial observer might have supposed that he had completely shaken it off. In society he appeared so cheerful, so animated in conversation, and so ready to join in a hearty laugh, that a friend who saw him only as a guest has remarked that he seemed a *bon-vivant.* Those, however, who had greater opportunities of studying him, knew that

the last caress of his little daughter at Grove Street, and that moment
of anguish in the early summer's morning at High Ashes were never
forgotten.

He was one of those who love the society of their children, and as we
were now thrown more together than before, I soon learned to look upon
him not only as a most indulgent teacher, but as a favourite companion :
and although he never joined in any regular game, he made the innumerable hours I spent in his society seem delightful.

He knew well the inestimable value of a school and university training,
but unfortunately for me, the catastrophe of his life, and the great crash of
all his theories made him shrink from sending his last child away from
home. He therefore . determined to ground me in what he himself
considered as essentials, and everything hinged upon his own ideal—
Elements and Accuracy, manual accuracy being included. He writes :—

" The peculiar excellence of skilful home teaching seems to me to lie
" in the earliest lessons being made *pleasant*. Beguile a child into his
" A, B, C, instead of beating him into it. Teach him to read so as to
" make him like the sight of a book rather than hate it, and you have done
" a *great* work. All attainment is difficult. Ill-tempered teaching goes
" near to make it impossible. As the child grows older idle fits will come
" sometimes, and there may be need of a little correction ; but, from what
" I remember, I think the parents are usually much more in fault than the
" children. They expect the little creatures to take pains to learn while
" *they* will not take pains to teach ; and so, for every cuff they give the
" children they deserve a dozen : and pretty hard ones too."

As early as I can remember I had been promoted (sitting in my baby
chair) to help him to fasten in his drawings with paste and paper, for the
exhibition, an opportunity for mischief and mess which he turned into an
elementary lesson in painstaking. Toys were very rare, but I scarcely
missed them, for there were a hundred little things to do, connected with
art, which he managed to make amusing. Few would have patiently borne
with the bungling of childhood in like matters, but it was an important
point in my father's method of teaching to set me things to do that really
wanted doing, and to point out that disastrous consequences would follow
failure. By this teaching, and by his own example, he gradually fixed in
my mind a conviction that whatever is worth doing at all is worth doing
well, and that few things can be done in a worthy manner without patience.
Elements, Accuracy, Method, Patience, Humility—these were the cardinal
points in my father's teaching.

He attached great importance to the regular lessons, which included
Latin, arithmetic, drawing, and English : but these were administered in
doses which, nowadays, would be considered infinitesimal.

K

I was attacked severely by entomological mania, and following the example of a friend whose enthusiasm found vent in collecting beetles, I spent many hours in the pursuit of butterflies and moths. Now, strangely enough, my father, even in boyhood, had never been smitten with the collecting mania in any form, and he seemed to be utterly without the fell passion known as acquisitiveness. Nevertheless, he allowed me to gloat over my captures, thinking that good might come in the shape of nicety of handling, and habits of observation.[1] I can remember, however, that when I sought to arouse his enthusiasm in the same direction by showing him my boxes and setting-boards, I was surprised by an indifference which I could not understand, and was told sometimes, in Pope's words, that "The proper study of mankind is man." Writing to the friend I have just mentioned, my father said, "Forgive my weakness about beetles, " only don't neglect the other B—Biography. It's biography that makes " moral muscle. All the great men have set venerated models before them, " and tried to work up to them."

It is worthy of note that, although keenly and vigilantly observant of so many natural phenomena, my father knew and was content to know but little of our native natural history. He could not have passed the most absurdly elementary examination in botany, entomology, ornithology, or geology.

For all worthy handicrafts and all mechanical tools he taught a reverence which he himself seemed to feel very strongly; although with the same kind of inconsistency as before, he had never cultivated manual dexterity. He says ". . . we might but too surely lament a moral debase- " ment, where a court dress was looked upon with more respect than a " carpenter's tool-basket. The things in harmony with religion and art " (not on any account confounding the two), are not fashionable follies, but " tool-baskets, spades and ploughs, house-brooms, dusters, gridirons, and " pudding-bags. Were the smell of soap-suds more exhilarating, I would " add the boiler and the implements of washing, in honour of that type of " lady-hood, the dear Princess Nausicäa who, in a warmer climate, " invoked Neptune for the laundry." My father forswore nice furniture and

---

[1] The study of natural history, within proper limits, is so invaluable a training for children, and so fascinating a recreation for their elders, that I wonder it is ever omitted in some form or other from the education of those who have the opportunity of pursuing it. The very least it does, is to bring them face to face with thousands of the most beautiful objects and the most marvellous events—objects and events to which they are otherwise absolutely blind. It gives a zest and a peculiar charm to every country walk; peoples the hills, the valleys, the streams and the very air, with innumerable friends; trains the mind to explore, little by little, the fairyland of science—trains the eye to see, the hands to handle deftly, and the feet to wariness. Yet how many are brought up blind, and deaf, and callous, to the teaching of this wondrous world and all that is therein, that they may enter so early the priesthood of the Great God Mammon.

other fittings for his study, in favour of rough, clumsy shelves, primitive palette-racks, mended chairs, and decrepit tables, because all this mending and making taught me, and encouraged me to do my best ; while at the same time, everything was a protest against what he was pleased to call " Cursed Gentility." In his study he intrenched himself against everything genteel, as he would have done against an insidious and potent disease raging all round him. There he felt at home, but among the drawing-room " Fal Lals " he was out of his element. The " staff " he carried in the garden was an ancient and worm-eaten umbrella-stick, clumsily whipped with string here and there. His old shoes were laboriously patched by an entirely original process of our own ; and worn-out garments, condemned by the authorities, were rescued and secretly repaired in ways unknown to tailors.

Now in boyhood he had been a bit of a dandy for a time (as he had been a bit of a free-thinker), bedecking himself in white trousers and flourishing a whangee cane ; but one day, when he was abroad in his glory, he came abruptly upon his full length reflection in a shop window. There was a pause, and then he said to himself, " No more finery for a gentleman as short as you ! " Thenceforth he gave up all pretensions to grand apparel, and in after life his dress, though always plain and sometimes eccentric, was made with due regard to comfort, hard wear, and pocket capacity. He often quoted the lines :—

> " Learn thou the goodness of thy clothes to prize,
> " By their own use, and not another's eyes,"

and as he hated affectation nearly as sturdily as fashion, he was safe from the temptations (whatever they may be) of the " artistic " or " æsthetic " style of dress.

He regarded ridicule very little in the attainment of any object he thought a worthy one. " It seems to me," he wrote, " that while nothing " is more silly than eccentricity for its own sake, few things are more " pernicious than the dread of being peculiar." And again, " How many " acquaintances can we tell off on our fingers, who will dare to be singular " —who will draw a line, and halt, and say ' No '? But to tell off those " who will be sure to ' follow a multitude to do evil,' if it be only a fashion- " able multitude, we need have the fingers of Briareus."

As far back as I can recollect, my father had generally worn on state occasions, a loose and lengthy broadcloth coat of a rather peculiar cut, and full of pockets so ample that, at a pinch, they easily engulfed a sketching outfit. A double-breasted waistcoat, buttoned high and close over the formal folds of an old-fashioned white cravat, added to a clerical appearance which was sufficiently great to cause a country clergyman, on one occasion, to request, through the clerk, his assistance in the service.

K 2

A pair of old-fashioned silver spectacles with very broad rims was used for distant objects; but on the state occasions aforesaid, these were exchanged for spectacles of the ordinary pattern, which once lost, he with his near sight, sometimes trod upon, and afterwards groped for with much grumbling at the prejudices of genteel mankind. Blake's great, round, steel-rimmed glasses, bleared by many a year of use, were among my father's very few personal treasures. This fewness was another of his peculiarities, for who has not a little collection of very favourite belongings? I never knew him to possess a single article of jewellery, and even of his family crest he was content to have nothing better than a single wax impression. So quiet and uneventful was the nature of his present life, that he found no use even for a watch. His pockets, however, were replete with chalks, lead pencils, charcoal, sketch-books, and keen knives, besides a certain old wooden snuff-box of rich, golden hue. This resembled the tint of some of Titian's flesh-colour, and was used by "The Ancients," in their visits to the Dulwich Gallery and other collections, as a chromatic Shibboleth. Three or four recently-received letters were generally carried in the ample waistcoat pockets, and on the envelopes many a design had its birth, the tiny "blot" being hardly larger than the postage-stamp.

My father seemed naturally nocturnal in his habits. He speaks of "Blessed Green-tea-time winding up to Hamlet and ecstacy"; of "early bed and early rising" being of all things most distasteful to him; and we have seen how "The Ancients" revelled in the small hours. Now, as then, the early tea was looked forward to as the fore-runner of a quiet time when he could take up a favourite author or a new design after the day's work, or indulge in one of his chief pleasures, letter-writing. Notwithstanding this, he was never a very late riser till the "drousie days" of age overtook him.

At this period of his life breakfast was generally over in good time and was invariably followed by family prayers, which were another symptom of his originality. He read the Bible and Apocrypha without regard to the Lectionary, and he often recurred to certain favourite chapters; but his selection generally had some motive. Over and over again, as years went by, he read us the story of Judith and other favourite episodes; but the greatest favourite of all was the history of Ahab, and especially the incident of Naboth's vineyard. Jezebel was established as a typical woman, to whom he compared, rather uncharitably, the modern woman of fashion. Indeed, so frequent were his allusions to Jezebel's supposed love of finery that, with his friends, "Jezebel Top" became a synonym for the small fashionable bonnet.

He abhorred few things more than quick reading and the modern custom of abbreviating the preterites, the last being in his opinion a barbarous innovation, destroying the rhythm of the old English. Even in church, I have seen his face darken with anger under the monotonous, scrambling drone of the young, high-church reader. He himself read in a very different way. Without any conventional religious tone, any affectation, or any effort, he sent the story home to the minds of his hearers, and brought the characters before them. But there were passages when his emotion mastered him time after time, and he had to lay down the book. One of these was the 11th chapter of St. John's Gospel,[1] which seemed to go straight to the heart of a man longing more and more for reunion with those whom he mourned. Although he loved the Church of England liturgy, for home use he preferred extempore prayer. This was highly original and intensely earnest.

In the summer he would generally spend half an hour or so in the garden after prayers. Then, having set me my lessons, he would retire to his study, and work till our early dinner-time with a concentration of thought and inflexibility of industry which would have done honour to a man of half his years. It was work of such a kind that had he continued longer without a break it would have been at the expense of what he had already done. A short siesta after dinner was often provoked by a pipe, and by some light literature, such as a novel, which he seldom allowed himself except at this time ; and then came work again, till our tea at five o'clock. Afterwards, we strolled out together in the long evenings, through fields of young corn, or grass, or sweet-scented trefoil, to see the sunsets. Few sunsets have seemed comparable in beauty to those he showed me, and when he could go no longer the twilights seemed to lose half their poetry. It was not merely that he so cordially admired or understood so well the beauties of the aërial tints, or that he could point them out with peculiarly well-chosen words. In the enjoyment added by his presence there was something far more subtle than this, and beyond the power of words to describe. It was probably akin to what he himself had experienced when walking with Blake.

His pleasure in thunderstorms was quite as keen as in the days when the peals, rolling from combe to combe among the hills, had called forth "The Ancients" from the Shoreham Cottage ; and now, as a tempest crept towards us in the twilight over the landscape—the flashes, to his delight, sometimes revealing stupendous chains of cloud mountains—we simply revelled in the sight, till the great drops upon the dust and the crash of near thunder drove us indoors.

In all our summer rambles, the abundant wild flowers delighted my father more and more. He did not study them botanically, or horticulturally, or altogether artistically. He knew scarcely any of their names : but he loved them so well that at last a corner was set apart for them near

---

[1] There are several allusions in his letters to Lieven's *Raising of Lazarus*, a work which, agreeing with Fuseli, he thought worthy of the subject.

his study window, under protest from the domestic authorities and from
that agricultural implement the gardener. But my father was inexorable,
and although his favourites were once or twice surreptitiously flung over
the hedge, he brought them back or replaced them.   He wrote to
Miss Redgrave (a very favourite correspondent of his), ". . . . I *will*
" have my weeds though !   The white convolvuli are commencing[1]
" their tortuosities (to speak in Reigate dialect), and Herbert has
" made a bench for the arbour.   Miss Mary [a new housemaid] com-
" menced weeding the other day, and pulled up both my hairbell roots,
" that I have been coaxing for three years into the garden."   This
was an incident which led to an unwonted explosion of wrath on my
father's part.   The "weeds" became a by-word, and nobody understood his
pleasure in them, or saw their beauty.   Some gave us infinite trouble, and
pined away, in spite of a system of artificial irrigation suggested by a passage
in the *Georgics.*   All we did was accomplished clumsily and with labour :
moreover the soil was so barren, our supply of water often so inestimably
precious (for we depended entirely on the rain) that everything was
against us.   I do not think I have ever seen my father do anything with
greater care and pleasure than, in the dry summer weather, the doling out
of a little water to his favourite "weeds."

The garden had other attractions for us than the hardly-earned fragrance of our wild flowers, and the songs of the birds which abounded
there ; for we cut lanes in the undergrowth of the shrubs leading unawares
to tiny, sylvan arbours, whence we could get a peep of distant country.
Then, by means of prodigious expense of time and toil, we raised a small
hillock ("The Specular Mount," as we call it), whence, over a very un-
classical paling, we could get a downward glimpse of the steepest slope of
the hanger, and imagine if we liked, that it was haunted by a Faun or two,
or perhaps by a beautiful Dryad.[2]   And so, in our own esteem, this very
little and very ordinary garden seemed to lose its primness and gentility,
gradually changing into a charming wilderness, and it pleased us as much
in its way as if it had been a garden of King Alcinous himself.

The wisdom of the head of a family may sometimes be guessed by the
way that family spends Sunday, and there are an infinitude of gradations between those who treat it as a holiday, or as an ordinary day of

---

[1] I do not think my father was aware that this verb or its derivatives is used certainly
once by Spenser and seven times by Shakespeare.

[2] My father was particularly delighted to use as part of the material for " The
Specular Mount " a large heap of the kitchen breakages.   Female destructiveness and
strength in destruction was a favourite topic with him.   " I could wish," he writes, " that
" the tender creatures had not contrived to split my strongest brass-backed saw, bent the
" very toughest of my carpenter's tools which they have borrowed, and sown successive
" cinder-heaps with snuffers.   But they know best."

work, and others who compose their solemn faces to a day of austerity
and straitlaced idleness: forcing their very babies to put away their toys,
and frowning down all merriment. With artists, especially, Sunday is
often regarded little. They paint, or haggle with some dealer, or show
their pictures to crowds of visitors, if it be at exhibition-time. None of
these things had my father done. He rigorously observed Sunday throughout his life, but with no fanatical austerity; and spent with him, I found
it the happiest day of the seven. While his health allowed it, he was
regular in his attendance at morning service, but afterwards there was
much that might be read, and much that might be done both indoors and
out. Unaffected piety was as marked a feature in his character as a
craving for knowledge; but he never attempted to cram either intellectual
or moral food down unwilling throats. The young mind was allured, but
never driven to its fairest pastures. The pursuit of wisdom and virtue
was inculcated much by precept, but more by example, while the knowledge
of baseness and evil, without being forbidden, was made to appear unattractive by the tempting beauty of the opposites.

The winter evenings brought their own resources, and were often
begun with a hit or two of backgammon, my father's only game. All
other games he disliked, as usurping the place of reading and conversation,[1]
and I can hardly imagine his handling a cue or a pack of cards. The
backgammon over, he would take up a novel by Scott or Dickens, or
oftener, his Shakespeare, Chaucer, or some other favourite old poet, and
read to us till my bed-time, when he returned once more to the congenial
solitude of his study; where he read, or wrote, or designed, till a late
hour.

There were occasional visits to London, all of which had some imperative object far apart from mere pleasure-taking. Perhaps it was some
notable exhibition of the Old Masters, perhaps the investigation of some
new photo-mechanical process, or the proving of an etching: but in the
pencil list of things to be done, there was always something printed in
large letters, which was of chief importance. On one occasion (my father
tells a friend), the object of the journey was the study of "a bit one inch
square, in a single picture."

The preparations for a day in town made by a very sedentary man who
sees little of the world around him are usually such as would amuse the
ordinary man of business not a little. Being sometimes allowed to accompany my father on these great occasions, I well remember the bustle
and circumstance attending them. For days, perhaps weeks, beforehand

---

[1] He wrote, "Burke complained in his day that it was difficult to meet with
"conversation--the discussion of some subject.' The odious ' music,' as it is called, stops
"conversation effectually."

a list of things to be seen, done, and got, was carefully compiled upon a
leaf of a small sketch-book, and the route was systematically planned out,
so as to economize time to the utmost.   On the eventful morning, the
broadcloth coat with long, flowing skirt was brought forth, and the white
cravat was adjusted with unusual care.   One or more sets of underclothing
was donned, according to the time of year, and sometimes indeed a second
pair of trousers in severe weather.   The silver spectacles were reluctantly
laid aside for those of thin steel, and a mighty silk hat was disinterred
from a box where it dwelt secure for months together.   What a hat it was !
But for his limbs my father would have been a big man [1] and I verily
believe that hat (though it fitted him) was the biggest that could be bought.
The label on the bandbox had been directed by the hatter to " The Rev.
S. Palmer " and there was certainly a sort of very venerable curl about
the brim.

Arriving at the station in a flutter of excitement, and not less than half
an hour or so too early, we patrolled together, my father quite unconscious
of the attention that his peculiar dress attracted, or if sometimes made
conscious, not in the least put out.   Once fairly in London he devoted
himself to showing me everything of interest that lay in our route, and it
was astonishing how much he knew of the history and the associations of
every nook and corner of older London.   Regardless of staring, laughter,
or jostling, he would stop dead in the middle of the pavement, or in a most
conspicuous place, to point out to me some classic spire or memorable
house, or the ancient haunt of one of his heroes.   On one occasion he
stopped thus, when he was walking with a young friend, before a milliner's
shop and began, with some vehemence of action, to declaiming his high,
tenor voice against the " Jezebel Tops " within.   A few passers-by, scenting
any eccentricity in the usual unerring way, also stopped ; and my father
happening to turn, found his companion fled, and himself the nucleus of a
growing crowd.

He did not confine himself to showing me the ordinary out-door sights ;
for, under his guidance, I saw the interior of many a notable building,
which his descriptions fixed in my memory.   As for his purchases, what joy
there was in them, small though they were and few in number !   An old
book, a print or two, a photograph of some favourite picture, or a miniature
antique bust from Brucciani's—these were the things that found their way
into his bag or pockets during the day, and they gave him that keen
pleasure known only to cultured men of small means who grievously pine
for an object for months before they venture to buy it.

I remember particularly, the courtesy of his manner to all with whom
our travels brought us into contact, without any distinction of class,

[1] He was barely 5ft. 3 inches in height, but was 40 inches round the chest.

or any nicely-gauged discrimination of relative wealth. In the pursuit of the chief object of the day he was tenacious and patient as a bloodhound ; and so, when we returned home in the evening, and dragged our weary legs up the steep homeward hills, we were able to reflect that not one single minute had been wasted.

In some of my father's letters allusions occur (not without pathos), to an exceptionally drastic annual spring cleaning. This was an event he used to dread, partly on account of the discomfort attending it, and partly because the precious contents of the painting-room—books, plaster-casts, papers, and portfolios, were bundled out upon the lawn, there to be diligently dusted, and afterwards returned to the shelves in an order unfamiliar to him. No corner was too sacred to escape the deluge ; no old folio volume too reverend to escape a banging ; and no treasured store of odds and ends (for all which he had a use of his own), too well hidden to defeat a severe, revising scrutiny. To avoid this hygienic but very painful visitation, my father fled ; and he usually betook himself either to London, or to "Elysium" as he called it, Mr. Hook's retreat at Churt. In 1869 he writes to Mr. Redgrave :—"Little did I think when Hook walked "into our Club meeting for the first time (it was at Creswick's), that "the privilege of his friendship and that of his most excellent wife "would be such an item in the consolations of my future being!" And again he writes in 1870 :—"I am so glad that Mrs. Hook has thriven "upon Norway. She is so discreet, so genial, and so good, that if "*Ecclesiastes* was yet to write, Solomon might say, "One of a thousand I "have found."

My father's sympathies were strongly bucolic. Loving dearly the breath of cows, the sweet smell of the new furrow, and all the wonders of the gardener's art besides, he looked forward for weeks together to this visit to his half artist and half farmer friend. Writing to Mr. Hook he says :— "Orchards and kitchen-gardens are to me more delightful than whole "mountains of dahlias, but foul were the mouth that could slander the rose "or the lily ; or loveliest of all, the woodbine." That he revelled in the scenery round Churt, his sketch-books, and letters testify. And returning from this to the prim, densely-peopled neighbourhood of Red Hill, the "Gothic" villa, and the tiny garden where every inch was of value, and every twig on the eastern side had its work to do in shutting out slate roofs, my father must have felt his heart sink within him. Nevertheless, within the sturdy covers of his old books, he knew that he had fairer estates than even "Silverbeck," to console him.

Such as I have described it, was the quiet tenour of this most uneventful and almost humdrum life. It was without hurry or the ordinary causes of excitement ; without the commonest forms of ambition ; and it lacked altogether those salient points beloved of the biographer. Indeed, unless the reader can, by some means or other, bring to bear a little sympathy, he will find it hard to understand that such an existence can be passed contentedly, by anybody but an avowed anchorite. So uneventful were the years, that little occurrences which an average man would forget in a few days were apt to become magnified in my father's mind into adventures, somewhat to the amusement of his younger friends.

Those who crossed the threshold of his room, found themselves centuries behind the times. In the place of the daily newspaper, or the latest novel, heavy old folios and quartos lay upon the table. The last scandal or the newest crime failed to awaken any curiosity; and although it is true that the greatest religious or political questions of the day (as reported upon by his friends) were canvassed, for the most part literature, philosophy, poetry and art, were the chief topics; if ancient so much the better; and if modern they were approached with interest, but with a prejudice little disguised.

Certain evenings of the week were set apart for the reception of two frequent visitors—the sons of an old friend of my father's then living in the neighbourhood. Naturally fond of young people, my father took to these boys almost as to children of his own : and finding their minds and tastes much above the average, he welcomed their visits, till in time these became a settled ordinance, interrupted only by school and university duties. Poems, essays, magazine articles, red-hot schemes for various sweeping reforms—all were brought and laid before him; but not always with the anticipated success in securing a straightforward opinion. That was a matter in which my father was habitually and, as we used to think, unnecessarily careful not to commit himself.

Among the many conversations which took place on these occasions, I cannot remember one which was not interesting. The singular animation, the infinite number of authorities appealed to, the wide range of subject, the keen sense of poetry, pathos, and humour which distinguished the trio, were as noteworthy as the vehemence and ability with which each would defend a favourite author or pet conviction, when (as was almost invariably the case) the talk glided into argument. Many of these arguments took the form of a defence of antiquity—of ancient authors, philosophy, and poetry, from ingenious but often feigned attacks by the two exponents of more modern thought. The sympathy of his adversaries was often with my father, but he courted attack, and knew how to provoke it to some purpose. Thus it happened that the disputants sometimes waxed more earnest than was consistent with perfect temper; as, for instance, when in his turn, he assaulted modern science, and openly averred that he preferred Aristotle as an authority on natural history, to the greatest modern naturalists.

A few instances of his convictions on subjects such as this, taken from his letters, may not be out of place. They show an incredulity which could be pronounced enough when occasion served : a bias which, considering he read little or nothing of the works he repudiated, and often knew less of those facts and theories which he dismissed in a contemptuous paragraph or two, amounts to injustice :—[*October* 20, 1864]:—" The influences of the day promise much worse things than paganism, with its " perverted truths and misapplied devotion. What measure of light was " permitted, *Pagans* would not have changed away for the wretched " *débris* of rotting skulls and flint arrow-heads. If so-called science bids " us give up our faith, surely we have a right to ask for something better " in exchange."

[*February*, 1868.] :—" I am lamentably stupid with this severe attack [of " illness], but not quite so far gone as to part with the LVIIIth of Isaiah " for all the geological, dismal millions of ages, or all the wretched flint " axe-heads, or all or any cavernous bone-grubbing whatsoever."

[*January* 2, 1873.] :—" As to the hopeful young gentlemen who do us " the honour to own our parentage, they are precisely as I was once, making " my way to pay a first visit to an old country house up a very dirty lane " in a quiet, grey moonlight. Looking on my left I saw what appeared " to be a perfectly smooth and clean pathway. I leaped out of the mud " and found myself in a ditch ! What *can* have maddened them ? When " did we, in our maddest days, *approach* the folly of preferring Mr. Darwin's " ' developments ' to these words :—' God created man in his own image ' ? " When did we imagine such debasement—*intellectual* debasement, as " would read that wondrous chapter, the raising of Lazarus, without " believing it ? . . The genus juvenis seems to be marching backwards " apace, with colours flying and a full band, and this they call " ADVANCE."

[*February* 15, 1879.]:—" The learning which is indeed exceptionable, is " that science, falsely so called, which would tortuously pervert the universal " language of God's glorious works into a disproof of his existence."

These passages speak for themselves, and I will therefore leave them without comment.

It was as evident to my father's auditors as it is easy to see from his letters, that he was no optimist ; that he thought many of the modern tendencies were downwards ; and that most of our boasted " progress " was little better than retrogression towards the universal catastrophe he seemed seriously to anticipate. " Have you really seen the last of " Margate ? " he writes to Mr. Richmond, " Can't you come down and have " a social groan over things in general ? " On one occasion, being pressed very hard to give some one instance of genuine progress in this century,

after an "agony of accommodation" he was able to call to mind only
the abolition of intermural interment. He upheld against repeated
attacks what we called his "undulatory theory," thus expressed in
his own words:—" Like everything else it [the theory of the earth's
" motion], has gone see-saw, which those who are at the upper end of the
" plank for a moment call 'progress': whereas the whole history of
" nations, and science, and art, has been see-saw (ill spelt I fear), or, if we
" *must* have a fine word, 'undulation.'"[1]   It will be found that he pointed
to many of the discoveries of the present century as evils and national
calamities : and he believed that, in many other respects, we were merely
on the summit of a wave which would subside, and rise again, and so on
till the fast-approaching day of visitation.

To what extent my father was in earnest, or rather, to what extent he
was secretly convinced as to the truth of some of his statements and
apparent beliefs, as expressed in these conversations and in many of his
letters, I am not prepared to say.   I have always suspected that he was
not convinced in all cases, because his mind appeared sufficiently logical
and sufficiently trained—his reading sufficiently wide, to guard him at all
events from so violent and unreasonable a kind of prejudice as that he
occasionally paraded, although he seemed unconscious that he was not the
least prejudiced of men.   I am inclined to think that of the many stout
fortresses held from his youth up by his affections against his intellect
(for it must be remembered that he was once, he says, a bit of a
free-thinker), several were undermined by proofs to which he could not
altogether remain blind.   Thus, perhaps, it has been in all ages ; and in
proportion to the amount of a man's knowledge and ability, he has been
compelled (often sorely against his will and often secretly) to march sooner
or later with the times in which he has lived.   Yet it is impossible to read
many of my father's letters without seeing that, in some notable cases,
prejudice held its own against all comers.   A fair idea of the relative
strength of his intellect pure and simple, and of his prejudice, will be
given by the few passages which follow. [*August* 1, 1856.]:—"There is
" an ancient brick house which stands back in the High Street of
" Margate, whence, eighty or ninety years since, my grandmother
" leaped in affright from a first-floor window.   Strange to say, it is
" reported that the people who now live there leave it every Saturday
" and inhabit elsewhere.   Only think of a restless spirit wandering
" about *one* house for nearly a century!"

[*April* 27, 1862.]:—" No one is less credulous than myself in accepting
" strange narrations of our intercourse with the unseen world—yet,
" independently of anything contained in the Holy Scripture, I think

[1] Letter to Mr. C. W. Cope. September, 1872. LXXXIII.

" that the occasional experience of men in countries and ages widest
" apart, from the earliest times, making innumerable subtractions, and
" admitting every reasonable doubt, do altogether *prove* this much, that
" *sometimes* the spirits of the departed know what is going on among those
" dearest to them on earth ; and if so, we cannot tell but that they always
" know it, although unable to manifest that knowledge. I *can* find *some*
" comfort in this."

[*October*, 1870.] :—" When at Margate with Herbert I had peculiar
" opportunities of collecting evidence as to haunted houses, and spent
" almost the most interesting evening in my life in a family meeting
" (convened for the purpose) of alleged eye-witnesses. My impression
" was that, making all allowance for imposture and mistake, there was
" a residuum of evidence which no candid mind could resist. I think you
" must have some curious information on the subject, and should like to
" talk it over with you."

[*December*, 1870.] :—" At last cumulative evidence has *compelled* me to
" believe that *sometimes* departed spirits haunt particular places."

[*August* 29, 1872.] :—" I know . . . certain particulars of five haunted
" houses, not reckoning that which was pulled down near Turner's house.
" There is still the first-floor window out of which my grandmother leaped
" There is still the mystic canary-bird, or the little toy horse. Who can
" pass a Saturday there? Not very comfortably, he must confess, Yours
" ever, S. Palmer."

[*October*, 1873.] :—" Please observe that I am not quite so absurd as to
" doubt of your little press [Mr. Hamerton's], because I have not tried it
" myself. This would be as bad as the hackneyed folly about apparitions :
" ' I will believe when I see one myself' ; just as if Self's eyes were
" sharper than any one else's ! (Pardon the grammar). What a picture !
" Self waiting for his own proper bogy to accredit the testimony of all
" nations and ages."

[*September*, 1875.] :—" I am inclined to concur in your opinion as to the
" credulity of men of science—i.e. until they come to the proper objects
" of Faith ; *then* they are all caution and cavil."

[1878.] :—" Without in the least disparaging the other system, I am
" inclined to think that there are cases in which the (globule) homœo-
" pathic treatment is quite efficacious. I believe in it, as I believe in the
" fact of their having been *some* haunted houses, because, if you sift both
" questions till you sift your arms off, there is still a residuum of evidence
" which you cannot get rid of."

[*October*, 1879.] :—" Ask to see Sir James Thornhill's Allegorical Stair-
" case. . . . I never saw it. It was at number 96 [of a London Street] that
" Mrs. Powell for many years made her pipe of wine from the grapes which

" grew in her garden. I never saw it. What of that ?—Other people saw
" it, and their eyes were as good as mine. There are two sorts of people :
" those who believe on evidence, and those who, in their omniscience, make
" a list of the impossibles, and believe even on the strongest evidence only
" such things as their expurgatory index has left open."

March 16, 1880. :—" Many thanks for telling me *The Athenæum* ghost
" story. I believe and KNOW that the dead have reappeared, but this
" case seems parallel with one narrated in a subsequent number, a
" phantasm of the brain ; or, to express it in high-class gibberish, an
" exceptional phase of psychological subjectivity."

I was present at the family gathering convened at my father's request,
and I remember it well. It consisted chiefly of ladies, all of whom were
such devout believers in the supernatural, that they related in perfect good
faith, and with as much *sangfroid* as if they were the incidents of every-day
life the most astounding occurrences. With an eager and boundless credulity
ready made for all emergencies they had, as they believed, been eye-witnesses
of certain events in places already abundantly provided by tradition with an
evil reputation ; and my father, with a credulity in my opinion little
inferior, urged on by a powerful imagination, absorbed what he heard as
" evidence." The truth seems to be that he was never at any time of his
life in the habit of subtracting the large percentage of exaggeration and
inaccuracy, that most people subtract almost unconsciously from what they
hear.

His credulity with regard to strange or romantic episodes in natural
history (as, for instance, the capture of a mighty sea serpent at Oban),
to say nothing of a firm conviction of the futility of modern science
generally, which was largely due to wilful ignorance of the evidence ; his
repugnance to taking up any book or to investigating any facts opposed to
his own impetuous and warm beliefs—all this leads to the conclusion that
he was, in his way, not only as biassed as most men, but as incapable of
seeing that he was so. Unless we can believe that a man's mind may be
divided into two sharply defined kingdoms or politics, the one ruled by his
impulses, affections, and imagination, the other by his intellect and
reasoning power ; each kingdom being distinct and sometimes able to act
independently of the other, it is impossible to reconcile all we meet with
in my father's writings and actions.

Quite as much of the amusement of the long series of conversations
with the two young scholars lay in this want of self knowledge, as in the
warmth of his convictions, the coolness of his incredulity, the ingenuity of
his defences, and the vigour of his attacks.

It must not be imagined that if my father was a prejudiced disputant, he
was unfair, impatient, or overbearing. He was an unconscious master of

the rare art of drawing people out to show themselves at their best, and after half an hour's conversation he would often sit passive, while some enthusiastic friend trotted his favourite hobby to and fro before him. He achieved this result partly by the pardonable Jesuitism of agreeing with his companion as far as agreement was possible without loss of self-respect, and he mentioned as a type of man to be avoided, an early acquaintance of his who met every statement made before him with a knowing look and " I don't know that." In himself there was nothing of this, and he preferred passing over palpable blunders and inconsistencies, as long as there was no trespassing within certain boundaries. His companion once within these boundaries, he took up his parable to some purpose. He was a good listener; and he rarely refused sympathy with an adversary's opinions, where he could conscientiously give it. This art of listening (for to listen well is an art), and readiness of concession had something to do with his popularity with men of widely differing shades of opinion, although such attributes may sometimes have brought him within a measurable distance of the accusation of trimming.

On the other hand, his views, as I have said, sometimes brought down upon him a series of attacks ; but however well these were marshalled by logic, or backed by an array of unimpeachable authority, or weighty evidence, he would rarely admit defeat. Towards the end of some tough discussion, when his antagonist felt assured of a decisive victory—suddenly, by some ingenious manœuvre, some energetic confession of faith, or an abrupt retreat into the strongholds of paradox (for which, like Blake, he had a liking), he would show that he valued the arguments, and the evidence, and the authority, not a snap of his fingers, against his own cherished convictions. Thus he often left his opponent with an angry eye and useless weapons.

Very few regular visitors found their way at this time to Furze Hill House. Of late years my father had made scarcely any new friends, although the neighbourhood was one where literature and art were said to flourish under the auspices of Societies which sketched and read and were lectured to, after the curious manner of country Societies in general. From these he held himself instinctively aloof. Since his loss, he had shunned mixed gatherings, and he had always disliked the formal hospitalities of etiquette. Thus it was that those who came at all were to some extent kindred spirits, and among them there were a chosen few who were admitted to my father's study. Thither, when domestic matters threatened distractions, retreat was made for the most notable readings and conversations. In his reading aloud my father particularly hated interruption, and asserted that it always came at some important crisis in the story or poem. Much to his friends' amusement, he invariably (and perhaps a little osten-

tatiously) stopped short, if there was any whispered instruction to a
servant, a tinkling of tea-things, or a rattle in making up the fire.

The study had a very pronounced sentiment of snugness about it ;
being neither too orderly, nor too empty, nor too large.   A bow window of
western aspect looked out upon Leith Hill, and the curtained shelves
which lined the opposite wall bore a heavy load of plaster casts from
antique gems and busts, wax models of the figures of designs which were
in progress, many colours, and very many books.   Here lay one of the
beautiful smock frocks once worn by so many of the peasantry, there a
relic of Mary Ward—her battered tin ear-trumpet ; and there again,
unstrung and silent, the old violin, once eloquent with many an ancient
air on the banks of the Darent.   Some much larger shelves on one side
of the room held, in classified portfolios, the innumerable sketches of
all sizes, all degrees of finish, and in all materials ; a long life's selection
from much of the choicest scenery in England.   Five or six box-
portfolios beneath contained the more elaborate studies, British and
Italian.

Next to the sketches, a chest of drawers bore upon it a home-made
cupboard.   This contained a set of well-used etching-tools with other
etching materials, and a few miniature antique busts in wooden cases or
calico bags.   This was the favourite corner of the room, and great was
my father's rejoicing when, one day, the "Etching Cupboard" was evolved
from an old packing-case.   Not the least important item among the
contents of the drawers was a tiny box labelled "BRIGHTS."   In
this there dwelt, protected from all contamination, and each in a white
paper jacket neatly fitted over the upper part of it, certain cakes of the
colours with which my father worked on the brightest passages in his
drawings.   As he sometimes attempted "a focus" which was "a well-head
of dazzling light," and often the very sun himself, such care was well
repaid.

Finally, there was one rarely-opened drawer holding a few relics of his
dead children, at which my father dared not look, though perhaps he liked
to have them near him.

Upon the plain, deal easel some disjointed words were chalked, each
being a clue to some truth or maxim which he wished to keep before his
mind.   For instance, the single word "PARSLEY" was the most conspicuous, and referred to an anecdote in Mr. Hamerton's *Intellectual Life*,
thus related :—" I happened one day to converse with an excellent French
" cook about the delicate art which he professed. . . . Among the dishes
" for which my friend had a deserved reputation, was a certain *gâteau*
" *de foie* which had a very exquisite flavour.   The principal ingredient,
" not in quantity but in power, was the liver of a fowl ; but there

" were several other ingredients also, and amongst these a leaf or two
" of parsley. He told me that the influence of the parsley was a good
" illustration of his theory about his art. If the parsley were omitted, the
" flavour he aimed at was not produced at all ; but, on the other hand, if
" the quantity of parsley was the least excessive, then the *gâteau*, instead
" of being a delicacy for gourmets, became an uneatable mess."

Next to the easel stood the painting-table, which on examination, revealed itself as an old wooden washstand ! Now, it creaked under an
unwonted load, consisting of a large rack full of china palettes ; under
brush-cases, mugs, saucers and gallipots ; most of them containing the rich
succulent masses of colour my father delighted to use, mixed with the last
of a long series of vehicles invented successively, since the days of the
notable " egg-mixture."

Many of these materials were, like the furniture, very different from
those usually found in the water-colour painter's studio. Some of the
brushes seemed large enough for fresco, though the series included the
tiniest sables. Throughout the room, till you came to the last of the
rough and heavily-laden bookshelves and a decrepit arm-chair, there was
nothing that was costly or conventional, or even what would be called by
many, " respectable " ; and there was little that did not bear evidence of
our clumsy tinkering.

The simplicity I have described was no longer a matter of necessity,
for my father's circumstances were easier now, his prices higher, and his
commissions constant. Society of course, or rather the small portion of
society's outposts with which we had anything to do, if it had not been
rigorously excluded, would have had the same opinion of his room which
it has held touching such things since the days of Diogenes. I think it
was my father's vehement hatred of pretension and show that took the
concrete form of a study furnished as I have described, and that such a
practical counterblast comforted him not a little. " There are States
where Visionary men are accounted mad men ; " and although somewhat appeased by the drawing-room " Fal Lals," I fear there were those
who took the master of the house for a harmless lunatic, living in
highly necessary seclusion. His habit of talking to himself had grown
upon him, and he was wont to discourse audibly with certain imaginary
persons on such subjects as his "weeds," the progress of his work, or the
composition of a design. These persons were addressed, and were
familiarly known as " Mr. Jackson," " Mr. Jinks," and " Mr. Jick ; " and
they seemed to play quite a natural part in our little circle. What the
housemaid and gardener thought of them, history sayeth not.

Sometimes when a friend was dining with us, my father would appear
at the table with a ring upon his little finger, which unwonted ornament he

would ostentatiously display. The guest was sure, sooner or later, to notice not only the ring (it was a plain, substantial-looking hoop), but a markedly genteel bearing and gesture. But, towards the end of the meal, a dangling screw would appear where the stone is usually set, thus showing that the jewel was nothing more than a new and highly lacquered picture-frame ring. This, the wearer would continue to show off with mincing attitudes, and " Reigate genteel " conversation. This was of course another practical counterblast. He was also wont to appear before his more intimate friends affecting great fragility and decrepitude. When one of them has been announced, I have often seen him seize a blanket, throw it over his head and shoulders and with a shawl or two superimposed, totter into the drawing-room, there to be greeted not by sympathy but by much laughter. Except in the hottest weather he was rarely to be seen outside his painting-room without his shawl ; and latterly, when he ventured upon railway travelling, he was, as he said, " swathed like a mummy."

It was in the cosy but shabby little room I have described, that my father's most ambitious works were completed, his letters written, and his literary recreations so ardently pursued. There it was, that, after his day's work, he lighted his small paraffin lamp [1] " Nancy " (for to many things he had given some strange name), and might be found by those privileged to enter, with his old books piled round the tea-tray. He writes to Miss Redgrave :—These old books go well with country associations, and I find " some solace in them ; less, however, than when I read them with poor " faithful ' Tab ' upon my knee, gently patting the leaves now and then, " that I might take some notice of her."

Nevertheless, although contented, he still remembered with a natural regret the resources of London—its libraries, museums, and galleries. He writes to Miss Redgrave in 1864, " After all your London treats, conceive " if you can, of the stagnation here. [The loss of] ' Tab ' is the only event " since we had the pleasure of seeing you, except that the creeping hours " are the more weary, as each creeps along with a hod of mortar on her " shoulders to multiply hideous, slate-roofed ' villas ' all over the place. " But all this comes of living in a GENTEEL RESIDENCE, with a " BUTLER'S PANTRY in it ! There is no stagnation about a farmhouse. " All is life there ; change—progressive change ; production. Of course I " mean an old-fashioned farm ; not those flat Yahoo-sheds they build now " and call ' model farms ' ! The natural ascent in the scale of beauty " from the real cottage, is through the farmhouse, the grange, the old " baronial place, to the cathedral.

" I long to see the first picture that is painted of reaping by steam. " ' O !' but they say, ' It's only want of imagination in the artist ; it is just

---

[1] Gas he loathed and continually railed against.

" as beautiful : did not Turner paint a train ?' To which the fit rejoinder
" is 'FIDDLESTICK!'"

Literature was at this time more than ever indispensable to my father's
happiness. In 1839 he wrote to his friend Dr. Williams from Italy, of his
longing to be back again among his books—to have a "Great Read" as of
old. Now, he writes to Mr. Edward Calvert :—"How dirt cheap are
" really good books, when we compare them with the price and intrinsic
" value of everything else we lay out money upon. Why, a suit of clothes
" costs a greenhorn from eight to ten pounds, and a knowing man five or
" six. Think of the gems,[1] think of the blessed books we can buy for that
" money ! Any one of which is worth all the toggery we ever put on our
" backs or ever shall, even if we lived to see the next 'revival of art.' " Only
a year before his death, we find him still rejoicing in books, as giving the
cheapest, the best, and the least palling of all secular pleasures. It was
seldom, even now, that he ventured out alone without some pocket volume,
and he had written of this habit to Mr. Gilchrist in 1861. " . . . the little
" book which I have carried in my pocket and read as I walked, has
" somewhat cheered the dreadful solitude I feel when walking alone. I,
" who used to love the wildest solitudes—for whom no glens were too
" savage, no woods too dark."

For more than half a century, my father and his first cousin Mr. Giles
had spent Christmas together. It is difficult to imagine two natures more
completely congenial ; and their minds, from their youth up, seemed
instinctively to follow the same channels. Permanently impressed by my
father's influence early in life, his cousin, during his visits to Shoreham as
one of the "Ancients," acquired an admiration for the same kind of art,
and literature, and music, and for the rich scenery, which he learned to
invest with the same associations. Even many years spent in the prosaic
atmosphere of the Stock Exchange failed to vitiate these early tastes,
which indeed intensified with time ; and what my father himself had long
admitted to be immoderate or eccentric in the art and the opinions of the
Shoreham period pleased the other all the more. A relic of a strict, bluff.
old school, Mr. Giles carried with his comely stature a sentiment of warm-
hearted geniality appropriate to Christmas. From the time of his arrival
he retreated to the study, where secure from all interruption, the pair conversed of the old days, deploring modern innovations, and extolling
antiquity. The plethoric "Shoreham Portfolio" was invariably in re-
quisition, full of the works of the Shoreham period by my father and one
or two other members of the clique. There was hardly one of these works
that was without its story, or that failed to call up a host of associations which.

[1] He means the exquisite little plaster casts from antique gems, of which he had a
collection.

even at second hand, had a charm of their own. To hear those two old men talking together over that portfolio, was to live the seven years of secluded happiness over again, to abandon oneself to the same enthusiasms, to see the same " visions," and to creep with awe or shake with laughter at the stories and adventures. The portfolio being ended, a little, dusty colony of Shoreham pictures were reached down from the highest shelf, and put one by one upon the easel for discussion. Year after year Mr. Giles's admiration for these pictures seemed to increase, and by degrees, he possessed himself of some of the best. The purchases usually led to some refreshing touches being given, for which it was necessary to re-open the ancient oil-colour box ; and it was evident that the artist was himself refreshed by the well-remembered smell of copal and spike-lavender, though it reminded him of disappointed hopes.

Among the very few new friendships formed by my father after his removal from London, there were two upon which he had especial cause to congratulate himself. Each of them led to a lengthy and very interesting correspondence, stimulating his mind and his imagination at a time when his isolation and failing bodily vigour might have caused the mental atrophy which threatens those who have no one to whom they can communicate their best thoughts. The friendships did more for him than this, for the one led the way to the realization of an old purpose which for years had seemed far beyond fulfilment ; while the other created a new hope, not destined to be realized, but beguiling him on an enthusiastic quest which death alone forced him to abandon.

In the winter Exhibition [1] of the Old Society held in 1863, hung a little drawing by my father called *Twilight: the Chapel by the Bridge*, and of this Mr. L. R. Valpy became the purchaser. Courteously suggesting that the light in the chapel was a little too strong, he asked if the drawing might be reviewed in that particular—a request which was granted with alacrity. " I have spent a morning on *The Chapel by the Bridge*," wrote the painter, " and not an unpleasant one, as it has made the difference of the last " few sun-glows which give the fruits their sweetness." These were words which he would scarcely have been foolish enough to write to an ordinary art " patron," but he had already discovered that his new correspondent was not to be considered in that disagreeable light.

Mr. Valpy was a man of a strangely-combined character. A serious and sensitive devoutness which suggested that of the old Puritans, a business-like shrewdness and caution worthy of a veteran merchant, and the astuteness of an experienced equity lawyer—these attributes seemed inconsistent with an ardent love of art and of poetry. His face—keen, stern, and

---

[1] The Society kindly allowed him to break the rule that sketches and studies only should be exhibited in the winter collections.

dark; his somewhat reluctant smile, and a deep, deliberate diction, seemed to forbid the associating him with any of the luxuries of life, or (save in religious matters) with its emotions. Yet he was a man who (to use his own words), "sought refreshment in nature's deepest and highest utterances as rendered by some of our English artists;" whose mental qualities and eclectic taste often made the intercourse with those artists as pleasant and as stimulating to the employed as to the employer. He was a man who could revel in the tints of a dying bramble-leaf, and who could fling his law, and his caution, and his seriousness behind him, before a beautiful landscape or a resplendent sunset.

A mutual mental harmony being assured, "sympathy expanded," (as the lawyer put it), "and acquaintance ripened into friendship." Of this friendship a great pile of letters is the index and memorial—letters which reveal, on each side, much of the inmost nature of the writers, their points of sympathy and of antagonism, their artistic and religious beliefs; and their keen enjoyment (each in his own way and degree), of the best poetry, whether found in nature, in literature, or in art.

It was not long before Mr. Valpy made the very singular request to be shown anything my father had in hand which specially affected his "inner sympathies." He received this answer:—". . . Only three "days have passed since I *did* begin the meditation of a subject [1] "which, for twenty years, has affected my sympathies with seven-"fold inwardness; though now, for the first time, I seem to feel in "some sort, the power of realizing it." After describing the subject in the words the reader will find in the letter from which I quote, he adds:—"I never artistically know, such a sacred and home-felt delight, "as when endeavouring in all humility, to realize after a sort the imagery "of Milton."

Many years before this, my father had left London for the purpose of attempting, in country retirement, a series of designs from *L'Allegro* and *Il Penseroso*, but had attempted them vainly.

Here and there in his portfolios I have come across slight sketches bearing the titles of the two poems, and he had occasionally painted other Miltonic subjects, and even sold them. For Mr. Valpy, however, was reserved the giving of the impulse which led to the realization of the old scheme. Before the preliminaries were settled, he became the possessor of another drawing or two, each of which led to further correspondence, and to a freer interchange of ideas which were not always in accordance. Finding my father ready to listen to suggestions and criticisms, his friend

---

[1] This design, like most of the earlier Miltonic sketches, is essentially a figure-subject. The figures are large, and a mere glimpse of landscape is caught through the lattice. It was an unfortunate composition; sure of being, sooner or later, abandoned.

sent him letter after letter full of little else, though the suggestions were
always dressed in the utmost courtesy of language. An artist accustomed
to begin his work tentatively, without a thoroughly definite preconceived
design, or without an ideal before him, would probably have become
confused, if not angry or discouraged ; but my father was saved from
this, firstly by his invariable practice of condemning to " seclusion
or the fire " everything he did which was not done as well as he
could do it ; secondly by his invariable refusal to be influenced by any
criticism whatever till he had shaped out his own course. He writes
to Mr. Valpy thus : -" Now, while in this train of thought, I feel that any
" criticism, even yours which I must value, would put me out, or at least
" might do so ; though the very same criticism might be valuable when I
" had *got to the end of my own tether.*" And again " . . . I would rather
" not show anything just yet, as I am convinced that it is injurious
" to receive the suggestions of another mind before one has satisfied
" one's own. After *that,* criticism is sometimes invaluable . ." A third
safeguard (and this point is a very important one, if an artist is to
maintain absolutely his originality), was the vivid intensity of the mental
" vision " that preceded the actual making of the design. Thus my father
writes of one drawing that it was " mentally, though not manually
finished."

After much discussion of size, proportion, and price, in which as
usual, and even more than usual, he sacrificed mere pecuniary gain to a
love of his subject, a definite plan was agreed to about April 1865, which
involved the making of eight drawings (each measuring 28 inches by 20)
whose themes were to be found in *L'Allegro* and *Il Penseroso.*

A sudden " impulse " to begin some of the subjects arose after a
deliberate mental review of " the whole, the parts, the relations " ; and, at
last, my father says, some of the designs came to him " unawares." Where
imagination is in equipoise with reason, this is not an unnatural kind of
artistic evolution. After years of pondering, years of unswerving devotion,
rendered nugatory by unpropitious circumstances, those circumstances
change, and the impulse to begin arises together with the wherewithal.
Each useless without the other, together they are potent.

He lost no time in securing after his manner the designs which he
describes as lying photographed just over his eyes, and " packed in their
bone box ready for use " : and his manner was to hint rather than sketch
them in sepia, or bistre, on detached pieces of drawing-paper or cardboard ; each subject measuring 11 inches by 8. These hints being intelligible only to himself, and perfectly useless even to him if carried any
further at that particular stage, a point naturally arose at the outset, which,
in the case of a less wary or sympathetic employer, would have led to

difficulty. However, I believe my father departed from his usual custom, and allowed Mr. Valpy to see these first indications, being rewarded for the concession by a very unusual degree of intelligent appreciation ; while the criticisms made were not hasty, but were the result of considerable thought.

From this time, a very copious correspondence (which treated of many other topics) kept pace with the progress of the work. There was abundant criticism, and not a little hypercriticism, while there were even a few decided collisions of opinion. Point after point was reasoned out between the two (much to the benefit of the national revenue) with a zest, in those cases where the translation of the text was involved, of which the few letters I have been able to choose give a scarcely adequate idea.

Although Mr. Valpy had definite notions of his own as to the rendering of Milton's imagery, they were somewhat realistic ; and where they differed from his friend's, he was compelled to throw the reins upon the neck of an imagination which he found so unusually strong. Both men were in earnest, neither disdained to learn from the other, and both had that reasoning faculty which my father believed to be so essential to the use of the "best images" by the imagination. Furthermore, the lawyer even seemed in some degree capable of sharing that clear "inward sight" which distinguished the artist : a thing, as the latter remarked, very different from mere speculation.

The story of the completion of the Milton Series may be partly conjectured from what I have related of my father's mental and artistic career ; but not altogether, without a knowledge of some peculiar aspects of the employer's character. For many reasons, the progress was extremely slow ; and, as my father says, while he was doubting about the place of a light or the shape of a shadow, a Church was disestablished, or an Empire overthrown.

A few passages will serve to show the spirit in which he worked, and partly to account for the fact that the series was some sixteen years or more in hand :—[*November* 21, 1867.] :—"While I was touching on the sheep in "*The Lonely Tower,* all of a sudden, I don't know why, the whole seemed "to come as I intended, so I packed it up in a paper and string to make it "difficult to get at, lest I should spoil it. In this state, a few breathings, "after we have had a final look at it, will be precious."

[*March*, 1868.] :—"I find that quiet looks in still seclusion have done and "are doing so much for the drawings, that it would be to their loss to leave "home till taking-in day. Only yesterday, I improved one of them "essentially by just a few touches of delicate grey."

[*November*, 1870.] :—"I am glad you are so indulgent as to give me a "little more time, for I think some gossamer films and tendernesses may

" be added, which are not always to be done at the proper time, but come
" strangely when one cannot account for it."

Again :—" If once in the doing, caution and fear get ever so little ahead
" of impulse and joy, a work is, I think, in its worst peril, though all four
" are good, each in its *time* and turn throughout life."

To describe more minutely how my father attempted to reach his
Miltonic ideal, is like endeavouring to describe how a poem was written.
I have often seen one or other of the series on the easel late at night,
lighted simply by the candle he held in his hand, as he stood pondering in
that dim light the suggestions a brighter light would not have given.
Many a time I have seen him pause just as his brush touched the cardboard, and then quite unconsciously lay brush and palette aside for hours
together, his eyes remaining fixed upon the drawing.[1] Possibly the result of
these hours of thought might be a single touch—perhaps not even that.

In a letter written to Mr. Valpy in 1879, after a misunderstanding in
which he was not to blame, my father sums up his share in the scheme as
follows :—" . . . I loved the subjects, and was willing to be a loser in
" all but the higher matters of Art and Friendship. I do not in the least
" complain that I have lost a thousand pounds by them. It was my own
" act and deed. In the same time, I could have made thrice the number
" of telling and effective drawings of the same size, but I considered your
" taste and feeling so much above the ordinary standard that, in order
" fully to satisfy them, I have *lavished time without limit or measure,* even
" after I myself considered the works complete."

The undertaking was in fact a costly luxury, which, had my father's
circumstances been less easy, he could never have afforded. This is proved
by the fact that, as it was, he found it necessary to keep more remunerative work going at the same time, and to work his hardest.

I have generally found it a difficult matter to explain to some persons
who look at his studies and sketches for the first time, what use he
made of them with regard to his finished works. Some suppose (if I have
rightly understood) that he copied portions, or even copied the whole of
some of these studies straight off, adding so much new matter as might be
necessary to completeness ; just as an author might copy an extract verba-
tim into his manuscript. I have also found it just as difficult to explain
that such and such a finished drawing which a visitor may have been good
enough to praise was purely imaginative ; and instead of being painted
direct from nature, or copied from sketches bit by bit, was evolved in the
artist's mind.

Now, in accomplishing the Milton scheme, my father's proceedings with

---

[1] In a letter to a lady artist he writes " When our work is on the easel, I wish we
were obliged to sit a quarter of an hour with our hands tied, to have time for forethought."

regard to his sketches and the use he made of them were thoroughly typical; so, at the risk of obscurity, I will try to describe what he did. We learn from his own words in the first place, that each Milton subject incorporated something or other of "picked matter" in his studies from nature; and again, that the best of these studies "pressed themselves," without his seeking it, "into the service." A thing may be incorporated in two ways; either as a brick is incorporated with a wall—a hard, tangible and visible fact; or as an essence or elixir is incorporated with any other fluid, a gas with the atmosphere—also a fact, but not so apparent as the incorporation of the brick. I can but compare my father's use of his sketches with the latter illustrations. They "pressed themselves into the service," and though their essence was absorbed, it was in such a manner that, perhaps with one exception only, it would be almost impossible, or at all events very difficult, to find in any of the Milton drawings, a single portion, however small, which we might recognize as having been copied from a sketch. Nevertheless, the influence of some of those sketches on his mind is as clearly evident as the influence of the essence on the other liquid, or of the gas upon the atmosphere.

One autumn day in 1864, my father betook himself to the glue-pot, and joined together with a broad strip of canvas two strong mill-boards. Next day this primitive portfolio had fixed upon it a great label bearing the letters "MIL." Then he began a thoughtful search through the other portfolios which lined the room, picking out from the classified divisions, sketches small and large; highly finished, or mere pencil indications with accompanying written memoranda, or tiny effect "blots." Henceforth this Milton portfolio stood on its especial chair by the easel, and was carried from room to room. Week after week, month after month, and indeed, year after year, it was added to little by little, and my father often became so absorbed in its contents, that night changed to morning before he went to bed. This study was collateral with the study of the sepia or bistre designs I have mentioned, and may be likened to the oil which fed their flame. They dwelt in the Milton portfolio, together with some other things which appeared to have no relationship whatever to the work, and indeed to be absolutely incongruous. But these incongruous things were there because they called to mind certain essential trains of thought, just as the word "Parsley" on the easel called to mind an all-important maxim: and their relationship to the scheme, though not outwardly apparent, existed in the painter's mind. A few designs (notably those by Mr. Calvert), found their way into the portfolio as "mind toners," just as my father pasted into his common-place book, as a curious example of all that he abhorred, part of a baker's paper bag, whereon was a remarkable poem called *The British Volunteers.*

A picture may be a transcript from nature outright, a more or less free or literal translation, a more or less careful compilation of isolated facts. It may also be as much an original work as a noble poem, and may in like manner absorb an almost infinite variety and amount of material—material neither paraded nor misapplied. I think this originality and fulness of matter may be claimed for the eight Milton drawings, whatever may be their shortcomings in other respects. Before a single sketch was drafted into the Milton portfolio, the embryo of each design had quickened, the ideal had been formed, or (to use my father's simile) the hare had been caught, what remained being merely the cooking and garniture.

As works of art, these drawings must not be viewed by an ordinary light. They show us the homely episodes of agricultural life, and even of English agricultural life ; but this is not all. Their author writes :—" The " work of a poet ' where more is meant than meets the ear,' would I " should think suggest picture-work where more is meant than meets the " eye." It is a haunted stream by which the young poet dreams away the summer's evening ; and it is a spirit, or some benign sylvan Genius, who sends the sweet music that gently awakens " Il Penseroso."

The relationship between the poetic and the pastoral was a theme my father loved dearly. We find it mentioned in the introduction to his *Virgil*, and in the descriptive lines appended to *The Eastern Gate* and *The Lonely Tower :* while in the *Morning* he tries to " unite poetic remoteness " with such homely reality as the smell of turned-up earth and the details " of the farm afford." No doubt it was one reason why he had always turned with such zest to our older poets, because, in their day, the sad divorce between romance and rural life was yet to come. Where now all is machinery and model buildings, the fairy tripped it on the ancient hearth, or the goblin, mindful of the cream-bowl that awaited him by the embers, plied his " shadowy flail " with all his strength.

Of " Fact and Phantasm " the author of these designs indubitably leaned towards Phantasm. His sympathies being naturally in accord with all that is romantic and poetic, and " sentiment" being, as he believed, " the end of art," his whole soul was thrown into this Miltonic work.

Early in the progress of the undertaking, he had written to Mr. Valpy as follows :—" . . . Till all the series are settled upon pretty clearly, I do " not see how we can well choose the first pair ; nor how, considering the " uncertainty lurking in the future, and the fragility of life itself, we can " *make sure* of the set."

In 1880 he writes :—" I wish in all of the Miltons, not to add a touch " without a thought : for having given them up to the present moment such " an amount of time, such a *ridiculous* amount, some would say (without

" reckoning illnesses), I think the best and in fact the least tardy way will
" be to do my very best to the last. Indeed, for several years, this ha,
" been my inexorable rule with every work, from largest to smallest ; having
" nothing to do with what less elegantly than expressively are called 'pot-
" boilers.'"

The artist's last allusion to the scheme he had taken so long to carry
out, the reader will find in a letter dated February 16, 1881 ; and after that
it was not long before the enthusiastic artist and the courteous lawyer were
gathered to their fathers.

In the most successful of the few photographic portraits of my father,
he is holding in his hand a small volume which he took to London for
that express purpose. This was a copy of Virgil's *Eclogues*, with a series
of figures of Virgilian plants ; and in 1863, he writes of it to Mr. Edward
Calvert :—"The photograph of that Virgil you so kindly gave, it is but
" fair that you should have, so I enclose it. You can cut it out and
" throw the old man who holds it into the fire. The old man was obliged
" to sit, as it was for a set of the Water-Colour members which Mr. Cundall
" in Bond Street has published ; so he took your Virgil in his hand ; which,
" indeed, is seldom long out of it. . . . I have been as a resource in the
" deepest distress of mind, employed for many months in endeavouring to
" sift the *Eclogues* thoroughly, to the last exactness of meaning and expres-
" sion. With the exception of a few verses, I have now gone through the
" whole ten, and long after the Latin is thoroughly construed there are
" certain difficulties, here and there, which puzzle all commentators."

This poring over Virgil led to an ill-fated project which grew in
time even more engrossing than the Miltons themselves. Long before,
and while my brother was living, the *Eclogues* had set my father longing to
translate them into English verse, with especial care that the " pastoral
essence " and the immeasurable wealth of imagery and suggestion should
not be "evaporated " into verbiage. And so if the friends who from time
to time paid us an evening visit at Furze Hill had closely examined the
piles of books which lay on my father's table, they would have found among
them one in manuscript—a manuscript so interlined, erased, and cut about
for the insertion of slips of new matter, that but little of the original
remained. He was never to be found by strangers with the volume in his
hand, for a knock at the door was the signal for its being put out of sight.
It was not long before this maiden effort in literature began to be connected in the author's mind with the seductions of printer's type. I think
the idea of having his name associated within the covers of a real, published
book, with the work of an immortal poet, betrayed him into unwonted
castle-building. It blinded him to the fact that the work of a tyro alike
in classical scholarship and English versification would not be likely to

hold its own against, still less to eclipse, some of the best translations already extant. He knew, however, that his strong point was the keenest appreciation of that "pastoral essence" he loved so well, and that to him the poet's imagery was unusually eloquent.

The project was kept a secret from all but myself, but the problem of the mode of publication proved to be one which my father found himself quite unable to solve. So in January, 1872, he took Mr. P. G. Hamerton into his confidence, whom he had known since the publication of *Etching and Etchers*, and whom he now knew intimately on the strength of a correspondence which had been kept up between them, although they had as yet never met. The manuscript was accordingly posted to Autun, and was returned with the wise advice to secure popular toleration, by the addition of illustrations. My father, like all would-be authors, had anticipated that his work would stand on its own merits, and we have his authority for believing that he "loathed the thought of illustrations." But Mr. Hamerton's sagacious remarks as to the form they might take suggested the possibility of designing some subjects which should be worthy of Virgil, and which at the same time should secure the circulation of the translation. So my father braced himself for the struggle.

By the month of May 1872 the verse was practically finished, and the prose essay which was to precede it was well in hand. The domestic barometer foretelling the annual spring deluge which so woefully discomfited him, my father packed up a store of pencils, pens, and Bristol board, and fled before the scrubbing brush to what might be thought the one place least suited to contemplation. He had formerly retired into the quietest country to attempt designs to Milton, but it was in one of the noisiest thoroughfares in noisy Margate that he applied himself to represent those solitudes where the Nymphs lamented Daphnis, and that romantic shore to which Galatea is invited by an Arcadian shepherd.[1] If other examples were needed to show how completely he could dissever his mind at this time of his life, from the distracting and depressing influences of untoward surroundings, the works he produced at such a place as genteel Red Hill may be adduced.

Returning home in due course with the ten subjects upon their cardboards, and one or two of them well advanced, my father plunged into investigations touching photo-mechanical processes. The supposed existence of an ideal process of that kind had betrayed him into trying to use pen and ink in a manner which was unnatural to him : that is, by endeavouring to

---

[1] The reader may remember that, years before, some moon-lit cloud behind a row of Margate Lodging-houses had suggested one of the most peaceful and poetic of his etchings, and that " The Margate Mottle " was far from being the only effect gathered at that once picturesque old town.

keep each line and touch separated from its neighbours—an attempt which his artistic feeling rendered futile. But just as he had once imagined that his drawings on wood could be faithfully translated, so in 1872, he imagined that some wonderful process would give him a facsimile of work to which even the perfected methods of to-day are, by themselves, quite inadequate. He was soon undeceived by a few experiments, and finding that his best work was uniformly "processed" into smudge pure and simple, he got, as he says, like a fly, more and more engulfed in the technical treacle-pot. I have spared the reader the voluminous correspondence with Mr. Hamerton, treating of dreary technicalities—of photographic mares' nests, and in numerable attempts to find among them something on which to build a theory. In the end, Mr. Hamerton suggested original etching as the most suitable method of interpretation, perhaps without knowing what meaning was attached to the word in my father's mind. My father was incapable by nature and training of doing anything whatever by halves, and he had throughout the whole of his life been mountaineering among the mental Alps that were always overtopped by some still more inaccessible peak. Since he had ceased to "loathe" the thought of illustrations, he had been haunted by one of his "visions," this time consisting in a small but very exquisite head-piece to every Eclogue; and to do these head-pieces, had Blake been alive, he would have commissioned him, as the solitary competent person. He had said of these :—" I myself should like to undertake them, " but it is hopeless. I have no spare brains and even less bodily strength, " and what I have is taxed to the uttermost." . . . "These things, so " quickly conceived, consume much time; not so much in putting the " work, as musing *where* to put it." His ideal was "poetic compression in antithesis to landscape diffuseness," with ample time for "dreamy half hours." The magnitude of the undertaking, therefore, was not to be gauged by the very small surface to be covered, amounting to only 240 square inches. I think in some respects it would have been better for him if he had kept firm, and had not attempted at the age of sixty what at the age of forty would probably have daunted him. The temptation, however, to resume his favourite employment, and by that means to secure the publication of his book, proved too great to be resisted. Remembering the episode of the earwig in the egg-plum, and his battles with mordants that refused to bite anything but skies, he ordered a dozen little plates of tremendous solidity, and laid in a stock of the most ferocious nitrous acid which money would buy.

It must not be supposed that he intended to attempt ten new etchings under quite the same conditions as those which had ruled the production of the ten plates representing him at this time : that number having been spread over more than twenty years. But a few quotations will serve to

show that although his opinions had been somewhat modified, he had not
forgotten the old traditions I tried to explain :—[*August* 1, 1871 : to
Mr. Hamerton,] "Were my subjects such as to admit of rapid etching,
" it would be simple enough. But I am not alone in discovering that,
" where tone is aimed at, copper bites into time as greedily as acid into
" copper."

    May, 1872 : to Mr. Hamerton] :—"Knowing by old experience what
" time an etching insidiously consumes before I can make the effect ring, I
" doubt whether the etchings of such subjects could be managed under
" from twenty to thirty guineas each according to size. . . ."

    [*January* 13, 1879 : to Mr. Hamerton] :—" . . . My etchings consume
" very much time, because, though I aim above all things at simple
" arrangements and fewness of masses, yet the progress is analytic, and
" matter aggregates within matter till the copper looks as large as a half-
" length canvas. An artist *dares* NOT flinch from his own conceptions,
" whether in the first impulse of invention, or its innumerable vibrations,
" widening like the circles when a stone is thrown into the water. Now
" all this is, I believe, the veriest castle-building, and doubtless I shall, if
" writ at all, be ' writ in water-colours,' instead of that delightful, durable,
" printer's ink, with a strong touch of brown in it. . . ."

    He also wrote thus :—" Process 1874 D.V., For etching get first the
" great, leading, *pathetic* lines, having first obtained the same in the figures.
" Work from the great leading lines, and to them recur. Make friends
" of the white paper." I remember his reiterating that, if he had but
known the value of what he had considered as disasters in his former
plates, and had he been as competent to turn them to account as he was
now, the qualities he had attained only by indefatigable patience, he would
have attained easily, and far more expeditiously.

    Once more then, the doors of the little Etching cupboard stood open,
the acid fumed, and needles were diligently sharpened. Colours and
brushes were not "pitched out of window," as he says they should be
in an ideal etching revival ; but the conversation ran on half a hundred
delightful technicalities, and if the angry mordant played him a trick or
two, and bit half through the copper (for reluctance of biting was a
thing now unknown), he rejoiced the more. The " Vs " became a by-
word between us ; a portfolio full of the most carefully-selected material
was promoted to a chair of its own : an old cigar-box was made into a
rack for the ten plates, and his " sole remaining hobby " took the bit
between its teeth to some purpose.

    But in spite of all this energy, and enthusiasm, and love, the progress
was slow. There seemed to be an especial fatality against the accomplishment of that one doubly-cherished scheme. Two other etchings of

a much larger size than the Virgils were completed and published, and yet the " English Version " remained in manuscript. Why my father, who was now mentally in the prime of his life, and who, if he loved anything, loved concentration, should have indulged in this discursiveness it is hard to say ; but one potent cause of the slow advance was his extreme fastidiousness. That which had stacked his shelves with half-completed pictures, plentifully besprinkled his portfolios with watercolours upon which he had lavished time and study, only to abandon them, and had turned his manuscript into a paper patchwork, was the same dire Nemesis which pursued, and still will pursue, the man who would sooner die than put a pinch of incense on the great golden altar of Mediocrity.

A few of the designs that were brought home from Margate, apparently so well advanced, were abandoned ; and even after they had been etched, one or two were given up. One only was completed as an etching—the plate known as *Opening the Fold.* As for some of the other designs, " vision " succeeded " vision," till the little V. portfolio grew quite corpulent.

Just before the series was begun, he had written thus :—" When an artist " sees at last what he ought to do, and gathers himself up for the effort, I " believe it is a sign that his days are numbered." He did not realize as he wrote this, how true it would be in his own case ; and as he neared his end, his hope of at last turning over the leaves of his book strengthened rather than diminished. Even on his death-bed he spoke to me hopefully of the " Vs," but he died leaving the manuscript unprinted, only one plate completed, and only four of the other designs begun upon the copper.

If I force myself to regard my father's achievements quite impartially. I am bound to admit that, with the exception of the introductory Essay. *The English Version of the Eclogues* is by no means one of his best : and those who have read the prose essay and the verse may perhaps regret that he attempted verse at all,[1] or at all events that he hampered himself with rhyme, but the attractions of the ten-syllable line, with which perhaps his admiration for the poetry of Pope and Dryden had something to do. carried the day.

As for the illustrations, they must not be judged too harshly, for the reasons I have given. By his earlier work on copper, he had established so high a standard, that even his best subsequent work will not bear comparison with that standard (except in a few important particulars), still less any work which was not entirely his own doing. Had he lived. however, not only to complete, but to *ripen* the unfinished plates, as he had

---

[1] His early attempts at poetry were far inferior to his contemporary prose.

ripened the Milton drawings, little by little, and touch by touch—to muse over them by the hour together in "undivided allegiance," they would have held their own against all his other work, early or late, for his whole heart and soul was thrown into the scheme in which he was so lamentably thwarted.

CHAPTER VI

FOR more than fifteen years, my father lived in his retirement at Furze Hill much as I have shown ; doing everything that was worth doing at all with a zest and a will and, among the daily tasks, invariably doing the most disagreeable thing first.

Over the once quiet and pretty neighbourhood, little villas with big names had multiplied by the hundred ; and genteel mansions, each with a smaller garden and a more imposing façade than its predecessor, engulfed field after field. The only old farm near us, to my father's double disgust, was turned by capital into a hideous " park," all trim roads and iron hurdles ; so by degrees his sense of solitude and isolation grew upon him, and his walks became more and more perfunctory till he set himself a certain beat with a gate-post at the end, which he always made it a point of conscience to touch before hastening homewards.

His sketching expeditions were long since over, and the dear Devonshire combes he would see no more. But, as his bodily strength decreased, his mind seemed to grow more vigorous, as was shown by the pithiness of his correspondence, the alacrity with which he entered into any topic which touched upon the deeper veins of thought, by his industry, and by the unabated fertility of his powers of design. He worked, he asserted, with more energy than at thirty ; and in 1878 he was able to say :—" . . . I do " daily, before dinner, about four hours' work *with my whole mind bent* " *upon it*, but cannot go on longer at a stretch. Sometimes the train " of thought is renewed when designing, or what not, in the evening." His strong but very near sight, like his hearing, had suffered very little by the approach of age ; and, as of old, he revelled in the delicate processes of etching, which are a crucial test of good eyes.

Not long after he had resumed his favourite art with so much vigour, I persuaded him to set up a press of his own ; and this being done, I was taught the mysteries of printing etchings by Mr. Goulding—a teacher of such zeal and efficiency that I was soon able to take all the necessary proofs. In 1878 my father made up his mind to begin two new plates of a larger size than any he had done hitherto. He says " The etching dream

M

" came over me in this way : I am making my working sketches [for the
" Miltons] about a quarter of the size of the drawings, and was surprised
" and not displeased to notice the variety ; the difference of each from all
" the rest. I saw within, a set of highly finished etchings, the size of
" Turner's *Liber Studiorum*, and as finished as my moonlight with the
" cypresses,[1] a set making a book, a compact block of work, which I
" might fain hope might live when I am with the fallen leaves." A
scheme within a scheme, this had little chance of realization, and only two
etchings of the ideal set were ever completed, *The Bellman* and *The
Lonely Tower*. The former was published separately, and the other
(ruined by bad printing [2]) appeared in the last work of the then languishing
Etching Club. Although these plates were carried on in a far bolder
manner than any of my father's earlier etchings, and undoubtedly possess
certain qualities unknown to those etchings, I think they prove that
smaller work suited him better. Executively *The Bellman* and *The Lonely
Tower* cannot be considered equal to *The Rising Moon* or *The
Herdsman*.

It was about this time that the solitary Virgil ever completed on the
copper was published under the title of *Opening the Fold ;* and no one
suspected that it was "hapless Damon" who leaned against the olive
stem.

Having incidentally touched on the question of the size of my father's
etchings, it may not be amiss to mention that, like the question of proportion, size was a matter to which he paid the greatest attention. The
dimensions and proportions of his works were rarely determined by any
accidental circumstance, but were most carefully thought out in their
relation to the design, and even in works as large as the Milton Series, a
quarter of an inch more or less, in length or breadth was not a matter to
be settled off hand. It will be found, however, that the artist's natural
bent was rather towards small than large work. He speaks of the marvellous "condensing power of art"—a power which enables a painter to
compress within a few square inches, as a poet does within a few lines, a
universe of beauty and suggestion.

Little by little, increasing weakness, and his old enemy, asthma, deprived
my father of his few outdoor pleasures. He could no longer pay an
evening visit to his old friends at Reigate, or join their Christmas gathering, or take a day's holiday in London. And now was proven the inestimable value of his early habits and tastes. At an age when many

[1] *A British Pastoral* or *The Rising Moon.*

[2] My father writes :—" So the dear old Etching Club revives on the 15th. I love it,
" though it has quite smashed *me* by the way my *Lonely Tower* has been printed. Full
" directions were sent to the printer, and a model proof, but in vain."

are a burden to themselves and to all around them, wearily halting through a peevish senility, it could be said, thinking of his cosy quietude," Stone walls do not a prison make."

When his work was interfered with by illness he "sprang upon his books"[1] and was comforted. He had a small table upon which, in very inclement weather, he could work while he was actually in bed, and he did this by the hour together, without impatience or loss of energy. How his constitution, strong as it was, stood the prolonged confinement to one room and the entire want of exercise, I am at a loss to imagine, yet he rarely succumbed altogether. His means being now comparatively comfortable and his tastes unaltered, he had every temptation to relax his labours in favour of literature, but it was just as he says. His love of work and his mental energy seemed to increase rather than diminish, and he seemed quite as incapable of idleness as on an occasion when a doctor had ordered him to lie on a sofa and do nothing. He tried it for one minute, "and started up with a howl."

Although, latterly, he could no longer devote the evenings to the severe mental strain of designing, he actually turned for light amusement to arithmetic and algebra, carrying about with him a bag of scribbling paper for the purpose. This was strange, as his want of success in arithmetic was a joke against him. After an hour or so spent in puzzling over his sums and problems, he seized his books and read till bed time. A local library supplied him with the chief reviews and with such standard literature as his own shelves lacked, but he was still faithful to the intimate companions of his youth, a pile of which in their strong, ancient binding usually lay side by side with his designs, and a new volume of his common-place book. The few pages of this volume that my father lived to write are strikingly characteristic, and show great clearness of thought, without the slightest sign of mental decadence. Nevertheless there are signs of tremulousness in a handwriting once so singularly firm. It ranges as it always did from very small to very large, and it is still legibility itself, but it shows that the end is approaching.

This seems to me to be exactly typical of his later artistic work. The ideal is the same as before, the sentiment and suggestion the same, and nearly all those more essential qualities which distinguished the artist in his prime from others are undiminished, but there is a tremulousness in the execution, and a diminished power of rendering the colours of nature[2] by

---

[1] He writes, "The true book-lover is all tiger. He tears open his prey, and slakes his drought with huge draughts from the jugular."

[2] It is said that the lens of an aged eye is liable to become yellow. When this happens in the case of an artist unwonted crudities of colour may, or perhaps must arise in his work, and notably, crude blues and purples.

pigments which show that the time is at hand when the brush must be laid aside.

In the common-place book and in my father's later letters there are indications of the kind of literature to which he now chiefly turned his attention. His choice was still varied, still guided not a little by prejudice, but it is evident how his mind seemed to retire more and more within its old entrenchments, sheltering there from the modern developments of theology, science, and philosophy. In these his last days, he seemed to me more and more instinctively to shun the present, and to nestle in the past. He longed more earnestly than ever for holiness and wisdom, deploring more often his own unworthiness, compared to those great and good men to talk and read of whom he never tired. Although his religious convictions deepened, he seemed to me to have none of that latent assurance of salvation which marks some pious people. He found in his religion consolation and hope ; and this being so, he strove to save others from the dark sea of doubt and perplexity, not as one assured of his own safety, but as a seaman reaches out his hand to a drowning man from a boat that itself lies in peril. Yet his appeals were rare, and though very earnest they were never in bad taste. The remarkable point about his religious faith was its unalterable stability. In a very early letter he says :—" I am a free-thinker in art, in literature, and in music ; but as I " read of but one way to heaven, and that a narrow one, it is not for me to " choose which way I will be saved, and make it a pretty speculation or a " matter of taste ; and run to seek my Saviour in holes and corners. . . ." Fifty years afterwards, he was still plodding onward, as best he might, on that narrow way ; and in the long interval, none of life's vicissitudes had been powerful enough to force him from it. He had been tempted by the ritual and the associations of the Roman Church, and he had been frequently and vigorously attacked by the fierce proselytizers of dissenting sects, having very near relatives on each side. The Sadduceeism and fatalism of the darkest despair had cast a shadow over his path, and he saw even his own beloved Church of England split up into vindictive factions. Still, he kept to the narrow path he had chosen so early. As to Rationalism, Agnosticism, or any other such form of modern religious thought, he put them impatiently aside (just as he put aside many of the truths of science), simply as " Infidelity with a fraudulent label."

He was a staunch, earnest Christian, who had never " held his dogma in solution," had hardly ever paraded his beliefs, and had never arrogated to himself a spiritual superiority over others, however much he might detest their views. This immutability of belief throughout a life-time, in the midst of all the temptations of religious controversy and religious faction, and all the varieties of heterodoxy and free thought, was partly due to a firm conviction of the personal existence of the Devil, and of the reality of his subtle attempts to overthrow the Christian by every variety of cunningly-contrived temptation. A man who believes in the existence of imminent peril from a terrific enemy who is close to him in ambush is more wary than one who merely suspects a far off danger. And one, like my father, who sees in every religious doubt or perplexity, a direct temptation by a personal Devil, leading to the utter destruction of body and soul, becomes habitually watchful.

Companionship in any quest or conviction often increases in a very marked degree the energy and strength ; and it was my father's lot to see constantly before him an example of faith, firm as his own, equally unwavering, and even simpler in its components. It was indeed a faith as primitive and unquestioning, in its way, as that of the patriarchs.

A devoted wife, indefatigable in her care and solicitously watchful over his health, my mother was latterly his constant companion. In the evening she read to him that kind of serious literature in which they both found edification, such as *The Holy War* and *The Pilgrim's Progress* (of which they probably knew much by heart), and certain sermons whose orthodoxy comforted them.

Such of his old friends as time had spared retained their affectionate cordiality, although their age did not often allow them to travel to Red Hill. One of them wrote to him, " We never meet, we never communi-" cate and yet, I believe, have such well-grounded trust in one another, " that if we met to-morrow, old love would revive, and grateful feelings " all come back again, as if we had never been separated."

As death took, one by one, many of these companions of his youth, and his own time drew very near, the great hope of my father's later life increased—the hope of reaching at his journey's end a fair country, where he would once more have his little daughter's arms about his neck, and grasp that hand he had touched for the last time at High Ashes Farm. " If I were *quite* certain," he wrote, "of rejoining my beloved ones, I " should chide the slow hours which separated me." Next to the happiness of this reunion he longed to enjoy, in a far more perfect manner than this life allowed, a state of spiritual and intellectual light. There, perhaps, in one of the many mansions of his Father's house, the righteous man might find not only an eternity of happiness far beyond human knowledge, but, the power of searching out the unexplored depths of wisdom and of learning all he had desired on earth, with no more sorrow or sin to hinder him. There, too, in radiance by the side of which their earthly lustre was a mere glimmer, might be seen worthies and heroes of all ages of the world. Such I think was my father's hope, and his idea of the Christian's future happiness.

Old age, inexorable but not unkind, crept upon him by degrees, mercifully sparing him some of those infirmities so often the portion of the last days of life. So gradual was the bodily decline, so great his mental vitality, that we never noticed the long shadows of the Valley of Death stealing across his path. He might still be seen rapidly sketching a fine cloud or sunset from the window, or pondering over one of the much-beloved Virgil designs in the evening. He might even be found, on warm days, leaning on his "staff," and sorrowfully gazing at the few wild-flowers that lingered on, pining for his protecting hand. He revelled in his old prints and Shoreham relics as much as ever, and plunged with all his old delight into an evening's argument. The folio volumes were yet piled upon the table, and still the etching-cupboard was kept sedulously in order.

A new pleasure partly took the place of many others, and consisted in long drives through the prettiest parts of the surrounding neighbourhood, far beyond the odious villas. My father and mother liked slow travelling, and in the matter of horses were unanimously nervous to a degree, so the equal sleepiness of the venerable fly-horse and his driver (both adepts in the work that is paid by the hour), soothed their prejudices, and allowed full play for my father's intuitive watchfulness for fine effects and beautiful lines of country or foliage. So they jogged along the lanes, or crept up the steep hills on summer afternoons, comparing notes on the vileness of railways and of modern inventions in general, and on the pretty country the skirts of which they were able to reach. Their favourite route lay through Gatton, once notorious as a pocket borough. The old park lies partly under the great range of chalk downs, and partly on the top, some seven hundred feet above the sea. Here, as at Shoreham, ancient yew-trees mark out the Pilgrim's Way, and the fine timber clothing the sweeps of the down reminded my father of Lullingstone. It was here in Gatton, and sitting in the fly, that my father made his last lines from nature, and slight as these are, they show that his hand had not lost its cunning in tree draughtsmanship.

He entered on his last winter's work with a full share of his usual energy—a winter which will long be remembered on account of its inclemency. After the celebrated snow-storm of the 18th of January, 1881, he was driven to his bed by the cold, and there (clothed in one of the rough flannel coats beloved of navvies) he continued his work for a time, more effectively than I should have thought possible. He even carried on towards their completion the three last-remaining Miltons, *The Bellman*, *The Prospect*, and *The Eastern Gate*, having also in hand (together with a few other little drawings) small replicas of *The Bellman* and *The Lonely Tower*. The large *Bellman*, lacking yet (in my father's opinion) the bloom of finish, was kept back for those last reflective touches which he always liked to bestow upon his work. These drawings being completed, and milder weather allowing him to resume his usual habits, he once more flew upon his Virgils as a schoolboy goes to his play, and finished in black and white the design to the 2nd Eclogue—one resembling, and in some respects superior to *The Rising Moon* etching. It is an instance of the ripeness and activity of the artist's mind after the decadence of his manipulative skill. He then sketched in with redoubled zest the subject intended for the 10th Eclogue, having abandoned the first attempt. This was my father's last work. Although carried but a little way, it is full of suggestiveness, and being in an early stage, there is no appearance of tremulousness of execution.

The patient struggle to continue his daily work, even when confined to his bed, may remind us of the episode that had so impressed him fifty-seven years before—his first interview with Blake.

Soon after the beginning of May, my father (who had been ailing for some little time) was taken seriously ill, and by the middle of the month we had given up all hope of his recovery. Only six days before his death he talked with me cheerfully on many matters; and apparently not realizing that his end was near, he even discussed the continuation of the Virgil scheme, cherished to the last. It was sad to hear him speak so earnestly and hopefully of the project upon which, off and on, for twenty years he had lavished his time in vain; sad to see his eyes brighten with pleasure as he spoke of the difficulties yet to be overcome. But a "peace that passeth all understanding" seemed gradually to throw a veil over all earthly matters, reconciling the gentle spirit to the parting with the now helpless body. My father bore the last hours of his painful illness with great patience, regretting the trouble he was giving. He was comforted by the presence of his old friend and tried companion Mr. Richmond, who shared the watch by the bed-side, and did much to soothe the dying friend he had loved so well.

On the morning of the 24th of May my father asked for me, but I could only guess the meaning of the few words he whispered. This was our farewell and it was then, as I touched his hand for the last time, that I thought what he had been to me. Everything in the room (for he died in his study), had some memory of the hours we had spent together in years past—of all our little schemes and plots, and of the work he had done so devotedly. There, just behind him, were some of the ancient books he had loved in his youth, his plaster casts from the Antique, and his small models in clay or wax. Close by, in an old cigar-box which I had fitted with grooves, stood the Virgil plates, a commentary on the futility of human schemes. When I entered that room next, I found Mr. Richmond reading some prayers by the bedside in a voice broken by sorrow, and I knew that at last my father had left us.

We chose his grave in one of the quietest parts of Reigate churchyard, and there we laid him on a warm, showery, spring morning of the very kind he loved most. Some elm-trees cast upon us his favourite "chequered shade," and just above us a skylark joyously sang till, as the last words of the service died away, it dropped silently into the long grass. Who could have wished a better requiem?

.   *   *   *   *   *

My father's character, in spite of its simplicity, is an easy one to misinterpret; but the reader (if he has followed my story attentively), will. have detected certain traits and peculiarities which, taken together, will form a clue to that character, and at the same time to the genesis of my father's art.

His early home training and the seven years' seclusion which followed it would have ruined many an ordinary man for life, even without the assistance of the little "independence." The youth, however, whose remarkable sayings and doings I have detailed, invested his time like his money, to advantage, succeeded in escaping mediocrity, kept his character unstained, and made himself respected and beloved by many good men and true. Nevertheless, after the Shoreham Arcadia had passed away, and with it those happy, youthful dreams which are never realized, his life became a struggle; not like the struggle of the average professional man to acquire wealth and position, but to follow up an ideal which absolutely barred the way to those universally coveted acquisitions. With the career of an elder son there grew up one great ambition—the hope of one superlative reward for all the father had suffered and renounced. Both were dashed away, and over the futurity which had once more seemed happy, settled a desolate cloud of weariness and despair. Then, little by little, the old loves of the shattered mind revived, the old ideals rekindled, and in the end, the life of this loyal man relapsed into that peacefulness and happy isolation from incongruous things which distinguished its beginning. From the beginning to the end, like the refrain of some song, we may find recurring that which more perhaps than all else leavened my father's life—its unaffected piety. At twenty he had written :—"Young as " I am, I know—I am certain and positive, that God answers the prayers " of them that believe and hope in His mercy . . . . and I now tell you, I " *know* that my Redeemer liveth." Within a year of his death he wrote again :—" In the kindly fruits of the earth, in physical and mental " pleasures, God has given more than sufficient to solace and sustain us, " while we daily present ourselves living sacrifices to His service, in the " whole of our moral being, in the bent and intention of our lives."

My father was far from being an ascetic, and in some respects he was an Epicurean, delighting in congenial society, and doubly delighting in cosiness. He has indeed been described by one who saw him only as a guest, as a *bon vivant*.

A somewhat singular feature in his character was the almost feminine want of reticence in matters relating to his feelings, griefs, and disappointments ; and things which some men would shrink from discussing with or confessing to their wives he discussed or confessed in letters to friends. This effusiveness extended to frequent allusions to his health or physical infirmity. The peculiarity may be regarded in two ways ; either as a form of effeminacy, or, I think, more correctly, as the impulsiveness and the confiding nature of childhood preserved to mature years by the want of those conditions which, in nearly every individual, extinguish them early in life.

Another peculiarity was the co-existence of what appeared to be a very remarkable amount of moral courage, with physical timidity ; though each of these qualities was sometimes absent. In some ways he appeared to be altogether insensible to ridicule, in others most sensitive. And while he had been known to meet the advance of a wild cow on the Campagna, with his wife on his arm, and by dashing his great sketch-book in its face with a shout, to put the cow to flight, he would make quite a to-do over a scratch or a little bruise.

Whether his prolonged battles to achieve certain conquests arose from determined courage or invincible patience, it is difficult to say ; but that patience of no common order was one of his most prominent attributes, is evident.

For an artist of his knowledge and technical power, he may be said to have egregiously failed in the battle of life and, in spite of his economy, he died far from rich. The greater part of his life had been spent in a struggle against what many would call poverty ; and though his labours were protracted to the end of his days his reputation is confined within very narrow limits. Moreover, compared with the achievements of many of his brother artists, and fellow-members of the Old Society, the list of his exhibited works shrinks into insignificance. The reasons for this are too obvious to require recapitulation.

He was one of those who live and die almost without an enemy, and who leave behind them a name upon which even an enemy would be unable to detect a stain. Rash as it may seem to say that he was without uncharitableness, seeing what an universe of vices is involved in that one, yet I believe such is the truth. His own innocence from youth up amounted, in some respects, to the simplicity of an old-fashioned child : and he seemed to find a real difficulty in believing any evil of others until unanswerable evidence forced the knowledge upon him. It may be imagined, therefore, what an easy prey the race of human falcons found him, and how he fared in matters of business ; glorying in, rather than deprecating, any catastrophe or discomfiture which followed some intensely unbusiness-like administration of affairs, if he had been led thereto by his conscience, or by his religious bias.

He had "a rugged side" to his character, readily evoked by such things as an act of brutish Vandalism, or the insolence of wealth to poor, deserving men.   He seemed to honour the poor with a genuine respect, uncontaminated by any secret feeling of superiority or contempt.

In summing up his character it would be impossible to find words more apt than his own used in describing Blake and Flaxman :— " He was a man without a mask, his aim single, his path straight- " forwards, and his wants few. . . . Declining, like Socrates, the common " objects of ambition, and pitying the scuffle to obtain them, he thought " that no one could be truly great who had not humbled himself 'even as " a little child.'   He knew that order and proportion are divine principles, " and of universal application : that, as they, governing the conduct of " picture or poem, can alone reproduce the unity of the first idea, so, without " them, the life of a man cannot be consistent or complete, or even a " single day, perhaps, be employed to the best advantage.   He could " distinguish gold from tinsel, the transient from the enduring ; assigning " to everything its proportionate value. . . .

" He represented well the dignity of his calling : there was nothing " mercenary in his diligence, or penurious in his economy, or mean or " contracted in that simplicity and humility of soul, without which the " Pathos of Art can never be conceived, nor its most touching results " accomplished."

His soul may be described not only as simple, but as symmetrical ; and as he himself once said, " a symmetrical soul is a thing very beautiful and very rare."

THE LETTERS OF
SAMUEL PALMER

Designs at Shoreham.

THE LETTERS OF
SAMUEL PALMER

1828

I. TO MR. JOHN LINNELL

SHOREHAM, KENT, *December 21st*, 1828.

MY DEAR SIR. . . . . I have begun to take off a pretty view of part of the village, and have no doubt but the drawing of choice portions and aspects of external objects is one of the varieties of study requisite to build up an artist, who should be a magnet to all kinds of knowledge ; though, at the same time, I can't help seeing that the general characteristics of Nature's beauty not only differ from, but are, in some respects, opposed to those of Imaginative Art ; and *that*, even in those scenes and appearances where she is loveliest, and most universally pleasing.

Nature, with mild reposing breadths of lawn and hill, shadowy glades and meadows, is sprinkled and showered with a thousand pretty eyes, and buds, and spires, and blossoms gemm'd with dew, and is clad in living green. Nor must be forgotten the motley clouding, the fine meshes, the aerial tissues, that dapple the skies of spring ; nor the rolling volumes and piled mountains of light ; nor the purple sunset blazon'd with gold and the translucent amber. Universal nature wears a lovely gentleness of mild attraction ; but the leafy lightness, the thousand repetitions of little forms, which are part of its own genuine perfection (and who would wish them but what they are ?), seem hard to be reconciled with the unwinning severity, the awfulness, the ponderous globosity of Art.

Milton, by one epithet, draws an oak of the largest girth I ever saw, "Pine and *monumental* oak" : I have just been trying to draw a large one in Lullingstone ; but the poet's tree is huger than any in the park : there, the moss, and rifts, and barky furrows, and the mouldering grey (tho' that adds majesty to the lord of forests, mostly catch the eye, before the grasp and grapple of the roots, the muscular belly and shoulders, the twisted sinews.

Many of the fine pictures of the 13th, 14th, and two following centuries, which our modern addlepates grin at for Gothic and barbarous, do seem to me, I confess, much deteriorated by the faces, though exquisitely drawn, looking like portraits, which many of them are ; and from the naked form, thwarted with fringes, and belts, and trappings, being generally neglected or ill expressed, through a habit of disproportioned attention to secondary things, as the stuff and texture of draperies &c. ; which ended at last in the Dutch school ; with this damning difference ; that in the fine old works the heads are always most elaborated—on the Flemish canvas, the least finished of any part ; and yielding to the perfected polish of pots and stew-pans ; a preference most religiously observed by the cleverest disciples of that style at present. An instance of this appeared in the last exhibition, where was a painting in which, against the sky and distance, beautiful, intense, and above the Dutch perception, there came a woman's head ; hard to tell whether quite neglected, or laboriously muzzled—the least perfect object in the piece, with a careful avoidance of all shape, roundness, and out-line. But nature is not like this. I saw a lovely little rustic child this evening, which took my fancy so much that I long, with to-morrow's light (God sparing me), to make a humble attempt to catch some of its graces. If I can at all succeed it will be nothing Dutch or boorish.

Temporal Creation, whose beauties are in their kind perfect, and made and adapted by the benevolent Author to please all eyes and gladden all hearts, seems to differ from images of the mind, as that beautiful old picture in the last British Gallery (I forget the name ; it is that I miscalled Garofalo) differs from the conceptions of the Sistine Chapel, or the tomb of the Medici : were both called suddenly into breath, the simple shepherds would, I think, as they ought, modestly withdraw themselves from the stupendous majesty of Buonarroti's *Night*.

So, among our poets, Milton is abstracted and eternal. That arch-alchemist, let him but touch a history, yea a dogma of the schools, or a technicality of science, and it becomes poetic gold. Has an old chronicle told, perhaps marred an action ? Six words from the blind old man reinvigorate it beyond the living fact ; so that we may say the spectators themselves saw only the wrong side of the tapestry. If superior spirits could be fancied to enact a masque of one of the greatest of those events which have transpired on earth, it would resemble the historical hints and allusions of our bard. I must be called mad to say it but I do believe his stanzas will be read in Heaven : and to be yet more mad—to foam at the mouth, I will declare my conviction that the *St. George* of Donatello, the *Night* of Michelangelo, and *The Last Supper* of Da Vinci are as casts and copies, of which, when their artists had obtained of God to conceive the Idea, an eternal mould was placed above the tenth sphere, beyond changes and decay.

Terrestrial spring showers blossoms and odours in profusion, which, at some moments, "Breathe on earth the air of Paradise" : indeed sometimes, when the spirits are in Heav'n, earth itself, as in emulation, blooms again into Eden ; rivalling those golden fruits which the poet of Eden sheds upon his landscape, having stolen [them] from that country where they grow without peril of frost, or drought, or blight—"But not in this soil."

Still, the perfection of nature is not the perfection of severest art : they are two things. The former we may liken to an easy, charming colloquy of intellectual friends ; the latter is " Imperial Tragedy." *That* is graceful humanity ; *this* is Plato's Vision : who, somewhere in untracked regions, primigenous Unity, above all things holds his head and bears his forehead among the stars, tremendous to the gods !

If the *Night* could get up and walk, and were to take a swim to the white cliffs, and after the fashion of Shakespeare's tragicomic mixtures, were amusing herself with a huge bit of broken tobacco-pipe, I think about half a dozen whiffs would blow down the strongest beech and oak at Windsor, and the pipe-ashes chance to make a big bonfire of the forest !

General nature is wisely and beneficently adapted to refresh the senses and soothe the spirits of general *observers*. We find hundreds in raptures when they get into the fields, who have not the least relish for grand art. General nature is simple and lovely ; but, compared with the loftier vision, it is the shrill music of the " Little herd grooms, Keeping their beasts in the budded brooms : And crowing in pipes made of green corn," to the sound of the

chant and great organ, pealing through dusky aisles and reverberat-
ing in the dome ; or the trombone, and drums, and cymbals of
the banner'd march.   Everywhere curious, articulate, perfect and
inimitable of structure, like her own entomology,   Nature does yet
leave a space for the soul to climb above her steepest summits.
As, in her own dominion, she swells from the herring to leviathan,
from the hodmandod to the elephant, so, divine Art piles mountains on her hills, and continents upon those mountains.

However, creation sometimes pours into the spiritual eye the
radiance of Heaven : the green mountains that glimmer in a
summer gloaming from the dusky yet bloomy east ; the moon
opening her golden eye, or walking in brightness among
innumerable islands of light, not only thrill the optic nerve, but
shed a mild, a grateful, an unearthly lustre into the inmost spirits,
and seem the interchanging twilight of that peaceful country,
where there is no sorrow and no night.

After all, I doubt not but there must be the study of this
creation, as well as art and vision ; tho' I cannot think it other
than the veil of Heaven, through which her divine features are
dimly smiling ; the setting of the table before the feast ; the
symphony before the tune ; the prologue of the drama ; a dream,
and antepast, and proscenium of eternity.   I doubt not, if I had
the wisdom to use it rightly (and who can so well instruct me as
yourself ?), it would prove a helpful handmaid and co-mate of art,
tho' dissimilar ; as mercury sympathizes with gold, learning with
genius, and poetry (with reverence to speak it), with religion.
Those glorious round clouds which you paint, I do think inimitably,
are alone an example how the elements of nature may be
transmuted into the pure gold of art.   I would give something to
get their style of form into the torso of a figure.   And I must do
my taste, if I have taste, the justice to observe that I consider and
have always considered your miniature of Anny, Lizzy, and
Johnny, a perfect, pure piece of imaginative art ; and I have a
pleasing hope that its beautiful living models will some day
themselves be poets or intellectual artists.   I care not how, or from
what a thing is done, but what it is.   Parmegiano's auto-portrait in
the last British Gallery, I can't help thinking not only superior to
his other works that I have seen, which have been rather
composite, but the finest picture of any sort I ever saw : we have

only the copy of Leonardo's, tho' I don't know what can go much beyond that.

I beg to be understood as not so much positively asserting anything in this half-studied scribble on a very difficult subject which is beyond me, as, for the increase of my knowledge, putting forth a thesis by way of query, that where it is rotten it may be batter'd, thus avoiding to choke the throat of every sentence with "*I humbly conceive—I submit with deference*," which had made these lines, if possible, more tedious than you will find them. I will not correct them, lest I overspend that time in talking which should find me doing. . . .

Mr. Richmond, in a letter from Calais, asks me very anxiously about your health. He heard from his father that you were worse. He says from enquiry, two might go to Rome and stay six months, for ninety pounds between them. Is this credible? I should like to hunt out some gems like the *St. George*, if I could go, and bring them home on grey paper, especially such works as we have no good engravings of. If, at any time, you feel the *cacoëthes scribendi* come upon you, I wish you would favour me with your opinion how, should I go Romewards, my time might be most profitably spent there. I have no prospect of travelling yet; but some time or other, God willing, most certainly shall, and wish to get together all kinds of information on the subject. . . .

With love to the little "Ancients," I remain, dear Sir, Your oblig'd affectionate Servant, SAMUEL PALMER.

P. S. I have just finished another attempt at a portrait on grey board in colours. I took pains, and it is a likeness, but whether tolerably executed or not, I cannot tell. I am desperately resolved to try what can be got by drawing from nature. I think the pictures at our exhibitions seem almost as unlike nature as they are unlike fine art. I am going also to try a little child's head: if anything would please me in the copying it is children's heads.

1829

II. To Mr. John Linnell.

SHOREHAM, KENT, *Saturday May* [17], 1829.

MY DEAR SIR. Pray accept my thanks for the trouble you have taken in getting me the colours: they arrived quite safely. I

N

have not been to town since you saw me ; but in a few days, when I have finished a bothering little job of a likeness, shall come and have a look at the exhibition, and I hope, have the pleasure of your company back to Shoreham. Nothing but such pleasure has been wanting to perfect my delight at the glory of the season. Tho' living in the country, I really did not think there were those splendours in visible creation which I have lately seen.

The ways of the Royal Academy are to me unaccountable—not that it is unaccountable they should reject six of my drawings ; but that they should hang those two which I thought far least likely. I expected they would reject the " *Whole kettle and boiling,*" as they have for these two years, and intended, with the patience of an ox, to prepare eight colour'd pictures for their rejection next season ; and if *they* were refused, a like dose on the year succeeding. As they condescended to receive any, I wonder they did not prefer the nature sketches, and perhaps the two little moonshines, in which, I think, there was more look of light than I have got before ; and less of my wonted outrageousness than in the *Ruth* or *Deluge.*[1]

I will immediately enquire about horses and asses. There are plenty of *brutes* in Shoreham, but no asses that I know of, except myself, and *I* don't answer the description, for I cannot say that I am yet *able* to *draw,* tho' certainly most willing.

The artists have at last an opportunity of wearing the beard unmolested ; I understand from the papers that it is become the height of the fashion ! I hope they will avail of this. . . .

With best respects to Mrs. Linnell, and love to the children, I remain, dear Sir, Your obliged and affectionate Servant, SAMUEL PALMER.

1832

III. To Mr. GEORGE RICHMOND.

Friday, September 21, 1832.

MY DEAR SIR. Pray do not fail if you see Mr. Knyvett, to tell him how sincerely and exceedingly I am obliged to him for his kind remembrance of me.

I will be in town on Monday or Tuesday at farthest, and in the meantime, if there is a desire to see some things of mine, my father

[1 The two accepted designs.—ED.]

will be so kind as to get my blacks, which were in the exhibition, conveyed to Miss Lawkins'.

I have been working very hard at art, which I now love more than ever, and recreating myself with good books, Sir Thomas Browne's *Christian Morals,* and the life of holy Bishop Fisher ; of which the first is a little casket of wisdom, and the second a most comfortable and blessed cordial in this cold, heartless, and godless age. I mean to get the print of the venerable Fisher, and one of his friend and fellow-martyr Sir Thomas More, and hang them cheek by jowl in my little chapel, that they may frown vice, levity, and infidelity out of my house and out of my heart.

I have greatly desired to see your little daughter, and indeed have already loved her though unseen ; and while so many children, innocent and beautiful at first, lose daily as they grow up the similitude of their divine parentage, and become weeds and thistles instead of olive-branches in the church ; what if, by the hearty prayers of. her parents and friends, your child should be like St. John the Baptist, filled with the Holy Ghost even from her mother's womb ; and like Samuel the prophet, minister while yet very young, in the temple of the Lord ? Yet, such glorious things can earnest prayer accomplish ! Nothing is beyond its power.

How is the situation of a Christian changed in becoming a parent ! An immortal soul placed under his control and guidance for eternity ; and that at his immediate responsibility ! All sanctimonious whining and canting apart, it really is a most awful thing ; and so indeed is everything influencing the salvation or damnation of a soul. It has now, I know, become quite unfashionable and unbearable to talk of Hell even in the pulpit, but none will fully enjoy the comfort and peace who do not know also the terrors of the Lord, the plague of their own heart, and the deadly evil of sin. If people knew how deeply the whole world lieth in wickedness, and how totally it is estranged and set in opposition against God, they would, I cannot help thinking, no longer wonder why all kinds of sects and schisms may not equally be termed the churches of Christ ; and think the robe of the true Church too mean and narrow, without tacking upon it the abominable vestments of Quakerism, Socinianism—yea the church of Mahomet, to swell it to the dimensions of modern charity ; but would gladly press into the sanctuary of the Apostolic Church for refuge from the wrath of God, and lay fast hold of the horns of her altars.   Once I was full of this lightness and folly ; yea, even to the present time, my old Adam can see no reason why the sleek and sober Quaker, or the meek and moral Unitarian, should be beholden to the Church, claiming the power of the kingdom of Heaven.   But blessed be God, I am changed ever since you saw me.   I am a free-thinker in art, in literature, in music, in poetry ;—but, as I read of but one way to Heaven and that a narrow one, it is not for me to choose which way I will be saved, and make it a pretty speculation or matter of taste ; and run to seek my Saviour in holes and corners : but to go at once where He is ever to be found, at the Apostolic altar of the Melchizedekian priesthood.   Elsewhere, whatever the uncovenanted mercies of God may be, we have no ratified charter, no sealed covenant of salvation. . . . I remain in great haste, dear Sir, Yours most affectionately, S. PALMER.

1834

IV. TO MR. GEORGE RICHMOND.

SHOREHAM, KENT, *October* 14, 1834.

MY DEAR SIR. As you are now become a great man, I will address you on a sheet of my best writing-paper ; not gilt-edged and delicate like yours, but rather too extravagant for me, who may perhaps be composing a set of King's Bench bucolics in the winter months. . . . I have no club or artist's Trade's Union to fall back upon ; and should therefore be much obliged if, as you kindly promised, you would let the little mezzotint flock [1] hang up somewhere where it can be seen, as it might be of some service to Sherman or myself, who are both at present pinched by a most unpoetical and unpastoral kind of poverty.   I seldom taste animal food, and know when I do that I am exceeding my year's supply ; so that, tho' sweet in the mouth, it turns sour on the conscience ; and therefore I prefer bread and butter and apples, washed down with a draught of my only luxury, weak green tea, which is about as cheap as bad table-beer. . . . Don't think I'm writing when I ought to be painting.   I'm just come from work after dark, and have cleaned my palette &c. with scrupulosity, and just scribble a

[1 This was an engraving in mezzotint by W. Sherman (one of "The Ancients") from a small picture by my father of a Miltonic subject.   Impressions are very scarce.—ED.]

little while the tea is drawing. I am in solitude and poverty, but very fat and well, and if I could but get a twenty-guinea commission, even if it were to take a view of Mr. Stratton's conventicle, or to draw the anatomy of a pair of stays, should be as happy as the day is long ; and [I] feel a kind of presentiment (I hope not a false one), that Providence will not suffer me to come into embarrassment.

I have a slowly but steadily increasing conviction that the religion of Jesus Christ is perfectly divine ; but it certainly was not only intended to be enthroned in the understanding, but enshrined in the heart ; for the personal love of Christ is its beginning and end. . . .

I feel for parents, but I feel still more for poor little children who, whether from the darkness or most cruel neglect of their natural guardians who do believe, are kept from the nurture and admonition of the Lord ; and are brought into the world . . . . that they may perish body and soul for ever. How fearful is the responsibility of parents, how urgent their call to set their children from their tenderest years an example of almost sinless perfection ; and that not negatively, but by a positive and visible devotion of the whole household to God—by openly delighting in Him ; by the seriousness of penitence and prayer ; by the merriment of hymns and spiritual songs, with which they should be waked and lulled to sleep : and we have the blessed assurance and promise that a child brought up in the way he should go will not depart from it when old ! But I am afraid that *Way* is nothing short of the devotional and openly holy life exhibited to their children by apostles and patriarchs, and in later times, by a few such devoted and affectionate parents as Sir Thomas More, whose house was as much a church as an academy of sublime wisdom and heroic virtue.

I feel more energetic and ambitious for excellence in art than ever ; but yet, I hope, with a more innocent and less selfish enthusiasm. Our purest and best motives are sadly debased with every kind of alloy ; but really a handsome income and personal influence do enable a man by his savings and his authority in society, to do a very great deal for those two great interests which ought ever to be nearest our hearts, the poor and the Church of Christ. Even base money will enable a man while sitting in his study at his daily duties, to be at that very moment spreading the light of the Gospel into the most distant lands. I do not think (tho' I am very likely quite wrong), that Christianity is meant to damp the spirit of enterprise or the desire of success ; but certainly, entirely, utterly, to change its ultimate object from vile all-absorbing self, to the Poor, to the Church, to the welfare—the eternal welfare of all around us ; to the promotion of the Kingdom of God, to the glory of the Lord Jesus Christ. And though the selfishness of ambition, that "last infirmity of noble mind," may linger for a good while after nobler things have entered the heart, yet it will soon, I should hope, be absorbed like the damps of morning into the beams of the rising sun. But it is a very trying situation in which I am at present placed—wishing as soon as possible to struggle up into repute. I have not the money nor the influence to do good with, and I am in danger of having all my thoughts and affections absorbed into the means. But I shall endeavour to use rational means, and I do not think I shall, if I send any pictures to the next exhibition smaller than kitcats and three-quarters. I hope I have already the materials for one kitcat, and two, perhaps three, three-quarters ; and, if I can but get time before the rain sets in, I hope to have two more kitcats. Where the frames are to come from I know not. I must try to hire them for the exhibition.

I have heard there is in one of the late Quarterlies a very interesting article on Coleridge : it was, I think, before his death. . . . SAMUEL PALMER.

V. To MR. GEORGE RICHMOND.

SHOREHAM KENT, *Thursday, 16th October*, 1834.

MY DEAR SIR. . . . I received your kind and welcome letter the next morning after I had scribbled the foregoing, and though I believe our old friendship can subsist very long without fresh nourishment, yet you afforded it a very pleasant and nutritive meal ; and I took it the kinder as you sent it to me from the abodes of the great, among so many alluring and attractive objects, where the simple and the poor are very apt to be forgotten or despised. . . .

With respect to the studious lamp, it is just what I wish, and hoping to be much more beforehand than usual with my exhibition subjects I shall be able to clean up the palette by dark, and devote, if I live, the winter evenings to the figure. I should like to tackle one or two very fine hands and feet, and to dissect an arm ; first finishing the old bust, if ever we can manage to get it quite in the right height and position again.

I thirst vehemently for your legend of the Rhine, and hope to hear it elaborately wire-drawn over six large bowls of Hyson, which I am glad to hear you have not learned to despise as I feared. Mr. Calvert told me something about the skies there which has set me all agape. If you were only to put down in your memorandum-book the names of places at which you arrived each day, before you forget them, it might help to keep in mind some of the minutiæ which may perhaps slip the memory, and I should like to hear an eight hours' description at least. I would not have been without the Devonshire reminiscences on any account. I hardly ever try to invent landscape without thinking of them.

You may go for five shillings now by the steam-boat to Plymouth, close to the cluster of little rivers that fall from Dartmoor, and see the wonderful Titian &c.—not as a deck passenger, as I heard before, but lie on a sofa in the cabin, and vomit quite genteelly.

I long to see some first-rate distances, and hope you have brought a line or two of some of the quaint, rocky, or wooded summits of the Rhine. I believe in my very heart (but the heart's a great liar tho' it's the truest part about us), that all the very finest original pictures, and the topping things in nature, have a certain quaintness by which they partly affect us ;' not the quaintness of bungling—the queer doing of a common thought, but a curiousness in their beauty, a salt on their tails, by which the imagination catches hold on them, while the sublime eagles and big birds of the French Academy fly up far beyond the sphere of our affections. One of the very deepest sayings I have met with in Lord Bacon seems to me to be, " There is no excellent beauty that hath not some strangeness in the proportion." The Sleeping Mercury in the British Museum has this hard-to-be-defined but most delicious quality to perfection. So have the best antique gems, and bas-reliefs, and statues ; so have *not* the Elgin marbles,

graceful as they are : but it is continually flashing out in nature ;
and in nothing more than in the beamings of beautiful countenances. But I begin now to be quite humbled, and to speak of all
things as modestly as an impudent man can speak. Every day
convinces me, with wise and good Dr. Johnson, that this life is a
state in which "much is to be done and little to be known ;" and
what is known is apprehended by doing ; and whatever *is* done
is wrung out of idle, fallen, wretched man by necessity, immediate
and foreseen ; and what is done at leisure is done wrong, and whatever is done best is done when there is hardly time given to do it in.
Talk of putting thistles under donkeys' tails to make them go!
Why *man*—imperial Man, unless he sits upon thorns will sit still
for ever. Dr. Johnson would scarce have written anything if he
had not been hard driven by want ; and as to Milton, he had plenty
of other business which he was obliged to attend to, and most
likely came to poetry as a relaxation : and as to artists who paint
to please themselves, perhaps they would get through ten times as
much work and improve thirty-fold if they were forced to sit half
the day behind a desk in the Custom-house. Happy the artist
who has half his time bespoken in commissions, and half to paint
what he loves.

I intend, if I live, to keep the lower Port Royal cell neat all the
winter, and work upstairs, and perhaps knock down the partition,
and carefully exclude every inch of prospect from the window, as I
purpose never again to see London by daylight when I can help it,
though I would gladly visit the great national dust-hole once more
if it were only to enjoy the grand Rhenish tea-festival I
remain, my dear Sir, Yours most affectionately, S. PALMER.

1835

VI. To Mr. and Mrs. George Richmond.

NEAR BETTWS-Y-COED, NORTH WALES, [*cir.* 1835].

MY DEAR MR. AND MRS. RICHMOND. It is midnight, when
the traveller's heart turns to those he loves. All is solitude and
utter stillness, except the fall of a mountain stream and the tick-
ing of a clock : and when there is much more noise than this, the
heart seldom plays its full music. Mine you will call a cracked
fiddle, not having heard from me yet ; but a real Cremona it is still,

I assure you, in matters of love and friendship; though my poor mind, in the process of eccentricity-cleaning, nature may perhaps serve as the housemaid did her master's violin one morning —scrub off the tone of centuries. My sufferings are like those of the " Friends ", " Considerable ". I am walked and scorched to death, and have then to make living pictures of dead nature . . . . I must be up betimes in the morning, and so wish you good-night.

Evening the Second. I have just received a letter which has put me into good spirits. O! what gracious people you married ones ought to be! Youthful passions at rest—mutual good example and most sage counsel; participation in prosperity, sympathy in adversity, and sugared-sweet tempers. And then the "dear pledges"!—" Good night, dear Papa." " Good night, dear Mama ", just before they cuff and scratch the nursery-maid all the way up-stairs, and kick over the basin as she washes them.—" Speak! Ye whom the sudden tear surprises oft."

As Mr. Calvert and I walked in a romantic dell, we saw a very young Welsh girl of more than ordinary beauty and loveliness of ex-pression. The features were softened with that delicate shade of pensiveness &c. &c. She timidly approached, and offered (I think for sale), a large, winged beetle, not yet impaled on a pin, but girt with packthread. It was taken from her and let fly, to her utter astonishment. O! for a safe passage to that world where undivorced beauty shall ever be the index and form of goodness! O! for a heart with none of the girl and beetle in it! We went astray from the cradle speaking lies. We killed flies at Church, and came home telling where the text was. See the worst of your children as they grow up : be yourselves, not the censors, but the caterers of their pleasures : while their pleasure is to romp, romp with them : hear their loudest and their worst, and whip them only for vice and dis-obedience. But don't think them saints because they lisp little hymns while they are cutting their first teeth. I am delighted when I think of your children (who I hope will, one day, be dear friends of mine), to know that both of you have the good sense to despise the maudlin, twaddling sentimentality—the Radical-French-Revolu-tion philanthropy—the super-Bible religion—the wiser-than-Solomon sagacity which would disuse the rod. I agree with you that frequent beating is barbarous and unnecessary, and ought to be bestowed on the parents themselves who have managed clumsily enough to find it needful : but depend upon it, fear of one kind or another, as well as hope, is necessary to move adults as well as babes to effective goodness and virtue. We go fast with sunshine before us, and a thunder-cloud behind. I believe the dread of ultimate bodily correction is the only real bugbear to children ; while, on the other hand, thousand are the pleasures and holidays which may be made for them—nay half their learning may, by great skill, be given them in sugar. . . . .

Evening the Third. I hope you have secured the proposed Saturday for favourite studies. I think it would improve your health and spirits, beside the intellectual solace and profit. How many blessings does the future promise ! How do the present and the future belie it ! How beautifully and usefully may the hours of the day be parcelled out in a moderate and sober plan of life ! But an allowance must be made for accidents and ugly etceteras. However, if the leading points of a good scheme be generally secured it will be more than one in a thousand is able to accomplish ; so few have any plan at all, or see the one, two, or three leading advantages which are worth securing at almost any cost. How does all animate and inanimate creation—all the range of high arts and exquisite sciences proclaim the immortality of the soul, by exciting, as they were intended to excite, large longings after wisdom and blessedness, which three-score years, or three hundred years would be too short to realize. We are like the chrysalis, asleep, and dreaming of its wings. The simplest division of our time seems to me to be into a portion first for religion, and its fruit, active benevolence ; secondly for business ; thirdly for bodily exercise ; and lastly, for soothing, intellectual recreation. It would be well if Christians in easy circumstances divided the poor of the neighbourhood among them, and each had a little circle of sick and indigent to visit by turns, say one every day. This might be done in an hour, and would secure the arrangement for bodily exercise. There are visiting societies, I believe, belonging to some of our Churches, which enter into the lowest haunts of wretchedness. Combination will do very much at the expense of very little individual labour. I am inclined to think that the happiest hours of many people are those in which they work at their calling ; and if recreation itself were something both useful and necessary, and not a mere hulling about and kicking of one's shins, it would be much more effectual relaxation than it usually is. I should think the amusements of Sir Thomas More and his family were, besides bodily exercise, little other than changes from the severe to the elegant studies. O! blessed biography, which has embalmed a few of the graces of so many great and good people! Perhaps, to those who are in earnest for improvement, no literature is so useful. Principle and precepts are the grammar of morality; example is its eloquence.

Though I have often talked of the importance of quiet, intellectual evenings to those who are fagged in the day, and though I think them a delicious and never-cloying luxury, yet I do not mean that we should make pleasure of any sort the aim of life; on the contrary, as every little self-denial and agonizing brings after it a "sacred and home felt delight," so, on the large scale, our whole earthly existence ought to be a short agony to secure eternal blessedness. But as, in a long and sultry walk, we choose out shady places now and then to sit down in, so, I think, none will agonize so effectually as those who take the mental bath and balsam of a little daily leisure. Blessed thoughts and visions haunt the stillness and twilight of the soul : and one of the great arts of life is the manufacturing of this stillness. The middle station of life, where more is demanded to be done than there are hands enough quietly to do, almost forbids it ; and the rooms of our houses are so crowded together that we less enjoy life than hear the noise of its machinery : it is like living in a great mill where no one can hear himself speak ; so I think the fewer wheels the better : but what matters what I think, who am thought mad upon these subjects? Mad I mean to be, till I get more light ; and wherever I find it, will turn to it like the sun-flower : for obstinate though I may have been in trifles (much to my shame), I am not stubborn in greater things, but like a little child crying for food, for which I expect kicks and buffets. However, I am prepared : and with a body and mind pretty well adapted, so far as that is concerned, to get through life with—oil outside and adamant within, but I hope less and less oil of vitriol every day of my life.

I have not seen a paper, but suppose things are going on as they have been for some time ; occasional reform of real abuses, accompanied (as good and evil always tangle together in this world), with a gradual demolition of institutions which Englishmen ought to hold sacred. Jews, Turks, Infidels, and Heretics have broken down the walls of bigotry, and I suppose will soon be throwing the stones at each other. In the meantime, as long as the still, small voice of friendship can be heard, believe me, dear Mr. and Mrs. Richmond, Ever your affectionate friend, SAMUEL PALMER.

VII. TO MR. GEORGE RICHMOND.

TINTERN, VERY DEEP TWILIGHT.   Wednesday, August 19, 1835.

THE address for letter is to us, at Mr. William Hiscock's Black Lion. Tintern Abbey. Monmouthshire.

MY DEAR SIR. Our Ossian sublimities are ended, and with a little more of Macpherson's mist and vapour, we should have had much more successful sketching ; but unfortunately, when we were near Snowdon, we had white, light days, on which we could count the stubbs and stones some miles off. We had just a glimpse or two one day, through the chasm of stormy cloud, which was sublime : however we have this evening got into a nook for which I would give all the Welsh mountains, grand as they are ; and if you and Mrs. Richmond could but spare a *week*, you might see Tintern and be back again. The Bristol stages start daily—the fare I believe is low, and there is a steamboat daily thence (only three hours' passage), to Chepstow, within six miles, I think, of the Abbey and such an Abbey ! the highest Gothic ; trellised with ivy, and rising from a wilderness of orchards, and set like a gem amongst the folding of woody hills. Hard by, I saw a man this evening, literally sitting under his own fig-tree, whose broad leaves, mixed with the hollyhocks and other rustic garden flowers, embower'd his porch. Do pray come. We have a lodging with very nice people under the walls, and three centuries ago might have been lulled with Gregorian Vespers, and waked by the Complin to sleep again more sweetly : but the murderer of More and Fisher has reduced it to the silence of a Friends' meeting-house. Mr. Walter was shown the inside, and says it is superb. After my pastoral has had a month's stretching into epic, I feel here a most grateful relaxation, and am become, once more, a pure, quaint, crinkle-crankle Goth. If you are a Goth come hither : if you're a pure

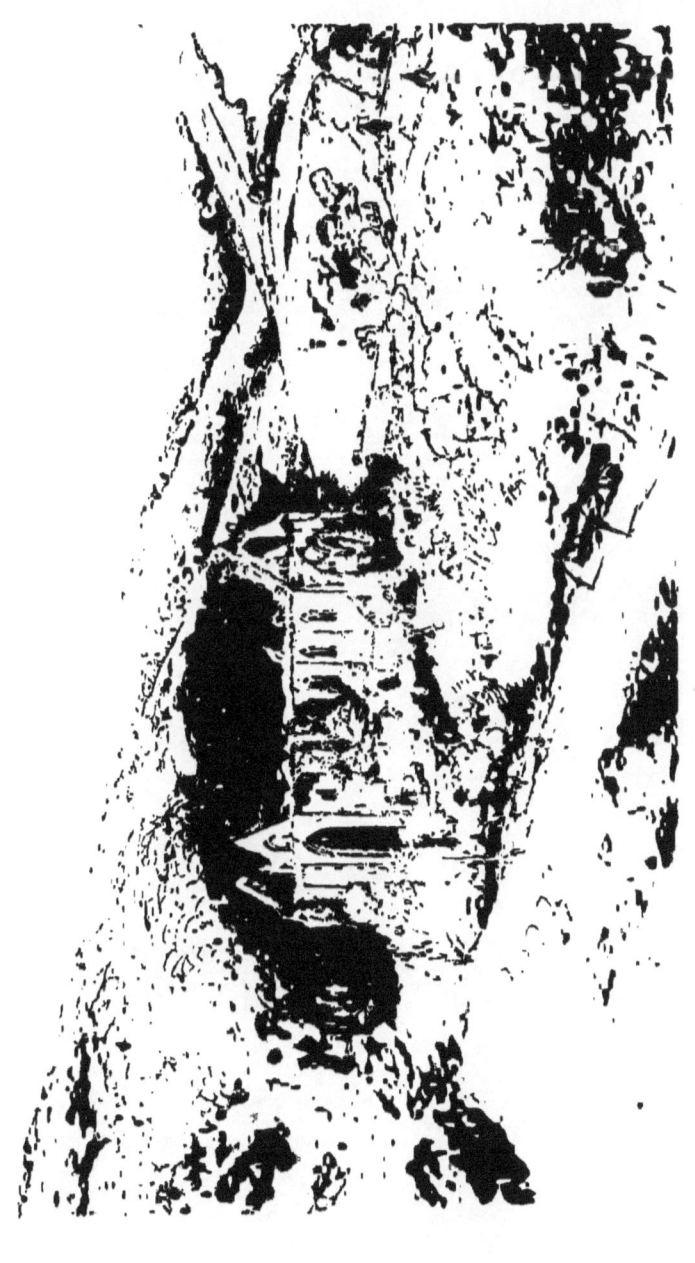

Greek, take a cab and make a sketch of St. Paul's, Covent Garden, before breakfast. Addison speaks of the Cathedral of Sienna (one of the richest in the world), as the work of barbarians—clever savages almost. What a " Spectator "! He could not bear too *lofty* and *pointed* a style: pity he died before the era of Doric watch-houses, Ionic turnpike-gates, and Corinthian gin-shops! His taste outran his age—ours hobbles after.

Thursday evening. Poetic vapours have subsided, and the sad realities of life blot the field of vision: the burden of the theme is a heavy one. I have not cash enough to carry me to London. O! miserable poverty! How it wipes off the bloom from everything around me. Had I conceived how much it would have cost, I would as soon have started for the United States as Wales: but I have worked hard, seen grand novelties, and enlarged the materials of imagination. If I could but sell a picture, or clean another Opie or two, or—but I am all in the dumps, " shut up and cannot come forth," and feel as if I alone, of all mankind, were fated to get no bread by the sweat of my brow—to " toil in the fire for very vanity." If you've a mangy cat to drown, christen it " Palmer."

If you could oblige me with the further loan of three pounds, my father will repay you I daresay, if you can call at Grove Street, but I shall soon be in Town myself, only—I want enough both to bring me home, and to enable me to stay a little longer, in case I should find subjects which it would be short-sighted policy not to secure. But I hope not to spend so much. If the Movement Party want a professor of drawing in the Marylebone Charity schools, pray canvas for me. Things are come to a crisis now, and I must begin to earn money immediately, or get embarrassed: horrid prospect —the anxieties of debt, on the back of perturbations of aspiring studies. The refuge, I know, is in faith and prayer: but is daily bread promised to those who overspend their income, which I am afraid is now my case? However, I was deceived by the strange misstatement about cheap living in Wales, otherwise my Muse should have donkeyfied upon thistles from husky Hampstead this summer, with a log at her leg. Well! I must come to London, sell my pianoforte, and all my nice old books, and paint the sun, moon, and seven stars on a signboard, I suppose: would I could get it to do!

I find I am writing strange stuff and boring you with my own

selfish troubles, so I'll have done.   If you can favour me with the
three pounds, would you have the further kindness to send it as
soon as possible, and with a very full and legible direction on the
letter : what if it should miscarry !   I must stay at Tintern, and go
to plough : could you send by return of post ?

The candle is going out, as did the light of my mind some hours
ago, so I must wish you miserably, good-night.

Mr. Walter desires me to give his love, and say that he wishes
to return directly, but not having the means, would be obliged if
you would make it up a five pound note.   I will pay the postage
of this when I see you.   With kindest love to Mrs. Richmond,
and such old friends as you may happen to see, I remain, my dear
Sir, Your affectionate friend, SAMUEL PALMER.

1838

VIII. TO MR. GEORGE RICHMOND.

NAPLES, *June*, 1838.

MY DEAR SIR.   We got into the *vettura* on Tuesday morning,
and encountered a torment of fleas (thought by some of the self-
denying Fathers so useful in the disturbing of sloth), which has been
increasing up to the present moment.

We saw the lake Albana, which I thought very tame, as well as
the environs of the town.   Whatever foregrounds the Campagna
may afford, the view of it from a height is anything but inviting.
I think we can bear barrenness better in a foreground than at a
distance ; for landscape should be the symbol of prospects bright-
ening in futurity.   I noticed the beautiful town on the hill you
mentioned, and liked it much.   We were much pleased with the
mountains on our left, going through Velletri ; and surprised at the
gigantic rock of Terracina.

Along the Pontine marshes, so well drained and cultivated, I
feasted my eyes on a quantity of English-looking copses and woods,
such as I had not seen for many months.   But the country assumed
an aspect more beautiful than anything we had seen, on approaching Itri through wooded ravines interspersed with blocks and tables
of over-grown rock : on seeing the town with its ancient, grey castle,
I was seized, fastidious as I am about scenery, with unmingled
delight.   Thence to Mola, is a rich Devonshire country, with two

or three very rich bits of ruin on or near the road side. At sunset
we entered the charming gardens of the hotel, an old villa, and
looked from among the terraced vineyards, over the bay to Gaeta,
" standing merrily by a haven side." I was agreeably disappointed
by the character of the first distant outline of Vesuvius, and by a
nearer view. I think the summits are grand and peculiar, and that
the tameness of the base is compensated for by the beautiful white
towns that skirt it, and the glittering villages that stretch to the
end of the promontory.

I think I have made quite sure of my drawing of ancient Rome
and the moment I cast my eyes on these mountains and on Capri,
which looks like an enchanted island, I said to Naples, " I think I
can grapple with you " ; though I have yet been out no farther
than to the Grande Bretagne, where Mr. Baring received us very
kindly, and told me of the Villa . . . . . where we are at present
lodged with Messrs. Lear and Uwins. We have a little room which
commands the bay, Vesuvius, Capri, and the whole chain of mountains, and which is quite cool at three in the afternoon. Indeed
though we were all day yesterday lodging-hunting (a most sudorific
employment), and had both slept the night before in a pestiferous
little den with only a thin roof between us and the sun, in a bed
not large enough for one person, with a window opening inwards
to the shaft or funnel of the house, ventilated only by blasts from
drains and kitchens, and in one of the most filthy streets, I do not,
in this blessed climate, suffer at all from heat ; but enjoy, rather,
the perspiration of walking, like a tepid bath ; and feel as if the sun
were only ripening me like the plums and peaches.

I quite agree with you that the interior of Naples is filthy and
uninteresting ; but surely on the shores of this bay one feels that
one has at last discovered the climate and the land of joy and of
enchantment. But what shall I say of Monte St. Angelo? Surely
all the mountains we have seen would kick the beam if weighed
against its ripe convexity, and yet clifted sides. The right wing
of the bay, certainly, though cultivated, is tame. But I should fear
that such a bay, such mountains, and such a climate, are rarely to
be found elsewhere. From the very little I have seen, I should
think that here may be found united the grandest mountains with
the richness of Devonshire valleys. We have just been along the
Vomera ; and tame as Naples is, surely the country seems made

for joy and love. My first wish, in the overflowing of my heart, was to know whether it was right to love the Devil. I could not bear the thought of hating anything; and I should have knelt down and prayed for him, only I was afraid it might be wicked. I think you must have seen Baiæ under bad effects or bad weather, or perhaps it is not so fine on a nearer view; but I caught a distant glimpse which realized the enchanted islands we have sometimes dreamt of, and "cried to sleep again." In a carriage you are obliged to go along the high roads, which always give the worst view of a country; but do pray bring Mrs. Richmond here in the early autumn. Take your dinner out in a basket, and explore every inch of the ground : such delicious air I have never felt; and hoping to enjoy it before long with you and Mrs. Richmond, ere we are again "stived up" in the Via Sistina, I remain, with kindest love to Mrs. Richmond, Tommy, and baby, dear Sir, Your much obliged and affectionate friend, SAMUEL PALMER.

When you feel disposed to write, be assured that it will be a great treat to us : and be sure to write small, and to give us a very long letter; for if, as I have sometimes fear'd, my long letters have seemed tedious to others (the suspicion of which has almost disgusted me with writing at all to anybody), be assured a long letter from you will be a great treat to me. My mind has for the last year been soured and choked with disgust at the thought of all the things whatsoever with which I have formerly taken great pains; because this is, of all times, the age in which pains-taking meets with the least reward. I wish I could get back again all the long letters which at sundry times I have written to sundry persons. That I might burn them in a heap? No, that I might elaborate them into the most polished mellifluence, and publish them for the benefit of the trunk-makers; and then in double disgust, leave the arts and literature altogether; and then in triple spite, take lodgings in the city, and work a little money about in the Stock Exchange, and turn a penny by the little daily fluctuations—and so, rot. I shall, if I live, begin Baiæ to-morrow, and give my whole soul to the work that the world may spit upon it the more scornfully.

But on the other hand, if I get on, I shall I hope become a good man, a wise, a temperate, and a just—do much good to others, and just grease my own wheels once a month, with the goose-club which I shall forthwith establish, of which you shall only be an "associate exhibitor" till you have learned to eat the richest bit of fat in the "apron." N.B. You will perceive, from its colloquial fluency, that this epistle has not been written from a rough copy. As I was in great haste, it abounds with extemporaneous elegances of bad grammar and construction.

IX. TO MR. AND MRS. GEORGE RICHMOND.

CORPO DI CAVA. Improviso and warm from the heart. *September* 16, 1838.

MY DEAR MR. AND MRS. RICHMOND. I am told that I behaved rudely on my travels. Now I have forgotten these things, but remembering that the heart that once truly hates never forgets, it struck me that because you took me for a monster you have not answered my letter from Naples, and I write again to tell you that Caliban still loves you, and is doing his best not merely by a blind copying of nature but by studying his art in nature, and endeavouring to get from that great storehouse substantial principles and philosophic views of his profession, to show you that your kindness in enabling him to make this great tour was not thrown away. If I can, by what I am doing, convince you of this, I shall be amply repaid for intense study and unwearied application. . . . At Naples, Mrs. P. made a panoramic sketch of the whole city from the gardens of a villa : studies of Vesuvius, St. Angelo, and the bay, from our window ; and a small copy of a most exquisite Correggio in the museum. I secured a large drawing of Naples, a smaller of the same, and a large view of Baiæ. At Pompeii I got five drawings, including the theatre, amphitheatre, and the street of the tombs : and at Corpo di Cava . . . I have got a large drawing of the town and convent, and about a dozen smaller subjects ; besides hints, outlines, and memoranda, in my little sketch-books, which I now always carry about with me.

In this place a load has been lifted off my mind which has hung upon me for more than a year, and has been as troublesome as John Giles's "loaf."[1] I now see my way, and think I am no longer

[1] My father alludes to the consequences of Mr. Giles having been beguiled by himself

a mere maker of sketches, but an artist. I only hope it may not turn out a delusion, and prove a " horse-shoe " at last.

If we are spared, we shall visit Amalfi and Ravella hastily, for motives and outlines, and return to Naples, where Anny will copy the other little Correggio, and I shall explore Baiæ. Then we hope to grapple with Tivoli, and [to] resume our labours at Rome, where we earnestly hope to see you in the winter ; afterwards, to have a fierce grapple with Terni ; then, to get some views of Florence, and return home laden with spoil, which we hope may not be mislaid or lost at the Custom-house before those " great gods " the Academicians come down and pass them.

You will be pleased to hear that Mrs. Palmer has had a dose of landscape-drawing at Corpo di Cava, and has made great improvement ; getting her hand into it, and working with great freedom and success. . . . My dear Mr. and Mrs. Richmond, my old and tried friends, believe me Ever yours most affectionately, SAMUEL PALMER.

X. TO MR. EDWARD CALVERT.

NAPLES, *9th October*, 1838.

MY VERY DEAR FRIEND. Ever since my arrival in Rome I have been thinking of you, desiring to write, and longing to hear from you. I wished also to give you pleasure by telling you about some of the grand things I had seen ; but filled more than the space of a letter with a really concise account reaching no farther than the Louvre ; so many novelties had presented themselves. This discouraged me, for if I were less particular, you would only have a catalogue which you might find in commonplace-books of travels. But I am so pricked with compunction that write I will, if there be only room to mention a few works of creation or art which impressed me with their novelty or beauty : though to you, who have travelled so much, it will be little more than the reviving of old recollections.

At Calais I entered for the first time a Continental Romish cathedral, and was delighted with its rich and furnished fulness.

and the other " Ancients " into bathing with them in the Darent after dinner. The victim was afterwards long troubled by a sensation which he described as an internal quartern loaf.—ED.]

Besides the great altar, there were smaller ones with their statues, pictures, marbles, and other enrichments, in every side recess ; and I then little thought that the same were to be seen in thousands even of the smaller civic churches of the Continent. The picturesque poor people also, leaving their avocations for a few moments, and kneeling about the doors, and in the dim recesses, added to the comfort and furnished appearance of the temple ; for which, I doubt not, in Other Eyes than ours, the religious poor are the richest of all decorations. We were much pleased too, with the high, strange towers, and old-fashioned market-places and piazzas, with their market-carts, and gay but rustic costumes, and the profusion of fruit and vegetables spread over them : very different in the painter's eye to Covent Garden, but perhaps after all, not containing so many or so good eatables.

The Louvre, in the gardens of which I was first delighted with the sight of statues in pure air and brilliant sunshine, contains a splendid collection of antique sculpture. Three-fourths of the pictures are of little interest ; but then, those which remain are in themselves a most noble gallery. They are, however, with the exception of two rooms (in one of which happily, hangs the *Marriage of Cana*), most vilely lighted : but there are Giorgiones and Titians which would *make* sunshine in any other darkness than the darkness of the Louvre. The *Marriage of Cana* is I think, in some respects, the most extraordinary picture of its size I ever saw. All is pitched in the highest key of light, and in the purest brilliancy of colour : not tinged with golden, evening light, yet all glowing with the joy of mid-day sunshine—full of brightness and full of depth ; having all the treasures of the palette, yet no weight of pigment—the last facility of imitation, yet no flippancy ; and though of immense size, and crowded with subject, bearing not a symptom of dulness, doubt, weariness, neglect, or delay. To see this alone, is well worth the journey to Paris. Then in the dark galleries or rather caves beyond, coruscate, rather to the mind than to the dilated, straining eye, " full many a gem of purest ray serene." But I cannot bear to talk or think of the barbarity which could place them where they are : it is a dark mine, but it is indeed a golden one. For the Luxembourg gallery we had no time.

Every one should see the Gothic Church of St. Eustache ; not so large as Notre Dame, but to my taste, of much finer art ; uniting, without mixture of the styles, in a remarkable manner, the proportions of Greek and Norman architecture. It seems to me a great master-piece of symmetry, giving length, breadth, and height ; without sacrificing either to the others. . . .

Almost our first glimpse of Italy was the dawn glimmering behind the mountains of Lago Maggiore, from a balcony of our inn, trellised with flowers. The pinnacles of Milan cathedral studded with sculpture, seem carved of ivory. Within, all is richness and poetic gloom. In the library, are some small, exquisitely-finished designs in chalk by Michelangelo, and heads, by Da Vinci, of which the features are turned with unrivalled subtlety and elegance. The picture-gallery we missed. *The Last Supper* is a wreck. At Parma I climbed up so as to be close to Correggio's dome, but it was so faint and damaged, that I did not enjoy it. Walking by moonlight through the arcades of Bologna, I was astonished at the vastness of its churches, and the terrific height of its leaning towers ; seeming twice that of our Monument ; but I then had not seen Rome.

We just lunched and slept at places whose treasures of art would have have occupied weeks to explore them. We had a glorious journey over the Apennines to Florence ; everywhere finding that beautiful characteristic of Italy, the village or city on the hill, cresting the woody summit or rocky precipice with human, and sometimes with historic interest. How different were Wales so ornamented ! The vast, cultivated plain of Florence, stretching away between the receding Apennines till they vanish in Italian air and Italian light, leave nothing to be wished. Descending to Florence, we looked up upon Fiesole, the watch tower of the " Tuscan Artist," and soon entered that blessed city so dear to the lovers of art and of the old philosophy. Its admixture of art, primitive and mature ; its dusky, semi-barbarous Cathedral ; its sumptuous Baptistry ; its turreted, baronial palace, with the colossal statues of Michelangelo in the court beneath, indelibly impress the mind with their sullen stateliness and strength. I think of this city as of a heavy, old-fashioned, yet rich and exquisitely-wrought golden cabinet, containing in its caskets and curious recesses, specimens of all in art that is most pathetic and sublime. May we have time to explore it on our return ! The gallery here is a splendid collection : the Pitti we did not see. Here are also twenty thousand drawings by the Old Masters, frescoes of the choicest age, and everything which can make Florence the kernel of art. We did not stop to see the falls of Terni, reserving them for a hard sketching week by and bye.

At last we saw and entered the Eternal City—that wilderness of wonders, of which it is impossible to say little, and needless to say anything, as you have seen that, and almost everything else which we have visited ; so nothing remains but a little chatter about ourselves.

The weather was for months very rainy, and (we being without a fireplace) so cold that I wore a waistcoat lined with flannel, and Mrs. Palmer wrapped up like a mummy. To me, our December was nothing like it, and it seemed rather strange, in a climate which, I had been told, ripened strawberries at Christmas. However, I bore it with an allowance of English grumbling, and learned in time to wade along the streets, avoiding the water-spouts which concentrate the rain on the tops of the houses, and hurl it down in torrents to scour away the filth. When the sun burst forth, out I popped, like the lady in the weather-box, and tried to draw white palaces so sunny that the white paper seemed " double smut " against them. Mrs. P., meanwhile, went every morning about two miles by herself to the Vatican, to copy the Bible subjects in the Loggia ; being occasionally annoyed a little on the way ; people calling after her " Piccola Inglese " &c. Then we met at our room in the twilight, and turning down a dark passage and opening a little door, found ourselves at our dinner-table, with Messrs. Gibson. Williams, &c., where the hour passed very pleasantly after our labours, in chewing, chattering, and laughing. *Conversation* you know, in the true sense of the word, is banished from civilized society.

Mr. Baring, through Mr. Richmond's kind introduction, commissioned me to make him a large drawing of modern Rome, with which Mr. R. told me Mr. B. was very highly pleased. I also much pleased Messrs. Gibson and Williams, with a drawing of Ponte Rotto, which I exhibited. I tell *you* these little things, because I know you are really pleased with any good that befalls me. Mrs. P. was very ill for a month soon after our arrival, but quite recovered.

At last we set out for Naples, and when we got upon the hills, and I saw it glittering through the gardens and vineyards, my heart opened, and I felt goodwill even for the Devil. It seems to me that all the choicest effects of shade and colour, all the happiest accidents—all the blooms and blushes of Nature hover about this enchanted region. But there is a summit farther on whence the whole panorama is spread out—Naples, Vesuvius, Baiæ, and Camaldoli—O ! such a scene !—It would have made " Sam Weller " sentimental !

We lived a month in Pompeii, dining in one of the antique vaults, and living for the first time in a room with an unglazed window : we had only to step out, and we were in the " city of the dead." Here Mrs. P. made thirteen sketches of the antique pictures, and we saw a slight eruption of Vesuvius, of which I gave a short account in a letter to Mr. Linnell which you have probably seen. We then stayed two months at Corpo di Cava, commanding the finest distant mountains I have seen, and are now in Naples once more, to get a second view of Baiæ, intending, in a day or two, to trace its beautiful shores.

I will, if possible, get a sketch of that white temple you saw while anchoring in the bay. How I should enjoy a long talk over it, and over a large cup of tea—pure terra-vert ! When shall we join again by an English fireside, over that intellectual, social, but long untasted beverage ?

. . . I have been thinking a great deal about the principles and practice of art, and endeavouring very much to increase my acquaintance with the phenomena of nature, as well as working hard and incessantly, with the exception of time consumed in travelling ; so I am in full energy, with my will and determination not a whit unstrung by time, and hope to bring forth fruit in my old age. Travelling, so far from unsettling me, has, I am sure, limited and concentrated my desires and on a few points, calmed my mind most sweetly. I never had a Haydonish rage for big pictures ; but now I have seen how even Raffaelle was set to paint dark chambers like a house-decorator, with a window coming in the middle of one of his finest ; how an altar is fixed up for months against the Charon group in *The Last Judgement*, and how the same kind of homage is paid to works of genius in most of the Churches which are fortunate enough to possess them, I look upon

a kit-cat panel as, after all, the most enviable field for exertion
Besides, I think the Great Masters themselves, with very few
exceptions, distilled more of their intensity into little cabinet
pictures than upon great walls and altar-pieces. Such wrought
and polished gems as Mr. Mulready's *Seven Ages*, the half of which
I was fortunate enough to see, leave a deeper dent in my memory
than many of the great Jupiters and St. Jeromes sprawling over
large ceilings and saloons.

It is moonlight, and the Bay of Naples fills up our window,
sparkling like diamonds on ebony : what a pretty thing to do with
our blue-black flake-white !

I was thinking the other day that opposites are not, as we may
have been used to consider them, at enmity with each other—
giving spirit to a work by their violent contention ; but they are
like the truest friends, manifesting each other's perfections. However, perhaps both views are right, though seemingly difficult to be
reconciled. Certainly, red manifests the beauty of green, and
green the beauty of red. It may be said that it is the same with
moral opposites, for that they also manifest each other ; but the
analogy goes no farther ; for though vice manifests the beauty of
virtue, virtue does not manifest the beauty of vice, but its ugliness.
Now the opposites in art make each other look the better—the
advantage is not merely on one side.

I have carefully examined the Pompeian pictures, which offer
much matter for consideration. Mrs. Palmer has copied the best
of those in the ruined city ; and as I was obliged to be with her,
here and elsewhere, to protect her from Neapolitan insolence, I
saw them well. I remember writing to Mr. Linnell, while they
were fresh in my memory, that joints and articulations were
shaken out of the pencil with the facility of a Gainsborough's pollards ;
and really if these [pictures], as is perhaps the case, were executed
by second-rate artists, the first-rate men must have possessed a
mastery over the figure of which later ages have shown very few
examples. They are also full of life and elegance, but show, I
think, no traces of those discoveries by which Da Vinci and others
added so much to the sciences of chiaroscuro and colour. The
pigment in the lights is remarkable for fulness and fatness ;
therein exceeding, if I remember well, the frescoes of the Cinque
Cento. There are a great number in the Neapolitan Museum,

where Mrs. P. is now copying a splendid, impasted little Correggio of the Madonna and Child with St. Catherine, which I think I have often heard you speak of. It cost eighteen thousand dollars, if I rightly understood the custode. Though the lights are so richly impasted, yet the dark, transparent shadows, and lucid, semi-transparent half-tints, project beyond them, when you look along the surface ; which, with other reasons, makes me think that the painters of that age used a great deal of vehicle in their shadows something like copal, not oil merely, or soft varnish, which I think would not stand up and remain as it was first laid on.

I have been out of practice in oil-painting for a year, but have endeavoured in my mind to analyze the process, and think I should go to work now with much more certainty. I often wish I could consult with you and ask your opinion on points of art ; for I reverence more and more, philosophical and ordered wisdom, though I shall always desire the liberty of doubting where I am not convinced, and of demurring at axioms which do not seem self-evident to me, though they may be clear to another as the sun at noon-day. I hope you will send me some account of what you have been doing since we parted, and be kind enough to communicate any great principles or trains of thought that may be strongly on your mind at this time, that all intellectual intercourse may not be denied me, though I am cast so far away. But as there are times in which one does not feel prepared for writing upon art, or has not time for it, do not delay a letter on that account ; but when I push my card through the post-office grating at Rome, let me be revived by the sight of your hand-writing, at all events. Give my kindest love to Mrs. Calvert (for I suppose a married man may send his love to a married lady without danger of being called out); and the same to the dear children who I hope are growing fast, both in wisdom and stature. Tell them I often think of them, and imagine how I shall enjoy to find a year and a half's improvement in each of their heads when I come back. I can think of scarcely anything that would give me greater pleasure than to see them grow up wise and brilliant men, and little Mary an elegant, accomplished woman, in the true sense of the words.

I hope you have not quite forgotten that " There is a plant grows in a wood," &c. ; for if I remember, you were getting rather lax on that point. I believe if an angel were to come down and whip us every Monday morning, it would give us a fillip, and do us all much good. Wishing you every happiness and blessing, and above all, those choicest blessings on which, as we differ so widely, I have forborne to speak, I remain to the heart's core, my dear Sir, Your affectionate friend, SAMUEL PALMER.

XI. To Mr. SAMUEL GILES.

POZZUOLI, *October* 28, 1838.

TO MY DEAR MRS. GILES, AND TO THE REST OF MY DEAR COUSINS IN KING WILLIAM STREET ASSEMBLED, GREETING.

An account of all the novelties which I have seen, if hung from the top of the Monument, would trail upon London Bridge ; therefore I will just mention a few things as they occur to me, and waive all introductories excepting an apology for having seemed to neglect you so long, occasioned by a continual press of labour and study, which has prevented my writing a line to any one, but in our periodical letters to Bayswater. Yet, many a time, have I sat down in spirit by your cheerful and intellectual fireside, where have passed some of my very happiest hours.

The inside of a Romish church was the first novelty which presented itself ; not a believer's band-box, in which the greatest quantity of lace caps and laces are crowded into the smallest possible space, partitioned out into dress boxes called pews, for the comfort of consciences too tender for the opera ; where fine ladies cover their heads with *Valenciennes* to play at hide and seek with the angels (by which, perhaps, were meant, says Dr. Gill, young ministers), and making what is called a *respectable* congregation—a *thriving interest*. Not this, but a refuge for the abject and the outcast, the peasant and the pilgrim ; with no *free seats*, where all are free, to publish his poverty—no brandy-faced beadle to drive Lazarus from the door, and waddle before Dives to the chief seats. A continental church is no whitewashed pantile shop for paroquet costume, where a picture or statue could not be tolerated for fear of worldly pomp ! But a temple enriched by the noblest talents of man for the honour of God, and opening its gates for him who has no other friend. I expected to find one great altar, gorgeously decorated, and no more ; but found an altar enriched with carved wood, statuary, pictures, and precious marbles in every side recess, and between the pilasters all along the side aisles ; so that service may proceed, without much interruption, in several places at once : and there are groups of poor market-people, who have laid down their baskets for a few moments (some still poorer), praying in oratories and dim recesses ; and others prostrate at the door.

Thus far all is right, tho' the Romanists have not been wanting in other means of money-getting ; but there are things more questionable. In the churches of Naples you see life-size figures of the Virgin, dressed out in the height of the fashion of the time when they were made ; with stay-tight waists, and Bond Street hips, and rings on their fingers. When an image of the Madonna makes a procession through the streets it is preceded by soldiers with fixed bayonets, and a military band playing merry tunes. An image which I saw carried in Rome, with seven daggers in her breast, was, I think, borne by butchers—at least it was the butchers' costume, which is said to be that of the sacrificing priests of Jupiter. Like the Pagan household gods, little ugly dolls of the Virgin and Saints under glass cases are kept in many of the houses; and votive offerings are hung in profusion in some of the churches, before the shrine of the delivering saint : horribly-painted little pictures too of remarkable deliverances from fire, drowning, or spirited horses, are suspended about them : and at a favourite shrine of Our Lady I saw innumerable knives stuck into leather thongs up the wall, which were the weapons of converted assassins. You see parents lifting up their children to kiss the foot of a Saint. That of St. Peter in the Vatican, though of brass, is much worn.

No one was ever more cruelly or unexpectedly disappointed than myself with almost all the church music I have heard in France and Italy. During the consecration of the Host, they play operatic music; and an organist once, who could not please the congregation by other melodies, played the air of "Go to the Devil and shake yourself," very much to their satisfaction. An eminent artist at Rome, who is also an organist, told me that after wearying a convent with fine music, he quite delighted them with "Bumper Squire Jones." At high mass I have heard the chant of the priest ac-

companied in the most frivolous taste ; and when after loud music
there comes an unaccompanied chant, the organ keeps the priest in
tune with a loud shrieking note now and then, all the stops having
been left open. The vocal choir of St. Peter's and the Sistine
Chapel is very fine, but in the gallery of the former the leader
stands in front beating time very energetically, and the cries of
"*Piano ! Piano !*" are rather *forte,* and much too distinctly audible.

We saw the grand Easter ceremonies, and were several times
within a yard of the Pope. We saw him wash the feet of the
thirteen priests (whom he afterwards waits on at dinner, girding
himself with a napkin), and after singing mass, bless the immense
assembled multitudes from the façade of St. Peter's. This is a sublime spectacle—thousands of country people in their picturesque
costumes, beating their breasts, holding out strings of beads, and
awaiting, in breathless silence, the great benediction. When the
Pope appears, all is hushed. He spreads out his arms over the
people and blesses them ; and then, all in a moment, the great guns
of St. Angelo fire, the martial bands distributed over the piazza,
strike up, and the bells of the city, which are silenced through Passion Week, ring out a peal. Before this, at the grand mass at St.
Peter's, at the moment when the elements are consecrated and all
are prostrate, a slow, sublime harmony of wind instruments peals
along from over the great western door, softened in this immense vault as in the open air. The dome, though much higher
and vaster than St. Paul's, is not, in my judgment, nearly so sublime ; and in sublimity and musical effect I think the grandest
ceremonials of the Vatican are far short of our cathedral worship.

We found the scenery from Calais to Paris pretty tolerable in
places, but the few villages on the high road looking very desolate
and deserted. Indeed, throughout our French journey, excepting
one single village in the south, all the little country places appeared
dismantled and wretched, with not a gleam of cottage comfort.
No rustic chimney "between two aged oaks" (for forest timber
we saw none till we came to Switzerland,, no "neat handed
Phillis" ; but houses in the taste of Walworth Common and Rother-
hithe, only without, or with broken, glass, and tumbling to decay ;
and instead of ruddy ploughmen, ragged, sallow, blue-coated mon-
sieurs ; the whole looking as if it had been purged, not purified,
through twenty, instead of three or four revolutions. This is not

caricature, or an exaggeration of the *general* impression made on my senses. Our modern philosophers say, I believe, that our ideas come only through the medium of the senses, and really the sense of smelling is by no means an inactive agent in forming one's idea of France and Italy ; nor the sense of feeling in the flea season, though happily for us, in Rome (to parody the kitten pie-man), *when frosts was in, fleas was out.* In Rome, where the bed-linen is shaken into the streets, we are told that in summer the fleas swarm you so as you walk that people are obliged to change their clothes when they come in ; and at Naples, those little creatures which in the language of Dante are called " pedoccii " so abound that they are sent home in the clean linen. However, a comb and soapsuds would sooner clean one of these, than the most stoic philosophy of the blue devils in lurid London. These vermin, though they certainly do not contribute to ease, are light and limber enough to grace the modern style of epistolary correspondence, which is said to derive most of its grace from facility of movement.

The fury and vociferation, and brutal, butt-end horsewhipping of French *diligence* drivers are a strange contrast to the quiet mastery of the " Mr. Wellers " of old England. But the movement-note of one of our charioteers was very curious: while he was beating away with all his might, he was exciting his cattle with a tone exactly like the cooing of a dove !

We arrived at midnight in Paris, and put up with a most dismal-looking room in a great hotel whose gates were guarded by sentries Nothing in travelling is so wretched as a night arrival in a strange city. We were surprised to find no soap on our wash-stands, but soon found it was an unheard-of luxury which we must buy and carry about with us through the whole journey. We found here several pretty nauseous examples of French filthiness.

At the risk of being every moment pushed down or run over, we began to explore Paris—were delighted with the Louvre, tho' the pictures are hung in the dark, but had not time for the Luxembourg. We were detained day after day by the shameful delays of the passport system, [and] our consolation was to creep now and then into the Louvre. We did not then know that by giving a few francs to the commissionaire of the inn, all would have been done for us. O ! the physiognomies that I saw in the public offices ! We were told that, some time since, the present *liberal* government took away from travellers on the frontiers the pistols which they carried for their private safety. The new king's soldiers form a guard of honour with a standard, over the graves of the so-called patriots who were killed in the act of dethroning the last monarch!

I shall not easily forget some grand old fortified and cathedral towns near the Swiss frontiers of France. We had just a glimpse of their grey fanes and mouldering battlements before we entered for the night, and left them before daylight in the morning; which, when we looked back, we saw glimmering upon them in the valleys beneath. Sometimes the morning mist filled up the vales and plains like an ocean with its friths and bays; while the rising sun, striking upon the island-like summits and mountains, fired with living gold here and there an ancient village or city on their glowing ridges. Sometimes what seemed to be sky opened and disclosed a patriarchal village nestled among the pastoral downs, and glistening like silver or pearl through the rarer vapour; or the cloud would partially vanish or rise like a curtain, and disclose a champaign country at our feet; while, on either side of the road, the village people were brushing away the dew from the ripe vineyards, and piling up the purple treasure in baskets, or loading them upon teams of cream-coloured oxen.

Then came the wonders of Switzerland; while, winding up and down among vast green or furrowed slopes, or shaded by luxuriant forest timber, we saw the hoary Alps at sixty miles' distance glimmering like sunny clouds across the horizon—above them, greyer or more vaporous colour, and the Alps again! Lausanne sweeps down with its terraces and gardens to the margin of the great lake as it seems, though a mile intervenes, which is lost in the stupendous scale by which the eye measures everything: being filled with the giant forms on the other side.

On the hilly environs of the Lago Maggiore stands the statue of St. Charles Borromeo as large as a tower, with his hand stretched out over the country, as if blessing all beneath him. There is a staircase inside the statue, and several people can dine in his head. Mr. and Mrs. Richmond and Mrs. Palmer saw it, and a room where this blessed saint and servant of God was born, with a cast of his face, some of his hair &c. I did not, being plagued with heavy boots, and unable to ascend to these precious relics, which I reckon a great loss. I however saw the statue at a distance.

Our first sight of the lake was from a flower-trellised balcony at the inn, with the first crimson flush of dawn glowing behind its mountains.

Milan cathedral is a wonder of holy, Gothic, inspired art, and its dim religious light gilds the very recesses of the soul. It is the antithesis of the new Post-Office, and not very similar to the National Gallery.

But Florence is the "city of my soul"—quaint, antique, stately, and gorgeous, and full of the gems of those divine and divinely inspired arts which, three centuries ago, lived there in wedded love with the old Platonic philosophy. Not the pot and kettle philosophy of The Useful Knowledge Society, beginning in steam-engines and ending in money and smoke, but visionary and ideal—the solid food of the soul. For money and beef are not, as people imagine, the solid things of the *mind;* but as unreal and unsatisfying to the immortal part, as a lecture on metaphysics would be to a hungry belly.

But what shall I say of Rome, of whose wonders a tenth part I have not seen, yet have seen what would fill a volume? Its churches are cathedrals, and its Vatican larger than the city of Turin within the walls. Rome is a thing by itself which, once seen, leaves the memory no more—a city of Art which one had dreamed of before, and can scarce believe that one has really seen with these ocular jellies——to which London seems a warehouse, and Paris a trinket-shop. What must it have been in its antique glory? You can only look at its dazzling palaces, blazing in Italian sunshine, with your eyes half shut. Indeed, Italian air and Italian light, and the azure of an Italian sky, can scarcely be imagined in England. It spreads its magic over streets and houses, and invests the commonest objects with a peculiar beauty : but the people do not, I fear, plunge into the Tiber after athletic games as heretofore, or wash their carcases as we do every morning in cold water ; for they leave a wake of unsavoury odour behind them as they walk the streets, which are strewed with filth.

We have lately been exploring the wonderful environs of Naples, are now at Pozzuoli (Puteoli, where St. Paul landed), and hope soon to be in Rome for the winter.

I grieve to pass another Christmas without our family meeting. It made me sad last year to think of it, and I do earnestly hope,

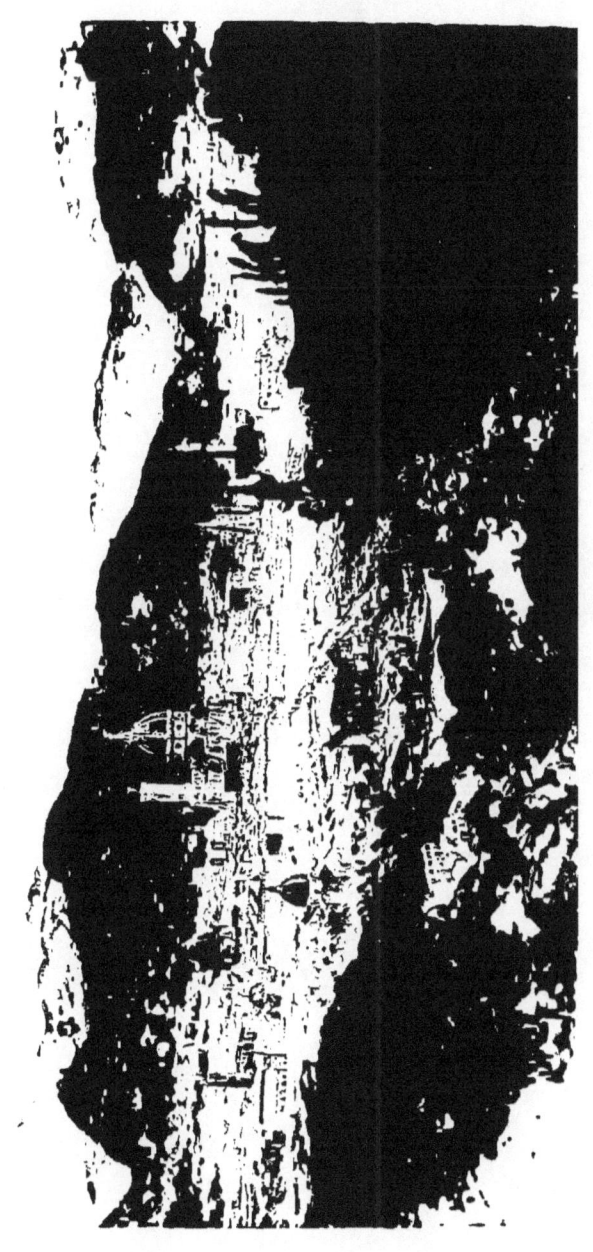

my dear John, that we shall spend next Christmas but one
together, and in company with our feathered friend, whom I have
not forgotten, though my last sight of him was in your company.
Green tea too, and the bookish evening have charms to draw me
to England, where I hope we shall often enjoy them together.
Pray write me a *long* letter . . . . and tell me what delightful
books you may have lighted on since my departure, and how little
Willy and Samuel get on with their studies, which I long to know.
Give my best love to them, and tell them they are not forgotten.
Pray begin to write as soon as you get this, and write five minutes
a day in a very small hand till the letter is full.

I saw Dr. Wiseman at the Easter ceremonies, with a purple
gown and fur tippet, looking as sleek and fat as ever, and heard
him preach once or twice. He has been getting up performances
of Shakespeare's plays by his pupils of the English Academy.
He sings, and is, I believe, fond of the arts.

I have been received with great respect by the first English
artists in Rome, who were much pleased with a drawing I exhibited
there. Mr. Richmond kindly introduced me to Mr. Baring, who
gave me forty guineas for a view of the city, for his father's, Sir
Thomas Baring's, collection. We met with a very pleasant and
intellectual friend in a son of Sir Thomas Acland, who passed a
good deal of time with us at Naples. I have said nothing about
Mr. Richmond as I know he has been in correspondence with
you : indeed, I am very anxious to know where he is, as I do not
much think he remained at Florence. Pray let me know, if you
have heard. Do not forget between you to get me up a long
letter. Give my love to all relations and friends, and believe me,
my dear cousin, Ever yours affectionately, SAMUEL PALMER.

When we were leaving Pozzuoli this morning, I saw a monk
getting the materials for a dinner in a very cheap and ingenious
way. He was presenting to all the old men and women in the
little fish-market a glazed, coloured print of the Virgin to kiss,
and was in turn presented by each with a small fish, which he
carefully deposited in his handkerchief. I think in Billingsgate
he would find himself as much out of his element as the fish
themselves.

We have just heard from Mrs. Tatham (their aunt, at Naples),
that the Richmonds are at Rome ; that Mr. R. is now quite well ;
that Mrs. R. has continued all along in perfect health ; and that the

Roman baby has cut six teeth and is a giant. Our children also are, I trust, pretty well. They are twins ; viz. Mrs. Palmer's drawings and my own. Dear little creatures ! They will I hope, support *us* instead of our having to keep *them*, which I hope will not be long ; for I desire speedily to launch them on the tide with a favourable gale. If they sail into the port of prosperity, people will begin to say, " What a nice young man Mr. Palmer is. Ah ! I always said *he* would get on." Perhaps now they say, " Do you know that old fellow Palmer, with grey bristles on his head—he's an odd fish, isn't he ? " If I get on, I mean to live most temperately, but to establish a monthly Goose Club, with a few select friends who appreciate that noble bird. The morning to be spent in reading our old poets, the bird to be discussed about two o'clock, and vivid green tea to be brought in at four, and kept on the hob all the evening ; during which, over a blazing fire, we can talk over our old times at Greenwich and Shoreham, and have a little bit of Fletcher's *Faithful Shepherdess* now and then, or some of your old sophisticated Catholic books, dear John, which you must bring in your pocket. Tell me where you spent last Christmas Day, and whether you mourned, as I did, that the old family compact was broken up.

My dear Albert, if you go on drawing, continue to study from the divine, eternal, naked form of man, even if you are driven out from the society of men, and obliged to pursue your studies in a hay-loft. Take the greatest pains to secure a beautiful outline, and study from the works of the finest masters. Every inch you gain in this way is a mile. The devout and holy study of the naked form purifies the imagination and affections, and makes us less pervious to evil temptation. Here, beauty is often the whited sepulchre of vice ; but in eternity that human form is, as it were, the body and symbol of goodness and truth. Seas may forsake their channels, mountains be shaken to their base, but the eternal form of man will survive the wreck, and, as it existed from eternity in the Divine Idea, will flourish in immortal youth amid the " clash of worlds." I again subscribe myself, my dear cousin, Yours most affectionately.   S. P.

Now ! Do you think I'm mad, all of you ? If I am, come and be bitten, for the vaccination of artistic madness is a good specific against the small-pox of worldly vanities.

Excuse bad composition, for I write in great haste.

1839

XII. To Dr. Walter Williams.

Rome, *March* 18, 1839.

My dear Sir. In case you should have forgotten that there is such a person in the world as S. P., he begs to inform you that he is still in the body, but that his spirit has often, during the last eighteen months, sat by your hospitable fireside when you little suspected who was there.

We peculiarly cherish the memory of those friends who have the power of catering for us a happy, intellectual, leisure day. This power you possess in a high degree ; and you must allow me, if ever a day's, or half a day's leisure comes again, to spend it with you. I do hope to afford a bookish day now and then ; having arrived at the age when man begins to simplify his projects, and find out that he has only two things to take care of—viz., to please God and to mind his trade. But how highly are *we* privileged, having professions so intellectual (and yours so benevolent), offering a boundless scope for curiosity and investigation. Still, much as I love my calling, I am a true bookworm, and hope on my return to find, about once a month, a whole day for a Great Read ! " Some place their bliss in action "—I in a dull, pattering, gusty, December day, which forbids our wishes to rove beyond the tops of the chimney-pots ; a good register stove ; a sofa strewed with books ; a reading friend, and above all, a locked door forbidding impertinent intrusions. There should be a light dinner about one o'clock ; then a little prosy chat (not too argumentive), just to help digestion ; then books again, till blessed green-tea-time winds us up for *Macbeth* or *Hamlet* and ecstasy. Late dinners spoil everything : they cut up intellectual evenings. But on my plan, you rise betimes the next morning, with alacrity, to those daily *duties* in which every good man ought to find his pleasure—robust disciplines which chasten and invigorate our fallen, idle nature, and without which, we soon become at once weak and mischievous. Happy are those who have an imperative daily occupation. *Respectable*, in the true sense of the word, are all those who do their best in that calling, be it ever so humble. Away with that libel on Providence which dignifies only the richer

P

members of society with the title of respectability. Is it not disgusting and almost blasphemous to talk even of *respectable* congregations in our *churches;* meaning that few poor people frequent them—those poor to whom it was the crowning glory of Christ's ministry that the Gospel was preached. Meaning that the clergyman's exquisitely-tied cravat, and sweet amalgam of Christianity and gentility, draw after it hosts of silly women, swimming and strutting into the presence of their *God*, with laces, and trinkets, and smelling-bottles, and birds' feathers? The whitest-winged angel of Heaven thinks the chimney-sweep and scavenger who twitch and trundle their brooms with energy and skill, truly respectable ; though their dirty fellow-sinners in shiny hats and superfine coats, think differently. As, however, you are in a learned and most truly noble profession, and I in one which even the stupid pride of fashion thinks tolerable, we are spared the insults which Dives has ever cast at Lazarus ; and have each of us the privilege of going to Hell like a Christian and a gentleman. You, however, have, I believe and know, declined availing yourself of this privilege, and are, by divine grace, toiling up the narrow hill-path which leads to Life. But alas, with all its blessings, how sore a temptation is the all-absorbing interest of a liberal or learned art : how often does it leave only the dregs of the mind, the sleepy or exhausted hours, for communion with God ! Happy are those who find Him and adore Him everywhere, as they investigate His beautiful creation ; and in whom (to murder Wordsworth's language, which I cannot accurately remember) the smallest flower that blows gives " Thoughts that often lie too deep for tears ! " Perhaps it is owing to the all-absorbing interest of the arts and sciences that " not many wise " are effectually called ; and that Religion, too sincere and too humble for polite or learned society, is often found sitting with the cobbler in his stall—turning the very clang of his hammer into music, or hiding herself from dons and dandies, among the butter-tubs in a chandler's shop.

If angels laugh at all, they must laugh till they shake the feathers out of their wings to see one poor insect scorning another because it is not dappled with such butterfly colours ; but our pride of dress is sillier still, for we do not even strut in our own plumage, but in the hides of beasts and the feathers of birds! Stripped and stark, Cæsar is as " poor, bare, forked an animal " as " Sam Weller."

But I have no more time to scribble ; and therefore, hoping that we may soon have a long meeting in England, and a longer still when this corruptible shall have put an incorruption, I remain with *very, very, very*, kindest regards to Mr. and Mrs. Williams, my dear Sir, Your ever affectionate friend, SAMUEL PALMER.

P.S. If I had another sheet to fill I would not say one word about luscious Italy, or its kernel Rome ; because expectation is so wound up about letters from hence that one is sure to disappoint it. Only, by the bye, please to take notice that I have not approximated one inch towards Romanism, though I hope to live and die an English Catholic of our Protestant Church. Also, I hope you have not swerved towards dissent. We ought to love the persons of dissenters and of the whole human family, daily more and more, and it is our *duty* to proselytize whenever we can, while we take care not to be ourselves entrapped, or to run the least hazard of " perishing in the gainsaying of Core."

1848

XIII. To MR. EDWARD CALVERT.

[LAIRA, DEVON], *July* 25, 1848.

MY DEAR FRIEND. I have this instant arrived at Laira, very tired, having risen at half-past three this morning, and travelled from the north Cornish coast ; yet I have seen so much within the last three hours to remind me of yourself and Mrs. Calvert, that I cannot refrain from just sending a line to tell you of the pleasure it has given me.

At this moment I am sitting within view of the woods of Saltram, with only the river Laira between us—that Saltram, of whose Titian we have spent hours in talking, at dear old Brixton. I have for the first time by daylight seen the streets of Plymouth, through which you must so often have walked with Mrs. Calvert ; and have enjoyed several distant peeps at Mount Edgecumbe, where it was, if memory fail not, that the relentless Archer first transfixed your heart. I have caught glimpses of the noble Tamar for some miles, before alighting at Saltash, with the dark woods of the castle which pleasure-parties go to see from Plymouth, with rich valleys beyond, closed by the desolate but, to me, inviting

Dartmoor; coming on by boat from Saltash to Plymouth, and getting a most significant hint of the strength of our navy.

What an interesting place is Plymouth! There can be no end of variety in the walks about it. Such an interchange of land and water ; the ocean, the harbour, the arsenal, the busy hum of men ; the most retired dells, the richest orchards and most sequestered lanes and valleys ; the mountain streams tumbling over the granite of the moors ; everything which may rouse, cheer, soothe, tranquillize the spirits ; a combination seldom, I should think, to be met with elsewhere. Really, with reverence be it spoken, I must call it a bit of perverseness in you to number Paddington among the four " beautiful cities," after living at Plymouth. What end is answered by confounding light with darkness—the omnibus office with Mount Edgecumbe, and Kilburn Road with the " thunder fraught " Hamoaze ?

I have been thinking much lately of the shortness of life ; and when I passed through your youthful haunts and "ancient neigh-bourhood," every turn of which seemed to speak to me of you and Mrs. Calvert, I could not help remembering how great and import-ant an addition to the happiness of my little life had been your united friendship. Memory would be much impoverished if she were robbed of Brixton, and grief in its bitterest anguish would have been still less bearable, but for your late sympathy and vividly-remembered kindness. From first to last—in youthful spirits, in toil, in adversity, in bereavement, you have both given me the best proofs of friendship ; and I lament that untoward circumstances have not afforded me an opportunity of evidencing gratitude.

. . . . I long to hear of our dear young friend who is upon the ocean, and when you get a letter we must have an evening over it. But first we must have a Plymouth night, and go over all the old ground again. I asked to be shown the Athenæum, but could not get a sight of it. I meant the Plymouth debating society which we used to talk of. I shall start D.V., early to-morrow morning for Collumpton, which seemed very rich from the railway going down ; and then homewards, by one puff of steam, in about a week hence or earlier, to your fourth " beautiful city."

The north Cornish coast is very wild, but the country above treeless and desolate. There is one most curious place on the

Pele Point, Land's End.

Study of Sea, Cornwall.

peaks of two cliffs, which are gradually tumbling by huge
fragments into the sea, viz. Tintagel Castle, the birth-place and
palace of King Arthur. It was a mouldered ruin in the days of
Henry the Eighth. Some turreted fragments which remain are
very quaint and strange. I found the people, as you said, very
human and civilized ; spending a very pleasant week in a lone
cottage among the hills, close to a rocky, sea cove. The goat was
milked in the kitchen, and two pigs always came up to be scratched
the wrong way of the bristles. It seems with them a pleasure
equivalent to honours and titles among mankind .... Ever, my
dear Sir, Affectionately Yours, SAMUEL PALMER.

1856

XIV. To Miss Louisa Twining.

6, DOURO PLACE, VICTORIA ROAD, *August*, 1856.

MY DEAR MADAM, Having spent a fortnight in the country,
where some friends live, I came back to the floods, and have
since been enjoying Kensington coast scenery from my windows!

I am very sincerely gratified to hear that you enjoy your
copy. Remember that the brush is sometimes to be used wet,
sometimes half dry—sometimes in a point, sometimes spread.
The same may be said of the sponge. Get a piece with an angle
in some part of it ; then it will act on large or small portions ; but
do not depend upon it : work as if you had no such resource.

When, by practice, you get the clue to processes which seem
mysterious, you will perceive that the right process is always the
most simple that can be devised, *relatively to the end proposed*.

A cedar and chestnut are just the best trees you could be
employed upon. *Do make them as like as you can.* But when the
drawing is settled, then work upon them only at that time of day
when they have the light and shade you have selected as the best.

Trees are sometimes very grand and solemn when there is no
positive sun-light. It is well to get the layers or plates of foliage
rather over than under defined at first, but always with a feeling of
gradation.

The kind of teacher you want is most difficult to find, and I do
not at present remember one, but will be sure to let you know

should anything occur to me. The very best thing I can think of is, in the meantime, to set the Teddington young ladies going *yourself*. Whatever may be their ultimate choice, let them by all means begin with the figure.

Gruner's Raffaelle's Bible, will make a bold beginning. If your published works are there, let them try some of the best defined figures with an H.B. pencil, and afterwards ripen the outlines with pen and ink. In short, anything which will soonest give the power of correct outline. This, according to the mental constitution of the pupil, will, in the acquisition, prove either a pleasure or a trouble ; but it *must* be done, and so the sooner the better.

If this could but be accomplished while pupils are young, so that they could readily draw the outline of any object set before them, it would simplify the whole future process ; and then occasional lessons from the best masters would keep them right ; and if they *worked diligently*, they could get some periodical criticism upon the amount of their intermediate labours. Outline requiring constant thought and comparison I think very young people should not sit at it too long together. You might try two half hours with a short rest between, letting them go on for the whole hour if so disposed ; making this the invariable rule, to secure daily practice, and letting them do as much more as they feel disposed for.

It seems to me that a great secret of early education is not to overrate the powers of attention in children. If they go to a church, for instance, where there are long sermons, I should let them have scripture history, or lives of the Saints full of pictures, to be administered during the latter half of the discourse, rather than knuckle their ribs or prick them with pins, to make them " attend to what the gentleman says."

Your own powers of attention are far above the ordinary standard, yet even *you* were wandering a little when you set your palette ; hence these cracks. Make the setting of your palette a morning's work, and you will save time in the end. Keep it *well replenished*, for I mentioned the method. It is this. Before laying any pigment for good upon the palette, put a rather full touch, dry, upon a piece of drawing-paper. When quite dry, it should have a slight gloss, but should not look at all dead : this secures its right effect upon the drawing. Then, to secure the palette and the facility of getting the colour off with the brush, try if you can move it somewhat from the paper I mean move it somewhat about *upon* the paper) with a brush dipped in water. If it dissolve and work about tolerably quite as much as you would wish it to do in your drawing), it is right, and not likely to tear up the palette:[1] if it does not, add a little honey, till it dries of the right consistency. Perhaps also, it would be well to lay, *very thinly*, a little honey upon the palette first and let it set, before laying on the pigments ; and if you want to lay your palette by for any time, a little diluted honey laid over each colour might tend to keep them moist. Perhaps flies out of doors might be attracted by the honey, and they are such lovers of art that it is impossible to keep them from it.

At Subiaco a nest of wasps swarmed about me, crawling about my face and spectacles, and eating little clean, round holes into the oil-paint, as I laid it on ; but never having, on any consideration, left off a sketch from external annoyances, I persevered to the end ; only moving my arm and hand very gently, as I knew they were insects full (as the novelists say) of "just pride and proper spirit ; " and by respecting their heroic instincts, I came off unstung.

Reflections in water are rather changeable, so I would recommend making studies on tinted paper, where you have the advantage of the white for the glittering light ; getting it as soon as you can, while it lasts, with crayons and black and white chalk ; and afterwards if it remain, or any part of it, you may go on with water-colours as much as you like ; but slight sketches themselves are most useful to those who carry on their studies as far as I suspect you will. When you have not time for anything but a pencil line, *write* the leading particulars and try to understand the leading phenomena. Beware of the notion that shadows cannot be cast *upon* water. It is, I believe, true of a perfect mirror, but when is water such ? I lately saw the shadow of a pier cast upon the sea, and its colour thereby totally altered by losing the warm sunlight, and reflecting to the eye only the blue of the sky above.

I think these are the leading points. 1. Water as a mirror, reflecting sun, moon, sky, landscape &c. 2. Water reflecting to the eye its local colour, taking cast shadows, obscuring the ground, weeds, &c. by its intervention. 3. Water as in different degrees a

[1 The palette referred to here, was of wood, with a white oil priming.— Ed.]

transparent substance, showing objects beneath it. The brilliant sunshine on beds of gravel, shining up to the eye through water, is a great beauty. Water *varnishes*, if I may so speak, everything it covers.

Pray let me hear of your proceedings from time to time, and I will write at all events a line in cases of difficulty. Believe me dear Madam, Your faithful Servant, S. PALMER.

1858

XV. TO MR. JOHN REED.

6, DOURO PLACE, W., *January* 26, [1858].

MY DEAR REED. Planets and systems rolling through millions upon millions of miles of dark, empty space are dismal matters to think on, and repulsive to our human feelings, as crushing man and his concerns into less than a point—an atom. Whereas the Torso Belvidere is more truly sublime than an infinity of vacuum ; and the Sistine Chapel, as an inspiration from the Spirit of Wisdom, than any of the material wonders of the universe. It is the work of God upon mind, which must needs excel His working upon matter, as the subject is greater, although the Infinite Wisdom the same. I have long believed that these vast astronomical spaces are real to us only while we sojourn in the natural body, and that the soul which has put on immortality will, so far as soul can be cognisant of space, find itself larger than the whole material universe.

How easily can the Divine Will annihilate, for a given time and purpose, the "laws," as we call them, of matter. Our blessed Lord although "clothed upon" with His resurrection body, came and stood in the midst of the disciples, "the doors being shut." "The Spirit of the Lord caught away Philip," and he "was found at Azotus."

And we find that the most powerful agents in the world of matter itself, are those which seem least to partake of material solidity. The electric fluid blasts the oak and shivers the battlement ; and to this subtile fluid and the elasticity of steam, we owe the two inventions which have abridged space and almost annihilated time. Probably the spirits of "just men made perfect,"

have no impediments of space and time to sunder them ; and if
the planets of this and other systems be the "many mansions"
of our Father's house, there may perhaps be no difficulty or delay
of communication between them. The rush of the autumnal
meteor may be a snail's pace compared with the motive Will
of interplanetary travellers.

At present however, after all the railways have done for us,
the case is very different, as engagements of one kind or other
leave us with time too little even to avail of the express train :
and thus it is with me, or I would certainly have run down to
see you long ere this. It is not enough to have you in my heart,
for I want to see your face, and feel the warmth of your smile :
or the warmth of your scolding, if *I* happen to smile on certain
occasions when you think I ought to look very severe indeed !
But thank you most cordially for your sincerity. You are one of
the very few who seem to care for my soul, and what kindness
is comparable with that ? I enjoyed much the paper you just sent
me—all but the Chinese affair.[1] To say nothing of the massacre
of an innocent populace, is it not like a big boy insulting a little
one ? Is this the first time that, on the shores of China, our
commercial greediness has played the fortune-hunting bully ?

Saul slew his thousands, David his ten thousands, but the
lust of gain its millions. Burke, speaking on the East Indian
Bill, describes Lahore as exhibiting for years, an unintermitted
but alas *unequal* struggle between the goodness of God to replenish, and the wickedness of man to impoverish and destroy.

I can sympathize with your fatigue after "many parties,"
having been obliged to go to several myself very lately. The
night after one of these meetings with really fine pianoforte
playing and Italian music, Mrs. P. read me George Herbert's life,
which, though I had often read it before, was better than a dozen
of these midnight dissipations. Cards and music are the great
destroyers of conversation. If I were an absolute monarch and
wanted to clench the people in a hopeless tyranny, I would take
off the duty on cards, and have thousands of reams of cheap
music at every stationer's. A poor soul enervated by opera music,
cares neither for itself nor its country.

Think of English daughters and English mothers, squalling

[1 Possibly the bombardment of Canton.—Ed.]

voluptuous love bravuras, while the household and the nursery are left to the tender mercies of hirelings !

Talking thus of parties, I must make an exception to some occasionally given by artists. Artists have a good deal of real humour in them, and see the point of a joke better than most people. . . . .

What poor, fun-loving babies we are—here, just upon the verge of eternity. All is a puzzle and heterogeneous heap of inconsistencies so wild and strange that, but for their daily experience, they would be incredible.

Thousands lavishing, thousands starving ; intrigues, wars, flatteries, envyings, hypocrisies, lying vanities, hollow amusements, exhaustion, dissipation, death—and giddiness and laughter, from the first scene to the last.

I remain, dear Reed, Yours affectionately, S. P.

XVI. To Miss Wilkinson.

6, Douro Place, *May*, 1858.

Dear Miss Wilkinson. I have taken the earliest moment, after all sorts of bustles and engagements, to see about your drawings. . . . As there is plenty of time before the Manchester Exhibition, I wish you would write a line to say whether you still wish to sell the *Florence*, for it gives so good a notion of the old sombre, delightful place, that, unless you have a duplicate, I think you may regret not having kept it as a memorial of your visit.

Why do you persist in using that rough paper on which the Roman study is done, for delicate architectural details ? It is fit only to play artistic, or rather *un*artistic tricks upon, and rasps both eye and mind like a great, coarse file. How much better to *make* the textures and qualities. As to trees, if there be a time suitable to begin your study of them, it is surely winter or early spring, when their bones are not too encumbered with muscle. One might draw the cypresses in the Villa D'Este for a year and not exhaust them. There are some good ones too at a villa a short ride from Rome. I forget the name.

You must have been much pleased with Mr. Glenny's beautiful drawings, which are now on the screens at our Gallery.

If you fall in with our excellent, kind friend, Mr. Dessoullavy, please give our kindest remembrances. Mentioning my name, I have no doubt he would be happy to show you his pictures.

I am too much of a stay-at-home to tell you any news artistic or otherwise, and have no doubt you get it all long before it reaches me. If I were asked for the best art advice I could possibly give to lovers of sketching, I should say what Joseph John Gurney said to a young man in whose welfare he took an interest, "If you wish to succeed, give your *whole mind* to *one* thing at *one* time." If your subject is more than a mile distant, ride to it. If you tire the body, the mind will not have fair play. Turner had a list of the implements he was to take with him, and wisely added "myself," well knowing that it was better to forget some of his colours, than not to take the whole man to the work. It is very difficult really to imitate anything, and the outside of nature, if ever so well imitated, is merely a shell ; or like the outermost lemon in the childrens' lemon toy, the innermost of which, in a bean-sized lemon, contains cups and spoons. Now, in tree drawing, many an artist has got two deep in his lemon, some three deep, some few, four deep : but among the landscape-painters, only Claude Lorraine has got at the cups and spoons. I remain, dear Miss Wilkinson, Yours most truly, S. PALMER.

XVII. TO MISS WILKINSON.

[KENSINGTON, *September* 17, 1858.]

DEAR MISS WILKINSON. I cannot at present answer your letter as it deserves, having sent it to Mrs. Palmer in the country, but I have before me a little abstract of its business contents in my commonplace-book, about which I may say a word or two, the matter having no sequence, which you will excuse.

You say you cannot embody a scene. No one can. That is the work of a Picture. A sketch can but make an abstract of some qualities. It is well when they are the most characteristic. Nor can you "go alone without some advice." Then imagine what they would say whose judgment you value. I have found this useful to myself; as also writing in cases of nicety, which I always practise. It forces us to think clearly. . . . For sunsets I would try a pencil or chalk outline on brownish-grey paper, tinted with soft crayons, and sometimes explained by writing on the parts themselves, or referring at bottom by A. B. C. &c., to parts so lettered. Sunsets are full of drawing; and the tints, without the peculiarities of form and texture, will not go very far. The Pincian Hill is a great battlefield for sunsets, and I think they are fine, off and on, through the winter. . . .

I am afraid, as you say, there is "no chance" of my coming to Rome, although I wish to see the southern vintages again, and am attempting one or two haunting memories of my travels. As a man, Rome is of course the attraction, but I am speaking artistically. Were I to go again, I would make hundreds of outlines of those rock-lifted cities on hills, from different points of view; some near, with strange antique gates, and mule-step road up to them; or a gentler incline, up which white oxen with bended necks drag the vintage wain. What a quantity of sketching matter turns up in near objects about every village. I think by far the quickest way of sketching is upon brownish paper, rather deep, for you are not afraid, as on white paper, to score out your lines with the black chalk; then heightening with white chalk, and tinting here and there with crayons, using yellow for instance just to discriminate trees or grass from buildings &c., you get almost in the same time something more explanatory than with pencil in a sketch-book of white paper. . . .

I really do not see how book illustrations can possibly be managed in the midst of interruptions. When you want as much expression as possible with as little labour, the mind usurps all that can be spared the fingers; and it will not do, just when you are turning a line on which the subject hinges, to be snatched up by a friendly foraging party for a ride to a flower-show, or an Exeter Hall spouting match! I do not mean that you frequent the arena of those spiritual gladiators, but merely name the Hall, as one of the London shows. I believe that, *literally*, ten minutes of close attention do more for a drawing than a day of semi-distraction.

I heard at my printer's the other day, that a first-rate hand bit in a little etching for a lady, with not much work in it, for seven shillings. He would also lay the ground. As it is so cheap, and as etching is so perfect a material, I think it would be best to try that. . . . If you get the ground laid and the etching bitten for you, there will be no uncertainty. Neither you nor I could bite it with certainty. Mine is a scramble of uncertainties from beginning to end. Yours must be neat and precise, with a sort of light, vignette elegance. I trust I can give you really copious information concerning the theory of etching, having lately added to my stock and, as I recommend, WRITTEN IT.

How delightful it must be to get out and sit, as you describe, at the top of the house. I wish we could all do it in Douro Place, for the sake of the skies (smoked though they be), and for the air, lifted a little more above the drains ; but both you and I would like an easier mode of access than you have probably seen achieved from the front attic of No. 6, by an aspiring student, who this day, September 17th, went for the first time to the grammar-school, and into the highest class. They have a capital head master now, which I was waiting for.

I do wish I had some news to tell you, but when you so kindly lent me *The Times* every day, I got such a stock into my poor head that I fear it will never hold any more. My newspaper is the Crystal Palace. There alone, we beat the whole world, ancient and modern, in treasures of all climes and ages. I took More there the other day, to give him a fill of music. There is music of one kind or other all the time. There was I, drinking in, so far as a half-civilized Englishman could, the wondrous beauties of *The Funeral Genius, The Torso, The Ariadne, The Polyhymnia*, while from the distant, great organ, sweet streams of melody spread like perfume through the halls. But for the Crystal Palace, I should heartily pity all who return hither from beautiful Italy. Of course I am talking the talk of the " natural man "—the old Adam. But however I may *practise*, I *know* better than to suppose that a Christian ought to seek his own happiness *here* (or a philosopher either), for to run after it is to lose it. Happiness is too swift-footed for us. We can never overtake her, but in the straight path of duty she will overtake *us*. There *is* a path (Alas, that I should be unworthy even to write of it), at the end of which martyrdom itself is but a goodly tree blushing with rose and amaranth ! " Another time looking out of his windowe to beholde one *Mr. Reynolds*, a religious, learned, and vertuous Father of *Sion*, and three monkes of the *Charterhouse* going forth of the Tower to their execution, . . . Sir Thomas, as one that longed to accom-panic them in that journey, sayde to his daughter, then standing besides him : ' Loe, doest not thou see. *Megg*, that these blessed Fathers be now as chearfully going to death, as if they were bridegroomes going to be married ? Whereby, good daughter, thou maist see what a great difference there is betweene such as have in effect spent all their daies in a straight, hard, and penitentiall life religiously, and such as have in the world like worldlie wretches 'as thy poore father hath donne) consumed all their time in pleasure and ease licentiously ? ' " [1] What a high ladder is that of Christian perfection ! This humble penitent was no other than that model of Christian laymen, the blessed Sir Thomas More. The Charter-house monks remind me of Camaldoli, about three miles from Naples. From the end of their garden is *perhaps* the finest prospect in the world. Ladies, of course, cannot enter ; but if you could see the enchantment anywhere outside the walls, it would be worth while climbing the hill on hands and knees for it ! Thence I saw the sun dip into the Mediterranean. There, Mr. Etty found among those happy hermits (for they do not live in cloisters, but in separate huts), some " who " (to use his own words) " loved learning for its own sake," not with the mental harlotry which loves learning for the sake of its scholarships, and fellowships, and canonries and bishoprics !

But I begin to be in earnest, which is very ungentlemanly ; and therefore it is time that I remain (that is, that what in me remains cool and discreet and fit for " good society," should remain), dear Miss Wilkinson, Ever yours truly, S. PALMER.

XVIII. To MISS LOUISA TWINING.

Kensington, October 28, 1858.

DEAR MISS TWINING. . . . . . I forgot to congratulate you on having been able to attend the meeting on Social Science to which you made so valuable a contribution last year. In my humble opinion, Social Science is worth all the other sciences put together, in the largeness of its working ; and indeed it is *the* great preliminary science ; for, to the thousands who are left half-paid and housed like swine, knowledge presents only a lamp which glares upon their own wretchedness.

[1 More's *Life of Sir Thomas More.*—ED.]

But I suppose the avowed principle of Free Trade, " Buy as cheap and sell as dear as you can," must work itself out until the " day of visitation," which an untoward combination of second causes such as the failure of the cotton crop, a bad harvest, a panic, and such like, occurring together, may bring about when least expected, I remain, dear madam, Yours very truly, S. PALMER.

1859

XIX. To THOMAS MORE PALMER.

HASTINGS, *June*, 1859

MY DEAR MORE. A man with no *aliud agere* is, as you say, likely to be a mere animal ; but so far as his worldly interests are concerned, he is often a very efficient animal. I allude to what are called " the plodders who get on."

A first-rate man is one who has taken quite as much pains as the plodder to attain excellence in some one thing, and has done *that* all the better for his general curiosity and varied information. The danger with young men is this, that general knowledge—a superficial smattering of many things is a much easier affair than first-rate excellence in any one thing ; it does not call out those peculiar energies and that discriminating refinement of judgment which can alone arise from a grapple with some one worthy subject.

As to a *livelihood*, concentration is all important. Where there are so many competitors there must be genuine excellence to ensure (D.V.) a slice of the bread and cheese which society deals round to the *workers*. We can work only according to our strength, but so far as that reaches, the great thing is to do our *very best.*

Emerson says, " Genius is patience." [1] Patience and painstaking are indispensable to *high* excellence. When you have the happiness to know any one who is first-rate in his way, you will find him, like Mr. Brown, [now head master of Charterhouse] harping upon " accuracy and elements " " elements and accuracy." This is what gives position in life. More or less of this defines the income and prospects of the scholar—makes the difference between the head master and the usher. There are much higher views of the subject, but I will now close my sermon.

[1 According to Lord Beaconsfield the saying is Buffon's. See *Tancred.*—ED.]

. . . . I am glad to hear you have the Beethoven, and the more so, as it is a work complete in itself. I did not think the microscope scheme bad. I doubt whether even upon the back of "a flea as big as a mastiff," you could hop quite so far as into the invisible world. You will best do that, by watching your heart morally as well as physically. "Keep thy *heart* with all diligence ; for out of it are the issues of life": and alas, alas, of *death* also, the physical again, being a true type of the moral.

But to return. The microscope would have been used comparatively seldom ; the music will (D.V.) very often amuse you. But *do* mind to secure your present great opportunity of being a good classic. It is far too great a thing to be done by halves ; and unfortunately, if we become but half-people, the halves will not become wholes, like those of the polypus.

How grand must be the Gregorian music at All Saints', with such an organ ! Were I young again, I should like to sing in that choir. How happy must Sir Thomas More have felt (laying aside the Chancellor's gown on Saturday) to don the chorister's surplice next day in old Chelsea Church, where, if you remember, we have before now worshipped together. "Blessed are they that dwell in thy house : they will be still praising thee."

In architecture, in music and the other arts, in society, in the different intellectual orders of men, you are now seeing a great variety. When we rise in thought by steps and stages from the trifling to the sublime, we scarcely perceive how far they are asunder ; but put them side by side, and they are like " Pop goes the weasel" on a cracked fiddle compared with the Gregorian choir at All Saints'.

If you come across any one who talks very freely about other people and laughs at them, *do* remember, if only from prudential motives, that to one who has his way to hew through the world such a habit is absolute *suicide*. Such a habit is both hateful and treacherous ; treacherous because the material of ridicule and scandal is often filched from its very victims in the confidence of social intercourse—perhaps under their very roof! While we listen to such tattle we are ourselves, perhaps, furnishing material for amusement at our expense. Nasty things are sometimes done by otherwise very nice people. Hence the danger. We should try to embody in ourselves a portion of each *good* thing we see among our friends, and so, as we roam, collect honey everywhere. The fly, unlike the bee, settles with satisfaction on every little heap of filth and refuse. Sometimes there is a good deal of drollery and even wit mixed up with what is wrong, and that makes it the more dangerous.

. . . . It seems to me, that all the eminent and considerable men have laid up *while young* a large stock of solid knowledge, which they have afterwards embellished by eloquence and fancy. But they had to make their ginger-bread before they could gild it. In light literature, think how much must go to make a book like *The Caxtons.* I do not allude to quotations, but to the texture of the general fabric. You may get your " trimming " from books of reference, but the wool or the silk must be homespun.

If you have time to write a letter of decent length, like the last, I should be glad of it. Incidents and adventures are pleasant. When you have something to tell, and feel that you should like to tell it, here I am.

Let me advise you amidst all you meet with, gay or grave, pleasant or irksome, to remember that there is also RIGHT and WRONG—*never to forget that ;* and that whatever present satisfaction many of the blessings of Providence throw in our way *gratis,* yet, as Mr. Brown quotes to you, " Nil sine *magno* vita labore dedit mortaiibus." I remain, dear More, Your affectionate father, S. PALMER

XX. To Miss Louisa Twining.

6, Douro Place, *December,* 1860.

DEAR MISS TWINING. Allow me to thank you for the pamphlet containing your powerful address on the work-house schools, which surely it is the interest as well as the duty of the guardians to render as effective as possible ; for anything which makes the poorhouse depauperizing must tend to lower the rates. A low view of the subject, but interest is a capital lever when goodness moves it. But when interest is blind as well as cruel, we almost wish for a despotic government which can devise and execute great designs without paltry interference. Would that you were the despot of the Unions for the next three years !

Q

But for the spendthrift war, think what might have been done with the taxes we have been paying through the last half-century. A country rich and unembarrassed, gracious and wise in council might, by massive combinations, make its work-houses and prisons self-supporting, and put them into *real* antagonism with destitution and with crime. A grand educational institute might be open to rich and poor, and the traditional thousands of Oxford be no more incredible.

Instead of this, we have, as the ballad says, "gone to fight the French for king George upon the throne," while matters of highest moment have been stinted and tight—cracked, patched, and cobbled in our treatment of them, for want of largeness of purpose and singleness of purpose, and national funds. Still there is left what, under God, has ever been the main-spring of great movements, *individual energy ;* hampered it is true in a thousand ways, harassed by opposition, or "encumbered by help," yet finally victorious.

The world's true heroes have fought after a strange fashion ; battering their way through difficulties with the very chains that bound them. I think your Cause is the more noble because it is not ambitious. It aims at no romantic results, and presents no theatrical contrasts. It has its dealings with those who are not "reckoned among the nations" ; it soothes the dying beds of those who have long been dead to society. Yet perhaps from these very schools that you are labouring to reform there may arise *through that reform,* some great and good man, in himself alone (could you look into futurity), an ample reward for anything you may do or suffer. And if not, is it nothing to "turn many to justice" ?—the direct result of a plain, practical, Christian education. From one who is *doing* so much for children, it is instructive to hear A FEW WORDS about them.

While ladies say that they can't trust their servants with their keys, we see that they *can* trust them with their *children :* trust them at the most impressible age to take their shape and bent of mind and soul from hirelings ! What then is the momentous business that can drag the mother from those dearest hours of her life, *her mornings with her children ?* No business at all ! *You* have answered the question. It is the hatred of conscientious painstaking in which and through which alone comes the delight of duty. The well is deep and the wheel is heavy which fetches up the living

waters of comfort. Even the sea-monsters draw forth nourishment
to their young ; but where are these genteel mothers of ours—what
are they about in these precious morning hours, with the bodies and
souls of four or five children in the hands of the young lady from
whom they lock their tea-caddy ? Not *surely* making morning
calls, or sight-seeing, or busy with the last new novel ! One of the
old-fashioned nurses was worth a hundred of *such* mothers. To
my dear nurse I owe the first movements of poetic impulse. Well
do I remember, while the long shadows of moonlight were stealing
over an ancient room, her repeating from Dr. Young :—

> " Fond man, the vision of a moment made,
> Dream of a dream, and shadow of a shade ! "

Often do I read in her well-handled but clean-kept Milton, given
me on her death-bed.

When a man tends upward, he moves towards the cherubic
state, that of hallowed intelligence. A woman moves, I really
believe, towards something still higher—seraphic love. When they
tend downwards, the man falls towards brutality, the woman towards
trumpery. Toys and trumpery, filigree and finery, with an insufferable dash of morbid sentimentalism, make an odious compound,
for which indeed the poor children might profitably exchange the
honest ministration of one of those old-fashioned nurses.

Do write a companion little book called *The Mother's Morning :
or Self-denial rewarded.*

I do not believe there is any solid, enduring pleasure which
does not walk hand in hand with self-denial. Nay more ; we may
say that the peculiar pleasures of any duty or study—that its
deepest, highest joys can be tasted only in conflict with its sorest
difficulties. So, in the work of early education ; but then it may
plausibly be said, how few mothers will be sufficient for these
things! Not so however, for it seems that, besides the general
measure of mental power, the Almighty has added an instinctive
sagacity for the fulfilment of natural duties ; and I think we see
this in the mother very strongly, when not perverted by folly. It
is her patience and tenderness in the first reading lessons which
make the sight of a book pleasant to a little child. Led by the
mother's hand, Wisdom's ways are ways of pleasantness. Not
so when a crinolined nurse, installed as pedagogue, shouts out,
drowning the nursery roar—" Now master 'Gustus, I've called you

twenty times to come and say your task, and I'm blest if I don't tell your 'Pa when he comes home, and no mistake about it!"

This is our early education!

We think ourselves civilized!

Perhaps we may happen to have heard of *another* civilized nation where all who could afford it kept in the house a master of morals and manners, who was the children's companion everywhere who took them to and from the public school, and taught, or strove to teach them *justia*.

These were Pagans. We call ourselves Christians!

Pray forgive all this garrulity. From a favourite subject or a sore subject it is difficult to abstain, and education with me is both.

If these loose, hasty words move you to write a little book, I shall not have been foolish in vain.

I see it as in a vision—the good mother in her nursery; the good mother *walking out* with her children : a whole bevy of nurses and under-nurses if she please, but still the mother there.

And now, out of breath as I am with my own cackling, believe me, dear Madam, Yours most truly, S. PALMER.

1861

XXI. TO MR. JOHN REED.

[KENSINGTON.]

MY DEAR REED. . . . . I must make a sudden transition to the house subject. The soil is all right, but DO make thorough research as to the drainage, upon which the health of every member of a family depends. . . . . Next to process in connection with colouring, drainage seems to me the most intricate, endless difficulty ; because builders go by receipt and don't master the principles of the unsavoury, or I should rather say, most savoury and sanitary science.

And now let me, ere I forget to write what I certainly do not forget to desire, wish you and yours, so far as domestic trials will permit, a merry Christmas and most happy new year ; as happy as any of us can find it in their hearts to be, forming part of the . . . grand climacteric of a great country, and elbowed as we are on the one side by exuberant wealth, and on the other by ghastly destitution. Which state of things, Lord Bacon tells us, has betokened the ruin of great nations. We go to the clever ones and they are at fault. Those who are knowing in everything but human nature may possibly be so far deluded as to expect a panacea through universal education. It is indeed a delightful dream, and the resources which knowledge opens up tend to keep people out of mischief as to their general habits, but to make them the more powerful for mischief when so disposed. Take the present London as it is ; assure to the children and descendants of every unit of those millions a good, plain education at least. Well, no doubt the boon would be inestimable ; but would it create a pure, peaceful, self-denying, charitable future? Are not the most educated people the farthest removed from each other in opinions and belief. Are not thousands of the best educated people back-bone protestants, and hundreds of the same Vatican papists ? Or, I might say, thousands ; for whereas the thinly scattered ruins of our old monasteries were, fifty years ago, visited principally perhaps for their beauty, but also as curiosities and something outlandish and obsolete, there are now it is said one hundred monasteries, or such like institutions in this our protestant England.

Well! But if education can't make people agree, does not it make them tolerant and loving? Give them a month's provisions, and shut up Dr. Manning and Lord Shaftesbury in a lonely tower, and see!

Milton and Locke were well educated, and far advanced as any of ourselves in the love of civil liberty, and yet both of them taught that the Roman Catholic worship should be prohibited. If then education will not make men either think alike or tolerate each other's disagreement, whence are we to expect the final victory over physical or moral evil—the everlasting kingdom of light, and grace, and love ? How will it be inaugurated ? Probably when He who rules and actuates matter as well as spirit permits some disruption beneath the sea, letting its waters into one of those vast volcanic regions which extend thousands of miles, and lie beneath the sea. Then the steam, suddenly generated, will blow everything to pieces that lies above it ; and as to devouring fire, every one knows that it has as it were honey-combed the under surface, and is only restrained till He shall say the word in mercy, that out of the ruins and ashes of these sinful and incurable ages, He may create a new earth, wherein dwelleth righteousness.

Any apathy we find concerning our blessed Lord's second coming is, I think, little to be wondered at. Why should modern Christians who are well-to-do in the world, and take pains to make themselves comfortable, like to be disturbed ? The old Heavens and earth have done well enough for them ; and though the whole creation *does* groan in pain together until now, they will feed *their* poodles upon chicken, and give away some blankets at Christmas !

Believe me, with kindest regards to Mrs. Reed, and kisses to the dear little ones. Ever yours affectionately, S. PALMER.

XXII. TO MR. EDWARD CALVERT.

AT JAMES LINNELL'S, ESQ., RED HILL, SURREY, *July* 11, 1861.

MY DEAR CALVERT. As you are the *first* of my friends whom I sit down to make partaker of my sorrow, I will not wait for black-edged paper, which is sent for.

You I take first, for you were first in kindness when dear little Mary was called away, and your *kind, kind* heart will be wrung to hear that at our lodging at High Ashes, near Dorking, on Leith Hill, my darling Thomas More left us at a quarter to six. It was effusion of blood on the brain.

I can write no more, dear Mr. and Mrs. Calvert, and do not know where I shall be for the next few days. Broken-hearted, I remain Your old, old friend, S. PALMER.

My poor wife is at High Ashes, where the dear fellow died.

XXIII. TO MRS. GEORGE.

[REIGATE], *November* 2, 1861.

DEAR MRS. GEORGE. To-day the first snow has fallen upon *our* dear boy's grave !

Is it not a comfort to find that his numerous manuscripts, and the contents of his private desk meant for no eye to see, are as unsullied as that driven snow ?

Yes ! he will lie to-night under his new winter shroud.

He whom his mother cherished so from his earliest infancy

with every forethought and device of devoted tenderness, to see
him always fed with the best, and clothed with the warmest, has
left our fire-side where he should be sitting now, musing with
poetic ear on the westerly wind which is moaning to me, as I
write, direct from Abinger. But it has passed over his grave, and
seems to invite me thither, and to sing to me that we shall not
very long be parted !

There is no sensation in the grave, so it is a foolish fancy ; but
I have always felt it so very sad that, while *we* are warm by our
winter fire-side, those precious limbs, mouldering though they be, of
our lost dear ones should be far away from us, unhoused and in
the damp, cold earth, under the wind, and rain, and frost. Thrice
happy those to whom the grave is a golden gate, and who *know*
that " though worms destroy this body," yet in their flesh they
shall see God. . . . But what am I writing ? the snow has set me
off, for " I cannot choose but weep, to think they should lay him i'
the cold ground." Believe me, Affectionately yours, S. PALMER.

XXIV. TO MRS. ALEXANDER GILCHRIST.

PARK LANE, REIGATE, *December* 9, 1861.

DEAR MRS. GILCHRIST. The dreadful truth which was gradually
broken to me, I knew in full on Saturday. My Sunday will not
easily be forgotten.

Any expressions of sympathy must be inadequate—any of
consolation premature ; and so utterly taken by surprise, so shocked
and stunned as I have been by these dreadful tidings, what can
I say which will not be incoherent and distressing ?

Yet *can* I be quite silent ? *I* can feel some small comfort, while
grieving over your sorrow, from knowing that *all* the future of
your life *must* be more bearable than the present time, for life's
worst calamity is passed nor can I forget that it places you in a
new, a peculiar, and very near relationship to our Heavenly
Father, who has declared himself specially, " the God of the
Fatherless and the Widow."

Poor broken reed that I have been under my own sorrow, who
am I that I should essay to staunch a bleeding heart ? I will not
attempt it, nor farther profane the sacredness of your grief.

Pray do not write, for it opens the wounds afresh, unless we can in any way comfort you.

Ere the worst was told me, I thought I ought to come to you and tender my help in nursing our dear, kind friend, but was so poorly and shattered as to be quite unable to leave home.

I have just recovered from my own dreadful sorrow sufficiently to see what these things should teach, and for what ineffable blessedness they are meant to prepare us. They empty us of what is most dear on earth, that we may "be filled with all the fulness of God."

Mysterious indeed are the permissions of Providence, and we may say with the Prophet, "Verily thou art a God that *hidest thyself.*" Lying still in His hand, may we say also with the Psalmist, "My flesh and my heart faileth : but God is the strength of my heart, and my portion for ever."

Believe me, dear Mrs. Gilchrist, Your grieved and affectionate friend, S. PALMER.

1862

XXV. To Mrs. George.

[REIGATE], *March* 10, 1862.

DEAR FRIEND. Worthless otherwise than as a curiosity, behold the handwriting of a real hermit. I always honoured solitude, and it is grateful. My dear, kind books gather round me in the evening, and in their sweet society I am as little miserable as one can be who, in this world, must never more be happy.

We English people feel the domestic instinct at tea-time very much, and would fain *then* see the family circle complete. The magic chain is broken ! Well, the remaining links ? They are away ; so I set a chair for " Trot ": up jumps poor puss, and between us we make a segment of a circle, at all events. Even the dumb creatures have gratitude and love in their measure, and the time will come when we shall know that the sagacity which finds a new planet is less essential to the perfection of our nature than gratitude and love. " Trot," like her betters, has a pair of eyes—an eye of love and an eye to the milk-jug. Like her betters, she purrs *for* her milk—*unlike* many of them, she purrs *afterwards.*

Yes, our family circles and our friendly circles get broken, and

like the poor spider, we hasten to mend the broken web. But the
spider beats us at this kind of work ; it is poor cobbling with us,
after all. *My* gallant barque has foundered, and *now*, like the
hunted witch, I

> " Sail in an egg-shell, make a straw my mast
> A cobweb all my coil."

This is our state. These are our *Facts*, as old familiar friends and
some dearer than friends fall off—all our coil a cobweb !

Then comes the voice from Heaven, bidding us open our
eyes and see, and stretch out our hands and *grasp* the ANCHOR
OF THE SOUL. . . . . Believe me, Affectionately yours,
S. PALMER.

XXVI. To MISS WILKINSON.

FURZE HILL HOUSE, *May 29th*, 1862.

DEAR MISS WILKINSON. Jacob told Pharaoh that his days
had been evil although Joseph was found. What must mine be
now ? Perhaps in mercy they may be made few ; therefore let my
words be few, and if possible useful to others—that is, in a very
humble way ; for aspirations, and poetic dreams, and even the
decent, moderate hope that a son might make amends for a father's
shortcomings, are no more. Still, I may perhaps not be wholly
useless if I can circulate little cookery receipts, or any—the most
insignificant hints which may help oil the creaking wheels of our
bodily life—hints jerked out in defiance of all style, or connection,
or elegance. Nay, as David said to his most decorous wife, " I will
be yet more vile," and at once suggest a *FLEAFUGE* (no useless
matter in Spain or Italy) in the shape of a great lump of camphor.
Any one who thinks it indelicate to say or write FLEA, on due
occasion, deserves to be most soundly bitten. Mosquitoes, I read,
may be banished by burning pieces of camphor the size of
a hazel-nut. Would that we had known it at Pompeii. I grieve to
think that you have again felt that difficulty of breathing. When
accompanied by obstruction in the throat, a few whiffs of tobacco
are sometimes most efficacious, not in the coarse shape of a cigar.
putting tobacco into the mouth. but through the rational and
refined medium of a CLAY PIPE. Clay is injurious to the lips,
therefore take a little thin paper, and gum it round the mouth end—
or, to be perfectly elegant, the oral end of the pipe.

I read with much interest and, I trust, not without improvement, your remarks on certain advantages which render advancing
years less depressing ; but here I have a sad advantage of you,
taking comfort in their very fewness. I hope and believe it will be
otherwise with you, when you have attained to my years ; though
before I was stricken down we had *then* this in common, not to be
without affliction ; and this, in moderate measure, is an essential
blessing. What a repulsive creature is a man who has had it all
his own way !—A creature without sense of social duty, who lives
to make himself comfortable. Men have puzzled themselves for
such a definition of their species as should clearly separate the
inferior species. I will not attempt a definition, but hazard
this. *A brute does what is pleasant, a man does what is right.*
No definition can be hammered out of this, for unfortunately
there are thousands of two-legged brutes, and very good-natured
ones too, who live for the very purpose of doing what is
pleasant. I think *all*, rich and poor, should work—do something
useful, five hours a day at least. I am *obliged* to work, for I dare
not leave leisure for such a grief as mine. There is a time for
prayer and a time for sleep ; every other *moment* I am obliged to
snatch from the monopoly of grief. But seeing the face of a
friend does us much good ; and we seem for the moment cheerful
and merry, so that if we had the pleasure of seeing you here, I do
not think we should make you gloomy. Matter for sketching
abounds, even from the windows, and they say the sea air may be
smelt as it sweeps hither uninterrupted from the Brighton downs
which bound our horizon.[1]

I am very glad to hear about your three drawings ; and, so far
as finished drawings are concerned, quite agree with you that they
cannot be too much finished, or rather let us say they cannot be
too much *studied ;* for the word finish has come to have an evil
meaning, such as the attempting to paint what nobody ever saw,
every leaf on a tree—such as the drawing attention to the genera
and species of vegetation in the foreground of a landscape, which
no one strongly impressed with a beautiful scene would so much

[1] In his occasional recommendations of the neighbourhood near Furze Hill to his
friends, my father may appear to have forgotten his old emphatic preferences. This was
far from being the case. His ideal of scenery was not to be found at or near Red Hill,
though it was approached, perhaps, by some of the exquisite country on the western
borders of Surrey.—ED.]

as notice. The art is, while thoroughly *knowing* the species, to render them truly, lest the eye *should* be attracted by them through fallacious drawing or colour—to give the lesser truth of their own identity, governed by the greater truth of their relation and subordination to the whole. No right line sufficiently extended can pass through the centre of a sphere without touching two points of polar opposition. Art is such a sphere. The best artist, in some two points of his work, will give the extremes of the definite and the indefinite if he can, and the lesser intensities of both elsewhere. When, where, and how is a life's study, to be helped by carrying in the pocket something like Reynolds's blot book. "The indefinite half is the more difficult of the two," as Millais said to me when we were looking at the Turner Gallery. I never looked at the slight sediment at the bottom of a coffee-cup without getting a lesson. When I think of a pocket sketch-book of soft printer's paper (plate-paper), a piece of charcoal, or very soft chalk, and a finger to blend it about, I think of improvement—mastery. Towards the art of giving a completed look to work, nothing helps more, I think, than the principle of emphasis and gradation (like a comet) in the relief of masses ; and, if you can, in every touch. This, with the polar quality of massive opposition, distinguished Titian.

You doubt whether hasty sketches are of any use for improving yourself. Quite agreeing with you as to what are usually called hasty sketches, allow me to suggest that the art of completed work is twofold. First the art of imitating what is before us with all its detail (I am speaking of pictures done out of doors), which imitation represents nature asleep ; and secondly the knowledge of the phenomena. These bring it to life. The latter can be treasured up only by continual observation, and a little memorandum-book and pencil carried always in the pocket. Often, the sketches *must* be rapid, as the effect is momentary. Thus alone can the action of moving figures be caught ; and the action and expression are almost everything. They are best caught by single lines ; [sketch] then you can by the side of the line go on from recollection, and then a little larger, with the light and shade, and writing the colours of the draperies. At home you can draw it about three inches high, unclothed, making use of an anatomical book or casts, till the main masses are right, and proceed to lay on the drapery.

[Sketch.] Of course the figure being draped in nature, you sketch it so but the lines of the limbs and body are the great things if you can get nothing else. At home, when you design a figure for introduction into your subject, after the first blot you should draw it faintly, undraped, so as really to know what the action is, and then add the dress. A little figure study always going on is of golden use to the painter of landscape or architecture, and gives an increased value, artistic and pecuniary.

Mr. Newman made me eight or ten of his cedar colour-boxes without partitions, and a little deeper than usual, in which I possess a fine sculpture-gallery, having filled them with casts from the finest antique gems. These are most useful for reference, when working out lines caught from nature. I assure you there is nothing far-fetched in this. All the best landscape-painters have studied figures a great deal. Mr. Rogers used to prize a Claude of his the more because the figure was painted by Claude himself. I would advise you to collect casts from the best antique gems whenever you can get them. The enamelled roundness of a well-modelled figure is invaluable as a foreground. To tell you all that is in my heart, I believe the two great parts of art to be SENTIMENT and STRUCTURE. Under structure, beginning with human anatomy, I include all the organizations and atmospheric or other visible phenomena of this material world about us. If you say, "Who is sufficient for these things?" I can answer only with a groan. But we must do our best, at all events apportioning our effort according to priority of claim securing what is most important first), and when we do not see what to do—doing *nothing* till we have *found out* what is to be done. *Writing* our difficulties; which writing compels us to think clearly of them, during which effort they will often vanish. Abhorring "muddle"—abhorring half work, and preferring play; not working on after the attention is fatigued; keeping by us a lump of tangled string as a visible representation of "muddle," and stamping upon it every morning directly we put our shoes on. We *may* hate and stamp upon "muddle," because it is not a living being. It is the negative pole of sin; and the Psalmist exhorts those who love the Lord to "hate the thing which is evil." I do not *hate* the Devil, though I fear him and hate his *doings*, but I *do* hate muddle, hurry, indecision of purpose.

Pray beware of sun-strokes. Pray do not work too long together. Pray do not over-tire yourself, but avoid triflers and morning callers, and take plenty of REST and SLEEP. Believe me, dear Miss Wilkinson, Yours most truly, S. PALMER.

XXVII. To MR. C. W. COPE.

FURZE HILL HOUSE, *Dawn of June,* 1862.

MY DEAR COPE. The sun has not yet risen upon the earth, but unable to sleep, and thinking of my poor boy, I begin the day's work by assuring you that though *my* lamp is "put out in obscure darkness," I am not so envious as to be insensible to the happiness of others, but very heartily congratulate you on your dear wife's safe passage through her hour of trial, and on the birth of another son. You must have been very glad of this, and will have reason indeed for thankfulness if he grow up to resemble his brother, whose progress at Oxford I sometimes picture to myself, and seem to see him busy over his books in that snug, quaintly-angled room he sketched for me from memory.

For me, the few dark months or years which may remain are the more distressing, as the work of a profession leaves so little time for doing good—positive good to others. Perhaps, however, I may do some good to *you,* if I can prevail upon you to come and see a tract of land close by, where ground is yet to be bought. It is not so high as to be bleak, yet commands a panorama : the soil is sand, and it is reckoned as healthy a spot as is, or can be. If the artists knew of it, it would soon be gone : and a little money invested there would be merely secured from the pockets of the doctors. It is a plateau on the top of the sand hill close to Cockshot Mill—not half an hour's walk for *you* from Reigate Station, whence it will soon be less than an hour from Charing Cross. There are plenty of trees about, but it is just so lifted up above them as to be perfectly dry, and open to the freest circulation of some of the finest air in England. It is quite away from the dismal sentiment of Red Hill, and close to the miniature Devonshire dells of Lord Somers' Park. Altogether, there is a continuous two miles run for the children along the hill-top. Those who do not take snuff say they can smell the sea air which sweeps without impediment from Brighton. Indeed, as James Linnell was saying the other day, you may travel about England for hundreds of miles without finding such a site for building. The ground is dear, yet cheap for the situation, £400 an acre (so I was told: it may be less): now half an acre is sufficient, and what a boon you would be conferring on your children if you were to build a small house just to run down to yourself, and to send them down to when out of sorts, or better, before they become so. I should think it the very place for your dear Emily, because of the dryness of soil, and sweet, genial quality of air, without *any approach to bleakness*. By building on a plan which allows for additions afterwards, you might have a house large enough to begin with, and a painting-room of the right kind (glass at top, and windows all round, closeable by shutters at pleasure), for five or six hundred pounds, and the value of the property would be sure to increase, for it is the only perfectly healthy tract yet unenclosed. It is secluded too, not haunted like Hastings with open-air novel readers. You will think I have studied under Mr. Robins, though I have abstained from his crowning attraction, the "hanging wood," which happily is unknown here.

Contrast this with the frightful environs of Wimbledon, Hounslow, and the damp, reeking "*Thames scenery*"! where you can't get along the towing-paths without treading into dead dogs; and remember that things are not likely to be flattered or seen all rose colour, by Yours affectionately, THE MOST UNHAPPY OF MEN.

P.S. I admire your ground-plan, which gives very picturesque angles. I have heard that the roof is great part of the expense of a house, so perhaps the cheapest way would be to let the first part built be under one simple roof, to which a corresponding piece might be added afterwards.

A friend of mine, a clergyman, built himself a house here (i.e. Hakewell designed it for him), which is extremely pleasing. The plan is one long passage, with the large rooms on one side, and the smaller on the other. [plan] * is the drawing-room. I do not mean a room for drawing in, but a primitive, apostolic, protestant drawing-room for the female apostle and "young ladies," and some very handsome "devotional chairs," a grand piano and other appliances tending to our English ideal of "Piety without asceticism," "Rational piety" &c. &c. This is not intended to refer personally to my friend's house, or any living clergyman's; in fact it is far too humble to adumbrate the splendour of the palatial mansions of many of the clergy. We English are *such* a sensible people—so little given to fanaticism! We know "where to stop" with a vengeance ! ! ! !

Every clergyman should have Butler's *Lives of the Saints*. O ! that such of the clergy as choose to deny themselves the whole of ecclesiastical history between the Apostolic age and Luther, would at least read Southey's life of Wesley ; just to see what curious things a man does who is thoroughly in earnest. Of course Southey dummyfies the rich points, and comes in like spoonfuls of nauseous soda in a lemon pudding ; but still we can get at Wesley through Southey. He (Wesley) was a real fanatic, like the glorious men of all ages. On looking into the derivation of fanatic, I find it ought to have a good meaning so far, rather than a bad. For a real, wild treat, read St. Athanasius's life of St. Anthony.

XXVIII. To Mr. C. W. Cope.

Furze Hill House, *June* 21, 1862.

MY DEAR COPE. I have twice looked at the land since writing to you, and think that if on the whole it is probable that you may build some day a place to run down to, and send detachments of your family, then you had better just look at this at all events. . . . . There is a particular *corner* close to Cockshot windmill yet for sale, which is most tempting. It is just the highest point, and I don't think others could build out any part of your view, which is a complete panorama. I am speaking as to health, for I don't much believe in scenery—that is, short of Baiæ or the sides of Monte St. Angelo. Yet hold !—these eyes, ignorant as they are, alas, never see a cast of the Belvidere Torso without revelling in that universe of hill and dale. Bracing walks too, the mind may take among the bold acclivities of the Hercules Farnese, hated by muffs. But I wander ; no uncommon thing now.

Pray don't think I am enamoured of a country life, or of life at all. (O ! far, *how* far from it !) or that this has *anything whatever* to do with my recommendation of Cockshot Hill. . . .

Think not I am enamoured of Surrey. In this county I began

my life, now seared and withered in its autumn. Keeping near the rail, I have looked for a dwelling almost through the whole length of the county, and know of no eligible spot but this. Guildford I explored : it is in every way a failure, and land £800 per acre.

There is one other consideration I would mention, but I just know and *love* the figure art so much as to speak with the utmost deference to one of its ablest living masters. I therefore spiritually roll myself in the sand, and rising all besmirched begin. Our *historical* painters have hitherto painted wholly from London models, and generally in the London atmosphere. Now I have for years been haunted by the vision of the pictures which I think they might produce by the use of country complexions in country light. When I say *they*, I mean only historical painters like yourself who, unlike the mere rustic figure-painters, would know what to choose and what to reject. I have often said to myself when I have seen the glorious complexions of the " Sun-burnt sicklemen of August "[1] (see *The Tempest* for a fine subject), and the delicious palpitations of bloom beneath sunny and sun-burnt glow, in country girls—how is it that, in their choice of models, the very artists who live to embody ideal beauty, *can* confine themselves to London skins ? With all my blindness, I do yet see within, something which none but a high-class figure-painter could *do ;* and which *done* would, or ought, in a lower view of the subject, to fetch a guinea per square quarter of an inch. My impudence now has had its swing and is ended, and I shrink into my own wretchedness ; and how deep that is, can be known only by Yours affectionately, S. PALMER.

Only think of Rebecca at the well, glowing in the sunset, with ripe, ruddy arms, and the Homeric elbows, and then of the *London Ladies* bleached by the dissipations of midnight parties !

XXIX. To Mrs. Alexander Gilchrist.

FURZE HILL HOUSE, *June* 27, 1862.

DEAR MRS. GILCHRIST. We are fellow sufferers. All yesterday morning I was trying to see my work through my tears. But of those matters by and by.

Directly I got your letter I sallied forth to try and borrow a

[1 " You sunburnt sicklemen, of August weary," is Shakespeare's expression.—ED.]

copy of the book for a couple of days, but as my request was in-
effectual, I had nothing for it but to sit down then and there and
make scribbles, intelligible only to myself, of all the designs, insert-
ing however, the first and last words of each illustrated page in
hope that you have by you a duplicate copy of the text, in which
case, if you will forward it by post, I will try to find out what the
designs mean, and perhaps can then furnish some brief description of the said designs, which, if I can describe them at all, I will
describe immediately.

My wife sends her kindest love and sympathy.

This world and its connection with the spiritual world is an intense mystery, so there is a strong *primâ facie* probability that a
beneficent Creator would give us some *clue.* When I am tormented
with doubts I ask myself where shall I get a clue if not in the
Gospel of Jesus ; I mean the written Bible understood according
to the grammatical meaning, which is what we endeavour to get
out of any other book. Had men ever a better clue ? Could any
one devise and invent a better ? Now a clue, by the very meaning
of the word, is not a thorough explanation, nor like a mathematical
demonstration, nor is such a thing possible in the present state of our
faculties. *Touching* are those words of our Lord. " Thomas, because thou hast seen me thou hast believed : *blessed are they that
have not seen, and yet have believed.*" This is our legacy—the blessing upon believing the unseen. And those who do so our Lord
will suffer, more effectually than Thomas, to touch his wounded
side and be healed. . . .

Admirable, I think Mr. Rossetti's verse. I have only just
begun, owing to bustle. What an admirable man Rossetti must
be ! Yours ever most truly, S. PALMER.

It is growing late, but as I know it is a serious thing to stop the
press, I send you the following very meagre catalogue from memory.
As I have not the letter-press to refer to, I must speak of the
designs independently. If this will do, it will save you the trouble
of sending me the letter-press ; indeed, Blake's letter-press, sometimes, does not illustrate the designs at all.

The Marriage of Heaven and Hell is a little book, the pages
within a fraction of six inches by four. All the pages are illuminated. The letters, in the copy I saw, were red for the most part.
The words of the title-page are surmounted by a strip of land,

R

bearing on each side scant and baleful trees, little else than stem
and spray. Drawn on a tiny scale, lies a corpse, and one bends
over it. Flames burst forth below, and slant upward across the
page, gorgeous with every hue. In their very core, two spirits rush
together and embrace. In the second design, to the right of the
type, there runs up an almost leafless tree. A woman clinging to
the thin stem, and holding by a branch, reaches its only cluster to
a man standing below. Distant are two figures, fallen I think, and
writhing on the ground. At the top of the third [design], a woman
rushes forward, pursued by devouring flame Beneath, lies a slain man.
Two murderers are rushing away. In the next, the sun sets over the
sea in blood. A spirit struggles and plunges. Another, in the midst
of fire, would fain rush to her, but an iron link clenches her ankle
to the rock. The fifth [design] resembles the catastrophe of Phaëton,
save that there is but one horse. Spines of flame are already kind-
ling below. Below the text of the sixth, an accusing demon with
bat-like wings points fiercely to a scroll—a great parchment scroll
across his knees. A spirit sits on each side recording. In the next
design, we have a little island of the sea, where an infant springs to
its mother's bosom. From the birth-cleft ground, a spirit has half
emerged. Below, with outstretched arms and hoary beard, an awful,
ancient man rushes *at* you, as it were, out of the page. At the top
of the 14th page, a spirit with streaming locks stretches his arms
across it—the arms extended, and pointing hither and thither. She
hovers, poising, over a corpse looking as if laid out—the arms
straight by the sides ; helpless ; uncoffined ; and flames rolling
onward to consume it. The ninth design is of an eagle gazing upwards, flapping her wings. Her talons gripe a long snake trailing
and writhing. Both are flecked with gold, and coruscate as from a
light within. The tenth gives us giants, as the text would suggest,
but the Ugolino story as it would seem, were it not for two extraneous
figures. The next is a surging mass of mingled fire, water, and
blood, wherein roll the volumes of a huge double-fanged serpent,
his crest erect, his jaws wide open. In the twelfth, the disembodied
spirit, luminous and radiant, sits lightly upon its late prison-house,
gazing upwards, whither it is about to soar. It is the same figure
as that in Blair's *Grave*, where you see also the natural body bent
with years, tottering into the dark doorway beneath. The
thirteenth and last design gives Blake's idea of Nebuchadnezzar in

the wilderness. I have very old German translations of Cicero and Petrarch, in which, among some wild and original designs, almost the very same figure appears. Many years had elapsed after making his own design, before Blake saw the woodcut.

The copy I saw was highly finished. Blake had worked so much and illuminated so richly, that even the type seemed as if done by hand.

The ever-fluctuating colour; the spectral pigmies rolling, flying, leaping among the letters; the ripe bloom of quiet corners; the living light and bursts of flame; the spires and tongues of fire, vibrating with the full prism, made the page seem to move and quiver within its boundaries; and you lay the book down tenderly, as if you had been handling something which was alive. As a picture has been said to be something between a thing and a thought, so, in some of these type books over which Blake had long brooded with his brooding of fire, the very paper seems to come to life as you gaze upon it—not with a mortal, but an indestructible life, whether for good or evil.

XXX. To MRS. ALEXANDER GILCHRIST.

FURZE HILL HOUSE, *July* 2, 1862.

MY DEAR MRS. GILCHRIST. Mrs. Palmer has looked at the original work and finds that the doubtful word is "Genius"— "Thou seest a portion of genius lift up thy head." I think there must have been a colon after "Genius," but Blake's punctuation and spelling always wanted watching, so it does not do to trust to hasty transcription in the copy which goes to press.

I have delayed the MS. for a day, as you wished me to look at the text, and as I am finishing works *against time*, it is with the greatest difficulty that I can snatch, or rather tear time to write; but such very grave suggestions arise in reading *The Proverbs of Hell* that I felt it a *duty* to give you my opinion about the matter, though I assure you I do not rate that opinion highly on this, or any other point. I shall give it you simply and plainly in the rough. Don't think me arrogant, but just simply expressing what strikes me, like a child for the first time in Madame Tussaud's "Chamber of Horrors."

But before I begin, just let me say that I have no wish to claim as my own the few paragraphs describing the designs. They are quite at your service, in any way you like. I am only very glad that, done under such fearful disadvantage, without the originals to ruminate over, you think they will do.

Now then!

Imprimis, what follows has no relation to my own opinions and belief, but I speak of what I think will be the prudential proceeding relative to the public, and *reviewers*.

Life is uncertain, and lest I die before I have time to say it, I will say *at once* that I think the whole page at the top of which I have made a cross in red chalk would at once exclude the work from every drawing-room table in England. Blake has said the same kind of thing to me; in fact almost everything contained in the book; and *I* can understand it in relation to my memory of the whole man, in a way quite different to that roaring lion the "press," or that led lion the British Public.

Blake wrote often in anger and rhetorically; just as we might speak if some *pretender* to Christianity whom we knew to be hypocritical, were *canting* to us in a pharisaical way. We might say, "If this is your Heaven, give me Hell." We might say this in temper, but without in the least meaning that that was our deliberate preference.

This is the clue to much of Blake's paradox, and often it carries its own explanation with it. Where it does not, without presumptuously recommending you what to do, I will just say what course *I* should think best. I should let no passage appear in which the word Bible, or those of the persons of the blessed Trinity, or the Messiah were irreverently connected. . . . . I should simply put * * * s; and in case of omitting a page or chapter, simply say "The ——th Chapter is omitted." This sometimes gives zest—a twinge of pleasant curiosity to the reader, the more attentive through not having the whole. I should state where complete copies could be consulted, I suppose the British Museum. Thus I should be guilty of no injustice to Blake, nor would I ever omit without asterisks; for it is not just to any author, living or dead, to join clauses when *he* has words intervening.

Now I have nearly done, but this one thing more occurs to me, that I think it would explain matters somewhat if the public knew that Blake sometimes wrote under irritation. Nothing would explain some things in the MS. Being irritated by the exclusively scientific talk at a friend's house, which talk had turned on the vastness of space, he cried out, "It is false. I walked the other evening to the end of the earth, and touched the sky with my finger."

In his quiet moments, he made the devil on the heath say what he (Blake) hated, and the angel among the hay-cocks, what he (Blake) loved.

His real views would now be considered extravagant on the opposite side to that apparently taken in the *Marriage*, for he quite held forth one day to me, on the Roman Catholic Church being the only one which taught the forgiveness of sins ; and he repeatedly expressed his belief that there was more *civil* liberty under the Papal government, than any other sovereignty; nor did I ever hear him express any admiration for the American republic.

Everything connected with Gothic art and churches, and their builders, was a *passion* with him. St. Teresa was his delight.

If madness and absurdity be synonyms, which they are not, then Blake would be as "mad as a March hare," for his love for art was so great that he would see nothing *but art* in anything he loved ; and so, as he loved the Apostles and their divine Head (for so I believe he did), he must needs say that they were all artists. You see a touch of this absurdity in his *Marriage*, where he makes the blessed Comforter the spirit of poetic invention. So indeed he is—that is, of the highest poetry like Milton's ; but Oh he is something more ! Else we should all be doomed to learn *The Proverbs of Hell* by heart in their own "printing-house." In the copy I saw, "printing-house" are the only black letters. They are very black. It has a droll and good effect.

If you have that edition without designs, of the *Songs [of Innocence]* published by Wilkinson, it would not be well to paste the type into your copy without looking it over, as I think there is a mistake in the grammar here and there, and if not more correct than Blake's own, there is an obfuscation as to the priority of the e and i in such words as "believe," "receive" &c. There is an ugly mistake in that line, "Where flocks have *took* delight," instead of "ta'en," but perhaps that is Blake's own.

I am sorry to write in such an off-hand, impudent way. It is almost as bad as Blake's naïve mention of Isaiah and Ezekiel dining with him! But it is near midnight, and I have had a hard day's work, and there was no choice but to write off-hand or not at all.

At any other time but a time of such bustle, I should have felt much at seeing your dear husband's hand-writing once more ; indeed if I once indulge myself in serious thought I shall sink down. Tears, tears, tears are your portion and mine. It is perhaps well for us that we are so much engaged. He whom you have lost is never out of my thoughts twelve hours together. In one of your letters you speak of the principle of reaction, I think. I could not but believe as I read it that you would find its blessing on the largest scale—reunion in eternity after bereavement in this short, vain life of ours.

Pray give my kindest regards to Mr. Haines, and love to the dear children. I hope Percy will buckle to his Latin grammar *because* he feels it disagreeable and dry, for he must remember that everything he has learned was so at first, and that the value of everything on earth is pretty much in proportion to the difficulty of acquiring it.

"Taking pains," *means* taking pains—putting oneself to pain in the first act of application, which habit afterwards becomes, in some sense, one of the greatest pleasures. I have always found among my acquaintance, that the more eminent are so just in proportion to their being the more painstaking. What can appear more fluently exuberant than Burke's prose ; yet, after he thought he had quite finished his manuscript, he went on correcting, and sometimes seven successive proof-sheets of a passage witnessed his unwearied pains. Emerson says Genius is Patience. I should be inclined to say, Genius is Accuracy. *Talent* thinks, Genius *sees;* and what organ so accurate as sight. Blake held this strongly. His word was "precision." Believe me, dear Mrs. Gilchrist, Yours ever truly, S. PALMER.

XXXI. To Mrs. Alexander Gilchrist.

Furze Hill House, September, 1862.

My dear Mrs. Gilchrist. . . . . I am *delighted* with the sixty pages, and do not know when I have found so much interesting matter within so small a compass. Your dear husband's charming and eloquent criticism rouses me, weak as I am.

I am glad to see that you have taken such skilful pains with the punctuation, and that the printer has rendered it so carefully, because it tends to the *sine quâ non* of all writing—Perspicuity ; especially in this age, when people read fast as a luxury, and expect to catch the meaning in a moment.

Burke used sometimes to correct to the amount of six or seven proof-sheets, after he thought he had finished, and I have no doubt punctuation was part of the business. Molière was not far out when he made his housemaid the measure of public perception.

I fancy we arrive at the expression of our thoughts something in this way. First by perspicuous vigour, so that, as to *quantity*, the alterations should be very inconsiderable. In the fair copy we mend the manner and mar the sense ; in the third, we unite both. Sometimes afterwards, coming with a fresh eye, we even make the first thought more lucid ; but woe to us if we throw away the first rough draft, which is after all, perhaps, better on the whole than all the intermediate attempts, though inferior to the "last consummate flower." That Shakespeare "never blotted a line," is only one nauseous particle of the mountain of nonsense with which his memory is overlaid.

If this beautiful work have fair play and a large impression, so as to get among all sorts of minds, the name of the dear biographer will never be forgotten. I do hope and believe that you are building him a perpetual monument, and it is this belief, that makes me hazard my impertinences about the quality and consistence of every trowel-full of mortar used in raising it.

This is joyful news—Mr. Rossetti's memoir. If Mr. R. were not so great a master of verse as he is, you would have had his translations back long ere this, but they will very soon be sent. What I should like is this—a beautiful, medallion-like, delicate portrait of your dear husband, immediately under the last lines of Mr. Rossetti's memoir.

No bright thoughts have come to me since my boy left us, but animated by reading the MS., *something did strike me* which may be worthy of consideration—a preface (however short) by Mr. Carlyle. I never saw a *perfect* embodiment of Mr. C.'s *ideal* of a *man in earnest*, but in the person of Blake. And if he were to write only thus much, " This was a good man and true," thousands would be talking of Blake who otherwise would not care two-pence for fifty Blakes put together.

You have, of course, this anecdote about the *Songs of Innocence and Experience*. Wordsworth said to a friend, " I called the other day while you were out, and stole a book out of your library— Blake's *Songs of Innocence*." He read, and read, and took them home to read, and read again. . . . Believe me, dear Mrs. Gilchrist, Yours ever most truly, S. PALMER.

I can't help you about the French, and am glad I can't. W. B. *was* mad about languages. Let me congratulate you on the admirable rendering of the mother's agony in the wood-cut ; also on the beautiful type, and the symmetrical distance between words and lines respectively.

I fancy that, next to the training of one's own children (*I* had *children* once !), the most delightful of all employments is the last correcting of last proof-sheets such as these.

XXXII. TO MISS LAURA RICHMOND.

[RED HILL].

MY DEAR LAURA. In case you should " cut " me when you marry, I " make hay " with my letter writing, " while the sun shines."

If any friends of yours want a large and beautiful house and garden close to a railway station, for three months, here they are. Lady Mostyn wants to let hers for that time. . . .

I have been in London for five days, and hoped to get to see you, but every moment was occupied, and it was impossible.

I was going to say " I think Fuseli's smaller picture (Œdipus) in the International, one of the finest works there," but I correct myself. We have laid aside diffidence nowadays, and drop the " I think." We used to say " Black is black, I think." Now we say "BLACK IS WHITE." We don't *think* it ; we know it ; and you will observe an equal advance in confidence of manner and originality of thought. I will therefore make a few assertions *à la mode.*

1. If the essentials of Art may be comprised in two words, those words are ANATOMY AND SENTIMENT.

2. We must know the construction of whatever we would imitate.

3. Claude was the greatest landscape-painter who ever lived ; and there is a grand picture of his from Sir Culling Eardley's at the British Institution, which enraptured dear Mother Radcliffe : see her journal. The drawing of the trees is sublime. In a smaller picture (Mr. Wynne Ellis's) is a bay, exquisitely painted. There is a long Cuyp, very fine.

4. Mrs. Radcliffe far exceeds Sir Walter Scott in descriptions of scenery.

5. Stories from the classics are peculiarly fit to be painted at the present time. Their connection with an exploded mythology has not in the least impaired their beauty and freshness ; for their freshness, being the freshness of first-rate poetry, is eternal ; and to every man gifted with imagination, they come home at once— fascinate and bind him as with flowery wreaths wet with the morning dew. If you tell such a man that they are obsolete, he will smile at you with a peculiar smile ; for, by the very constitution of his mind, he and they are contemporaneous, and you might as well tell him that beef is obsolete while he is in the act of eating his dinner.

Fancy any one talking this " stuff " to Nicholas Poussin !

6. Classical subjects are peculiarly fit to be painted just now, as a protest against the degraded materialism which is destroying art.

7. Hogs live in the Present ; Poets in the Past ; or with the grace of alliteration—The Past for Poets ; The Present for Pigs. The Present is not.[1]

8. Richardson is one of our best novelists.

[1] The reader may care to pursue the subject in a postscript to a letter written by my father to Mr. F. G. Stephens, in September, 1875. Ed :—

" . . . landscape of any kind is poor work without its persons, polities, and human associations, expressed or understood.

" In Yorkshire scenes, you get your landscape from the past ; and though it is, just now the fashion to say that great geniuses have been distinguished by their sympathy with the then present, I think their works have always synchronized with the past ; though as men

9. Sir Thomas Lawrence found Fuseli in tears, while contemplating the Farnese Hercules.

A test of Taste. Do I love Virgil, the Antique, Michelangelo, Milton, Nicholas Poussin and Claude? Or, more compactly thus, Do I love the Giulio Romano in the National Gallery?

It is easy to make assertions, you see. As a general rule, those who are best qualified make fewest. It is, however, a fact that Lady Mostyn's house is to be had ; at least it was so a few hours ago, when Lady Mostyn told my wife so. . . .

As I live in the deepest dejection of spirits, a letter would refresh me, but I like a long one full of matter. If much engaged, do not write at all. Believe me, dear Laura, Yours affectionately,

                                * * * *

The highest art is what you see in the Belvidere Torso—another assertion—I am getting on, you see !

But what is art, even the highest, compared with the " Cup of cold water given to a disciple in the name of a disciple " ?

Let those who drink water *give* water. Let those who drink claret *give* claret.

Let not those who drink claret give water, lest they should want a little to cool their tongue. This is truth—another assertion. Howard drank water and gave claret. He gave *himself* to those who were " sick and in prison." Read Burke's eulogy. Be often reading Burke. Read the finest treatise extant on political economy, Mr. Ruskin's *Unto This Last.* I wish I had time to learn it by heart. You will find Mr. Ruskin's papers in *The Cornhill Magazine.* . . . .

[The assertions in the above letter are scratched across with pencil, and the following words written. " I am not answerable for what is scratched out." The letter is not signed. - Ed.]

---

and moral agents, it is to be hoped they sympathized with the people about them, and did what good was in their power. A preference for the present as a matter of taste is a pretty sure sign of mediocrity.

"This modern definition of genius would exactly suit dogs and cats, who are eminently remarkable for sympathy with the present—the very present piece of cat's-meat on the skewer ; *that* is *their* preference. But Johnson teaches us that whatever makes the past, the distant, or the future predominate over the present advances us in the ranks of thinking beings. And the best poets and painters appeal to this faculty and instinct within us ; and I do not think that it is either the truth of his colour, or the charm of his trees (unrivalled though they be), or the gold of his sunshine that makes CLAUDE the greatest of landscape-painters ; but that Golden *Age* into which poetic minds are thrown back, on first sight of one of his genuine *Uncleaned* pictures."]

1863

XXXIII. To Mrs. Alexander Gilchrist.

FURZE HILL HOUSE, *January*, 1863.

My DEAR MRS. GILCHRIST. I ventured, on the strength of having your proof-sheets in my hand, to take a little walk *by myself*, and *our* dear Author annihilated space, and gave a short but perfect intermission of sorrow. How vividly has he recalled old times!

Such is my impression again on going through the description very carefully this evening. *The Author and his subject were congenial!*

Alas! Why was I obliged on page 298 to erase "*now and*"? Do let him stand on your pages "that *good* man Mr. Finch," with "good" in italics, for alas! where shall his friends find his fellow? He died just a few months back—my earliest friend!

In him we lost the last representative of the Old School of water-colour landscape-painting. They are all gone now.

This is remarkable, that if, among Blake's deceased friends, we were suddenly asked to point to one without passion or prejudice, with the calmest judgment, with the most equable *balance* of faculties, and those of a very refined order, Finch would probably be the man; and yet he, of all the circle perhaps, was most inclined to believe in Blake's spiritual intercourse. I do not state this as giving myself any opinion on the subject, but simply as a curious fact.

As a man's friends illustrate his own character, and as the dead may freely be spoken of, it occurred to me this evening that perhaps you might like, in a note or otherwise, to insert a short notice of this *very* old friend of Blake; for indeed among Blake's friends, he was one of the MOST REMARKABLE—remarkable for such moral symmetry and beauty, such active kindliness and benevolence as do honour to any profession, and may serve to show the employers of artists that sometimes they themselves might be benefited by the example of such men's lives.

If you like, I could furnish you with a very short testimonial to the virtues of a man whom Blake was honoured in knowing. . . . . Ever faithfully yours, S. PALMER.

XXXIV. To Mr. C. W. Cope.

BOTANY BAY-WINDOWS, *February*, 1863.

MY DEAR COPE. I have just read for the hundredth time, and at a sitting, *Paradise Regained*, perhaps the most perfect poem in the English language. This reminds me that Paradise Lost will be the portion of the ungrateful. Pray, therefore, let me thank you for your kind painstaking about those outlines, and for the invigorating aroma of your letter from the Academy. It was enough of itself to make anyone a pretty firm draughtsman, except such a blighted, palsied, parboiled creature as myself. O! that I had had the human bones broken about my stupid head thirty years ago; for I have come to the conclusion that the whole of Art may be comprised in two words; ANATOMY— SENTIMENT. I mean of course anatomy in the larger sense of Structure, which will include even colour. I should long to take home and anatomize every dead dog in the ditches, were I not myself a dog more dead than they—a creature that cannot rear its whelps, and may howl for them in vain! Jeremy Taylor says we *may* make a noise when we are hurt like this; and Isaiah —"We roar all like bears, and mourn sore like doves." . . . . .

How is an artist to be a Christian if, as Michelangelo said, "Art is jealous and demands the whole man"?

What an interesting little book might be made under the title of CURIOUS QUESTIONS. In the course of my life, now terminating so auspiciously, I have concocted twenty or thirty which I should like to contribute under the title of UNSETTLERS, for I rather think that experience and habits of patient thought will lead us to believe in Christianity as the one only truth, and to be sceptical about everything else whatever. I think Pascal came very nearly to this. *He was* a Christian. He did not keep the cross laid up in lavender, and take it out at prayer-time, and on Sundays to "glory in it," but he "took it *up*," and carried it upon his shoulders.

Many thanks for your kind mention of the Gaspar Poussins, but I think I have several of them—enough for reference. He was not a Giulio Romano or a Bonasoni, but he was a *dear* old fellow nevertheless.

I am given to understand that art in London is progressing with such ample strides that very soon all the old pictures will be going for a old song. If you should be bidding at the National Gallery sale, please bid up to ten pounds for me, for that *Nursing of Jupiter;* very bad I dare say, but it will please a simpleton like me none the less, and dearly should I like to hang it up and have it to look at over my tea. It was painted, they say, about five years ago! . . . . O that Vatican Gallery! I stuck fast on a staircase there, before a Greek female bust, and could neither go up nor down. I suppose I got down, or I should not be here living in this *delightful retirement!*

We are giving our best consideration to the matter mentioned by Mrs. Cope. We hoped to find a really good school (which would be far the best thing for Herbert, and for Harry too, if he were with us), but we can hear of no such thing. There is a small foundation grammar-school—a clergyman the master; but I am given to understand that the blacksmith's son goes there, and the sons of other useful people, and as we are very "genteel" here, our foul English pride snorts at it.

Whatever may be our national virtues, humility is not one of them. A lady at a party asked me in one word to name our great national virtue. I said, without a moment's hesitation, "Cleanliness." Yes! we may look down from the organ-gallery at St. Paul's, Knightsbridge in the London season, and say, "Every one of you has taken a tub this morning!" In what other country could *that* be said? Believe me, Ever yours most truly,
S. PALMER.

XXXV. TO MR. J. C. HOOK.

FURZE HILL HOUSE, *May*, 1863.

MY DEAR HOOK. "Canst thou not minister to a mind diseased?" Yes you can, and you have done so in your most kind and cordial letter.

You cannot "pluck from the memory a rooted sorrow"; but sorrow is soothed when a man is asked to spend some time with the very host and the very friends he would have chosen had he been dreaming out for himself an ideal visit. These are greater attractions than even the Devonshire junket!

And then, to talk about those islands—those wild Atlantic rocks, lashed for ever by long-backed breakers! To enjoy their memory tenfold the more by contrast, riding between the Surrey sand-banks, lapped and folded in by pastoral crofts and over-hanging orchards.

Why, from childhood onwards, are we ever dreaming of capes and caves, and islets and headlands, and the marriage of the land and sea? Yet what attracts us like Acrasia's bower, and Armida's gardens, and that *Isle of isles* where Calypso sang, and Ulysses built his ship?

But there are things yet higher than poetry and art. The painter does nobly when he plucks new thoughts with the dew upon them, and bids them live upon his canvas; but he does even better, when he takes thought for a suffering brother, broken by an irreparable loss; and so kindly attracts him to his hospitality, that nothing but being *quite below the mark* would hinder the poor worm from making a westward crawl.

Still I live in hope of a happy day at " Pine Wood," and of an ideal cruise with you among the " Isles." Believe me, Ever most truly yours, S. PALMER.

Tuesday Morning. At this moment the [Etching] Club are at full tear upon the rail, and you are looking for your pilot-coat to go down through the weather and bid them welcome at the station.

1864

XXXVI. To MR. L. R. VALPY.

FURZE HILL HOUSE, *June*, 1864.

MY DEAR SIR. . . . You read my thoughts!—It is really very curious. Here is the evidence. 1st. The last touch was put to *The Chapel by the Bridge* the moment before I opened your letter: 2ndly. All the time I was writing my last, Mr. Chance's name was on the tip of my pen, as the very man for the work; but I thought it hardly fair to introduce a rival to whomsoever you might usually employ. By the bye, my wife is Mr. Chance's cousin, she being Mr. Linnell's daughter, and Mr. C. his nephew: 3rdly, and most curious of all, you ask me to show you anything I may be upon " which specially affects my inner sympathies." Now only three days have passed since I did begin the meditation of a subject which, for twenty years, has affected my sympathies with sevenfold inwardness; though now, for the first time, I seem to feel in some sort the power of realizing it.

It is from one of the finest passages in what Edmund Burke thought the finest poem in the English language :—

> " Or, if the air will not permit,
> Some still removèd place will fit,
> Where dying embers [1] through the room
> Teach light to counterfeit a gloom,
> Far from all resort of mirth,
> Save the cricket on the hearth."

The lower lines a companion subject out of doors.

> " Or the bellman's drousy charm
> To bless the doors from nightly harm."

I am trying the former small—the size of your *Chapel.* The student, in his country, old-fashioned room, meditating between the lights : the room dimly bronzed by the dying embers (*warranted without "RAYS"!*) and a very cool, deep glimpse of landscape, and fragment of clouded moon seen through the lattice, just silvering the head and shoulders : the young wife in shade, spinning perhaps, on one side of the fireplace. Should I displease myself with it, the " dying embers " may revive within my own fire-grate ; if the contrary, it will give me much pleasure to show it you *by and bye.*

I carried the Minor Poems in my pocket for twenty years, and once went into the country expressly for retirement, while attempting a set of designs for *L'Allegro* and *Il Penseroso*, not one of which I have painted (!!!), though I have often made and sold other subjects from Milton. But I have often dreamed the day-dream of a small-sized set of subjects (not however monotonous in their shape yet still a set ; perhaps a dozen or so), half from the one and half from the other poem. For I never artistically know " such a sacred and homefelt delight " as when endeavouring in all humility, to realize after a sort the imagery of Milton.

Your strong feeling for the poetic in art will make Blake's *Life* a treat. It is abundantly illustrated too, and is a book to possess. I had the honour of knowing that great man, and can vouch for many of the anecdotes : disavowing, however, all adherence to some of the doctrines put forth in the poems, which seem to me to savour of Manicheism.

[1] My father quotes from memory, and although he knew *Il Penseroso* by heart, not only writes "dying" for "glowing," but (as the context shows) evidently thinks the word enhances the poetic sentiment. ED.]

Mr. Butts's visit to "Adam and Eve" had grown in the memory, I think. I do not believe it: it is unlike Blake. This and the above are all I carp at.

Mrs. Palmer and I spent an evening with Mr. and Mrs. Gilchrist, looking over a number of Blake's drawings; and were so riveted and unaware of time, that a first look at the watch told three in the morning! Our servants were frightened! As we are early people, they thought we must have been slain and disposed of in a ditch.

I hope to do myself the pleasure of calling when I venture to London, and am very pleased to think that your three subjects still interest you, and prove a resource in the intervals of your severer studies. What should I do without resources, writhing, as I have been now for three years, in agony for the death of my son, full of promise, and just going to Oxford? Believe me, dear Sir, Yours very truly, S. PALMER.

XXXVII. To Mr. L. R. VALPY.

RED HILL, *August,* 1864.

My DEAR SIR. . . . . For my word's sake, I send the clumsy little blot of The Shepherd, which I trust, for my sake, you will burn. I forgot a serious rule I had imposed upon my proceedings, viz., seclusion or the fire for everything, large or small, that was not done as well as I could do it at the time; and this yields the "peaceable fruit" of knowing that no one has anything of mine which is not taken pains with, be it good or bad : no *scraps.* The scribblings I can best paint from are, in the opinion of the artist, to all other intents and purposes *hideous,* therefore you cannot wonder that he invokes oblivion. . . .

You do me the honour to ask my opinion of Blake's Blair's *Grave.* It seems to me to contain some of his finest designs, and worth possessing were it only for that lovely thought, the beautiful soul leaving the body; with a look out upon hill slope and sky—nothing, yet everything. Howard the R.A. said he would give one of his fingers to design figures like Blake; and to me some of his background landscapes, and particularly those *Pastorals,* often suggest the chopper. I think you would not

regret the purchase; it is a mine of thought. There is great
inequality in Blake's drawings—genius in all. But I know none
like him, ancient and modern, when he lifts you off your feet and
out of yourself in a moment. He seems then quite up to the
mark (may I dare to say it?) of Milton's Death; or that
moonlight of moonlights with the Lapland witches. (*Par. Lost*,
Book 2. Line 662.) . . . .

I am never in a "lull" about Milton in the abstract, nor can
tell how many times I have read his poems, his prose, his
biographers. He never tires. He seems to me to be one of the
few who have come to full maturity of manhood; not however
to infallibility, which is superhuman   Yours most truly,
S PALMER.

XXXVIII. To Mr. L. R. VALPY.

RED HILL, *September*, 1864.

MY DEAR SIR. I am truly glad to hear that you have
escaped the perils of that dear, naughty county, where the rule of
the year is said to be nine months' rain and three months' bad
weather; and escaped it to meet dear friends in improved health.

Mrs. Finch has told me what kind attention you have
bestowed upon her little book, and communicated your remarks,
in all or most of which I quite concur, after reading them three
times most attentively. You attacked the advertisement in front,
and I in flank, so I trust we shall see no more of it.

The real subject-matter of the book is Mr. F.'s musings; but
somehow, each of the very few friends who have seen it seem to
feel the Memoir to be so, and they feel justly the want of more art
anecdote. It was I who suggested the title. Perhaps *Musings of
a Student* would have been better, as much of the book does not
relate to art; and perhaps *Some Memorials* should be substituted
for *Memoir*.

Still, I am glad that some memorial has been written, both
because it must in some degree have beguiled deep sorrow, and
because, whether the readers be few or many, the moral influence
surely will do them good.

I have nothing whatever to do with the theological part.
Swedenborg was a mystery, as I now begin to think most things
are. Kant, who knew him well, although he ignored the

s

supernatural (I mean the miraculous), yet confessed that there were things of that kind connected with Swedenborg which he could not refute.

His inward knowledge of that fire thirteen miles off at Stockholm was curious.

Just now I have been wholly engaged with other matter, and shall be for some time longer. But I have the Miltons, here within, safely photographed just over my eyes, and packed in their bone box ready for use before very long I hope. Believe me My dear Sir, Yours very truly, S. PALMER.

Two similar tables might be made showing respectively the opposites and varieties of colour and of effect.

P.S. As you wished it, I have sent you the rough lines. But I could not at all express what I mean without spending a day upon each; but with the aid of the voice and my new little Milton portfolio, I think all could be explained. The following will perhaps help to show how I propose to distribute the serious points among the subjects.

L'Allegro.	*Il Penseroso.*
No. 1. Sunrise. Fine Morning. Agricultural. Farm sentiment. Hunting. The Pastoral.	Grey morning. Grey moors. Shower. Wind. Yet not wretched, or sloppy. If you like this, I should be glad of any inventive suggestions. I think wind and wet are a variety worth securing. *Transient* rain.
No. 2. The upland sentiment. Freedom. Merriment; including the best points of the "Many a youth and many a maid." Song and fruitfulness, like 65th Psalm.	The *inland* sentiment. Deeply recessed. Cavern; waters falling. The one piece of glory pours down through the leaves, making the "arched walks" doubly solemn. The obscurity of the hinted figures, *hinting* that it is or may be a haunted forest.
No. 3. "Straight mine eye." Wide expanse, melting into fairyland, &c. Sort of dancing grace in the leading lines.	Wide expanse of blank water. Instead of bleatings of nibbling flocks, the solemn curfew, and the lowing steer.
No. 4. The amber sky. Meant for the quintessence of the remote and romantic in the severe sense of the word. Day rather dreaming than dying.	Mysterious suggestion. More meant than meets the eye. The sleeping fold a sort of comfort, so that there should not be desolation. Darkness. "'Thy hand, great anarch, lets the curtain fall."

Would you kindly read the text and just name to me what good *landscape* subject seems to you left, after the eight I have named are taken away: e.g. there is the "many a youth," to begin with. Then we may be said to have *ransacked* the whole. I think there are several, but I have stuck to the literal view from the first. The "dying embers" I think one of the very best, but don't see how it could possibly be treated just now.

XXXIX. TO MR. L. R. VALPY.

RED HILL, *September*, 1864.

MY DEAR SIR. . . . . . I hope I can give a good answer to your *L'Allegro* and *Il Penseroso* inquiry. They have occupied much time and thought; and viewed in the whole, the parts, the relations: then laid aside for work that was pressing, but not until the first survey was complete and I felt that I could do the whole.

Yesterday, some of the designs came to me unawares, and an impulse to begin the "Straight mine eye" and "Lonely tower."

How different is the inward *sight* of a thing to speculations about it! For years, off and on, has the former subject teazed me, owing to something in the text. I had been over it again, and at last given up the quest—when suddenly, as I could not go to the thought, the thought very kindly came to Mahomet, and unlike anything I had expected.

Milton's nuts are worth the trouble of cracking, for each has a kernel in it. Monkeys and illustrators are apt to make faces, when they crack and find nothing.

That mystery which cannot be commanded, that immaterial and *therefore* real image, that seed of all true beauty in picture or poem falls into earthly soil and becomes subject in a great measure to the conditions of matter, and fails or fares as the soil permits— the desert sand; the ploughed fallow; the rich, garden mould. To say that the seed does everything is fanaticism. Milton saw both; the former which in his prose works he expressly asserts to be divine; yet what a soil was *he* preparing who knew Homer almost by heart at sixteen!

I doubt whether the best images can be made use of by an

s 2

imagination which is not coupled with large reasoning power ; and we know what, in ripe years, was Johnson's verdict—that excepting Butler, there was more "*thinking*" in Milton than in any of our poets. He said, "I admire him more than I did at twenty."

Yours of the marble settings is indeed a refined and comely thought. It set before me a series of works "severe in" "beauty"; but such works as with their several marbles were to be fitted again into compartments of national or sacred buildings, rather than the veiled recluseness of pastoral or Georgic ; and should not what borders the work be quite even in tint ? If we had gone to that remarkable man—that great patron of British genius, if men had their dues—to Mr. Butts I mean, I think we should have come away best pleased if we could remember nothing about the frames. To do this, however, there must be good workmanship, for we may say of frames as of good men that they are at their best when they nullify themselves.

Blake often expressed a wish to take me himself to Mr. Butts', but ere a day was fixed, "came the blind Fury." What a show, with such a showman ! What a casket of a house ! What prince of his own choosing ever got together under his broad roofs so many precious thoughts ? Yes, so many, even if they had been bolted to the bran, and a third part burnt as refuse ?

You say "my thoughts were confined to the realistic aspect of the poet's thoughts. Would that it were given me to rise higher, but each must be content," &c. "It is something to be able to *feel* a degree of elevation, when examining such outpourings as those picture thoughts of Blake." Something indeed ! Something, it seems to me, with which you may rest not merely content, but thankful.

We are all of us more or less influenced by the fashions of the day, and the arts of the day are influenced, like its literature, by materialism : but you are *aware* of the influence, and anyone who loves Milton as you do, and does not *hate* Blake cannot be much tainted.

Truth in art seems to me to stand at a fixed centre, midway between its two antagonists Fact and Phantasm.

You have too much taste to like the fantastic, so that must not be set down against you, but on the credit side of the account.

Perhaps your very realism *is* imagination or something very like it
--something which will develope into it, as you become better
acquainted with the inner circles of art. Mr. Carpenter is the
chancellor of *our* university; our Bodleian is that quiet print-
room at the Museum. Below, in the Townley Gallery, is the sure
test of our imaginative faculty—the sleeping Mercury. More
than two thousand years ago the sculptor bade that marble live.
It lived, but slept, and it is living still. Bend over it. Look at
those delicate eyelids; that mouth a little open. He is dreaming
Dream on, marble shepherd; few will disturb your slumber.

We will go our ways, and feed upon our "facts"; our "bits of
nature"; our bits of fish; our fresh herrings or a deal board with
all the grain in it. "As nat'ral as life isn't it, master 'Gustus,"
says the nursery-maid—"And the herring, why it looks as if we
could scrape the scales off with a knife!"

> " So move we, each his own desire to find,
>   A substance, or a shadow, or the wind."

Believe me, dear Sir, Yours very truly, S. PALMER.

XL. TO MR. L. R. VALPY.

RED HILL, *October* 20, 1864.

MY DEAR SIR. Here I sit, with those two ivy-leaves and with
your comment before me—so sad, so poetical, so true; yet I must
needs rejoice to think that you have returned unscathed from dear,
spongy Devon, to dry, dirty London. Devon quite haunts me
now: I have been working all day at an *attempt* to get its
quintessence.

The Etching dream came over me in this way. I am making
my working sketches a quarter of the size of the drawings, and was
surprised and not displeased to notice the variety—the difference of
each from all the rest. I saw within, a set of highly-finished etchings
the size of Turner's *Liber Studiorum;* and as finished as my
moonlight with the cypresses; a set making a book—a compact
block of work which I would fain hope might live when I am with
the fallen leaves.

I was the more led to this, as I find that each subject will
incorporate something or other of picked matter in my studies

from nature, and be far removed from the pseudo-classical, which I hate. . . . .

Heartily do I subscribe to all you say against the figment of a new revelation or dispensation. Have we exhausted this? The Foundation can be but One; is then the superstructure meagre? The Spirit poured out at the Day of Pentecost a stinted legacy? Is it not that by our own lack of faith we have forfeited many of its privileges?

People have a notion, gorgeous and glowing like those leaves you "lifted off," of a moral millennium just beginning to rise softly like a summer dawn. A curious time for it, when almost all the periodical press is *influentially*, though but a smaller part of it avowedly, infidel, and the powers of good and evil are even now mustering for the battle.

The influences of the day promise much worse things than paganism with its perverted truths and misapplied devotion. What measure of light was permitted, *Pagans* would not have changed away for the wretched *débris* of rotting skulls and flint arrow-heads. If so-called science bids us give up our faith, surely we have a right to ask for something better in exchange!

I have some humble doubts whether the spiritual and physical can ever be made to appear consistent *in the present state of our faculties*, because they seem to exist under different conditions— the physical in time and space, the spiritual in some other media. It is happily true that though, as Lord Bacon says, science tends to atheism until carried very far, yet that, as in the case of Galen's study of the human hand, its erratic orbit wheels round again.

Busy as you must find yourself in resuming harness, do not trouble yourself to write; and as I am in like case, pardon silence on my part, Believing me &c., S. PALMER.

XLI. To Mr. L. R. VALPY.

RED HILL, *November*, 1864.

MY DEAR SIR. Many thanks from Mrs. Palmer and myself for your so kind and cordial invitation: from myself for the kind interest you take in my brain-work; which must needs be pleasant, and I should think beneficial, to artists and authors, if it leave them, as it ought to find them, as free from vanity as new-born babes.

A certain preacher once said from the pulpit, " Talk of the innocence of babes ? Why a new-born babe is one of the greatest hypocrites that ever set foot on British ground !" But I must differ from the Reverend Gentleman.

We shall not alas, be able to avail [ourselves] of your kindness, as I dare scarcely leave the room except for indoor exercise , although better, and in vigour of thought and work such as it is. *What* it is I never can tell when about it, or directly it is done, but can only conjecture from the sort of moral influence which is upon me at the time. If I'm in a " fine fellow" state of mind, then I suppose, it will be trash, but generally it turns out tolerable if I have the grace to suffer and to love. For the intellectual is a curious counter-part of the spiritual. Love stoops to suffering ; takes it up, carrying it in her arms,

"And makes e'en suffering sweet "

as St. Teresa sings—winding up each stanza so.

It is very kind of you to take an interest in the matted woods called *Going home at Curfew-time.* I can't say I suffered much over it, from my intense love of Devonshire, but it lay by a good while, and whenever I could get at it, I did so.

No artist has seen it except one of my brothers-in-law, and he likes it better than anything I have done ; but what will the public say ? What they said to George Primrose's Paradoxes ?[1]

The thought of exhibiting sketches makes me feel sea-sick. Yet what have I done ? Mr. Field spent an evening here and somehow made me promise to send a blot which he fell in love with, so *that's* gone to the Water Colour.[2]

In your North Devon cornfield, there is a bit of white left as a good place for a rabbit, in case of making a picture from it. Now, if I were to put in a good rabbit, it would unfinish the corn ; and work upon the corn would *ruin* the distance, which is the point of the case. For sketches and pictures are wholly different things. . . .

Directly you were gone, I terrier'd into the Milton Warren, and in a moment pounced upon the prey—sought for years, that shy animal the "curfew."

Handel has set that very finely ; and in the end, the lights in the villages seem to go out one by one, through the use of what I

[1 Vicar of Wakefield, Chapter XX.—Ed.]
[2 Near Clovelly—A page from the Blot-book.]

may call the double minor where, in the third, the semitone changes its place thus. . .

But I must not remain in the warren just now, having a press of things to do. . . . You shall see (D.V.) every Milton as soon as it takes intelligible shape ; meanwhile forgive this most incoherent scrawl from, my dear Sir, Yours ever most truly, S. PALMER.

XLII. To Miss Louisa Twining.

FURZE HILL HOUSE, *November* 22, 1864

DEAR MISS TWINING. If anything reminding me of the past *could* be very pleasing, after the blow which struck me down, it would be the sight of your handwriting again.

How differently we have spent the intervening time ! You, in " taking " as *dear* Burke says, " the gauge and dimensions of misery, depression and contempt "—I, in making marks upon paper to amuse the public.

If you can think of, or rather if you can set your heart upon copying anything of mine, let me know, and I will contrive some means of sending it. I don't wish it to be made a matter of business ; and please let the lending it be between ourselves. I don't mind sending two or three, as I know your conscientious carefulness and habits of order ; *but*, having carefully considered what you have done hitherto, I strongly advise you not.

You should now go on, as you would have done with me, to make *use* of the degree of imitation you had mastered ; to study the manner in which the best masters *applied* it to nature ; and how they simplified [nature's] intricacy and, when necessary, did the most in the least time ; which is particularly desirable in your case, whose time is so occupied with still better things.

If you could paint a robin red-breast perched on a twig, and finish it so highly as that we could tell what o'clock it was by the reflection of the dial of the village church in its eye, you would have done a work less noble and natural than Gaspar Poussin in that small picture in the National Gallery, with the sheep coming forward in the shady lane. Such works lead you to detect large arrangements of light and shade in nature, and so to take hold of nature in its practicable moments.

Don't think I am undervaluing detail and real finish; it is the preparation for everything that is noble. Claude, of whom Fuseli says that his characteristic is sublimity, one would wish to be studying day and night; but I am now trying to devise what is best *under the circumstances* to bring your hand in, *to make you free of your colour-box*, and ready for your tour work; and though I mention these first, as relating to the matter in hand, they are but the smaller advantages.

I am too poorly to write perspicuously, yet I really want to explain myself. However, it will be "confusion worse confounded," so I will take the popular method of dogmatism. Suppose yourself standing before that divinest of landscapes, Claude's *Enchanted Castle*. Lo! It becomes *real* (in the silly popular sense of the word), and you walk up and enter the gates. You find it full of the most beautiful paintings, and *long* to make some memoranda of them. You have only a fortnight to stay in the neighbourhood, and have permission to go to work. Now, with a like spirit of vigour, go to work in the enchanted schools of our National Gallery on fine days (for it is ill lighted at the best), and on dull days, to sweet, quiet Dulwich College.

Take hot-pressed *thickest* imperial [paper], and on about ⅛th imperial, according to proportion of picture, make little, rich, bold copies of a few of the broadest works. A *very* thin wash of white all over the paper will make the colour "take" at once. Take pains with the outline, and in all the nearer parts: put bistre into a *swan pinion*, ... and outline firmly. Have two saucers and two pens—saucers for distances with a mass of Cologne earth on one side, and a mass of cobalt on the other; at the bottom, make the tint you want, to feed the pen with by the brush; this gives you a great scale of inks, from cobalt, which is colder than you are likely to want, on to Cologne earth. Then, in the other saucer, have bistre.

I have tried this in sketching from nature, even in remote distances, and find it save *much* time. It is not indelible: so much the better. Keep on *refreshing* your ink outline as you go on. You can have pens for various colours. You will of course have pens *ready*, cut to various degrees of fineness, for the varying distances. Use the zinc-white (in tube) freely, whenever it is of use; only mind (and this is very important) when you use heightening lights, on a tree already painted for instance, do the lights first, delicately and sharply with white ; when dry, add the colour.

Above all, *use plenty of colour.* I mean that the smallest touch should be put from a tempting bit of paint just worked up with the palette-knife, and laid crisp and comfortable ; no scrubbing and fumbling from colour dried hard, and spoiling a poor brush in the effort. Until a vituperative dictionary is published, I can't tell where to find any epithet vile enough to hit this kind of work. Plenty of *paint*, and interstices of palettes cleaned every day, and kept replenished from the tubes before you go out. *Large brushes for large work.* The darkest touch in the original to be laid at once, as dark as it is to be at last, which will be helped by the pen outline. Try at the National Gallery the pictures I mention, washing all but the sky with Cologne earth, as a ground to work on. The rather long-proportioned Gaspar, I forget what it is called (this large Gaspar will do you vast good) ; Sir Joshua Reynolds's property and favourite, Sebastian Bourdon's *Return of the Ark*, if hung within sight. At Dulwich, a very fine Cuyp ; very few cows, one black, or spotted with black ; church tower I *think* on the opposite bank : you will know it by the amber sky. Yellow ochre bright enough I should think ; perhaps a *little* gamboge in it.

You may say, " But these are not the kind of things. I want to sketch from nature in Italy." I am quite aware of that.

On a small piece of paper half the size of ⅛th imperial, washing it all with Cologne earth before you begin (excepting highest part of light in sky), you might make yourself a little treasure to hang up, from that *Jacob's Dream* of Rembrandt.

You are the only lady I know, to whom I should recommend *dashing*, but I advise you to *dash* at these ; to turn your swan pen into an anchor, and then be bold and get these little copies, through thick and thin ; sometimes painting with your brush, then with your fingers. With his finger, they say, Titian put the last finish ; it is a wonderful instrument in painting. Don't forget a bit of sponge, only keep it away from the highest lights ; don't alter, but go right ahead, and do the next better. The first outline should be with softish pencil, lightly used in the distances, and having got your paper as nearly as you can to the proportion of the original, hold a thread diagonally across so that it intersects

the corners of the work, and see where the centre touch comes, and afterwards what objects coincide with the lines ; and having the corresponding lines delicately marked on your paper, you will find much time saved.

Get as much as you can the desired amount of force as soon as possible, and keep refreshing the outline. Weak outline is at once killed by the colour, but you will find work for the tubes with a firm line underneath. You will soon find that you will want more tubes for Italy than you would otherwise have taken.

Dark pictures are best drawn on brown crayon-paper (the tint of whity-brown, but a little darker) only you cannot scrub the colour about so well. Any time you can get for pen and ink copying of Claude's trees out of *Liber Veritatis* (at the British Museum print room) the better. Trees are so important. In the small picture of our Saviour appearing, which belonged to Mr. Rogers there is a perfect school of copse and ground painting : you might get a study of that, in black and white chalk.

Believe me, my dear Miss Twining, Yours most truly,

S. PALMER.

1865

XLIII. To MR. L. R. VALPY.

RED HILL, *Saturday, February,* 1865.

MY DEAR MR. VALPY. . . . . I shall be most happy to do what you mention as to the National Gallery. But alas, in many cases we should have to admire the past majesty in the present ruin. All the pictures unprotected by glass have succumbed to London dirt, and many to the London cleanings, far the worst of the two. Years ago, Sir A. Callcott told me he remembered the magnificent Bacchus and Ariadne far different to what it was even *then.* When you add to this, that the old rooms are vilely lighted, so that you cannot see what is in the pictures by any straining of the eyes, we shall find in a new sense of the words that seeing must be believing. The collection of Claudes was wonderful ; I have seen their gradual decay, and then the fearful cleaning which swept the dew, the light, the pearl, the golden influences into the pail and committed them to the sewers. The *St. Ursula* alone escaped, and happily abides, merely in its dirtiness. . . . . Believe me, dear Mr. Valpy, Yours most truly, S. PALMER.

XLIV. TO MR. L. R. VALPY.

RED HILL, *February*, 1865.

MY DEAR MR. VALPY. . . . . None seem to need a little spiritual help more than earnest artists. I have often thought that feeble ones are likely to enter into the Kingdom of Heaven before them : for there is a close and curious analogy between the really intellectual and the spiritual life—so close, that art is apt to become our religion. The very "experiences" are analogous—almost identical in sequence, though not in kind. There is, as Reynolds says not irreverently, the "becoming as a little child," the New Birth in fact, when the real artist abhors himself and esteems his best efforts as "filthy rags;" when, either by sudden conversion, or a protracted struggle like that of Bunyan's in his *Grace Abounding*, the painter in the loves of his mind (whether or not in *the power of his hand*), escapes "like a bird out of the snare of the fowler," from the NATURALISTIC—not from the natural, but *towards* the natural : escapes from "Hagar," his "Mount Sinai in Arabia," "which gendereth to bondage," towards his "Jerusalem," the IDEAL.

Like Tereus, he tries awhile the half-fledged wing—fluttering above his own old roof, "the house of bondage"; and then, in all his desires, and sympathies, and loves, wings his way to those distant ridges where "the morning" is "spread upon the mountains."

Unworthy as I am even to take his name upon my lips, I will venture to write two lines of one of Michelangelo's sonnets,

"Above the visible world she [the Soul] soars to seek
Ideal form, the universal mould."

Then come "experiences"; inward darkness, doubts, all but despair; seasons of refreshing. In short the thing is so thoroughly an intellectual *religion*, in its whole, in its parts, in its inward processes, that it is but too likely to supersede the renovation of the *Heart*, while it is in the highest degree refining and elevating the intellect. And what is most curious, there have been I think in every age the unconverted and converted, the Naturalistic and the Ideal working side by side; and with the farther most sad resemblance, that the unamiable converted have much to learn and much that they would do well to imitate in the amiable unconverted; if *really amiable*, *loving* people can be said to be unconverted. I *will not* venture to say it ; nor to forget that in the Heavenly Father's House are " many mansions," and that many shall come from the east and from the west and sit down in the kingdom.

That solemn tone and stately line which we see in the great Masters was no happy necessity of their time. I was looking at a picture at Hampton Court which had none of those qualities, but was a most dexterous example of the naturalistic and academic, when the friend who was with me said, " That was painted in the times of Titian !" . . . . There was a somewhat similar contemporaneity in Domenichino's time of a set of fast workers upon dark grounds and conscientious painters upon white grounds (just like Bunyan's Passion and Patience), and fine squabbles they had, if I remember rightly.

How delightful it is when the converted style of art is employed upon sacred subjects, as in that most touching *St. Jerome*, the Perugino *Tobit*, and the Mantegna—the Filippo Lippi too ; those holy doctors and confessors sitting together in a sort of garden. What a wonderful subject would it be (were there any one who could handle it), the conversion of St. Augustine—the final victory under that tree in his garden : " When thou wast under the fig-tree, I saw thee." It has the disadvantage of no action : perhaps Fra Angelico might have hit the expression.

According to the theologians, it would seem that there are varieties of degree among the holy angels, as to intellect and heart ; the Seraph, wholly absorbed in the direct ecstasy of love : the Cherub, loving through his intuition of the Divine Wisdom and Goodness.

The Tuscan Archangel (to pursue the parallel) knew well that art, even HIS art, was not in itself religion. In one of his sonnets he bewails, if I remember rightly, how art itself had led his thoughts and meditations from the cross. After a life of contradiction and persecution (the parallel again—" He that was born of the flesh persecuted him who was born of the Spirit "), it is delightful to know that his soul was illumined by the full glory of the gospel ; the princess Colonna, herself converted through the doctrines of Savonarola, having in their high and august converse " taught him the way of the Lord more perfectly." His last words to those who stood around were these, " In your passage through life, remember the sufferings of Jesus Christ."

Every one knows that Bartolomeo too was one of the fruits of his friend Savonarola's ministry.

But who am I, to gabble about blessed Savonarola? Pardon me, sacred memory!

What made me run on so I can't conceive; poor "Mr. Talkative" never got over the River. Dark, dark River!

Thank you again for your couple of oars, and believe me, dear Mr. Valpy, Most truly yours, S. PALMER.

XLV. TO MESSRS. WALTER AND JOHN RICHMOND.

RED HILL, *April,* 1865.

MY DEAR YOUNG FRIENDS. I have no seal (otherwise it should be at your service), but I *have* an impression, not on wax[1] but on memory, that I lent Mr. Giles my seal that he might have another made from it. The only seal I remember was made of steel, or iron, or some metal which looked like them.

My impression is perhaps erroneous. Should all vestiges be lost, I must go to Heralds' College and request them, with what sweetmeats they may like to add in the way of unicorns and griffins, to give me my pet crest, *A bull dog, patient.* I esteem the bull-dog, because whatever he lays hold on he does not willingly let go again.

Being much vexed at my printer's one day, because an etching did not "prove" as I had expected, I adjourned to an eating house hard by, that, invigorated by some beef and draught stout, I might endeavour to form my character anew. The ideal I finally fixed upon, was that of A CHRISTIAN BULL-DOG.

This, in much weakness, I have since been endeavouring to realize, but alas, with many lapses and frailties.

The human race may be divided into mumblers and holdfasts in the proportion of mumblers, 1000; holdfasts, 1.

"The spider *taketh hold* with her hands, and is in Kings' palaces."

Of the wise woman in *The Proverbs* we are told that "her hands *hold* the distaff."

[1 My father had and I still have a wax impression of his family seal.—ED.]

I have thought much of you, my dear John, during your long illness. If, by the Divine blessing, you can but regain your strength, you will perhaps have been no loser ; for there is something about affliction which gives us sympathy for the sufferings of others it acts like a vigorous stone-breaker upon the flint of our hard hearts. For my own part, I dread coming near any one who has never been in trouble ; he might tear me in pieces for his amusement ; as the old feudal lords (who look so pretty in poetry), coming home after a bad day's sport, would shoot down a few stray serfs to make amends. When, after a hard day's hunting, they came home very tired, it is said that they found warm human blood refreshing to steep their feet in, and tapped a vassal or two for the purpose. One of those gentry got into a scrape with the just St. Louis for *hanging* a very little boy for snaring a rabbit ! A boy at Eton refused to let the late Lord King, who was then his " fag," use a toasting fork in making toast for him ; for the thought that a human hand was scorching and withering made the toast taste all the crisper. Lord King's hand was maimed for life.

Now these propensities seem to be modified by affliction, and it is worth while to suffer a good deal of pain if we become less unjust and unkind. Then we shall turn away disgusted from these barbaric tyrannies, to that homage of LAW which distinguished the best times of Greek and Roman history. Depend upon it, dear Walter and John, that if the diapason of the moral universe do not, as we grow up, become sweeter to us than music over the waters, we shall have no music in our *souls*, though we " do our scales " till we can warble enharmonics like a cat upon a skylight.

" Shut up ! " says the contracting note paper. " I was manufactured to waft sighs and vent flatteries, and I can't a-bear this stuff about history, and liberty, and them sort of fellows. I was reared in a *slave* state, supplanted linen, was formed in a mould, and crushed into polish ; and as to Romans, and what d' ye-call-'ems, I'd have you to know that I am meat for their masters." O ! I'm so frightened—yet ever, Yours affectionately, S. PALMER.

XLVI. TO MR. L. R. VALPY.

RED HILL, *June* 3. 1865.

MY DEAR MR. VALPY. . . . I am happy to say the "dripping caves" have long been provided for in the subject we agreed upon for the passing shower.[1] I have no longer a difficulty about the brook : what I had, arose from attempting to combine it with the avenues of pine and monumental oak, which is distinctly another theme. Yet it is surprising how many indications, how much bye play (or by play) may suggest itself, if strict unity of main subject be secured. Thus, the cottage behind the aged oaks may find a place in the "Prospect" or elsewhere : and I fancy my temperament, or whatever we call it, would lead me rather to overfill with matter than otherwise.

Of course, if possible, I shall be glad to indicate that it is ancient timber which surrounds the brook dell ; but the avenue *subject*, like aisles of a cathedral, cannot be combined with the brook, without sacrificing one or the other.

It seems evident to me that poetry, being successional as to time and to suggestion of space, and as it can turn and look all round it, admits more objects than picture ; but that picture, although tied to the unity of one moment and one aspect, gives incomparably more illustration to each of the images.

But I perfectly agree with you as to what should be aimed at. "to use the minor, to lead up to and strengthen the major element of thought," nor do I think that it could be better expressed.

It is in the tertiary regions and masses that these attractive minors suggest themselves, which do not come within the scope of first sketches, the latter being something like skeleton school maps.

I wish I could have the pleasure of seeing Lord Ellesmere's collection with you. Besides the *Three Ages* of Titian there is a *real* Leonardo da Vinci, and a Palma Vecchio with the *lakes* (!), after three centuries, as fresh as when they were painted. Hallam thinks Leonardo altogether (not merely as a painter) the greatest man of the Middle Ages. Believe me, &c., S. PALMER.

[The *Morning* Milton —ED.]

XLVII. TO MR. RICHARD REDGRAVE.

FURZE HILL HOUSE, *July* 14, 1865.

MY DEAR REDGRAVE. I ought to correct a mistake of Mrs. Palmer's about the board I work upon. It is six sheet "London-board" of best quality from Newman's, Soho Square (which I think a most reliable place for water-colours), imperial or royal : the royal, they say, is made for or used by flower-painters.

I take off the gloss by rapidly sponging with water (a *little* alum dissolved in it might perhaps do no harm)—*rapidly* lest the paste should soften underneath ; thoroughly, so far as to see that it takes the water everywhere. I was driven to use it simply because, on the best modern paper (the only sort to be had since Creswick's was bought up), I found it impossible to get any one quality I liked.

At first I felt like a baby on a slide, but found that this might be avoided by using the colours less wet than on simple paper. Ultramarine especially, and the ashes, always difficult to [lay on in a] wash, will not bear a full, wet brush ; but a very thin wash of zinc white over the sky and distance part, before beginning, might facilitate. Several practised artists have done this.

These difficulties have their equivalent advantage in the ease with which a bit of sponge or even a wet brush will remove dried colour. In this respect the surface is intermediate between paper and ivory. I have done my largest things upon it ; getting it made on purpose rather than use paper. I fasten it round the edge with the smallest flat-headed brass pins (not passing them through it, which, if you avoid working much on parts already wet, prevents warping), upon a thin, light drawing-board of seasoned pine ; the screws which fasten on the cross bars, having room for contraction of wood. . . . A sheet of white paper is fastened on the front of the drawing-board, so that even if you have not much margin of the "London-board," you have a sort of white mount.

Some of the advantages are these. 1. If safe colours are used, they will not be liable to change, as on the newer papers. An artist told me that, in the course of a quarter of a century, drawings of his on paper were now and then sent to him to refresh or restore, if faded in parts, but never once on Bristol board, now called "London-

T

board." 2. It reflects light through the pigments.[1] 3. It shows the full depth of the colours laid on, and as you retouch with more colour the retouchings are still darker, as one would suppose they naturally must be. In the modern papers, you come to a full stop at a point far short of the depth of the pigment—in fact it is an ocular paradox. Believe me, Ever yours most truly, S. PALMER.

XLVIII. TO MR. L. R. VALPY.

RED HILL, *December*, 1865.

MY DEAR MR. VALPY. The pictures of *The Lonely Tower* and *Haunted Stream* have been in hand some time, and lately I have been at them *heart* and *soul*, wishing to get one or both ready for our summer exhibition.

I hasten to remove any anxiety on your part by mentioning, as I thought I had done before, that none of the subjects would be proceeded with about which we had not conferred, without showing you the designs. . . .

You, perhaps, have little of my own fastidiousness. After we had agreed about *The Stream* and *Tower*, the sketches underwent a rigorous examination by me before I transferred them to the picture papers.

Danger is likely to accrue rather from my own over-fastidiousness than otherwise ; and in art, that is sometimes more dangerous than rashness. If once, in the doing, caution and fear get ever so little ahead of impulse and joy, a work is, I think, in its worst peril : though all four are good, each in its *time* and turn throughout life.

I am the very "youth"!! of the biography upon whom Blake turned with the question, "Do you work with fear and trembling?" and I could tell him now, as I told him then, "Indeed I do." But I look cheerfully on the Milton set because my mind is in undivided allegiance to them and in their very arduousness I find my delight. . . .

As to the order of doing the respective subjects, I apprehend that each will be done best, whensoever its impression on the artist is most vivid. I should not have troubled you with all this if I could have borne to think that you were under any unpleasant anxiety. . . . Yours very truly, S. PALMER.

[1] A point my father esteemed most important. See his references to white grounds in oil-painting, and to transmitted light in nature.—ED.]

1866

XLIX. To Mr. L. R. VALPY.

RED HILL, *February*, 1866.

MY DEAR MR. VALPY. It is indeed gratifying to hear that friends who travelled so far and in such weather were not disappointed. Mrs. Palmer thought that the leaden light of that day quite spoilt the studies.

I will remember your wish, but studies made with a motive are of such useful reference that until parted with one does not quite feel their value. One such, containing the rocky matter of a mountain, the soil here and there, and a full clothing of heather &c., I miss to this day. I was prevailed upon to part with it along with that former set of waterfalls which I have sometimes referred to, and which I should like to re-purchase whole and entire had I any clue to it.

I went "beyond my last" in venturing conjecture as to the future of those pitiable ones who sin, not against a known gospel, but by the very force and virtue of filial obedience, parental command, earliest habit, unanimous consent and example of all around them : by all else scouted and hunted, and from the cradle to the grave—the thief's cradle to the pauper's grave, exposed to every variety of temptation, except indeed that of wealth, in itself perhaps of all the most dangerous. Blessed be God that even through *that* ravine of the "needle's eye," many *have* passed, though as it were, one at a time, to His great glory. Let us sing *Te Deum* for that glorious man who has given so munificently . . . . to afford the London workmen healthy habitations.

Vile were this hand if it wrote anything adverse to the "Faith once delivered." But its symbols, which have graven essential verities in adamant—such preeminently as the Lord's coming in the flesh, "Born of the Virgin Mary," and as we say again in the Nicene, "And was made *man*,"—these creeds have left large spaces for private meditation and pious hope.

If I mistake not, Jeremy Taylor in his *Liberty of Prophesying* inclines to a large scope, making the creed we name from the Apostles a competent measure of saving belief. Of this, who am I that I should venture to speak ?

In my ignorance, for it is no perverseness, I can sing in Church

T 2

those awful clauses of the Athanasian Creed and yet have little fear for such, for instance, as Mrs. Barbauld—her name happens first to occur to me. And now I remember to have heard of her husband, a German, who was ever dwelling as he taught in broken English, upon the love, love, love, of the dear Heavenly Father. The crystalline logic of that symbol seems to me to *imply* possibility of belief in those to whom the faith is proposed—moral possibility, and to denounce only the unbelief which springs from moral perverseness. It is in the moral perverseness that Taylor places the very essence of heresy. But "Taylor is *broad*," you may say.

Every day reveals to me more and more my own ignorance, and, "the Faith" alone excepted, makes me more doubtful of everything. Yet of *one* very serious matter I feel as fully persuaded as that the pen is in my hand : namely, that there are, from time to time, great mental and moral epidemics for good or for evil ; and that these are not reasonably to be accounted for, but by referring them in great part to spiritual agency : that there is *now* an epidemic of unbelief as real as the cattle disease, and somewhat resembling it in the dates of its recurrence : that we are *all* perhaps, even the most simple believers, in danger, nay I was going to say perhaps slightly influenced by it.

Myself you will perhaps think more than slightly tainted, and that an "*auto da fe*" would deal with me as a vigorous government with these cattle.

We love matter; we revel in subdivision, we glory in space, and we say, "If space and matter be infinite, what room is left for spirit, and for the Creator of spirits ?" There seems indeed to be no common measure by which the two can be apprehended or measured upon *together*. But happily, we have the witness in ourselves. Self-consciousness is an *a priori* impregnable by the whole universe of matter. If a man does not believe (and in this, I apprehend, lurks the virus of our present epidemic) that *spirit can move matter*—then, it seems to me that astronomy itself will draw him towards atheism ; but to him who believes that the *himself* who moves the wondrous mechanism of the hand (the hand which converted Galen), *is* spirit, and an emanation of the Father of Spirits, to this man the Heavens will declare the glory of God and the firmament show forth his handiwork. . . . I remain, my dear Mr. Valpy, Yours ever truly, SAMUEL PALMER.

P.S. This invincible repugnance in some men's minds to believe that spirit can act upon matter seems to be the obstacle to their belief of miracles ; but if we assent to it, then the whole of a miracle is as much cause and effect as ordinary phenomena ; differing in this, that the miracle includes and brings into contact two trains of causality ; the one spiritual, the other material ; and the former, being the more powerful, matter is forced by it out of its usual course. Perhaps in Miss Fancourt's case ʻwhich gave occasion to Dr. Maitland's essay in the *Eruvin*ʼ, the same process took place which in cases of ordinary cure, is the work of months and years ; although in her case it was what we called instantaneous : but then with the Lord one day is as a thousand years.   When once the miraculous *fiat* had set it going, the process which removed malformation in the " impotent man," had human sense been quick enough to follow it, might have been such as would have satisfied Sir Benjamin Brodie. By the bye, Sir Benjamin Brodie asserted that the evidence was irresistible for one alleged miracle so unpopular just now that I will not even venture to name it. Nay, the more ethereal kinds of *matter* itself acting on the grosser, force them sadly out of their usual, phlegmatic conditions ; witness the late lightning havoc at Falmouth. Nay, a bit of sealing-wax rubbed on the sleeve will seduce naughty little bits of paper from their allegiance even to the " laws " of *Gravitation*, that great goddess of the Ephesians.

Excuse the erasures of this little note.   Mine is a stammering tongue which erelong will be " silent in the grave."

L. To Miss Frances Redgrave.

Furze Hill, *July* 6, 1866.

Dear Preceptress.[1] I owe you apologies for never noticing your kind present, the photograph of the great Energizer.   O ! for the leisure to contemplate it an hour daily with knotted scourge in hand to lash myself into some semblance of his efficiency.

I paid a first visit to the Academy, but was fairly driven out by the heat before I had seen half the best oil pictures, having

[1 During Miss Redgrave's visits, my father used to amuse himself and her, by grotesque attempts at pronouncing French words and sentences. She corrected his pronunciation, and thus he came to call her his " Preceptress."—ED.]

moreover been waylaid in my approach to them by a beautiful drawing of your papa's which reminded me of the scenery about the brow of Holmbury Hill ; I mean the distance, particularly.

Pity and forgive when you hear that Mr. Frost's[1] picture gave me great pleasure. The poetic beat and movement of the feet upon the sands among other beauties. *Indeed* I could not help it ! Don't scold me ! His pictures always seem to me so refined, so quiet ; painted as if he loved the thought ; with no vulgar appeals, or knock-me-down-all-of-a-heap-execution. But when " costumes " " is in," fairies " is out."

No doubt you saw those noble works of Reynolds at the British Gallery. The very day on which I was looking at them, his countrymen were suffering the unique Wellesley collection, for which *he* would have bid so high, to be dispersed by auction !

It would seem then that we have not been idle during the century which has elapsed since that great man was in his prime, but have shown an " alacrity in sinking " which would have outdone the heroes of *The Dunciad.*

Mr. Woodburn told the artist who denounced Sir Thomas Lawrence's collection as " *Hortus Siccus,*" that he had heard of people who did not admire Homer, but had never been aware that it was Homer's fault !

Yes ! those dear, precious Claudes that Dr. Wellesley spent a life in collecting are with the four winds. What are we lusting after to fling away such a banquet ?

Once more accept my thanks for Mr. Cole's much-valued image and believe me, Yours most truly, S. PALMER.

LI. To MR. L. R. VALPY.

RED HILL, *August* 27, 1866.

MY DEAR MR. VALPY. Refreshing myself with another read of your last kind letter, I found that I was asked to " report progress." What a monster I must have seemed to neglect so kind a wish ! . . .

I have just got up from a very pleasant musing upon *The Haunted Stream,* which I hope before *very* long will be in a showable

[1] Mr. Frost's tardy election to the full honours of the Academy was a very sore subject with my father, who seemed to see in that tardiness an affront to Imaginative Art.— ED.

state. I have been kept from it through wishing to get a couple of drawings done . . . . and having got through the hard work, can now hope, D.V., for a little Miltonic solace ; for, exquisite as are some of the favoured aspects of nature, no facts nor representation of facts alone can give *rest* to the mind which has humbly dwelt on the works of the ideal masters. Though sight is the most refined of the senses, yet sight of colour and shade is a sensual pleasure, unless the visible suggest the historic and poetic ; and it is perhaps the very intensity which belongs to sensual appetite that makes us fasten with such appetite upon sketches done at once from nature. But He who gave us the senses wills that we should use them in measure, with thanksgiving. We have sensual pleasure in smelling a honeysuckle, but of so refined a class that it almost suggests poetry. What can be more attractive, as to the present pleasure we derive from it, than the journal of some quick perceiver and bright describer, written day by day off hand while exploring beautiful country, and among interesting races of people. *While reading* it, the grand, old, stock thoughts of the poets seem almost conventional and musty in comparison, and their personages rather stiff and old-fashioned—Ariadne, and Procris, and Psyche, and "all those fellows," as a very unpoetic person once called them.

But yet, long after the journal has been forgotten, we catch ourselves wandering with Gallus along the margin of Permessus, though scarcely daring to hope for a glimpse of the sister who led him upwards. Yours most truly, S. PALMER.

LII. To Miss Julia Richmond.

FURZE HILL, *September the something*, 1866.

MY DEAR JULIA. I would do anything I could to please you, but a LETTER is really quite out of my power. Letters should be so artless, you know, so negligently elegant ; they want the natty native-grace-Gainsborough-kind-of-a-touch : at least so the critics say, and I really don't think we want any more of them—letters I mean ; or either. We have Pope's, and Cowper's, and Gray's. Cowper's name is with me the synonym of elegance, and some say that Pope's smell of the lamp ; but I like oil, and would recommend you to breakfast upon Betts' cocoa, with oleaginous globosities bobbing about as you stir it, like porpoises of the deep.

And if this is "too rich" (for gross it is *not*), then a slice of roast beef and a pint of home-brewed. Perhaps we grow, both in mind and body, to be somewhat like our diet ; therefore, though it should never be gross, it need not be nervous, vapouring fantastical, like strong green tea : much less narcotic (by the bye, they are now making cigarettes for the ladies), like that detestable tobacco—the substitute for food which they cannot afford to buy, with our half-starved field-labourers. I am told that the target practice is in every case impossible until cigars are relinquished. London-season-ladies go to opium at once. The labourer's pipe smells comfortably in a country lane on a chilly, autumn evening, as he is plodding home from the furrows ; and we have no reason to complain of Milton's single pipe and glass of water before going to bed, for he rose early and soared without roaming (see the last couplet of Wordsworth's [sonnet] to the Lark—one of his best, I think) : but all these things have their mental analogies. There is a kind of green-tea poetry and smoky philosophy of which we may have too much. Shelley, if I remember, in his ode to the lark, assures that bird that, after all, he is no lark at all, but a spirit ! a spirit ! " I say—none of that !" the bird might have replied, as the Tower warder to dear Mr. Finch, when he saw him sketching the armour.

Poetry may be *too* transcendent, and so may music, may it not ? Are paradox, muddle, and bombast the "three graces" of literature?

"What have ladies to do with literature?"—Who said that ? O you brute ! Tell me, barbarian, are there not *many* ladies in England who have made Cowper a pocket companion ? And who can read Cowper without being the better, morally and mentally ? "He's flat."—Is he ! What, because he doesn't bother you about the "mystery of Being" and that kind of thing. Flat, I suppose, as fine music is flat, after the barbaric crash of unprepared German discords.

I beg pardon, dear Julia, I was rebuking that demon who whispered something about ladies not reading. O *don't* they read. Did not they rush to hear Carlyle lecture against all sorts of vanities, with rings on their fingers, a French novel in the carriage, and a poodle looking out of the window ? Besides, they read Milton—O yes! *Once—quite through,* as a pious duty; and think the battle of the Angels "awfully sublime"—as it is.

Upon the whole, I think women when not rebellious) better creatures than men—less irreligious, less selfish, and self-indulgent; but their views of the sublime are peculiar. I remember that John Varley, whose lady pupils were legion (*angelic,* legions you will understand), was dreadfully put out by this peculiarity. "Why, they think Salvator Rosa more sublime than Claude!" he used to say, and rub his face, and look as cross as he *could* look, for he was the soul of good-nature. . . . .

As ladies *read,* let me recommend you Fairfax's *Tasso* even though you may have read the original. He was born with music on his tongue, and moreover was Queen Elizabeth's godson ! ! ! ! ! ! ! ! ! ! ! ! ! ! ! ! ! *There's a chance !*

Perhaps he kept a gig . . . .

Now, dear Julia, write me as many letters as ever you like ; they always give me pleasure.—O yes ! you'll write me *such* Devon descriptions that I shall seem to be sweetly smothered in cream. Do tell me all about that dear country: but I really *can't* write anything rational ; so you see, unanswered letters of yours will be a virtuous iteration of returning good for evil.

Many happy returns of your coming birthday, with all my heart. Yours affectionately, S. P.

LIII. TO MR. R. REDGRAVE.

RED HILL, *October* 1, 1866.

MY DEAR REDGRAVE. I must trouble you with one line just of thanks for your great kindness to *mine* who are solaced under your roof, as the pilgrims of old at the "House of the Interpreter" . . . .

With this, or within a post or so, you will get one of Dr. Maitland's mud-carts. There is a procession of them, like Mr. Darke's. That man spent his life in carting mud out of men's minds, and in eliciting out of utter confusion the present Lambeth Library. His reward—dismissal, on accession of Archbishop Sumner. The great mud-cart-man of antiquity had better fortune, and very beautiful carpets, as we know from the peculiar recognition with which Diogenes favoured them.

It is very kind of you to send a word of advice to such a lost wretch as I. "Change of scene." Yes! would I could get it—but where? I must still take myself with me, alas! Yet I *should* like *one* peep at the Southern sun before I look my last at him. Just a glimpse of Naples perhaps, from the Vomera, glittering like a mosaic of gems, but with innate living light from a sea of beryl.—O! this won't do! I am going off! This morning my family went to that respectable and salubrious green-mud-side resort, *The Marina St Leonards*. I *can't* make the letters slant enough. Margate *is* a nice place (Turner knew it well), but people won't go there : for if they do, they see poorish folks enjoying themselves, which of course is quite shocking!

With many thanks to Mrs. Redgrave and yourself, and love, if I may say so, to the dear young ladies, believe me, ever Yours,
S. PALMER.

LIV. TO A. H. PALMER.

RED HILL., *October* 14, 1866.

MY DEAR HERBERT. . . . . Your mother's account of the new lodgings would, if I were movable, bring me down for a day, but there is no fear of my coming. *I* should prefer a room built imminent ; bumped from beneath by the booming brine ; or, to avoid vulgar alliteration, a tambourine for Thetis, which, though alliterative, is not vulgar. By vulgar I mean coarse, not common ; for some of the commonest things are the best ; light, air, bread, for instance.

All secular and much moral wisdom is taught by the epic poets. The *Georgics,* though not an epic, teach the wisdom of all life and the mysteries of intellectual discipline under the veil of agriculture, vintages, cattle, bees, so that the veil itself is glorious—the diamond is set in gold. Take, for instance, this simile, on the danger of a little remissness after long perseverance :—

> " Non aliter, quam qui adverso vix flumine lembum
> Remigiis subigit, si brachia forte remisit,
> Atque illum in præceps prono rapit alveus amni."

How many might this have saved from ruin! Fools call these things folly : I have done.

When we meet (D. V.), remind me about the occasional growth of our English rats to the bigness of a good-sized cat.

All facts are worth having, and should be investigated with patient accuracy ; though a mountain of facts will never make even a mole-hill of truth.

We may teem with facts and yet be deplorably ignorant. But I am going off again ! Subject to fits, you see ! While foaming, I will finish with a bit from Heraclitus, I think, given loosely :—" The knowledge of many sciences will never give wisdom, but the voice of the Sibyl, by the divine Power, shrill with unadorned Truth, is heard after a thousand years ;" and the root of all—the first word of wisdom is GOD. All things are innocent which do not grieve Him. And we find that, where the conscience has been at peace, there has been to the last, even with the martyrs, a lambent sprightliness and humour like the harmless play of summer lightning. But, as Addison observes, what would have been shocking levity in another sort of man was lovely in Sir Thomas More. He is speaking of his joke about his beard and the scaffold.

I take no credit to myself for not being full of the gossiping stuff which makes a " nice letter." In fact the supply has been cut off, as no one has been here.

I dearly love solitude, but miss poor " Tabby." If I could but have taught her to read, what a comfort she would have been to me. You may be, please God, a balm and cordial to my heart —but I fear the odds are against it. Men of my turn do not please the neighbours about them, and disrespect is catching : and not being a bold, pushing, blustering, black-whiskered " fellow," in a blue coat and yellow buttons, elbowing everybody I meet, you can't look big upon the strength of it, and say, " As to *my* father, he *is* a *REAL WINE-MERCHANT.*" You know the story.

Carry with you through the week these words of Balaam. " He hath showed thee, O man, what is good ; and what doth the Lord require of thee but to do justly and to love mercy and to walk humbly with thy God ? " (from the Sunday's lesson, Micah the 6th). Remember in your prayers, dear Herbert, Your loving father, SAMUEL PALMER.

LV. To A. H. PALMER.

RED HILL, *Sunday Evening, November* 4, 1866.

MY DEAR HERBERT. . . . . It is high time you got to the end of the syntax, and then the daily readings through the month will be sure, I *hope*, to keep it in memory. . . . The total difference a liberal education makes in a boy's habits of thought, style of speech, and general demeanour makes me most anxious that you should secure the principal points at all events, and a thorough acquaintance with the Latin grammar makes other things easy. I think, with our Vicar, that girls should learn it too ; for a knowledge of Latin gives a mastery over English which nothing else will give. . . .

Jane and I get on together like a pair of silver doves :—

> " — not a breath disturbs the deep serene,
> And not a cloud o'ercasts the solemn scene."

She is most attentive to make me comfortable ; and I hope that never by any unintentional rudeness, [do] I omit to show the high respect I feel for her.

When my room was being done and all my things were out in the "*Hall*" (for one *must* be genteel writing to *Brighton*,)[1] who should pop in but Mr. Collard. It amused me much. I was driven from " dibbing " work for that day, and all the " fal-lals " were off the drawing-room table, replaced by a mighty mass of Virgils ! Then, indeed, I felt that things looked " respectable " in the true sense of the word, and not in the sense of " keeping a gig."

This is a gossiping letter, is it not ? What different things go by the same name ! Think of St. Paul's letters, to which the dying Grotius said he would devote ten years, if they could be spared to him ; and to descend to a lower sphere, what an elegant correspondence was that which Charles Fox carried on with Gilbert Wakefield when Mr. Wakefield was in Dorchester gaol, as to whether the nightingale's note expressed joy or grief. Then, how the classics were ransacked !

Jane thinks I had better leave off now and have my dinner and I am like a lamb in leading strings.[2] " Wise as serpents and harmless as doves," the Apostle says. If we once lose sight of GOODNESS as the PRINCIPAL THING we are adrift without an anchor. If we merely ask ourselves what will people say of us, we are rotten at the core.

I have done as I was bid—eaten my dinner, and in public too,

[1 The words in italics are written in a most genteel and flourished hand.— Ed.]
[2 Not intended as praise to myself, but to the strings, for a man may be too much of a lamb after all.

like the Kings of France. Miss Thomas called. . . . and is only
just gone. I told her I was not up to the politeness of the French
Court in the reign of Louis XIV. When the king would show
a particular mark of favour, he took a morsel of something, a
sweetmeat perhaps, and having bitten off a piece for himself, sent
the rest down the table to the favourite guest. Soldiers then were
the only "gentlemen," and when besieging a refractory town their
favourite pastime was to catch some of the town-folks' babies,
impale and roast them, if I remember rightly. So much for the
fashionables of the most fashionable reign of the most fashionable
age. I am not clear whether they did not sometimes eat the
roasted babies.

These and a thousand other piquant mischiefs vary the
administration of Satan's kingdom, and to a corrupt heart make
it more *entertaining*, however shocking sometimes, than religion—
religion as observed from a false point of view by the children of
this world, as a *negative propriety*, or a grim demeanour; but not to
those who esteem conquest of self as real a siege and struggle as
the taking of a city—nay, not to those who are sufficiently read in
ecclesiastical history to see all the elements of heroic poesy, nay
even of spiritual romance and chivalry in the story of the Church ;
whether grappling with sin in the courts of princes, or hewing a
way with missionary hands and axes through dense forests among
the wild beasts ; draining marshes, confronting and converting
ferocious barbarians ; and eventually, round each retreat in which
they had planted the symbol of suffering, causing the desert to
" rejoice and blossom as the rose." . . . . The way to praise our
Lord acceptably here is to *learn to pray*. " Lord, teach us to pray,"
said the disciples : and our Lord then gave them that divine form
of prayer which goes by His blessed name, but was wholly or in
part used before, I believe, in the Jewish liturgy.

Now I want you ever to remember, that saying—repeating any
form of prayer, is in itself no prayer at all, if the heart do not go
with the words : and believe that Satan and his agents are ever
busy to thrust in distracting thoughts. A boy who has endeavoured
to " place himself in the presence of God," and in the fewest words
really asked forgiveness of faults, thrown to Heaven one loving
glance of thankfulness, and asked God to help all His creatures,
and His whole Church, and then goes merrily abroad, in his young

friskiness turning somersaults half down the street, is more likely
to have the protection and blessing of God through the day, than
another boy who has been to matins, very demurely kneeling, but
never once sending up a real prayer, his mind being occupied with
other things. This is no fault of the holy liturgies which we have
received from the Apostles and Fathers (our divine Communion
Service is supposed to be very nearly that used by St. James,
Bishop of Jerusalem), any more than it is a dinner's fault if we eat
without chewing it. But the Church which contains and teaches
ALL TRUTH, and is thereby distinguished from other bodies
which teach parts of truth, has never discouraged private extempore
prayer, and I wish people, especially young people, practised it
more. The words will be in a literary point of view poor stuff
probably, compared with the inimitable forms we are used to (the
exquisite second collect for Evening Prayer, and the prayer of St.
Chrysostom for instance), but what has literature to do with private prayer ? The loving, filial eye is the thing—the tear in that
eye ; the pang for having offended ; these are what the Father loves ;
and all art and literature are as inferior to these great and *eternal*
transactions of the heart, as education, literature—what in short
the Scotch call the humanities are, in turn, incomparably superior
to the objects of worldly ambition. With love to all, believe me
dear Herbert, Your loving father, S. PALMER.

Don't forget to pray for me daily.

LVI. To A. H. PALMER.

RED HILL, *November*, 1866.

MY DEAR HERBERT. I am not going to write you a letter, but
just to mention one or two things as refreshers to memory. When
I found that you were likely to stay so long, I told you to learn
daily one of the little portions of the new syntax, besides reading
over the daily portion of the old, and I hope you have not failed to
do so. This will leave at least 23 hours out of the 24 for sleep,
eating, and holiday making.

Would it not be a sad thing to lose what you have been at so
much trouble to learn and I to teach ? This very light exercise of
memory will just be what a mininum of daily exercise is to the

body. If, for several weeks, you were obliged to lie perfectly still through the whole twenty-four hours, I doubt whether you would be able to move a muscle when you tried. It is an ignoble thing to receive of God the light of His sun, and the fresh, sweet air, and to be quite useless in the world—to live, as the Apostle says, "to ourselves," instead of "to him who *died* for *us*."

Young people must be trying to learn some one thing at least ; to learn some one thing thoroughly. *You* are upon Latin grammar, which wise men consider the best first step to efficiency in after life. Now I wish you to spare me the trouble of reminding you, by being your own Mentor.

Howard, and Inglis Richmond have just taken tea with me. and I enjoyed their visit. Of the two I prefer the society of boys who are in earnest about their learning, to that of grown people, who often lose their young ardour for progress, and become stationary or retrograde. Inglis thinks my plan of the daily grammar reading excellent, and says that Mr. Giles did much the same with him, but with three points of difference : first, after the daily repetition without book (the second point), which lasted an hour and a quarter, Mr. Giles used to present him with a couple of the finest possible oranges, and with half a dozen, on the wind up of Saturday's exercise. Thirdly, they divided the grammar into six instead of three portions, so that the whole grammar (one about the size of Valpy's) was repeated without book from beginning to end, every week.

Now I have done my duty (which, please God, I will do till I am put away), and it remains for you to do yours. Usually I fear, the less is asked the more difficult it is to get it done.

Having no time to compose letters, I merely talk with my pen, and it was in this way that I called the drawing-room-table books "fal-lals." I merely spoke of their outsides—all that gilding and stuff, and their solemn parallelism with the sides of the table, which Jane sedulously cultivates, not forgetting the central nosegay, a red rose in which, she observed, was the very first thing which attracted the Miss Wilkinsons when they called the other day. . . .

I have a letter in several sheets from Mrs. Finch addressed jointly to your Mamma and myself, from which I extract a little bit to show you the unexpected and important uses of acquired knowledge, when there is a virtuous disposition to use them for good, as in the case of my quondam pupil.

"I am going to-morrow to spend a day or two with Mary Humphry, wife of Professor Humphry of Cambridge, their home being one of the rendezvous of the savants of the place. She also remembers you with interest and kindness. Such a pair, I ween, are seldom seen, as she and her husband. When he was about to bring out a work on the human bones, she set herself to learn to engrave, and illustrated the volume with plates, not from copies, but from the bones themselves—dry work, some people would say; and now all his lectures are enriched with her illustrations, magnified by herself to gigantic proportion. Are you not proud of your sometime pupil?"

I hope not, for pride will have a fall. But I want you to notice what follows. I always remarked in that family a thoroughness in the education. Nothing was loose or slippery, and there was no show or parade. The little I did for her would have been quite thrown away upon most people, but *thoroughness* was in that house.

Observe too that any important branch of study is found *dry* only by dry minds. If I am getting too serious again, I may vary pleasantly by observing that for some days the water has declined to go down the sink, and that I am going to get Mr. Nightingale to look at it. This is what people call a substantial fact—no moonshine or nonsense about it. Also I have not missed my monotonous walk every morning. There's another fact for the benefit of the whole human race. Now comes another with a more pleasing sentiment about it. Miss Thomas has brought Jane a very pretty coloured glass smelling-bottle, with which she is much pleased.

Now to stuff the mind with a legion of little facts makes it stupid and heavy as a bed is made heavy by its fulness of light feathers; and the very facts are useless, because we have no main study to which they minister. Then, if we take up Sunday's epistle, *that* will seem hollow to us—fanatical even, though we may not dare to indulge the thought. It speaks of a hope laid up in Heaven for such of the Colossians as the Apostle addressed. Now, if we become carnally-minded we shall say, "For my part, I prefer a bird in the hand." . . .

This is a dull boy's letter; nothing of cricket, boating only incidentally; but this house is a centre of dulness—a becalmed pond with neither ducks nor drakes to splash about in it. With love to all, and commending you to the Divine blessing, I remain, dear Herbert, Your loving father, S. PALMER.

DON'T FORGET JANE'S SEA-WEED.

LVII. To Mr. L. R. VALPY.

FURZE HILL, *September* 13, 1867.

MY DEAR MR. VALPY. I wrote one line to acknowledge the safe arrival of *Religio Medici* . . . and chiefly to apologize for my rudeness in never so much as thanking you for sending *The Times* . . .

Those church-breakers exploded me. Next morning. . . lapsing into a sweet tranquillity, I took out *The Haunted Stream* for the first time. I think you will like it, as I am touching it with pleasure to myself, in a much-musing mood which is not always one's experience. . . . You cannot tell how much I like the plan of written annotation : it leaves one at peace to do a little now and then as one feels it, without fear of forgetting.

Allow me strongly to recommend (his theological bearings excepted) Mr. Matthew Arnold's Oxford lecture on *Culture and its Enemies* (printed in *The Cornhill* of July) as a work of real thought and perception. I hope his " Philistinism " will become a household word, and tend in some measure to civilize our dear country. He is trying to teach us that man is to be estimated not by what he has, but by what he is ; and that " sweetness and light " are even sweeter than sovereigns ; but with a change of dynasty in France, and its not impossible alliance with America against us ; in the present state of our defences—our navy, and our artillery, we should perhaps not survive to take the lesson. Believe me, with best regards, Yours very truly, S. PALMER.

LVIII. To Mr. L. R. VALPY.

September, 1867.

MY DEAR MR. VALPY. Many thanks for your sunset, which is particularly interesting to me as I have sketches of various phases of the near greys, separated or rent, and have used them for

U

several subjects. When rent sufficiently, I have seen all the palette, or rather choir of greys which lie between blue, or violet, and copper colour (in one case all the splendour of rose and purple, orange and gold), far away in the horizon, with the dark nimbus near and detached.

I was a little disappointed with the Wye, as far as four miles up beyond Tintern, but most likely it improves as it becomes more of a mountain stream.

I was anxious to mention what I read the other day, that Herefordshire contains many unspoiled, ancient granges and manor-houses, which are to me the gems of England, the landscape around being a setting for them. When you are well up the Wye you might perhaps find a little belting tour of Herefordshire well worth a day or two's experiment. You might find some relics of the most ancient machinery and implements for cider making, and a few of the grand large cottages (for grand they are), some five or six hundred years old, buttressed with stone and ribbed with heart of oak. These reminders of the "dark ages" (! !) vanish right and left before the railroads, and give place to the new lights of lath-and-plaster, stucco, and whitewash. The sentiment of real English remoteness is therefore the most precious, and with all its sacredness of human, and sometimes divine association, seems to me more truly grand and entertaining to the imagination than a good many "Loch Lomonds." With an intelligent countryman as guide, and the ordnance map, I should like to explore that part of Hereford for old farms and buildings of all sorts. . . . How nice it would be to get photographs of some of the remote Hereford farms, granges, cider-presses &c.—a Miltonic *roller* or two, and such like. The great poets, with whom MAN is always expressed or implied, seem to have preferred such imagery to lumpish mountains and leaden lakes ; e.g. the "cider-press" in Keats's *Autumn.* Believe me in haste, Yours most truly, S. PALMER.

LIX. TO MR. L. R. VALPY.

RED HILL, *October* 21, 1867.

MY DEAR MR. VALPY. . . . The other day, *at last*, I think the true "vision" came of *The Prospect* Milton, "Straight mine eye hath caught new pleasure" &c. It is a very curious subject, for there seems no medium between a mappy, Buckinghamshire treatment, and a genial, poetic swoon. Between ourselves, and trembling to say it, I think that Milton (with him a most exceptional case), was a little halting between the two. The mountain's "barren breast," and the "meadows trim with daisies pied," seem to jar a little.

Hard work must be some apology for my tardy correspondence.

I am very glad to hear of your Hereford explorations, and the turning up of those old "manor-houses" which add to landscape a history, and humanity. The finest green-grocery gets a lift when we imagine some of it gracing "King Alcinous' Feast."

We rise thus from ordinary landscape to the bucolic and poetic, where "more is meant than meets the" eye. With the poet, a single adjective has power to lengthen and dignify a river course, suggest city and citadel at its estuary, and farther up, disputed fords and foughten fields; then, upward still among the rocks and falls, the spirits of woods and streams, the fairies, and the good old river-god. As an instance out of many, we may take " That ANCIENT river the river Kishon " . . . Yours, &c., S. PALMER.

LX. To MR. L. R. VALPY.

FURZE HILL, *6th November*, 1867.

MY DEAR MR. VALPY. . . . Added to the result of our discussion on *The [Haunted] Stream*, I found out something after you left which has put it all in my power. I have worked on it a little to-day, most tenderly breaking those delicate crimson tones which, in the little sketch, depress the saffron to a focus, and merging the extreme distance, as in the sketch, to a more mysterious purplish gloom, and the result is that the city, which never pleased me, has sprung up and asserted itself (I fancy) as the poetic eye of the drawing. Your *rock* suggestion I am delighted with.

I shall want the little sketch as long as the drawing is in the house and indeed for some time, as I hope to make a small drawing with that sky and mountain as they are, according to my

first wish as to the use of it for the *Penseroso*, for what I think is
the finest suggestion in the poem, Saturn and Vesta solemnly
reposing in the Forest—secret shades of " Woody Ida's *Inmost
Grove*." That, to me, is worth a great many " Towered Cities."
Think of the cedars ! [sketch]. Yet I think I have among my
studies a sky which would suit it even better than the amber.
That and " The Bellman's drousy charm " have an unutterable
going-in-itiveness.

What a foolish digression ! You may depend on my attention
to the remarks, as in the former case.

That " Hymen " who has been the plague of my life, must be
turned as if going round the corner to the right. . . .

I had rather take time about *The Stream*, doing a little as I
quite feel it, for the last subtleties are so much better done this way,
while other subjects are going on. Believe me ever, my dear Mr.
Valpy, Yours truly, S. PALMER.

LXI. To A. H. PALMER.

21st Sunday after Trinity, 1867.

MY DEAR HERBERT. If we rank in the moral scale above the
noisier four-footed beasts, surely we shall be touched by the collect
for to-day, " ——pardon and peace . . . and serve thee with a
quiet mind."

The violets of the Lord's garden, the sweet, retiring souls who are
to be traced but by the fragrance of unobtrusive charities, have
been refreshed to-day by that collect, in many a remote dependency
and distant isle. As sometimes in mid-ocean, sometimes when
traversing the desert, men have plainly heard their native village
bells ; so, to-day, far on either side of the equator, to the Lord's
little ones has that sweet collect chimed of " Heaven which is their
home." But suppose it should please our Master to convert us
wholly to Himself, so that you and I, dear Herbert, should one day
live together merrily in Heaven ; suppose we make up our minds at
once to start together on pilgrimage—no sooner are we afoot, than
all sorts of hindrances molest us. First there's the Devil, for he is
not quite dead yet, though the German critics think they have made
away with him. Then there's the old man within us: the law in

our members warring against the law of our minds. Then, evil influences of example, and not least perhaps, to make a kind of " bull," the evil example we set to ourselves Then the habits of modern domestic life, so arranged as to leave the least possible time for all which is of the utmost possible moment. You are beginning to learn a profession (a great Christian duty), and know how difficult it is to get time free from interruption for that and the simplest necessities of education.   I call Latin a necessity of really good education, for without it I do not think the best English has ever been written or spoken : and as speech pre-eminently distinguishes us from the brutes (I mean them no disrespect), we ought surely to speak well. Some relish too of ancient and, still more, [of] ecclesiastical history, and of heroic poesy, tends to make us less despicably selfish than we might otherwise be, scraping carrion each to his own kennel: teaches us that we are members one of another, and of the rational polity : expands us ; pulls us up out of the ditch ; takes us up hill, and gives us a wider prospect, and shows us why and how we should utter with yearning hearts, " Thy kingdom come."

Your new acquaintance " Uriah Heep " would have been the better for something of this, would he not ? Don't let us grovel, but let our word be, " Upward—upward ! " Pray for your poor ailing father, S. P.

LXII. To Mrs. Richard Redgrave.

My dear Mrs. Redgrave. I have been blessing every one I could think of whose name begins with an R. for giving me a rich evening's treat in Mr. Lowe's speech. You were the first friend I thought of; the " R. R. " fitted, if it had not been for that puzzling " M " in the middle. To-day, Mrs. Palmer has solved the difficulty by telling me that you have two given names. It was read again last night, aloud, by a young friend who called, while I sat coiled up before the fire blinking and almost purring, like a large cat. An *ad libitum* of raspberry tarts is not more relished by a little boy in the holidays.

It is delightful to meet with any intellectual quality in its per- fection, and Mr. Lowe seems to me to be the very sublime of *clever-*

ness. One cannot help transporting oneself to the lecture-hall, and imagining the sharp practical eyes of the utilitarian majority of the audience, who devour the whole as incontrovertible, sparkling with triumph as he pours out his skirmishers upon the flanks of poor Antiquity :—

> " None of these ancient heroes e'er saw a cannon ball,
> Or knew the force of powder to slay their foes withal :
> But our brave boys do know it, yet banish all their fears,
> With the Tow row row de dow of the British Grenadiers."

There is no muddle about Mr. Lowe ; he is so clear-headed and logical that you are much pleased if you much differ.

Grant his minor, and his famous reform speech was conclusive. This on education is no less so, if we attach his meaning to the one word "usefulness." But here people differ. King Alfred himself was anything but a useful person in the eyes of the good housewife who entrusted her cakes to his watching.

There is certainly much that is indefensible in our educational system ; the shameful waste of time over Latin-verse making for instance ; but Milton has gone into everything in his little *Tractate on Education*, and I think we may there see how a master of the Ideal, and he alone, can best treat of the expedient and the actual.

With many thanks, believe me, dear Mrs. Redgrave, Yours most sincerely, SAMUEL PALMER.

1868

LXIII. TO MR. JOHN GILES.[1]

MY DEAR JOHN. Lest they should have put me away and got the house tidy before then, I wish you a Merry Christmas, 1868, and a Happy New Year, 1869. But as it is, I am turned out neck and crop for a couple of days or so ; for the " Helps " are going away, and they say my den *must* be cleaned out before the new ones come, and it is declined, the taking one step towards it, while I am in the house, lest I should interfere with what of course I don't understand. So I write, as you kindly bade me, to ask if you would house me for a couple of nights if I come on

---

[1] [Written on filigree paper stamped at the top with the Christmas and New Year's greetings in ornamental letters.]

Friday, but pardon me if, after all, combined hail and east wind befall and stop my progress.

When I am "not Stephano" but a cramp, the unattached blanket is precious ; our cook Jane, whose only fault was drinking, told me of it, bless her heart : do *I* judge her ?

Could we get up a Maitland evening ? I fear not. Twelve onions were got for that bullock's heart, and you know the result.[1] I'm sick of it all ; not of bullock's heart, or of onions, but of the draw-ing-room-genteel-life-servant-keeping system altogether ; and if I were alone again, would build a vast, airy hut on a dry soil in an old fashioned town, where there was a wholesome cook-shop, and be my own house-maid and char-woman.

Servants have been made what they are by the foolish example of their "betters ;" but they are killing off their mistresses by wholesale with the incessant worry. To think that, loving peace and a simple life, one should be entangled in these things like a fly in a tar-barrel—no settlement, no safety ; no improbability of the house being set on fire any night in the week, by the "helps" falling asleep over "*The Illustrated Police News !*" Well, it's work for patience, and one in which patience may have her *perfect* work.

O ! happy Barrys ! thrice happy Alexander Selkirks, "if only their happiness they knew"! Well might Jansenius say that with his Bible and St. Augustine's works, he could be perfectly happy in a desert island. O ! what unspeakable pains do people take in elaborating their own misery ! Rich subject-matter for reflection, which I hope we shall follow up in this very room together ere long, for horrors are becoming my pastime. In the meantime believe me, Dear John, Yours affectionately, the wretched S. P.

My pet narcissus, the eye of the garden, gone ! Virgilian nose-gays basketed off to Reigate to make bouquets for butcher-boys. Do I then despise butcher-boys ? Heaven forbid ! One of the "helps" nearly fainted from tight stays the other morning, and at prayer-time too. I like that ; it's a sample of our modern Chris-tianity. A text for a sermon that I should like to preach the Sun-day after next, from the pulpit of Reigate church : but they've gagged the laity.

FILIGREE FOLLY, *May* 1868.

[1] None were used.—ED.]

LXIV. To MR. L. R. VALPY.

RED HILL, *September*, 1868.

MY DEAR MR. VALPY. . . . I wish the Lucys had sent [to the
Leeds Exhibition] the pair of long Titians mentioned in my last note,
and that you could have seen Claude's *Enchanted Castle*. After all,
there is nobody like him when we get him at his best and uninjured,
I mean among the painters of pure landscape. Two things always
affect me in a great picture-gathering ; first—the vast amount of
power and knowledge ; next, a regret that it should comparatively
seldom have been devoted to the embodiment of sentiment, in the
higher sense of the word—that the love should seldom be found
in measure quite equal to the skill. I cannot but feel with you
that there is a sweet refreshment in the scenes of Fra Angelico :
nooks and dells of Paradise, where emulation, and power, and
learning and greatness, have become empty sounds. We can rest
there awhile, and return to the genuine sublime in design and
chiaroscuro, all the better for our retreat—if indeed the humble
heavenly love which he depicts be not of all great things the
greatest. . . . S. PALMER.

LXV. To THE REV. J. P. WRIGHT.

FURZE HILL, *September* 1868.

DEAR MR. WRIGHT. I can't let Herbert's letter go without one
line to thank you for your kindness to him on this and on other
occasions.

Happy are those who have whooped and measled satisfactorily,
and had small-pox three times, like the Rev. Vice-Principal of the
English College at Rome.[1] These things are not in my depart-
ment, nor do I interfere with the sanitary jurisdiction, but I am
not without hope that A. H. may one day investigate Winchester
cathedral under your guidance.

Upon some matters whereon pulpits are strangely silent, it has
pleased Him who "girded Cyrus" to make *The Saturday Review*
a "preacher of righteousness." I hope you will read *The
Fashionable Woman*, No. 667, August 8th, 1868, page 184. This,
and the next following article, *Sermons on Sermons*, p. 186, indicate

[1 Mr. William Giles, my father's cousin.—ED.]

such a widely-spread declension in faith and morals as to suggest in vulgar phrase but sad reality, that we are "going to the Devil" very fast indeed.

If, with connivance or only feeble protests from the clergy (observe the "if"), educated Christians are becoming less religious than the average Pagan of antiquity ; if they are becoming almost as licentious and far more frivolous and foolish, the evidences of Christianity become practically damaged ; met with a formidable *cui bono* ?

What some call the "sins of folly" entail more misery and ruin than sins of malignity, because there are so many more sinners. How many acquaintances can we tell off on our fingers who will dare to be singular ; who will draw a line, and halt, and say "No"?

But to tell off those who will be sure to "follow a multitude to do evil," if it be only a fashionable multitude, we need have the fingers of Briareus.

I think we should earnestly thank God for having influenced the hearts and guided the pens which have laboured of late in *The Saturday Review* to stay, if it be possible, the deterioration of our fair country-women; for, unless the care of young children be wholly deputed to hirelings, the mothers of this generation make the morals of the men and women of the next.

I was much interested by Professor Tyndal's address at Norwich, reported in *The Athenæum*, and hope the latter part will repress the flippancy of many a young materialist. Even if we grant that the crystal, the passion-flower, the mature man even, are built up by atoms acting by purely mechanical laws or chemical affinities and antagonisms (and we cannot yet define either "chemical" or "mechanical"), it redounds but the more to the glory of His wisdom who devised such laws and made such atoms. Except figuratively, however, the word "law" is sheer nonsense, for law can only act upon an intelligent patient.

The "laws of nature" are the usage or habit of nature put into poetry, I think. The atoms which compose an apple falling to the ground or a pickpocket knocked into the kennel are not really obeying a law, but gravitating by an impulse : nor did Newton conceive that gravitation could do its work without a Divine Omnipresence.

A bit of rubbed sealing-wax applied to scraps of paper suspends the LAW of gravitation with impunity, and are we to *demand* of the Almighty *how* he made the iron swim? Believe me in haste, Yours most truly, S. PALMER.

1869

LXVI. TO A YOUNG CLERGYMAN.

February, 1869.

MY DEAR   * * * The matters touched on in your letter being *all-important*, I take a large sheet. If I put what strikes me in the form of assertion, it is merely for brevity's sake.

I so fully intended to acknowledge my pleasure in reading your article in the —— that I thought I had done so. What if you took Bunyan's *Life of Badman?* As a scarcely-known work of an all-known author it might fairly class with curious old books. I have it not, alas! . . .

I wish some clerical Alcides would slay that three-headed Cerberus the "Sermon." The word has gradually changed its meaning, narrowing from a discourse into a particular kind of essay. And "discourse" itself is not large enough to include preaching in some of its best senses—exhortation, persuasion, &c. However, it is our constant tendency in backing from an obstruction on one side of the way to upset into a ditch on the other; and he is to be pitied who undervalues our exegetical divinity, so much of which as was extant in his time was venerated by Lord Bacon. And how much have we had since, down to our own times! Take Bishop Horsley's sermons—naming one example at random among multitudes. We are most prone to this backing when we are angry, and then it is, I think, that we should seek for the DRY LIGHT which Pythagoras preferred—intellectual perception not obfuscated by the passions.

I quite agree with you that when a clergyman has not had time to write a sermon, and is not in energy for the extempore, he should take a printed one into the pulpit; telling the people who wrote it when it is finished; which will keep alive curiosity and therefore attention—Attention the daughter of Curiosity, who seldom can be prevailed upon to go anywhere without her mother. Why are *The Homilies* never read? There is an excellent one upon dress. By the bye, Mr. Giles told me that one of them was by Bishop Bonner.

I think that he should have been moderately whipped who said that orthodoxy was (one almost trembles to write it) the sin against the Holy Ghost. Surely hyperbole or any other rhetorical figure is out of place in such connection : and, to digress from *such* rhetoric, I remember my father many times expressing his wonder that divines should have raised such a mischievous, nay poisonous dust about a subject so dreadfully clear. *They* were not to be forgiven who, seeing our Lord's miracles, attributed them to Satan. Now I remember having, when a child, been taken to visit a lady who had been in a madhouse, distracted with the fear that she had committed that sin. So much for impertinent inferences, however balefully ingenious, drawn from Scripture. As to the thing meant by your rhetorician, orthodoxy (doubtless you remember Bishop Warburton's definition of it), like everything else, is a bad thing in bad hands. It is a weapon of petty persecution in the hands of petty bigots, and the most orthodox man in the world, if he be not a dullard and a dummy, is liable to the charge of heterodoxy and even atheism, if he write an original and brilliant defence even of orthodoxy itself. I believe Cudworth may be instanced.

Without defending *The Tale of a Tub* it may be mentioned as at once the most powerful satire upon Romanism, and the handle by which Swift was excluded from the Bench by a protestant archbishop—the internal evidence making it more than probable that Swift was the author. I can never think of that great man without nauseating Thackeray's depreciation. Think of *Gulliver's Travels*. Who would not have crawled on his hands and knees across Central Asia to have written that book ?

To be safe, a clergyman must be dull—any man must be dull, or else supremely wise. "The point of danger is the point of victory," but if we love this side of the medallion very much it may not perhaps be amiss to inscribe on the reverse, "The point of victory is also the point of danger : " too headlong a pursuit of the enemy has sometimes exchanged conquest for disaster.

The sorrows you express are such as ought to find sympathy in every Christian breast. "We have not dared," you say, "to rebuke them for their sins." Does not this arise in part from a compliant partnership with their levities? What clergyman can "rebuke" at noon his partner in the dance at two o'clock of that very morning? Should not a pastor be at least rather a drag upon the wheel of Fashion than her running footman?

Might not Law's *Serious Call* be looked into a little by district-visiting ladies and others. If we bend the bow too tightly, are not things in such a state just now that nothing less will get them right. I do not know that ladies would think the better of it for Dr. Johnson's verdict, who said it was the finest piece of hortatory theology in our language. It used to be, and probably is circulated by the Society for promoting Christian Knowledge.

Deplorable, however, as are the encroachments of a tasteless dissipation upon all that is most precious in English domestic life, there is yet a viler and more alarming defection: I mean that air of independence of God which leavens so much of our periodical literature: difficult, as a negative, to find in any paragraph, yet as to the tendency of the whole, expressed by the prophet Daniel "—the God in whose hand thy breath is, and whose are all thy ways, hast thou not glorified." The superstitious reluctance of the Romans to begin great undertakings without careful auguries were a blessed piety compared with this self-sufficient godlessness, of which, sown broadcast over Europe, we have the blade and the ear in the late French poisonings: and God grant that ere we see the ripened crop of this hellish harvest, His Blessed Son may come and visibly take those honours and that kingdom which we pray Him to hasten every time we say the prayer which Himself put into our mouths. As to the moral amelioration of the world by education and the like, it is fanciful rubbish concocted in the darkest ignorance of the human heart.

And now, your frank, earnest and much-valued letter (which I show to no one, leads on to something very serious indeed. You say, "I believe He has given me *personally* a certain message to God's people." And again, "He has given me a word to speak and I will not keep silence." Now if you say this, not rhetorically, but as a simple statement of fact, surely there is no cause for "grief;" but rather for thankfulness in that He who has already bestowed on you that MORE EXCELLENT gift of Charity, is adding a Pentecostal gift of prophecy (in the large sense of the word, and putting a word into your mouth which you may deliver in the power of the Spirit.

As however these living waters, passing like a mountain affluent into the turbid current of our own fallible wills and understanding, are always subject to deterioration, evil spirits will be on the watch to pervert the whole. Hence is the wisdom of God most manifest in putting the tests whereby we are to "try the spirits" into the mouths of St. John and St. Paul. The "beloved disciple" surely knew "the mind of Christ," and he gives the test of the Incarnation. St. Paul also, who was caught up into the third Heaven, MUST have known what doctrine was heavenly, and he says let even an angel from Heaven be anathema who teaches any other gospel. Many speak as if the ONE gospel into which the angels desire to look were narrow and contracted. To me it seems so vast a universe of truth and love as only eternity is long enough to explore. If you receive a message which seems inconsistent with some isolated text, perhaps it is not more so than some other isolated text which elsewhere might be found.

That wondrously beautiful passage in the fifty-eighth of Isaiah describing the inner part and "thing signified" in fasting, may seem to clash with Lenten abstinence and Lenten services; but does it do more than bring to light the meaning—the soul of which they are the body?

Prophetic gifts seem to clash and may really clash with the fallible maxims of a visible Church, particularly with those of a national one, but I would rather look at the Anglican Church as a protected orchard, in which the gifts of the Spirit *may* be permitted to ripen, if that submission be observed towards those who sit in the Apostles' seats, which our Lord commanded towards those who sat in Moses' seat, and were soon to crucify the Lord of Glory. Nothing under the sun is new, and the Jewish Church, as a corporate body, always held the Prophets in antagonism, just as a newly-sent prophet now *must* be unintelligible to a public school head master promoted to be a Lord Bishop. But a certain degree of antagonism is wholesome; and real revelations have sometimes, perhaps, degenerated into fanaticism for want of due restriction, humility and obedience.

The glory of the poet's art is that he converts the BONDS of metre into indispensable conditions of perfect beauty. You speak of "old formulas": being old myself, excuse me if I do not quite relish this. Why are they the worse for being old? If they are as old as the Apostles they are the more likely to be genuine. And if old formulas be unsatisfactory, what STUFF new formulas would be! If we want a new gospel there is a beautiful one made to our hands—Swedenborgianism. My natural man delights in it (the natural man loves pleasant visions): no wrath in God, no Vicarious Sacrifice (the universal belief of all ages and countries), but an entirely benevolent system according to *our* notions of benevolence. Now *our* notions of a benevolent Creator are upset at once by the physical phenomena: the late earthquake at Quito for instance. *We* should not have permitted such a thing: but "My ways are not your ways, saith the Lord." We MUST humble ourselves, and believe, and WAIT.

I would be the last to sneer at Swedenborg. Many are the beautiful things in his writings. I doubt not that he saw and conversed with the spiritual world. But it may be that in the spiritual world there are spirits which are fallible—partly in error though not malignant. Swedenborg thoroughly believed that our Lord came in the flesh. Blake was I think misled by erroneous spirits. I knew an instance in which an accomplished mind could not be persuaded to accept as an article of faith the "coming in the flesh." The final result was a devout paganism. I do not use the words reproachfully, but literally, and without comment.

You say, "I believe in an inspiration of all God's people, as true and as real as the inspiration of the writers of the Bible." In a certain sense this is very true. Our blessed Lord says, "He shall teach you all things." But it makes me uncomfortable, because it is so like the talk of the *Mountites*, who use our Lord's blessed sermon as a wall behind which to *skulk* while they are throwing stones at St. Paul.

In the early part of your letter you express just indignation at falsehood. What, I would ask, is the falsehood of taking a lithograph sermon into the pulpit to the dishonesty of holding up the Bible as a text-book—annotating on and preaching from it, when teaching a religion palpably opposed to its letter and if possible even more to its whole meaning, and spirit, and tendency? As surely as Hippocrates wrote on medicine and the *Georgics* treat of agriculture, so surely is the Vicarious Sacrifice the very spine and marrow of Holy Scripture, from the day when it was promised that the seed of the woman should bruise the Serpent's head, to the apocalyptic hymn, "Worthy is the Lamb that was slain."

I delight to think that you have "passed the Rubicon," and by your distinct avowal, have separated from the *respectables*—have become in short, what they would call a fanatic ; but I think you will do your congregation most good by not informing them of it, lest, to your own annoyance and their own greater hurt, you should have to say with Milton,

> " —— this is got by casting pearl to hogs."

I do not mean "conceal your message," but only honour it with all circumspection and prudence. At the same time I *must* crave pardon for saying that your letter brings to my mind what may be read in the *Bacchæ* of Euripides, when Pentheus met his mother and her comrades in the wood,

> " Then Pentheus saw that he was near calamity."

However, he who leaves the mud for the mountain is nearing calamity in the very act. The more needful to be provided with spiked pole and mountain boots ; and supposing that Providence had provided him with an INFALLIBLE CHART, it would be unwise to leave it behind, even though he had a direct inward assurance of safety. For in both the physical and moral universe, assured ends are realized by conditional means. St Paul's [ship's company] was to be saved ; yet he says, " Except these abide in the ship, ye cannot be saved."

Letter writing is most distasteful to me, much more the apparent egotism of so long a letter as this, but it was forced from me by a sense of duty, lamely as I was aware I should discharge it.

One or two of your expressions which seem to me exceptionable are, in the very letter, what dear friends have expressed to me years ago ; and in some of these cases, with all apparent spirituality, the outcome was such as it gives one pain to remember.

As you can best "glorify God in your body and spirit" when your body is in sound health, I hope you will not abate one jot of that soundness by intemperate fasting. I know a Roman Catholic dignitary who is obliged to have a dispensation and to eat meat, simply because he cannot do his work without it.

Probably you saw that extraordinary pamphlet by a learned Roman Catholic against papal infallibility &c. which was reviewed in *The Times* about Christmas-time. He shows that, whereas they charge us with lay subjection, his own Church has been even more king-ridden. I cannot recollect the author's name. It is in the form of a letter to Dr. Manning. It was placed immediately on the Roman Index.

Please remember me and mine sometimes in your prayers, and believe me (writing perhaps for the last time), Yours most truly, S. PALMER.

LXVII. TO MR. L. R. VALPY.

RED HILL, *March* 16, 1869.

MY DEAR MR. VALPY. . . . . I should have much enjoyed the meeting you so kindly asked me to attend, for though I do not think our blessed Christian Sunday is the Sabbath Day (seeing, among other reasons, that the primitive Jewish converts kept *both*), yet I fear that the opening of exhibitions would lead to the opening of theatres, and in the long run produce the Parisian Sunday, which is a day of rest for nobody : and the Christian Sunday was doubtless meant to number the weekly rest among its blessings, though many of the early Christians were obliged to work all through it, going early in the morning to the " Breaking of Bread."

The Church, unlike the hypocritical Pharisees, permits the reaping to go on in critical weather, and does not prohibit the doing of good.

Judaizing notions have made Sunday very miserable to children, some parents having actually put away the toys on Saturday evening. A little child brought up in this way asked its mother what Heaven was like. " My love," said mama, " Heaven is a perpetual Sabbath." On which the poor little thing expressed a wish that, when she died, she might go *elsewhere !* Martin Luther, on the other hand, writes to his little child that if he went to Heaven he would have toys and drums and hobby-horses, as many as heart could wish (I quote from memory) ; and he declared that he would go out hunting on Sunday, if people would insist on confounding it with the Sabbath.

If it did not involve keeping so many attendants from their

weekly rest, I should like to see august cathedral services in pure
air and in the most beautiful buildings, richly furnished with high
art, where the people could either take their food with them, or buy
it reasonably on the spot ; and I would select the ablest extempore preachers to deliver short addresses.

Yet I have always set my face against the indiscriminate
opening of galleries on Sunday, and refused to sign petitions in-
dustriously circulated with that object.

. . . . Only think, the British Museum has bought Mr. Pye's
variorum Liber Studiorum. I shall not forget the delight with
which he showed us some of them at Mr. Field's.

With best remembrances to Mrs. Valpy, believe me, Yours most
truly, S. PALMER.

LXVIII. To Miss FRANCES REDGRAVE.

September, 1869.

MY DEAR SISSY. I must thank you very heartily for the kind
pains you took in getting the *Anatomy.* It *is* the same which I
saw and, so far as the bones and muscles go, invaluable : as to the
manner of finally clothing them the author's views are singular,
and would not quite meet Michelangiolo's views (thus dear Fuseli[1]
spells him), but that is of little consequence, as it is for those bones
and muscles that we want it. I wish I had been well flogged
when somewhat younger, and made to copy every one of them.

We have also a fine copy of Albinus ; so we are like—or to
speak for myself, I am like a young minister who went to a
venerable elder to ask what books he should read : "O Ivemy,
Ivemy," said the big-wigged dignitary, "You don't want books—
you want brains!" I have just brains enough to perceive that
books are the cheapest things to be bought in this world, beyond
all comparison. Only think that one can buy that Fau's *Anatomy*
for a quarter the price of a swallow-tailed dress coat to sip coffee
and make oneself ridiculous in. . . .

Good Words, July 1, 1869, contains an excellent lecture by

---

[1] To this day I remember vividly his small picture of *Psyche coming to the Fates.* With
much mannerism and *some* bombast, he yet indelibly impresses the memory, and it is
a most touching and gratifying compliment to be thought a fool for admiring him.

Kingsley on *The Two Breaths*. It is, I think, the duty of everyone who reads it to recommend it to every young lady he sees, for he deals with the TIGHT LACING CURSE. Yes, I say *CURSE*, and I mean it, and wonder how Kingsley could have done his duty so thoroughly and at the same time have kept his temper so well: he is leniently inclined to excuse it on the plea of our very incomplete civilization, yet he says forty years of warning have proved useless, which argues much moral perverseness. He is amused at the peals of laughter with which a tight-waisted female would have been greeted by the ladies of Attica. I have the honour to have long shared this ludicrous vision with Mr. Kingsley, and to have imagined the very fish-women of the Piræus pelting her with sea-weed.

Excuse great haste, and with love to all, believe me, Ever truly yours, S. PALMER.

LXIX. To Mr. George Richmond.

[RED HILL.] *December, 1869. Almost to-morrow morning.*

MY DEAR FRIEND. It is too late almost to reciprocate your kind Christmas wishes, but not [for] those to yourself and all in York Street as to a new year; with like remembrances to the young lady who has "sloped her westering wheel" towards Bayswater. [1]

All this from the bottom of my heart! As for affairs in general I hate to write, and hate to speak, now that English words mean just the reverses of what they used to signify.

Plunder, sacrilege, infidelity, have become the synonyms of philanthropy and intelligence, and one is considered a born fool for not perceiving it immediately.

I was told that a "leading journal" can muster from among its contributors enough professed atheists to form a cheerful dinner-party.

When we are instructed that there ought to be a few infidel bishops by way of variety we feel humbled, like the Devonshire rustic rebuked by his neighbour just returned; "Y'm a fool mun; you've not seen Lunnon."

[1 My father's old pupil, Miss Julia Richmond, now Mrs. Robinson.—ED.]

However, we are not quite so far advanced just yet, and I was pleased to hear that a newly appointed prelate, directly the *Essays* appeared, advised his sixth form not to read them, and expressed to the other masters his deep regret for being mixed up with them.

There is nothing really new about Rationalism; it is only infidelity with a fraudulent label. But the infidels of the 17th century did not call themselves advanced Christians, and get Church preferment on the strength of it.

To patronize Christianity as a thing that was very useful for the dark ages but is now behind our requirements argues a folly equal to its profanity. Surely the Bible is either infinitely true, or a persistent aggregation of the most audacious falsehoods which were ever palmed upon mankind.

How is it that educated—highly educated people, don't see this? If St. Paul were in error as to such fundamental truths as the Vicarious Sacrifice and justification, then it follows that he was converted and selected to be sent to the Gentiles with lies in his right hand.

But why should I run on thus? Perhaps it is bad temper, vexed to find that the little I thought I knew of the English language has all to be unlearned, and that every one must wait for a new dictionary. I keep four in my room, including Johnson's *in extenso*, but they must all go into the fire, and I must go to bed forthwith, with many apologies for my garrulity. Applying to myself the words of the wise man, "a prating fool shall fall," I remain, with best love to all, Yours affectionately, S. PALMER.

1870

LXX. To MRS. GEORGE.

RED HILL, *October,* 1870.

MY DEAR MRS. GEORGE. I can't grub about here like a hog crunching acorns, without feebly endeavouring to express my sense of your generosity. It is said that souls like yours feel as much pleasure in giving, as mob-made souls, whether royal, patrician, or plebeian, in receiving. But I have been wondering whether it is possible that even *you* can have felt as much delight in sending Herbert that splendid fowling-piece as he in its fruition. . . .

It was a grand moment yesterday, the showing it to the Alma

veteran, Herbert's drill-master. The Sergeant thought the stock quite a master-piece, and kept fondling it after the manner of a doll.

Would that the French and Prussians were playing with dolls at this moment, instead of waging one of the most needless, reckless, and profligate wars which will have to be recorded in modern history ; rendering, through all time, the hatred of these contiguous nations equally intense and inextinguishable. Since the moral millennium people about 1844 were prophesying, in their blind ignorance of human nature, a lasting and almost immediate pacification of the world, there have been little else but wars and tumults, and I think there is every reason to fear that it will grow worse and worse, till the end of the present dispensation.

The majority are not good : Education may make them wiser, but not better ; for though it may refine and elevate the intellect it can never change the heart.

Now "knowledge is power." Therefore, by educating, we increase the power of a creature who is not good. Hence it will result that though people will become too wise to suffer encumbrance of national debts for wars like *this*, they will be more warlike and more formidable than ever where there seems the certainty of a very great gain, or a very great revenge.

Not that I depreciate education : on the contrary, the subject is my hobby ; but mere secular education, though it will withdraw people somewhat from the more gross and vulgar vices, will rather increase than assuage pride and ambition, two great movers of war. Great knowledge is always humble, but among the masses of the best educated few will ever attain to greatness ; and it is as symptomatic of the vastly clever, well-informed man to be proud, as of the great man to be humble.

You seem to be, like myself, "lashed to the helm" of home ; yet it is a pity that you should not get a glimpse of our green fields ere they are mantled in snow. How I should enjoy another morning among your books.

Only think of your rat family in the dresser drawer ! I knew a very poor old man in Kent who had been a smuggler. Life had passed roughly, yet he had one, only one comfort left, *a rat-pudding!* He took no steps to catch them ; but, governing his appetite by patience, calmly awaited the desired return of the village rat-catcher. Then, having carefully cleaned, skinned and prepared his delicacies, the difficulty was always where to borrow a saucepan ; for the petticoat government of his wife and daughter debarred him from the use of his own utensils. However, he always found some neighbour or other kind enough to supply him, and at last he sat down, with a thankful heart I believe, to the only solace left him until that last one of the sexton and the spade. We are such geese of routine, such fools of fashion, that if rat-pie —I beg pardon, *tart*[1] is the genteel word ;—if rat-tart became a favourite at Balmoral, in a short time they would be seen on every dinner-table in London, with the tails elegantly coiled and arranged outside the crust, like the claws on a pigeon pie—there I go again—pigeon *tart* I mean. What a thing it is to be naturally vulgar !

When at Margate with Herbert, I had peculiar opportunities of collecting evidence as to haunted houses, and spent almost the most interesting evening of my life, in a family meeting (convened for the purpose), of alleged eye-witnesses. My impression was that, making all allowance for imposture and mistake, there was a residuum of evidence which no candid mind could resist. I think you must have some curious information on the subject, and should like to talk it over with you. Meanwhile, believe me, Yours affectionately, S. PALMER.

LXXI. To MR. L. R. VALPY.

[RED HILL.] *December* 13, 1870.

MY DEAR MR. VALPY. Recovered sufficiently to get to work again, though not to write much, I just send this line to say that every day henceforth of delay in sending *The Curfew* will be a day in some part of which it has been actually ripening. Having detained it so long, I make a point of conscience of looking at it the first th'ng every morning. It has been much worked upon since we saw it together, and it is in a state corresponding with *The Comely Cloud*[2] just before its last completion, and I think it will quite reach the same mark.

It is now getting more and more at every touch of the solemn

---

[1] How beautiful a thing is refinement ! What a difference between "Rump-steak-pie" and "OX TART !"

[2] Known also as *Morning and The dripping Eaves.*—Ed.]

fusion belonging to the theme ; and directly it reaches that point at which it is an even chance whether another touch would do it harm or good, I will send it. But a good many dreamy half hours may be indulged in before there is a chance of harm.

The eye now rests undisturbed upon the minster tower, which looks quite another thing though not a touch has been added to it.

I am too weary to write more, but, with kindest remembrances to Mrs. Valpy, remain, Yours very truly, S. PALMER.

1871

LXXII. TO MR. L. R. VALPY.

RED HILL, *January* 1, 1871.

MY DEAR MR. VALPY. Your very kind letter was brought me just as I had succeeded in pleasing myself with a passage in *Waters Murmuring*, which would have been finished some time ago, but that I thought, by preliminary study, I could make it hang upon qualities which would perhaps turn out an original work. . . .

I must, if possible, get a glimpse of the Old Masters, and yet I must not catch cold. . . . No student of eighteen could be more loth than I to lose any opportunity of improvement by the study of the Great Masters, and I manage in the spring and summer to see the most eligible collections that are open ; and in winter am not without means of reference by prints at home. I talk thus reluctantly about myself, lest a friend whose good opinion I so much esteem should suppose me apathetic—as good suppose that I had taken to drinking !

It is curious to find how a habit of quick observation may be engendered by the briefness of opportunity ; and it is thus perhaps, that the brevity of this life should urge to vigorous preparation for the next. Though a new year should be begun in thankfulness for a twelve-month of mercies elapsed, yet it always affects me with awe. Indeed the little hand of a watch which marks the seconds does the same. Time is *so* relentless, he will not stop for us a single moment. " He who works against time "—no, I think it is " He who runs a race with Time," says Dr. Johnson, " has an antagonist who is not subject to casualties."

I feel nearly sure, by the manner in which it affects you, that the forty-five thousand pounder is apocryphal. The nine thousand pounder always affects me in the same way. It is Raffaelle's design and is beautifully done ; but "beautifully done" is not exactly what we say of a real Raphael or Raffaelle—Raffaello is best). In all his genuine pictures there is an unction in the doing. I heard a first-rate judge say, "I can't bear so and so's works because they are so perfect." This spurious kind of perfection is vastly popular with the populace of picture-buyers ; partly because it makes such neat furniture, and goes so well with the uphol-stery—with chignons, crinoline, "corsets," sonnets to deceased lap-dogs, and sermons to "respectable" congregations in pro-prietary chapels ; but I think neither you nor I have ever been taken with it.

I think the *Pope Julius, II.* which hangs aloft, is a genuine Raffaelle ; if a duplicate, yet relishing unmistakably of his own handiwork. The tassels of the chair are impasted like Rembrandt. I have seen it close, and once began a copy of it.

Excepting when he was under strong Florentine influence Raffaelle was either soft and tender, as in his early pictures influenced by Perugino, or rich and full, as in the little picture of *The Vision of Ezekiel.* Nay, there is a charming richness in the handling of some of his early pictures, as in *The Agony in the Garden,* though Rubens-minded people would think it drier than burnt bones . . . S. PALMER.

LXXIII. TO MR. BRYAN HOOK.

RED HILL, *June*, 1871.

MY DEAR BRYAN. You and I are such old friends that I quite missed you at "Silverbeck": however, your brother did every-thing that was kind to console me. I saw the magic boat, which transformed your visitor into the "Lady of the Lake,"[1] and, for my own purposes, should prefer a venture in the Norwegian craft. The tree-frogs are flourishing, and in fine voice.

[1 Mr. Hook's amphibious sons, never happier than when in the water, used some-times to tempt visitors into some more or less crank craft on the ponds. The attendant catastrophes are, to this day, proverbial. —Ed.]

I have been train-waiting twice at Guildford, but in school hours ; so it would have been useless to call at the school unless they would have taken me in and taught me something, which would have been a great temptation, for the older we get the more we lament our own ignorance and lost time when we were young and *had* the opportunity. However, Flaxman used to say, " It is never too late to become wiser and better," and Herbert and I had a great treat these last winter evenings, brushing up our Arithmetic out of Colenso.[1] For it is all a mistake about Grammars or mathematics being *Dry* (I put a capital G. by mistake, but it is so momentous a word that all its letters should be capitals) : they are as wet as a plum-pudding-cloth when it comes out of the saucepan, if we were not loth to untie it that we might *get* at the pudding. But supposing that they *are* dry ; so is the shell of a walnut, or of a cocoa-nut ; yet we crack and hammer away to get at the good stuff inside. I believe there are no school studies which would not be purely delightful if we would only form the habit of fixing the attention. The late Joseph John Gurney said to some one in whom he took an interest, " If you would succeed in life, give your whole mind to one thing at one time."

I would add, whenever there are two things to be done, do the more unpleasant first. Just try this for a year. But what am I saying ? Perhaps you are doing it with a will, much better than I, and will call me a fusty, rusty, musty old " fogy " for my pains.

I fear that " fogy " is slang ; it is in Webster but not in Johnson. Webster's definition is " a dull old fellow " ; but if we take that of a pocket edition, " a stickler for old things," it is not a term of reproach, unless the old things are also bad. But a stickler for mere secular education is a fogy : Eve tried it, with the Serpent for her tutor. An atheist is a fogy ; he is a stickler for the old creed of David's " fool," who " hath said in his heart, there is no God."

He who gainsays or slights the miracles of holy Scripture is a fogy ; he is a stickler for ancient Pharaoh whose heart was hardened, even after the seven plagues. He who says there is no Devil is a fogy—a stickler for the old Sadducees who said there was " neither angel, nor spirit."

There is nothing new in infidelity ; suppose that I read in some new book that men were once baboons ; it is merely a slight im-

---

[1] My father succeeded in making even Colenso palatable.—Ed.]

provement on Lord Monboddo who, more than a century ago,
fancied that men once had tails.

The vamped up arguments against miracles were familiar to me
when I was fourteen, and perhaps I thought it manly to be a bit of
a free-thinker! But at that time, unbelievers were honest enough
to avow their unbelief: some of them now profess to be advanced
Christians! What is Rationalism but infidelity with a fraudulent
label?

I rejoice to hear that you are about to be confirmed, for with
that ordinance *rightly received* you will gain two kinds of strength;
strength of conscience to resist temptations to sin, and power of
spiritual discernment to detect the hollowness and sophistry of
" oppositions of Science falsely so called " ; of experimental science
for instance; which, being conversant with material phenomena,
ventures to gainsay those of the spiritual world, with the conditions
of which they have, perhaps, nothing in common, except the relations of subjects to a master ; for spirit has the power of commanding matter and sometimes of suspending its ordinary conditions,
commonly called laws ; law, as applied to matter, being a conve-
nient term, purely figurative ; for literal law can act only on a
sentient being.

It would have been furthest from my thoughts to touch upon
these subjects, did I not know that our whole mental and moral
atmosphere is just now *reeking* with infidelity. Our colleges, our
schools, and alas, some of our pulpits are full of it. I take up a
so-called religious book ; I read beautiful things about our Lord,
beautiful things about the Sermon on the Mount, but ere long I
discover that the writer has entrenched himself behind the Mount
to throw stones at St. Paul. I meet with some stranger who talks
very finely about the *New* Testament and does not believe a word
of the Old. Another tells me (I shudder to write it) that the
Gospel of the New Testament was good enough for the people of
those times, but is now behind our requirements ; but a third
wiseacre steps in and is good enough to *patronize* the Gospel ! —
suggesting that it is really in its nature elastic, and meant to be
drawn out of shape at pleasure, so as to fit our improving stature
through every vagary of abnormal growth.

This is no laughing matter to *us*, but will not He that dwelleth
in Heaven laugh them to scorn who fancy that they have given

the go-by to a faith which commanded the supreme reverence of such intellects as those of Augustine, Anselm, Bacon, Milton, Dante, Barrow, Pascal, Newton? Would these men have thrown away their Bibles because coral-reefs took a long time in forming, or somebody fancied himself the grandson of an ape?

There is one view of confirmation which will commend itself to the young Englishmen of our grammar-schools. We are a warlike people, and our young men do not like sneaks, but prefer a fair stand-up fight. Now Christianity adapts and hallows this instinct of our nature. In confirmation you personally enlist as "Christ's Soldier." You burnish up your armour, above all things taking the Shield of Faith (whatever efforts may have been made to rob you of it), and in God's strength wield for yourself the sword which was laid up for you in baptism.

And never was there a time when the army of God stood more in need of soldiers, of *young* soldiers too. I think it was Dr. Arnold who said "Shame be to the boy who is ashamed to say his prayers"; we may add, all honour to the brave Christian boy who "rejoices to suffer shame" for Him to Whom he has given his heart. Religion implies no grimacing or hypocrisy; a peaceful conscience makes a merry heart, and penitence itself is but like the showery morning of a bright, spring day.

Forgive this long preachment, written in haste, and I dare say full of mistakes, and believe me to be, Affectionately yours,

S. PALMER.

LXXIV. TO MR. P. G. HAMERTON.

FURZE HILL, *July* 8, 1871.

MY DEAR MR. HAMERTON, "The Little Corporal" would have upset two or three dynasties while I have been debating with myself whether or not it is possible for me to find time for the etching. Inclination says, "If you can't find the time, *make* it;" and a subject has occurred to me which would be the very thing for the purpose.

If this kind of needlework could be made fairly remunerative, I should be content to do nothing else, so curiously attractive is the teazing, temper-trying, yet fascinating copper. But my etchings consume much time, and I am not alone in discovering that, like the cash absorbed by bricks and mortar, the final amount often doubles the estimate: and this time has to be withdrawn from commissions which are really lucrative. I can get 100 guineas for quite a small drawing which does not occupy nearly the time of some of my etchings; but I am purchasable, perhaps, not only for one, but for a small series of larger etchings, which are in contemplation, on terms which would be just to my family. . . .

As to skies we are fellow-sufferers. I have been in the habit of sketching clouds in pencil as they passed; and perhaps the shadow we are thus obliged to put in rapidly and delicately may suggest a simple and natural method for etching; besides keeping in our memory the structure, and *linear*, as well as the aerial perspective of the various layers of cloud.

Bonasoni is to me the great copper master of shadows: he never commits the grievous fault of making shadow, as such, rich and of a positive texture; and his lines, if not etched, as I have sometimes suspected, are more like etching than those of any other engraver.

I am inclined to think that, in cloud-shadowing, long lines should be avoided, and that the short ones would naturally vary somewhat in direction, and that cross hatching should be used very sparingly. In complicated skies, I doubt whether much can be done without frequent stoppings-out and rebitings. The most precious thing I was ever taught seems to be this; "One day of stopping-out is worth five with the needle;" and this, quite irrespective of the style of work as to more or less pronunciation of line. Directly we think of a real *organized* sky, the whole condition of work is changed, and quite a new scale of study and force elsewhere is demanded to support it. I believe it is now discovered that Rembrandt spent years upon his etchings; but, being himself essentially "picturesque," he never shows painful labour, but seems to be amusing himself after a delightful manner.

I shall be anxious to see your new work, having derived so much pleasure from the former one, the practical part of which I was consulting with much care only the other day.

I have just watched cloud-cast shadows over a distance, from my window, and see that the way to etch that common but beautiful phenomenon would be to draw the subject-matter completely; then to bite it in; and having laid a new ground, to etch the shadows upon that, with a *tint* of lines—a *wash* by virtue of its quiet parallelism: so each line of the shadowing would be a little fainter than the preceding outlines.

Your suggestion of a "short paper" now and then rouses another of my hobbies. If I love any secular thing better than art it is literature. Would that even now I might serve a late apprenticeship to it! Surely the direction of a line or the gradation of a colour are not more interesting than the structure of a paragraph.

Of the "dead masters in water-colour" I know less than of the oil painters, being myself a water-worker by accident, and liking to regard water-colour as it appears in tempera and, on a small scale, in the old missals. With the exception of my letter in Blake's *Life*, my only scrap on art subjects has been my recollection of a few facts in Flaxman's life, which bore chiefly on his moral symmetry, and which, if not wanted by the friend to whom I gave it, would be at your service. Believe me, Yours very truly, S. PALMER.

LXXV. To Mr. P. G. HAMERTON.

[FURZE HILL], *October*, 1871.

MY DEAR MR. HAMERTON. I can quite sympathize with you about etching uncertainties. My standing grief has been the unaccountable stopping of the biting, after two or three—sometimes after one stopping-out ; and it may be useful to know that you are subject to this with the Dutch mordant ; which, never having tried it, I hoped was reliable, till the other day I learned the reverse from one of our finest etchers.

Your thin ground difficulty obliges you to do what seems to me the best thing possible, viz. to remove the ground after completing the outlines and the organic markings. I should like an outline as deeply bitten as those in the *Liber Studiorum ;* and believe that if we were to make an etched copy of a bit of near landscape out of one of Albert Dürer's wood-cuts, of the same width of line, and then, on a new transparent ground, to add what we wished of shade, the lines would scarcely be too powerful to support them. And the purely liquid quality of all shadow, to which anything like richness of texture is destruction, coming over the textured richness of the lines would give that fulness of quality which in art, as in everything else, can result only from the union of opposites. He is great, says Pascal, who touches the poles with his grasp.

Let any one look at a fine impression of Albert Dürer's Holy Family going through the wood, with the palm-tree on the left, and think what a comfort it would be to have such a preparation ready bitten on the copper, the ground removed, and a transparent one laid on for beginning the shadows. But somehow or another, I fancy we have all of us more or less the notion that because an etching should be spirited it should be done in a hurry. I grant that there is a sort of vigour and a very agreeable texture got in this way, which delights the eye for a short time, but beyond which the work never grows upon us : but Rembrandt's, many of whose etchings are, in the leading points, very highly finished, which he was constantly revising, sometimes to the extent of organic changes, retain their hold long after the first ocular pleasure is over.

I am no great believer in etching direct from nature ; or in doing anything but through the medium of studies. Callcott told me he thought that a picture done out of doors must needs be false, because nature is changing every minute. But if a pen and ink drawing is made out of doors, there is more left for selection, and all that is most attractive can be faithfully transferred to the copper ; very near objects [being] worked at the same hour of each day. Grand tree-trunks and the like seem excellent subjects ; but distances and mountains never know their own minds ten minutes together, so we are obliged to have two drawings, one of the parts— one of the chosen phenomenon seized at the moment.

The pen drawings I have seen by Titian and other great Italians, when carried only to a certain point, ignore local colour, and would be true sketches of scenery in plaster of Paris ; yet these are the very men unrivalled in richness of local colour and splendour of effect. And indeed, their power of figure-drawing enabled them to extract so much form and modelling from land-scape nature, as to fill the eye with a certain richness and brilliancy, before any masses of shade came in.

What would I not give to see etchings, or any landscape copper work, by Sebastian Bourdon ?

You will see that I am not etching, by my running on so glibly : may the humbling copper soon shut my mouth! . . . . Believe me, Ever truly yours, S. PALMER.

LXXVI. To Mr. L. R. Valpy.

Red Hill, *November*, 1871.

My dear Mr. Valpy. . . . Knowing your feeling and perception of high art, I believe that what you gather in your own mind from Mr. Haweis is perfectly true and wholesome, but I must say I should guess *him* to prefer Shelley's *Queen Mab* to *Paradise Regained*.

With you, I believe it is the sort of yearning which all who really feel entertain towards reaches of unattainable beauty— unattainable till the earth "and the works that are therein shall be burned up." And in the new earth, all the powers which God has given to man will be consummated.

It seems to me that the author proceeds upon assumptions which are untrue, and that Music has not indeed her rival, but her greater sister, I had almost said her Queen, in Verse ; that while Music waits upon her and learns of her she goes right, but breaking loose from her, plays the wanton in a luxurious effeminacy which a wise commonweal would forbid. Would Handel's *Messiah* affect us as it does without the divine words? Is not music, as a medium of "emotion," excelled by eloquence ?

Of ancient music we know little or nothing ; not even its scale ; but has any music we can name produced such powerful emotion as even modern oratory ?

Was ever music played that affected the soul so deeply as the highest poetry read—read even to ourself ?

Where is the music without words that can affect us like Milton's allegory of Sin and Death ? For indeed, two of music's three powers exist in perfection without musical notes, in such verse as Virgil's or Milton's : viz., melody and rhythm ; "harmonious verse " being a false expression for melodious.

Few people love music more than I, revelling as I do even in the peculiar tone of each individual instrument, independently of melodious succession. It was from boyhood my favourite amusement : also how many hours have gone to the violin and to singing ! But surely, any man in whom reason and the higher imagination bear sway will be more deeply affected by a well-acted tragedy than by the sweetest or most solemn combination of sound—will have most "*emotion*" excited, which is the point in question.

I can only understand what Mr. Haweis says about colouring by supposing him ignorant of what has been achieved. If we look around us and behind us at the marvellous works of man in the various arts: at works and monuments modern and ancient, is there any greater measure of attainment than Titian's as a colourist; or of spiritual symbolism than in some of the more Southerly Italians, and of Blake in his best and most highly-finished drawings? Did not the Venetians "constitute the colour art"? Was not Titian peculiarly master of its phraseology? "Instruments were invented" more complete than with all our modern chemistry we possess.

I think perhaps the author has in his mind's eye something wholly beyond the reach of mere colours, viz., real light. This, added to the pigments in little bottles of sunbeams, would make matters very different: Now, as Mr. Hamerton says in his paper on Tain (I think that is the name), in the last number but one of *The Pall Mall Budget*, it is impossible to paint a red autumnal cherry-leaf with the sunlight on it.

What inspired young ladies think they may accomplish after a course of lessons is what can barely be approached by life-long study. If they have any real fancy they imagine light and colour in equal force.

I fear you will think me very controversial, but I will ask you to read my assertions as queries, being sceptical on all subjects but ONE, which is the object of faith. Faith, as St. Paul teaches us, is the SUBSTANCE of things hoped for: sight is conversant only with phenomena. Experimental science, though it may distantly tend to it, can never be knowledge; for if we know, what need for experiment?

With what grand modesty does Sir Isaac Newton speak of his vast attainments; in difficulties ready to suggest other than his most favoured solutions. He compares himself, I think, to a child gathering a few shells or pebbles by the margin of the ocean of truth. But there is no hesitation, or qualification, or reserve in his avowal of faith in the word of God. What a contrast to the incredulity of flippant sciolists, who believe only in what they can handle!

A female atheist, lecturing on the sea beach some time since, said, " For my part, I make a point of believing nothing which

I can't see." "What do you say to the wind, Ma'am?" said an old sailor who stood by.

Why do I run on so? Yours, S. PALMER.

LXXVII. To Mr. L. R. VALPY.

RED HILL., *November* 11, 1871.

MY DEAR MR. VALPY. Until the last day or two I have been very poorly ; part of the time, however, thinking the more perhaps, through being able to work the less. There are moments of lassitude which, removing our work to a distance, reveal its main scope and general proportions, too apt to be lost sight of in application to particulars.

I hope to send to the winter exhibition one of the studies you mentioned, the waterfall in shadow, which I do not care to sell, as it is so useful for reference : however, I have put 80 guineas on it. With it goes also a little drawing of quite a different character.

I have been imagining you by your fireside, talking over your autumnal forest walks. There is a vividness in present impressions which memory lacks, but then it bolts everything from its bran, and clothes the selected essence in a soft, harmonious unity very congenial with a contemplative turn of mind. . . .

We trust that the deep sadness which overshadowed your path has yielded to those consolations of which you so well know the value ; and that many happy years are before you, subject only to those wholesome fluctuations which are needful to remind us that "this is not our rest ;" though it may, in God's good providence, afford us many resting places in our upward journey. Believe me, &c., S. PALMER.

LXXVIII. To Mr. JOHN RICHMOND.

RED HILL, *November*, 1871.

MY DEAR JOHN. I thought that the pleasant duty was unexceptionably discharged : no insult, no savageness, no blood drawn ; and Mr. C. is a model of the breeding which the English prize so highly, being quite undemonstrative and incapable of warming with his subject.

Perhaps, for a moderate honorarium, he might be prevailed upon to attend private families occasionally, to their manifest advantage.

The cat, like the steam hammer, has a wide scope of gradation between feathering and flaying, and if each member of a household kept respectively a little private account of peccadilloes, one attendance would suffice for several of them, which would be economical. Two lashes, we will say, for any words of detraction or slander ; three for novel-reading by daylight, or after 11 p.m. ; five *good ones* for abbreviating the preterites in reading the Scriptures or Liturgy.

I like impartial justice for rich and poor, and think it quite unfair to the middle and upper classes to deprive them of Mr. Calcraft's services, which seem to be comparatively wasted on poor creatures who have never been taught, or taught nothing but evil from their cradles. No, let him flourish the scourge over sinners against light—over highly educated sophists who hunt for souls.

Suppose now, for a moment, that the heads of a great university obliged the students to "get up" for their "moral philosophy" course (facetiously so called) certain books which tend to confuse all distinction between right and wrong (the most deadly cruelty which can be perpetrated on the young), might not the hearts of these "Heads" be made better for a little counter-irritation between the shoulders ? Shall we say thirty lashes with the "Pentonville" cord, which is a little thicker ?

It is a distinguishing mark of God's children that they hate sin, and live in a constant, holy fear of falling into it ; and you will find it equally characteristic of those who, in a plain spoken OLD BOOK, are called the children of the Devil, that these latter have become seared against any sensitiveness to sin, as such, and try with miserable sophistry to explain away its guilt—nay, to deny its very nature and essence, calling it the accidental result of imperfect faculties, of cerebral structure, of a neglected education, or such like. Now if, by bad example, I lead a young man into sin, my guilt will be great indeed, yet neither of us are out of the pale of repentance. But what if I enjoin him carefully to pore over works of elaborate argument tending to ignore the sovereignty of conscience, to make it appear that pleasure is, after all, the real

motive of our actions, or that expediency must over-rule principle
—that the just and right is not obedience to the Divine Law, but
what *we think* will be on the whole best for the greatest number of
people ?   If I were to do this I should not be defiling the streams
of action but poisoning the fountain.   It would be "robbery with
violence"; an irreparable outrage and mutilation of conscience.   I
hope I am wrong, and that no such books are propounded at
such an university ; otherwise the professors of Laputa were
more hopefully employed in trying to extract "sunbeams from
cucumbers."

From silence to the contrary, it gives me much pleasure to infer
that you are all well.

Outis[1] has been half-way to jaundice, Dr. Holman tells him ; to
which imputing his moroseness, you may perhaps allow him to
subscribe himself, yours affectionately, though he *is* such a
croaker.

1872

LXXIX. To P. G. HAMERTON.

FURZE HILL, January 26, 1872.

DEAR MR. HAMERTON.   Had I thanked you earlier for your
[Etcher's] *Handbook*, which came long ago, I could not have thanked
you so much ; for it is the test of good books as of good pictures that
they improve with acquaintance.   I had a little *Milton* bound with
brass corners that I might carry it always in my waistcoat-pocket :
after doing so for twenty years it was all the fresher for the
porterage.

Your invention of the positive process is equally useful and elegant : useful because the reverse method lessens the pleasure of
work ; elegant, because the materials are delicate, and the process
cleanly and expeditious.

On the whole, there are only two points in the book against which
I am inclined to except.   You call the copper acid "nitric," which
I think ought to be nitrous,[2] nitric being the mordant of steel.
Secondly, if Mr. Fagin may step into the witness-box to speak to

---

[1] A name my father assumed.—ED.]

[2] In reply, Mr. Hamerton explained that the French use nitric for both steel and
copper, weakening it for steel.—ED.]

In Clovelly Park.

character, I would suggest that the prisoners at the bar, however much they have erred, have not been guilty of clipping—that they have attempted rather to bow the guitar than to pizzicato the violin. I don't defend either, and, with some fear of merited chastisement, beg your acceptance of the accompanying guitar performance *con arco*. Impromptu graces were out of the question, as it was begun years ago to illustrate a classical subject ;[1] but finding that I could no-how clip my poodle into lion-shape, I even let the hair grow, and christened him for the Art Union, *The Morning of Life*. I must try to be a better boy next time.

Most likely you are full of engagements when in town, yet I sometimes hope that you will spend a day here in spring-time. If you would like to do so as an act of penance, I would annoy you with inquiries as to the best way of disposing of a completed verse translation of Virgil's *Eclogues* which, right or wrong, I am resolved (all being well) to print. Whether they would be eligible one by one for any periodical I don't know, or whether there would be an opening for the disposal of the copyright.

It seems desirable that those who do not read them in the original should have some version from which the pastoral essence has not quite evaporated.

Whatever my version may be, it is a work done *con amore* in the superlative degree ; but so is murder by a zealous " Thug." It has been " bread eaten in secret," as no one but my son knows of it.

If Blake were alive and I could afford it, I would ask him to make a head-piece to each bucolic.

How exquisitely he would have done it we know, seeing that perhaps the most intense gems of bucolic sentiment in the whole range of art are his little wood-cut illustrations to Phillips' *Pastorals* in Dr. Thornton's book. They seem to me utterly unique. But enough and more than enough of myself and my dreamings.

Etching out of doors finds, I think, its most eligible subjects in what you have chosen—tree trunks. They are indeed very congenial to the resources of art, which some things equally or more attractive seem not to be. I do not see why a month should not be spent upon a grand group of stems, working each day while the light falls at the same angle. How prominent they are

[¹ Hercules and Cacus. Hercules was altered into the kneeling woman. —ED.]

(were alas !) in the *Peter Martyr* and other works of the great historical landscape-painters.

If they or anything else can be " done at a sitting," so much the better, because life is short ; but Macbeth's famous receipt for cooking beef-steaks demands emphasis on the " were."

What you have done at a sitting to illustrate the biting process is, I think, quite satisfactory for the purpose, though the advantage of farther work is evidenced by the other examples, in some of which you have taken several. Believe me, Very truly yours, S. PALMER.

LXXX. To MR. F. G. STEPHENS.

FURZE HILL, *May* 4, 1872.

DEAR MR. STEPHENS. We deeply sympathize with you. How should we do otherwise, having more than once drained a like cup of bitterness ? What *can* I say, what *can* I think of to comfort you ? It is distressing to stand by and witness such a sorrow, with no power to alleviate it, and it seems a mockery to fill the page with stale topics of condolence.

One of the stalest, however, is so precious that it can never be worn out : I mean the precious hope which both nature and Revelation have written indelibly within our hearts—the hope of rejoining our beloved ones when the hideous discrepancies which sin has brought into the world shall be done away for ever.

Mrs. Stephens' loss has been precisely my own ; a beautiful young life full of purpose and promise plucked up by the roots. To this day I cannot bear to dwell upon mine ; but the Divine Comforter can sometimes apply well-known words with new and strange power to the wounded heart. It was only last year, I think, that walking down to the Red Hill station on my way to town in the deepest dejection of mourning for my poor boy I was *confronted*, on entering the waiting-room, with these words on one of the large-print Scripture placards. " . . . He will dwell with them, and they shall be His people, and God Himself shall be with them, and be their God; And God shall wipe away all tears from their eyes ; and there shall be no more death, neither sorrow nor crying, neither shall there be any more pain, for the former things are passed away. And He that sat upon the throne said, Behold I make all things new. And

He said unto me, Write ; for these words are true and faithful."
Revelation xxi.

Well ! I did not sorrow any more that day. This was the solution of all the moral and physical discrepancies around us indicated by those discrepancies themselves, if rightly understood. This
" making of all things new " [is] a necessity, if we may so speak, of
Divine Love, after the wreck and débris of a great moral catastrophe
have strewed the face of a once beautiful earth—types of a worse
confusion in the hearts of men. The very axis of the earth
[seems] somewhat to have changed in its relative position to the
sun, making vast tracts inclement which once were genial, if we
may credit the explorations of so young a science as geology ;
which, however, must not be taken on trust for a century to come,
as all new sciences go through some ages of self-contradiction
before they can right themselves.

I was a free-thinker at fourteen, and spent much time in controversial reading which ought to have been given to painting. It
would be affectation in me to deny that I am acquainted with the
whole scope of popular sceptical reasoning ; and can therefore, after
my poor little storm-beaten skiff has shifted about among quick-
sands and treacherous, floating isles, green to the eye but fatal to
the feet—after all this I can the more assuredly find an
anchorage, where Pascal, Bacon, Newton, and Milton lowered their
cables. From this spiritual harbour of refuge we may look forth
on the material element without terror, albeit perhaps, with the
deepest grief. Your dear treasure is there ; mine is mouldering in
earth which I can almost see from this window : but the precious
words return upon us like the refrain of some heavenly music.
" There shall be no more death, neither sorrow nor crying—Behold
I make all things new."

Through untimely illness, caused, my doctor says, by the late
trying changes of temperature, my year's work came to nought ;
or rather, stood over ; and I must now, all being well, go away for
a week or two for change of air. On my return I do hope that
you will bring Mrs. Stephens and dear Holly down for a long day ;
if by that time you have sufficiently recovered from this dreadful
shock ; for you will come to see fellow-mourners, who will not
" sing songs to a heavy heart." . . . .

In the presence of such a sorrow as yours, I should not have dared to name anything so utterly futile in comparison as etchings, or the like ; but as you have done so, I must very kindly thank you for the trouble you have taken in transmitting mine to the Museum, and with our united sincere and anything but formal condolences, subscribe myself, Gratefully yours, S. PALMER.

LXXXI. TO A. H. PALMER.

MARGATE, *June*, 1872.

MY DEAR HERBERT. Independently of their divine pathos, the 13th to the 16th verses of Sunday morning's second lesson [1] seem to me, in our version, to be a flawless gem of narrative English. From this brief, barn-door-fowl flight I drop at once to lower but not base matters. In one of Sir Joshua Reynolds's *Discourses* he quotes with all reverence, or alludes to, the 15th verse, as not less truly indicating the conditions of all high excellence in art. The higher the aim, the more child-like must be the disposition of the aspirant. Sir Isaac Newton compares himself to a little child collecting a few pebbles or shells by the margin of the ocean of Truth.

Poetic art, expressing itself by verse, by marble, or by picture is one of man's loftiest pursuits. He will do well in such to resume his pinafores. The means also are arduous : structural knowledge of the figure, and an all-embracing study of the Antique. Pinafores still ! As he descends to practical geometry and perspective he may change his pinafore for a paper cap and working apron, and tuck up his sleeves, to get through them as soon as he can, consistently with thoroughness. . . . . Art is so long and life so short that I could wish you were well rid of this "geometry," as they call it ; and as it is too bulky to batter, you had better descend to the mining, pickaxe in hand, and work out so much as you comfortably can per diem, but not *over* work. Labour such as this, which, unlike the higher things, can be accurately measured, can be accurately apportioned. This "geometry" reminds me of the sudden check presented when you are taking a field walk in Cornwall by one of those high stone-wall hedgerows. There is nothing for it but to get over. . . . Your affectionate father, S. PALMER.

[¹ Probably Mark x.—ED.]

LXXXII. To Mr. P. G. Hamerton.

Furze Hill, *August,* 1872.

Dear Mr. Hamerton. . . . I wonder that the French, the countrymen of the world's greatest landscape-painter, the countrymen of such a triumvirate as Claude, N. Poussin, Sebastian Bourdon, should rejoice, as they seem to do, in blue mounts and blue whites.

We English are just as bad. A philosopher to whom I am indebted for some rudiments of civilization stood still suddenly one day while we were walking and talking and uttered these words, " Light is orange." They have never been forgotten.

All being well, I go to Town at the end of this week to get a little brain embrocation from some old pictures, but principally to see Mr. Cayley, whom I know well, about these pending autotypics. If I could but get the TIME, I would give Mr. Seeley another chance for *The Portfolio* by making and lending him a pen and India-inkite done exactly as I am doing the Virgils ; but somehow or other, let a design be never so studiously simple in the masses it *will* fill itself as it goes on, like the weasel in the fable who got into the meal-tub ; and when the pleasure begins, in attempting tone, and mystery, and intricacy, away go the hours at a gallop. They seem to take fright, like the nervous animal you were leading. Well says the Volume which contains all truth and the germs of all wisdom and knowledge, "An horse is a vain thing for safety." At the risk of imputed consanguinity, I confess a preference for the donkey, which, in old times, was specially used by persons of dignity ; and the Persian ass is, I think, abstractedly from associations of strength and speed, more beautiful than the horse. " Speak, ye that ride on white asses," we find in that grand lyric of Deborah and Barak. A horse is never to be relied upon, and no horsemanship is an assurance of safety : think of Sir Robert Peel ! Under the present dispensation the horse is a necessity and a great gift to man ; but war is a necessity, it would appear, and yet I never wish those for whom I have a deep regard to have much converse with either.

After this explosion of monomania you will agree with me that it is time to wind up ; so with very hearty congratulations on your escape, ... believe me, dear Mr. Hamerton, with many thanks for the interest you take in my doings, Yours very truly,

S. PALMER.

LXXXIII. To Mr. C. W. Cope.

September, I forget what, 1872.

My dear Cope. Many thanks for Mr. Galloway's most interesting book just returned.   To pass judgment upon it is for those who have read Newton's *Principia*, &c., &c., &c., &c., &c., &c., &c., &c., &c., &c. ; but "a cat may look at a king," and my feline eyesight can see in the dark that the inclination of the moon's orbit is remarkable.

In utter ignorance I "guess" that the supposed nucleus of the earth, surrounded with fluid, would very soon adjust itself to the new equator of the outer crust : there is such an entirety in the direction of bodies in rapid movement.

Of course I can't guess whether the earth moves round the sun or *vice versâ*.   The greatest mathematicians in various ages have been divided about it, and it amounts to the same thing in calculations.   Like everything else it has gone see-saw, which those who are at the upper end of the plank for a moment call "progress" ; whereas the whole history of nations, and science, and art has been see-saw (ill spelt I fear) or, if we *must* have a fine word, "undulation."   Is it not evident that any "advance" beyond the tombs of the Medici must be sheer bombast ?   Was it not the FACT ? Newton, by the bye, was a less staunch Newtonian than his followers : see his doubt about vacuum.   *He* did not sing the hymn which has this remarkable couplet,

> " My Buts and Ifs I've laid aside,
> And now in Shalls and Wills confide."

Nor another, of more rhetorical peculiarity, enriched with this gem,

> " Without an If to foul the stream,
> Or Peradventure here."

What a treat for geologists, Mr. Galloway's cannon embedded in solid rock !—with Lyell for its purveyor !

But physics and morals will never be reconciled till they are seen to be the opposite, not contrary poles of a vast whole ; and he alone is most truly great, says Pascal, who can touch each pole with either hand.   Pigmy-like I cling to the moral pole, and believe that any youth who can stand an examination in *Sandford and Merton* is more fit for civil appointments than a crammed sciolist. . . . Yours ever, S. PALMER.

LXXXIV. To Mr. T. H. Wright.

"DIFFIDENCE VILLA," *October,* 1872.

MY DEAR HOWARD. Like "Giant Despair" I have my fits occasionally, and then a little truth comes out. Perhaps, however, with characteristic timidity, I have been too mealy-mouthed. I car therefore your own Professor in the preface to his Lectures on Sculpture.

"Notably, within the last hundred years, all religion has perished
"from the practically active national minds of France and England.
"No statesman in the Senate of either country would dare to use a
"sentence out of their acceptedly divine revelation, as having now
"a literal authority over them for their guidance, or even a sug-
"gestive wisdom for their contemplation.

"England especially *has cast her Bible full in the face of her
"former God;* and proclaimed with open challenge to Him, her
"resolved worship of His declared enemy Mammon."

Here is the sound of the trumpet! If, after this, I repeat that to dress in high merinos while the sun is up, and in low muslin when he sets is a compound of decivilization and cruelty worthy of the Feejees who eat their aunts, you will see at once that Apollo has twitched my ear, and that, leaving higher matters to Mr. Ruskin, mine has been a playful descant on the pastoral flute. Yours affectionately, OUTIS.

LXXXV. To Mr. Richmond Seeley.

FURZE HILL HOUSE, *November* 2, 1872.

MY DEAR SIR. Many thanks for the two copies of *The Portfolio* containing such excellent impressions of my etching on such picturesque paper. I sit down to thank you before reading what has been said about me because it is so very difficult to advert properly to anything concerning No. 1.

I am sure everything will be well written, and kindly written; and if corrected in the same spirit I shall be ready to kiss the rod, for it struck me only the other morning that the most calamitous of our birthdays was that on which we had become too old for whipping.

There is no hurry, but please send me that identical impression from which the mechanical process autotype was done. I shall then be able to reason accurately, and, I hope, to circumvent the said mechanical into a virtual production of ten *etchings*, much more truly etchings in public opinion than anything done on steel or copper ; as the British Lion is unalterably persuaded that pen and ink drawings are etchings, and that all etchings are drawings in pen and ink   I want, if I can, to make them so attractive that people will say " Hang Corydon, and Thyrsis, and Venus, and Ceres and all those ' fellows,'[1] but here are no less than ten of the man's etchings, and they are worth the money."

Not to give unnecessary trouble, I have tried to condense my *sine qua nons* (shade of Cicero pardon the plural !) into a brace— 1stly, the printing upon a luminous paper, without a tinge of grey, blue, or green. 2ndly, entire disuse of lamp-black, and the substitution of ivory black as printing-ink.

Lemma, or rather *di*lemma as I have found it made by human perverseness. If we should think it desirable to mix a little brown with the ivory black, that the brown should not be umber, but Vandyke brown.[2]

From time to time, at your leisure, you might get light, perhaps, as to the probability of these two very little matters to the doers, but *everything* to me, being realized. As, however, every true Englishman is a compound of rectitude and rut, I scarcely expect it.

Stir a *workman* in his rut and he feels in a moment that Magna Charta, trial by jury, blood-bought liberties, &c., &c., are in jeopardy. Yours truly, S. PALMER.

You will find the brace of " nons " most useful in printing what *we* call etchings.

LXXXVI. TO MR. RICHMOND SEELEY.

November 6, 1872.

MY DEAR SIR. Some little children were trying their eyes at a puppet-show when one of them asked, " Please sir is that old Boney, or the Queen of Sheba ? " " You pays your money, and you takes your choice," said the benevolent showman. If I were you I should not trouble myself about the etching [In *The Portfolio*]:

---

[1] This is fact and quotation.

[2] [When a copper-plate press was afterwards introduced at Furze Hill, I tried the substitution of Vandyke brown for umber. We found, however, that so much more brown had to be added to the black in order to produce the desired tint, that the quality of the ink was materially affected.—ED.]

probably it is as like sunrise as sunset, more shame for *me*: nay, who knows but that some " British Lion " is at this moment pointing out to Mrs. Leo and her purring progeny how subtly the artist has discriminated between the two, so that no one could possibly mistake it for a sunset ?

A painter must use his very utmost energy to *move* the public, but he never can quite forsee the direction of the movement : the best full moon I ever did sometimes passed for a sun ; but had I not taken my utmost pains, it would have passed for neither, to anyone's satisfaction.

All the drawings are in progress in various states of advancement ; none yet finished, and though I *ardently* wish they were complete, I *dare* not hurry one of them. It will be some time yet ere one of them is fully ripe. Directly one of them is so I will send it you.

Supposing that there should be a lucid interval in this vile grey and blue paper system, and that the mechanical process authorities shall have some really white or creamy paper on which they could print, I should think it would be well, if the first subject came well upon it, to have enough for an edition secured at once, but this you will consider. My case is rather hard : I want nothing *done*—only some pernicious adjunct omitted. I have this moment placed one of the mechanical process impressions beside a piece of London board (Newman's), and it is evident to me that something has been done either to blue or bleach the paper. If we asked the paper-maker to *make* us a creamy tone we should rue the day. All I say is, after you have washed them, make up the rags pure and simple or impure and simple, into paper, just as they are, and let them alone : no bleaching-acid, please, no blue-bag, no toning . . . . Yours very truly, S. PALMER.

The very nice paper upon which you have printed these last reminds me of *Etching and Etchers*, but with this difference, that something has been done to *cure* (! ! !) the natural colour of the rag, and that has chilled it. The maker of that lovely paper of Mr. Hamerton's went to sleep and forgot the bleaching. . . . . . .

My demurs as to paper-making are a trifle. I was told at Mr. Colnaghi's that a chemical agent was used in making the paper for a large and expensive engraving, which, after a good while, absolutely turned it BLACK.

LXXXVII. To Mr. F. G. Stephens.

Furze Hill, *November* 6, 1872.

Dear Mr. Stephens. When a judge "sums up" as favourably as you have done in *The Portfolio* the first impulse of the gentleman in the "dock" is to thank him very heartily: yet, perhaps. he is hardly in the right, for it half implies that the judge has been warped by feelings of personal kindness: but he may justly be grateful for the skilled elaboration with which every particle of evidence in his favour has been noted. Now your notes of my works are so vivid that I could paint a picture from any one of them without reference to studies and sketches, although much of what you remember I have half forgotten.

It would be a yet additional kindness if you would get one date altered in future copies of *The Portfolio*. I am quite positively certain that my first exhibited work was in 1818, or 1819. If catalogues say otherwise, there must have been another S. Palmer. The first R.A. exhibition I ever saw was in 1819.

In 1809 I had not long emerged from long clothes, and the constellation of the Fork had not yet loomed in the horizon. What promotion in after life equals breeching? There were then no knickerbockery gradations, but we emerged at a bound from short petticoats and blue legs into blue trousers and sugar-loaf buttons—and—O rapture! into *pockets*; a bi-sided potentiality for gingerbread-nuts, story-books, toffy, squirts, and pop-guns. How different the obverse of the medal; yet, under happy auspices, not less desirable when

> "The soul's dark cottage, batter'd and decay'd,
> Lets in new light through chinks that time hath made."

Maugre the elements, we have not yet given up the hope of your promised visit, when something presents itself more cheery than these leafless trees beaten half down by the rain.

I suppose, by this time, you are numbered among the favoured few who have seen Mr. Holman Hunt's picture. I have a longing desire to see it, but shall not reach town till the spring, if spared to do so.

Fearful as the floods have been in many places, I trust you have not been contemplating the reflection of that enchanting Michael Angelo bas-relief, in the extended Thames.

Pray give my best regards to Mrs. Stephens and love to the Golden Holly, and excuse the haste of this scrawl, as I am obliged to seize the moment as it flies. Ever, dear Mr. Stephens, Yours faithfully, S. PALMER.

P.S. I think there must have been another Palmer, as I never exhibited a portrait.

LXXXVIII. To Mr. P. G. HAMERTON.

FURZE HILL, *November*, 1872.

DEAR MR. HAMERTON. Just as you have been saying in *The Portfolio* certain kind and touching words about me which tended to moisten the eyelids, I find that you are taking no compassion upon yourself. We have read of those who, while guiding some rapid machinery, have been caught by a part of their dress, dragged in, and cut in pieces. These importunate engagements are just the superfluous dress which I *beseech* you to tear off at once. A wife is self-knowledge ; unpleasantly so sometimes, when lifting up the forefinger of admonition against our little foibles ; sometimes still more unpleasantly, but most savingly. I ask you, as a personal favour to myself, to read this poor, homely, but hearty protest to Mrs. Hamerton against what is nothing less than self-destruction, and to consult with her about some steps to be immediately taken for securing you one twelve-month of rest. I don't mean idleness, but one great, broad, unexecutionized, Bonasoni mass of shade, concerning which, if I have said anything worth quoting, make what use you like of it, or anything I may write, *provided always* the matter quoted contains no names of living men, women, or children, and no libel upon the dead : begging as a favour that you will supply defective punctuation, and see that the relatives and antecedents agree in number.

Bonasoni seems to me the greatest master of shadowing upon copper. " Well, but it is like baby's work : there is no execution." —That is it : that is precisely what I mean. " But there is no richness of texture." I have yet to learn that, unless after flagellation, the human skin is much granulated. Let any one who can draw, copy exactly in pen and ink some boldly-shadowed limb of Bonasoni's, and afterwards turn it into a tree-trunk by vigorous line work expressing the textures of the bark, and he will then see texture in its proper function, and shadow in its poetic sleep.

Claude, the supreme tree master (his mother must have been a
Dryad ?) never transgresses the neutrality of shade, though, from the
intricacy of his matter, the science is less obvious than in Bonasoni.
Textureless shadows, composed of parallel lines in gentle unaffected curve, will be found, I think, in **Titian's** landscape
sketches, and in the drawings and etchings of all landscape-
painters who have founded themselves upon the human figure ;
textural shadows in those who, without such discipline, have
struggled after the picturesque ; and, as a meretricious accomplishment, in almost all the line engravers since the time of Woollett.

This, if you think fit, may be spliced on to the passage you
wish to quote. I think it clearly expresses what I mean—that (for
a wonder) it is perspicuous. My writing on such subjects is usually
so much the reverse in the first draft, that nothing short of the
shock your letter has given me would have waked me up to it. A
lady told me that her husband's work (literary) had been brighter
and more forcible ever since a pitch from his phaeton which nearly
fractured his skull.

Now I am going to be saucy. Mere amateur as I am
in literature, and scarcely that, one of the charms of your prose
has seemed to me to be this, that if you walked you walked,
and if you ran you ran ; but that you were never to be detected in
a hurried gait. Can you retain this leisured manliness, this noble
rhythm, if you suffer the publishers to lure you to over-production ?
I hope you will consider this very rude at the first reading, and
what I have said above, very rude, and that you will be very angry,
and that, like the fat boy in *Pickwick*, I shall succeed in making
" your flesh creep "—anything to create a sensation ; to stir you
up ; that with a fresh eye you may turn round upon your over-
work, and take some calm but determined step while it is yet
not too late. The break down of health comes *suddenly—
irremediably.* . . . Yours most truly. S. PALMER.

LXXXIX. TO MR. P. G. HAMERTON.

FURZE HILL, *November* 9, 1872.

DEAR MR. HAMERTON. I have just sent off my letter of
November 7, but this discomfiture of your Autun project haunts
me. There's not exactly beauty or picturesqueness in the usual

sense of the word, but there *is* a something or other about an old French town which nothing comes up to : and with strenuous old Rome "cropping up" here and there, Autun must be to our tastes as satisfying as a huge plum cake to a schoolboy's. . . . This piece of paper may as well lie ready in my writing-case in case anything suggests itself : just jotting down each " notion" between lines, without inflicting upon you any more of my long-winded commentaries—remaining, Yours most truly, S. PALMER. . . .

I am trying the crow-quill for evanescent passages : it is yielding and tender, and apt for dreamy delicacies : it belongs, of course, not to the great organ, or choir organ, but to the swell.

I regretted sending my last letter when it was too late, fearing that the rod had been deserved for busybodying in other men's matters, but am cheered by finding in your answer just received abundant tokens of forgiveness. A suggestion or two, offered with THE UTMOST DIFFIDENCE, I shall write down in the shape of positive assertion, merely as the shortest way.

Oil-painting seems wholly incompatible with the vocation of an author, as it is a lifelong study in itself. Reynolds insisted that it must be studied as a *lost art* of which we find that each of the most successful artists manages to recover a fragment sufficient for his immediate need. By marvellous perseverance, much agony, and many prayers, Etty accomplished this. Sham oil-painting (relatively sham to Titian) works with slow-drying oil pastes of many colours, and, if employed upon subjects not much above the perceptive powers of the buying class and very dexterously executed, may " lead on to fortune." The artist feels that he has given the Old Masters the "go-by," and partakes the innocent rapture of Jervas, who cried out, having put the last touches to a copy from Titian, " POOR LITTLE TIT : HOW HE *WOULD* STARE !" But this dexterity again demands the whole time, and seems wholly incompatible with authorship. The same holds good of the exquisite materials tempera and egg. From my old practice in tempera I TRY, as much as in me lies, to make my drawings tempera pictures.

I think that every sort of practice that a man has had ought to tell somewhat upon everything he does in whatever material. The Old Masters came to oil-painting through fresco and tempera.

Water-colours upon paper hued like the lightest whity-brown paper (I have a sketch-book of whity-brown paper which Mr. Newman got hot-pressed for me: it is very thin however) and with use of white, are most useful for registering passing effects, and soft [coloured] crayons still more so (the *Fixateur Rouget*, sold somewhere in Paris, quite fixes them ; even the soft Swiss, which are the best) : and they are most valuable, I think, to the *etcher*, by enabling him to desist in a moment from his detailed work, when the right effect presents itself, or the right figures or cattle are passing, and to register those transitory but all-important suggestions in a moment. And in etching at home I don't think a line should be scratched before, at the cost of whatever study, a little sketch is made, showing the general effect (I care not how smudgy), in which the masses and trains of dark are right, and the emphatic lights and darks in their proper places. And this, whether the etching is meant to be worked into tone, or suggested almost by line.

All the kinds of art we are busy with depend, I think, for *their hold upon the eye*, upon the right construction of lights and shadows. I know the vast importance of the above, from having often and shamefully neglected it. Reynolds's BLOT practice from the Flanders and Holland pictures seems to me invaluable. The little effect sketch for the proposed etching may be done best with charcoal, I think, fixing as you get certainties, for you may fix and refix with the *Fixateur* as often as you like.

The only quite certain way of making money by water-colours is, I fancy, to do such figures, fruit, and flowers as William Hunt did, and to do them as well. This again wants a whole life.

ETCHING seems to me to stand quite alone among the complete arts in its compatibility with authorship. You are spared the dreadful death-grapple with colour which makes every earnest artist's liver a pathological curiosity. Take, for instance, only a unit of the milliard—the painting of but one bit of human flesh under one given influence of light and atmosphere. Well I remember Mulready's saying to me, "To get one quality of flesh is comparatively easy ; to get two is difficult ; to unite three is *very* difficult."

Etching does not necessarily demand more than individual or local chiaroscuro, and the crayon will seize brilliant phenomena.

But the great peculiarity of etching seems to be that its difficulties are not such as excite the mind to "restless ecstasy," but are
an elegant mixture of the manual, chemical and calculative, so that
its very mishaps and blunders (usually remediable) are a constant
amusement. The tickling sometimes amounts to torture, but, on
the whole, it raises and keeps alive a speculative curiosity—it has
something of the excitement of gambling, without its guilt and its
ruin. For these and other reasons I am inclined to think it the
best *comptu* exponent of the artist-author's thoughts.

(Quite abruptly, as it occurs to me, I would suggest that it is
sometimes best, when you have much near matter, not to etch
delicate sky or distance at first, but to put them in after two or
three bitings : you then are in no terror, and can overbite and get
a good rattling first proof. My best first proofs were those which
quite frightened me ; and I foolishly began softening, instead of
laying a ground for intense, dark lines like those in the *Liber
Studiorum*, which would soon have brought the first biting to reason.
If you work from an organized effect in your little sketch, you don't
want so much to see your effect on the copper.)

Now I'm going *ultra crepidam* into the impudent vein again,
telling you what I should do in a matter I know nothing about.
Were it my blessed privilege to be an author (for, after all, what
comes up to a good book ?), and an author of your calibre, I should
try to make that my Fortunatus's purse. The Reviews, such as
The Edinburgh and *Quarterly*, are lucrative, and contributions to
first-rate periodical literature would *buy the time* for the slower
elaboration of such standard works as were intended for " Prince
Posterity." Who knows, however, but that *The Portfolio* may span
the globe—that its etchings may sparkle in Australia ? The great
thing to bear in mind, as you have done, is that the many are
sluggish ; that *indifference* is your enemy—to give the British Lion
a series of gentle electric shocks. Perhaps it will become the
accredited etching organ. Some of our very best English etchers
have not yet appeared in it. Where are the great capitalists who
prefer giving three thousand pounds for a single picture to giving
three hundred ? Here we are, with our coppers and acids all ready.
The price of one picture would set thirty coppers going at £100
each : or, much better for the Etching art, fifteen at £200. Why

z

should original steel or copper work be so miserably underpaid compared with engraver's copies on those metals? A moderate capitalist might get some picking out of us if he had the wit. Going his rounds he might say to himself, "There's a promising young man at Red Hill, with remarkably light hair: I'll invest in him." O! the joy—colours and brushes pitched out of the window; plates the *Liber Studiorum* size got out of the dear, little etching-cupboard where they have long reposed ; great needles sharpened three-corner-wise like bayonets ; opodeldoc rubbed into the fore-head to wake the brain up ; and a Great Gorge of old poetry to get up the dreaming ; for, after all, *that's* "the seasoning as does it." Not while he was tarring' his sheep, or counting his woolsacks, but while Endymion slept on Latmos, did Cynthia pause.

In answer to your commercial question I will hazard something which has occurred to me ; premising that, in private negotiation, drawings are better sold in the summer than just now, when the dealers may guess that we are expecting our annual bouquet of those little sweet Williams which "come in" at Christmas ; the rule, adjusted by the nicest "sliding scale," being to offer less in exact proportion in which more would be acceptable—"political economy" in short; the Golden Rule of Greed, *Give to the Rich ; grind the Poor.* And what with modern habits, the waste of modern servants, and the decreased and decreasing value of money, who is *not* poor under two thousand a year? What occurs to me is the transmutation into cash of the most improving possible practice ; the seizing of transient effects by the best—the only perfect way, soft [coloured] crayons and charcoal; which I think should always be in the artist's pocket. Suppose you had made a first sketch of one of your Autun subjects thus, upon ⅛th imperial or less, snatching the best effect, and chose to copy that the same size, ... [fixing] it between each sitting ; you might take it to the spot, and finish the depths with water-colours, using the colour rather dry if the paper were absorbent (you may load on the crayon), using crayon-paper of a cream-colour or a light buff tint. I should think such drawings would go down delightfully at the Dudley Gallery. Charcoal—the very (average) colour of near, cast shadows, used for a fine tree, finished as if you did not intend to colour it, would be an excellent preparation to colour over with

transparent and semi-transparent tints; and then being able to
fix charcoal or crayon between each sitting keeps all progressive.
Still, as this would be an experiment, I should not advise spending
much time upon it. I would trust no crayons (but the Swiss)
which I did not make myself, as they mix lead (flake white)
with the crayon white and light tints. I have a study done with
————'s crayons in which the high lights on a cloud and the flash
of lightning are the emphatic darks. I usually try to catch
transient effects and passing figures with pencil, writing the colours
and various remarks on the several parts; but, as a sketching cam-
paigner, I think soft crayons and charcoal are the sheet anchor.
Turner was said to have made ten thousand studies of skies alone.
So now, unawares, I have come round in this precious piece of cir-
cular advice to what is clearly incompatible with the demands of
authorship. In fact, though at the risk of wearying you I have
tried to touch upon the points you mention, I don't think myself a
good adviser as to affairs. I am looking into my mind at this
moment, and can only find one bit of wisdom there—I mean the
advice I constantly give myself, and usually follow, " Whatever
things you have to do, always do the most disagreeable first." If
that were my own invention I should be a little conceited : it was
stolen somewhere no doubt.

Your own plan of study seems to me quite beautiful. And
what a blessing to throw it off when you are tired, and to become
paterfamilias in a moment. What so charming as to be with little
children, whose simplicity, and faith, and love are models of our
own *highest possible attainment ?*

One hint only I will venture. Intense study is not, I think,
properly balanced by violent exercise either on horseback or on
foot. Those who are constantly grappling with brain efforts,
should in physical discipline lean, as Lord Bacon says, to the
benign extreme. I don't think that either author or artist could
bear the discipline of a boxer in training. " Boxer," by alliterative,
reminds me of biscuit. Woe to the man who dines late, and who
does not take some little luncheon about twelve o'clock ; the neglect
of this has " slain its thousands."

One word about the Virgils, as you so kindly advert to them.
When you " commanded " me to make illustrations I loathed the

thought. But I took "the disagreeable first," and now it is my all-engrossing study. They take a long time for the very reason that I am longing to see them done, and know that the shortest and only way is to aim at no mechanical finish and to put only touches of love. . . .

Pray do not answer this long rigmarole. Would that I could write more incisively and to the purpose : At the end of a long letter these words usually occur to me, " A prating fool shall fall." But with many thanks for your indulgent interest in my Hobby— a double Hobby now, believe me, Yours most truly, S. PALMER.

P.S. Ere you reprint *Etching and Etchers* I should like you to see Holman Hunt's little etching of the Sphinx and the tent. . . . . You would *delight* in it. It seems to me to be a precious, little gem of sentiment, and perfect in the executive. I entirely love it.

XC. TO MR. L. R. VALPY.

RED HILL, *November*, 1872.

MY DEAR MR. VALPY, . . . There is a superlative treat at the Print Room, British Museum, (that is there would be, if we were in any proper sense of the word a civilized nation) fine photographs of all the Vatican sculpture. But what do pheasant-popping squires care for Vatican sculpture ? . . .

I am so eccentric as not to worship the dog like my country-men and the old Egyptians, but do endeavour to keep steadily before me the tenacity of the *bull-dog*. It is a great example ! Our reason for dog-worship lies in the depths of human nature. Praise is sweet, but from a human creature we can never be sure that it is quite sincere. Now the veneration of a dog for his master is entirely so.

To their respective dogs, Alcibiades and Mr. William Sykes were the ideals of perfection. Dogs worship us, therefore we worship dogs ; an idolatry which has something equitable in it at all events, and considering the dog's faithfulness and intelligence, much more rational than the worship of gold, which has no intelligence and maketh itself wings and flieth away.

Roger Ascham says truly, that men are more careful of their studs and kennels than about the culture of their children ; and I take worship to mean the extreme devotion of the affections and intellect to any given object.

"My son, give me thine *heart*." Here seems to be the danger of poetry, in whatever way developed, lest those who have any portion, great or small, of its influence, should love the gift more than the Giver.

Much should I enjoy a talk with yourself and Mrs. Valpy about your late tour. Alas, the weather was unfavourable and though storms are poetical, a skinned umbrella is apt to disturb a train of thought . . . .

I scribbled this hasty line . . . . and must now go to bed. Sleeping or waking, Yours, S. PALMER.

> " These are our drowsie daies, in vain
> We do now wake to sleep again.
> O come that hour, when we shall never
> Sleep again, but wake for ever."

XCI. To Mrs. Robinson.

[Formerly Miss Julia Richmond.]

FURZE HILL, *December* 9, 1872.

MY DEAR MRS. ROBINSON. Your Iona passage gives me more pleasure than Dr. Johnson's, though it is one of his finest, "To abstract the mind etc." Read it in the *Journal.* I should not be inclined to encourage the young lady's walking efforts, but should prefer crawling and kicking, which are with the strongest children the first natural movements, and in the stronger sex an important element of advancement in after life.

What is statesmanship but successful crawling and kicking ? With a view to this, at our public schools, the fag crawls to be kicked, and in his turn kicks the fag who crawls to him : and the ruling powers are far too cunning to abolish a system which so perfectly represents and so admirably prepares for the requirements of public life.

Politics however often reverse the process. Pulteney kicked long and lustily before he crawled into the Earldom of Bath ; and this is found to be very successful in detail: you kick and squabble a little with the givers of good things, just to make moral capital by it, but always let your stubborn honesty be convinced by their arguments.

Illness apart, parental anxieties begin when a child begins to walk; for beginning to walk is beginning to tumble. It is a defiance of gravitation, and Newton is sometimes avenged. By " natural selection " they come down upon sharp corners, edges of fenders or coal-scuttles; or, if precocious ambition prompts them to rise by crawling, a little head is seen near the top of a steep stone staircase, while the " square of the distance " is growling for its prey at the bottom.

Fastened into my little chair, screwed into its stool, I can just remember the whole coming down with a crash; my mother screaming; Riga balsam applied (sovereign for cuts); and here I am, alas, writing nonsense in my old age, no chair of discipline it would seem having been screwed into the " stool of repentance."

But, seriously, Margate is a noble place for air is it not? I heard all about Iona's weighings, and her daily increase of gravity, which had reached its acme when I sought and found her on the cliffs. She was entirely polite, and more in sorrow than in anger seemed to say, " Your manners are plausible—your principles inadmissible." Her fair junior, *whom you maligned*, seemed rather interested in the " singular old gentleman."

He, in turn, is really pleased and more than pleased that you should sympathize with the simple details of his pilgrimage.

Sorrow, in its saddest phase of bereavement, has followed him; yet, perhaps, without sorrow there is little sympathy for others. By sympathy I do not mean any amount of good-nature, but fellow-ship in suffering.

Without free street-fellowship, open air all day, and gambols by the kennel-side, with negation of brain work, London is a sorry place to bring up children in. " Alexandrina, you little muck, come out of the gutter! " a mother exclaimed. It would have been to little purpose had she set the little muck to grind decimals, which are said to be so cultivated in one of our Reigate schools as to leave the poor little girls scarce any time for plain needle-work. Can there be folly more infatuated than that which would leave the children of the poor ignorant of household management and practical duties? Muriatic acid, is it not, which now so pervades the London atmosphere as to render building impossible without speedy corrosion of the stone? Before the east end of West-minster Palace was finished, the west end had begun to rot;

and what will peel a stone wall is not likely to put flesh upon a baby. Then there is the filthy gas. Muses of Phlegethon assist the mortal who would set forth half its loathsomeness! Destroying vegetation (the noble suburban elms which Milton celebrated, rotting to pieces), ancient muniments, and toughest parchment; and yet, forsooth, through blind subserviency to custom, admitted into our dwelling-houses; and, incredible as such wicked carelessness may seem, even into our nurseries! Such, with the visible typhus steaming up through the drain vents in the street, is the atmosphere in which we strive to rear the tenderest infancy. No horse-breeder or dog-trainer would consent to rear his whelps or fillies in such a medium.

But in everything which does not relate to dogs and horses, our national idols, we follow each other like sheep to the slaughter-house. Life itself we hold cheaply, if it may not be preserved by precedent. "I would rather die," said a lady, "under Sir Henry Halford, than be cured by any one else."

Often and often I bless my father's memory for making me repeat almost daily, "Custom is the plague of wise men, and the idol of fools." . . . . I will just remark that, in the article you read, there is a mistake of ten years as to the date of my first exhibited picture, as in 1809 I had not very long emerged from long clothes —not long enough, at least, to approximate the hope of pockets and "inexpressibles." The first exhibition I saw (in 1819) is fixed in my memory by the first Turner, *The Orange Merchant-man on the Bar;* and, being by nature a lover of smudginess, I have revelled in him from that day to this. May not half the Art be learned from the gradations in coffee-grounds? . . . . Believe me, Ever affectionately yours, S. PALMER.

1874

XCII. To MR. P. G. HAMERTON.

FURZE HILL, *February,* 1874.

DEAR MR. HAMERTON. Your son's etching has given pleasure to other than "parental" eyes. "What a sweet little etching," said my wife, who saw it lying on the table, "It is like an old master." There is something touching in the sight of a beginner full of curiosity and hope. My yearning always is, "O! that he may escape the rocks on which I split": years wasted, any one of which would have given a first grounding in anatomy—indispensable anatomy, to have gone with to the antique. The bones are the master key; the marrowless bones are the talisman of all life and power in art. Power seems to depend upon knowledge of structure; all surface upon substance. Knowing *this*, and imbued with the central essence, we may venture to copy the appearance, perhaps even imitate it. It does not seem to me that we have the alternative of copying or imitation, but that copying as upon oath precedes and is the condition of imitation.

Minus the *name* pray make what use you please of the barrowful of *débris* which I sent you from a mountain of doubt.

Thank you for the newspaper extract,[1] which is curiously the reverse of what you have been teaching the public, viz. the scope and compass of etching, its unlimited power of expression, and ductility in the hand of every artist to his individual purpose. Here, is the extract, it is curtailed to a function much better realized by lithography. Surely a rather uncertain chemical process on metal is not the medium in which to render "a few lines" "sternly clear," especially if pencil or charcoal quality is wanted, and pen line to be eschewed. It is some time since I saw a fine collection of Rembrandt's etchings, but my impression is that, in every instance, they are the better in the ratio of the labour; some of the finest being exquisitely finished, and as etchings, the more essentially precious. What wonder, if the labour be a labour of love? Are not Jacquemart's fine in the ratio of his labour of love? Would Veyrassat's *Crossing the Ford* [a plate in *The Portfolio.*] have been bettered by slightness? Is not tone the prerogative of etching, and chiaroscuro its territory? . . . . .

You mention mezzotint in connection with etching. It seems to me that, in some degree, the deep shades of mezzotint differ for the worse from those of etching, in much the same way as the shadows of an oil picture painted on a half-tint ground from the shadows of one on a white ground. I mean when a year or two has done its work with the former. The cases too are analagous as to time; mezzotint, beautiful as it is, and low-toned grounds, bad as they are, being more rapid and cashy. One of the finest qualities of etching seems to me to be a certain luminousness even

[1 Ruskin's letter on Etching addressed to *The Architect.*—ED.]

in its dark shades ; in all but the very darkest : and, if this be a "bull," it is the fault of the fact.

Etching, regarded from your point of view, does seem to be the finest of the metal methods ; and it can easily be shown to be better than wood-cutting, which lacks variety in its dark shadows, though the sparkle of its light is joyous. Then let its flashes illuminate etching ; let all be inclusive and cumulative. What is any art but that which genius has made it by extending its boundaries, while criticism demurred at every venture ? Whence this strange gratification in scraping art with a potsherd, and paring the eye-lids of Regulus ?

I have been reading again Fuseli's *Lectures* (our best, I think). Your son would enjoy them if he is fond of reading about art. He wrote in vain, it seems, as for the last thirty years we have been walking backwards, not towards nature but naturalism.

The Philosophers, who are by no means too imaginative, can set us right. Lord Bacon says it is the office of poetry to suit the shows of things to the desires of the mind.[1] We seem to aim at suiting the desires of the mind to the shows of things. Does not the former imply a much more profound and inclusive study of the "shows of things"—"nature," as we call it, itself? What was it but his ideal of Helen which obliged the Greek to study all the most beautiful women he could find ?

When I was setting out for Italy I expected to see Claude's magical combinations. Miles apart I found the disjointed members, some of them most lovely, which he had suited to the desires of his mind. There were the beauties ; but the Beautiful—the ideal Helen, was his own : and the sense of this ideal is so lost and forgotten by a materialistic age that Claude himself is considered rather as an accomplished master of aerial perspective, or what not, than as the genius, equally tender and sublime, who re-opened upon canvas the vistas of Eden.

But is not all this gaseous rhodomontade about the Ideal exploded by the fact that every artist worthy of the name finds it almost impossible to render one tithe of its beauty when he sits down either to copy or to imitate the simplest object ? I think not ; and it seems to me that, in the present state of our faculties, any system which is without its paradoxes is, by the same token,

[1 *The Advancement of Learning.* Book 2, IV.—Ed.]

as suspicious as the exact correspondence of several witnesses in a trial at the Old Bailey.

As a discipline of exactness Mulready recommended the copying sometimes objects which were not beautiful, to cut away the adventitious aid of association. A very inaccurate imitation of a bunch of grapes will be pleasing in virtue of the subject ; but when I have gone to school to a potato in black and white chalk, I have found it difficult to make it unmistakably like.

Would other demands upon time permit, it seems to me that, at any stage of a painter's progress, it would be useful frequently to copy some simple object of still life, that exactness which is the common honesty of art might never be on the wane.[1] It would seem to be negation, or a contracted power unable to reach the opposites, that makes cold, unimpassioned art. In its relation to landscape, Fuseli says :—[2] " The landscape of Titian, of Mola, of " Salvator, of the Poussins, Claude, Rubens, Elsheimer, Rembrandt, " and Wilson, spurns all relation with this kind of map-work. To " them nature disclosed her bosom in the varied light of rising, " meridian, setting suns ; in twilight, night and dawn. Height, " depth, solitude, strike, terrify, absorb, bewilder in their scenery. " We tread on classic or romantic ground, or wander through the " characteristic groups of rich congenial objects. . . ."

I extract also the following : it may be perhaps useful to your son, if he follow the art and desire to catch it. He says of Titian, who was sent in his tenth year to the school of Giovanni Bellini, that, under him and Sebastiano Zuccati, he acquired while a boy " a power of copying the visible detail of the objects before him " with that correctness of eye and fidelity of touch which distinguish " his imitation at every period of his art. Thus when, more adult, " in emulation of Albert Dürer, he painted at Ferrara Christ to " whom a Pharisee shows the tribute money, he outstript in subtlety " of touch even that hero of minuteness. The hair of the heads and " hands may be counted, the pores of the skin discriminated, and " the surrounding objects seen reflected in the pupils of the eyes ; yet " the effect of the whole is not impaired by this extreme finish : it " increases it at a distance . . . ." &c.

[1 Taken in conjunction with my father's other opinions on art, this is a noteworthy passage.—Ed.]

[2 Lecture IV, " Invention," part 2.—Ed.]

This will not be new to you, nor anything I have said above. Then why did I say it? Why indeed? In my last, I performed Morgiana among the oil jars "by particular desire"; this latter looks very like garrulity, so please accept the apologies of Yours most truly, S. PALMER.

P.S. By way of one last word à propos of the "shows of things," I will add that I saw the arrangement of your sunset river from a boat near Chelsea, and noticed it as a first-rate landscape theme—the dazzling silver, or rather diamond-flakes of tumbling water under the golden sunset. Now here was the "show of things"; but inasmuch as the falling water, looking quite pure by reason of its polish, was evidently, from its position, and some deplorable brickwork seen partially between the trees, nothing more nor less than the issue of a sewer, or filthy factory slush, into insulted Father Thames, the "desires of the mind" were far from being completely satisfied.

The mountain stream fulfils them.

XCIII. To Mr. George Richmond.

Furze Hill, *June* 1, 1874.

MY DEAR FRIEND. I wish you were here this morning, the first genial one almost for the last two months, after those blighting east winds.

First and foremost, let me congratulate you on dear Willy's success (he'll knock us down if we call him "Willy" now); it is delightful to think that so much study and enterprise should have its reward.

Should The Right Hon. William Pitt [1] to quote the Academy Catalogue) be invited to join the new ministry at Trafalgar Square, we should both be glad, as it would in a manner consolidate Blake's identity in our archives. You did your utmost during a season's administration; placing him on the Botticelli Treasury benches (what a treasury that room was!) but now his name flits about again with no beseeming register, and if he be singled out from the host of British Painters as being unworthy of a place in the

[1 *The Spiritual Form of Pitt guiding Behemoth*, a picture by Blake. It appeared in the catalogue as quoted in the text.—ED.]

Gallery of his native land, I do think it time for his native land to buy a "fan" and blush.

As to the *Pitt*, I can truly say that I have scarcely thought of pounds, shillings, and pence in connection with it; yet it is the farthest from my thoughts, as a political economist would say, to "pauperize" the British Lion by making him a present of what he might think scarcely worth a wag of his tail if he took it in alms.

Now that Mr. Burton is at the helm, who knows but that even a Fuseli may be brought into port? How I should delight to see there my love of ancient days, *Psyche coming to the Fates*.

"What is that?" said a lady to her mate, as I was drinking it in at Somerset House. "O! that's *imagination*," said he, with a most contemptuous emphasis upon the word. "Come along!" giving her a vigorous pull to the next picture.

It is one of the curious paradoxes in which the world of fact differs from the world of theory and logic, that though Fuseli is often bombastic and usually mannered through insufficient study of the visible, yet he is essentially poetical and sometimes sublime. I remember your saying of him years ago, "The expression may be imperfect, but its intention is right." No painter of our time gathered about him such a host of of non-admirers. Coleridge, I think, nicknamed him "Fuzzle," or "Fuzzly." Again, after many years, I have been reading his *Life and Lectures*. *Such* a reminder of old times. Where are stowed away all his hundreds of designs on paper, like that pen and ink line of Balaam of which Mr. Linnell has a lithograph?

But "where" is a sad word. Where is Banks's bas-relief lately over the doors of the quondam British Ga lery; where is that grand cartoon of Michelangelo which you and I used to visit together? Where is that *essence* of Rome in Turner's Loggie with La Fornarina—utterly ruined through sparing a few pounds-worth of glass? Where will be the poetic mystery of St. Paul's dome when they have succeeded by mosaics, or what not, in their frightful purpose of "filling it with *light*"—doing away with Thornhill's painted architecture which binds all together, and completes the perspective (otherwise somewhat questionable), in the concentric slope of the pilasters over the Whispering Gallery; faultless at present. Where is Marc Antonio's print of part of Leonardo's cartoon *The Battle of the Standard?*

To pass from "where" to "when," my wife wants to know when we may expect, what would delight us both, a long day's visit from yourself and Mrs. Richmond. There is just a bit of myself left to help to receive you, convalescent from my old acquaintance the asthma, which, with my other ailments, the doctor lays to the weather, saying that these late east winds find out such patients, even in their beds.

I am much concerned to hear or rather read, if I read aright, that you have been for some time unwell: having asked several friends, from time to time, and had a good account, it takes me by surprise.

How these ailments hinder locomotion! No exhibition seen yet—no Churt visit, after such a kind invitation from Hook.

Those who are now nearly at their journey's end leave the world at a crisis of its history. Wars of interest have their term, but a war of principles, being international and universal, is terrible to think of. To me there is a blessed solace in the belief that the present dispensation is near its close, and I cannot without wonder hear big children vaunting about "progress," just as things seem to be coming to a dead lock. It seems to me that no national conjunction can be more perilous than that of gigantic enterprise and wealth with a spirit of godless independency. Even the Pagans considered such implied boastfulness dangerous and unfortunate. Yet, during the last half century, men have been disabused of much prejudice and error, and, in a few centuries more, might redeem the calamitous errors of the past, on one single condition— no less than a total change of their nature! Those who believe in its perfectibility through improved circumstances without wonder at the failure of all their efforts, and will continue to wonder: but those who believe, look forward with a cheerful and unwavering hope to the "new heavens and a new earth, wherein dwelleth righteousness."

How strangely the pen wanders from subject to subject. Steel pens are excellent correctives of digression, as they make the act of writing disagreeable and restrain sudden sallies with a catch or a splutter. Having a goose-quill in hand, I will check the contagious tendency of that pompous bird to wander over a wide common of topics, and yours affectionately S. PALMER will say at once, with the clergyman at Lullingstone, "This is the end."

P.S. *June* 3, 1874. After all, I have not approached your ques-

tion : "Winifred Jenkins" would have spoken more to the purpose !
I do not wish to "fix it rigidly" at £500 and I think the nation
ought not to have it for less than £300.   I think it is worth £500
to the nation ; but if Britannia, while I am in my present mind,
held me out a cheque for 300 guineas filed on the end of her
trident, I would approach cautiously, lest it should be a ruse to
spike me, take it with a long pair of tongs, and invest it.   As a sum
between five and three I will leave it wholly to your better judgement.   It would seem to depend somewhat upon the style in which
the Directors are used to traffic.   There are some who don't like to
buy anything at the price asked, nor without the pleasure of
beating it down.

I would buy a blushing-fan bigger than Mr. G's if it were
I, simply, for whom you were taking trouble : but you are seeking
(to speak paganishly) to soothe the shade of Blake, which we seem
to see hovering about the Gallery's portico, and hitherto, though
not NOW, regarded unfavourably by the police.[1]

XCIV. To Mr. T. H. Wright.

FURZE HILL, *Late on Friday night, October*, 1874.

My DEAR FRIEND. Mr. and Mrs. [John Wright] have just
departed, and our Reverend friend has read me some passages from
Herbert Spencer's *First Principles*.

These philosophers want to make our minds as acute as
possible.   Shortly after I was breeched, I wanted to have my first
penknife made as sharp as possible, but it was explained to me
that it would do nothing but shave ; and that, used for any other
purpose, the edge would turn.

Lord Bacon thought that even a lawyer's mind might be too
acute, because "whatever sharpens narrows."   A man who says, " I
think, therefore I am," will proceed to the next question.   " As I
am, what ought I to *do ?* "   And will set to work.   But a *very*
acute man says, " I think, therefore I seem to be."   Is not this
rather a moonshiny way of beginning a life at the longest very
short, and yet with so much to be done in it ?

A more serious matter is this : to receive the teaching of these
gentlemen we must *hypothetically* deny Christianity ; and is there

[1 The picture referred to was ultimately bought for the National Gallery.—Ed.]

not danger that he who watches to seize every opportunity for
evil may try to make out of this hypothetical denial a real
apostasy, and convey doubts into our minds which may cause us
many agonies of remorse. They say the "Absolute is unknow-
able." The Bible says—our Lord Himself says, "And this is life
eternal, that they may *know* thee the only true God, and Jesus
Christ whom thou hast sent."

St. Paul says, "And even as they did not like to retain God in
their *knowledge*, God gave them over," &c. ; and again, "The Lord
Jesus shall be revealed from Heaven with his mighty angels, in
flaming fire taking vengeance on them that know not God and
that obey not the gospel of our Lord Jesus Christ."

Is it not perilous, even hypothetically, to entertain propositions
which profess to lead upwards (?) through the physical sciences to
a conviction that we can never know God? Moreover, this
elaborate system of negation requires half a life to get together its
scientific apparatus, which is to end in paralysis of doubt, dimming
our best perceptions, and removing all the most stirring and noble
incentives to labour.

I have been reading the life of John Stuart Mill, and have been
struck with the result, after all their knowledge and thought, in an
incapability for worthy *action*, nay, in imbecility on their own
strong points, both in father and son. The father's political
ultimatum was the widest possible representation even with our
present untaught constituencies.

David Hume treating of *Morals* treats the chastity of women
as a mere fudge except where it happens to be expedient

Now a labourer's son at a Sunday school who has been carefully catechised and really is trying to do his duty to God and to
his neighbour as set forth in the catechism is, I think, farther
advanced in real education than a master of negations, though he
may have learned languages, attended lectures, and walked
hospitals, to elaborate, in the most ingenious propositions, his own
and everybody else's nonentity.

All this is so much more demonstration (if more were wanted)
of the truth of God's words, "The world by wisdom knew not
God." "But the natural man receiveth not the things of the spirit
of God for they are foolishness unto him : neither can he know
them, because they are spiritually discerned."

We are told also, which is exactly to the point, that man cannot "by SEARCHING find out God," but that God reveals these things by the Spirit to the spirit of man : and that the way to "know of the doctrine, whether it be of God" is to do the will of God.

Mere human success and mastery of any art is not to be attained by first knowing all there is to be known about it, but by trying to *do*, while you are trying to know how to do better.

"He that cometh to God must believe that he is," says the Apostle. Now is not the influence of a book, to say the least, perilous, which tends, when we kneel down to our prayers, to cast over the mind flying doubts, or at least momentary misgivings, whether we, baptized Christians, are after all not praying to a shadow ?

My spirit is stirred, and hence these hasty and probably ill spelt and unstopped sentences—but pardon Yours affectionately,
S. PALMER.

1875

XCV. TO MR. L. R. VALPY.

FURZE HILL, *February* 1, 1875.

MY DEAR MR. VALPY. "I have done the deed. Didst thou not hear a noise ?" A noise of my groaning when, according to Herbert's advice, I was "girding up my loins" to attempt the enclosed descriptions [of the Miltons] or whatever they may be called.

It was no fancied difficulty ; for in trying to describe the motive or impulse of a picture, which is or ought to be fervid, it seems to be implied that the painter has realized his idea, else, what is the use of describing it ? And whether he has done so is for others to decide. "Let another man praise thee, and not thine own mouth."

If the painter says : "From the skirts of an ancient forest the eye is led to a parapet of granite mountain stretching far away, through a break in which there is a glimpse of a vast champaign, while the golden moon is just emerging from the more distant ocean", it is hard to discern that he is not complimenting his own picture, for an equivalent in *painting* to those few words demands great mastery. As my father-in-law once remarked, it is easier to *say* "Jack Robinson" than to paint "Jack Robinson."

Vastly different were the task, or rather pleasure, of comment-
ing upon another man's picture : the string of one's tongue is loosed ;
at every inspection, if it be really fine work, we find new beauties ;
and what we do not find we fancy ; so that if the artist were to
come to life, he would say with Socrates, " What does not this
young man fable of me ? "

I remember a learned D.D. who, when people asked him
whether some eloquent preacher did not " bring a great deal out of
a text," was wont to answer, " Yes : a great deal more than ever
was in it ! "

But the real charm of art seems to me not to consist in what
can be best clothed in words, or made a matter of research or discovery. Its technical means are conversant with several branches
of science ; and it demands lifelong investigation of phenomena ;
but I do not think that the *result* is a science, though Constable
very truly said that every picture was a scientific experiment. The
result I take to be not interpretation, but representation—its first
appeal not to the judgement but the imagination.

Lord Stafford's house-maid stood leaning on her broom before
that wondrous Claude, not because it excited or gratified her
curiosity, but because " she thought she was in Heaven."

No man, perhaps, more perfectly rendered his genuine perceptions than the elder Cuyp, in those groups of milch kine beside a
brimming river, with maid or swain ; all bathed (if a river can
be bathed !) in amber light. Now here is ample matter for ex-
cogitation—hydrostatics, cattle-breeding, &c. ; yet I doubt whether
any one who could feel his charm ever *excogitated* at all before the
works either of the elder or younger Cuyp. Painters excogitate to
find out how it was done. Turner based much of his colouring
upon these masters ; but this is an after affair ; if we are gifted
with the seeing eye we feel before we think . . . . Yours, S.
PALMER.

XCVI. TO MR. T. H. WRIGHT.

FURZE HILL HOUSE, *April* 15, 1875.

MY DEAR MR. WRIGHT. Many thanks for the extract, which I
have carefully put away for you until you are furnished with an
indexed commonplace-book like Herbert's.

A A

Who would have thought that Swift was less English than Johnson? Yet from one single language (the Latin) Johnson probably adopted more words than Swift or Gibbon. Fewer words, if they are all from one language, leave a more exotic impression on the memory than a collectively greater number from several languages.

Moreover, Johnson liked to teaze the Celtic-simplicity-people, now and then, with a sonorous Latin trumpet-blast, and one of these impresses memory more than twenty muffled explosions.

To me, the most curious thing is the moderate extent of Milton's vocabulary ; seeing that it is perhaps, effectively, the richest in our tongue. In the poetry of prudence a word is a word ; in the poetry of (Plato's) madness it is many ; and all the best poets are out of the body while they write, though the bodily hand holds the pen. Yet on referring to the most superhuman passages we find the words simple : so placed, however, under the divine frenzy that one word does duty for many. So, in *real* music, the simplest change of key occurring at the right time in the right place, effects everything ; as the "shadows *brown*," in Handel's setting of *Il Penseroso*, are solemnized in a moment by descending one semitone upon the adjective ; going into the key of the 4th, if I remember rightly.

The barbaric blurters of unprepared discords could not have effected it by any amount of hideousness.

A friend of mine of exquisite musical taste [Mr. F. O. Finch], who was one of the mourners at Sir Thomas Lawrence's funeral, always remembered, as the procession entered the west door of St. Paul's, a flattened seventh in the bass of the organ, then solemnly rolling : it was in its *right place*. The mere thing itself occurs continually.

But moderns who have stimulated their musical appetite with burrs, and thistles, and prickles, find everything else insipid ; Corelli's harmonies are "*thin*" they say. "Make the gruel thick and slab."

Well ! these things are all vanity compared with the "things which are above " ; yet, perhaps, things which are in good taste bear the closer analogy with things morally good and holy. By the bye, what an absurdity it seems to seek for the things that are above, in physics, or the laboratory, though that will furnish beautiful analogies. Our so called "philosophers" seem like perverse little boys who go to the butcher's for toffee and to the sweet-shop for kites, and then put their knuckles into their eyes and run down the street howling, because they can get neither kites nor toffee. Yours ever, S. PALMER.

XCVII. To MR. T. H. WRIGHT.

FURZE HILL, *May*, 1875.

MY DEAR FRIEND. Too much of the ludicrous enervates the mind, yet who can repress a smile when a gentleman is running after his hat, or a philosopher after an "invariable law," which, by the terms of the game, he can never overtake till it is stopped by the outer wall of eternity ?

A spice of the droll sometimes flavours very serious matters, such as the deposition of an eastern magnate when we assure him that he is not deposed on account of misconduct of which he has just been acquitted ! Our dear and Reverend friend begged me to write to you on the subject, remembering a conversation which took place in this room a few weeks before the upshot.

I do not take credit to myself for anticipating anything so ridiculous, having merely suggested generally that few obstacles are suffered to stand in the way of political expediency—" of commercial expediency either," I might have added. We have an instance of each in the same reign, the massacre of Glencoe, and the breach of faith with the settlers at Darien, whose bleached skeletons long whitened the coast.

To change the subject, what a refreshing thing is good sense lucidly expressed. Here is a morsel from *The Spectator,*[1] No. 110. (Addison doubtless, from other marks, although that paper has neither of his distinguishing initials "C. L. I. O.") After ridiculing rustic credulity, the author says, "At the same time, I think a " person who is thus terrified with the imagination of ghosts and " spectres, much more reasonable than one who, contrary to the " reports of all historians sacred and profane, ancient and modern,

[1] Note.—Adverting to microscopic criticism, we may observe that it does not follow from a sentence being wrong when we take it to pieces that it is not quite right when put together : the sun has spots ; the flame of a farthing candle has none.

A A 2

" and to the traditions of all nations, thinks the appearance of
" spirits fabulous and groundless."

This is the motto of Dr. Lee's new book, *Glimpses of the Supernatural :* in which, by the way, he mentions some Oxford under-
graduates of 1829, who found a shorter cut to godlessness than
boring to it through physical induction. They formed a Hell Fire
Club which used to meet twice a week at Brazenose ; each trying
to outdo the rest in blasphemy. The authorities suspected
something, but could not discover their whereabout. Towards a
midnight in December, 1829, one of the Fellows of Brazenose,
returning home down the narrow lane connecting the square in
which Brazenose faces All Souls, with Turl Street, saw what
appeared to be a tall man *helping* some one to get out of one of
the fenced windows of Brazenose. Rushing forward he saw a
student, his form and features distorted with agony, being forcibly
dragged out between the iron stanchions. He rushed past, to the
chief entrance, and fell down in a swoon. Just then there arose a
cry from a crowd of students rushing out from a set of rooms
immediately to the right of the porter's lodge. They were
members of the " Club." In the utterance of a volley of blasphemy the occupant of the rooms had suddenly broken a blood-
vessel, and was lying dead upon the floor. " The account was
current in my days (1850)," says Dr. Lee. A version of the story
is also in *Odds and Ends*, London, 1872. Dr. Lee has the Glamis
story too. Yours affectionately, S. PALMER.

XCVIII. TO MR. L. R. VALPY.

[*May*, 1875.]

MY DEAR MR. VALPY. How happy you must have been at Wells
under such favourable circumstances ! When the love of God
makes sunshine within a house, we can bear with wet weather
without. I will not say

" Earth hath not anything to show more fair,"

but earth hath not many things to show more fair than the west
front of Wells Cathedral. It shows what Christian art might
have become in this country, had not abuses brought it down with
a crash, and left us, after three centuries, with a national preference

of domesticated beasts and their portraits, before all other kinds of art whatsoever.

I must have ill expressed my meaning if it seemed that I would exclude geological drawing from art drawing. It seems to me that art drawing includes it, as figure drawing includes anatomy. Probably the confusion arose from those who seem to me the great rock and earth Masters being supposed by others to be geologically incorrect.

The visible characteristics of the various rocks were as patent to artists before their history (?) was attempted, as since the conflict of opinion began as to their modification by fire, water, ice, and what not ; the great "discovery" that the earth made itself and was never created by the Almighty not being, I should suppose, of any particular service to the painter !

I do not know whether the rocks upon which Nicholas Poussin has seated Polyphemus have ever been gainsaid. They affect the imagination, and if they failed to affect mine, I should feel that I had gained a loss, by any supposed knowledge which had lessened their impression. Had this happened to me after much study of geological diagrams, I should feel that my knowledge was disproportioned, and that I wanted much more of some other kind of knowledge to set me right.

Last year, at Margate, I made several observations and memoranda upon certain reflections of sky in sea, which seemed to violate the most obvious optical "laws" ; and I think we shall never see rightly unless we bring science and knowledge of the individual refinements and niceties of nature into contact with an equal amount of art knowledge, and the phenomena which modify individualities.

Nature knowledge and art knowledge ought to be in harmony, but they are two distinct things. Nothing would please me more than to spend a year in resuming my old studies of botanical minutiæ. It would replenish the mind with a world of delicate refinement, but it would not give that perception which "laps me in Elysium" at the sight of a fine (uncleaned) Claude : nor would any amount of geological diagrams bring my soul in unison with Nicholas Poussin's *Polyphemus :* rather, perhaps, it might incline me to pick holes in it.

I think that the great landscape-painters used as much of literal truth as was necessary in order to " make the ideal probable," and that minute criticism will never be more prone to object than when they showed the chief mastery of art in knowing what to omit. I think the *Callisto* rocks should be studied in order to *see* nature.

I have heard one of the most eminent living painters express his gratitude to art for the specific reason that it taught him to *see* nature. Turner, who of all men was the most pronounced disciple of Claude (painting large pictures of avowed companionship with certain of his great masters'), learned from Claude, Poussin, &c., how to see nature; to see nature in its proper aspect and position relatively to art. I remember some Savoy pictures by Turner in which he was bringing to bear very evidently what he had been learning from the Poussins.

It is thus, I think, that the great original painters and poets are made. They differ from inferior men by having at once more of their own and more of other people's: more of their own and more of their masters'.

I dislike writing about art because the comparative ease of talking twits me with the difficulty of doing: and nothing is more true than the "*de gustibus.*" If a youth of seventeen is not charmed by a fine Claude, no amount of art or nature-culture will avail him: but Turner, in common with the maid who leaned on her broom at Stafford House, had the faculty to which Claude never appeals in vain.

Next time I hope not to talk shop. Excuse hasty first words, and with our united best regards to yourself and Mrs. Valpy (who saw with you the Cheddar rocks, I hope), I remain Yours most truly, S. PALMER.

XCIX. TO MR. L. R. VALPY.

FURZE HILL, *May*, 1875.

MY DEAR MR. VALPY. When we had the pleasure of seeing you, I said something concerning the principles of art which may need a line of explanation. Perhaps that may be better done by a statement of my belief, than in an argumentative way. If I make positive assertions it is because it saves time to put suggestions in that form; and besides, it is quite in the fashion!

We cannot, as Mulready said, proceed a step without anatomy ; and in landscape, without what is analogous to it.

We cannot rightly see or imitate what is before us without understanding structure.

"Rock foregrounds." Geological drawing is not art drawing, though the latter includes as much of it as may be wanted.

The last skill of imitation is to know what should be omitted. Rocks should be studied from the Poussins : *e.g.* in the Callisto. That is the finest mass I remember. I remember reading a critique questioning the truth of a peculiar mass of rock in one of Claude's pictures. I had seen none like it, but I did not measure Claude's knowledge by my own ignorance. In my next tour, I came upon the very thing and sketched it.

Very extensive knowledge of nature is requisite if we would apprehend a tithe of what is contained in Claude and the Poussins.

If we are chiefly conversant with the tints and patterns of nature, Gaspar will be a sad disappointment to us. We shall say "Bless the man ! He seems to have tried how much he could leave out."

In the painting of ground I think Claude is at the top. Indeed, where is he not ? His knolls, so softly clad, are round and figure-like. As to trees he is indeed pre-eminent. Titian alone may compare with him. Whether with pen or brush, in drawing, in conception, in colour, they so imbue us with delight, that even laudatory criticism is out of place. . . . I wonder less and less at Reynolds's saying, "The world *may* see another Raffaelle, but never another Claude."

Claude, Poussin, Bourdon, did not attempt to satisfy that curiosity of the eye which an intelligent tourist ever feeds and never sates ; nor did they attempt to reproduce a scene : for they knew that every hedgerow contains more matter than could be crowded into a picture-gallery ; and that, supposing they could deceive the eye, the real impression could not be completed but by touch and hearing—the gushes of air and the singing of birds. They addressed not the perception chiefly, but the IMAGINA-TION, and here is the hinge and essence of the whole matter.

I have observed all my life long that where there is imagination, either among the greatest artists or those ignorant of art, and whatever they like or dislike elsewhere, there is enchantment for such minds in Claude.

His works, as Thomas Warton says of *Lycidas*, are a sure test of imagination.

Ordinary landscapes remind us of what we see in the country ; Claude's, of what we read in the greatest poets and of *their* perception of the country, thus raising our own towards the same level.

"To Titian," says Fuseli, "to Mola, Salvator, the Poussins, to "Claude, Rubens, Elsheimer, Rembrandt and Wilson, nature dis- "closed her bosom in the varied lights of rising, meridian and setting "suns ; in twilight, night and dawn. Height, depth, solitude, strike, "terrify, absorb, bewilder in their scenery. We tread a classic or "romantic ground, &c." Lecture 4. Works. Vol. 2, p. 217.

C. To Mr. P. G. Hamerton.

FURZE HILL, *November* 2: 1875.

DEAR MR. HAMERTON. It's rather like having a tooth drawn : however, here I am in the chair, so pull away ! The "I consent" has gone to Mr. Seeley.[1]

One thing I must ENTREAT you to do for me. Make it clear that all is suggestion, not assertion ; though for brevity's sake it may have taken that form. With this proviso, the oil-colour hints are at your service. . . .

The scruples as to my own part involve no cowardice. The few things I *do* know I am ready to assert though the parish laugh in chorus at me ; but Art unites things in themselves remote ; Vision, Matter, Science, for instance ; and so it came to pass that of some of its wisest saws the reverse is equally true ; and this suggests catholic scope and delicate handling.

We lose a great deal of truth, however, if we refuse to believe some things which, *in the present state of our faculties, are contradictory ;* verbally so I mean, for there are niceties of thought and feeling which words, however well chosen, do but inadequately express.

[1 Mr. Hamerton's request had been for some technical notes for *The Portfolio.*—Ed.]

I am very glad to hear from you, having had some misgivings that you had worked yourself to death, a kind of industry I decidedly object to ; and I am sure Mrs. Hamerton will agree with me on this subject ; with best regards to whom and to yourself, believe me, Yours very truly, S. PALMER.

1876

CI. TO MISS FRANCES REDGRAVE.

[FURZE HILL.] *January,* 1876.

DEAR PRECEPTRESS. Many thanks for your kind remembrance of an ailing friend ; especially at this time when advanced philosophy is contriving for them the means of a painless quietus. Political " Science " is tending this way, but does not speak out because of some lingering prejudices against homicide. Owing to this, some time may yet elapse before aged farm-labourers who are past work will receive from their Board of " Guardians " a few drops of prussic acid to stop the demand of their now unproductive muscles for a little food and raiment out of the pockets of the rate-payers.

I have much reason to be thankful that my working power remains, and that my head, after the measure of its clearness, is not more muddy than of old.

The doctor's horror of cold-catching confines me to a corner, where there is room only for small work ; but upon that I energize some hours in the forenoon, and after tea, by Silber's lamp-light.

As to imprisonment, it is only a pleasant " hermitage," as the poet says, where there are many resources ; and books enable us to keep the " very best society " without the trouble of going about to seek it.

Many thanks for your mention of Casaubon's life. That of his son would be interesting, were there sufficient material, from the changeful times—the offers of Cromwell, including that most tempting one of restoring to him his father's library, &c.

We owe the cartoons to Cromwell : he had a wide scope of perception for whatever was sterling and noble ; and it is well that attached members of the Church of England like you and me should not suffer our notions of English history to be stultified by the Divine Right politics of advanced ritualists. Dr. Neale published a boy's history of England which I think the Star Chamber would have pronounced to have been inspired!

An able friend of mine, rather high-church too in his views, described the leaders of advanced ritualism as, for the most part, men of weak heads and strong wills. Ritualistic art too is very poor stuff—skinny saints and starved Madonnas. And as to architecture, if St. Paul's could speak we should find it [could] scarcely articulate, from the agitation of its narrow escape. Fancy the putting frescoes into the dome to give it light, when its essence is gloom and mystery!

Westminster Abbey is as unritualistic as can be. All is ideal symmetry and design; nothing of filigree, and scraps, and patch-work, lace fringes, or flummery. A *Romanist* bishop (French), not long ago, finding in his cathedral an ornament of devout ladies' needlework, ordered it away immediately saying, "This place is a church, not a theatre." It seems to me that all ornament of surface should be based upon structural grandeur.

If Christians love the "*beauty* of holiness," why should they seek it in rag-tag; and not rather, as Bishop Thirlwall suggested, in noble architecture, music, and eloquence? What havoc ultra-ritualism makes of the two latter is best known to those who have got cramp in the tongue in the effort to keep pace with the profanely-gabbled responses, or slept under the Oxford drawl. This is now the fault, as it has long been the misfortune of Oxford, as they refused the endowment of a professorship for the purpose of teaching them to read.

I shall never forget the service at Exeter Cathedral some years ago, where time and rhythm were observed, as well as melody.

The love of unrhythmical melody is I think the sure mark of a barbarian. In this kind of music the cats are beyond all competition unrivalled: no *prima donna* can approach their subtle enharmonics.

I am grieved to hear of your dear uncle's continued indisposition; a friend who never gave me an unkind word or look, and concerning whom my only regret was that I could not see more of him. Believe me, Most truly yours, S. PALMER.

CII. To MR. RICHARD REDGRAVE.

[FURZE HILL.] *March*, 1876.

MY DEAR REDGRAVE. Ever to you and yours the heartiest reciprocation of your good wishes for the sand-martins!

You should write a tragedy, for you can make the spirit leap and the flesh creep, the former with Burlington House, the latter at the very hint of a shop-prepared ground. No! let the colourman paint the picture rather than lay the priming. . . . I hope the James Ward tradition will be left by his son. The father told me that his *Bull*, impasted as it is, would *roll up* without the least cracking. His sons made the vehicle that he used, and alone are acquainted with the method. . . . . .

Rich painting with copal and amber will leave a first-rate shop gesso ground, dropping clean off in large flakes. They make no reticulated tooth in successive layers to lay hold of the touches in whatever direction they may come. When this is delicately done it yet leaves the ground quite smooth enough, and the brush has always something to feel. The best oil grounds I ever saw were brilliant with the best flake white used stiff, but with a little oil copal in it; not enough to make gloss, but enough to make it in some degree homogeneal with the paint of the picture. But doubtless you know all this and much more, so I have besmirched myself with "carrying coals to Newcastle."

One word more. It is not pleasant to order absorbent grounds (tempera I mean) at a first-rate shop, and to be supplied, as a friend of ours was, with tempera grounds indeed, but washed for the nonce over oil grounds!

I miss that friend much, for I learned much from him and it was my own fault that I learned not much more. . . .

Ah vanity of vanities! The Colin blue struck me just as it has struck you; so keeping it for flowers and little touches on little figures, the trouble was almost for nothing. But it was right, I think, to take pains about it, because of its resemblance in *powder* to the queen of hues, verditer—so like the infinitely retiring eastern sky during the western after-glow. So one went back to dear old Mother Ultramarine and her three less showy but inestimable daughters the 1, 2 and 3 Ultramarine Ashes, bless them! Verditer, I think, will stand in tempera under varnish; not so (judging from a single experiment) verdigris.

I was trying, last night, to design something in charcoal with a view to your cherished fixing fluid, and could not help feeling what a different art etching would be if we could have the variety of point, from sharp to very blunt, which we enjoy in charcoal. Perhaps three or four of the finest etching-needles, or of strong, common needles, welded close together, side by side, would do it. . . .

I was delighted to hear from Sissy's very kind letter that our friend Haden had not relapsed. What a shock to the whole system such a shock must be! I blessed the fair catalogue-sender from my heart. Artists and the public are much indebted for the pains you have taken in purveying them such a feast.

March 3rd. Swathed like a mummy, and at the risk of my worthless life, I went direct to Burlington House and back again, with the exception, happy as it turned out, of a look at the Dudley Gallery : for I was delighted with a drawing of yours which has remained in fond memory ever since. It is part of the Evelyn Woods I think, with a little deep-blue, fine-weather sky, and is very intricate, attracting the eye into the recesses : there is part of a pond or mere seen under the trees. Surely without this poetic *intricacy*, landscape loses nine tenths of its charm. . . . At Burlington House the picture I was trying as for my life to investigate was the Nicholas Poussin *Callisto*. Now one cannot stand for an hour or more before a picture, without hearing a running commentary from the BRITISH PUBLIC. With the single exception of a bright young lady who told her party at once that Arcas was the individual who saw Diana bathing (! !), *every one*, male and female, began with this formula : " Very strange!— O ! *A landscape, with the story of Arcas and Callisto. Nicholas Poussin.* I don't know what that is." A perceptive lady—one of those terrible creatures who can detect your character from your signature said, pointing to the Jove, " That figure sitting upon the eagle is doubtless Our Lord. Yes, it must be so from the glory round him :—but —but—the *bear*—I confess I can't make that out." A " gentleman," after going through the formula, was much tickled with the cloud. After enlarging on the absurdity of the whole affair, he showed how nicely the cloud was shaped into steps for the convenience of the non-gravitating passengers. Of all who looked, not one loved, not one admired, not one approved.

And these seemed to be otherwise well educated people : the cushioned and chicken-fed poodles left in their carriages were perhaps at that moment on their hinders, making teeth at wayfaring Christians out of the windows. O ! how different their masters from the working men I have heard talking together with tasteful alacrity before the Turners at South Kensington ! But then they do that horrid " rattening."

I thought that stately Altieri Claude had been at some former time injured by cleaning. That and a companion picture were offered in Rome many years ago to a deceased friend of mine for 1,300 scudi. Only think ! About £160 each !

It is a very fine collection, and not the less gratifying for that one has seen most of the pictures before, either with their proprietors, or at the British Gallery ; for they improve by repetition. One feature is entirely new, the seeing them in so good a light ; and how well they bear it.

I should have enjoyed a long look at the Leslies, but when I thought it was about three o'clock my watch bade me instantly depart to catch the last daylight train. . . . With best regards to both houses, believe me, Most truly yours, S. PALMER.

CIII. TO MR. T. O. BARLOW.

RED HILL, *September* 30, 1876.

MY DEAR MR. BARLOW. Accept my thanks for informing me, through my son, of some very interesting propositions, otherwise confidential, relating to the Etching Club. For myself I doubt whether etching in the old sense of the word is not almost superseded by the new art of *retroussage* added by the printer upon a comparatively slight fabric. Sometimes it has been very effective, but, in most instances, is so inferior to linear etching as to become quite another art : but then, as it produces an effect quite as satisfactory to the public eye in about one fifth of the time, it beats linear etching out of the market. It seems to me that the charm of etching is the glimmering through of the white paper even in the shadows; so that almost everything either sparkles, or suggests sparkle. Now this is somewhat like the effect of a purely white ground under an oil painting. The *demonstrable* difference may be

small, but the real deterioration of a dark ground is universal ; and
not to quote irreverently, is "a darkness that may be felt" if it
cannot be proved. Well, *retroussage*, if not kept within narrow
bounds, extinguishes those thousand little luminous eyes which
peer through a finished linear etching, and in those of Claude are
moving sunshine upon dew, or dew upon violets in the shade. I
remain, Most truly yours, S. PALMER.

1877

CIV. To the Rev. J. P. Wright.

FURZE HILL, *May*, 1877.

MY DEAR MR. WRIGHT. I should have written long ago had
anything occurred to me which might have cheered your solitude,
but for news of this district I was wholly dependent upon *you ;* and
all else you have had in the newspapers.

Many thanks for your DAY IN DETAIL. What much com-
forts me is your sticking close to the " publicans and sinners."
When the " respectable " people have done with these poor creatures,
especially the women, their one only tie of sympathy with their
kind is through the clergyman. I hate cant, but I really cannot
see how any of us can be quite sure that we are better than they ;
so much depends on surrounding influences and early habits.
Sin, however, lies heavily at the door of those who have suffered
their poor to live in pig-sties and have filched from them their
gardens. I have just met again with the statement (to us almost
incredible) that the act of Elizabeth forbade the building of any
cottage which had not " four acres " of land attached to it.

" For whom would they work," we should say, " if they had so
much land of their own ?" What we esteem "so much" our
fathers set down as the minimum.

Mr. Tooth, you will have heard, has returned to his vicarage
like a "giant refreshed," and officiated in his church at 8 a.m. last
Sunday in a " richly embroidered chasuble " the day after the
vestment-prohibiting judgment had been given ! . . . .

Ever since a very brief account of the new judgment which I
met with in *The Globe,* Mr. Giles has continued to irrigate the
drought of my ignorance, 1st by *The Times* of Monday, 2nd *The
Daily Express,* and this evening, Thursday, by a closely-printed
octavo volume. . . . .

I suppose the "vestments," or simple surplice worn next Sunday will manifest the intention of the respective wearers as to obedience to the (secular) law, or its manifest defiance. The Apostles disobeyed, I think, their own Sanhedrim, but it seems hardly worth while to pull this dear old Church of England about our ears for vestments of any kind ; though how the Lords can pronounce the cope illegal which was always worn in the cathedrals till Warburton (afterwards bishop) threw his aside one day in a pet because of some difficulty in getting it on is hard to see.

Dr. Irons wrote *at once* in *The Daily Express* beseeching for patience on the part of his brethren. Hoping soon to have something more to communicate, I remain, Affectionately yours,
S. PALMER.

CV. TO THE REV. J. P. WRIGHT.

FURZE HILL, *June* 2, 1877.

MY DEAR MR. WRIGHT. Adverting to your interesting narrative, I suppose your experiences have long ago suggested that no mere moral suasion, nothing indeed but the preaching of Christ unto them, can move those who have long been in the fetters of evil habits—nothing short of that miracle wrought by the Holy Spirit when he shows to each true penitent the Saviour crucified, not merely for all, but for *himself* individually, and thence awakens that love and gratitude which can move mountains ; which can say to this heap of guilt "be thou removed and cast into the sea." It is only the love of Christ which can reverse the "tenfold-nature" power of habit.

This alone renders credible the conversion of those Gentiles into "Holy Brethren," "Members of Christ." Philip went down into Samaria and "preached Christ unto them." Is there enough of this in our pulpits?

This marvellous power of the love of Christ, enduring through nearly two thousand years, astonished Napoleon and made him think little, in comparison, of military and imperial objects.[1]

It was the sense of a Saviour crucified for him (so strangely impressed or suggested) which converted Col. Gardiner on the

[1 I am at a loss to imagine my father's authority for this statement. See Letter CXVIII.—Ed.]

very evening of an assignation with a married woman. See Dr. Doddridge's *Life of Col. Gardiner;* a "Tract Society" tract, I believe.

It was indeed, as our friend said to you, a marvellous change wrought upon those Gentiles; and now, to change the subject with only this link of transition. Last Tuesday afternoon Mr. Palgrave himself appeared; looking, I thought, younger than when he left for the Palace. All his family seem to get on pretty well in that Westminster air of evil repute, but then they all go away four months in the year. We went at it "hammer and tongs" for $1\frac{1}{2}$ or 2 hours on all sorts of subjects. He says Carlyle, it is thought, must have been hoaxed with some utterly false report when he wrote that Eastern Question letter to *The Times*, in which he said that Government was going to do something which would bring down all Europe upon us.

. . . Doubtless you sometimes have the sense of loneliness drop suddenly upon you like a pall, or Dante's leaden cowls. But the time will come when a pastor, who is a pastor indeed, will feel anything but lonely; meeting again, where there is no danger of relapse, the fruits of his ministry, and can say, "Behold me and the children whom thou hast given me."

If you feel lonely—a shepherd with a little flock upon a hill, *concentrate* yourself upon that flock, and you will find that "There is society where none intrudes"; and think of my loneliness, frozen up and crippled up from the haunts of men, from my London friends—from that dearly-longed-for Blake exhibition, which was a severance indeed; and, now that *you* are gone, I know of the two, perhaps, rather more of what happens in the moon than what happens here. . . . Affectionately yours, S. PALMER.

CVI. To the Rev J. P. Wright.

FURZE HILL, *June* 9, 1877.

DEAR MR. WRIGHT. I got *The Life of Stirling* for the sake of the Coleridge sketch. I was much surprised to read of the view of London, "big Paul's" &c. from Mr. Gilman's. By his kind permission I saw all the Coleridgeiana there; went into C.'s study; sat in his seat in the garden; and so far from seeing anything distant, found the garden view, beyond a little meadow land, quite blocked by

Lord Mansfield's woods; the view in front across a piece of spare ground, backed by other Highgate houses. From what I noticed of the position of the row of houses, one of which was Mr. Gilman's, it seems that nothing short of the instrument described by Mr. Weller Junr. in the witness-box could give a glimpse of London, or any other distance, from any part of the premises.

What a dismal book it is! A history of "Littlefaith robbed of his jewels"; not by foot-pads, but by the bad set of friends among whom he had fallen, till they left him nothing to die upon but Hume's "Leap in the dark." It is painful to see him hustled along by them in their stumbling scuffle towards the outer darkness. How soothing after this to hear, as a few days before Bishop Butler's death he was walking in the garden with his chaplain, "I feel that my feet are upon the Rock." This book seems to me altogether to ignore belief, and to remove it as an intermediate from between unbelief and hypocrisy. Wretched is man if these are the poles between which he is doomed to waver. But I *know* that this is not so. I knew *scores* of dissenters (*the old fashioned ones*) who, in the literal sense, believed the Bible narrative [1] and I hope there are many Church people who do so, notwithstanding their sleek living, and frequent "hops," and midnight *soirées*, and worldly conformity, tending to interpose a somewhat thick veil on the hither side of the objects of faith. I dislike what is called ritualism, because it offers to such silver-slippered Christians a substitute so specious for real devotion, in outward prostrations, rote prayers, and the like; but odd things are to be found in odd corners at all times—Nicholas Farrers, Edmund Laws, &c.; and amid the very whirl of business, himself in servile employment, had we not very lately Thomas Wright of Manchester, whose "name is like a civet-box"?

Your reason for public catechising, as to its indirect effect on the *parents*, strikes me much. How powerful is indirect influence for good or evil, and how widely may unsuspected consequences spread, like the circles when a stone is thrown into the water, from a single wholesome or indiscreet word!

O! that we might recall the idle words of our youth; but they are spoken for ever. . . .

[1] How absurd it seems to be asserting such a palpable truistic fact: but really I emerge from the book as from an exhausted receiver, thankful to remember that there are and have been people surrounded with vital air and with lungs to make use of it. . . . . .

Mr. Ridsdale of Folkestone is going to disuse the vestments, &c., for the present, having procured a command and DISPENSA-TION (! ! !) from Archbishop Tait. . . .

You are quite right about the warm colour of the young oaks. Why should not clergymen inform themselves through their eyes as well as through the ears : what are both, but gates of the under-standing. Why should a fine, antique statue be to the *illiterate eyes* of a senior wrangler, as one said, merely a big, stone doll ? Simply because at our universities the eyes are left untaught. A pastor who had been taught to use his eyes might teach much to farm-labourers from his poetic perceptions of farming. See Flavel (one of the learned—the ejected Puritans), his *Husbandry Spiritual-ized.* . . . Yours affectionately, S. PALMER.

CVII. To the Rev. J. P. WRIGHT.

July 17, 1877.

DEAR MR. WRIGHT. As you *invite* criticism, I will suggest that, however valuable your essay may be as author's material for future use, it might possibly, in its present state, be misunderstood by some readers, who would not always see whether you were in jest or earnest. This, if it be true, is hardly your fault, for it is the office of satire to guard men against the specious side of error by exposing its ridiculous or shameful side. But what is satire to do if Error *prides* herself upon her ridiculous side, and turns it outwards ?

Spenser had to strip his " Duessa " ; but now-a-days " Duessa " dances stark naked. If she, while you depict her filthiness displays it for public approbation dull people will mistake you for one of her admirers perhaps.

Progress, in the nature of things physical and moral, is never so rapid as when it is down hill ; and such a race of this kind has been run by really learned and accomplished people that Satire's " occupation's gone " ; she must sit down exhausted and confess herself beaten : she has been beaten with her own weapons, and can transcribe only the absurdities which she would not have ventured to imagine.

Let us take a few at hap-hazard, all from great "lions," German, French, and English, abridged from memory.

Philosopher 1. "*The Iliad* is not a unity or work of art, but "shreds of old songs quilted together into a scroll or book, after the "savage natives had been taught to write."

Philosopher 2. knows that the inferior animals are mere automata, and rather thinks that Homer and Milton were nothing more.

Philosopher 3. "So far from seeing any divine design in the "human eye as an implement of sight, I would have returned "upon his hands my optical instrument-maker's workmanship, "if he had sent me such an one—a contrivance so clumsy."

Philosopher 4. "As to the arrangement of the solar system I "think I could have improved upon it."

Philosopher the 5th is a benevolent sage who, regarding "more in pity than in anger" the slow emancipation of thought, warns us that "no country can be considered as really civilized in which we may not go into the street and stab the first comer whenever a body is wanted for scientific purposes."

Now people will hardly understand an essay in which such like monstrosities are attacked with the mock gravity of satiric prose, if they have heard them maintained in sober earnest, perhaps at public lectures.

I should try in everything I wrote for the *present* age to excite CURIOSITY. Secondly to give some story. Thirdly to move some passion. Fourthly to create some surprise—treating the British lions like children.

Were I an author, I should not venture into long essays, but try to found everything, jest or earnest, upon some plot or story, however simple. How much *Gulliver's Travels* gain by this. I would not trust the public patience : people *will* have amusement, and will not read twice to gather the meaning. The above may be all a mistake. Pardon the invited freedom of, Yours affectionately, SAMUEL PALMER.

CVIII. TO MR. F. G. STEPHENS.

FURZE HILL, *October* 4, 1877.

DEAR MR. STEPHENS. I was reading to my wife *The Athenæum* critique on the Holkam Hall Claudes when she said, "Claude is so beautiful that the very description of his pictures is music."

On this, I bethought me of the *musician* and how long it was since I had heard of his welfare. If he and those most dear to him are quite well, one line to say so, at any moment of leisure would gratify, His very sincerely, S. PALMER.

P.S. Wild and vigorous as he was, I do not think that Salvator was so supreme a master of landscape as Claude, though his grandeur is of a kind more obvious to the many. It was a standing puzzle to my old friend Mr. Varley, which he several times expressed to me, that his lady pupils, one and all, thought Salvator more sublime than Claude—Claude whose distinctive essence was sublimity, in the estimation of no less a critic than Henry Fuseli. But it is difficult to read your account of the pair of Salvators in your " Sivinton [?] Park Collection " (*Athenæum*, September, 29) without feeling a stimulus to invention ; and, having twice read it, I discover that were the " conventionalities " omitted—that monster tree and the like, there would be no stimulus whatever.

. . . . How well you describe the " purposes " of Gaspar Poussin and Salvator—the " conventional conditions." These conditions had *become* conventional because of an universal agreement that they were conditions of the most excellent beauty.

What a treat awaits you at Farnley ! But I must repress the baleful passion of envy. . . . .

1878

CIX. TO MR. T. H. WRIGHT.

FURZE HILL, *March* 4, 1878.

DEAR SATIRIST. You know my tooth and have sent me a bonbon. I was in the middle of a letter, but away it went, and down I pounced upon my favourite Goldwin Smith, who always knows what he means, and expresses what he knows. I read aloud to the " head," and we agreed that there was as much sense in a page as some of our literary gold-beaters would have spread over twenty.

He ought not to have abused the façade of the National Gallery ; to do so is to " go with the multitude to do evil." What is Wilkins' own is wholly elegant ; all else was compulsory, and, I believe broke his heart.

We have been at it again. Capital! Capital! Not a fuzzy conception, not an obscure passage or phrase. Mr. Goldwin Smith is a thorough modern, and would not have willingly spent a week at "Cobweb Castle"[1]; but then he loves modernism on its truthful side, as I hope we all do.

I read in *The Athenæum* of a fortnight back that the Quakers, having become proprietors of their own nonconformist Campo Santo and wishing to build over their ancestors' bones, have with difficulty found workmen to grub up their remains, the place having been for some years a pleasant garden ; that they have rummaged the dust of John Bunyan ; torn up in gobbets what fleshly remains there were of William Blake (William Blake was buried by his own desire—will you call this a bull, I wonder—with the rites of the Church of England), and hundreds of others ; got them into a heap, soused them with carbolic acid, and then tumbled them into a great pit in the corner.

Now this is just what I am sure Mr. G. S. would not sanction. Nor would Aristotle call it magnanimous. When you have full time, some day, please send me that passage.

Herbert has finished my head[2]; an *alter ego*, if some may be trusted who have seen it.

Our united much love, in this tiny space which is left for it, by your too loquacious old friend, S. PALMER.

P.S. The Goldwin Smith scrawl I scribbled on the instant and enveloped. I disenvelope it, as the "Friends" have just disenveloped William Blake, to add a yell on your news from Oxford. Of course it is "scientific" to prefer a beverage chemically prepared with half a dozen deleterious compounds to your own first-rate beer, brewed of malt and hops in your own college ; but as to the *library*, the proposal you mention just pairs with the Bunhill Fields exploit, as an outrage on the dead, with the addition that it is a swindle on the living.

Modern exploits must be described in modern words—our old language breaks down under them.

The proposal to tamper with Merton library implies a boundless

---

[1 Mr. Wright, having heard from his boyhood all about "The Ancients," wrote a parody of their strange doings and opinions, in which he made "Cobweb Castle" their head-quarters. The title was, I think, *Noctes*.—Ed.]

[2 The portrait at the beginning of this volume.—Ed.]

impudence ; but a three-syllable word is too rhythmical—too grave, in fact, for a proposal which should be withered by some slang monosyllable. What do you think of "*check*" ? I wish we could add, " Don't you wish you may get it?" But I fear they will. Your college has money and ground : build a large room for " useful" books by all means ; and a large laboratory (for chemistry is a noble science) ; and, if needs be, a light, cheerful vivisection-room for the amusement of the ladies, to alternate with the art lectures elsewhere ; but for decency's sake keep your hands off your own books ; the hoofs of wild boars out of the vineyard of your fathers.

When I read what you have told me, the old proverb rings in my ears, " It is a villainous bird that fouls its own nest," and has so rung ever since I first opened your letter.

I hope you have read the second article in January's *Quarterly* on *Scientific Lecturing*. Prof: Virchow's speech you have doubt-less heard of. It seems that the very earliest fossil remains of man are dead against the ape theory . . . .

Is there no monosyllable that fits the library affair ? Well, it's A STENCH in the nostrils of S P, and should be yet more so in yours.

CX. TO MR. L. R. VALPY.

RED HILL, *September* 8, 1878.

MY DEAR MR. VALPY. With many thanks, I return your very interesting notes, feeling almost as if I had enjoyed personally the Veronese exploration. In Italian cities I think the English eye enjoys *physically* a rest from right angles and perfectly straight lines which harass it in every square rood of London buildings.

I remember, young as I was, presuming to demur to an assertion of Mr. Blake's that our old cathedrals were not built to rule and compass ; but I now see that, like many of his art state-ments, although literally a stretch or violation of truth it contained or suggested a greater truth.

Moreover I am told that the corresponding sides or arches of Winchester cathedral do not *exactly* correspond. It has been dis-covered that the apparently straight lines in the finest Grecian architecture are really subtle curves ; and in the street architecture

of Rome we have a simple disregard of exactness ; for Mr.
Cockerell found that there was scarcely a house there at right
angles. Now I do not mean to assert that irregularity is beauty,
but merely that emancipation from rule and compass lines is a
visual comfort. Those columns we saw together from Diana's
Ephesian temple all *looked* as if they were hand and eye work.
I suppose that art superimposed its charm upon the preparations
of arithmetic.

What discovery is this—of another *Assumption ?* Have we
no prints of it, even in Messrs. Colnaghi's collection, or at the
Print Room ?

Henceforth, since, or I may say during the most profane and
barbaric demolition of the Wren churches, Englishmen of any
feeling or compunction must reckon themselves aliens, perhaps
intruders in their own country.

There are many exceptions, but an innate barbarism is a
national characteristic. We cannot be civilized beyond a certain
point : we should have relished another Russian war ! We have
reason, however, for thankfulness that Christianity has done so
much to civilize and soften the *heart*, which is a greater thing than
any intellectual polish ; even if we might hope to rival the Athe-
nian culture, for it left many of them sad rogues in other respects.
With our united kind regards, believe me, Yours most truly,
S. PALMER.

1879

CXI. To Mr. P. G. HAMERTON.

FURZE HILL, *February* 17, 1879.

MY DEAR MR. HAMERTON. . . . . I have little doubt that you
have chosen for the best in using oil-colours for autotype : however, if you find reason to change, water-colour has the one great
and weighty advantage of the pen line. Without its equivalent in
etching, I doubt whether Turner could have made his monochromes
so attractive. Line seems to me like the cymbals in a band, as the
dashes of shade are like the great drum : we scarcely miss the
colours where line pervades everything in its mysteries and its might.
The precision of its delicacy clears things up, like that tiny flute
which announces the melody, with no unpleasant shrillness, in a
full orchestra. But it is so important to use a material congenial

with the chemistry of autotype that I should be loth to change what I found could be faithfully rendered.

Now as to your kind wish to see me at the etching once more. Well! My foot has slipped, and I have been for some weeks neck deep in nitrous acid.

Four of the poor little V's have been bitten and proved, and I am just finishing two etchings almost the size of the *Liber Studiorum* drawings, 9¼ inches long. One plate, alas, by an old compact is parted with ; the other, an essentially Palmerian affair, I wish to keep in my family, and the amount it will realize by sale of impressions will enable me to make some guess as to *market* values. I am re-approaching etching not from the line-engraving side, but wholly from the racy and picturesque ; yet it makes havoc of my time, and I must shortly break off to finish long-standing commissions. Yet, if I live to finish them, I would from that day forward refuse all future ones, were etching only sufficiently remunerative.

The fact is that outline, with its *local* shadows, can be etched rapidly ; not so that mystic maze of enticement ideal *chiar-oscuro*, of which I think you will agree with me that etching is the best exponent. Mezzotint is the more obvious ; but, however well done, it lies in some degree under the disadvantage so fatal to oil-paintings, of a dark ground, by which the pictures of a whole nation have been disfigured ere now. Like that cruel Othello, it puts out the light and then puts out the light ; eclipsing the sun before it closes the shutters. Though, with Ben Jonson's witches, etching says to a shadow, here and there, "Deep, O deep, we lay thee to sleep ;" yet, like those deepest of the deep yet clearest of the clear early Flemish pictures, there is the virgin white of the gesso ground behind. All this, however, you have expressed in other and better words ; and I thank you much for having called my attention to it : it influences the whole of my work. As to reconcilement of interests, &c., I have a design ready for transference to the copper (which probably will never be transferred), with the advantage of essential brightness in its structure, and suited to the increased size of my present work (9¼ inches) ; and, all being well, upon the copper it might go, if I were guaranteed the price of a certain number of impressions ; and just so my ten poor little V's, more deeply thought out than anything else I have done, might see the light, if anyone would make a bid large enough to provide beef during the remainder of the siege, while my private means furnished the potatoes : but as my approaches, like "a death from Spain," give a long reprieve, the rations of beef must be proportionate.

Once more let me entreat you to see for yourself that your autotypes have not those middle-tint mounts, which I should call, from their destructive power, Satanic, but that I believe in, and am experimentally certain of, the personal existence of Satan, whose deepest artifice, it has been well said, is to infuse a doubt into men's minds whether there is any Devil at all. . . . . . Yours most truly, S. PALMER.

CXII. TO MR. P. G. HAMERTON.

RED HILL, *August* 4, 1879.

DEAR MR. HAMERTON. Pricked already with etching like a full pincushion, your latter letter burst my side as with a packing-needle ! How can I possibly touch copper again for eight months to come, with drawings in hand which ought to have been sent home years ago ? Etching, that wheedling hussy, like another Millwood has already made me rob my long-suffering employers of time which really belonged to them. It is true that I have not yet, like my prototype, shot an uncle, neither have I eaten an aged aunt like the Fejee Indians ; but there's no knowing.

Some have fancied themselves to be tea-pots ; others fragile glass. What am *I* but a broken etching-needle with its wrong end wedged into a paint-pot ? . . . .

It is *my* misfortune to work slowly, not from any wish to niggle, but because I cannot otherwise get certain shimmerings of light, and mysteries of shadow ; so that only a pretty good price would yield journeyman's wages. Happily, I think I could realize something more, in quarters to which I have myself access ; this will perhaps soon be in some measure tested, as to what I have already done, because there seems to be a lively demand. . . . .

I am very glad that you like my *Bellman*. . . . It is a breaking out of village-fever long after contact—a dream of that genuine village where I mused away some of my best years, designing what nobody would care for, and contracting, among good books, a fastidious and unpopular taste. I had no room in my *Bellman* for that translucent current, rich with trout, a river not unknown to song ; nor for the so-called "idiot" on the bridge with whom I always chatted—like to like perhaps. But there were all the village appurtenances—the wise-woman behind the age, still resorted to ; the shoemaker always before it, such virtue is in the smell of leather ; the rumbling mill, and haunted mansion in a shadowy paddock, where sceptics had seen more than they could account for ; the vicarage with its learned traditions ; and Wordsworth brought to memory every three hours, by

> "— — the crazy old church clock
> And the bewilder'd chimes."

Byron would have stuffed his ears with cotton had he been forced to live there.

I must again thank you for the pains you took to enlighten me as to publication. I love calculation in the abstract—quite understand why Johnson put Cocker into his pocket to amuse him in his travels, equations having been, off and on, my daily amusement for some time, but when it comes to the concrete—oh then,

> "Thy hand great" Dulness "lets the curtain fall,
> And universal darkness covers all."

With our united best regards, believe me to be, Ever faithfully yours, S. PALMER.

CXIII. To MR. P. G. HAMERTON.

RED HILL, *October* 13, 1879.

DEAR MR. HAMERTON. Do not be alarmed. This is not one of those scorpion letters which entail an answer, like my late column of queries which you so kindly and so copiously answered. Your advice has been taken, the etching has been published by The Fine Art Society, and the poor Bellman is gazing out of the window at the shops in Bond Street.

. . . . I have been reading with much interest your notes on Æsthetics : in the last you are approaching the deep matters of placing : placing of lines, of shadows, of colours. This art, under the name of composition, is probably despised by the naturalistic school. Yet what is composition but the art of placing things naturally ; a result, however simple, of most subtle knowledge acquired in the course of a life-long comparison of nature with art? If the lights and shades are finely disposed, as in Tintoret, for instance, the work, irrespectively of subject, will gratify the eye, turn it upside down, or whichever way you will. I have often wondered whether such men could define in words the *Grand Specific*, or give us more than the few golden traditions which they have left, such, for instance, as "Few lights, many shadows, much middle-tint."

Surely you have an acquisition in Mr. T. S. Townsend : I find myself recurring to his Gothic Tower [an etching in *The Portfolio.*] I may be quite wrong but it seems to me no small thing to achieve aerial gloom with a needle point, and to discriminate the qualities of light and shade ; avoiding in the latter the besetting errors of rattle and texture. I judge from only a single impression, and know not how much is *retroussage ;* but, with such feeling, there must surely be some amount of inventive power, which perhaps may be inherited, if he be a son of our poet-etcher whose " shadowy flail " in The Etching Club *L'Allegro* can never be forgotten. . . .

. . . . But surely you do too much for your health, and so many things ? Variety is refreshing, but multiplicity may overwhelm. This is not said in malicious envy ; though perhaps if, like St. Martin, you could bestow upon me a moiety of your multiplicity-mantle it might do no harm to either of us.

It *does* sadden me not to have touched a needle since Mr. Bellman's suit was stitched together, nor to have any chance of doing so for some time to come. Some of my large drawings, long since due, seem jealous of the poor, harmless coppers in the cupboard, and determined never to get finished. Then there are new commissions ; but if I once get free and have my present reasons for thankfulness as to health, then welcome once more dear, teazing, tickling coppers ; may we never part again till the great change come when Æsthetics and the Intellectual will be of little moment, and the MORAL all in all.

I am glad that, in the outset of your essays, you have so distinctly separated the three ; for I fear there is many an ardent art-student who is likely to make Art his Gospel. If half-educated, the more likely to mistake analogy for identity, the analogies of religion and *ideal* art being copious indeed. It is by a most unnatural disseverance, in this our fallen state, that truth and beauty, wisdom and goodness, do not always co-exist. By and bye they will, but, meanwhile, a murderer whose name need not be perpetuated having prepared a poisoned supper for his sister-in-law, whose life he had insured, went forth with his paint-box and sketched a fine sunset from Waterloo Bridge.

On the other hand some of the greatest men and greatest artists have been good. Among the moderns the greatest of the great was converted by his friendship with Vittoria Colonna.

Please give our kindest regards to Mrs. Hamerton, whose image, with your own, is often recalled. My mind, so much or little of it as is left, walks frequently in your neighbourhood, and sometimes takes a header into the trout-stream at the end of your garden.

Always curious to guess what you are engaged upon, and hoping that you will not catch many colds in a studio which I think you proposed building in your garden, ... Believe me, Ever sincerely yours, S. PALMER.

CXIV. To the Rev. J. P. Wright.

FURZE HILL, *October* 17, 1879.

DEAR MR. WRIGHT. Men, rats, and pike are distinguished in natural history by their propensity to prey upon their own kind. The "rights of man" are the right of the less voracious to restrain those who are more so ; the rights of the poor majority are pure air and pure water, and sufficient space to walk about in, when the rich minority are befouling the air with manufactories, poisoning the rivers, and, as in the neighbourhood of Foots Cray and St. Mary's, adding "field to field, till there be no place" left, and the villagers cannot step out of the dusty high-road without a trespass.

The rich and the middle classes for ages befouled the air by retiring into their coffins beneath churches which were frequented by all classes ; and when, by an agony of accommodation, I was trying to please our "learned friend" [Mr. T. H. Wright, now a barrister,] by naming some instance in my own time of undoubted progress, fortunately, I thought of the abolition of intermural interments.

This *is* an advance, but I think our dear, cheerful, peace-loving Virgil says in the *Georgics* that "all things are always tending to the worse," and that in trying to row upward against the stream we may be tumbled all over back again by remitting one stroke of the oar.

Cleanliness is active, dirt passive. Fallen nature, therefore, which among other things is idle, prefers dirt ; not indeed with that passionate preference which makes a washed lapdog roll himself in the first filth, but with the quiet, inevitable habits of " heredity "—the first time I ever used the word. So that your travail and warfare, hard as it seems, is really a bright exception to the usual somnolency of boards and committees ; which latter are best composed of a couple—a seer and a doer, or " two single gentlemen rolled into one " (Colman's *Broad Grins*—a curious book to quote from !), and less and less effectual in proportion to the number. . . .

I am very glad, and very sorry—glad that Mrs. John is so much better ; sorry to lose dear friends at St. David's. Hoping to have at *last* one more talk with you ere long, and with my wife's love, who means to write, and lamenting that, according to the article, the poor Club, during forty years, did nothing for etching, I remain, having another letter to write against time, Yours affectionately. S. PALMER.

CXV. To MR. T. H. WRIGHT.

FURZE HILL, *October*, 1879.

MY DEAR MR. WRIGHT (I can't " Tom " or " Jack " an Oxford Don, can I ?)[1] Here's a bad style, beginning with a parenthesis ! Well ! Mr. Williams lived at 104.[2] Ask to see Sir James Thornhill's allegorical staircase. Excellent was its condition in 1829. I never saw it. It was at 96 that Mrs. Powel for many years made her pipe of wine from the grapes which grew in her garden. I never saw it. What of that ?—other people saw it, and their eyes are as good as mine. There are two sorts of people ; those who believe on evidence ; and those who, in their omniscience, make a

[1 Our friend, having known my father since his childhood, objected to being called " Mr. Wright," a formality adopted by his correspondent after his becoming a Fellow of Merton.—Ed.]

[2 I believe this refers to St. Martin's Lane.—Ed.]

list of the impossibles, and believe, even on the strongest evidence, only such things as their expurgatory index has left open. Even Mr. Huxley says that the word impossible is impossible with a philosopher.

I said the other day trying to illustrate an uncouth absurdity, that it was like "blotting-paper sandwiches, pensive cheese, or grated consciousness": but, after sending off the letter, I remembered that there were few indeed who, at one time or other, had not known the flavour of grated consciousness.

Now my poor consciousness is sadly grated when that same infallible list rubs against it.

That bag of impossibles is a big one by this time : curious matters tumble out when you shake it ; poor dear Homer among the first. Now what is meant by saying that Homer did not write the *Iliad* is this ; that no man wrote the *Iliad*—in fact that it "*developed*" : that it was self-developed out of fragments.

But it is as impossible that a first-rate poem or work of art should be produced without a great master mind, which first conceives the whole, as that a fine, living bull should be "developed" out of beef sausages.

If I could call the most august authorities to give judgment they would be unanimous.

It would be cruel to call Homer, as he would be "Burked," *i.e.* critic'd, in the street. Well, these might suffice.

Virgil, Milton, Dante, Michael Angelo, Blake. All, in every age, *who had made the article* would testify that an idea of the whole was indispensable to the adjustment of the parts.

If, on the other hand, the *Iliad* be not a work of art, all the world has been drivelling for three thousand years, or thereabouts. . . . . Yours affectionately, S. PALMER.

CXVI. TO MISS LOUISA TWINING.

FURZE HILL HOUSE, *November* 18, 1879.

DEAR MISS TWINING. You asked me why I had never *written* what I said to you about St. Paul's. I have just been invited to a meeting about St. Mark's at Venice which reminded me of a peril so much nearer home.

There is a fund, amounting, I am told, to no less than fifty thousand pounds, for what is called the " completion " of St. Paul's.

There are also the echoes of Sir Gilbert Scott's three words of wisdom—"LET IT ALONE!" But dilettanti with half a plum in their pocket will let nothing alone, and these "completers" of St. Paul's are particularly attracted by the cupola, as giving the widest scope for their fancies and experiments.

Sir Christopher, having kept the deeply-set windows of that sloping wall between the dome and the Whispering Gallery narrow —so nicely dispensing the "dim religious light" as to leave the cupola in a sort of poetic mystery, mosaics were proposed, not long ago, to make the dome more cheerful, and metallic reflectors to brighten the mosaics! The slope of the pilasters is continued upwards, at present, by the architectural divisions in the chiaroscuro of Sir James Thornhill, so that the eye does not detect the artificial perspective ; but directly the chiaroscuro is removed, and horizontal layers of any kind substituted, the secret will out ; the dome will seem to be fifty feet lower, and the wall which supports it about to topple upon the spectator.

Perhaps in all literature a single word was never made to tell more effectively than the "*circumspice*" in Wren's epitaph, which was composed with a view to its proper place in the cathedral, but is futile in its present position ; for who can "look around" him when he is against a wall ?

If, however, the gentlemen of the committee once begin to manipulate that peerless cupola, the most sublime though not the largest in Europe, we shall not desire to look around us any longer, but shall exclaim with Fuseli, when a fellow-traveller in the stage-coach mentioned that his daughter painted on velvet :—"Let me get out !—Let me get out !"

Wren insisted on such nicety of proportion, even on that vast scale, that I believe he refused Father Smith an additional seven inches in the width of the organ-case.

Now, in their own sacred profession, the Dean and Chapter of St. Paul's reverence the symmetry of Truth, and know the peril of an illiterate and slapdash theology. Surely, as members of the completion committee, they must have noticed something analogous in the lower, though not low, region of æsthetics. . . . .

Believe me, with our united best regards, Yours very truly, SAMUEL PALMER.

CXVII. To Mr. W. Williams.
[The younger son of my father's old friend, Dr. Williams. —Ed.]

RED HILL, *December* 26, 1879.

DEAR MR. WILLIAMS. This is Boxing-day: kindly accept six words: DO THE MOST DISAGREEABLE THING FIRST—pantomimic words, transformable into competency, freedom, and fine weather in the conscience: useless five years hence, for then the Habits will have been formed, and habit, as The Duke said, is not second nature but "ten times nature." You see I set the example of doing the disagreeable first, namely giving advice ; and so proceed unencumbered to less nauseous though melancholy matters of the confession that, yesterday, I strangely omitted to read, as was my wont, Milton's *Ode on the Nativity,* and the confession that I have not learned by heart *Paradise Regained;* "a charming poem," says Bishop Warburton, "nothing inferior to *Paradise Lost.*"

As to advice, am I so inexperienced as to suppose that any one will take it ? Well, there is just the millionth part of a chance, and at all events I have washed my conscience.

As matter of fact, I have, during a pretty long life, taken advice two or three times, and with advantages which abide with me to this day. When very young I did not consider the hours between breakfast and dinner sacred to work ; to education, with a student until he graduates ; to his profession or business, with man settled in life.

Now when about eighteen, I gave some little part of the sacred daylight to music ; but a friend, only a little older than myself, warned me, and I *instantly* left an amateur musical society, and thereafter sang or fiddled only in the evening.

" In the sweat of thy face thou shalt eat bread," is, as Burke has somewhere beautifully shown, a dispensation of mercy in our fallen state ; and surely afternoon and evening are long enough for our exercise and recreation. With you and me choice books are the favourite amusement, but woe betide us if we are indulging our taste when we ought to be doing our work. How well Buonaparte knew the value of time ! He said of some of his Marshals, "They do not know the value of MINUTES."

Much may be learned of him ; much also of the Devil, who watches opportunities, and *makes* opportunities. . . .

You may read of Thomas Wright, to whom I alluded in my last, by getting Smiles's *Self Help*. I read it once, and think we should all read it twice. It helps much to explain what you were inquiring after, the nature of greatness.

Before we quite dismiss Buonaparte, I may mention that a gentleman who had conversed with him at St. Helena told me that when he otherwise smiled his eyes never smiled. Much may be learned of him. "KNOW WHAT YOU HAVE TO DO AND DO IT," said Mr. Mulready. This was Buonaparte's way, and had he been king of England, and absolute, many things would have been done in a year or so which we have been half a century fumbling after.

He never PROCRASTINATED I think until his fatal morning of Waterloo. Satan also is a most wonderful person, and it will be the worse for us Christians if we underrate the stupendous compass of his intellect and energy. I suppose, if the truth must be told, that he is the "natural man's" favourite hero; and no wonder, for is he not the "god of this world"? . . . . .

In answer to your question, I think that if Swift (as I believe he did) wrote *The Tale of a Tub*, it must take rank next to *Gulliver*. With objectionable matter, it contains the most pungent satire on popery I ever met with. Through other parts Swift lost a bishopric.

There was so much dirt in the writings of one or two of these gentlemen, that I should fear there was still more in their conversation : not so in Bishop Berkeley's, I think ; to whom Pope assigns "every virtue under Heaven." Walpole is said to have detained thirty thousand pounds from Berkeley's American Mission.

Much as I admire Queen Anne's Wits, I cannot venerate them as I venerate the pre-Restoration men. When your age I read the very men you are reading, and learned from the satirists to despise folly and vice. Some years after I found in the seventeenth century matter to admire and imitate, sanctity, and ideal beauty. Yours &c., S. PALMER.

CXVIII. To MR. W. WILLIAMS.

RED HILL, [1879.]

MY DEAR MR. WILLIAMS. I rather think that Burke admired Ximenes for his goodness even more than for his greatness, so far

C C

as I could gather from that after-dinner talk ; and it is owing to a dreadful twist, a *sprain* of the perceptions, if *we* do not admire goodness more than greatness.

What a vulgar scoundrel was Buonaparte [1]—what a butcher, what a brute, compared with Thomas Wright the clerk and warehouse-man at Manchester.

I make it a rule to write or speak evil of no one, but there *are* exceptions, and they are said to manifest the rule. When we are *not* comparing Napoleon with Thomas Wright, or with the martyrs, we can admire his misdirected genius, the Greek chiselling of his features, his aquiline eye, and electric movements. . . .

Miss Burney's day at Sir Joshua's Richmond villa was pleasant reading ; much more so than her novels. I think I met with it in Lord Minto's life. How Burke rejoiced in Lord Minto's successful speech when he was only M.P.! . . . .

As to "great men's greatness," from what I have seen, heard, or read, they seem to be distinguished from other men by their energy, patience, and accuracy.

Accuracy of itself is not greatness, but as essential to it as the air we breathe is essential to life. I have observed that in proportion as men approach greatness they are observant of little things, that they do not think much about themselves, but are absorbed in their great aim, whatever it may be ; and that the motive spring of energy is devotion to that aim, and not at all that they may be called or thought to be great men.

The greatest man it has been my lot to know insisted most on our becoming like little children. Newton compared himself to a child trying to collect a few shells, or pebbles.

Some one says "Patience is genius:" If a genius could be made, he would be made by the words, "Whatever you do, give your whole mind to it."

A great man told me that all *work*, inventive or otherwise, was equally pleasant to him. Dickens says, writing to his son Henry, "I should never have made my success in life if I had not bestowed upon the least thing I have ever undertaken the same attention and care that I have bestowed upon the greatest." Dickens's *Letters*.

---

[1] "Nothing was more debased than his soul." See *Athenæum*, November 22, 1879, page 653. Middle of the 3rd column.

Most of the great men have had bodies strong in endurance if not in muscle ; most have been early risers. None, that I know of, have begun to see things " dreadfully clear " at eleven at night, and have then brewed gunpowder tea, or strong coffee !

I would strongly advise young men to adopt a wise regimen of diet and exercise, with a view to that wondrous blessing a sound body.[1]

Your mention of our individuality, our essence, almost makes me tremble ; for mine must, in the course of nature, soon be called away to give an account of the things done in the body, whether good or bad ;—the things which IT has done through the body as its instrument. Can we wonder that Kant never thought without awe of the starry heavens, or of our moral responsibility ? Sometimes I cannot write for weeks together, so please do not feel hurt if I postpone at any time. With our united love to your dear father and mother, sister and brethren, believe me to be Yours faithfully, S. PALMER.

1880

CXIX. To MR. W. WILLIAMS.

RED HILL, *July* 20, 1880.

DEAR MR. WILLIAMS. Although generally in agreement with your letter I will mention, merely as a fact, that the French peasantry are in much better circumstances than before the Revolution. This however is no result of atheism, but of a more equitable distribution of property, and deliverance from unbearable oppression.

With ourselves, neither principles nor practice are satisfactory : where there is no belief there will be no conscience ; and those who know best speak the most sadly of our dishonest speculations, our fraudulent commerce, and an export of " Devil's dust," loaded silks, wooden nutmegs,[2] and the like, which have sent and are sending our foreign customers elsewhere.

Political reform has done so little to make us better that the

---

[1] See Lord Bacon on this subject in his *Essay*. [*Of Regimen of Health.*—ED.]

[2] The people of Connecticut have been credited with such astuteness that it has been called "The Nutmeg State" on account of their supposed capability of passing off wooden nutmegs. Webster's Dictionary.—ED.]

old maxim which the liberals used to laugh at so much, " Let each reform himself," seems respectable advice after all. As to the blessing of liberty depending upon the character of the free, no one has spoken more strongly than John Stuart Mill.

Who does not love to see animals disporting at large? Yet we do not open the cages at the Zoological Gardens. My hope for our country lies not in our wealth and enterprise but in His mercy who would have spared the guilty city for ten's sake.

Every young Christian who has " conquered the natural man," and, being strong by the indwelling Spirit, has " overcome the wicked one," is, in result, the wisest politician, the best citizen, and defender of his country. Can we name a hero more noble than the youthful warrior whose armour shows many a dint and bruise of that most terrible contest, the warfare with *himself*, and of the victory? For him alone remains a manhood and serene age

> " —— whose course is equable and pure,
> No fears to beat away, no strife to heal,
> *The past unsigh'd for and the future sure.*"

I never saw the St. Paul's sermons, but should expect much from the author of *Fundamentals;* which, I think, would have had a wide sale with a wise public. I wish you had time and eyesight (for the type is bad) to read an eighteen-penny book, the Rev. Joseph Cook's *Boston Monday Lecture* on *Life and the Soul.* His aim is to show that the exactest science and logic are not only not at variance with Divine Revelation, but must result in its acceptance. Talking of type, may I recommend you to write larger, with good broad letters, so much insisted on by Lord Palmerston? It is only near-sighted persons like myself who can read small writing without pain. Of *course* you never cross-write—that is felony!

Bear in mind Mr. Cook's lecture, and with our united love to all, believe me, Yours faithfully, S. PALMER.

CXX. TO MR. C. W. COPE.

RED HILL, *July* 27, 1880.

MY DEAR COPE. Many thanks for the Milton, a model of condensation. This makes the sixth life of him which I remember to have read. Others are probably forgotten. Each was a whet for the next. Masson's I have not time for. No one treats Johnson quite fairly. What *could* he say more than that Milton's epic is even finer than Homer's? This is implied in saying that the *Paradise Lost* "is not the greatest of heroic poems, only because it is not the first." Johnson's *Lives*.

Johnson was not touched by *Lycidas* because he had a defective sense of the essence of poetry, though a sagacious judge of its machinery and concomitants. Over and over again have I read Gray's *Eton College* with Johnson's critique in my mind; yet I still love it, and cannot persuade myself that it is more specked and flawed than many charming things. I have heard that difficult passage in *L'Allegro*, "Then to come in spite of sorrow" &c., thoroughly discussed; and certainly Mr. Pattison is right as to the grammatical meaning; but that Milton's was the other, and that, for a wonder, he expressed himself ungrammatically I finally believe.

Milton's notion that "one tongue was enough for a woman" hardly accounts for the general neglect of his daughter's education, when he was living close to Whitehall, and in a social position not inferior to that of Sir Arthur Helps or the like. Neither Milton nor Scott, nor a greater than Scott, dear Edmund Burke, founded a family. Milton's ended with his grand-daughter, who kept a chandler's shop, and for whose benefit *Comus* was performed; and Sir Walter's is already extinct. His last relative died about a year since in a Kentish parsonage: Keston I think.

Mr. Pattison clearly perceives that Milton's descriptions are not scientifically accurate. It seems that poetic perfection and feeling are passive. Pindar's Eagle is passive under the influence of music; he does not count the aerial vibrations. Perception looks at the front of a picture; "Science" begins with the back, and by the "Method of Zadig" (see *Nineteenth Century* for June) discovers in Thomas Brown of 163, High Holborn, a marvel of versatility and productiveness, compared with whom Shakespeare was a mannerist and Michelangelo an idler.

Before Herbert was strong enough to use his press it went to London to be altered; and is now like all things else, including the British Constitution, under *considerable* alteration; but he will see to the burr if there be any, and forward the plates to Mr. Goulding, who was his printing-tutor.

Our " spring cleaning " this time has been unspeakable. Hall and drawing-room *wholly* covered with a better carpet than Brussels—namely Wilton—price altogether something short of £40!!

We can only reconcile ourselves to these awful wash-ups by remembering the opposite alternative ; two villages seen by Captain Burnaby in Asia Minor, wholly possessed by fleas ; the inhabitants, fairly beaten, living in tents at some distance.

A medical cousin of mine at Coggeshall, Essex, found a patient watching at his window for hearses, and longing for his turn to come. " O ! Mr. Giles," he said, " I have married a cleanly woman ! ! ! If I sit down in this room it is about to be swept ; in the next—it is to be scoured ; in a third they are taking up the carpets ; there is no rest for the sole of my foot." . . . . . .

With our united best regards to yourself and Mrs. Cope, who I hope has not forgotten poor me altogether, I remain, Yours affectionately, S. PALMER.

CXXI. To MR. J. C. HOOK.

RED HILL, *August* 13, 1880.

MY DEAR HOOK. Welcome back to the " spongy South " with all its lassitudes. With us there came with the new moon a change to dry weather, of which I once had three weeks in Cornwall.

I was much interested by your remarks on that difficult subject, publication. As those who are not rich can only obtain works of art in the shape of engravings and etchings, might there not be a reserve for them after the richer people have got their remarque proofs, &c. ?

Cutting the plate so as to make the margin a little narrower would be an unmistakable guarantee of genuine proofs to the holders of them. There is no doubt as to what are early proofs of the old etchings and engravings, yet they are said to have been afterwards quite hackneyed in the book-markets, and even printed in the streets ; and so hundreds of young artists have borne home half-crown's-worths of invaluable suggestion from the trays of the old London print-sellers. And to many of them a guinea is now not more than a couple of shillings were then. If the plate-destroying system had then obtained, Marc Antonio, Bonasoni, and the like, could have been seen only now and then in the museums.

In one of my Club works there is bound up one of those ghastly sights, an etching in an excellent state, all ploughed over. To me it gives real *pain ;* seeming like the murder of a *mind.* It seems to me like trying to increase the zest of a banquet by assuring the guests that all they leave will be destroyed, neither servants nor poor neighbours being suffered to taste it.

Excuse me for diverting, for a moment, your attention from Tol Pedn Penwith, Treen Castle &c., and with kindest regards from all to all, believe me, Yours affectionately, S. PALMER.

CXXII. TO MR. W. WILLIAMS.

RED HILL, *August,* 1880.

DEAR MR. WILLIAMS. What has the creature of an hour to do with "*the whole range of philosophy*"—with the wisdom, and folly, and confusion, and vagaries, alternating through a compass of three thousand years—when he has only just time enough to master the elements of education, to learn a profession or business, and to save his soul ? These things make me sick ! What can he want more than just enough geometry to flush the sewers of his brain, Aristotle to teach him how to think, the sacred Scriptures to direct his thoughts, and the indwelling Spirit of God to quicken these thoughts into action ? Milton's *Tractate* is the ideal of education, and if people were twice as wise and good as they are it might be practicable. He says himself, "it is not a bow for every man to shoot with who counts himself a teacher."

I strongly recommend you to read this, and his *Areopagitica.* You have hitherto enjoyed what, in rough distinction, may be called our colloquial literature, or rather our colloquial *style ;* and I think you might now take a step of advance to the heroic, particularly to Hooker, who will make a man of any one who absorbs him.

I can never forget reading through Barrow's folio on the Creed in the recess of a Kentish village ; and, by the bye, it is curious that the step from the strenuous to the more colloquial style is distinctly marked in the transition from Barrow to his friend Tillotson, who published Barrow's works. And Tillotson is no less a prose writer than the same on whom Dryden professes to have founded his style.

The fearful depravity you mention may be blessed to the children of God, by frightening them into a close shelter beneath the Almighty wings. Life is short to all of us, and it is well to lose no more of it in halting between two opinions.

When we have read how men were given over to a reprobate mind, because "they did not like to retain God in their knowledge," let us turn, as from a noisome cesspool, to the twelfth of *Romans*, and find there an universe of blessing cheaply purchased by the loss of a right hand or eye. In the kindly fruits of the earth, in physical and mental pleasures, God has given more than sufficient to solace and sustain us, while we daily present ourselves living sacrifices to His service, in the whole of our moral being, in the bent and intention of our lives.

In everything it holds good : no sacrifice, no success ; no cross, no crown. This "living" is no annihilation, no mystification, but a quickening of every faculty by the touch of a living coal from the altar ! Away then goes the "ME" ; Pascal's "me," which he regards as the pest of the moral universe. Yet there is no loss of individual character ; on the contrary, each temperament becomes more distinct by receiving that particular spiritual gift which it is best fitted to sustain. Where is individuality more evident than in ecclesiastical history ; in the saints, missionaries, champions, poets, and sages of the Church ; in an Augustine, a Boniface, an A'Becket, a Fénelon, an Anselm, a King, or Butler ? For I think we may regard *Telemachus* as a Christian prose-poem in a pagan binding.

Do stick to your large writing, and keep your letters broad : oblige yourself to preserve the loops in the Es ; which I do not always myself. With love from all to all, believe me Yours faithfully, S. PALMER.

CXXIII. To MR. T. H. WRIGHT.

FURZE HILL, *November* 17, 1880.

MY DEAR HOWARD. "Dis is vonders above vonders," as the Dutchman said, when, after visiting the "learned pig," he took his seat in the "*Reading* fly," and waited for the performance.

I read some time ago about the audible shadow, neither gulping nor gainsaying, and supposed it to be the *ne plus ultra ;* but must now consider it as one of the slopes of an ascent, on the very summit of which you yourself stand illustrious. Proceeding by the method of climax, I think the keeping of tame adders ranks above it ; next the continuing to keep them after being bitten ; and then, " with a great interval," the triumph of wonders in your belief in the harmlessness of that animal. Now, my dear friend, we are quits : alated snakes and injurious effets kick the beam ![1] In this happy thaw of incredulity we may extend our inquiries in the direction of those dog-headed men without necks, and with long hair hanging down behind, " who, as a cacique told Raleigh, had of late years slain many hundreds of his father's people, and in whom even Humboldt was not always allowed to disbelieve."

Now that we can hear a shadow we shall soon be able to see a sound. We shall hold up a telephonic bottle of parliamentary or forensic oratory, and see through it in a moment—the last thing intended by the speakers.

Who now will dare to question the continuity of progress, or waste a thought on such trifles as Ireland, Eastern Europe, Indian famines, famished peasantries, and monster armaments ?

> " Ye feather'd songster Chanticleer
> Han wounde his bugle horne,
> An told the early villager
> Ye coming of the morn."

" Stranger."[2] " It is *not* the chanticleer, it is the Cameron "[3]— and thus he crows :—

" If we consider the number of centuries that it took to produce the literature and art of the Greek nation we shall see that far more stupendous works are undertaken, more beautiful pictures are painted, more literature worthy of abiding to the latest time is written in *one year* in England in the Victorian era, than was ever the case in the days of ancient Greece."

In my phenomenal investigations I observed that the light in the sky for some time before sunrise increased by sudden yet gentle flushes. So it is with the great intellectual sunrise

[1 This refers to the Shoreham stories I have alluded to previously.—ED.]
[2 One of the characters in Mr. Wright's *Noctes.* See p. 373.—ED.]
[3 In *Our Future Highway*, 1880. You see we are up in the newest !

which we are now, every mother ape's son of us, agog to witness.

"Things is coming to a crœsus," as Winifred Jenkins says. Every one has his question, and demands an answer and forgets what he asked.[1]

"—*O, qui me . . . . sistat*" in the quietude of Maignan's cell whence the persuasions of monarchy could not remove him. "He is said to have studied even in his sleep, dreaming of theorems the demonstrations of which would awaken him with joy."

In a sphere more exalted, shines your western namesake ; a star of the MORAL FIRMAMENT. You would not marvel at the words "Dear Mr. Wright" if you knew *how* dear they were to me ; recalling the ever-cherished memory of your father, and of Thomas Wright of Manchester, at the utterance of whose name angels touch their harps.

Some day, when quite at leisure, tell me something about yourself ; also whether you have yet discovered the Chancery Court, and believe me to be, Affectionately yours, A SUCKLING AT THE BOSOM OF TRUTH.

CXXIV. TO MR. T. H. WRIGHT.

[RED HILL] *December* 21, 1880.

MY DEAR HOWARD. I shall be delighted to see you, and meanwhile wish you every blessing of the approaching season, and of the new year ; hoping for the sake of my fellow creatures that this may be the last Christmas of the present dispensation.

Social relations have long been a sad sight, but now they are a great STENCH.

What combinations of the burnt oil of the steam-engine with soap-lees, carts and *many* cart-loads of mangled human meat from city churchyards, could revolt us like the aggregate of modern progress ? Think of the swine who have rent, ravaged, and defiled the books and parchments of thirty-seven "valuable libraries" of which they have plundered so many monasteries in Italy—Italy the land of Cicero and Virgil ! "Uncounted thousands of volumes have

[1 Here follows a passage quaintly erased and curiously blotted, with words as follows in the margin. "If Ben Jonson says that Shakespeare ought to have blotted a thousand lines *I* ought to blot everything. Please accept this little instalment. Some would apologize ! ! ! !" —ED.]

disappeared, no one knows how." "Eleven thousand kilogrammes of books were sold as waste-paper at from three to eight sous the kilogramme. A cheesemonger had many works of great rarity, including even parchments, and that celebrated and very scarce book ' *Il processo degli Untori di Milano.*' . . . But these are only a few of the astounding facts," &c. &c. &c.

See *The Times* weekly edition for December 17, page 2.

I always thought the English language copious and forcible, though marred in its sound by the consonants and the ever-hissing S ; but it has suddenly become poor in vituperative power when it attempts to characterize combinations of sacrilege, felony, ultra-barbaric outrage, wanton waste, and crushing taxation, with which "the march of mind " is blasting the fairest regions of the earth.

I suppose, when "Liberalism" is yet a little more advanced, the above will be hanging matter, so I will sign myself Yours affectionately, A BLIND BABY FEEDING FROM THE BOSOM OF TRUTH.

1881

CXXV. To MR. L. R. VALPY.

RED HILL., Posted *February* 16, 1881.

DEAR MR. VALPY. It is cheering to hear of the safety of one's friends after the late frost ; during the snow, I was advised to keep to my bed (sitting up in it to work), and my room in the severe cold. Coming forth at last I got out *The Eastern Gate*, and was busy upon it when your letter arrived this morning. I am anxious to do my all for it, whatever that may be, as it seems to have impressed several persons more than anything I have done. Thank you for the information about the two frames. I think it would be better to send two than three large drawings to our Spring Exhibition ; but I wish to bring all to a close.

I do not know how to describe that which is in the Winter Exhibition otherwise than the rush of a flock, just let out of the fold, upwards towards the eye, with a ravine behind and distant mountains : it is nearly the same as the etching now in the hands of the Fine Art Society, 148 New Bond Street.

I wish, with you, that "brightness with some sense of beauty " might more often cheer the walls both of houses and public institutions ; but apprehend that beauty of form must come before bright-ness ; and that beauty can come only from the Beautiful. Now putting aside moral beauty, "the beauty of holiness," the English are not a beautiful people as those sad rogues the Athenians were beautiful. Some of the best people we know and the most benevolent of both sexes are quite void of taste, and would rather have a bit of still life, or a chromolithograph, than Raffaelle's *Vision of Ezekiel ;* and it is to the next generation that we must look for improvement, if we look for it at all.

The one thing, I think, is to improve the taste of the young by surrounding them from infancy with beautiful objects. With this view, for our National Schools &c., Mr. Gruner, forty years ago, published both versions of Raffaelle's Bible History, in the Vatican. But where were they hung up ? Now there is a plethora of beauty waiting to be hung up in our schools and nurseries, in the autotype establishment in Oxford Street : but where are the school-masters, clergy, district-visitors, &c., who would not prefer a kitten in colours ? And I fear you would be terrified at the colours placed upon the walls as you propose.

But though we are not a beautiful people, but very ugly-minded as to form, we like colour of a certain kind very much. When Mr. Rogers the poet was showing me his pictures, he said that the universal voice of his visitors was for the Rubens over his dining-room fire-place ; and that, because of the colour. Now these were some of the most clever people about town : though the choicer eyes prefer Titian.

Well, let our nurseries, school-rooms, &c., public and private, be hung with the Oxford Street autotypes of the Sistine Chapel ; that will help to expand our ugly minds from infancy upwards, if they *will* expand without cracking. But •three hundred years ago, foreigners remarked that we were a war-loving, semi-barbarous people : no less barbarous now perhaps, if we have become a money-loving, "peace-at-any-price" people. We suffered the Poles to fight themselves out, and the Danes, and the Circassians, and need not expect pity when *our* turn comes.

Many thanks for a sight of Mr. Ruskin's address. I am reading his *Letters*, which like all his works which relate to political economy and national policy seem to be very weighty. His *Unto This Last* is a grand book though a little one.

February 15. After four days' work on *The Eastern Gate*, is it framed removably, and put up for occasional inspection ; and to-day has been spent upon *The Prospect*. Believe me, with our united kindest regards, Ever yours sincerely, SAMUEL PALMER.

EXTRACTS FROM LETTERS TO MR L. R. VALPY.

. . . Surely we want domestic reform in England. It is the vulgar fashion to decry a classical education, but how many households would be the happier for Aristotle's distinction between pleasure and happiness ! It seems to me that while nothing is more silly than eccentricity for its own sake, few things are more pernicious than the dread of being peculiar. The Quakers " took the bull by the horns," and became " wealthy and wise " ; and it is curious that while depriving themselves of holy privileges, yet the daring in matters of life to follow New Testament precepts has saved them from the exhaustion of fashionable folly, and placed most of our wheat, and a great many other good things in their hands. They have not been wanting in benevolence, nor sleepy in getting the means. One of them said to me, " Friend Palmer, I never knew a Quaker absent about money matters."

. . . The art teacher's competency to his task depends upon his power of drawing the figure ; and if that be quite wanting the shortest way is through the school at Brompton (if he have some power), then at least a year's study of the Antique at the Royal Academy.

But, in nine cases out of ten, people don't want real teaching for their daughters, but some fine, touched-up drawings to show, in which they do not repeat themselves, but their masters. I have no reason to complain, having always, in London, had as much teaching as I could desire ; but it is my full conviction that a good bold quack with plenty of tact, a comely presence, and well-cut Hoby boots, would beat any real artist out of the field—as a teacher. I mean as to the figure he would cut on Schedule D.

J. M. W. Turner tried teaching a little, but was discharged for incompetency !!! His lectures were curious, for he was always losing his place. But he knew something which no one else did.

In the great social organ nothing pleases like the "SWELL" stop.

Your friend being the reverse of all this, what a pity it is that he can't turn his literary accomplishments to account. There must be much more pleasure in teaching Latin Grammar than drawing, for it is a thing that *some* will take the pains to learn; but what amateur will learn, or has time for, among all the other "accomplishments," the grammar of Art? And, after all, in the sciolism of so-called education, originality and natural character are so repressed that scores of young ladies (charming as they are in other respects), "*Come out*" at last as like each other mentally as a batch of rolls out of an oven. And all this after such a fag at Multi-science (which Heraclitus has warned us will never teach wisdom) that if you put down on paper the sum total of the time demanded by the masters, each for his "accomplishment," every day, I happen to know that they amount to rather more than twenty-four hours; leaving an absolute minus for eating, drinking, sleeping, and exercise : indeed nothing short of days thirty hours long would suffice them.

In entering at the Brompton Schools, the pupil explains his aim. In this case it would be, of course, the figure; because the plaster teaches drawing in a tenth of the time required by other courses of study : nor do they answer the end after all. Of course success requires energy—bull-dog tenacity. "O! well and happy shall they be" on whose funeral tablets we might inscribe, each by each, HE WAS A CHRISTIAN BULL-DOG.

If there had been no Christian bull-dogs the Church and the World would have been in a doleful case by this time. . . .

. . . The still small voice is *everything*. What is prosperity, without it, but a violated responsibility.

Let the rich (that is those rich ones who do not heed that voice) rejoice "in that he is made low," says St. James " because as the flower of the grass he shall pass away." So as to parting with worldly goods, even to the last shred, it is only a matter of time. What prosperity spares and accumulates, death swallows up in a moment.

The secular view seems to suggest two things among many. Firstly, whether the very adversity itself may not be turned to advantage ; as they say Sir Robert Peel's first ill success at college wrought a self-revenge which was the making of him.

Secondly, on any disappointment, it seems wholesome some times to begin again as it were : eminent artists have had to do this. Etty spent his early life in it. I remember Collins saying "Why don't we begin again?" Mulready replied, "*I do* begin again." Mulready was one of the few who realized Lavater's advice to devote ourselves to each new undertaking as if it were our test—our first work and our last. It seems to me that, in this competitive age, we must not allow ourselves to "take things easily"; but as Sir J. J. Gurney advised his young friend, "give *our whole minds* to one thing at one time."

Of course we should lay hold of a thing by its readiest handle, but that is another matter.

If Fortune (as they say) hurls a rough rock at us, and misses by *ever* so little, what if we turn ourselves about, and make it the first stone of our breakwater ? As to the storm itself the sailors teach us very well—taking in sail *betimes*, and making the ship "snug," as they call it. The battle of life demands a combination of various qualities, and some that seem contradictory : "wise as serpents, harmless as doves." Once I thought that I had hit it and that one should try to be a Christian bull-dog. The Christian element would make it harmless, and the bull-dog would come even upon the best things with the advantage of "holding them fast." . . . I would fain hope that everyone is always "beginning again," and never trusting to another what he should do himself. I think I found benefit from reading Foster's essay on Decision. Foster's *Essays*. He was a preacher among the "Baptists."

. . . I am torn to pieces with the quantity of matters which want seeing to, and I find this [writing] a truer rest after severe study, then doing nothing. A doctor once ordered me to lie upon the sofa and do nothing. I did so for a minute, and started up with a howl !

. . . Both Mrs. P. and S. P. are so thoroughly exhausted, and dead-beaten by the sight of really fine pictures, as to be the most wretched company in the evening. So few as three genuine, uncleaned pictures, say of Raffaelle, Claude, and Titian,

wake me up so thoroughly, that sleep revenges himself afterwards
like a mighty giant and knocks me down with his club.   An
"exposition of sleep" like Mr. Bottom's, which Titania and all
her Elfin revelry may not disperse.

CXXVI. To Mr. W. Williams.

RED HILL, *March* 14, 1881.

DEAR MR. WILLIAMS. . . . . You ask for my "judgment of
Carlyle."   If I felt equal to such an effort it would probably
resemble your own.

He tried to make the purse-proud English ashamed of their
gentility, respectability, and rubbish.   He taught that work was
noble, idleness shameful ; that ladies and gentlemen who live to
please themselves live the life of a beast—of the poodle on their
hearth-rug ; that duty, not pleasure, was "our being's end and
aim" ; that realities were better than shams.   But to make the
"upper-middle classes" swallow all this, he was obliged to disguise
medicinal truth, not exactly in nectar, but in a Scotch porridge
manufactured for the purpose, a notable "sham" of his own.

This was the dialect long since known as "Carlylese" ; a mode
of expression which, to any degree, would obscure, magnify, and
colour the thought, or the subject ; would mist-magnify it, like
something seen through a haze.   He knew that "the ancients had
stolen all our best thoughts" and most of the best subjects, and
that the second-best must be dealt with paradoxically to be sufficiently piquant for the loungers of the "London Season."   Every
one knew all that could possibly be known concerning Dr. Johnson :
here, therefore, was a fine opportunity.   His audience came out of
the lecture-room persuaded that hitherto they had seen nothing
but Johnson's skin, and that Carlyle had shown them the Man.
This, however, was the mist-magnified and many-coloured Johnson,
whom Francis Barber would not have recognized, and from whom
"Hodge" would have fled for his life.

Mr. Carlyle was one of the leaders of the Wonderful School.
Almost to the last page of an essay he keeps you on the tenter-
hooks of expectation for some discovery—some rocket-like explosion of a thousand discoveries ; some ultra-Solomonic wisdom,
which will make Hooker, and Bacon, and Milton, and Newton,

and Butler, seem like a bench of old daddies warming themselves in the sun. It is true that the wisdom-rockets never explode, but there is some strange attraction in Carlylese which beguiles you through the next essay and the next, with like expectation and with like result, till you are weary of it at last.

As to rhythmical prose (to change the subject), it was only revived by Dr. Johnson. It was supreme from Hooker's days down to Barrow's, inclusively. For the Queen Anneites (Addison for instance) it was not sufficiently colloquial. I think you will find Johnson's "we were now treading that illustrious island" &c. quite rhythmical and melodious.

It is long since I read the review of Jenyns, but it can never be forgotten. Doubtless you know Jenyns' retaliation epitaph:—

> " Here lies Sam Johnson ; reader have a care,
> Tread lightly or you'll wake a sleeping bear :
> Religious, moral, generous and humane
> He was ; but self-sufficient, proud and vain ;
> Fond of and overbearing in dispute,
> A Christian and a scholar, but a brute.

With love from all to all, believe me in haste, Yours affectionately, S. PALMER.

CXXVII. To MR. B. HOOK.

RED HILL, *March* 26, 1881.

MY DEAR BRY. I am in daily fruition of your delightful almanack, which really adds an item to every day's happiness ; or, as some would express it, subtracts an item from each day's misery ; and I very sincerely thank you for it, more especially as it reminds me every morning of the giver, and the dear friends at Silverbeck : and so much [that] I have been intending to write, ever since my first hour's enjoyment in pulling off leaf after leaf till I came to the right date. Yet this did not seem matter enough for a letter ; and until this moment (inclusive) I have been too stupid to think of anything whatever.

> " I knock my head to try if sense will come,
> Knock as I will, there's nobody at home."

My wife says " Only *sit down to it* and I am sure you will find something to write." But I reply " Nothing can come of nothing."
It is not wilfulness either, or a dumb demon such as occasion-

ally possessed a little cousin of mine, then at home, busy with the first elements. There would be some *one* word in his spelling-lesson which he knew how to spell rightly enough, but by no persuasion could be prevailed upon to do so. They gave him a cold bath, whipped out the demon for a time, but he came again. *Once* I prevailed upon him to spell the word in question, which, after much tender persuasion, he did ; and I reported that he had done so, hoping to save him from punishment ; but soon after he was up the next morning he was playing hare to the hounds round and round the garden, till they caught him at last and brought him in for a birching. The birching was blest, as the ordinances of God *will* be, and I saw him the other day, a worthy, cheerful, old gentleman.

O that there were time to collect from a copious dictionary all the epithets of disgust, abhorrence, and contempt, with which to designate the pernicious folly of those whom the Devil has persuaded to banish the rod from the nursery,[1] and to substitute "moral suasion " ; the words make me sick at the stomach !

Moral suasion for babies !

A birching for such gabies, is the involuntary rhyme. However, it is part of the epidemic infidelity of the age, rich in facts and phenomena, and just as deplorably poor in foresight, right reason, and knowledge of human nature. How men can have the patience, energy, and penetration to collect and arrange so many facts, and yet be so childishly weak, or fantastically absurd in their inferences, it is indeed hard to conceive. It reminds me of what Sir Humphry Davy makes " Poietes " say of Erasmus Darwin (the poet) in his *Salmonia.* " POIETES. I think Halietus is quite in the right to be a little angry at your observation, Physicus, in making him the disciple of a writer, who, as well as I can recollect, has deduced the *genesis* of the human being, by a succession of changes dependent upon irritabilities, sensibilities, and appetencies, from the *fish:* blending the wild fancies of Buffon with the profound ideas of Hartley, and thus endeavouring to give currency to an absurd romance by mixing with it some philosophical truths."

Dinner is up—if that filthy " moral suasion " will suffer me to eat. Believe me, with united love to all, your nauseated but affectionate friend, S. PALMER.

[1 It is singular that although, throughout the whole of his life, my father strenuously advocated corporal punishment, the rod was quite unknown in his own house. He rarely punished, and when he did, the punishment was slight.—ED.]

CATALOGUE OF
EXHIBITED WORKS

D D 2

A Kentish Hop Garden.

A CATALOGUE OF THE
EXHIBITED WORKS AND THE ETCHINGS
OF SAMUEL PALMER

THE ROYAL ACADEMY

1819.	1.	257.	LANDSCAPE WITH RUINS.
	2.	259.	COTTAGE SCENE : BANKS OF THE THAMES, BATTERSEA.
	3.	414.	A STUDY.
1820.	4.	185.	WOOD SCENE : A STUDY FROM NATURE.
1821.	5.	49.	A STUDY FROM NATURE : BATTERSEA.
1823.	6.	32.	VIEW.
1824.	7.	504.	LANDSCAPE : TWILIGHT.
	8.	706.	STUDY OF A HEAD.
1825.	9.	384.	A SCENE FROM KENT.

1825.	10.	410.	A Rustic Scene.
1826.	11.	570.	Late Twilight.
	12.	714.	The Skirts of a Wood.
	13.	849.	A Rustic Scene.
1829.	14.	516.	The Deluge: a Sketch.
	15.	641.	Ruth returned from Gleaning.
1832.	16.	493.	The Sheep-fold.
	17.	497.	Scene near Shoreham, Kent.
	18.	547.	A Pastoral Scene: Twilight.
	19.	605.	A Pastoral Landscape.
	20.	614.	A Harvest Scene.
	21.	816.	Landscape: Twilight.
	22.	818.	Late Twilight.
1833.	23.	48.	The Gleaning Field.
	24.	64.	The Harvest-moon.
	25.	166.	Landscape: Twilight.
	26.	356.	Rustic Scene.
	27.	657.	A Kentish Scene.
1834.	28.	49.	Landscape: Evening.
	29.	119.	The Flock.
	30.	280.	The Harvest Field.
	31.	419.	Landscape: Twilight.
	32.	517.	A Rustic Scene.
	33.	1010.	The Cottage Window.
1835.	34.	90.	Scene from Lee, North Devon.
	35.	153.	The Corn Field.
1836.	36.	656.	Pistil Mawddach, near Pistil-y-Cain, North Wales.
1837.	37.	553.	Near Pont-y-Pandu Mill, Bettws-y-Coed, North Wales.
	38.	574.	Pistil-y-Cain, North Wales.
	39.	670.	Caernarvon Castle, North Wales.
	40.	932.	The Chudleigh Rocks, North Devon.
1840.	41.	1005.	Pompeii: the Street of the Tombs.

"Where are the golden roofs? Where those who dared to build?"

1841.	42.	677.	A Street in Rome: drawn on the spot.
	43.	702.	Cattle at the Brook: a Scene at Norton, near Faversham, Kent.
	44.	1197.	The Bay of Baiæ.
1842.	45.	183.	Landscape from near Silton, Dorsetshire.
	46.	896.	The Ponte Rotto, Temple of Vesta, and Palace of the Cæsars, Rome.

1865.	47.	872.	EVENING PASTURES : *Etching.*
	48.	876.	"THE PLOUGHMAN HOMEWARD PLODS HIS WEARY WAY" : *Etching.*
1873.	49.	1283.	THE MORNING OF LIFE : *Etching.*
	50.	1296.	THE MORNING SPREAD UPON THE MOUNTAINS : *Etching.*

THE BRITISH INSTITUTION

1819.	1.	141.	BRIDGE SCENE : COMPOSITION. [25 × 21 inches.]
	2.	169.	LANDSCAPE : COMPOSITION. [39 × 34.]
1821.	3.	156.	STUDY FROM NATURE, AT BATTERSEA. [24 × 20.]
	4.	278.	LANGLEY LOCKS, HERTS.
1822.	5.	101.	A LANE SCENE, BATTERSEA. [24 × 20.]
	6.	106.	HAILSHAM, SUSSEX : STORM COMING ON. [40 × 36.]
	7.	195.	ON THE THAMES : EVENING. [30 × 25.]
1834.	8.	10.	LANDSCAPE. [12 × 10.]
	9.	205.	THE REAPER. [17 × 15.]
	10.	315.	A STUDY FROM NATURE. [24 × 16.]
	11.	342.	EVENING. [33 × 27.]
	12.	400.	LANDSCAPE. [11 × 9.]
1835.	13.	147.	A SCENE NEAR SHOREHAM, KENT. [21 × 18.]
	14.	154.	AT FILSTON FARM, KENT. [20 × 17.]
	15.	341.	THE LANE SIDE. [31 × 25.]
	16.	502.	COTTAGE WINDOW. [17 × 16.]
1837.	17.	275.	THE CATARACT OF PISTIL-Y-CAIN, NORTH WALES. [45 × 39.]
1843.	18.	115.	PASTORAL LANDSCAPE IN THE SOUTH OF ENGLAND. [28 × 24.]

THE ROYAL SOCIETY OF PAINTERS IN WATER COLOURS

ASSOCIATE, 1843-54. MEMBER, 1854-81.

| 1843. | 1. | 56. | THE COLOSSEUM AND ALBAN MOUNT. |
| | 2. | 114. | HARLECH CASTLE : TWILIGHT. |

"The moon is up, and yet it is not night."

	3.	131.	AT DONNINGTON, BERKSHIRE ; THE BIRTHPLACE OF CHAUCER.
	4.	197.	OLD FARM, NEAR THATCHAM, BERKS.
	5.	218.	RUSTIC SCENE, NEAR THATCHAM, BERKSHIRE.

1845. 22. 306. PORTA DI POSILIPO AND THE BAY OF BAIÆ, WITH ISCHIA
AND THE PROMONTORY OF MISENUM.

"The balmy spirit of the western gale,
Eternal breathes on fruits untaught to fail."

23. 337. AT SUNSET: THE MOUNTAINS BEHIND PÆSTUM AND
SALERNO, AND PART OF THE SALERNIAN GULF,
FROM THE SLOPES OF MONTE FINESTRE.

1846. 24. 108. THE AGED OAK.
25. 111. THE CORN FIELD.
26. 113. CHILDREN GLEANING.
27. 120. A LANE SCENE.
28. 122. THE LISTENING GLEANER.
29. 141. CROSSING THE BROOK.
30. 201. A FARM-YARD NEAR RISBOROUGH, BUCKS.

1847. 31. 148. THE BROKEN BRIDGE.
32. 176. A LANDSCAPE : SUNSET.
33. 241. THE CORN FIELD: CLOUDY MORNING.
34. 253. THE GIPSY DELL : MOONLIGHT.
35. 259. THE SKIRTS OF A VILLAGE.

1848. 36. 5. SION HILL, UNDERRIVER, KENT.
37. 51. MOUNTAIN FLOCKS.
38. 122. WOODLAND SCENERY.
39. 175. THE RUINS OF A MONASTERY : STORM COMING ON.
40. 204. CHRISTIAN DESCENDING INTO THE VALLEY OF HUMILIA-
TION. *Vide " Pilgrim's Progress."*
41. 217. MERCURY DRIVING AWAY THE CATTLE OF ADMETUS.
42. 228. CARTING THE WHEAT.
43. 251. CROSSING THE COMMON : SUNSET.

1849. 44. 88. FAREWELL TO CALYPSO !
45. 100. SIR GUYON, WITH THE PALMER ATTENDING, TEMPTED BY
PHÆDRIA TO LAND UPON THE ENCHANTED ISLANDS.
Faery Queen.
46. 149. SUN AND SHADE : ARESTORIDES.
47. 175. SHELTERING FROM THE STORM.
48. 222. KING ARTHUR'S CASTLE, TINTAGEL, CORNWALL.
49. 244. SYLVAN QUIET.
50. 255. CROSSING THE HEATH.
51. 334. GLEANERS CROSSING A SHALLOW STREAM.

1850. 52. 58. CHILDREN NUTTING.
53. 177. WIND AND RAIN.
54. 205. ST. PAUL LANDING IN ITALY.
55. 217. ROBINSON CRUSOE GUIDING HIS RAFT UP THE CREEK.

1850.	56.	304.	CATTLE IN THE SHALLOWS : SUMMER EVENING.
	57.	326.	CARTING THE WHEAT : SHOWERY WEATHER.
1851.	58.	192.	THE WINDMILL.
	59.	303.	SHEEP IN THE SHADE.
	60.	321.	THE BREEZY HEATH.
	61.	107.	A SHOWERY MORNING : SCENERY OF WEST SOMERSET.
	62.	237.	THE FORESTER'S HORN.
	63.	251.	SHADY QUIET.
	64.	263.	THE APPROACH OF DINNER.
	65.	275.	THE SKIRTS OF A COMMON.
1853.	66.	18.	THE RUSTIC DINNER.
	67.	210.	CHILDREN AND SHEEP.
	68.	228.	HASTE AND PATIENCE.
1854.	69.	241.	FAST TRAVELLING.
	70.	252.	THE FOLDED FLOCK.
1855.	71.	73.	THE DELL OF COMUS.

> "This evening late, by then the chewing flocks
> Had ta'en their supper on the savoury herb
> Of knot-grass dew-besprent, and were in fold,
> I sat me down to watch upon a bank
> With ivy canopied, and interwove
> With flaunting honey-suckle, and began,
> Wrapt in a pleasing fit of melancholy,
> To meditate my rural minstrelsy,
> Till fancy had her fill ; but ere a close,
> The wonted roar was up amidst the woods."

	72.	251.	THE RUSTIC CONVERSAZIONE.
	73.	255.	SUNSET OVER THE GLEANING FIELDS.
	74.	277.	THE BAY OF NAPLES.
1856.	75.	147.	THE BROTHERS, GUIDED BY THE ATTENDANT SPIRIT, DISCOVERING THE PALACE AND BOWERS OF COMUS.

> "*Attendant Spirit.* Immur'd in cypress shades the sorcerer dwells.
> You may
> Boldly assault the necromancer's hall ;
> Where if he be, with dauntless hardihood
> And brandish'd blade rush on him, break his glass,
> And shed the luscious liquor on the ground ;
> But seize his wand ; though he and his curs'd crew
> Fierce sign of battle make and menace high."

| | 76. | 153. | THE BROTHERS IN 'COMUS' LINGERING UNDER THE VINE. |

> "Two such I saw, what time the labour'd ox
> In his loose traces from the furrow came,
> And the swinkt hedger at his supper sat ;
> I saw them under a green mantling vine
> That crawls along the side of yon small hill,
> Plucking ripe clusters from the tender shoots."

1861. 109. 232. THE STREAMLET.

1862. 110. 241. THE PATRIARCH OF THE ORCHARD.

> "They climb and fill their baskets grey ;
> Swing by the boughs, and pelt and play ;
> So played, in its maturity,
> Their grandsires round that hoary tree."

111. 251. IN THE COUNTRY.

> "The sunshine over hill and dale,
> The fresh field and the foaming pail."

112. 259. A POET.

> "The sisters listening to his verse were moved,
> And Madeline the simple goatherd loved."

113. 267. THE FISHERMAN'S WIFE.

> "The storm and anxious night are passed ;
> The wished for sail appears at last."

114. 291. WRECKED AT HOME.

> "Th' occasion met, the peril braved,
> A brother and a husband saved."

WINTER EXHIBITION.

115. 390. THE FURZE-FIELD.

116. 407. FINISHED STUDY FOR A PICTURE : "THE SHADOWY POOL.

> "The thirsty oxen from the sunshine wind
> Into the shadowy corner of a pool."

1863. 117. 229. THE BROTHER COME HOME FROM SEA.

> "Awake ! awake ! our Robin is come home ;
> Just landing by the bay, no more to roam !"
> Brothers and sisters answer to his cheer,
> And 'twill be merry in the cottage there :
> Pullet and junket, and the old brown ale,
> And all agape to hear the traveller's tale."

118. 238. THE SHEEP-SHEARERS.

> "But who, from England's olden time,
> Sent Jason's freight to every clime,
> With generous wealth and plenty blest,
> Our loom-built cities of the West?
> Poor shepherds shearing in a row,
> Upon some sunny upland brow."

1863. 119. 285. THE SACRED RUIN.

> " Upon the marish in the vale
> A vapoury sun look'd wan and pale,
> The Abbey rose—the ground was till'd,
> The sun on golden harvests smiled :
> And still he loves that ruin grey,
> Making it golden in decay,
> And lends a colouring of his own
> Where once the deep-stain'd windows shone."

WINTER EXHIBITION.

120. 65. THE CHAPEL BY THE BRIDGE. [Known also as " Twilight."]

> " There was a little oratory by the bridge foot, and as we approached in the dying light we could hear the chanted responses."

121. 303. A DREAM IN THE FOREST.

> " In such green palaces the first kings reigned—
> Slept in their shades and angels entertained."—WALLER.

122. 316. " ON SUMMER EVES BY HAUNTED STREAM."

123. 323. " THE TRAVELLER'S REST."

> " They help the girls and children down,
> Belated from the market-town ;
> The cheer is good, the fagot bright,
> Within the oaken screen to-night."

124. 358. MOUNTAIN PASTURES.

> " The milkmaids on the mountain brow,
> The heather fleck'd with fleecy snow."

1864. 125. 150. A DREAM IN THE APENNINE.

> " Suddenly, at a turn in the mountain road, we looked for the first time on that Plain ; the dispenser of law, the refuge of philosophy, the cradle of faith. Ground which Virgil trod and Claude invested with supernatural beauty, was sketched—but ' with a trembling pencil."

WINTER EXHIBITION.

126. 189. THE EARLY PLOUGHMAN. [Known also as " Dawn."]

127. 196. LYCIDAS.

128. 320. STUDY OF A WATERFALL NEAR TREFRIEW, NORTH WALES.

129. 366. " THE RIVER GLIDETH AT HIS OWN SWEET WILL."

1864. 130. 368. NEAR CLOVELLY : A PAGE FROM THE BLOT-BOOK

       131. 421. GOING HOME AT CURFEW-TIME.

> "And now wind homeward in the dying light ;
> Homeward, my flocks, for Hesperus is bright."

       132. 434. HOVERING CLOUDS.

1865. 133. 111. THE GOOD FARMER.

> "Careless their merits or their faults to scan,
> His pity gave ere charity began,"

       134. 271. THE CLOSE OF A CLEAR DAY.

> "That promises each pastral lawn
> A starry night, an amber dawn."

       135. 273. THE GOLDEN HOUR. [Known also as " The Glorious
                   Sunset."]

> "Though heaven and earth with August glow,
> Our island streams unstinted flow."

WINTER EXHIBITION.

       136. 105. A SKETCH IN CLOVELLY PARK, LOOKING TOWARDS THE
                   CLIFFS ON THE FURTHER SIDE OF MOUTH-MILL RAVINE.

       137. 111. STUDY OF A MIDDLE DISTANCE : CLOVELLY PARK, NORTH
                   DEVON.

The boundary line is the abrupt edge of high cliffs which
have little or no table-land, the ground inclining thus in
woody slope.

       138. 348. HOPE, OR THE LIFTING OF THE CLOUD.

> "The day at first was sombre, like the shadowy turrets we
> were to explore. Then there was a distant gleam ; the breeze
> began to stir, and the rain-cloud, slowly rising, disclosed the
> mountains."

       139. 352. THE HAUNTED TURRET.

> "All day the clouds had hovered over the mountain, but about
> sunset they parted ; the cumuli rested far off, and the turrets glim-
> mered in a more genial light."

1866. 140. 253. STORIED SUMMITS : FROM THE "LEGENDS OF WEST
                   SURREY."

> "Who dropped the rock upon that central hill?"

1866. 141. 305. A DAY-DREAM OF SALERNO, WITH THE OLD LIBURNUS, FROM THE SLOPES OF MONTE FINESTRE.

> "More pleasing than the fitful gleam,
> With storm behind and gathering nigh,
> Still to frequent the temperate shade,
> Look far and see the prospect bright."

WINTER EXHIBITION.

142. 60. A STUDY AT TINTERN : DRAWN ON THE SPOT.

143. 194. FLORENCE : DRAWN ON THE SPOT.

144. 237. A STUDY OF WOODY HILL AND SLATE MOUNTAIN NEAR FESTINIOG, NORTH WALES.

145. 353. ARTHUR'S GATE : A LEGEND OF TINTAGEL.

> "They say that under that postern the body of King Arthur passed to burial."

1867. 146. 252. AT BACKWAYS, NEAR TINTAGEL : DRAWN ON THE SPOT.

1868. 147. 16. FROM "IL PENSEROSO." [Known also as "The Lonely Tower."]

> "Or let my lamp at midnight hour
> Be seen in some high lonely tow'r,
> Where I may oft out-watch the Bear,
> With thrice great Hermes, or unsphere
> The spirit of Plato, to unfold
> What worlds'or what vast regions hold
> The immortal mind, that hath forsook
> Her mansion in this fleshly nook."

148. 93. A TOWERED CITY : FROM "L'ALLEGRO." [Known also as "The Haunted Stream."]

> "There let Hymen oft appear
> In saffron robe, with taper clear,
> And pomp and feast and revelry,
> With mask and antique pageantry.
> Such sights us youthful poets dream
> On summer eves by haunted stream."

149. 193. MORNING. [Known also as "The Dripping Eaves."]

> "Not trick'd and frounc'd as she was wont
> With the Attic boy to hunt.
> But kercheft in a comely cloud,
> While rocking winds are piping loud,
> Or usher'd with a shower still,
> When the gust hath blown his fill.
> Ending on the rustling leaves,
> With minute drops from off the eaves."

1868. 150. 200.   POMPEIAN MEMORIES.

1870. 151. 97.   THE CURFEW.

> "Oft on a plat of rising ground
> I hear the far-off curfew sound,
> Over some wide-water'd shore
> Swinging slow with sullen roar."

    152. 105.   THE NEAR AND THE DISTANT: FROM SOUTHERN ITALY.
[Known also as " Italy Far and Near."]

1871. 153. 161.   THE FALL OF EMPIRE. [Known also as " The Colosseum."]

> "There is given
> Unto the things of earth, which Time hath bent,
> A spirit's feeling, and where he hath leant
> His hand, but broke his scythe, there is a power
> And magic in the ruin'd battlement,
> For which the palace of the present hour
> Must yield its pomp, and wait till ages are its dower."

    154. 205.   AN ANCIENT MANOR HOUSE, BENEATH

> "The western downs of lovely Albion."

WINTER EXHIBITION.

    155. 317.   A CASCADE IN SHADOW, DRAWN ON THE SPOT, NEAR THE
JUNCTION OF THE MACHNO AND CONWAY, NORTH
WALES.

    156. 378.   PAPIGNO ON THE NAR, BELOW THE FALLS OF TERNI.
[Bistre.]

> "Fluminaque antiquos subterlabentia muros."

1872. 157. 245.   CROSSING THE BROOK: SCENERY OF WESTERN SURREY.
THE CUMULUS IN MINIATURE.

1873. 158. 79.   A GOLDEN CITY.

> "Oh, Rome! my country! city of the soul!
> The orphans of the heart must turn to thee,
> Lone mother of dead empires! and control
> In their shut breasts their petty misery.
> What are our woes and sufferance? Come and see
> The cypress, hear the owl, and plod your way
> O'er steps of broken thrones and temples, Ye!
> Whose agonies are evils of a day—
> A world is at our feet as fragile as our clay."

1873. 159. 112. LYCIDAS.

"Together both ere the high lawns appear'd
Under the opening eyelids of the morn,
We drove afield, and oth together hear l
What time the gray-fly winds her sultry horn,
Batt'ning our flocks with the fresh dews of night."

1874. 160. 91. OLD ENGLAND'S SUNDAY EVENING.
1875. 161. 272. THE TRAVELLERS.
1877. 162. 5. THE WATERS MURMURING : FROM " IL PENSEROSO."

"There in close covert by some brook,
Where no profaner eye may look,
Hide me from day's garish eye,
While the bee with honied thigh,
That at her flowery work doth sing
And the waters murmuring
With such consort as they keep
Entice the dewy-feather'd sleep.'

163. 100. TITYRUS RESTORED TO HIS PATRIMONY.

"O fortunate old man !
Then these ancestral fields are yours again ;
And wide enough for you. Though naked stone,
And marsh with slimy rush about upon
The lowlands, yet your pregnant ewes shall try
No unproved forage ; neighb'ring flocks, too nigh,
Strike no contagion, nor infect the young.
O fortunate, who now at last among
Known streams and sacred fountain-heads, have found
A shelter and a shade on your own ground."

WINTER EXHIBITION.

164. 380. AUTUMN.
165. 402. IN MEMORIAM: A RECOLLECTION OF THE BURIAL-PLACE
OF KEATS, NEAR THE PYRAMID OF CAIUS CESTUS.
ROME. [Sepia.]
166. 431. PLOUGHMEN.

" Man goeth forth to his work and to his labour until the evening."

167. 435. CROSSING THE BROOK.

1878. 168. 238. RIVER BANKS AT EVEN.
1879. 169. 240. HASTING TO COVERT : A THREATENING RAIN-STORM.
170. 257. MOUNTAIN STREAM AND AN ANCIENT FORTRESS.

WINTER EXHIBITION.

1879. 171. 352.   WESTERN SHORES.

172. 360.   GOING TO FOLD.

1880. 173. 218.   SABRINA.

> "Still she retains
> Her maiden gentleness, and oft at eve
> Visits the herds along the twilight meadows."

WINTER EXHIBITION.

174. 313.   AURORA.

> "Now with her rosy fingers had the dawn
> From glimmering Heaven the veil of night withdrawn,
> And folded flocks were loose to browse anew
> O'er mountain-thyme and trefoil wet with dew."

1881. 175.   18.   THE PROSPECT : FROM "L'ALLEGRO."

> "Straight mine eye hath caught new pleasures,
> Whilst the landscape round it measures ;
> Russet lawns and fallows gray,
> Where the nibbling flocks do stray ;
> Mountains, on whose barren breast
> The labouring clouds do often rest ;
> Meadows trim with daisies pide,
> Shallow brooks and rivers wide :
> Towers and battlements it sees
> Bosom'd high in tufted trees,
> Where perhaps some beauty lies
> The cynosure of neighb'ring eyes."

176.   56.   THE EASTERN GATE : FROM "L'ALLEGRO."

> "Right against the Eastern gate,
> Where the great sun begins his state,
> Rob'd in flames and amber light,
> The clouds in thousand liveries dight ;
> While the ploughman near at hand
> Whistles o'er the furrow'd land,
> And the milkmaid singeth blithe,
> And the mower whets his scythe,
> And every shepherd tells his tale
> Under the hawthorn in the dale."

WINTER EXHIBITION.

1881. 177. 364. EVENTIDE.

1882. 178. THE BELLMAN : FROM " IL PENSEROSO."

"——the Bellman's drowsy charm
To bless the doors from nightly harm."

THE SOCIETY OF BRITISH ARTISTS

1836.	1.	45.	THE HOP PICKERS.
	2.	586.	PISTIL MAWDDACH, NEAR PISTIL-Y-CAIN, NORTH WALES.
	3.	640.	TREFRIEW MILL, ON THE ROAD FROM BETTWS-Y-COED TO CONWAY, NORTH WALES : DRAWN ON THE SPOT.
1842.	4.	86.	SCENE AT ZEAL'S PARK, WILTS.
1873.	5.	369.	A RUSTIC SCENE.
	6.	371.	GLEANERS RETURNING HOME.

L'EXPOSITION UNIVERSELLE, PARIS, 1853

1063. ULYSSE S'ÉLOIGNANT DE L'ÎLE DE CALYPSO.

THE MANCHESTER ART TREASURES, 1857

[Water Colours.]

1. 607. WINDMILL. (Lent by Mr. F. Dillon.)
2. 608. THE BROTHERS : ("COMUS.") (Lent by Mr. S. Palmer.)

INTERNATIONAL EXHIBITION, 1862

[Water Colours.]

1. 1081. RETURNED FROM INDIA. (Lent by Mr. T. Williams.)

1873.   2.   1107.   THE RISING MOON.   (Lent by Mr. F. Robinson.)
        3.   1115.   AFTER THE STORM.   (Lent by Mr. W. Quilter.)
        4.   1116.   THE BALLAD.   (Lent by Mr. F. Craven.)

L'EXPOSITION UNIVERSELLE, PARIS, 1867

1.   78.   LABOUREUR MATINAL.   (Appartenant à M. L. R. Valpy.)
2.   79.   LYCIDAS.   (Appartenant à M. L. R. Valpy.)
3.   80.   LA CHAPELLE PRÈS DU PONT.   (Appartenant à M. L. R.
            Valpy.)

THE GROSVENOR GALLERY, 1879

1.   881.   MEMORIES OF POMPEII.   (Lent by Mr. C. L. Collard.)
2.   882.   THE GOLDEN HOUR.   (Lent by Mr. G. Gurney.)
3.   1074.   LYCIDAS.   (Lent by Mr. G. Gurney.)

        "Together both ere the high lawns appear'd
         Under the opening eyelids of the morn,
         We drove afield, and both together heard
         What time the gray-fly winds her sultry horn."

4.   1082.   GOING TO EVENING CHURCH.   (Lent by Mr. J. W.
             Overbury.)   [An early Shoreham Work.]

AT MANCHESTER, 1887

1.   1169.   CALYPSO'S ISLAND.   (Lent by Mr. J. Haworth.)
2.   1679.   OXEN PLOUGHING.   (Lent by Mr. J. S. Bolton.)
3.   1762.   HARVEST FIELD.   (Lent by Mr. R. R. Ross.)

THE ROYAL ACADEMY WINTER EXHIBITION, 1891

1.   139.   LYCIDAS.   [23 × 15½ inches.]   (Lent by Mr. G. Gurney.)

1873. 2. 140. THE GOLDEN HOUR. [13½ × 10.] (Lent by Mr. G. Gurney.)

3 145. TITYRUS RESTORED TO HIS PATRIMONY. [27½ × 20.] (Lent by Mr. G. Gurney.)

IN THE HISTORICAL COLLECTION OF ENGLISH WATER-COLOUR
DRAWINGS AT SOUTH KENSINGTON

538. GOING TO SEA. (Ellison Gift.)

—

ETCHINGS

The Plates marked * are destroyed.

—

1. THE WILLOW. Probationary Plate on election to the Etching Club, 1850.

2. THE HERDSMAN'S COTTAGE; or *Sunset.* Published in *The Portfolio*, November, 1872, as *Sunrise* (see letter to Mr. R. Seeley, No. LXXXVI), and in Hamerton's *Etching and Etchers*, third edition.

3. CHRISTMAS; or *Folding the Last Sheep*, from Bampfylde's *Sonnet.* Published in *A Memoir of S. Palmer*, 1882.

*4. THE SLEEPING SHEPHERD. Published by the Etching Club, 1857.

*5. THE SKYLARK. Published by the Etching Club, 1857.

*6. THE RISING MOON. Known also as *A British Pastoral* and *Evening Pastures.* Published by the Etching Club, 1857.

*7. THE VINE; or *Plumpy Bacchus* (two subjects on one plate). Published by the Etching Club, 1852.

*8. THE HERDSMAN; or *Tardus Bubulcus.* Published by the Etching Club, 1865.

9. THE EARLY PLOUGHMAN; or *The Morning Spread upon the Mountains.* Published in Hamerton's *Etching and Etchers*, first edition, 1868.

*10. THE MORNING OF LIFE; or *Work and Gossip.* Published by the Etching Club, 1872.

11. THE BELLMAN, FROM "IL PENSEROSO." Published by the Fine Art
    Society, 1879.

*12. THE LONELY TOWER, FROM "IL PENSEROSO." Published by the
    Etching Club, 1880.

13. OPENING THE FOLD ; or *Early Morning.* Published in *An English
    Version of the Eclogues of Virgil,* 1883.

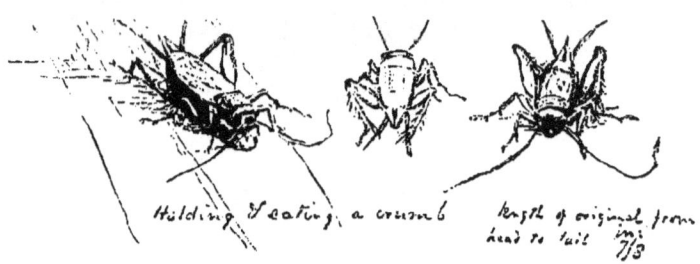

Holding & eating, a crumb   length of original from
                                 head to tail $\frac{in.}{7/3}$